CURSED SPITE

a novel
by

Douglas G. Noakes

Douglas G. Noakes

Printed and bound in the United States of America

Published by: Noakes Press
740 W. Pebble Beach Drive
Ashland, Oregon 97520
website: cursedspite.com

First Edition Printing: November 2006

Printed in the United States of America.

International Standard Book Number
ISBN 13: 978-0-977-44870-3
ISBN 10: 0-977-44870-3

Cover design, Text Layout and production by Roberta Great
(greatgraphics@charter.net)

10 9 8 7 6 5 4 3 2 1

Prologue

"There are few crimes as foul as murder. Yet a murder has taken place that to me is as foul as anything you can read about in a newspaper or see depicted on stage or screen. I speak of the murder of the reputation of William Shakespeare.

"He should be remembered as the greatest poet and playwright in the English language. But, some, including my worthy opponent to my left here, have claimed another person of that time wrote his great legacy of plays and sonnets. They have reduced William Shakespeare to the status of mere front man.

"It is murder of reputation committed in the name of snobbery and in the zest many have to weave fantastic conspiracy theories to subvert the plain truth. Sir Francis Bacon, The Earl of Oxford, Christopher Marlowe and even Shakespeare's wife, Ann Hathaway, have been picked by various pseudo-scholars as the real author of "Hamlet," "King Lear," "Othello," "Anthony and Cleopatra" "As You Like It," and the great historical plays of the War of the Roses, the wars of Prince Hal and the immortal Jack Falstaff.

"But Shakespeare was no front man, ladies and gentlemen. He was a genius and a hardworking artist. It's just that his accomplishments are too great for some to accept that his work came from a man who began his life in a unremarkable locale and was the son of a glove maker. But genius knows no barriers of class or race or gender, no matter how hard it is for some to believe.

"I will readily admit that the man William DeVant, Earl of Grantum and cousin to Queen Elizabeth I, did indeed know and befriend Shakespeare when he first came to London from Stratford-On-Avon. But to believe that the nobleman wrote his plays is nothing but a hoax, designed to sell my opponent's books. And, sadly, he has misled many readers.

"I will now have my assistant, Carolyn Mason, begin the visual presentation on the screen above me here. These documents I am about to present to you are copies of writings in the original hand of William DeVant. They have laid hidden for nearly 400 years and, since being discovered in Scotland, have been authenticated by scholars in the United States and Great Britain. When this presentation is over, I am confident you will find that William DeVant's journal entries from 1597 are authentic and that Mr. Warbeck's evidence is based on a fraud committed by the earl's grandson, who tried to cash in on Shakespeare's fame decades later.

Now if you'll observe the first slide..."

Note to reader: These notes are from the intended opening remarks of Jack Benchley, noted stage and film director, in a debate for a Strunk Network Television special, "The Shakespeare Controversy." They were found in his hotel suite following his disappearance a few hours before the taping of the broadcast.

Table of Contents

Chapter One

Dave McCreedy was my best friend. We had grown up next door from each other, starting at Roosevelt Grade School and Moreland Little League Baseball in San Jose, California. He was my best friend then and, after an interval of going in different directions in young adulthood we were best friends again. After I lost my job as a cop in Sutter City (a suburb of San Francisco) I took his advice and moved up to the medium-sized town of Rogue Falls, Oregon. Dave helped me get back on my feet. That move had been four years ago in August of 1997 when I was thirty four years old. I say Dave 'was' my best friend because he turned up dead a few days after we talked in a bar about a case he was working on.

For three years he and I shared a line of work—as contracted investigators tracking down and checking up on deadbeat daddies (and sometimes deadbeat mommies) who ran afoul of the Rogue County Family Support Bureau—and a line of recreation: drinking beer (mine had to be non-alcoholic 'brew') and watching basketball games on the televisions at O'Leary's Sports Pub. Tonight we were seated at a table across from the middle of the bar, engaged in both pursuits.

The saloon, with walls of stucco painted green and a decor of neon and back-lit beer brand advertisements, also had three televisions, one a big-screen. There were also a couple well-worn felt pool tables beyond the bar itself and, beyond the tables, a small back room, "The Leprechaun's Lair," for parties. The "Lair" had all the ambiance of a picnic site at a state park.

There was a crooked line of wooden stools at the bar, a dozen of them, about half the available number, occupied. The majority of bar hounds on this night were boisterous, twenty-something males from the local college. Rickety wooden tables lined the wall, one of which Dave and I were using. A table near us had an obsolete Pac-Man computer game built right into the top. (The machine had long been out-of-order.) Scattered illumination came from the green-shaded overhead lamps above the pool tables, the televisions, a couple track lights above the big mirror behind the bar, and the occasional flaring up of a butane cigarette lighter from a patron unconcerned with the Surgeon General's Report.

The place smelled of stale booze and cigarettes. Peanut shells were strewn about our feet on the floor. (There were always peanuts shells on the floor at O'Leary's, gathered in little clumps from the Wurlitzer Jukebox in front, below the brass rails under the barstools all the way to the pool tables in the back.) On television, the Portland Trailblazers were at home in the Rose Garden tonight, playing the Seattle Supersonics. My friend Dave was bringing me up to speed on what the local (and national) media were calling the Benchley Disappearance.

No one in Rogue County was neutral on the subject of Jack Benchley. He was a native son of Southern Oregon and the most famous living resident in the area. After a successful career as a screenwriter and director in Hollywood, Benchley left the motion picture business—his career curtailed by one too many unprofitable feature films—and returned to his hometown. A wealthy local man, and boyhood friend, appointed Benchley Artistic Director of a then modestly successful live theater company, The Northwest Shakespeare Festival. That was in the early seventies. Twenty five years later Benchley's artistic genius—at least I thought he was a genius judging the films I had seen—and the famous actors he lured to the festival had made the NSF a tourist trap for the culturally needy from all over the West.

The theater company put on at least four Shakespeare plays a year, plus another half dozen works divided between modern American and European plays. Before Jack Benchley, Rogue Falls had been a sleepy mill town whose chief exports were lumber and young people looking for decent jobs. After Benchley (and the loss of the mills due to plant automation and environmental laws) the town had become a trendy, chic little nook overrun with Californians for the six months of the year the festival ran. People who came to enjoy *Hamlet* and *Loves Labors Lost* also liked the woodsy, mountainous terrain that ringed the town. Many of them came back to retire or open up businesses. Some came to the area with just a car or the clothes on their backs, looking to escape the sprawling, crime-ridden cities and suburbs of California. And there was the rub: the town had changed too quickly for the old-timers. To them, Jack Benchley was the whipping boy for all the ills the influx of strangers had brought with them. Half the town cheered when he rode in the Fourth of July parade in front of some impressive float the Festival Art Department created. The other half either booed him or offered a stony silence to his smiling, hand-waving presence.

So the fact that it was now Spring and the Festival was opening and no one had seen Benchley for a solid week—not his friends, family supporters or detractors—nobody—made a ripe subject for speculation. I thought if anyone could find our resident VIP it would be Dave McCreedy, a man fifteen days older than myself.

Apparently the Benchley family, specifically his daughter, the actress Ann Benchley, shared my confidence. He was on her payroll to track her father down and bring him back, preferably alive.

Dave wiped a trace of beer foam off his mustache and glanced over at the television situated above the bar. A Portland Trailblazer guard had drawn a foul trying to strip the ball from Shawn Kemp of the Seattle Supersonics. "Damn it, Anderson!" Dave shouted out, his voice muffled by the chorus of guttural ejaculations coming from other patrons also glued to the final spasms of the contest. From his profile, my best friend bore a resemblance to the actor Jack Nicholson. Perhaps not the lean shark-like Nicholson of *Chinatown* but a more heavy-set incarnation from *Terms of Endearment*, *The Border* or *The Witches of Eastwick*. Dave looked in his forties, not his mid-thirties; the result of a life spent avoiding moderation. The semblance to the celebrity was enhanced by his unfashionably-long dark brown sideburns (with a slight fringe of gray hair near the temples), large front teeth and a receding hairline.

"That was a clean steal," Dave huffed. That remark drew a laugh from Wendy, Dave's wife, who was tending the bar that night.

"Tell me more about this young woman he was with," I asked Dave once he managed to pull his attention away from the game. I wanted as much detail on this Benchley case as he was willing to confide. I also had to get it out of him soon because Dave had a rendezvous with a couple pals at the VFW club after the game.

"Yeah, what about her?" Dave said in a tone of resignation, his eyes focused on the drink coaster in front of him. "I wish I knew. I spent three days bopping around San Francisco trying to get a line on her. All I know for certain is she came with old man Benchley to this Forest of Arden Retreat down near Santa Rosa. According to the Mexican kid, Rosales, they were hot and heavy for each other. At least he had the hots for her."

"If you can imagine a 76-year old man being able to get hot in the crotch," I said, then remembered the reputed effects of the Viagra pill.

Dave continued, "Then sometime the night before the last day of this wing-ding, in the middle of the night Carlos Rosales was on duty but he can only guess it was about two in the morning, Benchley and Carolyn Mason left their bungalow and then the two got in his white '66 Ford Mustang. They headed right out of the gate, toward Highway 101. The only way at the interchange down the road was south toward the city. Benchley was scheduled to debate this Warbeck guy the next day in the Globe Auditorium there, so why did he leave? For a couple days, Ann Benchley assumed he was just off on a gallivant. But when the Frisco cops found the old man's car with this woman in the trunk over on the west side of Golden Gate Park, dead as a mackerel and not smelling so good..."

"And no trace of Benchley in the last five days," I added, something anybody who had read the newspapers would have known. Dave shook his head and sighed deeply. "I wish Jack had let me go with him as a bodyguard. He'd have been safe and so would Carolyn."

"But Benchley turned your offer of free security down,

remember?" I reminded my friend. "Dave, whatever happened, it's not your fault."

"Right," Dave said, rubbing the emerging brown and grey stubble under his chin and looking up at the faded color map of the Emerald Isle that hung on the wall above us. He pulled out a small brown spiral notebook. "This is all I got in three days," he said after he flipped through a few dog-eared pages, then read aloud.

"I've got her name and the fact that she worked as a waitress at the Cliff House over on the west end of the city, not far from where they found her. Her sister back in Oklahoma told me on the phone she had spilled to the cops and wasn't going to talk to any private investigator. So, I have a lot of public-access information on her: Carolyn Mason, age 36, college degree in sociology, single but divorced, no kids, a brother and a sister in Oklahoma City, no arrest record and no speeding tickets. There is one thing about her basic records that's damned suspicious."

"Lay it on me," I said.

"She lived on Telegraph Court. 344 Telegraph Court to be exact. I couldn't get in the place thanks to the doorman but its an apartment building in a very ritzy part of town. There was a great view of the Bay Bridge and Treasure Island near the place. Now tell me what a waitress is doing living up on Telegraph Hill?"

"Benchley was subsidizing her. It was their love shack."

"That's what I figure," Dave said.

"What did she do before she went into the food service game?"

"She worked for Preferred Office Services at 479 Grant Avenue in Frisco," Dave said, flipping up another page on the notebook. "I got the secretary there to send me a record of her past assignments. Secretary is a cute young thing. Nice body. Don't think getting those records snuck to me didn't cost."

"Did you have to show the girl the tattoos you got in the Army?"

Dave winced, then smiled. "Not so loud," he said with mock seriousness. "Wendy thinks I'm a married man." With that, he looked over at his wife, made a whistling noise at her, and lifted his beer glass up. That was his signal for a free refill. I was not happy with the way Dave treated his wife, especially in public situations. He was not mean to her, not in public that is, just impolite. I imagined she resented it, but her feelings were kept to herself. Wendy was a strong woman and you would have to be to live with a man who had as many demons inside him as Dave.

"Fortunately," Dave said to me after getting Wendy's attention, "Ann Benchley pays well so I can afford to throw some green information lubricant around."

"What's she like?" I asked, then silently cursed myself for getting our conversation off track again.

A slight, thin-lipped smile creased Dave's well-worn, wrinkled face. His dark brown eyes twinkled in the subdued light around us. A devilish Nicholson-style grin formed on his lips. "I forgot you were a big movie buff. I should give you the inside gossipy stuff instead of boring you with all this grunt investigating work."

I blushed. "No. It's not that. I just..." Dave was smiling at me and shaking his head: the way he used to when he came over to my house as a kid and found me watching some movie like *Bride of Frankenstein* or *The Magnificent Seven* on a bright, warm Saturday afternoon instead of practicing my hookshot on the basketball court above the garage door. It was a look I well remembered.

"Oh, hell," I said. "Yes. I'm fascinated by people like that. So, what's the fat ugly bitch like?"

Dave smirked. "Well, you got one out of three right on her, pal." Then Wendy arrived with a fresh beer for her husband. Since Ann Benchley was not remotely fat or unpleasant to look at, I guessed the b-word fit her as far as he was concerned.

"Can I get you anything, Harvey?" Wendy asked me, after some small talk with her husband.

"No thanks, Wendy?" I said. I put my hand over my glass of 'non-alcoholic brew containing less than ½ of a percent alcohol content' and smiled. "Thanks anyway."

"Are you keeping an eye on him?" Wendy asked me.

"He won't leave my sight," I replied. This was an old routine we had. Dave enjoyed the notion that he was a whirling dervish who could careen out of control at any moment and Wendy and I played to his ego. Wendy was five years younger than her husband; a tall, svelte woman with a lovely mane of dark brunette hair, a pleasing oval face and only an appreciable bump on her nose shy of being objectively pretty. The bump came about when Dave punched her in the nose one night a year before when he came home from parts unknown soused to the gills. It was the only time he ever hit her.

He sobered up enough that night to say he was sorry several times before Wendy recovered enough to throw her unstable husband out the door. I was let in on the domestic crisis shortly afterward when Dave showed up at three in the morning at the single-wide trailer I shared with my wife, my then soon-to-be ex-wife. It was a week before Wendy agreed to meet him and accept his *mea culpa*. I gave Dave quite a lecture myself on avoiding ever physically hurting Wendy again. I think it took.

Wendy brushed her husband's hair into place and then went over to other tables to see if she could drum up some refills. Two white male college frat rats in buzzcuts from the table down asked for Budweisers. Wendy checked their identifications. They passed.

"How'd this Carolyn Mason die?" I asked, trying to get the discussion back on track.

Kenny Anderson, the Trailblazer guard, fouled out of the game. Dave duly noted the blow to his team's fortunes, then returned to me. "Didn't the papers say?" he asked.

"Foul play was the only information given," I said.

"She was strangled," Dave said, lowering his voice. "Strangled by someone using gloves. Her thorax was completely crushed."

"Holy shit," I said.

"That's one of the main reasons Ann hired me," Dave said. "I need to find Daddy Jack before the cops do. That little bit of information cost me money, too. Naturally, the detectives won't talk details but the attendant at the city morgue was less scrupulous."

"Do you think he did it?" I asked. Actually, it was not a question beyond Dave's realm of expertise. Six years earlier, after he started subsidizing his pay from the Family Support Division by working as a private eye, Jack Benchley had hired Dave to locate his only grandson. The grandson, Tyler Benchley, had been kidnapped from the Benchley Ranch late one night while his adoptive mother, Ann Benchley, was visiting her dad. The kidnapper was one Michael "Rusty" Williams, an ex-movie stuntman Benchley had befriended years earlier after a "gag" he did for a Benchley Western—featuring Steve McQueen—went wrong and Rusty wound up trampled on by a team of horses. A ransom note left behind in the child's bedroom demanded one million dollars. Jack Benchley and the fitful mother hired Dave based on a recommendation from a lawyer who had worked in the local District Attorney's office.

In a fairly short period, Dave had tracked down the father and the five-year old at a rundown motel in Tonopah, Nevada, something the authorities, including the FBI, couldn't pull off. The child was returned safely and Mr. Williams none the worse for wear outside of being maced in the face by Dave when he tried to make a getaway with the kid. "I would have slugged him," Dave explained later, "but I try not to swing on a gimp if I don't have to." "Rusty" is now doing ten to fifteen in prison. It was because of Dave's success—and Jack Benchley's money and endorsement— that Dave's 'McCreedy Investigations' had gained notoriety and clients. My friend then left the county payroll—which was diminishing with every local election—and started free-lancing. Jack Benchley had taken a personal shining to him as well. He had even offered Dave the position of Security Manager at the festival. My friend turned it down because he liked his independence. Dave had been invited several times to the large Benchley Ranch, situated a few miles out of town in the pine-crested foothills above Rogue Falls.

It was at one of Benchley's outdoor July 4th parties that Dave introduced the seventy-year old director to his sister-in-law, Rochelle. Wendy's sister became Benchley's wife a year later

"Do I think he did it?" Dave replied, mulling my query over. Before I got an answer, he stood up and called out to someone who had just come through the front entrance. I turned around to find my worst fear confirmed: it was Cletus, one of the Bomber Boys. I knew my fascination with the Benchley Case would have to wait.

The Bomber Boys were a couple of rednecks in their late fifties that Dave had befriended at a saloon that doubled as a betting parlor for horse racing out of Multnomah Downs up in Portland. Both men had served in the Vietnam War: Cletus as a noncom in Company C of an infantry battalion, Ferlin in different units of the Air/Sea Rescue wing of the Air Force. And besides having had active military service, Dave and the brothers shared a yen for all types of low-stakes gambling, particularly the video poker machines that the State of Oregon had so generously supplied in every drinking establishment in the state to lure the gaming-addicted to part with their hard-earned money. Since I did not have a VFW membership or an interest in gambling I was precluded whenever Cletus or Ferlin entered Dave's sphere.

"Stay around for a few minutes, will ya?" Dave asked me as he got up from his seat to join Cletus over at the row of bright, neon-blue machines. "I got a little job to throw your way here."

"What about my question?"

Dave shook his head. "Jack Benchley might be a dirty old lecher, but his hostility to pretty young ladies is zilch. The old bugger's been set up; take that to the bank. Can you loan me a ten?"

I did. For the fifteen minutes or so I nursed my brew while occasionally glancing backward to see how Dave was doing at the machines. The amount of coins he kept pumping into the poker machine he hovered over indicated to me it might be awhile before I saw my ten spot again.

Every now and then I watched Wendy watching Dave and Cletus. Her face bathed in the neon glow of beer logos, Wendy's pale complexion looked fetching, and forlorn. I knew that last week, just after he had gotten the Benchley assignment, Dave had gone by himself up to the Cow Hollow Casino on a Nawooka Indian Reservation near Crater Lake and blew a considerable portion of the advance from Ann Benchley. A couple of times, between filling orders, Wendy would glance over at me. I smiled back.

During a lull at the bar, I transferred myself up to a stool to keep Wendy company. I'm somewhat deaf in my left ear, thanks to another Sutter City Peace Officer's gun going off ncxt to said ear one night a few years ago when a stake-out to intercept a major crack dealer behind a seafood restaurant went ballistic. So it was hard to hear the question she posed to me over the music as I sat down. But without really hearing it, I knew what it was.

"No, I haven't heard from Jennifer. I did hear from her lawyer."

The reference was to my ex-wife. Legally, we were still married—a fact that caused consternation to me whenever I opened the mailbox and I saw a pile of bills—but she had sent me divorce papers from Powell, Arizona, and I had dutifully signed them. Our coupling had started to come apart when I lost my police career thanks to several black marks I had earned against myself with my drinking problem. I stopped drinking when I came to Oregon and got into an in-patient rehab clinic that Dave had used and recommended to me. He had lent me money to get in there after I lost my civil service insurance, a fact that opened my wallet whenever he asked. Jennifer and I had been stable until about a year ago when I was cut back from a full-time child-support investigator to part-time.

Dave had helped me by giving me more investigating assignments with his agency. I did foot work for law firms, surveillance gigs for insurance companies, process serving, and bodyguard stints for Jack Benchley's VIP friends when they came to Rogue Falls. But the extra work didn't help my marriage, Jennifer and I grew apart.

After tolerating my absences more than most mates, she went south on me with a rotund extrovert named Arthur Phelps, who had worked for the same accounting firm she did. The compatibility was there: they both liked Neil Diamond songs and quarterly spreadsheets.

I was slow to catch on to the loss of affections between us. I guess I was more irritable and uncaring than even the average guy gets when he feels himself slipping economically. About the time I realized she and this Artie character were a tandem, I blew my stack at Jennifer and said some things best left unsaid. The upshot was she left that night and, apart from her and Artie coming over one Hot August Night to get her belongings, I never saw her again.

That had been eight months ago. I still missed her, but I was still sober.

"You should consider yourself lucky," Wendy said, smoothing up the green apron she was wearing. She tossed her thick shoulder-length hair back, revealing the lines of a graceful, lightly-tanned neck as she shook her head.

"I'm lucky, you say?"

"Yes," she said, rubbing her shoulders by bending her

arms so her fingers could get to the area around her shoulder blades. "A single guy, still fairly young, ready to have a whole new series of life experiences..."

She waxed along on the joys of a singular existence, this woman with a two and a half year old daughter she loved deeper than all else, but hardly saw thanks to the dictates of a full-time job and nursing classes at the college and the local hospital.

"You can't tell me *you'd* enjoy being single," I said after Wendy finished trying to build my ego up. "You have a family: Dave and Jill. A family is what life is about, right?"

She laughed: a sardonic chuckle, not the soft, carefree laugh she usually emitted. "You right, Harvey. I've got it all," she said. "Keep reminding me of that whenever possible." She turned away to bring out some clean glasses from under the bar. I was about to come up with a new, more impersonal topic of discussion when the second member of the Bomber Boys, Ferlin (the one with crooked, brownish front teeth and poked, leathery skin on his face) appeared. He offered salutations to Wendy along with a request for a round of Bomber beers. The brothers always ordered that economy beverage. From what Dave had told me, they drank it by the case up in the underdeveloped acreage they called home. It was situated somewhere down a dirt road up in a unincorporated boondocks east of Rogue Falls known as Hazard Valley.

Wendy served up the beers, then looked at her watch, then over at her husband. "Dave went through his money now. He'll be headed over to the Veterans for a couple hours of pool now. How much did you give him, Harvey?"

"I spotted him a five," I replied. She shook her head. "Maybe it was a ten." I volunteered.

Wendy emitted her softer laugh. "Wendy Ann McCreedy and Harvey George Wells, the Professional Enablers. We ought to go on one of those sleazy daytime talk shows. Stop us before we enable again!"

Seeing that this line of subject matter was not bringing out the best in either of us, I changed the subject to a review I read in the Sunday paper concerning yet another biography of the late Diana, Princess of Wales, one sympathetic to old Prince Charlie. Normally I was not intrigued by the infidelities of the British Royals but I thought it might be of some interest to her. Wendy had been into such trivia at one time for her flights from the mundane. Months ago, I had even been boning up a bit on the Royals for her benefit. It turned out that Diana's death had put her totally off the British Royals. Instead she was reading a recently published "unauthorized" biography of Jack Benchley. Wendy had once been Jack Benchley's sister-in-law. This happened when Rochelle, her older sister (then named Rochelle Watkins) had been introduced to Benchley by Dave. The two hit it off and were married a year later, then divorced two years after that. I had read the book, although I did not give *Jack Benchley: Man and Legend* the same weight as I did Benchley's autobiography for truthfulness. I had read Benchley's own *Rise and Fall of Me* twice since it had come out two years previously, even managed to get it signed by the old boy himself when Dave got me a job bodyguarding Benchley during a book tour through Portland and Seattle. What the biography lacked in total accuracy it made up in salacious speculations about the film and theatrical director. I have to admit it was fun to recount the more adventurous and gossipy passages of *Man and Legend* with someone else.

"He was quite a womanizer in his time," Wendy said. "I guess he never wanted for female variety in his day: Natalie Wood, Audrey Hepburn, Jean Seberg, and that French actress he had an illegitimate child with back in the seventies. What was her name? Mimi Dupont?"

"Bebe," I said. "Bebe Dupont. I don't know if I would take all those presumed affairs as gospel. He did direct those actresses in movies, but—"

"But nothing," Wendy said. "He was a horn dog—between and during his four marriages. Didn't you see the photograph of him and Bebe Dupont that they had in that book? The two of them practically doing the wild thing vertically under that bridge in Paris? And don't forget, he hung out with John and Bobby Kennedy in the Fifties and Sixties. Case closed, Harv."

"I'm not saying that some things in that book aren't accurate," I said. "But that all happened in the Fifties and Sixties."

"*And* the Seventies," she remarked, holding one index finger down with another as she leaned over the bar. "*And* the Eighties. And even the late Nineties, when he was in over seventy." Three fingers were now held down by one. Wendy got closer to me, lowering her voice. "You know the stories about what goes on at this Shakespeare Festival over here—actresses who get parts in plays he directs for their off-stage talents."

This was a sensitive point for Wendy. Although Rochelle was thirty-some years younger than Jack Benchley, the dissolution of their two-year marriage was caused by the older mate having an affair with the aforementioned Carolyn Mason.

I've heard," I said.

"I mean, Rochelle left him three years ago," Wendy continued, "so I don't blame the old goat now. But he was a gold-plated philanderer."

I nodded

"Look Harvey, I love my sister, but she's a lousy actress. Jack cast her in plays anyway. And then he cheated on Rochelle with a twenty-eight year old, way younger than his own daughter! That's why that Carolyn Mason thing looks so bad for him: the tabloids figure he killed her because she was seeing a younger guy with more stamina. The papers say the police in San Francisco are only after one suspect—him."

I shook my head. "With all due respect to the *National Inquisitor*, a guy wouldn't kill a woman and hide the body in the trunk of his own car. Remember I was a cop for a couple years, Wendy. I think if Benchley killed her, which Dave doesn't believe by the way, he'd have at least dumped her somewhere remote. Leaving a corpse in your own car? That's less than brilliant."

"Maybe he never intended to kill her. Maybe it was just jealous rage, unpremeditated. He strangles her in some fit, then he panics. Maybe his brain was out of wack, senility coming on, something like that."

We went back and forth on the subject. After a few minutes, Dave came over to the bar. As predicted, he was headed to the VFW with Cletus and Ferlin. "Can you pick up Jill from the babysitter's house on your way home?"

Wendy nodded, kissed him on the cheek, and gave him some money from her purse for his pocket. He and I went back to the table we had shared.

Dave glanced over at the Bomber Boys, then back to me. "I got something for you," he said, reaching into his jacket pocket. "I'm going out of town tomorrow. Gonna check out that Forest of Arden Resort if Rosales can get me in there, then go back to San Francisco, then fly to L.A. to run down a couple leads." He looked around to be sure no one was taking note of our conversation, then handed me a folded-up sheet of fax paper he had pulled from his jacket.

"This is the list of Carolyn Mason's job assignments from that temporary agency," he said. "I need someone to gather background on the companies she worked for, especially the ones she worked for more than, say, a month or two."

"What are we fishing for?" I asked.

"Anything unusual. Ann Benchley doesn't even know where or when her old Jack met a nobody like this Mason chick, nor why her Dad accepted an invite to the Forest of Arden? The Benchleys and the Strunk family aren't exactly close, not after what happened to Ann and Sherwood Strunk's brother fifteen years back. Remember the Honeymoon Homicide?"

I nodded, remembering what was, until the O.J. Simpson murder trial, the most hyped celebrity trial in recent American history.

"I thought that went down as an accident," I said. "Ann Benchley was acquitted from what I remember. They were tussling with the gun because she was going to shoot herself because he was seeing some other woman, on their honeymoon, no less. The gun went off accidentally. Talbot Strunk got it and died. End of story."

Dave nodded. "From what Jack Benchley told me up at his ranch, the Strunks never bought that verdict. They see Ann Benchley as the Angel of Death, even if Ann's daughter is half Strunk by blood. Now, out of the blue, Jack goes down to Strunk's estate as a guest of this family. Ann says he did it because he wanted to bury the hatchet with the Strunk family and do this Shakespeare debate with some guy named Trevor Warbeck. You know about the Strunks, right?"

"Sure," I said. "Sherwood Strunk the Third is a media magnate. Father made big money all over the world in offshore oil deals. Talbot, the younger brother, is dead of course. The surviving son owns a couple satellite television networks, a radio network. Got his hooks in a couple big newspaper chains, too."

"Yeah, that rich asshole," Dave half-sneered to me. He then turned to the young guys behind us and bummed a light for a cigarette off one of them, then continued. "Anyway, Benchley and Warbeck were going to go at it for some television special. Warbeck's supposed to be an ex-movie actor or something. I'll bet you've heard of him."

"Yeah, he's an English guy. Good actor in his time; won an Oscar for Best Actor one year. He was good box-office from the mid-sixties to the early seventies. He worked with Jack Benchley on a couple pictures. Benchley fired him from one project. I can't imagine from what I've read that those two are the best of friends. A couple years after he and Jack Benchley parted ways Warbeck stopped getting good parts. He fell off the Hollywood map and dived into politics. Ran for the Senate down there a while back. I haven't heard much about him lately."

Smoke billowed out of Dave's nostrils. "This debate between Warbeck and Benchley was going to be in that Globe Auditorium the Strunks have on the compound. All the business and political VIP's who were invited were supposed to be in the audience. No newspaper people or cameras allowed in, except for Strunk's own outfit. The Vice-President was there—that's Vice-President of the United States I'm talking about. The FBI Director was there. There was Secret Service naturally, security a-go-go. Yet Jack and his girl-toy just leave the place and nobody sees them again until Carolyn Mason turns up dead down in San Francisco a couple days later in Sugar Daddy's Mustang."

"And Sugar Daddy is nowhere to be found. Doesn't look all that good for Jack Benchley, does it?"

Dave shook his head. "Ann Benchley says her old man was chomping at the bit to debate this Warbeck guy, something to do with a new take on William Shakespeare."

"Warbeck wrote this book that has a theory that some Baron or Earl was the secret author of William Shakespeare's plays," I said, recalling an article Jack Benchley wrote a month back in the *San Francisco Chronicle* that refuted Warbeck's findings. "I imagine that he wanted to defend Shakespeare's reputation. Benchley's high on Shakespeare being the author of his own plays. He devoted a whole chapter of his autobiography to a put-down of anybody who ever wrote or said otherwise."

I was now reading Shakespeare's plays in my spare

time—halfway through *Henry IV, Part One*—at the time this talk took place. It was a plunge into literary material I had avoided or skimmed over back in my high school and college days when plays and poetry seemed irrelevant to my life.

"He never talked about that Shakespeare stuff with me," Dave said. "We talked about war, team sports and hunting. I guess he knew I don't give a shit about that literary stuff."

"Yeah," I said. "You should read his autobiography though."

"What the hell for?" Dave said in a tense, abrupt manner. "I know the guy. He gave me a copy of the book, but hell, I don't need to read it. I know all his stories. He told me them himself out on his verandah. I don't have time for that stuff. Anyway, I know the guy."

"You don't have to get worked up about it," I said defensively. "You rescued the guy's grandchild. You went up to his ranch and drank together. O.K., so you don't need to read his book."

Dave nodded, realizing that his reading habits were no big deal with me. "Yeah, shit, I'm sorry Harvey. I just got things on my mind. Too many things." Dave's tone then softened, as it usually did when he needed something.

"The thing is, I need more on this Carolyn Mason. I got this list so late from that temp place I didn't have enough time to run down these businesses to see if anybody remembers her. Use that old computer of mine in the office to get what you can on-line. Make some follow-up calls on places I'm going to check out. Use the phone in my office. Do some research on these companies in the library, red flag any of them that have anything to do with Sherwood Strunk."

"You smell a set-up?" I asked.

Dave nodded. "It's a possibility. Possibilities aren't worth shit in a court of law, but it's a line that Ann Benchley wants checked out. You're better at that research stuff than I am. I'll leave messages on my office machine so check in over there every day. I might find something I need researched. You'll see a nice check out of this no matter which way it goes down. Believe me, this will be worth your while. Ann Benchley is a bitch, but she's a top dollar client."

I glanced down the sheet, reading the underlined names of companies and the dates Carolyn Mason had worked for them. "I can tell you one thing right now, according to this list, Carolyn Mason was assigned for three months back in '95 to the Institute for Factual History as a secretary. I read Benchley's article rebutting Warbeck's book about a month back. Your drinking buddy laid the wood to the Institute for Factual History. He said the outfit was responsible for a lot of crazy conspiracy books. And guess what outfit published Warbeck's book?"

"That good," Dave said. "You sure about that?"

"I can double-check, but I'm pretty sure the article said the Institute was based down in San Francisco. You ought to check the place out while you're down there."

"That's good for some money the next time Ann Benchley writes me a check. I know you can use the money what with Jennifer sticking you with all those bills after she split the state with that other guy. Plus the county cut your hours, I hear."

"Yeah," I said. "And if this next county tax levy doesn't pass, I might get cut to zero. Thanks, man." At that point, with Dave's track record, I'd have been happy to get my ten bucks back.

"Oh, one more thing, Harv. I want to repel off Pilot Rock this next weekend now that the snow has melted. My buddy Larry is still laid up from that skiing accident. I want you to go up the North Face with me this time."

My jaw dropped. "Excuse me, Dave. I thought for a moment there you suggested I go climbing up Pilot Rock?"

"Yeah," he said. "We'll go up the North Face so we won't have to sweat the amateur climbers. I got all the ropes and equipment. Just bring yourself."

I shook my head. "You've known me since I was a kid, right? Have I not mentioned to you, several times in fact, that I have acrophobia? I don't fly in airplanes. I don't look down from tall buildings or bridges. The only time I've ever flown was in a Huey Chopper when I was in the National Guard. And I was damn scared. And I'm sure as hell not going climbing up some butte that overlooks the whole frigging valley."

We went at this for a couple minutes. Dave finally halfway convinced me that the only way to cure myself of this phobia was to conquer it flat out. He also implied I had gone soft from being out of real police work too long and that I needed the challenge.

"If you're not comfortable with it as we go up the first fifty feet, we'll stop. But you'll conquer it, and thank me later. Trust me."

I agreed to the excursion, with a good deal of reluctance.

"I want you to call up some of these places where Mason worked down there. Pretend to be a grieving relative trying to get closure or some detective hired by the Mason family. You know, something unethical like that. Also, FYI, I got a line on a reporter for the Santa Rosa Republican. She's doing a book on Strunk and these Forest of Arden bigwig gigs he does every year." He glanced up at Wendy, who was mixing-up some Margarita in a blender down at the other end of the bar. "The reporter's name is Christy Mathewson. Sounds like a foxy thing over the phone. Don't mention that part to Wendy."

He patted me on the shoulder then said something to me I could not hear from the over-amplified music blaring on stage nearby. Wendy saw him going and, looking up from her service-industry duties, waved good-bye. She looked so sweet and vulnerable in that green apron that it made me wonder what reptilian part of Dave's brain allowed him to strike her so savagely.

I left shortly after Dave did, after leaving Wendy a good tip, and headed down Main Street to Highway 99 in my '89 Toyota Celica. My trailer was a few miles north of Rogue Falls in a low-rent, unincorporated town called Gasburg. I drove past the Shakespeare Plaza with its chic up-scale bistros and clothing stores that were situated in retrofitted 19th and early 20 Century brick buildings with beautiful hand-done facades and fancy cornices. The Plaza also had some nice bars: the kind with parquet floors free of peanut shells and piano players who play Gershwin and Cole Porter tunes and all the booze is expensive and imported.

It was just out of town that I remembered that my refrigerator could use some restocking. I pulled into a Safeway Market located just past the city limits. It was after ten in the evening and the shoppers were few. I entered through the automatic doors, selected a shopping cart with four operative wheels, and headed toward the bakery section for some bread. There, next to the cookie display, I ran into The Sheepman. He was an old homeless man I had seen a few times sitting on a bench in the Shakespeare Plaza or at the electric typewriter at the Rogue Falls Library, working on some project.

The man looked sixty, a lean and grubby sixty, with a wizened and sunburned face. He had sunken grey eyes, almost hidden away by a permanent squint and folds of wrinkled skin that sagged down to the deep, diagonal creases across his ruddy cheeks. His nose was red, red enough for gin blossoms to come in at any time. His outstanding facial feature was a puffy grey/brown beard that made him look scholarly despite his baggy brown corduroy slacks and his series of dirty crew-necked shirts that he wore under an open yellow and brown windbreaker that had the logo of the local public bus system on the back. Every time I had seen him he was wearing the same outfit.

The locals called him The Sheepman, perhaps because the beard made him look like an old agrarian hermit. *The Rogue Falls Daily News* happened to have done a feature story on homeless locals in one edition a week earlier. The old man told the reporter that he had once been a teacher in some town around here, and for some reason he left his position before he was eligible for a pension. That was all I knew about him, other than that his means of survival consisted of some rock-bottom insurance benefit and from gathering soda pop cans and plastic bottles for the deposit money.

Sheepman was in the bakery section at the front of the store, his shoulders stooped and his whole vertical posture looking like it could topple in a high wind. His gnarled hands were clutching a clear plastic box of oatmeal raisin cookies with a green mark-down sticker on the box. He turned at the sound of my shopping cart and said hello to me like I was an old friend.

I had never given him any money. I had seen other people slip him a dollar or two from their cars when he held up his 'Will Work For Food—God Bless You' cardboard sign at busy intersections around town. I had a lot of excuses for not giving him or any other homeless person a hand-out and I took full advantage of every one of them. Tonight I told myself that I might lose my job soon and I needed to save all the money I could. That won out over my guilt at Sheepman's 'hope-springs-eternal' attitude toward me. I simply said "hello" back.

"You're Dave McCreedy's friend, aren't you," he said in a

voice that sounded like he was well-educated.

"Yeah," I said, surprised.

"Say hello to him for me, will you?"

"Sure," I said, then passed him by. There but for the Grace of God was I, or would be I someday, but I just said 'sure' back like that acknowledgment would somehow satisfy either his need for money or my guilt at holding on to every bill in my pocket.

I gathered up my provisions—milk, bread, t.v. dinners, a few granny smith apples and bananas, a 12-pack of diet cola and a box of store-brand vanilla wafers that were cheaper than the national brand—and headed for the checkout. I was pushing the cart through the produce section when I happened to glance down toward the wine-and-beer section. Usually a glance to that area would evoke deep longings in me for the old days when I could drink real alcohol. This time those thoughts were headed off by the sight of a tall, lissome woman with big eyes (heavy on mascara), angel-fine blonde hair that caressed her narrow shoulders, and a look of preoccupation on her face. She was wearing a coat that came down to the middle of her thighs and showed off two tanned, well-toned legs. The woman was coming out of the glass door which separated the wine section from the beer displays. She came out carrying two wine bottles and put them in her half-filled shopping cart. After putting the wine in the cart, I noticed that she hugged her arms close to her. That seemed strange because she was wearing an oxblood leather coat, and that should have kept her torso warm.

I knew who she was: Rochelle Millman, Wendy's forty-something older sister. She was also Jack Benchley's ex-wife, now married (on a quick rebound) to Leroy Millman, a successful rancher, land developer and local big-fish-in-a-small-pond. They lived on a big cattle ranch in Hazard Valley, the last portion of flatland before the foothills of the Cascades rose up about twenty miles east of Rogue Falls. Wendy had mentioned a couple times in the last couple weeks how jealous she was of Rochelle because she was going by herself to The Cape Blanco Holistic Retreat and Spa, a posh resort on the Oregon Coast. It was Saturday night, so Rochelle should have already been at the resort.

But she was about 120 miles from the coast.

Chapter Two

Rochelle Millman and I were acquainted via her visits to see Wendy at O'Leary's Bar and the apartment Wendy shared with Dave. But Rochelle hadn't seen me watching her. She quickly grabbed a couple six-packs of beer, put them in the hamper with the wine, and moved briskly out of my line of sight toward the check out area. As she moved, I got a quick peek at the upper portions of her legs thanks to the rather long stride she took and the looseness of the leather belt around her waist. She must have been wearing a very short skirt because from my angle was all bare-legged save for a flash of red several inches above her kneecap. She was sporting a bright red, lacy garter belt; not exactly standard wear for a trip to the supermarket.

My need for food was suddenly outweighed by my sordid curiosity. I abandoned my shopping cart.

After going through the only open check out stand, Rochelle took her grocery bag out to a black Lexus EX parked just beyond the handicapped slots. A teenaged bag boy carried another sack for her. The kid gave her a big smile and a loud thank you, his eyes resting on a place below her face. She returned the teenager's smile, shook her head, and, as he started to walk away, whistled at him. The kid turned around to look at the customer. In a flash, she undid the belt about her waist, threw open her coat, and gave the young man the benefit of a quick flash. From my angle of observation—crouched down behind a pillar next to a pallet display of dog food—I couldn't see her in full display, but I saw enough to tell that the color of her lacy negligee matched the garter.

"Wow," said a hoarse voice behind me. I turned around to see The Sheepman standing above me. He had the oatmeal cookies under one arm and a bottle of fortified wine half-covered in a paper bag. He must have gotten the beverage from a convenience store and hid it away somewhere when he went in to buy the cookies. The Sheepman had seen the same thing I had.

"She gave him pleasure," he said. "Spinoza would say that young man has gone from a lesser state of perfection to a greater state. Joy consists in this."

Sheepman had read his Spinoza. I guess he did more in the local library than just type. He was one up on me. I wished I had a better angle to see more of the pleasure. Despite our shared experience, I still didn't give the old guy any money.

The Lexus pulled out onto the street. I jumped into my refinanced Toyota and took off after her, accelerating until I was just within sight of the back taillights on the Lexus. This was part and parcel of my line of work: following a deadbeat parent to see if he or she were really working only one job or if they were moonlighting at a second job, or had a business on the side where their income went unreported, thus cheating the Rogue County Family Support System. I had also chased and tagged speeders as a patrolman in Sutter City down in California. Tailing someone required a bit more finesse, but it was a good deal more exciting than just sitting in a car by the side of a county road with a radar gun glued to your chin.

She drove right through Gasburg, past the mobile home park I lived in, and headed up the local metropolis, Middleburg, population approximately 40,000. When she reached the city limit sign, she took the next available right turn, drove past the Wal-Mart on the recently completed winding, well-lit four-lane corridor that connected the state highway to the Interstate, and pulled in at the Four Star Hotel and Convention Center. The parking lot was crowded with vehicles because the hotel had 200 plus units and adjoined a Country/Western line-dance hang-out called Bob's Two-Step Lounge. She parked near the hotel entrance, but did not go in the building through the lobby. She walked toward a side entrance, carrying two brown bags of alcoholic beverages up in her arms and walking briskly in her red low-heel pumps. I followed from a short distance, staying roughly parallel to her. I dodged in and around the cars, trucks and vans, trying to keep up with my strutting target.

When she got to the side entrance, I ducked behind a mini-van then looked about to make sure no one was watching me. She paused for a moment to glance at the headlines in a newspaper rack, then laid down her second bag of groceries and threw open the single wide glass door. She held the door open with her foot, picked up the second bag—the bottles making a rattling noise as they jostled inside the bag—then she went inside. I got to the door myself just a couple seconds after it closed.

I peered into the door from one side, watching Rochelle's willowy form traveling down the thin, commercial-grade blue and green carpeting in the hotel hallway. There were doors every few feet on both sides of the hall. She turned a corner, and that's when I opened the door and jogged down the hotel wing. A bald headed man in a robe carrying an ice bucket opened a door and stepped in front of me. I put on the breaks, smiled at him, and changed my gait to a brisk walk. The man gave me a puzzled look, then went in the opposite direction.

When I got to the corner where I had last seen Rochelle I put on the breaks again. She was only a few feet away from me standing diagonally from the corner I had stopped at. Her back was to me, one bag was on the carpet, and she was swiping a card to open the door. I heard the sound of a basketball game as Room 206 opened.

"Could you help me with the bags sweetie?" Rochelle said in a soft tone I had never heard her use.

"Sure, babe. I just got out of the shower. You wanted me clean this time out, right?"

The latter voice belonged to Dave. He had overshot the VFW Hall and somehow lost the Bomber Boys along the way. Until that moment I never knew that Dave had actually cheated on Wendy with anybody, much less the sister she grew up with.

I decided to go out via the front of the hotel—it would look less like I was skulking around—and I followed the aqua-green carpeting out to the triangular shaped lobby. An older couple—the man wearing a ponytail, the woman with frizzy hair like a middle-aged Janis Joplin—walked by me. Their first names were 'Coyote' and 'Dawn' according to the sticky name tags they wore on their fronts. Above the felt-marker names were the words 'Psychic Fair.' I passed a display board next to the open public phone booths that told me the Shasta Psychic Convention would be taking place in the Shasta Room, starting at ten tomorrow morning. There was a list of speakers. I pretended to be interested in the list for a moment so I would seem less conspicuous coming out into the lobby. It also gave me a chance to get over the shock of what I had just discovered.

There was a jungle-thick display of ferns in the center of the lobby area. As I passed by the tall, healthy green flora, I was brought to a stop by a man I spotted up at the front desk. He was a tall, paunchy man with a reddish-tanned face and severe creases under his eyes and outlining his cheeks. If his nose had been a bit longer he could have passed as a cross between a human and a basset hound. The heavy bags under his eyes brought out that description. He looked around sixty and sported a waxed mustache of salt and pepper hair. His head was covered by a white Stetson, his pear-shaped body attired in a charcoal grey sports jacket and matching slacks. He wore cowboy boots; they looked expensive and spotless. He was standing in profile to me, waiting at the front desk, drumming his thick fingers on the shiny wood counter top. His prosperous-looking belly hung over a gilt-edged, shiny silver belt buckle that sported the engraving of a big letter M with a smaller outline of a branding iron cutting diagonally through it. I knew the guy.

He was Leroy Millman: the December half of the May-December marriage between himself and Rochelle Millman.

"Hey, there, fella'," he said jovially to me after glancing in my direction. We had only met once or twice at O'Leary's. Millman owned the 600-acre Double M Angus Ranch up in Hazard Valley. The locally famous geologic landmark, Pilot Rock, bordered his property.

We faced each other as two mere acquaintances. I might have even turned my head away before he saw me were it not for the circumstances of what was going on in Room 206.

I walked up and said hello to him.

"Hey, you're that fella' what's living off us taxpayers, ain't ya." He had the Texas drawl of his native state and a way of chuckling after he said something he thought was funny that was grating to my nerves.

"That's me, Mr. Millman," I said with a forced smile.

There was a chubby-faced, red-haired woman in a crisp blue blazer working the front desk. She was smiling at Millman, trying to keep him satisfied with her non-vocal customer service skills while she talked on the phone to someone trying to confirm a reservation.

"You hot on the trail of some runaway daddy? You getting some overtime outta this, boy?" The good old boy *par excellence* popped my right shoulder with his open hand. I would have liked to have popped him back, but I took it as a friendly gesture and muzzled my reflexes. "Somebody in this hotel trying to run away from Big Brother, are they?" A little crease of a yellow-toothed smiled flared on his face. He smelled of a musky man's-kind-of-man cologne that his liberal use of made breathing near him difficult.

I started some impromptu alibi about visiting friends up from California, but before I could get into some phony details the front desk person was off the phone and asking Millman what she could do for him.

"My wife's checked into this place somewhere," he said in a friendly voice. "I'm Leroy Millman. Could you tell me what room she's in?" As he leaned his elbows on the desk, I caught sight of a bulge under his left armpit.

He had a gun.

While the clerk turned and started pecking away on her computer keyboard, Millman turned back toward me. I got another smile, and, as if he had noted my interest, opened his coat up on his left. He was carrying a Taurus .44 revolver nestled in a suede belt holster.

"American-made," he said proudly, patting the stock. "You still carry that little Bolivian derringer?"

"My .38? It's a Rossi. Very accurate weapon. The company manufactures out of Brazil, I believe."

"Shouldn't even let that foreign-made stuff in this country," he said. "That what comes from all that free-trade crap." He turned to the clerk. "You got a fix on my wife there, little lady?"

"She in Room 206, sir."

"And just where might 206 be?"

The clerk gave him directions. Millman and I parted from each other with a brief exchange, and then, as soon as he was out of sight, I asked for a house phone. The clerk directed me to a white phone at the far end of the desk. I grabbed the receiver and punched up 206. It rang a couple times, and then Dave answered.

"Get the hell out of there," I said in an edgy whisper. "Leroy is coming down the corridor right now. If there's a back terrace or something, use it fast."

There was a scant acknowledgment from the other end of the line, just a quick "oh." The line disconnected.

I sat down on the padded bench next to the display of ferns. I pretended to read a section out of a discarded *USA Today* all the while waiting to hear the echo of a gunshot or two coming from the north wing.

Time passed.

No gunshots. No loud shouting. No screams. Just a little piano Muzak tinkling from a speaker on the ceiling right above me.

Then, after about five minutes, came Dave. He emerged into the lobby from the south wing entry. He was stuffing his shirt into his pants, a look of apprehension on his face as he came out of the corridor. Seeing the lobby was clear, save for myself, that apprehensiveness changed quickly to a Nicholsonesque smirk of confidence. He gave me a quick thumbs-up, then went right by me knowing that I would pick up and follow.

A couple minutes later we were driving back to Rogue Falls via Interstate Five. Dave wanted to be dropped off at the VFW. The Bomber Boys were going to be coming back for him in about ninety minutes, anyway, he told me.

"Rochelle wasn't even in the room when you called. She went to get some ice and Seven-Up down the hall. She left the door ajar. I heard her come back. Boy was that bitch surprised to see old Leroy in the room instead of me." He laughed in that curious cackle Dave had, as if the unexpected arrival of Leroy upon his wife in a local hotel room was an event quite impersonal to him.

"Rochelle wanted an all-nighter, of course," he casually explained to me. "But I have Bonnie in town right now. Want to hear something funny? Leroy Millman hired me for a surveillance job a week ago. He wanted to find out if his wife was cheating on him." He told me how deftly he had scooped up his clothes, opened and slipped through the sliding glass door, jumped into his underpants, and bounded over the railing of the first floor terrace.

I said nothing.

"Thanks, again," Dave said. "That cowboy was probably packing a horse pistol. Rochelle told me once he had a concealed weapons permit."

"You can believe that," I said. I spoke again after a pause. "Dave, can I ask you something?"

"No sermons, Harvey."

"No sermons, then. Your private life is your private life." I wanted to say a whole lot more, but what was the point? Dave was Dave. I jacked up the radio a little bit on a sports call-in show. The rest of our talk was about the upcoming baseball season and how well Dave's favorite team, the Oakland Athletics, were going to do in the coming season.

"Do you know this guy Sheepman?" I asked Dave as we came within a block or two of the VFW.

"Sheepman?" Dave said. "Oh, yeah, I might have dropped him a buck or two when I've been flushed. How'd you know about that?"

"I just saw the guy a while ago. He told me to tell you hello."

"Oh," Dave said. "Well, he's a nice guy—for a bum."

I dropped Dave off at the VFW and reiterated that I'd work on the Carolyn Mason personnel background checks. Dave knew he didn't have to tell me not to mention tonight's little real-life farce to Wendy. To have asked would have meant we weren't friends.

"See you Tuesday or Wednesday night, Harvey. I should be back around eight in the evening. Be at O'Leary's about then. We'll compare notes. And don't forget to keep your Saturday open. We're going to climb Pilot Rock together. It'll make you feel one with nature, friend. Trust me."

"O'Leary's then," I said. "And then we climb Pilot Rock next weekend? You promise this will cure me of my fear?"

"Imagine oral sex with Mother Nature. That's what it will be like."

"Whatever," I said, not relishing the 'conquest' of my acrophobia. Something else bothered me, too.

"Dave, be careful down there. Be very fucking careful."

"Always," Dave said with a lopsided smirk, and walked away from me, his shoes making crunching noises on the rock-filled driveway in front of the hall.

It was the last time I would see Dave alive.

I headed back to the Gasburg Trailer Park and home. Gasburg was only a few miles down the highway from Rogue Falls, but it was a completely different environment. Like going from suburban California to rural Tennessee. A direct illustration of this could be found in the large Confederate Flag that flew above the carport of the double wide trailer space next to my own space, which was single-wide. There were a lot of good ol' boys and gals in Gasburg: Leroy Millman-types without the big ranch, and for most of them the college and theater attractions offered down the road in Rogue Falls might as well have been a thousand miles away.

The Stars and Bars from the American Civil War flying over Space #34 were historically appropriate. The town had been founded in 1858 by Jedidiah Horatio Gasburg, a fellow who found gold in the nearby Rouge River, shot more than a few Native-Americans, and later built a flour mill and a saloon when the rest of the pioneers started streaming in. He went back East in 1861, served as a Colonel in the Army of Northern Virginia, and came back shy of one leg after getting it blown off during General Grant's siege of Petersburg, Virginia, in 1864. After the war ended, he returned to Oregon. He shot some more Native-Americans, got elected to the State Legislature up in Salem, passed laws against Chinese emigration, then died.

I pulled into my own carport next to my mobile home. The roof leaked and the aluminum side panels that were supposed to cover the foundation had been plundered by the last occupants of the place. I was renting the place from a nice old lady who looked familiar to a *Sweet Charity*-era Shirley MacLaine, only this lady was named Alma Ritts and she was not an actress/dancer or a New Age Icon but one half of a property management team at The Wagon Wheel Trailer Park. The husband—Bob, jack-of-all-trades—was the other half. Neither of the Ritts were shy about espousing their hatred of all forms of government within the United States: local, state, federal as well as the United Nations. According to Mr. and Mrs. Ritts, the current Secretary-General of that transnational body was in league with Japanese bankers, Arab sheiks and our own Federal Reserve to create a world government that would outlaw Christianity and private gun ownership. I was a bit skeptical about several government agencies myself, but equally skeptical of Mrs. Ritts and her husband's take on Things To Come.

The porch light over my narrow door had burned out a week earlier and I had to fumble with the keys and curse myself for forgetting to buy light bulbs again.

I checked my phone messages once I got the rusty lock on the paper-thin wood door open. There was a message from some lady who did not identify herself, giving me an 800 number to call her back. A credit card company, tightening the noose on me. I vowed to give them Jennifer's post office box in Arizona. She had been the shopper in the family.

The trailer I was renting had four basic components: a single bedroom big enough for a queen-sized bed if you could forego a dresser for the sleeping chamber; a bathroom featuring a shower just the right size to properly wash a chimpanzee; a kitchen/breakfast nook area with Formica so old I should probably tear it all out and send a big sample to the Smithsonian Institution, and a living room with the requisite pulp board ready-to-assemble entertainment center that held the 13-inch television set and stereo rack system Jennifer had taken the 25-inch set with her and her new guy. I kept the bedroom television set and VCR and whatever tapes and books she left behind after that faithful Saturday. In the living room, you could sit either on the floral-patterned love seat or the dark blue slightly-stained and lopsided imitation leather sofa and set your T.V. dinner or Hamburger Helper meal on the marble-topped cherry wood coffee table I had inherited from my late Aunt. The table Jennifer had really liked and somehow summoned up the ethical stamina not to take.

There were still empty places on the walls from where Jennifer's family pictures had stood. Only my parent's pictures and my police academy graduation picture from 1986 remained. Jennifer and I had not had any kids because she couldn't have any, and wasn't into jumping all the hoops to adopt a healthy child. To be honest, it was one of the reasons I was more than happy to marry her. I still missed her, but it wasn't the all-aching loss I had felt a few months previously.

When Jennifer and I were together the trailer had seemed cramped. Now it seemed like I was the only passenger in a submarine whose entire crew had gone AWOL just after reaching port.

I didn't have to jump out of bed for work the next day, so I watched some of the David Letterman show and did some bench presses and arm curls with my weight set. I had moved the equipment into the house from the carport after my wife had left. Despite this, I was using the barbell and weights very sporadically. A good deal of the self-motivation I had relied on to get me through the police academy and keep me alive and functioning on the street had left with Jennifer. It was only in the last month that I could tap some inner reserve to make myself care enough about myself and my future to stay in shape.

After twenty minutes of this, I glanced over the morning paper with my feet propped up on the coffee table. Then I went to bed and tackled some more of Sir John Falstaff and Prince Hal and Hotspur until I couldn't keep my eyes open. Then I drifted off, the lamp next to the bed still on. I was awakened a couple of hours later by the phone. It was Dave, drunk, wanting to know if I would drop by his office when he was on the case in California and check his fax and his mail. I agreed, making no protest to being woke up over a redundant request. In the background I heard Jill, his daughter, crying, and Wendy saying something unintelligible to me due to the crying.

"Everything okay, chief?" I asked.

"Sure, Harv. See you in a few, man." His speech was slurred. He must have pounded down a few beers at the VFW to make up for what he didn't get in the hotel room. We said good-bye, then he hung-up. I went back to bed, unaware that I had spoken directly to Dave for the last time.

Chapter Three

My friend David Francis McCreedy was found dead beside an old log on the bank of Cramner Creek, a tributary of the Klamath River. Dave's last stop was a couple miles west of Interstate Five, and just a couple miles north of the California-Oregon border (and a dozen miles south of the first Rouge Falls turnoff) in a practically empty old lumber town called Bowman. His right temple had been drilled, the temporal bone on the other side of his skull blown apart, apparently by a slug fired point blank. He could have used his .38 Colt Detective Special or maybe his back-up gun, a nine millimeter Golan automatic.

Or maybe it wasn't a suicide at all.

It was "an apparent suicide," or so Rouge Falls Detective Russ White said. I got the news on Dave via a call the evening of April Fourth from White, who had been a friend of Dave's and an acquaintance of mine. It was around eight-thirty, and I was at home in my trailer having just turned my stereo on, collapsing into a chair and starting in on the latest copy of *Baseball Weekly*. About an hour earlier I had played my weekly three games of pool with Bob Ritts, one-half of the Ritts property management team at the Wagon Wheel Trailer Park. We played Eight-Ball. Bob beat me two games to one.

While I read, I had the radio on. Some local public radio station was playing some selections of music by the film composer Bernard Herrmann, the composer who did most of Alfred Hitchcock's classic films of the 1950-60's. Somehow the eerie tone of the music from *Psycho* and *Vertigo* matched well with the articles I was reading on the rapid decline of Major League Baseball's popularity against other professional sports leagues in the United States and the slim chances that my team, the San Francisco Giants, had in capturing a playoff spot when October rolled around.

The radio station interrupted their Herrmann fest for a pitch to get listeners to pony up money "to keep public radio a vital part of Southern Oregon," or something to that effect. By then I was in the kitchen, doing bench presses with the weight set. I turned off the public radio pitch and put on an oldies rock and roll station. Chrissie Hynde of the Pretenders was singing *Back On the Chain Gang* when the phone rang.

Detective White gave me some details that the deputy sheriffs had given him. Dave had been found in a small ravine adjoining the creek. His Harley-Davidson V-Twin motorcycle was parked above him on the shoulder of the road that wound along the stream. He apparently took the bullet then fell head first over an old log. There were powder marks on his temple and his hand tested positive for traces of gun powder. Nothing suspicious, no other footprints in the area. No one heard any shots but the nearest house was over a mile away and, since Bowman Lumber had shut its doors two years ago, there wasn't a lot of traffic in Bowman proper, much less on the old creek road.

"Any marks on the body?" I asked Russ. "Contusions to the face?"

"There was a good-sized abrasion on his upper right cheek," Russ told me. "It was consistent with the kind of fall he would have taken after the impact of the bullet. The body is headed up to Middleburg. Dave may be at the county morgue already. The Crime Scene techs are going over the place tonight. I was up there myself for about an hour. Unofficially at this point, it looks like your friend committed suicide. I'm sorry, Harvey."

I did not believe Dave killed himself. I told Russ myself over the phone. Russ discounted my hasty conclusions as being biased by friendship.

"The guy had a drinking problem and a gambling problem, Harvey," Russ said. "He was in debt. He had a shitty home life. His wife did the 911 route on him a couple times because he was beating on her. Add that to his temper and his wild side. And the fact that he just up and left his first wife and kids, plus a great civil service job in California... Jeez, I mean the guy's a good candidate for, you know, winding up like he did."

"You blaming this on his ditching his first wife?" I said. "That's a reach, Russ. Dave was a survivor in my book, and a long way from going to the wall."

"Dave told me his Dad committed suicide," White said.

"Yeah, Dave's dad killed himself. But Dave's dad was stressed-out and wouldn't see a doctor. He smoked and drank and even got into dope. He was a cop in San Jose and when the booze and dope and all wouldn't kill him fast enough, he took a shotgun and put it in his mouth. But Dave wouldn't have taken that way out. He was stronger than his dad. My dad always told me Dave was different from his old man, and they worked on the police force together."

I went on, knowing it was futile. Of course, the evidence said otherwise and evidence said it all in an investigation like this. Besides, I was just a child support investigator working under contract with the D.A.'s office. I was not a full blown detective like Russ White but an ex-patrolman who had left fifteen years shy of a retirement party.

According to Russ, there were apparently no witnesses in Bowman who saw Dave, much less anyone else in that area at the right time the County Medical Examiner determined for the death—between five-thirty and seven in the evening. A deputy sheriff had responded to an anonymous phone-call about a gunshot in the area. The deputy was driving by the creek around seven thirty and saw the motorcycle parked just off the road. On his way back down the dead-end road, he stopped to investigate, and shined a flashlight down on Dave's body.

Officially, the case was still open but, from Russ' information, I figured it would go down officially as a suicide. Unsolved murders then to be a big blot on a rural county law enforcement team's record. To the People That Mattered, Dave McCreedy was a nobody who had a record of alcohol-related scrapes with the cops in Rogue County. He had also been a cop, first an M.P. in the Army, then he joined the San Jose Police Department. After seven years on the force he was on his way to becoming a Detective Sergeant. But one day he had up and quit all that, for reasons even I wasn't totally clear about, and ran off with Wendy. He left a wife and two kids behind. He had told me he had spent an afternoon with the kids, David and Carrie, on his way back from investigating the Benchley Case. Yes, he had up and left a good job and a stable home life. But that just made Dave a person given to excess. He saw Wendy and he fell for her. And the other life wasn't enough for him. He was tired of the traffic in the Bay Area and the hassles of his job, and tired of his first wife. So he changed his life, to his economic and domestic detriment.

"Why did you do it?" I asked Dave once, referring to his decision to leave it all behind.

"I was bored," he said, and let it go at that.

Bored. Was he bored again and decided to go out totally? No, not Dave. He'd leave and go elsewhere but he wouldn't kill himself. He had been through too much to die young in any way but an accident—or a disease—or a homicide.

The day Dave was found dead had been a typical one for me. I spent the morning trying to track down a couple deadbeat dads at their last known addresses (without luck), then worked on a case spying (i.e., gathering evidence) on a father of three who worked on the books at a feed store who was trying to get off paying child support on a off-the-books job he had planting trees for a landscape company on his days-off. Unbeknownst to my victim, I took some zoom lens photographs of him planting trees in front of a new apartment complex going up on the east side of Rogue Falls. I took the shots hiding in some bushes across the street. My evidence gathered, I stopped by the Family Support Office to add the pictures to the case file one of the women in the office was laying out on him, then, after some paperwork duties, and faced with my shortened hours, I left for the day. Around two thirty I walked the few blocks from the Family Support/Victim Witness office to the main library in Middleburg. The library was in the center of a park across from the Post Office. While the Federal building was large and post-modern in look, the library was a relic from eighty years previous, a small Greco-Roman style two-story building with a affair with a flight of steps leading to the main entrance. It was built in 1912 from an endowment from Mr. United States Steel himself, Andrew Carnegie, who donated his tax-free millions to such public-spirited endeavors. Near my destination, a large group of people, mostly gray haired, were gathered around a gazebo. They sat on folding chairs and chaise loungers or on picnic blankets on the lawn, watching a dozen-piece Dixieland jazz band. A few in the audience looked very old, but very trim and fit. Alas, from the look of the fat legs and pear-shaped bodies on most of the senior citizens, they would have been better off going to the park for brisk forty minute walks or at least tai chi classes.

Whereas Rogue Falls was the area for the culture vultures, Middleford was increasingly becoming a mecca for retirees. Twenty years ago, so Wendy told me, it was a middle class town for young families and affordable housing. Now, with the aging of the population and the large number of well heeled retirees headed to Oregon from the suburbs of San Francisco and Los Angeles, southern Oregon had become like much of Florida and Arizona: one of "God's Waiting Rooms" as Wendy put it to me. I was certain I would never be able to afford to retire around here, but at least the retirees were beyond the crime-perp stage and they certainly helped the service and medical side of the local economy.

I used one of the personal computers in the library's main floor to get what information I could gleam for Dave on the Institute for Factual History, the group that published *Shadow on the Crow* by Jack Benchley's rival, Trevor Warbeck.

I studied their website and found it dismaying. This was an odd little group. At first glance it was just your average political think tank that produced books on economic and political affairs. But it was what they stood for that set them apart. Their stated goals for the United States in the Twenty-first Century seemed neither Republican nor Democratic nor Libertarian or Green-Party in tone. More elitist than any of them, and very reactionary. No political party I was aware of wanted to limit the voting franchise only to families who paid the highest three-percent of taxes in the nation in the preceding year before the election, but the Institute for Factual History did. No political organization I knew of wanted United States Senators elected to office for life, but the IFH did. Nor did any political party I know of want "a North American Monarchy established, with a King or Queen to be given limited but real authority to call for elections every five years and form a government of ministers based on limited-franchise results of state elections for national representatives."

But the IFH did.

A monarchy? Redrawing the Constitution? Politicians elected for a lifetime? Disenfranchised voters in the tens of millions? Were these idealistic loons from outer space?

I gathered from some of the titles of the books—*The Articles of Confederation: A Reassessment* by some guy named Wayne Schroeder and another by a woman named Kelly W. Wong entitled *Wrong Turn: Why the 1787 Constitution Has Failed America*—that this group had intellectual mouthpieces for their weird views. And there was Sherwood Strunk, the owner of the Strunk Hotel where Jack Benchley was last seen, listed as its Chief Executive Sponsor. Trevor Warbeck was listed just below the Chief as "an award-winning stage, screen and television actor, now the editor and president of IFH." The lionizing continued with "...Mr. Warbeck is one of the most articulate spokesman for returning the United States to a more traditional government in the style of our British political forebears. His latest book, *Shadow on the Crow*, has been eagerly awaited by millions as the definitive book on the real identity of the plays falsely attributed to the rustic and barely literate actor William Shakespeare."

I could see where Jack Benchley and Trevor Warbeck would have had much to debate about. I wondered what prompted him to leave the Strunk Compound so abruptly right before their encounter.

I took a few minutes off and went to the book stacks, paying particular notice to the 790-799 section of books in the Dewey Decimal System. You could find books on motion pictures there, and I was on the look-out for anything new.

A pretty brunette library volunteer named Kimba (it said so on her name plate) came through with a rolling cart and returned a few books to the area while I thumbed through a book by a film critic that drew comparisons and contrasts between the Westerns of Sergio Leone, Anthony Mann and John Ford. One of the books she returned to the shelf was one I had never read. *Jack Benchley: Hollywood's Last Maverick,* was an unauthorized biography written by Jim Sutton, a writer in the proud tradition of the tell-all bios that Kitty Kelley and other "dirt-diggers" wrote on celebrities. I set the other book down and opened the unauthorized biography to the middle where the pictures were. Most all of the photos I had seen before. They were in Jack Benchley's autobiography, *The Rise and Fall of Me*, a savvy and humorous memoir of his growing up as the son of the film star Walter Benchley, his harrowing experiences flying over Japan in wartime and the first twenty five years of his career as a writer and director on the New York stage and a successful career (for the most part) in Hollywood. A second volume, covering his last films and his two decades of work at the Northwest Shakespeare Festival, had yet to be published.

The man himself had given me a hardcover first edition of his book two years ago after I had accompanied him up to Portland and Seattle for book signings and television interviews in the two major media markets of the Pacific Northwest. I provided security for the older man when he made those public appearances. Apart from sharing a quick room service dinner with him in his suite at the Hilton in Seattle, his schedule had left me very little time to me to talk to him. What time I did spend with him, and seeing how he treated reporters and fans, convinced me the old guy was down-to-earth and more good-natured about being intruded upon by strangers than I could ever be. The reason for my bodyguard duties were due to anonymous letters and e-mail death threats against him by a person or persons claiming to be representing a white supremacist group. Their threats on Mr. Benchley were "justified," the letters said, because of all the African-American and Asian actors Benchley had hired that year for the Festival's productions of *King Lear* and *Hamlet*. Unlike the disaster of San Francisco, Dave had convinced him that he needed protection for the tour.

The back of the Sutton book had a brief chronology of Benchley's professional life: from his birth in Los Angeles in 1925, growing up in Hollywood with father Walter Benchley a major star for MGM, Warner Bros. and other studios, to his military service in the Second World War as an aerial-gunner on a B-29 Superfortress, to his return to Hollywood in 1947 and his early success as a young screenwriter at three major studios. By the age of thirty he had become a writer/director of such films as *City of Night* with Robert Mitchum and Gloria Graham (1955), *Sir Francis Drake* (1956) with Burt Lancaster, et al, to a string of major films starring James Mason, Audrey Hepburn, Kirk Douglas, Eva Marie Saint, Henry Fonda and Marlon Brando. He actually fired the great Brando from 1960's *Macbeth* for "his non-professional attitude" after three weeks to the consternation of the Paramount Pictures brass. The film went on to be a modest success with a young relative unknown named Sean Connery in the title role. A director who tried hard to mix box-office friendly action "popcorn" films with the occasional "literary" effort Benchley won an Oscar as Best Director for his adaptation of *Middlemarch* (with Hepburn, Mason and Ralph Richardson) and was nominated for, and received other awards at every film festival from Berlin to San Francisco.

As for his social life. Natalie Wood was a Benchley "good friend" after her divorce from Robert Wagner. Audrey Hepburn and Jean Seberg were also "good friends." He had (so far) four marriages, three of them to lesser-known actresses, the last being the already mentioned Rochelle Millman. Benchley worked with Steve McQueen in two films—*The Yuma Kid* in 1961 with Tina Louise as the love interest and 1968's *The Smoking Gun*—and Trevor Warbeck in *The House of the Dead*, a 1969 adaptation of Fyodor Dostoyevsky's memoir about life in a Czarist-era gulag, Trevor Warbeck later became the second major star to be fired during shooting for a Benchley film; this time it was a film version of the Maxwell Anderson play, *Elizabeth and Essex* in 1972. Both Warbeck and Benchley refused to discuss the reasons for their rift on the shoot then and still were publically silent thirty years later.

I drove back to Rogue Falls to avail myself of Dave's telephone so I could make some long-distance calls on former employers and friends of Carolyn Mason.

McCreedy Investigations was located in an old three story brick edifice known as the McLoughlin Building. The place was unfashionably located near the Southern Pacific Railroad tracks and had stood there since 1908. I knew the exact year because of the bronze plaque attached to the building by the Rogue County Historical Society. That plaque was the classiest thing about the building. Dave's small office was on the second floor, above a furniture store that was hurting for clientele. (Since I had been in town business had changed hands three times in that space. I had even taken some refresher karate classes at 'Han's Martial Arts Academy' before Mr. Han's school folded and the space became the current 'Midsummer Night's Dream Bed and Futon Shop'). The building was the centerpiece of what was called the Railroad District because it was near the dilapidated depot that had seen its last passenger sometime in the 1950's.

Dave's office was one of three tenants that occupied the small offices on the upstairs floor. There were two other offices, both vacant. The other two were a Comic Book/Sports Card store that, according to a sign on the door, would open next week and a chiropractor's office. There were several apartments on the third floor, lived in by single people living on Supplemental Social Security checks and Veteran's benefits. It was a fairly clean building, but an eyesore compared to the businesses located in the posh Shakespeare Plaza area near the theaters.

To get into the office you had to have two separate keys Dave had entrusted the only spare set to me and you had to immediately input a five-digit code into a telephone-sized console that was located on a wall just inside the office and next to the power box. A year earlier, Dave had done some surveillance business for a guy named Spence Muldoon, who owned a used car dealership and an alarm company in the area. Muldoon was concerned about the theft of a couple Cadillacs, each stolen off his lot a couple weeks apart. Dave caught the two young men, ex-employees, who were doing the thievery on the third attempt. The businessman had been short of ready cash to meet the extra work above Dave's initial fee, so he had an expensive electronic alarm system set up, *gratis*, in Dave's office.

I opened the doors, and got treated to a few seconds of shrill alarm sound until I entered the code.

The office had two grainy, color-faded framed pictures of Dave and some of the other men from his military police unit back in his Army days. The pictures hung on a wall next to a Portland Trailblazer basketball team photograph, framed in plastic. There was a recent picture of Wendy and Jill with their Dad on the desk in his office. The second-hand grey metal-top desk—with Dell personal computer, the phone set-up and a stack of papers and old newspaper clippings on top—Dave's swivel chair and the two rattan chairs in front of the desk pretty well made up all that was in the office. There was a small closet Dave kept locked with a padlock and a hasp. This was where he kept his video camera; Nikon 35 millimeter camera with zoom attachment; his two-drawer metal file-cabinet; a gun safe , his porno magazines and a stash of whiskey and bourbon. A smell of booze usually pervaded the room and today was no exception.

There was a message from Dave. He stated he was going to ,"sell some insurance to an interested customer." This was code: it told me that Dave was going undercover into the place he was staking out. In this case it had to be The Institute for Factual History. Then, not in code, he said afterward he would head up to Santa Rosa to talk to the journalist, Christy Mathewson. He gave me a number to call him, he was staying at the Ocean Vista Hotel on the Great Highway in San Francisco. I made a couple of calls to places that Carolyn Mason had worked as a temp down in San Francisco. We worked on a case in a two-step approach—Dave breaking ground on foot and me calling in a seemingly-unrelated matter later on—and pooling the information later. After a couple go-nowhere calls, I struck gold when I called a restaurant called Rock and Roll Hamburgers where Carolyn Mason had worked for a time as a waitress and got hold of a woman who had been friends with Carolyn Mason while she worked there. She had apparently visited Mason at her apartment on Telegraph Avenue. She told me quite a lot about Carolyn Mason, and a few things about a man who would call her in the middle of the night and try and talk to her.

"She said she had worked for this IFH place and this man from there kept calling her," the woman, who called herself Jane Willey, said. "Carolyn wanted nothing to do with him, but he kept calling. She called the police, but they couldn't do anything unless he made a threat. That's what they said."

"What was the guy's name?" I asked her.

"No name," Jane Willey said. "Carolyn said he had a foreign accent. East European maybe. And he never gave out a name of course. She said she thought he worked for somebody else, some guy named Warbeck. She said she met Jack Benchley through this Warbeck guy."

Trevor Warbeck again.

"Did you tell the police about these calls? After Ms.

Mason's death, I mean?"

"Yes," Jane Willey said. "For what good it did. From what the papers and the TV news have come out with, the cops think Jack Benchley did it."

I talked more with her. She told me she had once roomed with Carolyn "until she went to live in this fancy Telegraph Avenue apartment that this Benchley guy set up for her. I used to go up there a lot and see her because she was lonely when he wasn't down seeing her. All of her family is in Oklahoma."

"Did you ever see Jack Benchley there?"

"Of course," she said. "I met him a couple times. I thought he was a nice old man. I don't think he killed her. The papers down here want to make it sound like he did it, but I can't believe it. I mean, he gave Carolyn this neat apartment to live in and everything. He adored her. He was way too old for her, but love is love."

Then I heard her make a plaintive sob over the phone. Memories of a deceased friend were getting to her. "Who...who did you say you were again?"

I said I was Michael Miles, a private investigator from an outfit called DBS Investigations. I added that the company was based in—of all places—Oklahoma City. DBS (which stood for Dependable Bull Shit) I explained, had been hired by Carolyn's family to look into her death. Ms. Willey believed this bold fiction, which was good. She had to get back to waiting tables however, and could no longer talk about her late friend.

"We have a private detective right now in San Francisco. Would you mind if I had him stop by and talk to you personally?"

"I get off late," she said. "Could he come by tomorrow afternoon?"

I got her address. "Anything you could share with one of our agents would be a big help," I told her. We said our goodbyes and I put the phone down and immediately picked it up again to try Dave's room at the motel he was at. The phone call to his room rang back to the desk and I told the desk clerk there to have Mr. McCreedy call me at my home number when he got back. I was anxious to get in touch with Dave because I now had some new information for him that tied Carolyn Mason further up with Strunk Enterprises. I was anxious: Dave would want to hear about this.

⊗ ⊗ ⊗ ⊗ ⊗

A few hours later, Russ White told me Dave was dead. "I sent Juanita from Emergency Services to their apartment to deliver the news," he said. "She just called in. Said nobody's home."

That was when Russ asked me to call Wendy and give her the bad news. I silently cursed him, but accepted.

"Wendy's over in Klamath County," I said. We ended the conversation shortly after that.

It was a terrible time all-around for Wendy. The day after Dave left, she had to pack up Jill and rush across the Cascades to Klamath City, 80 miles east of Rogue Falls, in the McCreedy family car, a Honda Civic, to be with her mother who had had another angina attack and had to be rushed to the local hospital. Wendy had left me her mom's phone number in case of emergency. With great trepidation, I called it. Surprisingly, a frail female voice answered. Was this the mother? No, it was an aunt of Wendy's. Wendy was out for the evening. Wendy's mom was feeling much better now, thanks for asking, and she was home from the hospital. Aunt Ruth was just in from back East somewhere and she was giving Wendy a break from watching over her mom. Wendy was out to dinner and a movie with an old girlfriend. She would probably be back in a couple hours.Was there a message?

I didn't share the news with Aunt Ruth. I told her to have Wendy call me as soon as she returned, and gave her my number. She could reverse the charges if she wanted to, but I emphasized I needed to speak to her. I said good-bye to Aunt Ruth, put the phone down, and felt a strange vibration all the way through my body. I had dealt with death on a professional level before, but never where it concerned a relative or even a close friend. I turned off the music and aimlessly leafed through a magazine waiting for a call back. I checked my watch: 9:17 in the evening. The news didn't seem possible for about an hour and a half. I continued to leaf through the magazine, not comprehending anything but the pictures, and not absorbing those for more than an instant. The more time dragged by, the more I dreaded talking to Wendy.

I stopped reading entirely, and paced the narrow confines of my private submarine.

Part of me wanted to go up to the site where Dave was found, hoping there was somebody up there from the Crime Lab I could talk to. I was supposed to talk to Wendy, though. I felt a stinging in my eyes; the realization was coming home. I would not be seeing Dave again. I sat down at the table in the kitchen, wondering if I would start crying.

A knock came at the door. I had rationalized the situation enough to imagine seeing Dave standing there, a big grin on his face, telling me it was all a joke and then exploding in laughter at my discomfort.

What I got were two guys in white Stetsons who let themselves in like they owned the place. One of them had a gun pointed at me so I put up no protest. The fellow with the gun was Leroy Millman, and the other a barrel-chested, younger version of him. I was certain this was not a social call.

"Sit the fuck down," Leroy said.

Chapter Four

I kept my eye on the barrel of the gun and groped my way back to the chair at the small kitchen table. I tried to keep myself outwardly stoic, even though my legs were already vibrating from the shock.

"I know about ya now," Millman said, standing a few feet away from me. "I know why you were at the hotel the other night." He turned to the younger version of himself. "Chad, you lock the door there and stay by it."

Chad had the same jug-ears and wide, leathery nose as his father, plus two beady grey eyes from whoever the first or second Mrs. Millman had been.

"Where's my wife?" Leroy Millman asked.

"I don't know," I said, trying to keep my voice from betraying my fear.

Millman leaned back against the kitchen counter. He was not so formally dressed as at our last meeting. This time he was in blue jeans and a thick green jacket open enough to reveal a plaid work shirt. He also had a different belt buckle on, this one bearing the emblem of an NFL football team. His gut roll covered the top of the buckle so only the bottom of the team logo on the buckle was visible.

"You were there at that hotel," Millman said, "because it was you who was poking my wife in that hotel room. You were on your way out when I was coming in. So you pretended some shit to throw me off the track. You lied to me, boy. Now tell me how long you and my wife been poking each other 'hind my back."

"I never went near your wife," I said. "Then, or ever."

"Why do you lie to me?" Millman replied. The barrel of his gun seemed to get bigger.

"I'm not," I said. I tried a different tack. "Let me ask you something. Why do you come into my house waving a gun?"

"You call this a house?" Millman said, chuckling. He turned to his son. "Look around," he said to Chad. That the son did, rifling through my drawers in the kitchen and living rooms and then disappearing toward the back of the trailer. I stared at Leroy and Leroy's American-made gun that I wished he'd put back in its brown suede holster. Leroy stared at me. I had to endure the sound of my drawers and closet being thrown open, then Chad returned to the kitchen. He was carrying my .38 inside its shoulder holster, the straps balled up in his hand. He set it down on the kitchen counter where his dad was leaning.

"Made in Brazil," the son said derisively, echoing the father's earlier pronouncements against imported firearms.

"Find anything of hers?" the father asked.

"Nope," Chad said. "But they could have done their thing somewhere else when they did it. If he's not off with her, then he probably knows who is. I say we take this one up to the ranch and talk this over." The younger man, who bore the cockiness only the immediate effects of cocaine and the future prospects of inherited wealth could create, was talking like he had rehearsed on the way over.

"Maybe we should," the elder Millman said, running a tongue over his chapped lips. I could see the gun he was holding remaining perfectly still. He was comfortable aiming a lethal weapon at someone.

"Where's your coat, boy?" Leroy asked.

I had to make up my mind on this one. I decided that whatever deep shit I was into, going to some ranch would not get me above it.

"I'm not going anyplace," I said, hoping this was a bluff, hoping that somebody in this half-empty mini-necropolis of a trailer park would have seen these two come in, hoping that they had seen them, too, and weren't going to press the matter.

The elder Millman reached into his jacket pocket and took a silencer attachment out. It was at least a foot-and-one-half long. He didn't put it on his gun. He just held it out so I could see he had it. I could have told him he was looking at six months in jail just having that little do-dad, but this didn't seem like the time to be quoting statues. The 'bluff' was starting to look rather serious.

"I'm not going anyplace," I repeated, trying to keep my voice from wavering. "And I don't think you want to shoot anybody, even if you could do it quietly."

Millman's eyes narrowed. "Why wouldn't I?" he said. "You think I'm afraid of the cops around here?"

I ignored the last question. "Because what you really came here for is information," I said. "You're smart enough to know your wife wouldn't fool around with a piece of Trailer-Trash like myself. I mean, I don't know your wife very well, but I do know her sister. And Wendy has always told me Rochelle has to have things that are first-class. Look around you here, Mr. Millman. Do you see anything that looks first class?"

Millman looked about. He looked at his son, and watched as the younger man slowly shook his head. Finally, perhaps, being in poverty was going to pay off.

"Okay," Millman said, jamming the silencer attachment back into his jacket pocket, "So you're covering for somebody else. Who? You had to be on the look-out for somebody?"

"I had nothing to do with your wife, or anybody who could have been with her" I said. "I was visiting two friends up from San Jose. They were at that Psychic Festival. I stopped off to have a drink with them in the lounge."

Millman rubbed one eye with a fat knuckle. "You're the friend of that no-good louse who's married to my sister-in-law. And to think I hired that bastard to check who my wife was seeing. Was Dave McCreedy the boy you were on the lookout for?"

I permitted myself a shake of my head. "As far as I know, Dave was over at the VFW with some of his old buddies. I had a drink with him at O'Leary's about an hour before I went to see my other friends in Middleburg. Then he went to the VFW and I did my thing."

"Anything else?" Millman asked.

I shrugged. "Nothing. We watched the Blazers play the Sonics. Blazers got a lousy call at the end and lost. We talked about the Benchley disappearance. Nobody mentioned your wife."

Millman mulled over my impromptu deposition. The gun stayed pointed at me.

"When is your friend coming back from California?" he asked.

"He's not," I said. "A deputy sheriff found his body about two hours ago off a dirt road just inside the county. Dave's dead. He put a bullet in his head. Looks like a suicide."

I gauged Millman's reaction. There wasn't much reaction to gauge. His eyes blinked a little faster and his brow furrowed when the news of Dave's death came to him, then he looked over to his son. The son just stood there leaning against my door, his tongue poking up the skin of one cheek. Neither man doffed their Stetsons nor bowed their heads so I didn't offer to lead them in a prayer.

If there was a moment that solidified my idea that Dave hadn't killed himself, that moment had just occurred. Now I was afraid I was going to be the second victim. Millman looked back to me, eyes cold and pale. "This McCreedy guy, was he the one seeing my wife that night?"

"He was at the VFW that night, and before that, he went and saw his wife and me at O'Leary's," I said. "I was his friend, but I didn't follow the guy around all the time."

"He's lying," Son of Leroy said. "You hired McCreedy to find out who Rochelle was seeing. It was this asshole and McCreedy covered for him."

"Look," I said. "I got my own life. But Dave never talked about Wendy's sister to me except as her being Wendy's sister and nothing beyond that. Nothing."

Millman nodded. "OK," he said, finally returning his gun to the holster strapped under his jacket. "Right now, I'll buy what you're selling, boy. But I'm also checking you out, you and what your friend was doing for the last couple weeks. If I find out you are lying, I'm coming back to you. And don't try and squeal to nobody over at the D.A.'s office. I got eyes and ears all over the law enforcement community here, and I'll be down on you hard. I have a lot of friends, Wells. And," he said, moving away from the kitchen counter, "if I find out you did just lie to me, then the best thing you can hope for is that I just ruin you for making a livin' in this area. And the worst thing is that I mess you up real good in some other ways I got.

You got me?"

"I got you," I said, looking him right in the eye.

One corner of Millman's mouth went up in an expression of smugness, then he broke eye contact with me and headed to the door. Chad kicked my door open with a boot and only the chain near the top of the hinges kept the thing from slamming against the side of the trailer. His dad stepped out of my place without hardly breaking stride. It was the son's hard little eyes I had focused on me like a laser just before he closed my door. He shut it with a surprising gentleness. I just sat there for a few seconds, then I got up and looked out the kitchen window at the overflow parking lot a couple spaces down and across the street from my trailer. The two men got into the truck and pulled away. I put my gun and my holster on.

I had something else to worry about now. I knew Millman was a big-time political player in the area, head of the local Cattlemen's Association. I knew that Leroy Millman was a keen supporter of the local law enforcement and that he donated plenty of campaign money toward keeping Sheriff Parker and my boss the D.A. on the public payroll. He was the head of a civilian auxiliary outfit called the Sheriff's Posse. Tales of Millman's big Fourth of July parties at the Double M Ranch for local cops and selected business and political types were legendary around the County Justice Center. I had also read in the newspaper that he was the leading candidate to win the local Congressional Seat now that Representative Orland Hathaway was retiring. How much trouble could he make for me? Lots.

Could one of the Millmans have killed Dave? And if so, why not kill me? Somebody could have seen them drive up with his son, and maybe that changed his plans. Perhaps he never intended to kill me, just throw a scare into me. If I didn't scare so well, then maybe he'd go further. If the Millmans did kill Dave, how did he get him out to some remote spot like Bowman? That dead little town was a couple miles off the Interstate. Would Dave be stupid enough to go meet the man whose wife he was having an affair with in some remote spot with no witnesses around? I didn't think so.

And then there was the enmity between Trevor Warbeck, who basically worked for Strunk, and Jack Benchley. I knew from Benchley's autobiography, *The Rise and Fall of Me*, that he and Warbeck were not the best of friends, particularly after the former had fired the latter from the role of the Earl of Essex in *Essex and the Queen* in 1972, a role later undertaken by Charlton Heston.

Jane Willey had told me that afternoon that a guy Carolyn Mason thought worked for Strunk was bothering her on the phone. Somehow, Mason, who worked at the IFH for a short time, was a link between Warbeck and Benchley. And she was dead. Jack Benchley was the prime suspect, of course, but where was Jack Benchley? Dave had gone looking and not come back alive. Dave had almost made it home, however, and it seemed strange that if somebody in the Strunk orbit did him in, they would wait until he got back to Oregon. But, then again, maybe somebody in San Francisco wanted to make it look like a local murder. Sitting there, still shaking from the encounter with the Millmans, I resolved to find out just what had happened to Dave.

The phone rang at 10:18. It was the call I dreaded.

"Wendy," I said. "This is not a joke...I wish it was...are you sitting down?..ok...ok. I got a call from Russ White. They...they said...yeah, something happened to Dave. He was found. He's not...what I mean is, he's..."

Wendy had to finally guess the catastrophe I couldn't articulate. I eventually got out the details that Russ White had given me. Wendy cried and cried. Eventually, her Aunt came on the line and asked me to pray for Dave's soul, and for Wendy and Jill. Jill was not even three years old yet. She wouldn't remember her father and Dave would never see her grow up. I put down the phone and felt a heavy knot of despair well up inside me. I cried.

I could have gone out and got very drunk very easily that night. Instead, I settled for insomnia and a long rambling walk in the middle of the night around the neighborhood. I finally conked out about an hour after the walk, catching maybe two hours sleep to face the next day.

Wendy spent the night in Klamath City. I had told her about the necessity of identifying the body. She said she would be back in town about eleven the following morning.

I went to the county morgue the next day right at eleven and met Wendy standing in the basement corridor of the

Justice Center. She had her hair tied back and was wearing a black dress that made her look shapeless. I accompanied her into the cold, sanitary white tile and stainless steel room where the dead were stored. The attendant was a skinny dark-haired guy in his twenties wearing a white smock, a hep-cat goatee, acne-scars on his pencil-thin neck and a look of disinterest. He was chewing gum. The room contained an x-ray machine in the middle of the room and the three gurneys, only two of them occupied. One of the gurneys had a small body on it, with a few strands of bluish-tinted hair extending out from the hem of the white sheet that was strewn over the body. I guessed that the corpse was that of an old woman, probably sent over recently from one of the local nursing homes. On the other side of the woman was a bigger body in a black plastic bag. That had to be Dave. A small amount of light from a small pebble glass window high on the far wall reflected a shaft of light over his covered torso.

The attendant unzipped the plastic bag on the stainless steel gurney and the ash-grey specimen of soulless skin and bone that had been a pretty nice guy was revealed to his wife.

"That's my husband," Wendy said in a halting tone. She looked away and walked out of the room rather shaken but nowhere near hysterics. I lingered over my friend a while, observing the small entry wound in his left temple and the large exit wound that had torn his flesh and bone above the right ear. His eyes were wide open, they seemed to be imploring me to do something. I had seen dead bodies before—some very fresh—but I had never felt the sense of disorientation and unreality of seeing a friend in that condition.

I looked up at the attendant, watched him chew his gum, then resisted the urge to take it out of his mouth and perhaps bop his chops around in the process.

"Thanks," I said, and took my misplaced anger out the door. When I got to the corridor, I saw Wendy calmly calling from a public phone. She was arranging to have Dave sent to a funeral home for cremation.

I walked her out to her car. Her eyes were glassy. She had her initial emotional outburst, but there was more to come. It had hit her what happened to Dave, but she was not over the worst of it. She looked like a zombie. I knew sometime soon it would hit her harder than it had already.

"You shouldn't be alone," I said to her.

"I won't be alone. I'm going to meet Rochelle. We're going to the funeral home later on after she tries to get me to eat. I've already talked to Dave's mother down in San Jose. She's paying for everything. The ashes are going down to California. The service will be down there. Rochelle is watching Jill now. She's checked into The Four Star. I guess her and Leroy are having problems."

"Can I do anything for you," I asked as she got into her red Honda Civic.

"Will you be going down to San Jose?" she asked.

"Not unless you need a ride," I said.

"Rochelle is going to fly us down there. She's going to hold my hand down there. God, I'm going to have to face his first wife and those kids he had with her. Thank God for Rochelle right now. I never thought...I never thought my sister would be there for me, you know. She was always so self-absorbed."

"She's family," I said. "This is what brothers and sisters are for." I spoke with the experience of an only child.

"Dave told me several times he never wanted a service. He just...he wanted just to be...burned away. Burned away."

She broke down and cried. I hugged her.

"He's going to have a service," Wendy said, after she blew her nose into a tissue from her purse, then wiped her eyes with her thin fingers. "His mom will see to that." Then I watched her get into the car and drive away.

After Wendy left, I went back to work. After I finished running down a couple leads on some fathers who, it turned out, had left the area, I drove up to Bowman at around four o'clock that afternoon.

It was a cloudy day and dark rain clouds seemed to cling to the line of mountains, called the Siskiyous, that separated Oregon from California. I drove up Interstate Five and took the last Oregon Exit and found myself in Bowman. I wanted to go first to the place where Dave's body was found. Bowman was a small town that had once been larger and bore the scars of crumbling sidewalks, dilapidated buildings and potholes so big you would have to be the village idiot not to drive around them. The place had only a combination convenience store/gas station near the off-ramp and a beauty parlor and cafe in a single strip mall. All other commercial activities were extinct. Past that and you only had a few trailers here and there and a lot of abandoned buildings. I saw a brown-coated, white-tailed doe and her small offspring grazing in what had been the playground of the old elementary school. The school was boarded up, as was the Klamath River Bait and Tackle Shop and the Cascade Theater, the latter with a marquee advertising *Bronco Billy*, a Clint Eastwood film that came out twenty years earlier.

Once through the town, you turned onto a dirt road. I stopped when I saw the familiar yellow tape with black lettering that denoted a crime scene. The tape was lying on the ground across the road; one end of it had apparently come loose from a tree along the road. I parked well ahead of the tape and got out. I noticed all the vehicle tracks in the dusty ground as I approached. I figured the Crime Scene group had taken pictures of all the tracks so I wasn't concerned about obliterating anything. I walked up to the edge of the bank and looked down. The log that Russ White had mentioned was down there, a few feet away from the water. The body was, of course, gone. I walked down there. I suppose I thought I was going to comb over the crime scene and find something the professionals missed. I was going to prove Russ White wrong, find some overlooked bit of evidence that pointed to a second person at the scene. But I never even bothered to take out my magnifying glass. Just from the naked eye, I could see everything had been swept. Except for the footprints the place probably was as it was twenty-four hours earlier. There was no sign of blood even. There must have been blood and brain matter judging by the look of what was left of Dave's head back at the morgue. But all that had been cleaned up now. The lab technicians had their little blood and tissue samples lined up in test tubes on little plastic trays back in the forensic lab in Middleburg.

The creek itself was running swift from the spring runoff. It was not far from here to where Cramner Creek ran into the Klamath River which eventually wound another hundred miles to the Pacific.

One thing was puzzling. There was a large blackened circle about six feet in diameter, at the edge of the embankment. It looked like someone made a small bonfire there. I bent down to touch the scorched earth. It was still warm. As I got up from the charred ground, a woman's voice told me I wasn't authorized to be where I was. I looked up to see a willowy young woman in a tan-colored Rogue County Sheriffs uniform, the dark brown hair that stuck out under her brown baseball cap blowing in the breeze. She was standing on the opposite bank of the creek, her gun belt slung over her narrow hips.

"What are you doing?" she asked above the sound of water rushing along, water rushing over large rocks in a continuous torrent destined for sea level. Her voice was strong and forceful. She had to be that way to do her job.

I told her the truth, even about my being an ex-cop.

"He was a friend of mine," I said. "I just want to make sure."

"Stay there." she said. She carefully crossed over the creek, which was between five and seven yards wide, over the protruding rocks. I noticed the other side of the creek was made up of a rocky embankment. I remembered hearing about the "Big Flood of '75" and figured the quarry-sized stones were put there to shore up the creek.

The woman's name was Lee Westphal. She was a deputy sheriff and I didn't know her. She must have been a new hire because I knew a good number of the deputies but this woman, who was maybe twenty-five, had escaped my notice. She took down the identification numbers off my driver's license and looked me over to make sure I was the same guy on the identification. She also looked over my Oregon Private Investigator's License.

"The guy who was found dead here was my friend," I said to her after she asked if my address was still current. "You can check with Russ White. He's a detective with the Rogue Falls City Police. He committed suicide. I just wanted to see the place."

"I don't know Detective White," she said. "Why are you up here? This was a restricted area."

"He was my friend," I said, somewhat exasperated. "Look, run me in if you want, but I'm just seeing where my friend died. Dave McCreedy worked for the D.A.'s office at Family Support. You do know Officer Reynolds, right?"

"Yes," she said.

"So do I," I said. "And he knew Dave McCreedy was a friend of mine. Look, if I knew anybody from your department was still up here, I would have left it alone. But I saw the tape on the ground there so I figured the place was swept over."

I noticed she had part of a clear plastic envelope sticking up from a fanny pack she had on the other side of her weapon.

"You find anything over there?" I asked. "What do you make of this big burned circle in the road?"

She ignored my questions. "Mr. Wells, I would advise you to keep clear of this area. You're not officially involved in this investigation. I'm afraid I'll have to report this to the District Attorney's Office."

"Do that," I said encouragingly, "because Mr. Masterson and I know each other well." The truth was that Peter Masterson, the District Attorney, knew me from the times I had been in his office reporting on something Dave or I had uncovered in our investigations that went beyond a child support infraction and into criminal non-support. Masterson certainly knew and respected Dave and I was sure he knew me enough to be able to understand why I came out to Cramner Creek.

"I'm just asking you to leave this scene," she said, her tone becoming a bit less haughty. "The investigation isn't altogether finished."

"Last night, Detective White told me it was a simple case of suicide. Are you saying there's a new development since last night?"

"If you were a policeman like you said, you should know I can't discuss—"

"O.K.," I said, putting my hands up in the air. "If there's nothing else, can I go now?"

I also checked out the town of Bowman, trying to see if there was anybody who might have seen Dave ride through on his Harley. I came up empty at the restaurant and at the one prosperous-looking business in town, the local convenience store/gas station called, not without logic, The Bowman Store. I first tried making small talk with the owner, a sixtyish, balding grey-haired man with a skeleton-like frame, cagy brown eyes—that looked me up and down from behind his wood-paneled counter like I was a familiar face in a police line-up—and a sour, puckered expression on his wizened face.

"You a cop?" the man asked, after I gave up on the small talk and showed him the photograph of Dave.

"A friend," I said. "Any cops come around asking questions before me?"

"If you're not a cop, then I'll sell you something. But I won't talk."

"You won't even tell me if any deputies have talked to you?"

The man shook his head. A customer in a red-and-black plaid coat came up and plunked down some long strips of beef jerky and a six pack of Budweiser. "I won't talk," he repeated to me as he rang up the sale. I thanked him for his time and left..

The short, stocky woman at The Elegant Look Beauty Shop had a flat, round face with eyes like the doe in front of the school, a long train of dark brown hair, and a Roman nose with an outward curve in the middle of the bridge. She was considerably more friendly than the bald guy. Her name was Wanda Truax. Her shop was empty and she hung over the front counter of her two-chair shop. I watched the large pendant with a quarter moon dangling from the front of her open-necked white sweater and a glimpse of the top of the ravine-like cleavage of her breasts. I asked her how her business was doing.

"Not too good," she said. "I'm just hanging on. My mother used to run this salon back when we had real traffic."

"Before the local lumber outfit shut down."

"Yes," she said. "That was a long time ago. My husband has worked at the Towson Mill down in Middleburg for the last sixteen years."

"That's a long commute," I said.

"Yeah, and lately his hours are lousy. Either he's working twelve hour days six days a week when there is lumber, or he gets his hours cut back to nothing. Some judge in San Francisco decides to rule against a timber sale up here and then, sooner or later, the mill shuts down. We got two kids and we have to send them all the way to Rogue Falls just to go to school. We'd sell this place but we'd get nothing for it. We could sell the house here but we'd barely make enough to pay off the mortgage. We're trapped. If it wasn't for the business I get from the folks over the California Line who don't want to go all the way to Yreka I'd be shutting down."

I told her who I was and my business. Then I showed her

the photograph and asked if she might have seen him Monday around five or six.

"He looks like Jack Nicholson," Wanda said.

I agreed.

"I saw him," she said, "but not yesterday. I was closed on the Fourth. But I saw him around here a couple months ago. He was with a woman. They came into my shop and asked if there were any real estate offices in town. They wanted to rent a house."

"What did the woman look like?"

"Hard to say," she said. "She was fairly tall."

I am 5'11". "About my size?" I asked.

"About two or three inches shorter," she said, describing a woman who could have been Wendy, in height at least. I asked what she looked like.

"Hard to say," she said. "She was wearing a wig and dark glasses when she came in. She hung on him like she had too much to drink and this was the middle of the afternoon."

"How did you know it was a wig?"

"I know about heads," she said with authority in her voice. "I know what's natural and what's fake. This babe had a wig, a platinum blonde wig she must have put on herself. Plus she had on a black motorcycle jacket and I think a leather skirt. Somebody dressed like that tends to stand out in this town, that's why I remember him and her."

I never knew Wendy to dress outlandishly. Rochelle was tall, like her sister, and she was also a former actress who had spent a couple years down in Southern California not making it in the film and television business and then a season or two at the Northwest Shakespeare Festival. If this woman was right, then either somebody who looked like Dave had been around Bowman with a tipsy lady on his arm or Dave had been hanging out here with Rochelle.

"You look like you could use a haircut," she said.

"I probably do," I said. "What do you charge?"

"Seven bucks," she said. "I'll even trim your eyebrows for free."

I couldn't pass that up. While I got my sides trimmed and the back of my neck tapered and cleaned up the stumpy, buxom Wanda filled me in on more about Bowman than I thought I'd ever needed to know.

That was all the business community Bowman offered. All that was left were a few houses back up on the scrub-oak covered hills above the town, but of the five or six places I went up to there were only three answers if you didn't count barking dogs. One house had a grey-haired woman who barely opened the door to me, asked if I was here to deliver her refrigerator, then shut the door as soon as I told her I wasn't. Another door at another house was answered by a tall dark-haired teenager with a wispy beard that barely covered his jawline and a vacant stare. There was a faint, but peculiar smell to the inside of his house. I noticed it when I handed him the picture. I recognized the smell as he looked it over. Marijuana. He shook his head and sent me on my way.

The last house I tried was a ranch-style place with a wide porch and a garage made out of cinder blocks. An old bald-headed man in overalls answered the door. He had a chin to spare just behind his original one, a day's growth of beard around his jowls and the scowl of a man who valued solitude. Grey chest hairs hung out from the top of his overalls. He wore thick rimless glasses and had an expression like a confused bulldog.

"Are you a cop?" the old man asked me after I introduced myself and showed him the picture of Dave.

"Never seen nobody like that," the old man, who was wearing a tattered baseball cap advertising a casino in Nevada, said. "I worked for Bowman Lumber for 28 years. This used to be a good town. We had our own baseball team. The Bowman Millwrights. We were the best small town team in Oregon. Had dances over at the Eagles Lodge every Saturday night. That's where I met my wife. You say your brother died?"

"No, he wasn't my brother. He was a friend."

The old man dug his hands into his overalls. "Lost my brother in the mill; gonna be twenty years ago this fall. He was climbing up on a load of logs. Some green punks didn't stack them the right way on one side. They all gave way when he was rigging up piping for the sprinkler system. A couple dozen logs rolled over right on him."

"I'm sorry," I said.

The man carried on as if he had a set speech.

"A few men died cutting up in the timber holdings, and a few lost a hand or a couple fingers down at the mill, but my brother died. He was a Marine. He fought the fucking Chinese at the Cochin Reservoir in Korea and he came back and got killed 'cause a couple college punks working short-time didn't do their jobs right. I gotta go. I'm getting ready to give my wife her medication." My photograph came back to me.

"I'm sorry to bother you. Have a nice day."

"Too late," the old man said and shut the door on me.

When I got home I called Russ White. He was still at his office. I asked him if he knew anything about the course of the investigation into Dave's death.

"Sheriff's Department is handling that," he said.

"I ran into a deputy searching around up at the creek. Kind of unusual for a deputy to be up there almost twenty-four hours after the incident took place. That is, if it was just a suicide."

"The Sheriff probably just wanted the whole area scanned over in daylight. Maybe they were just trying to find the shell casing from the automatic."

"But she was on the other side of the creek. A shell casing wouldn't travel that far after ejection. And there was a large circle of burned ground near the crime scene. What the hell, Russ, were the crime tech guys having a bar-be-que?"

"Look, Wells," White said testily, "I've had a long day and it might turn into a long night. There was a robbery at the Rogue Federal this afternoon. I've got a suspect being booked right now I'm going to have to grill. If you don't mind, I have to go. I'll check with the Sheriff's Department tomorrow. If there are any changes I'll get in touch, okay?"

I said goodbye and hung up. I was pretty sure Russ, who only knew me through Dave, was not exactly going to move heaven and earth to find out what Deputy Lee Westphal was looking for.

That night I had a dream about Dave. He was riding very fast on an icy winding road well up in the mountains. For some reason I thought we were in the Swiss Alps, a place I had never been. I was trying to catch up to him, but I couldn't get the car which I was driving to get near him. I kept catching little glimpses of Dave from behind as I went around a curve in the road and Dave and his motorcycle went around the curve in front of me. Then, finally, I drove down into a valley where I could see the road clearly winding for miles. But Dave was gone. I drove on but could not find him. I woke up from that dream knowing I needed to get answers.

Chapter Five

I did not travel the 400 miles or so south for Dave's service. I had been to San Jose on a visit to the Bay Area the year previously and to see the habitable city I grew up in turned into a overdeveloped mass of endless strip malls, glass-and-steel corporate blockhouses and endless entanglements of jammed expressways was a mental injury to the memory of the western fringe of the city I had grown up in and dreamed my dreams. Dave hated San Jose worse than I did, and my absence would be no affront to his spirit. Most of the other kids I had grown up with had long left the so-called Silicon Valley or the South Bay for places more open or more cosmopolitan. Besides, the funeral was for the family and for those who knew Dave from his days either in the active-duty military or when he was a cop with the San Jose Police Department.

Wendy told me she felt like an alien life form in San Jose. Dave had only taken her there once earlier and that was before they were married. All the people who attended the service knew the Dave who had a different wife and a different life. They probably never understood why he left all that—first wife Mindy and the kids—and started anew in Oregon. I knew part of the reason was dissatisfaction—and drinking. Dave's drinking problems had hit him earlier than my own, but it had been just as devastating. "I felt I had to get away, make a clean break," was all he ever said whenever I entreated him to tell me why he left his job on the force. Unlike me, Dave had lost his fight with the bottle. He had gone through rehab and stayed clean for a time with Wendy. And then their baby came along and the drinking began again.

In any case, I had no desire to return to the place I had spent my formative years and try to help strangers and half-forgotten acquaintances grasp a Dave McCreedy who, in the final analysis, wouldn't have cared what they thought of him now. Going down to San Jose at that point would have been a bad move for me, anyway. My mind was dealing with the loss of my best friend—in childhood, adolescence and later adulthood—by bringing forth a plentiful amount of memories. Dave and I had been close friends since the fifth grade. We were as close as non-relations could be. Dave McCreedy had been my compensation for growing up without siblings. And, later in life—when I was down on my luck—he had come through for me with help gaining employment and getting sober. He had done all that and I had thanked him, but I felt I couldn't even begin to feel closure until I could satisfy myself with what had happened to Dave that night along Cramner Creek.

❖ ❖ ❖ ❖ ❖

"I never would have got through that ordeal without Rochelle being there for me," Wendy said. We were sitting in the living room of the two bedroom, white-stucco apartment she and Dave had shared, a unit on the third story of an old three story apartment building just off Highway 99. She was sitting on a black vinyl sofa, the same one I had helped her carry up two flights of stairs after she brought it from Sears last Summer. She had bought the sofa while Dave was down in Las Vegas attending a Security and Investigators Convention. He had actually won a few hundred at the blackjack tables, which came in handy when the bill for the new sofa arrived in the mail. Wendy looked pale and older, her figure hidden in a shroud of baggy sweats she must have worn on the flight back to Oregon. I was sitting across from Wendy, a maple-colored coffee table between us. The table had scratches on it courtesy of Rufus, a long-haired, powder-blue and grey Persian Cat.

"This Mindy woman was there," Wendy explained, "and her two spoiled little kids. And all his old friends looking at me like I was some kind of tramp. I'll never go back there."

"Dave kissed them all off long ago, except for his parents and his kids," I said.

"What about Jill?" Wendy suddenly said in a tone of sorrow. "She never knew her father. She's too young to have lasting memories. She asks about daddy. I told her that daddy had a big ow-whee. That's the word I use when she falls down. She nods her head, but I don't think she understands he's not coming back."

"At least she has part of Dave inside her," I said. It was a stupid thing to say to someone in grief, I suppose, but I felt being silent would have been worse.

Rufus, a fat cat, now lay at his mistress' feet, back lying on the faded two-tone brown rug. Rufus was angling for a belly rub that never came. Wendy's long brunette hair was now cut short, only a couple inches below her ears.

Jill was on the living room floor, watching a video of *101 Dalmatians*. She was on her stomach in a two-piece red outfit, kicking her bare legs one over another. Every now and then she would get up and go over to Wendy and demand attention.

Suddenly a spell seemed to break and we started talking about Dave. We remembered his negative traits—his temper, mainly—but there was also the part of him that was off-the-wall and downright exciting to be with. I used to call Dave 'The Man Who Dared' because he did things—skiing, rock climbing, white-water rafting—because he had an impulse to be on the edge. The edge for me was doing my job well and not making a bad mistake, which I eventually did. Before the mistake that ended it, I was content with getting through a shift in my LTD police cruiser, tag some speeders, keep a few fender-bender accidents from escalating into brawls, and, when I got into the narcotics unit, putting some crack and methamphetamine dealers into the cage into the back of a cruiser and hope the D.A. could send them up to Folsom, Susanville or some other nice California Prison for a good long while. (That was a rare joy, however. The drug trash, thanks to their lawyers, were often out on the street faster than myself or my partners could get the dope we had obtained to the Evidence Room. Either that or the judges would slide them out of the overcrowded prisons in a matter of a few months and they'd be back in business as before.)

Dave's desire to be on the edge even off-duty translated into his social dimension. Dave would say anything to anybody if it was how he saw it. I tried to emulate that, but never could. That made him enemies, but it also made him a rare spirit.

"When he was in an up mood, his energy was like no other person I'd ever known," Wendy said. "She told me Dave stories I'd heard before and I told her mine and, gradually, we were almost both smiling, almost near laughing. We were interrupted by Rochelle's arrival. She had gone shopping for herself, Wendy and Jill. I helped her get a couple shopping bags out of the back of her Lexus. On my second trip to bring in groceries, I overheard Rochelle telling Wendy that she and Leroy had "split up for good this time." Wendy nodded her head. She was back in that spell I almost had her out of, numb to anyone else's bad news. If it was bad news. From the older sister's casual behavior toward me, I felt pretty certain that she didn't know I had followed her from Rogue Falls to Middleburg for her meeting with Dave the preceding Friday night. Once I was through with the lugging of sacks and plastic milk jugs, Rochelle, whose presence seemed to take over the room, practically pushed me out the door. As she was doing so, with Wendy out of earshot in the kitchen, I put in a word for myself on the Leroy Millman matter.

"Your husband came by and saw me the night Dave was killed," I said. I'd appreciate it, when you see him again, if *you'd* tell him I never had anything to do with you outside of being acquainted."

Rochelle looked at me like I was putting her on. "Does Leroy think that you and I...?" She pointed at a spot between her breasts, then shook her head. A smile formed on her face. The very thought of her and I jumping into the sack together must have been too funny for words.

"I may not be seeing my husband for a while," she said smugly. "We're separated right now. Why he would think there was anything between you and I frankly astonishes me. I'll give him your message if the topic comes up when I see him again."

I'd also appreciate it, for Wendy's sake, if you don't come clean about your meeting with her husband a week or so ago at the Four Star Motel in Middleburg. Your husband just about caught the two of you. I was the poor sap old Leroy saw in the lobby while he was trying to track you down. I called Dave to get him out of the room before he barged in on the two of you."

That took the smile off her face. "I don't know what the hell you're talking about?" she said. "Are you trying to imply—"

"Save it," I said. "I know you were shacked up with Dave. Probably more than once, too. I'll keep my mouth shut, but you tell your husband I had nothing to do with you. Just tell the truth. I trust you can manage the truth, Mrs. Millman."

"Go to hell," she said. The door shut. It probably would have slammed if Wendy had not been in the kitchen. I walked down to the stairway and to the parking lot to get in my car.

The next night, the passing of my friend was duly noted at O'Leary's Sports Pub. An informal wake was organized, though the mourners would be shy the body. The Bomber Boys were the stars of this more upbeat ritual with plenty of ribald and profane stories centering on Dave as the Star Reprobate of our group. I sat across a table from Wendy and her sister, feeling like I needed to put up a good front. Somebody asked Rochelle where her husband was. She replied that Leroy was hosting some sort of party for agribusiness men up at the ranch and sent his regrets. No mention was made by Mrs. Millman of our last conversation, which was fine with me.

I was supposed to celebrate my friend in life but inside of me there was still the emptiness of loss. I found myself focusing on what had obsessed me for the last couple days: was there any connection between Dave's "suicide" and his business with the Benchley case? Or with Leroy and Chad Millman?

"How are you holding up?" I asked Wendy, mustering up all the positive energy I could.

"Better," was her reply. Indeed, the strain was off her face. She was coming out of that shock that comes over a person at a great loss. I wondered if she had begun to feel relief that Dave was no longer around to spend too much money and bat her around from time to time. The redness in her eyes was less noticeable. She would have no trouble down the road getting a relationship going with someone else, if that's what she wanted. In the subdued neon-accented light, her light brown eyes, creme complexion and oval face gave off a beauty that grew on you. This was in contrast to first-glance beautiful Rochelle, the one who went into acting and married well. Rochelle was more traditionally beautiful, like a younger Susan Sarandon with thinner hair, but she seemed cold and distant compared to her slightly shorter sister. I had felt that way about her before I found out about her and Dave.

Wendy got up and went to the bathroom. This left her sister and I with the necessity of either talking to each other or, under the circumstances, just ignoring each other. Rochelle, flicking a half-inch of ash off her cigarette, decided to brake the ice.

"Wendy tells me you used to be a cop down in Sutter City," she said.

"True," I said. Our little group of a dozen was situated in the back area, just past the pool tables. The sound of cueball against a cluster of round targets gave me a second to think about how I would handle what was for me a sensitive query.

"Yes," I said. "I was for about ten years. I left. Got sick of it." Good, I thought. The answer covered any further pursuit into why I might no longer be a cop.

"Did you see a lot of suicide cases?" She was playing her part, making casual conversation. I casually conversed back.

"Usually, you'd see a suicide in a motel every so often. People who want to end check into some economy room. It got so I dreaded calls to a motel. Men are the worst to deal with in that situation."

"How so?" Rochelle asked. She took a bottoms-up gulp from her drink. The ice cubes dislodged from the bottom of the glass and fell against her upper lip. She put the drink down. Her eyes were not quite the luminous orbs of Ms. Sarandon's, but in different circumstances—her not screwing my best friend or laughing at the thought of anyone thinking we had an affair—I would not have kicked her out of bed for eating crackers. She ran her tongue over her wet upper lip. I lost my train of thought for a moment.

"Well," I said after a pause. "The thing about men is they usually shoot their brains out. Then you've got skull fragments all over the place and all the brain matter. Messy. I pitied the poor housekeepers who had to go in and deal with a room after a guy took that way out. Women, on the other hand, tend to go with pills. We saved a couple women with CPR, that is my partner and I, and later the paramedics, in a motel room once. They had some kind of joint suicide pact together.

"They were lesbians, of course," she said flatly.

"The subject of sexual preferences didn't come up." I said. "They might have just both been despondent heterosexuals and wanted to split the cost of the room." I waited to see if she would chuckle at this. She took it straight, like I was a tax preparer informing her that she was going to get audited by the IRS.

"Seriously," I continued, "a woman usually will try and get help if she makes an attempt. Not always, of course. Also, women leave more interesting suicide notes. Men usually leave curt notes; women sometimes go for the complete whole-life recap."

"Dave didn't leave a note for Wendy," the sister said matter-of-factly. "He did have a picture of Jill in his hand. I think that's interesting." It was true. Russ White told me about that, and I had told Wendy. Rochelle did not seem too broken up over her brother-in-law/lover's hasty exit off this mortal coil, but maybe the two of them had been with each other just for the sex.

Wendy returned from the bathroom. Her close-cropped hair made her look older somehow. I could tell she wanted out of there.

"Hey, Harvey," Cletus called out from the table behind me, "tell everybody about the time up in Prospect you and Dave had."

"Yeah, tell that one," Ferlin, the other Buckhorn Boy, asked. Ferlin had both front teeth missing and there was little sign he would ever replace them. He had the identical 'John Deere' baseball cap on as his brother did, but Cletus rebelled when it came to his brother's example of a tank top shirt. It was long-sleeve red-and-black plaid for Cletus on this sorrowful evening.

"The Prospect case?" I said, trying to recollect. "Oh, the one where Dave and I served that deadbeat a subpoena and he took a swing at Dave?"

"Yeah," Cletus said, "and Dave dropped him with one fist. Tell that one."

I told it, even though the punch line was gone.

Wendy got into a conversation with a girlfriend who came to offer support. After I told a couple more Dave vs. Deadbeat Dad stories, I got up to get another Dr. Pepper and ran into Detective Russ White. Up to that point, I didn't know he was there.

"Hello, Russ," I said. Russ was a thin guy in his early forties with thick reddish-blonde hair, freckles and a hatchet face. He had prematurely greying sideburns and high prominent cheekbones that gave him sunken cheeks. Like Rochelle, he was a smoker and his light complexion already showed a good deal of wrinkling for a guy barely into middle age. He was wearing a blue suit and had a worried look on his face, a look enhanced by the bloodshot eyes of a cop who had put in too many hours on his beat.

"I have somebody that wants to talk to you," Russ replied. "Can we go outside?"

After he paid his respects to the widow, I followed Russ out to the wooden deck that served as an alternate drinking and carousing area for the patrons during the warm summer months. There was someone waiting out there: an average-sized man with wide, sad-looking Peter Lorre eyes, coal-black hair thinning back between a tuft of hair over his forehead, and an alert gaze that screamed cop. He was dressed in a dark pinstripe suit and was leaning against the redwood railing on the landing just outside the back entrance to the bar. He offered his hand in a stiff, formal manner. As we briefly shook hands, he introduced himself as Detective Kayama of the San Francisco Police.

"Detective Kayama is with the Homicide Division down there," Russ added.

"I'm looking into the matter concerning Jack Benchley and the late Carolyn Mason," Kayama said in a calm, even voice. "I'm sorry if this is coming at a bad time for you, but I have to leave to fly back to San Francisco tomorrow. I was hoping you could answer a few questions."

It was about six-thirty in the evening, nearing dusk, and a light rain was falling on the deck. The cloudiness cast a gloom over the vista of old brick buildings and parking lots in the area. Just below us was an alleyway, a one-way drive enough for one vehicle but usually used by teenaged kids for skateboarding. I never came in or out of O'Leary's from this entry. I'd had a very bad experience in an alleyway years ago in Sutter City. I found the body of a teenaged girl—a runaway turned hooker—sliced up in a garbage dumpster. She had been butchered. That was the first time, outside a forensic lab where I had to see an autopsy during training, that I had seen a person hacked to pieces. The destruction of the woman's body—the blood, the expression on her face, her eyes—it was still something I had nightmares about, and it was the second most vivid thing that happened to me as a peace officer.

Detective Kayama cut right to the chase. "I want to know what Dave McCreedy was working on before he died." he said. He folded his arms just beneath his chest.

I folded my arms the same way, and thought a bit. I pondered the question for a few seconds, then decided to play it narrow.

"Dave had an Oregon State P.I. license," I said. "What he was working on as an investigator is privileged information outside a courtroom."

"Save the crap, Wells," White said. Obviously, he was putting on a tough-guy act for this big city suit.

I looked at White. "That crap as you call it is standard procedure in business like this," I replied. "My friend had a client. I suggest if you want to find out what Dave was working on, Mr. Kayama, you might try asking her."

"I already have," Kayama said. "The reason I came up here from the city was to talk to Ms. Benchley. I was hoping you could add something. We are talking about a homicide case here. If there's anything you know, you should be aware that withholding evidence in a —"

"Save me the statute book," I said, "I was a cop myself."

"I'm aware of that," Kayama said, scratching his nose. "You were a patrolman in Sutter City down in the Bay Area. You were terminated from that job six years ago. Now you are a child support investigator working outside the civil service for the local district attorney. You also have assisted your late friend in his past private investigations."

"Very good," I replied. "Did Detective White tell you all that, or did you log on to my world wide website?" I didn't mean to wax sarcastic, but being verbally pushed against a wall tends to bring it out in me.

Kayama was not ruffled by it. He glanced at his watch, then he continued:

"I would think a public servant in any law enforcement capacity should be forthcoming when a crime is being investigated."

"Well," I said, "the fact is I don't work for you, Mr. Kayama. I don't work for Mr. White or the Rogue Falls Police, either. I haven't committed a crime and I have no knowledge of Mr. McCreedy or anyone else doing so. Mr. McCreedy is dead, by the way, in case you didn't notice the wake going on inside. I will tell you, in the interest of not withholding information, that I have no knowledge where Jack Benchley is. Therefore, I have no relevant information on the matter you wish to question me on. Therefore, I don't have any need to be questioned on this matter by you, Mr. Kayama, or by you, Mr. White."

I glanced over at Russ White. He shot me back a look of disgust.

I continued. "I will give you what my friend Dave told me about the Carolyn Mason business. Jack Benchley didn't kill her. So, I get the feeling your investigation is probably going in the wrong direction if you're trying to nail Jack Benchley for this woman's murder. I could point you in a couple other directions Dave was working on, but not without hearing first from his client."

"How do you know Jack Benchley is even a suspect?" Kayama asked.

"I can read the papers," I said. "The local newspapers, the San Francisco papers, and all the other media outlets are full of this story. Somebody at the San Francisco Homicide Bureau is leaking little tidbits of rumor to the press. Let's see...I've read that Jack Benchley is hiding in Mexico; Benchley may be in Europe; that unidentified sources in your city police department say Benchley is the only person who can be tied in any way to the crime. No formal press conference. Just leaks. I know how the game is played. And, of course, the press and the television stations are eating it up. Your department is laying the groundwork to bag the old man because you have nothing better to go on. Well you go ahead and do that. Now, if you'll excuse me, I'm going back in. Mr. McCreedy died five days ago. He was a close friend of mine. Some other friends and myself are having a little remembrance inside."

Kayama didn't take the hint. "Your colleague, Mr. McCreedy, was down in San Francisco a few days before he committed suicide. He didn't phone you or discuss the case with you? Detective White tells me you were close friends and that you were quite probably assisting him on his investigation."

"That's right," I said. And I just went quiet.

"So you won't talk to me?" Kayama said, getting the non-verbal hint.

"I'm talking to you," I said. "I'm just not able to help you."

"You have no information that David McCreedy knew, at any time, of the whereabouts of Jack Benchley after March 25th of this year, when Ms. Mason was found dead, to the present time?"

"If Dave would have found Benchley, I imagine he would have brought him home to his client, Ann Benchley. The fact that Jack Benchley is not home would indicate to me Dave didn't find him. I assume if he'd have made contact, then he would have told Ann Benchley. So what did Ann Benchley say when you talked to her?"

Kayama sighed, and checked his watch again. He leaned back against the railing again and rubbed one set of fingers over the other. He looked at me like I was giving off a bad odor.

"Can you tell me what Mr. McCreedy was doing specifically down in San Francisco in the days before his death?"

"Just plugging along, checking out leads the police weren't interested in."

"You realize you may be subpoenaed at some point to answer questions," Kayama said in a direct tone. "A Grand Jury will demand specific answers."

"I was a cop," I said. "I know all that."

Kayama gave me a quick nod, then said good-bye to Russ White and walked down the stairway. White followed him down after giving me a nasty look. He caught up to the big city detective as he was getting into his nice shiny rental car. I stayed on the porch to try and see what was happening. They talked a bit more, with Russ taking a glance up at me once or twice. Kayama drove off. I stayed on the porch until Russ came back up the stairway. He stood a few feet away from me, his arms resting akimbo.

"You pissed him off," Russ told me.

"I'm deeply saddened," I said.

"There's a lot more to this than you think," Russ said. He paused for a moment, then walked over to the railing. A large black poodle was rummaging around the garbage can, his front paws on the rim of the open can. Russ stared down at the animal.

"That's a big poodle," Russ remarked.

"That's Charlie," I said. "The guy who has the restaurant down the alley owns him. It's a good breakfast place. Good muffins."

"Any reason you're taking ten days off from work?" Russ said casually.

I had to laugh. Russ had come prepared. "Oh, you know what a big baseball guy I am. The Athletics and the Giants are going to have their Trans-Bay two-game series down in the Bay Area, just before the regular season starts. I thought I'd head down there for a few days, see a couple ball games, catch up with some old friends."

Russ kept looking at the dog. "If I was a little poodle, and I saw that big poodle running around, I think I would just stay on my porch. Little poodles have to watch where they go and what they get themselves into."

"Didn't know you were so into dogs, Russ." I said.

Russ tried his luck solo and fired off some questions. "Did Dave make contact with Jack Benchley? Did he try and help him get out of the country? He knew Dave was in tight with the Benchley family, so what did he really tell you about that was going on in Frisco?" I didn't say anything. I just waited for him to play his hand. He didn't disappoint.

"You know what happens to guys who hide murder suspects?"

"Russ, I'm not hiding nobody. Neither was Dave. I have no idea where Jack Benchley is. You want to get a judge to give you a warrant to search his office, go ahead. You want to drag me downtown? The answer I just gave you on Benchley won't change."

Russ snorted. He drew a cigarette out of his shirt pocket, broke off the filter and lit up with a disposable butane lighter. He fixed me with a gaze right out of the Fuck-With-Me-Not school of interrogation.

"Remember, Wells, you got a job with the County D.A. It's a crummy job, but I'd bet you'd miss it. The least you can lose is your job if you hold out on me."

That last remark, a familiar one, gave me a chuckle. "That your idea of a threat? From what I read in the papers, Measure 19-6 is going down to defeat. I expect to lose my job, so your threat is rather underwhelming just now. I'm giving you the truth. Jack Benchley could be in Rangoon or dead for all Dave knew, or I know now. If I get anything, I know your phone number."

"Dave told me you used to be a cop down in Sutter City. I didn't realize before I checked into your records that Sutter City was near Sacramento?"

"Between Sacramento and San Francisco."

"Oh," Russ said. I knew what was coming next and I dreaded it.

"Dave said you got into trouble when you were a cop. I guess you got pushed out. I couldn't find out the specifics but you were pushed. I'll bet you never would have even got that crummy contract job in the Family Support Bureau if it wasn't for Dave." Even in the semi-darkness, I could see a couple veins bulging out of Russ's forehead. His face betrayed frustration.

"I know we weren't friends, Russ, but we both liked Dave. So why are you coming down on me about all this? Is there an Atta-Boy award with Chief Holden in it for you because your boss is a retired Frisco cop? Dave never told me you were an apple polisher."

"Look, Wells—" Russ began.

"Look yourself," I said. "You put this big town homicide dick on my case five days after my best friend dies to show off your stuff. You know Dave would've stonewalled him; did you think I'd cave in under a little heat? Try this, Russ: tell Chief Holden or anybody else you're trying to impress to find another guy to lean on. If you want anything else out of me, call me during business hours. And don't try and tell me to lay off the Benchley Case. I'm going to California tomorrow and pick up where Dave left off. I'm going to make sure his suicide was just that, a suicide."

"It was a suicide," Russ said.

"Then why hasn't there been an official finding issued by the Medical Examiner?"

Russ took a long draw on his cigarette. "Because the case isn't closed yet."

"But you said that night—"

"It's going to come down as a suicide," Russ half-shouted, then lowered his voice out of respect for the widow inside.

"Look, you want all there is on Dave McCreedy's death. O.K., smartass, here's what I know. The M.E. did a body temperature check on Dave at the site. Body temp is inexact, of course, but all things equal he puts Dave's death at around six o'clock that evening. The fingerprint people have been all over his motorcycle, all over the gun that was found in Dave's hand. The County has had officers checking out any tiremarks, any signs of other footprints in the area. As far as I know—and I'm not a deputy sheriff—there's no indication of anything but suicide."

"What about that circle of burnt ground?" I said. "What about ballistics tests? Have they checked the gun to make sure it was the gun used in the death? Do they have enough of the slug intact to run a—"

"Burnt ground?" Russ said. "Probably just kids playing with matches. They recovered the slug. It's gone to the state crime lab in Salem."

"To Salem?" I said. "They would only do that if there wasn't a match to Dave's gun. What the hell is going on, Russ?"

"That stuff is the sheriff department's business," Russ said, testily. "When they want to make it all public, they will. I've told you all I know. Now tell me what Dave was up to down in San Francisco."

"I don't know anything, Russ. We just did this drill, didn't we? That's why I'm going down to San Francisco; to retrace Dave's steps and see what exactly he was looking into. It may be the suicide was a set-up. I want to know for sure."

"I wouldn't advise poking your ugly nose around down there," Russ said. "S.F. cops are all over that case. The FBI has been brought in for consultations. They want Benchley and they want him before some part-time pseudo-cop from Bumfuc, Oregon, can get to him and help him beat the murder rap."

I let the 'part-time pseudo-cop' phrase slide, much as I would have liked to do otherwise, and stayed on the subject.

"You proved my point: Kayama and the gang down there think Jack Benchley knocked off that Mason lady?"

"What else could they think?" Russ replied. "I just hope, for your sake, you don't know what's happened to Jack Benchley."

"I know zero, Russ," I said. I then excused myself and

started back into the bar. Russ stepped in front of me.

"I think you're bullshitting me, Wells," he said in an unfriendly tone.

He was pushing it, all part of the fun of wearing a clean blue suit with a gold-plated badge tucked somewhere in the inner pocket of that clean blue suit, all snug in an alligator-skin wallet.

"And you're shitting me, Detective White. This isn't a simple suicide case anymore, and you damn well know it." Again, I could see blue veins pop up on Russ' forehead.

"You're headed for big trouble, Wells. I mean it."

"I'll ask again, officer," I said as calmly as I could muster. "Would you mind getting out of..."

We were both distracted by a commotion from inside the bar.

"You don't tell me to do nothin', asshole!" a shrill voice shouted out. "Now get your dumb Limey ass out of my face!"

I recognized the voice. It belonged to a character named Sweeney. I didn't know his first name, nor did I care to. He was a loudmouth, a skinny weasel of a guy who usually could be found at the pool table trying to hustle some unwary college kid. He had been a child support case of mine a couple years back. He supplemented his job pumping gas with doing some auto detail work in a garage. Trouble was he tried to keep the income from his second job under the table, not bothering to tell his former common law wife about it when he had a court order to pay out a portion of all his income to keep his two 'love children' fed and in clothes. I knew other things about Sweeney. He had tried to hit on Wendy a couple times before she straightened him out. When he persisted, Dave straightened him out with an unsubtle threat to rearrange his face if he even spoke to Wendy for anything other than asking for a beer.

I had a very good idea who he was calling a 'dumb Limey,' too. There followed some scuffling and grunting noises, then a sharp thumping noise. A few seconds later, I saw Sweeney coming through the hallway. Ray Harrison, bartender and bouncer at O'Leary's, was carrying him down the hallway. Harrison, a tall and barrel chested guy with dark hair greying around the temples, had one hand on the back of Sweeney's denim pants and the other gripping the collar of the smaller man's brown leather jacket.

"Coming through," Ray said, as he crossed the threshold of the back entrance, lugging the rowdy customer out to the deck and down the wooden stairway. Sweeney was kicking his legs and struggling, swearing like a Merchant Marine, but it wasn't doing him any good. When Ray and his cargo reached the bottom of the steps, the bartender heaved the customer unto a pile of plastic trash bags that were situated next to a locked metal dumpster.

I looked over at Russ for his reaction. He looked over at me, a slight smile forming on one corner of his mouth.

"That's your third and last time, mate," Ray said forcefully. His voice was rather high-pitched for a big guy, but it was forceful anyway. "Get out and stay out. If I see you in here again, you'll get the same if not worse." Ray turned and walked back up the stairs. Sweeney got up from the trash, brushed his ugly tasseled leather jacket and denim pants off, and looked up at us.

"You guys are cops or something, right?" the shrill voice implored. "You saw what that guy did. Do something."

Detective White did do something: he took another drag on his cigarette.

Ray came back up the stairs like he was reporting for just another routine day at work. "There's a phone call for you, Harv," Ray said casually. "It's on the bar phone. A woman's voice."

"My soon to-be ex-wife?" I asked.

"No, mate. Some other dollybird," Ray said, in his London Cockney accent.

"Excuse me," I said politely to Russ, who stepped back and let me pass.

Chapter Six

The woman on the phone was Bonnie Noel. She was an executive assistant for Ann Benchley, Dave's former client. I had contacted her through the offices of the Northwest Shakespeare Festival. I was hoping to get an interview with Ms. Noel or, preferably, Ann Benchley, to help me get to the bottom of Dave's 'suicide.'

"I understand you're an assistant for Mr. McCreedy," the voice on the other end of the line said. It was a nice voice, soft and throaty. Her tone, however, was firm and business-like.

"Yes," I said. "I'm trying to gather up any information that Dave gave to Ms. Benchley. I realize the confidentiality of the information, but I have some doubts about the preliminary verdict of—" I paused. I had slipped back into my official-style cop-voice for dealing with Kayama outside. Now that tone failed me. I couldn't say the word 'suicide.' It hurt too much.

"You don't think Dave McCreedy committed suicide?"

"Yes," I said.

There was a pause. "Are you saying Mr. McCreedy was murdered?" she finally said.

"I'm saying I'm not sure," I replied, cupping my hand over my right ear to muffle the chatter and television noise from the bar. "There are a few points I'd like to clear up on behalf of the McCreedy family. I also have some relevant information about Carolyn Mason. I think it might throw some light on the disappearance of Mr. Benchley."

Ms. Noel's voice took on a steely tone. "Mr. Wells, Ann Benchley is no longer a client for McCreedy Investigations. The

FBI and the San Francisco police are hard at work trying to find her father. If we need any more private services, we have contacts in the Bay Area."

I matched her tone. "The problem is that the San Francisco police are going to find Jack Benchley, if he's still alive, and then the Frisco D.A. is going to try and hang a murder rap on him. I just got a visit from a detective named Kayama. I suppose he has seen you and Ms. Benchley sometime today?"

"Yes," Bonnie Noel said. "A rather irritating gentleman."

"You know Dave believed Mr. Benchley was set up for the Mason murder. He's either in the clutches of the real killer or he's in hiding. I want any information you have on what exactly Dave was working on. I think your boss would want the information I've got on Carolyn Mason. It might explain why he's missing and she's dead. And by the way, Ms. Noel, I'm not angling for a job from your boss. I'm my own client when it comes to Dave."

There was another long pause. A peal of raucous laughter broke out from some loudmouth male kids sitting at the bar. The outburst drowned out whatever it was Ms. Noel told me next.

"I'm sorry. Can you repeat that?" I said.

She complied. "This information you have, does it have anything to do with a certain N.P.O. based in San Francisco?"

"If you mean the I.F.H., Ms. Noel, then I think you can see why I want to talk to Ann Benchley."

The steel went out of her voice. "I'll convey your request to Ms. Benchley. In any case, I think we should have a meeting on this. Can you be reached at this number in the next fifteen minutes?"

I could. After hanging up, Ray came over from the other end of the bar.

"Bonnie Noel, huh," he said. "She Ann Benchley's secretary."

"Did she tell you that?" I asked.

A smile crossed Ray's craggy dark-browed face. He was in his forties and had the build of a football player, or a soccer player, given that he had grown up in London's East End. He was about forty-five or fifty. His dark hair, streaked with the coming of grey, was perpetually tousled, and a five o'clock shadow was always on his mug anytime you saw him. He always wore t-shirts with a red-checkered vest and the same pair of faded, patchy jeans he had worn since the first Bush Administration. People were always surprised, from the look of him, that he had once worked at the Shakespeare Festival. Ray had been a Costume Designer, in addition to utilizing a special talent he had for bizarre or grotesque special effects projects. He had been fired for a rather sordid reason.

"I knew her from when I worked at the festival," Ray said. "She started out as an actress and somehow she wound up as Jack Benchley's personal secretary. Now she works for the daughter. I recognized her voice. A voice like that is easy to remember."

"You guys ever go out?" I asked.

"Once. About three years ago when she played Regan in *King Lear*. She's a little too frosty for me. We just went to the movie, had drinks, talked. She never warmed up to me really. I decided she was a bit of a tight-arse. Not for me."

Or vice-versa, I thought.

"Let me know when she calls back," I said. Ray nodded and I went back to the wake. Somebody had put on a CD of the Chieftains, Dave's favorite band. Dave liked those slow ballads of lament and sorrow. Sadness and loss appealed to his Irish spirit. "'Any of those Chieftains have more soul than a pack of Black Popes,'" Dave would say. Personally, I thought Dave's opinions had more to do with ethnic chauvinism than any objective 'soul-meter' he possessed. Wendy gave me a smile as I sat back down. She reached her hand out to me and announced that she felt tired and wanted to go home. I offered to take her home but her sister was going to do the duty.

"You were Dave's best friend," she said, giving my right hand a squeeze. "And I mean 'best.'"

I winced a bit at her remark, considering the fact that the Bomber Boys and several of Dave's other friends were in earshot. I got up and gave her an awkward hug as she was leaving. I would have left for home myself but I had to wait for Ms. Noel to call back.

After discussing who would reach the Final Four in the NCAA Basketball Tourney with Ferlin and a husky fellow Dave went deerhunting with whose name escapes me I was called to the phone again by Ray. It was Bonnie Noel, right on time. She told me that Ann Benchley was too busy to see anyone, but she had authorized her to meet with me. There was a performance of *Anthony and Cleopatra* scheduled to go on at 8:30 in the Ryskind Indoor Theater. Could I be over at the Ryskind in a half hour?

I could. This was working out well, since I wanted to start down for San Francisco the next morning. The only hitch was to get over to my trailer and get out the material I needed regarding the investigation. I guess at some point in our second conversation I must have said Ann Benchley's name out loud due to the volume of the music. Ray took note of this and hovered over me at the end of the bar until I hung up.

"Was that the warm and friendly Ms. Noel?" Ray asked.

"Yeah," I said nonchalantly. "She sends her love." I could tell Ray wanted me to elaborate on the conversation, but that wasn't going to happen. Ray was a very nice guy, but telling him anything confidential had the same effect as putting an ad in the newspaper. I suppose it is an occupational trait for good bartenders, even part-time ones. I wasn't giving out information to anybody if I could help it. Ray, however, was not of the same mind.

"You gotta go up to the Benchley Ranch and pick up Dave's effects, right?" Give credit to Ray, he lowered his voice so the college crowd didn't pick up on what we were talking about.

"What do you mean?" I was genuinely puzzled.

"He never told you about . . . about him and Ann Benchley?"

"What do you mean?" I repeated. "I knew he went over to see the old man a few times. They were drinking buddies. They talked about sports and hunting. That's what Dave told me."

Ray shook his head. "I'm surprised he never told you. After Dave found the kidnapper and that Tyler kid of hers, they started..." He trailed off, not sure if any of Wendy's friends might still be around. "They had a...a fling."

"*Fling?*" I said, as if the word came from a forgotten language. This was news to me, and not good. "I thought she was based in Los Angeles most of the time."

"She was," Ray said. "But you know last couple years she's been doing Shakespeare in her old man's company. Dave used to go out to the cottage she stayed in on the Benchley

Ranch. He even went down to L.A. and saw her last July."

I recalled Dave being down south last summer. He was supposed to be at a Security and Investigations Convention in Vegas, however. Wendy had a newborn and classes, so he went alone. This seemed way out; Dave with Ann Benchley, a famous multi-media actress? It wasn't plausible.

"What did Dave tell you?" I asked Ray.

One of the guys at the bar, a short chalky-faced kid with a pointy chin and long front bangs that made him look like Moe Howard of the Three Stooges, asked Ray for another round of Henry Weinhards.

"I'll be back in a minute," Ray said.

"I have to go, man. Can we talk about this later?"

"Whenever you like mate," Ray said as he walked away to the taps to fill the order. "I go off-shift in a couple hours."

I had to hurry to drive the dozen miles over to Middleburg, get the papers, and get back to downtown Rogue Falls, where the Ryskind Theater was. As I drove, I had a chance to let the news of the Dave and Ann Benchley tryst roll about in my head. At first glance, the union was preposterous. As a working stiff, Dave was way out of his league with a film and television star. On the other hand, Dave McCreedy was a handsome guy, and certainly self-assured, not a man easily intimidated. And, from personal experience, I knew it was impossible to understand the workings of a woman's mind, especially in the romance department. And Ann Benchley, although famous, was not a superstar. Maybe she had come close to that dizzying height, but now she was just a well-known actress rather than a household word. She had won an Oscar playing a aristocratic young Frenchwoman in her father's screen adaptation of Henry James' *The American*, which was his last film to date. But that had been fifteen years ago. Her biggest commercial hit had been as an interplanetary gunslinger Belle Kilroy in *She Came to Europa*, a film that was rumored to be ripe for a sequel. That film put her on the brink of being a major star. I had seen *Europa*. It was one of my ex-wife's favorite films, a high-tech allegorical space opera about a female law enforcement officer cleaning up a rowdy male-dominated one-spaceship town on one of Jupiter's moons. It seemed the corrupt, brutal boss of Jupiter's fourth largest moon—played by Dennis Hopper—had made the mistake of raping Belle's mother in an earlier phase of his character's life of crime and also did unkind things to Belle's sister in the film's present time. (Suffice to say, for those of you who missed it, Belle got her revenge.) More recently, she had been involved in some forgettable comedies and as the female ornament in male-dominant action films. Her only solo starring roles lately had been in direct-to-video theatrical features or made-for-cable fare.

Perhaps to shore up what remained of her professional prestige, Ann Benchley had taken leading roles in her father's Shakespeare plays in each of the last three years. I missed her Lady Macbeth in the first year, but did see her as Rosalind in *As You Like It.* I liked Ann Benchley as a screen actress and I was curious as to how she would come over on stage. Even though she was too old for the part, she had the audience cheering her at the curtain.

So the thought of actually meeting her was both intimidating and stimulating all at once. Assuming I would make it past her secretary.

I got back to Rogue Falls around 6:30 or so. The sun was setting so there was a nice glow of twilight filtering in gold shades around the old brick buildings that made up the Plaza. Because it wasn't Summer, and the tourists had not arrived in droves, there was still parking available within a couple blocks of the theaters. I parked up on a hillside, curbed the wheels of my Toyota Celica, and walked down the steep sidewalk past the main theater, to the outdoor Elizabethan Auditorium. The Elizabethan, or 'The Lizzie' as the locals called it, was supposed to be a replica of the sort of theaters that Shakespeare and his peers performed in. I had been inside the auditorium, but only as a tourist. This was because it was only opened in the summer, and by June I steered clear of the whole downtown plaza area with its swarms of tourists. Those who flocked there were comprised of drama-oriented high schoolers sent by busload to Rogue Falls from all over the West for exposure to Shakespeare; retired types who showed up in nicer busses, brightly colored double-decker ones with the name of the private tour company emblazoned across the streamlined sides of the vehicle; and upper middle-class folk from all over hell and gone.

A light rain was still falling when I reached the center of

the plaza area. It was once called Pioneer Plaza, but now it was called—what else—Shakespeare Plaza after the cash-and-credit-card cow that Jack Benchley had helped develop in his hometown. In the center of the plaza was a small, well-lit kiosk building where a pretty young lady sold programs and souvenirs to a crowd of theater goers and bystanders who were gathered for the Green Show. The show was an assembly of singers and musicians dressed in English Renaissance costumes: doublets, hose, breeches, floppy cloth caps, long billowing skirts and bodices, etc. The dozen performers were on an elevated stage and played madrigals and folk tunes and danced to warm up the ticket buyers for the theatrical experience. I noted a few new offerings at the kiosk; a sweatshirt which had an image of Shakespeare wearing cool-looking shades and a couple posters, one displaying photos of the Elizabethan Auditorium and another of the alluring Ann Benchley in full Cleopatra regalia.

I walked up the stairway leading to the theatre. I stopped because a television camera crew was ahead of me on the steps: a cameraman, a lady with headphones next to him, and a reporter in a blue blazer and matching skirt holding a microphone to her face. It looked like they were doing a "live feed." "Jack Benchley has now been missing for fifteen days, Chet," the woman said into the camera. "Still no break in the case in the search for the film director and Artistic Director of the Festival. Ann Benchley is appearing tonight for the first time since her father disappeared. This is Tawny Wilson, Eyewitness News...."

As I walked past the Eyewitness News crew, I heard Tawny Wilson say to the cameraman, "I'll bet they never find him. Never."

Once past the stairway I went down a sidewalk, past an Italian coffee bistro, then, on the other side of the walkway, the glass-enclosed front of the Ryskind Theater. The place was named for Morton Ryskind, a friend of Jack Benchley who had originally founded the Northwest Shakespeare Festival about forty years earlier.

The theater was a palatial pile of bricks, something like a big-city opera house, round and multi-storied with a lobby area big enough to park a couple dozen Cadillac DeVilles and lots of fancy woodgrain paneling and crystal chandeliers hanging from the cathedral-sized ceiling. I nudged myself through a crowd of patrons, young and old, waiting to get in and grab their programs and seats.

"I'm here to see Bonnie Noel," I told the thin, perfectly groomed elderly gentleman in the red blazer who was standing guard at the lobby entrance. "My name is Wells. Harvey Wells."

The old gent picked up a phone and speed dialed. He said a "Harold Wells" was here to see Miss Noel. I didn't bother to correct him on the first name. He told me to go down the stairway on the far side of the concession area and then straight on to the third office on the left. I did so, passing a long concession stand with a rectangular glass facade showing off wine bottles and paperback books of all the plays on display for the season. A young man and woman were behind the counter. Both were nicely dressed in matching formal red aprons and black ties and were busily setting up plastic cups, soda cans and imported beer bottles for the first-nighters who were presumably about to be let in.

The third door on the left was marked "Staff Only." It was half-open and a woman was seated in front of a large rectangular table, with several empty metal folding chairs around her. She looked up from her clipboard and her large eyes, green like a baseball field, jolted me from being nervous into being intrigued.

Chapter Seven

She was maybe 5'8" with frizzy, copper-blonde hair just brushing down to her shoulders. She could have been any age from thirty-five to forty, and had a graceful way of moving her head. Bonnie Noel had a soft demeanor and a full figure. Her waist a bit thick, but she had a generous bosom to compensate. Her face was oval-shaped and pleasant to look at. Her dark green eyes were large, and accentuated by light contours of mascara. She had a rosy complexion, with a thin layer of lipstick across her full lips. Her nose was slightly upturned, stubby and a bit wide. She had a strong chin and her cheekbones were not prominent but you didn't have to go looking for them. She had a face like an elf—a cute lady elf. She wore long gold earrings depicting some Mesoamerican Sun god, a white blouse cut low enough to show off a pearl-shaped amulet but, regretfully, stopping short of exposing any cleavage.

"Hello, I'm Bonnie Noel," she said, standing up. Her soft, throaty voice on the phone matched her presence well. She wore acid-washed blue jeans, not too tight but not baggy. "You must be either Harold or Harvey Wells." We exchanged a quick handshake. I got a smile from her.

I detected a sense of humor. I played on it. "Actually, you can call me either name," I replied with nonchalance. "I sometimes use two different first names in my business. It promotes confusion in my dealings with the Internal Revenue Service. There are amazing tax advantages in being two separate people."

"You can file a joint return with yourself," she said in a wry tone. "Wish I'd thought of that. What name would you like to be for this meeting?"

"Harvey," I said. I took a seat on the single aluminum chair across the table from her. She returned to her seat. I placed a folder of papers that represented my research on the Benchley case, and Dave's reports to me on the table.

"Mind if I take a look?" she asked. I told her I had no problem. "I'll elaborate on them after you've had a look." She reached down under the table for a compact black purse. Out of it came a soft case and out of the case came a pair of glasses with thin, light green frames.

"I just had my corneas zapped by laser treatments a couple months ago," she said after getting her glasses on. "It's called radial keratotomy. I still need glasses to drive at night and to see fine print after a long day. You should have seen how thick my lenses were before."

"They look nice on you," I said, then realized that was a bit forward. Oh, what the hell, I thought: I'm after information, not a job. As she scanned the material I looked around the room. The place had the feel of a meeting room. The decor to the place was a series of photographs depicting dramatic scenes from stage plays. There was also an old framed poster advertising "Sir Laurence Olivier as *Coriolanus*." The advertisement featured the actor in Roman-style dress on a platform appearing to shout down on a crowd of toga-clad, fist-waving male spectators just below him. He still had some dark strands of hair, cut in the bowl-shaped Roman-style. Olivier projected strength in his pose. He looked the same age as when he made the film "Sleuth" with Michael Caine. Next to the depiction of Olivier was a large black-and-white print of Ann Benchley in a white gown and spiked crown. She had her hands together and looked spaced out. That must have been from the *Macbeth* production I had missed. The thick, dark rings under her eyes and the intense, disturbed look she had, made her look very scary.

"I have to get back to Ms. Benchley shortly," Ms. Noel said. She looked up from the papers. "There's a lot of information here. Can you summarize your material?"

"I can," I replied, hoping I wouldn't be too rushed. "There is an organization called the Institute for Factual History. The

IFH puts out books, videotapes and CD-Rom material of a political nature. That nature is, from what I've surmised from the titles and synopsis available, is that the United States Constitution is a joke. The I.F.H. says it needs to be replaced with an old-style British government, monarch and all."

"That part we know about," she said, checking something off the paper on her clipboard. Was I being graded?

I continued; "The leader of the IFH, the founder in fact, is a fellow named Trevor Warbeck. Mr. Warbeck is a former film and stage actor from England who has turned his hand to writing books and doing a weekly syndicated radio program that promotes this, ah, shall we say, a... a..."

"The man is a demagogue," Ms. Noel commented. "He is no friend of Mr. Benchley. They had worked together in the past, and developed a mutual dislike. I take it you have something on the IFH my employer can utilize."

"Carolyn Mason was employed at the IFH for about three months back in 1995," I stated. "According to information Dave McCreedy dug-up, she later took a job as a waitress at the Cliff House in San Francisco. According to staff people, she met Jack Benchley there on several occasions. From an employment agency's records on Ms. Mason, she was working as a fill-in assistant to Jack Benchley for about a week when he was serving as a judge at the San Francisco International Film Festival two years ago, about the same time as her employment with the IFH. They probably met at that time."

Bonnie Noel just nodded and looked me dead in the eyes. She would have made a good poker player; I couldn't be sure this was new information to her or not.

"According to the same sources," I continued, "she had an apartment on Telegraph Hill and that Benchley either owned the apartment unit or was subsidizing her rent. It appears they were lovers."

Ms. Noel's eyes widened, then she nodded and put down the clipboard.

"How does, or did, he know that?" she asked, sounding interested.

"A friend of Mason's, a woman named Jane Willey, who worked at the Cliff House for awhile and was a close friend of hers. I contacted her a few days ago. I've tried contacting her since, but apparently she took a few days off. I've tried to find her residence and phone number in the San Francisco Area phone directories and city guides but there's no information. She did confirm the fact that Jack Benchley and Carolyn Mason were lovers."

Bonnie Noel's eyebrows arched nicely.

"The roommate also says that some guy with an Eastern European accent called Carolyn Mason at all hours of the day and night. The roommate took messages—nothing very revealing—but Mason seemed to get the most calls from this unidentified man shortly after her dates and weekends with Jack Benchley."

"Hmmm," Ms. Noel remarked. She set down the pen she was using, and leaned forward slightly, resting her chin on the palm of her right hand. "Interesting that you should say this mysterious caller had a East European accent."

I noticed she had no rings on her left hand, and only a little brown garnet ring on her right ring finger. "Do you have somebody in mind who might fit that voice?"

"There is certain information I'm not at liberty to share, Mr. Wells. Ms. Benchley wants to help you in your quest to clear up your friend's death, but not at the price of disclosing things she has learned in confidence from other sources."

"Sources like San Francisco Homicide?" I asked.

Ms. Noel nodded. "Ms. Benchley has been asked both by Detective Kayama and Special Agent Watson from the FBI to refrain from any public comments."

"How'd the FBI get involved in this—if I may ask?"

"I believe Director Hardy has taken a personal interest in the case. He was at the Forest of Arden as a guest of Sherwood Strunk when Jack Benchley left the compound. He was in an adjoining bungalow from where Mr. Benchley and Carolyn Mason were staying."

"Ms. Noel—"

"Yes, Mr. Wells."

"Call me Harvey," I said. "Quite frankly, the problem Ms. Benchley has is that the FBI and/or the San Francisco Homicide Unit are looking to find her dad, and if they find him, promptly place him under arrest for the murder of this Mason woman."

"Nothing has been stated by the Bureau—"

"Nothing needs to be stated," I interjected. "I'm not unfamiliar with homicide cases. This case has been well-documented in the media. They need a suspect and relations between the FBI and the Benchley family have not been exactly smooth or cordial. During the 1950's, Mr. Benchley's father was blacklisted thanks in part to J. Edgar Hoover. In his autobiography, Mr Benchley made some unflattering statements regarding FBI activities then and in the more recent past."

"Director Norville Hardy is not J. Edgar Hoover," Ms. Noel stated flatly. "This is the year 2001, not the 1950's. I'm sure the authorities are working on a variety of leads other than making Ann's father a prime suspect."

"With all due respect, if what you just said is in line with what the Feds are feeding your boss, I'd say she's being snowed. As I said, the Frisco cops need a suspect. If the FBI is in on this as things stand, so much the worse for Jack Benchley. He was the last person to be seen with Carolyn Mason. She was found strangled in the trunk of Jack Benchley's Ford Mustang. Jack Benchley is missing. That could be interpreted as his being in the clutches of kidnappers, but it is just as likely that skeptical law enforcement types are concluding that Benchley is on the run."

"We are assuming Mr. Benchley has been kidnapped."

"But has there been messages to Ms. Benchley from the supposed kidnappers?"

"We have had contact," Ms. Noel said, then immediately clammed up. She seemed to look me over for a few seconds and then proceeded. "There has been a message received by mail. It is rather cryptic. Ann turned it over to the local police. They sent it down to San Francisco to be analyzed." She changed the subject, wanting, I suspect, to get off the subject of the message. She took those glasses off and rubbed the top of the bridge of her nose.

"How much are you aware of the rifts between Mr. Benchley and Trevor Warbeck?" she asked.

I tapped the folder I had brought with me. "I've followed Mr. Benchley's career with informal interest, long before this recent turn of events. Particularly his film career. Benchley and Warbeck were both successful in Hollywood. Back in the late sixties, Benchley made a film about Dostoyevsky's little stay in Siberia."

"*The House of the Dead*," Ms. Noel offered. "One of his

best films."

"Exactly," I said. "A cute little prison camp picture. Trevor Warbeck was the lead. It helps make him a star. Four or five years later, they work together again on *Essex and the Queen*, which is considerably truer to history than the Errol Flynn—Bette Davis movie Warners did in 1939."

"You mean the Bette Davis—Errol Flynn movie," Bonnie Noel said. "She had billing over Flynn; it was more her picture."

"As you wish," I said, recognizing a Bette Davis fan.

"Trevor Warbeck is Essex. Glenda Jackson, in heavy make-up, plays Elizabeth. Anyway, the first scene Jack Benchley shoots is the part where the Earl of Essex goes to the block for trying to bring down Queen Elizabeth," she interjected, then picked up the story:

"Mr. Benchley looks at the rushes. Decides that Warbeck might be a great actor, but he's not swashbuckling-rogue material. Warbeck gets canned. Charlton Heston comes in. Warbeck's reputation suffers. And perhaps his confidence. He gives some rather nasty remarks in interviews about Benchley. Tries to become a film director himself. Does three or four box office duds and he's no longer a major player. Would you like a little Pepsi. It's diet."

"Thank you," I said after she poured some fizzing cola into a Styrofoam cup. "I guess you know the rest, Ms. Noel. Warbeck pulls a Ronald Reagan and goes into politics. Runs for U.S. Senator from California. A lot of high-rollers in business back him up because he's got great diction and wants to eliminate the graduated income tax. He wins the G.O.P. primary, but loses the general election. Jack Benchley does all the opponent's campaign commercials and gets his liberal pals to kick in big bucks to help defeat Warbeck."

"So, I guess you're familiar with Mr. Benchley's life. Call me Bonnie, by the way."

"Thanks."

"Are you familiar with the articles Mr. Warbeck claims to have written concerning the Benchley family?"

I've looked over a book I got at the library that Warbeck co-authored. He cuts pretty hard into Walter Benchley's reputation."

"That came out of The Institute for Factual History mill of

lies," Bonnie said passionately. "I doubt he even co-authored *Red Star Over Hollywood.* Walter Benchley went to jail and basically lost the last fifteen years of his professional life because he wouldn't name names in front of that committee. He belonged to some anti-fascist groups in Hollywood, but Mr. Benchley can cite a multitude of people who know his father was no Communist. He just didn't want to rat on his friends."

I remembered Ray saying Bonnie Noel had once worked for Jack Benchley. Obviously, she was quite loyal to him.

"Do you know about that Anti-Stratfordian book Warbeck claims he wrote?"

You mean *Shadow on the Crow*, I replied."

"Right," she said.

"Dave told me a debate was scheduled between Warbeck and Benchley."

Bonnie, as I now was permitted to call her, brushed a lock of hair back over her ear. "I helped Mr. Benchley prepare for the debate," she said, a tone of sadness in her voice. "He was trying to resolve that Earl of Grantum business. Warbeck says this Earl, who had been an early patron of Shakespeare's, wrote all thirty-seven of his plays, plus most of his poetry. Mr. Benchley has evidence that Warbeck's main buttress to the Grantum theory—the supposed journal the Earl kept—is nothing more than a hoax, and not even a new hoax at that. The grandson of William Devant, Charles, wrote the journal himself and tried to pass it off as his grandfather's work. All this happened in the 1660's, after both William Shakespeare and William Devant had been dead for fifty years."

"So did people back in the 1660's know that the grandson created this phony diary?"

"A good question," Bonnie said with a trace of a smile. "The authenticity of the plays and poems has always been subject to speculation by certain renegade pseudo-scholars. There's always somebody, somewhere, trying to prove that somebody else wrote Shakespeare's plays besides Shakespeare himself. Grantum is only one of several candidates." She took a sip of her diet drink, then continued. "You have Edward De Vere, the Earl of Oxford; Sir Walter Raleigh; Sir Francis Bacon; Christopher Marlowe, a playwright who died long before Shakespeare stopped writing plays. I even perused a book that said Queen Elizabeth herself found time to write Shakespeare's plays for him. Well, to answer your question: the reading public of the Restoration Era never had a chance to find out. You see, the print shop where Charles Devant took his phony journal was burned to the ground in September 1666, during the Great Fire of London. And the journal supposedly was destroyed in the fire. For centuries, all historians have had to go on were a couple letters that Charles Devant wrote to his friends around 1665 claiming that he had found this journal of grandpappy's in the cellar of Grantum Hall. Charles Devant asserted that his grandfather alluded to writing the plays in several parts of his journal, but no written copy of the journal had survived—until recently."

"And that was what Warbeck found," I said.

"Yes," Bonnie said in a tone indicating disbelief. "Sherwood Strunk owns an estate north of London called Sobel House. Sobel was built at the same site as Grantum Hall after the old hall had been torn down around 1670. Warbeck claims he was poking around the foundation of the house and came across a priest-hole left over from the original site. Inside the hole—supposedly—was a 17th Century printing of several passages from what Warbeck claimed was William Devant's Journal. His conjecture is that the printer in London had run off one copy of the excepts from the Journal and sent it to Charles Devant to look over. Naturally, the excerpts were in support of the grandson's claim that William Devant—the Earl of Grantum—wrote Shakespeare's plays, or at least he claimed to. The hype Strunk's media machine put on this business was enough to make *Shadow On the Crow* a best seller here and in Great Britain. That's what the debate was going to be over—the veracity of Warbeck's book versus what Mr. Benchley had found himself over in England."

"So what did Jack Benchley find?"

Bonnie took another drink, then checked her watch. "I have to wrap this up quickly, but here's the gist: Mr. Benchley went over to England a few months ago and found the original copy of the Journal. You're probably not interested in the details, but Mr. Benchley would have presented evidence at that debate that William Devant, the 15th Earl of Grantum, no more wrote Shakespeare's plays than Queen Elizabeth did."

"Kind of strange," I remarked, "that all of a sudden Jack Benchley could find the original journal after all this time. Did he say where he found it?"

"In a small private library in Scotland," Bonnie said. "Mr. Benchley told me he wasn't at liberty to reveal the person who possessed the journal. But he got it and had it analyzed down in Pasadena by several rare book experts at the Huntington Library. I only saw a few pages of it—what Mr. Benchley was taking to the debate—but he told me the whole journal appeared to cover William Devant's life from roughly 1591 to 1612."

"But its a hoax," I said.

Bonnie nodded her head. "The copy Mr. Benchley found recently had been handwritten, and, according to handwriting and documents experts at the Huntington, the parchment used was not available during Late Tudor or Early Stuart times. What's more, according to several expert graphologists, it had all been written in a matter of a couple weeks instead of twenty-one years. And, to cap it all off, the hand writing itself was in a style closer to that of Charles Devant than what writings we have of his grandfather."

"The grandkid tried to pull off a forgery," I said.

Bonnie nodded. "Charlie Devant was a big high-stakes gambler. Lost a lot of money playing a card game called Primero. Once his money was gone, all he had was Grantum Hall and he was looking at having to sell that. King Charles II was ticked off at him because his father had been a Roundhead—one of the Puritan faction that supported Oliver Cromwell and sent Charles I to the execution block—so he couldn't hope to get any help in that direction. He had to make money to save Grantum Hall. This was the Restoration period and Shakespeare's plays were being revived, badly revised in some cases, but revived in some form similar to the original texts. There was a bit of a legend in the family that William Devant was William Shakespeare's first patron when the writer came to London as a young man. So Charlie Devant came up with this idea to make up a hoax and sell a phony journal that would give him money and gain prestige for his family. There was enough interest in Shakespeare's plays then for him to make some money out of the hoax. When the analysis proved him right, Mr. Benchley had the proof to refute Warbeck's theories. The Forest of Arden debate was going to be the first time—"

"Bonnie!"

The air was filled with a loud female voice in a tone of distress coming from somewhere down the hallway. I looked over at Bonnie. She had her eyes shut tight, her mouth partially open, and her large straight teeth clenched. She looked cute that way.

"Bonnie, where are you?" the voice called out. I now recognized that the voice belonged to Ann Benchley herself. When I saw her on stage as Rosalind two years earlier, my wife and I had been up in Row Z, the cheap seats of the Ryskind Theater. Now the actress swept into the room and was maybe ten feet from where I was sitting. The effect of her was flat-out breathtaking.

"Notes! Notes! The goddamn little Berkeley drama twerp is still giving me notes!" Ann Benchley was fuming. A little Asian lady with an eyebrow pencil was just behind her. I guessed she was her make-up person.

It was not Ann Benchley, late 20th Century movie and stage presence before us, but the Queen of the Nile. This Cleopatra was not the petite, shimmering, silk-clad vision that Claudette Colbert offered up in Cecil B. DeMille's coy erotica of the early thirties. Nor was Ann Benchley sporting the top-heavy splendor of Liz Taylor in the recklessly-extravagant 1960's cinema offering. This stage queen was attired in a top as a warrior queen with an outfit of leather fitted to the advantages of her willowy figure. Her natural red hair was covered by a long mane of brunette wig. The Egyptian motif was enhanced by a narrow gold-colored crown that came to about the middle of her forehead and just above the ears. An intricately designed figure of an aroused cobra stood guard above her unlined brow. Her eyes had enough black liner on them for an inner-city prostitute, but I'm sure this was intended to enhance her visage for the stage, and not for close contact.

There was a man hovering at the threshold of the doorway. He was a tanned white guy brimming with good looks—a nouveau gent who looked like a young Bruce Springsteen on steroids. He had a good build indicative of regular iron pumping, dark curly hair with sideburns trimmed down to his earlobes, hard black eyes and a stubby nose that wouldn't have looked out of place on some soap opera ladies man. He had a couple days' growth of dark whiskers around his chin and sunken cheeks and I had the feeling that was an effect rather than tonsorial carelessness. He was dressed like a *Gentlemen's Quarterly* hoodlum in a black and grey herring-bone Italian-style men's suit with a square-knot in his cloth tie. I knew him by acquaintance from O'Leary's Bar: Ralph Bates, an ex-cop from Los Angeles who was Security Manager at the festival. Bates got the job after Dave turned it down a couple years back. I recalled Bates and Ray Harrison talked a good deal together.

Despite her initial distress at the sudden intrusion, Bonnie had regained her composure quickly. This showed me she was used to verbal buffeting.

"I thought you spoke with Roger after the dress rehears-al last night," Ann said in an excited tone to her assistant. "I thought this business with trying to warp my character was over with."

Bonnie replied back in a calm but direct tone. "Ann, I did speak to Roger. He was to confine written critiques to the other principals, and not to you. You need to take some deep breaths here."

Ms. Benchley took a few deep breaths, turning around to face the mirror to the side of her. It was obvious that Bonnie was not a simpering sycophant. The other people in the room waited for the star to speak again. Turning back around, she sent a quick glance my way. She looked at me as if I were a chair in the wrong place.

"Would you excuse me?" she said.

I stood up and introduced myself. "Hi, Wells," the actress said coolly. "Bonnie will be with you shortly. Would you and Mr. Bates please wait outside."

"Yes," I said, not wanting to miss my exit cue a second time. The make-up lady went out of the room in front of me. I followed her and Bates looked me over as I went past him. He did not seem, or want to, recognize me.

"Hello, Ralph," I said. "How are things going?"

"Fine," Bates said. He sounded apprehensive, like I was a threat.

The make-up person and myself sat ourselves a few yards down the hall, where a small upholstered bench had been placed. The hallway now featured traffic: men dressed as Roman soldiers in metallic chest plates and leather aprons;

older men decked out in flowing togas. The women, African and Caucasian, dressed in harem outfits with billowy pantaloons and not much coverage on top. These I took to be the supporting cast. One man was mumbling to himself as he passed, and a pale buxom woman in harem garb was leaning against a notice board at the end of the hallway. Her eyes were closed and she was drawing deep breaths. Other performers filed out of another door across the hallway from where Bonnie was bunkered in with her boss. From somewhere down the hallway, toward the stage, I heard music, eerie, ancient-sounding flute and drum compositions, trying to simulate ancient pop tunes for the playhouse audience filtering in.

The make-up lady's name was Nina, and we chatted about the weather and the excitement, for her of the opening of the theater season. She explained she was usually working in the wardrobe crew, but a genuine big-name presence in the production had relegated her to the status of dresser and make-up person for Ms. Benchley. Non-star performers handled their own make-up at the Festival. Her supplementary wardrobe duties at the festival kept her working almost every night because there were two more productions starting up that week, to be complimented by three more consecutive plays starting in the summer at the Elizabethan.

"Do you know Ray Harrison?" I asked her. "He used to work in the Costume Department here."

"Yes, I know Ray well," she said in her flute-like little girl voice. "He...he's..."

"Different?" I said, trying to help her out.

"Yes," Nina said. "He had a weird sense of humor. He had a flair for designing all the gruesome props we'd need whenever we did something like *Titus Andronicus* or *Doctor Faustus*. Ray liked to scare the actresses by leaving gory plastic arms and legs in their dressing rooms. Or disembodied heads. I think he has a thing for some of them, and that's his way of showing it. He was fired by Mr. Benchley a year or so ago. Too bad; he was talented. I wonder where he is now."

"Tending bar down at O'Leary's," I said. "He owns a half-share in the place."

Our formal talk was interrupted suddenly by an Ann Benchley tirade, the sound of which came high volume out of the closed door.

"You talked to him, Bonnie, I know that! But, lo and behold, that did no fucking good, did it? I'm not an escapee from a community college drama lab! I've been a pro for twenty years! Roger Rafferty is the tyro here! Five years ago he was a Scenic Designer in some dinner theater in Vermont, for God sakes! Then my dad sees this dreary Strindberg thing he directed Off-Broadway a couple years ago, and he thinks this theatrical abortionist actually has talent. Dad recruits the little shit and now the little wanna-be thinks he's Kenneth Branagh. Two years from now he'll be history. Five years from now he'll be Hack-in-Residence at some rural playhouse above the Arctic Circle! I want him out of the director's job! Let him cool his heels until *The Devil's Disciple* opens this summer. He's over his head with Shakespeare."

"I don't think she took her pills today," Nina said to me.

Pills? Apparently there were few secrets at the Northwest Shakespeare Festival. That notion was reinforced by the reaction of the actors and technicians who were going back and forth down the hall. People took note of the high-pitched shouting coming from the room, but a crowd did not gather around the door. The star having a fit apparently was not a novel event, judging by those who briefly stopped near where Mr. Bates was standing in front of the door and reacted with smirks or shook their heads.

Once in a while, Ann Benchley would have to draw breath, and that is when I could hear Bonnie's voice. Her tone was in a more discreet mode, so it was hard to hear what was her end of the dialogue. I heard Ann Benchley loudly exclaim, "Get her on the phone then!" There followed Bonnie saying something, then Ann speaking a decibel or two softer than before.

The door opened. "We will get Bea Ryskind on it tomorrow," was Ann's comment as she crossed the threshold into the hallway. The star was breathing heavily and her hands, bejeweled with rings, were shaking. Bonnie came out just behind her, clipboard in hand. She looked a little buffeted but not overly-stressed.

Nina stood up as the Queen of the Nile flowed up the hallway. "Ms. Benchley, we have about thirty minutes to curtain. I need to finish your make-up." She gave Nina a quick nod of her head, then turned her attention to a chubby red-faced fellow with tousled strawberry blonde hair. He had on a headset, a green-and-gold University of Oregon sweatshirt and blue jeans. I noticed his forehead was sweaty and he looked like the messenger of bad news.

"Where's Roger?" Ms. Benchley asked.

"He's up on the catwalk over the stage. Somebody forgot to double-check the lighting cells. We'll be starting late." The chubby fellow said the word 'late' softly.

"Shit," was the hissed reply of the chief principal. "If my dad was here..." She stopped herself, then rubbed her forehead. "Oh, God," she moaned, "for this blistering migraine I am about to receive, let me be eternally grateful."

Bonnie looked at me with a sort of half-smile. Apparently, that touch of humor in her boss' voice meant that the crisis had passed. The show, even with faulty light cells, and a director bound for the Alaskan tundra, would go on.

"I'll talk to Roger tomorrow after I see Bea Ryskind," Ms. Benchley said to the chubby man. "She's the one in charge of this menagerie until my dad gets back. Chris, you assemble the cast. I want to say something to everybody before we go on. Nina, let's finish getting my face on." The actress started walking away, then looked squarely at me.

"You're Dave McCreedy's friend, right?"

"That I was," I said.

"I'm very sorry about Dave," she said, sounding genuine. "He was a good soul. He even fixed my Harley for me not long ago."

Probably not the only thing he worked on for her, I thought, assuming Ray's gossip was correct.

"Do you think he really killed himself?" Ms. Benchley asked.

That last part brought me up short. If Bonnie was direct, the lady she worked for was flat-out blunt.

"No I don't," I replied after a pause. "I don't think Dave was the type to kill himself."

"Nor do I," she said. "Dave talked about you. Said you were smart. Do you want to be hired to take Dave's place? Is that the purpose of this visit?"

I didn't like the idea of getting into the case with two outsiders right next to us. Ms. Benchley realized this and told Chris and Nina she would catch up to them. Bates remained hovering nearby, but with a quick nod of her head he moved down the hallway. Once all three departed, I answered her.

"It's not a job that brought me here. I have some information on what Dave was working on down in the Bay Area. I wanted to share information. I'm going toward San Francisco tomorrow to check out a few angles."

Bonnie chimed in, "I think he may have something viable on this Carolyn Mason business, a connection from her to IFH and a certain party."

Ms. Benchley nodded. "You know," she said in a soft voice. "The FBI Director, Norville Hardy, is a good friend of Trevor Warbeck. I don't think the FBI or the city cops down there have explored the Warbeck interest in my father's disappearance." She flipped a few strands of brunette hair out of her eyes with a quick motion of her head. If Dave had had an affair with her, he was one lucky bastard.

"Ms. Noel tells me you received a letter indicating your father had been kidnapped. Has the FBI given you any analysis?"

Bonnie clenched her teeth again, and her boss shot her a look lacking in amusement. "Oh, Bonnie, you told Wells about the note. Looks like that exchange of information is going very well."

"I'm sorry, Ann," Bonnie said. "The Special Agent said not to talk about it, but..."

"Forget it," Ann said to her. "Director Hardy, or that nasty man Kayama is going to put my dad in the gas chamber if we don't find him first. What have any of those bureaucrats with badges come up with, anyway? Jack shit, that's what. Hey, Wells, have you ever seen *Anthony and Cleopatra*?"

I was beginning to adjust to the Benchley style: disjointedness. She expected a snappy reply so I gave her one. "Yes," I said. "I saw the movie Heston made back in '71 or '72 with Hildegard Neil."

"Heston directed that," Ann Benchley said. "Might have been a good film if they had a decent budget. You can't do 'Tony and Cleo' with all those scene shifts on film without a big budget."

"I agree," I said

"I had a crush on Chuck Heston," Ms. Benchley volunteered. "I had a little part as a lady-in-waiting in my dad's movie, the one where Chuck plays Essex." She sighed, presumably lost for a moment in the memory of her missing father or a schoolgirl infatuation. "Well, Chuck's old now and I don't like his politics on assault weapons. Anyway, let me ask you: do you think Cleopatra should be played as a simpering, lovesick schoolgirl or as a strong, no-bullshit power player?"

I guessed what the right answer was. Fortunately I had read the text of the play earlier in the year.

"I suppose it was Marc Anthony who behaved like a school kid," I said. "He loved her so much he forgot how to take care of business with a punk Octavius Caesar. Cleopatra should have been the Roman Emperor."

Ms. Benchley smiled. "A good answer. You know exactly how to play the courtier, yet you don't want a position in my little organization. Well, we'll see about that." She turned to Bonnie. "Has Wells here given you all the information he's got?"

"Not yet," Bonnie replied.

Ms. Benchley pointed a finely-manicured index finger at the folder of papers I was carrying. "Is that the fruit of your investigation?"

I nodded. Within two seconds, the boss lady had snatched the folder from under my arm.

"I have some off-time when Anthony goes to Sicily to meet Octavius," the boss lady said. "Can you hang around here at the playhouse? I may send Bonnie out to you with an offer worth suffering through a couple hours of blank verse." She smiled again. Ann Benchley has a hell of a smile. I had no choice but to acquiesce.

Chapter Eight

I sat quietly in Seat 43, Row Z, watching Ann Benchley kicking at a fellow thespian and shouting at the top of her lungs. The actor was in a fetal position at her feet, howling and moaning. It was quite a scene, although I preferred the incarnate Cleopatra's earlier performance before the play. the one she gave in the make-up room.

We were somewhere in the second act of the play. Cleo had just found out that her Anthony was married to another woman, Octivian's sister, and she was giving the underling a pasting for bringing her the bad news. I was impressed by Ms. Benchley's performance. She seemed to have her teeth into the role and, if her display of temper backstage was an indication of her normal behavior, then portraying the imperious Egyptian monarch was no great stretch for her.

The theater, which probably had a capacity between seven hundred to eight hundred seats, was nearly full. Since the summer season was usually the busiest season for tourists, the near capacity boded well for the success of the play, and was a testament to the drawing power of Ann Benchley.

Her histrionic fit abating, the Queen was held up from collapsing by her female attendants. The Queen held her forehead with an open palm, as if that migraine was coming on again. "Bring me word how tall she is. Pity me, Charmain," she said, "but do not speak to me. Lead me to my chamber." The ladies went off-stage. The footlights and overhead spots dimmed down slowly to darkness. A smattering of applause broke out, buoyed up by others, including myself, who joined in so as not to appear unappreciative of the leading lady's efforts. It struck me that this spontaneous eruption grew out of seeing a well-known actress from multi-media live and in person. Would an "ordinary" actress have drawn that brief spurt of hardy clapping or was Ann Benchley like a goddess from our two-dimensional electronic temples who has deigned to appear before her worshippers in the flesh?

Thrown into darkness, the audience was treated to a whirring noise from the direction of the stage. I could dimly make out the existing set: a throne room decorated with colorful Egyptian hieroglyphics, rotating slowly stage right and a new set of indeterminate design taking its place. The lights came up, this time much brighter and bluer in hue than the preceding backdrop. The stage now resembled a barren High Desert plain. A young man appeared. He had been in several scene openings before, dressed for some reason in a prep school uniform, decidedly 20th Century. "The parlay of Sextus Pompeius and the forces of Anthony and Caesar. We are in Misenum, south of Rome." With that, the young man walked off-stage. A moment later, the actors playing ancient military adversaries entered from opposite wings.

I had been so taken by the scene change that I did not notice that Bonnie had suddenly appeared behind me. I looked around after she tapped me on the shoulder. She was wearing her glasses again. "Let's go into the control room," she said, a trace of her beguiling perfume gently registering on my nostrils. "We can talk in there."

We did not have far to go to reach the control room. It was just up the stairway behind Row Z. Bonnie removed a rope barrier that separated the entrance to the stairs from the section where the audience was allowed. I followed her up the dozen plush-red carpeted steps to a narrow doorway. She rapped gently on the door, and the heavy-set Chris opened it. I stepped into a rectangular shaped, dimly-lit room which looked like the control room of a television station; computer consoles covered the whole side of the glass-enclosed section that faced out on the auditorium. Chris returned to his swivel chair. Before him was a panel crammed with levers and rows of buttons. Just to the right of the panel was a monitor which permitted a high-angled view from somewhere above the front tier of seats. The dialogue from the resonant voices of the actors came through the small speaker system adjoining the monitor.

Another man was in the control room. He was a tall, bespectacled African-American man with a delicate face. I could see the redness in his eyes as we passed him. Bonnie and the man exchanged quick hellos and then he continued his preoccupation: standing over Chris' back, gaze fixed on the monitor, with his two hands slowly tearing apart a Styrofoam cup.

"That's Roger, the director," Bonnie whispered to me as we sat down in a small office area at the opposite end of the room. "He's a bit harried right now. This is opening night of his first production."

"Poor guy," I said. "Is he the one...?"

"Ann wants his scalp," Bonnie said quietly. "But she'll get over that. He's really quite talented, a super-perfectionist. Ann, I'm afraid, is venting her distress over the loss of her dad. And Roger is just having his turn today."

"When's your turn?" I asked.

Bonnie ignored that. "I talked to Ann between her scenes. She had a look at your research and what Mr. McCreedy sent you. She wants to put you on retainer for the period you are down investigating Mr. Benchley's disappearance."

"I thought I was investigating McCreedy's murder?"

"Don't you think they are related?" Bonnie said. I nodded my assent.

"What does she want me to do?"

Bonnie lifted her glasses off the bridge of her nose, rubbing the reddish marks between her eyes where the glasses had sat. "She wants you to do exactly what you were going to do, anyway. Do surveillance on The Institute of Factual History. Find out what Trevor Warbeck is up to. Follow him. Get information anyway you can."

"I accept," I said. "Same rate as Dave got?"

"Yes," Bonnie said. "The stuff you gave me on this apartment Carolyn Mason had on Telegraph Hill was fresh to her. Her dad had never mentioned Carolyn Mason to her before."

"What does Ms. Benchley know about this guy Warbeck?" I asked. "You said he's tight with the Number One at the FBI. And Sherwood Strunk is bankrolling his little IFH outfit. But everything I've read about him or by him makes me think, outside of his acting talent, he's a crank. Frustrated director. Frustrated politician."

"A supposed muckraking journalist who doesn't write his own books," Bonnie added.

"Exactly," I said. "So why does he have such important friends?"

"Important people can use him," Bonnie said, her voice hushed. "That's how he got into politics. He has ties to a lot of major players because they wanted an articulate, seemingly intelligent guy as a mouthpiece for their hyperbole. I think part of it is the man's presence. He has charisma about him: the handsome profile; the thick barrel chest: the above-average height, and those big black eyes that don't seem to blink. Add to that his English Oxbridge accent and he was quite a package of *personalismo.* Of course, he's a fat pig now, but twenty years or so ago.... I was in California when he ran for the Senate and I knew several women who voted for him just because he was a turn-on."

"Sort of a mature, but not yet heavy, Orson Welles."

"Close," Bonnie said, removing her glasses and rubbing the bridge of her nose. I'd say he was closer to Laird Cregar, crossed with that British actor Alan Rickman. Forgive me, you probably don't have any idea about Laird Cregar."

"I do," I said. "Heavy set American film actor from the 1940's. He was in *Hangover Square*, playing a rather emotionally unbalanced composer. He also played the Devil in the original *Heaven Can Wait.*"

"The Ernst Lubitsch version, with Gene Tierney."

"Right," I said. "He played Jack the Ripper in a movie as well. Good actor. Alas, died very young."

Bonnie smiled. "A fellow Laird Cregar fan. There's not many of us around."

I could hear Ann Benchley's voice coming through the speakers. I also heard Roger say something from a few yards away. He directed the remarks to his assistant.

"She's wrong. She's doing it wrong! Her whole character is pitched too overwrought. She'll have nothing left for Anthony's death scene! Why the fuck didn't she just direct it herself!" There followed quick footsteps. I peered out from the corner of the room divider just in time to see the director stomping out the door.

Bonnie shrugged her shoulder, then went on. "And then there's the Shakespeare debate. How convenient it is for Warbeck that Mr. Benchley happens to disappear just the night before their debate at the Forest of Arden. It was going to be taped for broadcast on the Strunk Culture Network."

"From what you told me, Jack Benchley had Warbeck over a barrel on that Devant Journal business."

"I thought so."

"So now Ralph Bates is working full-time as Ms. Benchley's bodyguard."

Bonnie nodded. "That note the police are analyzing contained a death threat against Ann. She's a famous person, and unfortunately crank letters come with the territory. But since Mr. Benchley's disappearance, Ann's not taking any chances. The only problem with Bates is that he's a conceited little creep. Ann doesn't like his attitude. She's even tried to lose him when she goes off on her motorcycle trips just to make his job harder to follow her."

"She tries to ditch her bodyguard?"

"Crazy isn't it?" Bonnie said. "Ann is a little different."

"Why doesn't your boss just get a new bodyguard?"

"Because her father picked this guy out for her. Bates' father worked as a security man when Mr. Benchley made movies at Paramount. She's stuck with him out of loyalty to Mr. Benchley, for right now at least." She checked her watch. "I've got to get back to Ann before the end of Act Three. She stood up quickly, adjusting the lapels on the maroon-red blazer she was now wearing over her blouse. The inevitable clipboard was scooped up just as quickly. "We need to go to Mr. Benchley's office for a moment. That's where I left the papers you brought. I hope you don't mind my making copies?"

"No," I said. "How do you want me to report in while I'm in San Francisco?"

"I'll cover that in the office." We left via a door marked for emergency exits, then I followed her and the maroon blazer and acid-washed jeans down a corridor lined with blow-ups of actors and actresses cavorting in past productions. Another emergency exit followed. Now we were on an iron grated catwalk suspended over the broad stairway I had used to get to the theatre. At the realization that we were suspended over a walkway maybe five floors up, I kept my head looking forward and did my best to shut down my peripheral vision.

I do not like heights. It's called acrophobia, hence my discomfort at Dave's invitation to go rock climbing.

The office Bonnie took me to was in an old three-story building that made up part of the restored 19th Century buildings that fronted The Shakespeare Plaza. We entered the building from the backside. Bonnie undid a couple doors with a set of keys and we entered a dark room. I felt it must be large, but could not see well enough to gauge its size. Once she got the overhead lights on, I knew instantly that this was Jack Benchley's office.

What was the giveaway? It was the glass-enclosed case in the middle of the room. The case was long and displayed inside it were a variety of statuettes and plaques arranged on a velvet base. The case served as a room divider for the room, which had obviously been some sort of storage loft in earlier times. The ceiling was high and the brickwork around the walls gave the impression one had stepped back in time. While Bonnie shuffled papers on the massive oak desk across the room, I soaked up the photographs on display at all points along the walls. Among those displayed in frameless acrylic covers was Jack Benchley, with his craggy granite-hewed face featuring piercing dark eyes and sunken cheekbones, sitting next to one of his ex-wives Was she number two? I knew Ann Benchley lost her mother in a car accident. Benchley was lined up with Peter Sellers and some other celebs as the Queen of England and the Duke of Edinburgh gave their Royal inspection. Must be the premiere of Shakespeare's bio-film, back in 1972. Surprising that he would want to remember that one. Benchley with Tennessee Williams and Arthur Miller; Benchley with Laurence Olivier; Benchley on some sort of hunting expedition with John Huston and some funny looking little guy. Was that the legendary 'Truffie', the ex-British Army Major who had become Benchley's assistant director and best pal in the sixties?

Another 8x11 glossy had Benchley with a light-eyed alabaster-skinned woman—Ann Benchley's mother, I presumed— on a movie set somewhere; a production crew shot, that included John Wayne, with a steep mountain range in the background; Benchley, now older, crouched down behind the cockpit of what looked like a Huey attack helicopter. This must have been taken during shooting of Benchley's controversial Vietnam documentary, *The Long Twilight*. He was right next to a black soldier hunched over a machine gun. Benchley held a movie camera. Over the shoulders of the two men could be glimpsed a dense canopy of green jungle stretching out below the copter; then there was Benchley on the Ryskind stage directing two actors dressed in Cavalier outfits and holding swords; then Benchley, now looking as old and haggard as when I saw him sign my copy of his book a year earlier, joking it up at some party with Robin Williams and a young woman standing between them. I recognized the young lady from a recent picture in the San Francisco Examiner. She was Carolyn Mason. The picture probably was taken a year or two earlier. A sign in the background of the group announced, 'Welcome to the San Francisco International Film Festival,' an event Benchley attended frequently. Rumor had been Benchley had a slight stroke and was hospitalized down there. Perhaps he made up the stroke story to spend more time with her.

Bonnie must have noticed my looking at the display.

"Do you know a lot about movies?" she asked.

"You could say I'm 'well-viewed', as a friend of mine would say."

"Ever in the business?"

I guessed that by the 'business', she meant show business. "No, never" I replied. "Well, wait a minute. One time when I was a cop down in Sutter City, I did some off-duty security for a Vietnam movie that was shot out in the marshes along the Sacramento River. I was an extra. Played a dead marine."

"Errol Flynn played a corpse in his first American movie," Bonnie said. "But I take it you weren't discovered by this brief fling into the cin-e-ma." She pronounced that last word in a tone of mock affectation.

"Sadly, no. How about you, Bonnie? Somebody told me you were—"

"Oh, yes," Bonnie said glumly, as she stuffed something that looked like a cassette tape case into a manila envelope. "I was an actress. I've done every kind of theater. Everything from Shakespeare and Samuel Beckett, some cabaret and musical-comedy, a soap opera shot out of New York, even a few non-recurring shots in prime-time shows down in L.A.. But I got tired of all that unemployment in-between. If it wasn't for Mr. Benchley, I'd probably be waiting tables down in California someplace. You will help us find the guy, right?"

"Yes," I said, not mentioning that I wanted to find out all I could about Dave's last visit to San Francisco while I was at it.

"He's given jobs to a lot of his old friends in Hollywood who ran out of work, and helped their kids get started in the business up here, if they had any talent. He's worth saving."

"If he's alive," I said, then regretted the frankness.

"Oh, he's still alive," Bonnie said calmly. "I have a sense about that." She held out the manila envelope to me. "Inside this you will find three things. One is the original copies of the papers you gave to Ann. The second is a small white envelope containing your advance payment. Six hundred dollars. Cash. I hope your being renumerated without benefit of federal withholding won't upset you."

"No problem," I said. I was looking into her eyes now, lost in the green luster around her pupils. I was enjoying a close-up view of the soft, dewy underside of her chin so I didn't immediately catch the last relevant item she said was in the oversized envelope.

"I'm sorry. What did you say?"

Bonnie's eyebrows, delightfully narrow by the way, lifted slightly upward. "I said the box contains the listening device. You will be contacted by a man who will give you further instructions on where we want it planted."

"Huh?"

"I'm sorry I'm dropping this on you now," Bonnie said. I absentmindedly took the envelope as she held it up slightly higher than before. "But I couldn't talk about this part where anyone could hear us. There is another person who will contact you in San Francisco. He will be the one who will do the actual electronic surveillance. All you have to do, in addition to your planned surveillance duties, is gain access to the office where—"

"Wait," I said, handing her back the envelope. "Are you talking about planting a bug somewhere? Somewhere like the Institute for Factual History? You realize this would come under the heading of a black-bag job? We're talking breaking and entering for starters, plus burglary first or second degree, plus—"

"Okay," Bonnie said, placing the envelope on the desk. "I made a misjudgment here. I assumed you realized that you were not going to be paid just to pad around San Francisco, trying to get information out of office staffers or somebody's roommate. Ann Benchley does not have time to play it by the book. You've helped convince her more strongly than before that Warbeck is at the bottom of her dad's disappearance. You claim you want to catch the people who supposably killed your friend. But if the risk...."

She stopped talking when I picked up the envelope.

"What's the deal on this? Bottom line, I mean. I'll do it, but I need to know what—"

"You will be contacted," Bonnie said, a more affirmative tone returning to her voice. "Give me a number where you can be reached down there. Be at that number tomorrow night at 10 o'clock. The man will contact you then. He has an English accent and will refer to himself as Kipling. He will refer to yourself as Mr. Stoker. You're Stoker, as in Bram; he's Kipling, as in Runyard. If anyone else answers, he will hang up."

I gave the number of the friends I was planning to stay with. I knew I was getting into something that could blow up in my face, but I also knew a couple six hundred dollar paydays would go a long way to pay some overdue bills.

"I have to get backstage in a couple of minutes," she said, glancing at her watch. "Do you want to sit through the rest of the play?"

"No," I said. "Give my apologies to Ms. Benchley. I enjoyed what I saw of the show, but I need to get prepped. I'm making an early start for San Fran tomorrow. I want to check out the IFH office and a few other things, before my call comes in."

"I take it the advance was sufficient?" Bonnie asked. We brushed against each other as we turned and started walking toward the door.

"You could have had me for half that, times being what they are. I trust there will be more reenumeration forthcoming when the main task is successfully accomplished."

"Ann takes care of those who look after her interests," she said coolly. She put the lights out on the panel with one swipe of her hand, leaving only the overhead hallway light on. The top of her copper-blonde hair glowed softly. I was afraid, despite the potential peril of the illegal activities assigned to me, that I was smitten by the lady who had talked me into the potential peril.

"Do you mind if we go out another way?" I meekly requested. "I have a mammoth case of acrophobia. Sort of what Jimmy Stewart's character had in *Vertigo*."

"I won't treat you like Nim Novak then," Bonnie said in a mildly flirtatious way. "We'll go this way then." She pointed to a stairway that led in the opposite direction from the walkway. "When did you discover this fear of heights?" she asked as we descended the stairs.

"When I was nine," I said. I went to a baseball game in San Francisco with a YMCA group. The group of us had to sit in the upper deck at Candlestick Park. Anyway, after a while I couldn't look down on the field without feeling dizzy. I slipped away from the other kids and the counselor and went down and sat in a vacant seat in the lower reserved section. At the end of the game, I couldn't find the group I had been with. The counselor noticed I was gone. Finally, a cop found me. Needless to say, I've had better days at the ballpark."

"I'm surprised you didn't get booted out of the reserved section," Bonnie said as we went down the stairway. She went first, affording me a couple nice sidelong glances of her gait. "Weren't you sitting in someone's seat?"

"No, this was a San Francisco Giants game in the Seventies," I said. "They didn't draw very well down there unless the weather was perfect and the Giants were at or right near first place. I probably could have sat in the Owner's Box and got away with it."

"My phobia is closed-in places," she said as we reached the landing.

"Claustrophobia?" I said.

"Yes," she replied. She held her small black purse with one hand, fumbled for her keys with the other, and held the clipboard under one arm.

"Can I hold something?" I asked.

Bonnie looked up at me. A slight smile crossed her face. "You mean 'may I hold something?'" She pulled her hand out of her purse and handed me the clipboard.

"So when did you know you had claustrophobia?" I asked as she located the small key chain she had been scouring her purse for.

"About the same age as your ballpark trauma. I was at my ballet class. A couple bigger girls who were jealous of my leg extensions pushed me into an empty street locker. I was a bit more svelte back then, needless to say. Anyway, I was in there yelling my head off for several minutes before somebody got me out." She opened the door, prepared to relock it and return to the theatre through the catwalk. I was now disappointed in myself that my fear of that catwalk would prevent us from having some extra conversation.

"One thing, uh, Bonnie," I said as I looked back at her standing at the door.

"Yes," she asked. Her eyebrows went up again. Her eyes seemed to flash a bit. Did I interest her? Or was I projecting? Was it just a tiny flash from the illumination of the street light across from the parking area?

"Is this like that old television show? If I am caught, or killed, will the secretary disavow any knowledge of my actions?"

Two skinny high school females, dressed like background extras for a movie about the plight of anorexic young women, walked by. One was wearing metallic blue hair, the other had a coiffure that featured purple as a highlite. We stopped conversing until they passed. I noticed one girl had a line of earrings that extended all the way up the outer rim of one ear.

After they passed, Bonnie sighed. "Some people on our side tried this bugging job once already, and things went wrong. Nobody got arrested, but it was a botch. Don't get caught, Harvey. And the answer, by the way, is yes I would disavow. That's my job. It's the price I pay for not having to wonder where I'm going to get money for next month's rent."

"The question is," I replied. "Would your boss disavow all knowledge of you if there weren't schmucks like me to cut the corners for her? I'll bet you'd be the one carrying the little gadget in the envelope, otherwise."

She cocked her head, and gave me a smirk. "I gotta go," she said. "Oh, but one more thing: don't feel too sorry for yourself, Harvey Wells. You wouldn't want my job. Trust me on that." Even with that smirk, she looked like an elf.

We exchanged goodbyes. She went back to the rarified air of the fine arts. I headed for my car contemplating a lengthy stretch in a California prison. As I walked away, I noticed the homeless guy everybody called "The Sheepman" sitting on a park bench at the entrance to Pioneer Park. I decided to walk over to him and let him know about what happened to Dave.

"I already know," he said to me, looking up from a cup of noodle soup he was eating. "Dave was a good man. Give my respects to his widow for me, would ya?"

I said I would.

The wind was kicking up a bit and I zipped up my two-ply green nylon jacket coat. I had parked about sixty feet away against the sidewalk. The closest street light was about fifty feet further down the street where the Pioneer Plaza began. My mind was on auto-pilot, too full of speculations about the preceding conversation, to bother with being alert to my surroundings.

I got into the car and turned on the ignition. The radio station was playing *Walk—Don't Run* by The Ventures. I put the car into drive and then Chad Millman popped up from somewhere in the backseat and put a pistol to my head.

Chapter Nine

I drove for about ten miles with both hands on the steering wheel. Chad Millman told me to do so. He had a gun pointed at my head so who was I to argue? Soon, we were off the main roads.

My own gun was in the glove compartment. Considering all that had happened in the last few days, I should have been packing it. Not having my .38 in the holster, now hanging empty under my arm was inexcusable. I felt scared and like an idiot all at once.

Nancy Sinatra was now singing *These Boots Are Made for Walkin'* on the radio. I had paid little attention to the previous selections on station KLJB. But I took note of this song. I always found it a guilty pleasure. Now it could be the last tune I ever heard.

"Make a left," the young man behind me said.

He wasn't trying to hide his face so I figured he was planning to kill me. Not scare me. Not beat me up. Just leave me dead somewhere. It was late at night and we were driving through a two-lane road that skirted along two long rows of young Douglas fir trees. We were up in the foothills of the Siskiyou Mountains, west of the town of Rogue Falls, Oregon. Then I saw an open field bordered by a long row of two-tier wooden fencing.

"Another left," Chad said. I did it. The car I was driving went through an open gate, passed over a narrow wooden bridge and a metal cattle crossing and then wound around a bend. The road was now single-lane and there were no lights either behind or in front of us. I could smell cattle dung and cut alfalfa.

Then I saw a large garage-like building up ahead. The only reason I could even see it was because a bright sodium light was mounted just below the apex of the roof. That was the only building in the area. As I drove up to it I could see, far off in the distance, another larger structure—a house, no doubt—very well lit. It was about a quarter of a mile away and could only be partially seen through a break in the trees where the road continued on. My kidnapper told me to park just behind the truck. He had more instructions for me when we were parked.

"Shut off the engine," Chad said. I did. He got out of the car first via the backseat. He told me to get out. I did.

Perhaps I'd get pistol-whipped to find out what I knew, then this guy—or some minions inside the garage—would finish me off while I lay on the ground. Either way I knew the ending; I would be dumped off somewhere, perhaps in a way to make it look like I was the victim of a car jacking. They could dump me in Pioneer Park and fake a robbery by taking my wallet.

I could smell the revolting cologne of the young man as he put a hand on my shoulder and steered me toward the building. As he directed me I could feel him also poking me in the back with the gun. I knew his gun was right up behind me. No one else was around and this was an opening. I took it. Planting my left foot to the ground, I thrust my whole right side backward, leading with an elbow thrust, hoping to knock the gun he was holding out of his hand.

The good news was I didn't get shot. I had deflected the gun. I heard a popping sound go off as I spun around and got a grip on Millman's right wrist and forced his automatic to aim at the ground. That first bullet hit the dirt.

A second shot went off, hitting more dirt. I would've preferred to have taken the gun out of his hand, but this was better than dead. I got a second hand on the man's wrist. We struggled for the gun.

He was taller and heavier than me. I'd even say more muscular. A momentary thought flashed through my mind: I should have worked out more often in the last few months. I don't think Chad knew much about self-defense, but I was out of practice and in the clinches like this my attempts at leveraging him off his feet were offset by his superior strength. I tried prying the gun loose and got my finger on the inside space between the trigger and the grip. He landed a blow from his free hand into my lower jaw that knocked me backwards. Pain filled my mouth. As I fell, I had just enough lead in my butt to leverage him over with me. I still had the gun pointed away from me, but I no longer had a finger where I could jam his trigger. Lying on my back, I looked up and saw a faint gleam from the fist that was set to strike another blow.

The bastard had a ring on one finger the size of a German cockroach.

I stopped his second blow with a quick forearm block. That move forced me to lose my double hand-grip on his gun, and gave him enough momentum to pull me down to where my head was just off the gravel. I held his right wrist—the gun hand—up with my left hand while he pressed his left hand down on the upper part of my throat. You can do a lot of things with a broken wrist; you can't do quite as much with a broken neck. He still had the gun, too.

I heard a truck coming at us from the direction of the house. Then I heard the tires roll to a stop. A door opened, a familiar male voice called out a name, and then I heard the sound of heavy shoes crunching into the gravel driveway. Help was on the way, for the wrong guy. Leroy Millman was on his way.

I looked up as best I could and saw that Chad Millman had his legs spread apart. All the better for me. My knee had a nice impact on his groin and that resulted in breaking his grip on my throat. I gave him another kick to where his nerve endings would take the most notice, then swung him over on his back by grabbing a wrist and yanking his right arm behind his back. I got up fast enough to get a kick into his rib cage and pull the pistol free of his hand. I next smashed the heel of one shoe down on his solar plexus.

"Be very fucking still," I said to Leroy Millman, who stopped his advance when he saw me come up from what for him was the far side of my car. His hand was halfway into the coat he wore. He had his mind set on drawing out a weapon and I told him I would shoot him if the hand didn't come out empty from his coat.

He did as I told him, a refreshing change from a few days ago at my trailer.

I backed away from my car, giving myself an angle to shoot either man if one or the other made a sudden move. Chad stayed on the ground. The father, after two appeals to his better nature, put his hands up.

"You won't be able to prove nothing," Leroy said. "I got five friends back there at the main house that will swear I'm at the party I'm throwing down the road there right now. Right now."

Chad Millman lay on his back, his hands to his chest, struggling for air.

"Roll over, Chad," I said. "Roll over on your stomach, arms and legs spread apart. Do it now!"

"Do it!" Leroy barked out.

Once I had the son prostrate, I asked the father what the deal was.

"I wanted to talk to you," he said. "I wasn't going to hurt you."

"Like hell," I replied.

"No, no you're wrong," Leroy said, a more congenial tone to his voice. "I admit I wanted to scare you."

"Scare me from what? From the dangers of driving a foreign-made car? From parking that car in a dark place? Scare me into getting more vegetables into my diet? Scare me from what, Millman?"

Under the light from the sodium lamp, I could see Millman's thick lower jaw quiver. "I...I think you're the guy who was fooling around with my wife."

"Aw, Jesus!" I exclaimed. "Did your wife tell you that?"

"She admitted it," he said." She's gonna be my ex-wife now. The bitch came back and packed up her stuff. I say good riddance, but that's not the point. The point is I went into that hotel room of hers and it looked like two people had been in there. When she came back to me to pack her bags she told me you were the one who she was messing around with."

"Enough of this shit," I said. "Don't you know your wife had nothing to do with me? It was a goddamn coincidence I was even in the hotel. Do you understand? I was seeing friends from out of town, Millman. Coincidences happen. I don't even like your wife, Millman."

"Don't shoot us," Chad said. Both Leroy and I told him,

simultaneously, to shut up.

"It's pretty obvious you were going to work me over in that garage or whatever it is in there, you and your kid. Is all this just over Rochelle?" I glanced down at the son on the ground. He had the good sense to not move.

"Yes," Millman said. "I want you to tell me if you were porking her. I want to know it! I want to know for sure. I want to make sure Rochelle's told me the truth and that there's not some other guy walking away bragging about bagging my woman. Listen, Wells, I got five friends back at the ranch will swear I'm there right now. I got all the law on my side. The Sheriff knows me, your boss knows me, you can't prove any of this happened and if you made a charge I'd get it dropped and then sue you."

Tell me something I don't know, I thought.

"Come over here," I said.

"What...what are ya going to do?" Millman asked in a nervous tone.

"You going to come over here and spread eagle against the trunk of my car. I'm going to collect all the guns you have, then you will hit the ground next to your son, your arms and legs spread out like his. Then I'm going to get into my car and drive out of here."

"I won't," the inquisitive husband said.

"Then I'll shoot you," I said. "Do you have five friends who'll bring you back to life?"

"I was just going to scare you," Millman said as he bent over and spread his hands across the trunk of my Celica. I kicked his legs out further than he probably would have liked them to be, searched him up and down and pulled out the gun he had shown me back at the hotel in Middleburg.

"It was all to do with my wife," Millman said, too adamantly to be altogether convincing. "I just wanted to scare you."

"Lay down over by your kid," I said.

The big dog-faced man complied, sinking slowly down to one knee and then the other. After he was on his stomach next to his son, I went over to my car and got my own gun from the glove compartment along with a pair of green latex gloves I kept in the compartment as part of an investigation kit. Setting my own gun on the roof of the car, I put on the gloves and then used a piece of shammy cloth to wipe off any prints I might have left on either of the Millman's firearms. I then threw both guns into the tall brush near the driveway.

"Don't try this again," I said to the prone men as I got back into my car. "I don't care who you know, you cross me again and one or both of you will catch a bullet. And that's the least of what could happen."

I slammed the door and drove off, both hands shaking as I gripped the steering wheel. From what I could see in my rearview mirror, the son got up first. He was helping the more rotund Leroy to his feet as I turned a corner and my view changed to darkness.

What had I learned? Other than the need to wear my gun on me or have it in arm's reach every second of the day and night, nothing tangible. I could either accept the fact that Big Leroy was telling the truth—that Rochelle actually had the gall to say I was her lover—or, more likely, that he knew the real truth about her and Dave. That would mean Leroy Millman's undue interest in me was designed to keep me from investigating Dave's death, either by putting a scare into me or by killing me.

No doubt, Leroy Millman was a likely suspect in Dave's death. However, it was no good going to the cops. With Millman's influence, no lawmen around Rogue County would believe he'd bother with having anyone kidnapped. I would have to watch my back every moment I was in this town for the foreseeable future.

Slowly the adrenaline levels came down in my system and my arms and legs stopped shaking. I breathed slowly in and out, felt a pain in my jaw. I examined myself and discovered I still had all thirty two teeth. I had a bruise just below the gumline on the right side of my jaw. But I would probably live.

Chapter Ten

"Crikey! What the hell happened to your face, Harvey?" Ray Harrison asked as he opened the front door to his house. He lived in a single-floor three bedroom stucco tract hacienda.

"I accidentally banged into the weight bench I have in the house last night," I replied, trying to be as nonchalant as possible. "Fell flat on my face."

"Come on in," he said standing away from the door. "And don't tell me you're drinking alcohol again. You still go to your AA meetings, right."

"Every Tuesday night at seven," I said. "But this week we decided to just say 'screw it' and everybody went to a bar. The whole group had a great time, excect the folks who weren't allowed to smoke."

On my pass back from the joys of Hazard Valley by night, I decided to stop by Ray's place and take him up on continuing our conversation about Dave having an affair with Ann Benchley.

In addition to the stock of graying salt and pepper hair, rarely combed, a tall frame and a thick upper body from weight lifting, Raymond Harrison had bad teeth, a good sense of humor, and a girlfriend named Kathy who lived with him. She was maybe in her early thirties, about fifteen years younger than Ray, and she once was a stand-in for Ann Benchley on a couple films she had made down at the Burbank Studios in Los Angeles. Ms Benchley had taken a liking to the lady who had stood in the hot studio lights for her while the cameras set up for the star's next scene on the sound stage. According to Ray, she offered Kathy a job at the Shakespeare Festival. That's where she and Ray had met.

Ray had been at the festival for a few years before I came up to Rogue Falls. His mother was Irish and his father Cockney English. He came from a part of the East End called Whitechapel. He also claimed to be the great-great grandson of some crazy medical student who purportedly was the real Jack the Ripper according to a couple books my bartender friend had lent me. The Ripper angle was all crap, as far as I was concerned, but it got Ray attention which was what he craved as much as most people.

Ray's local "claim to fame," other than being fired from the Shakespeare Festival, was that he had been married back in the 1990's to one Susannah Ryskind, one of the twin daughters of festival promoter/physicist Morton Ryskind.

He spent his teen years in the "Swinging London" of the mid-Sixties, working in off-West End theatricals. He emigrated to America and lived in the Haight-Ashbury section of San Francisco, bartending in a dive bar called The Experience which was frequented by LSD-addled, flower-power hippies who had flocked to the area because of the relatively tolerant atmosphere. "When in Rome..." Ray told me in comment to his personal drug consumption habits at the time. He also attended UC-Berkeley, majoring in Theater Arts. He went into the behind-the-scenes craft work needed for stage, film and television jobs in Los Angeles, New York and San Francisco. Judging by the photographs on his living room wall, his pre-Festival forte was mainly as an FX (Special Effects) artist in horror and fantasy films. According to what he had told me, Ray had done just about everything from heavy-duty make-up work to scenic designing to costumes. He had been Shop Manager of the Costume Department at the Northwest Shakespeare Festival when he got the ax and went back into bartending.

He had also directed some low-budget schlock horror films, mostly on locations in and around San Francisco. Ray had had a couple of his early 1980's directorial efforts transferred to video. One of the local video rental stores even had a copy of one of Ray's horror efforts, and I had seen it at Ray's behest. I am no great fan of the modem splatter-and-sadism horror film, but I liked Ray's film, a horror comedy called *Orangoutangy*, loosely based on the Edgar Allen Poe short story, *Murders in the Rue Morgue*. The setting for the film was contemporary San Francisco and not the Paris of the 1840s. Ray liked to point out that his cinematographer on the low-budget film was none other than Jack Picasso. The latter gent was now an A-List director and a former boyfriend of Ann Benchley.

A few years later, after failing to interest any major distributors in a screenplay about zombies who take over a hospital and later an entire California suburb, Ray went up to Oregon and landed a job with the Northwest Shakespeare Festival. His flair for all types of behind-the-scenes artistry had allowed him to advance quickly, and according to Ray, made people with more specialized talents within the company feel jealous.

But his work on stage was not all that comprised Ray's efforts at the festival. He had also clandestinely set up a video/film studio of his own, without the knowledge of Jack Benchley. He recruited minor actors and actresses from the festival and amateurs from the local area and set about making "adult" films for the porno market. It was this politically incorrect work that got him fired from the Northwest Shakespeare Festival.

When I arrived, I requested a Dr. Pepper and sat down on the rectangular butcherblock table across from Ray. We were in the kitchen, a kitchen that was being remodeled and had been in a state of flux for the two or so years I had known him. Exposure to backstage craftsmanship had made Ray into an amateur carpenter, and he was always tearing up rooms in his house, supposedly to get it ready for sale. Ray was attacking the baseboards this season. The Formica countertop next to the sink was strewn with tools, a wood shaper, and little heaps of sawdust.

We were not alone in the kitchen. Kathy Quisted had a tawny complexion and a twig-like figure, probably in her thirties, with doe-like brown eyes and chestnut-brown hair that hung down to her waist. She was getting a make-over courtesy of Ray. There were make-up brushes and powders in little white plastic containers strewn about the table. She was wearing a baggy blue and white Hawaiian-style shirt I had seen Ray wear about his house a few times. The shirt had splotches and smears of paint all over the front.

"I'm going to bring the ends of your eyebrows up a bit." Ray said to the woman. "You have nice eyes, Kathy; you need to accentuate them."

"I still want to look intimidating," Kathy, whom I had never seen before, said. "Don't make me look vulnerable here. This is not about looking vulnerable, remember?"

Ray laughed. "Luv, you're going to wind up looking about as vulnerable as a stalking lioness." He looked over at me. "I'm just finishing up here, Harvey. What do you think of little Kathy here?"

What did I think of her? I had only been in the room with her about a minute. Was I expected to gush about her emaciated figure or her long slightly crooked nose that did nothing for her face? "Very...attractive," I finally said after Ray looked back at me, imploring an answer with his eyes.

Ray shook his head. "Attractive, eh? That's the best you got?"

I looked over at Kathy. She was staring at herself in a portable mirror angled up at her from the table. "Attractive is good," she said, giving me a bit of support. "Attractive needs to be part of the package here if I'm...that is we, are going to pull this off." For about another minute, Ray put some heavy shading under her lower eyelashes, then lightly powdered her cheekbones to make them look fuller. Then he stood back, and cocked Kathy's face toward him for a close look using one thick index finger under her chin.

"Get up and show the man from the District Attorney's office what you look like, kid," he said to Kathy.

Kathy got up from the rattan chair she was sitting on. She gave me a quick nervous smile, then off came the bulky shirt. She was wearing a skin-tight black leather outfit with black fishnet stockings. The outfit gave a boost to what she had in the way of cleavage, which wasn't much, and the lower part of the outfit featured a V-shaped crotch area that maximized her legs, which were surprisingly shapely for a skinny woman. Around her waist was a black—what else—utility belt with a coiled-up whip on one side of her hip and some other apparatus with stainless steel hooks on her other hip.

Ms. Quisted walked around some more. She had a shapely back and the cut of her outfit about her behind was snug and high but not so high as to look vulgar. I also noticed she was wearing black stiletto pumps with high thin heels. The heels were stainless steel, too, save for a rubber tip on the lower end.

"Do you still think the word attractive covers her," Ray said to me. "Or would you like to be a little more descriptive."

"She looks attractive...and exotic," I said.

"Exotic is good," Ms. Quisted agreed, looking down at herself, then holding her hands out in front of her.

"I have to get my nails in shape," she said. "I need those artificial ones that make you look like a cat with claws."

"Possibly," Ray said. "Why don't you go into your room, luv. Practice with your accessories for a while. I'm going to talk something over with Harvey here. After that, we'll do the photo and video shoot. First the naughty one, then the audition video for your legit work."

Kathy gave Ray a quick peck on his stubby-haired cheek, then practically pranced off down the L-shaped hallway, turning to go down to the far bedroom, a room I knew Ray had previously rented and was currently unoccupied.

Ray sighed after he heard the door shut. He looked at me. "I can't do much about the face, I'm afraid. Kathy wants to look like a young Angelica Huston, or her old boss, Ann Benchley but she doesn't have the intangibles. It's not just the body and the face, there has to be something else...a spark. She lacks spark. Not that that's going to deter a lot of customers. Most guys who want to be dominated will just be looking for the figure and responding to the tone of voice."

"Ray, what is this all about?" I asked, half suspecting I already knew.

Ray explained that Kathy was game for something. Ray had suggested that she become a part-time psuedo-dominatrix. Apparently, while grandma watched her kids from an earlier marriage the young mother was going to spend her weekend evenings entertaining 'clients' in Ray's backroom. Ray was furnishing the security for his girlfriend, and Kathy was doing the dominating. Ray was also going to coach her, putting his years of expertise in horror films and startling theatrical imaging into use.

"Her father was of Armenian stock," Ray said wistfully.

"That's why she has that nice olive coloring to her skin. I'm going to go with a late-period Ottoman Empire motif in that room, drag out some of my mother's old lurid red curtains, and get some ropes to make tassels with. I have to hook up a pulley in the room. That means reinforcing the ceiling. I've got the hardware for it, I just have to get up to the attic on my next day-off."

Music floated down from the hallway. It was clarinet and string music, but a long way from Benny Goodman or Artie Shaw. Ray saw my puzzled expression.

"Turkish music," he said. "My mum had some old 78's of Sukru Tunar. He was the Louis Armstrong of Turkey in the 1920's. We're going to use the music in the sessions. I'm not going to be in the room, of course. I'm going to be sitting here in the kitchen. No electric lighting when the clients arrive. Just candles. I'll do some alterations on my old Nehru Jacket to make it look more Turkish." He picked a towel off a photograph that was lying flat on the kitchen table. It was a picture of a no-nonsense looking guy with an aquiline nose.

"Recognize the bloke?" Ray asked.

"Omar Sharif?"

"Wrong. Mustapha Kemal Ataturk, the dictator who modernized Turkey. Tough-looking hombre, huh?"

I've heard of him. Hero of the Siege of Gallipoli back in World War One. He was the driving force behind the Turkish Revolution. His hobbies included putting lots of people under arrest for political reasons and pushing the Greek Army around. I guess you can't get more Turkish than old Whataturk."

"Ataturk," Ray said, putting the picture down. "I'm going to go Turkish myself for a little color. I've got a fez left over from that production of *Comedy of Errors* I worked in three years ago at the Lizzie. I went with an Ottoman design for the director on that show. Kathy's costume is from a prostitute's outfit I designed for the production.

"You really plundered the costume department when you left, didn't you, Ray?" I said. That was an established fact from the articles on display in the near-by garage which served as Ray's den/bedroom area. He had fixed up the garage after Benchley had fired him to rent his rooms. Ray had a trove of property from the Shakespeare Festival property department he had purloined in spite after his resignation: costumes, wigs, weaponry, imitation jewelry, clothing dummies, life masks of actors he had created to make molds for masks, etc.

I jokingly asked if he had secured permission to take any of the props.

"Hell no," Ray said with no trace of remorse. He reached into the refrigerator, popped open a Guinness, and sat down in the chair Kathy had occupied. "I didn't need permission from those bastards. I *created* a good deal of the stuff I took. I either created it or I supervised thé creation. And I was married to Susannah Ryskind, remember? I deserve some compensation for staying hitched to that ball-buster for five years. Besides, artistic license takes precedence over legal ownership.

"Good luck getting a judge to buy that," I said.

"What?" Ray said with that smirk across his face. "You going to turn me in for stealing a few props and costumes on my way out of Jack Benchley's sweatshop? Once a cop, always a cop, eh?"

I laughed. "You know I wouldn't do that, Ray. Now as to the pandering charge..."

"Excuse me?"

"I'm sorry. Pandering is a loaded word. You're going to be a pimp. I can see you in the county courthouse now: fez on your head, smoking a water-pipe, while your lawyer tells you to cop a plea to the lesser charges. By the way, how do you plan to plead if the neighbors find out about your Best Little Whorehouse In Istanbul?"

It was Ray's turn to laugh. "You don't know the bloody difference between a whore and a dominatrix, do you, Harvey? God, what a sheltered life you've led."

I picked up my Dr. Pepper and we went into the garage. Amidst all the props and shelves of old figurines and latex heads and limbs—and old production pictures of Ray at work—was a narrow open space with a television, a rug, and three chairs. The chairs faced a television with a video-recorder on the top and a video camera on a shelf above that. I looked at the display of videotapes on the shelf as I sat down and wondered how many of the tapes were filled with simulated sex acts he had needy actresses and actors perform for him after hours in the costume shop next to the Ryskind Theater.

I tipped my rattan chair backward so my upper back could lean against the wall. It eased the dull ache I had, and that periodically flared up, in my lower back.

"So give me the whole picture on what Dave told you about him and Ann Benchley."

"Dave was a son of a bitch. You know that." Ray said, following a quaff on his beer.

"Some people thought that way of him," I said, not liking the way Ray was starting.

Ray waved his hand at me. "You trying to break my last good chair?"

I leaned forward, putting the rattan on all four legs. Then Ray continued.

"From what Dave told me he and Ann Benchley were involved for about nine months. He went down to see her at her house in Santa Monica when he was supposed to be at a security convention in Las Vegas."

"We covered that at the bar," I said. "Did Old Man Benchley know about the affair?"

Ray nodded. "Dave told me Old Man Benchley thought he was the best guy Ann had ever been with. That's Dave talking, though. Dave was at the bar that night, putting the beers away fast and feeling no pain. He told me he and Ann had broken up. That was last month. He said she was starting up with a film director who was hot for her. Name of Jack Picasso. Ever hear of him?"

"Yeah," I said. "Makes splatter horror flicks and violent prison melodramas. He used to be an Alfred Hitchcock-Brian DePalma wanna-be; now he's a Don Siegel-John Frankenmeimer wanna-be. Wait a minute. Didn't you say you once worked on a movie with that guy?"

"Believe it or not, I got him one of his first professional jobs. It was back in '81, when I was making my Edgar Allen Poe film in San Francisco. He was fresh out of the U.S.C. Film Department. The old man had named him after Jack Benchley. Do you know why?"

I did. "Jack Picasso is Silvio Malatesta's son," I said, remembering bits and pieces from Benchley's book and articles on the Italian-American film writer-director in cinema magazines. "The old man was blacklisted in the 1950's from Hollywood courtesy of the House Committee on Un-American

Activities, or Joe McCarthy's Committee or whatever. After he was blacklisted, Malatesta directed low-budget movies in Italy and Spain until some shady producer ran off with all his money in some crooked deal. It was the early sixties, the blacklist against pinko leftwingers was still on, and he was broke. Jack Benchley hired him to write a screenplay for a film he was making on Simon Bolivar. Malatesta had to work under a pseudonym because John Wayne was playing Bolivar—a great feat of miscasting there—and Duke Wayne would have split his guts if he knew some blacklisted artist was writing the script."

"And the name the old man used was Diego Picasso," Ray said. "That was because Jack Malatesta's dad had been a socialist sympathizer. He raised money for the Republicans—the Commies that is—during the Spanish Civil War. He greatly admired Picasso's mural *Guernica*. He had lost a brother or something who was fighting for the Abraham Lincoln Battalion."

"That right," I said, remembering the rest of the story. "Jack Picasso was just a kid back when his dad was doing the Bolivar job around 1962 or '63. Jack was born when Malatesta was, hell, at least fifty-five. When he grew up and hit it big in Hollywood, he legally changed his last name to Picasso so he'd always carry around the memory of what the blacklist had done to his father."

Ray nodded. "After the blacklist ended, Benchley also hired Malatesta to collaborate on the screenplay for *Essex and the Queen*. Benchley also had his buddy direct a couple plays up here when the Shakespeare Festival started to take off."

"It was nice of Jack Benchley to keep him working all those years," I said.

Ray chuckled. "Benchley wasn't the only guy who remembered him. He was just the only guy who gave him work after he came back from Europe. Malatesta did go down to L.A. a couple times before the cancer got him. The Hollywood Left gave him a couple fancy award dinners to honor his work and the big shots all said what a shame all those things from the 1950's happened.

"Anyway," Ray continued, "all the rich Hollywood Lefties cried their bloody phony Actors Studio-trained tears for him, being that the Red Scare sort of screwed old Silvio out of a full career. Came from a well-educated family in Genoa. Mussolini ran his left-wing family out of Italy in the early Twenties and he came to America. He got to be a well-paid screenwriter in the Thirties, then went to Spain in '38 and made some documentary to raise money for the Loyalists. Anyway, that made him a big hero with the Far Left, but a pre-mature anti-Fascist when people saw what the Commies were really about. Anyway, he was a big icon with the limousine liberals down in Hollywood, one of their martyrs. Funny thing is, none of those big-time left-wing actors or actresses would agree to appear in any projects he tried to get off the ground. I think the last actual movie he directed was in Europe about '75. He was the Italian/American Orson Welles. Everybody wanted to give him a dinner and an award, but nobody would give him a job. Except Jack Benchley. He let him write and co-produce the movies he directed as well as direct plays up here."

"You don't care much for liberals do you, Ray?"

"I don't care for conservatives either," he said. "Democracy is a suckers game. The masses are asses. Give me a monarch, a guy like King Charles the Second. Greatest Englishman ever."

Ray got up and went to the kitchen to get another beer. I stared at the shelves of his trade: gruesome masks of gargoyles and demons left over from his film career as well as the head from the orangoutang costume he wore in his film. There were also various body parts on display between his stacks of books: arms and legs and severed hands in various states of synthetic decomposition. Ray had more than a touch of the Grand Guignol in his style of theatrical designs. There were also wig stands with thick bushy hairpieces and small models of various sets. Framed pictures set around the artifacts depicted Ray in his earlier days, working with actors in applying latex prosthetics to their faces, ears, torsos and legs.

One thing stood out from the other objects on display:a solid white bust of a beautiful woman that had been taken from a life mask. The subject was Ann Benchley. Next to the bust was a color photograph featuring the actress standing between a beaming Ray and an equally-happy red-haired gentleman with bad acne scars on his neck. Ann Benchley was holding up the life mask in her hands. Just below the big picture, in the lower left-hand corner was a close-up of a woman whose head was completely covered in something that looked like plaster of paris. The main photograph bore the signature of the woman I had met earlier that evening. "To Ray, thanks for covering me with all this sticky white shit. Best Wishes, Ann Benchley."

Ray returned not only with a beer but with another Dr. Pepper. I accepted the latter. The door leading to the kitchen was open and, from the back bedroom of the house, I heard the faint sound of a woman singing a mournful song in a foreign language. A zither-like instrument accompanied her. There followed a sharp crack, like a whip snapping in the air. Ray gave me a diabolical smile, then we got back to matters at hand.

"Anyway, we were talking about Jack Picasso, weren't we? He changed his last name after his father died. He got his first professional job doing some low-budget movies with me. Picasso was my cinematographer. He actually was quite a good lighting man. Well, you saw a couple of my movies here with Dave, didn't you think the sets were lit well?"

"Yes," I said, giving the opinion of a non-expert. "I guess they were well-lit."

"He went on to bigger and better things, needless to say. His last couple big features have been duds at the box office, but that's because he co-wrote and directed them. He shifted from straight horror movies to this fetish he has for doing pictures set in prisons. Did you see *Three Against Alcatraz*? *The Warden's Agenda*? And that weird science-fiction one, what was it...oh, *Moon of the Forgotten*, right. That one was really bad."

"I only saw the Alcatraz picture," I said.

"Except for that one, which Picasso didn't write, they all suck. He's gone from first-rate lighting man to, like you said, a third-rate director-writer. Somebody in Hollywood is blowing smoke out his you-know-what and now he thinks he's a writer-director. He's a great lighting man, and he has had some box-office success, but I could direct him right out of his chair in a fair system."

"Let's talk about Dave," I said. "I have my own self-pity waiting for me at home."

"O.K., back to Dave," Ray said. "I have to admit I can't feel too sorry for old Dave. He broke Wendy's nose, right? You know that."

"Uh-huh." This, sadly, was established fact. "Tell me more about Dave and Ann Benchley."

"The funny part of the story is that Ann Benchley broke up with him because Dave had started seeing someone else on the side instead of just her."

"That is funny," I replied. I had to laugh. "Our boy Dave was getting bored with Ann Benchley's company?"

"The woman Dave started up with was Rochelle Millman, Wendy"s sister. Leroy was dumb enough to hire him to watch her. I guess they hit it off according to Dave."

I played dumb. "No kidding? Jeez, Rochelle is a looker, but she's no Ann Benchley."

Ray took another swig from his can, then continued. "Dave told me Ann was messed up in the head. She's got one of those bi-polar disorders. She would be great one day, free and easy, then the next day she'd want him to ditch his wife and kid and move in with her; next day she'd accuse him of getting ready to sell the story of their affair to the tabloids, which wasn't Dave's style; and the next day she'd say he was a lowdown punk and that she could do better picking up a wino in Pioneer Plaza. Ann Benchley's a looker, but a head case. Dave knew he could have Rochelle anytime he wanted her, with no headaches. He and Rochelle knew each other a long time. He introduced Jack Benchley to her. That's how she and old Benchley had their brief marriage. Now her husband is an old cattle rancher with a lot of money, but he spends a lot of time travelling back and forth from Klamath City to another ranch he's got in Amarillo, Texas. From what Dave told me, the old cowboy can't get his *polska kielbasa* up so good anymore, so Rochelle makes some excuse and stays behind when old *Lee-Roy* (he pronounced the name in a good impression of the rancher's twang) goes to Texas so she can drive over to Middleburg and wing it with Dave. So really he was playing around on his wife *and* his mistress. He'd still be juggling the three of them if either Leroy Millman or Ann Benchley hadn't shot him in the head."

That last remark set me back. "Wait a minute...are you telling me there are two suspects in Dave's death? According to what I heard from Russ White, the preliminary finding from the Medical Examiner was a suicide." I didn't go into my own doubts about the 'suicide.'

Ray downed the last of his beer, belched, then gave me a crooked smile. "O.K., which theory do you want first, the fat boss rancher offing Dave, or Queen Cleopatra offing him?"

"Let's start with old Leroy," I replied. "I'm still getting used to the idea that Dave even slept with Ann Benchley."

"Dave was shot with his nine-millimeter handgun, right?"

"A Golan," I said.

I did not tell Ray what Russ White had said, that the State Crime Lab was still trying to identify the slug that went through Dave's head.

"Do you know who might also have one of those firearms?"

"A few thousand other people, maybe?"

"Leroy Millman," Ray said. "My old mate from the festival, Ralph Bates, tells me that Leroy is a pistol champion or something. He saw the old guy at a National Rifle Association deal up at the Middleburg Pistol Range. He was in the bar a couple weeks ago and told me he was a South State target champion in the Nine Millimeter Division."

"I happen to know he's into Taurus guns," I said. "He the 'Buy-American' type. The Golan comes out of Israel, Ray."

"He probably has an arsenal over at his ranch. Most ranchers have lots of weapons. I'm sure he'd tell you he only plays with American-made guns. Leroy is a red, white and blue guy, that's why he's running for Congress this year. Then your buddy shows up dead, and you already have Millman eliminated because the gun was an import."

Ray had a point. It was unproven, but it was food for thought. He continued.

"Dave was screwing around with Rochelle. Leroy Millman is an old-fashioned guy. He told me personally one night at the bar that he had caught one of his migrant workers porking his Elvira. She's his teen-aged daughter. They were doing it right in her bedroom when the old man caught them. Do you know what happened to that guy?"

"There was a shotgun marriage and he's going to inherit the ranch?"

"He's still on the ranch," Ray said. "But all he inherited of it was a little space six feet underground. Leroy shot the little upstart and buried him somewhere out on the back forty."

"You telling me he shot this guy in cold blood and bragged about it to you?"

"It happened a few years ago," Ray said, "before he was married to Rochelle, his trophy wife. Nobody knew about it except the daughter, and she got sent back East to college right after the incident. There was no police report because the guy was just a migrant. Leroy knows every cop in Rogue County, and he's tight with the Sheriff. Even if one of his migrant buddies wondered what happened to Romeo, the law wouldn't lay a glove on Leroy. Not over an undocumented Mexican fruit picker."

I shook my head. "Even if this Millman character popped that poor guy, it's irrelevant to Dave's case unless you can put him around Bowman or near Cramner Creek where Dave's body was found."

"Nobody's asked Millman where he was that night," Ray said.

"That's because the case is still officially a suicide? How can you have suspects in a suicide?"

"Maybe if you get through running your wheels off for Ann Benchley, you go over to the Double M Ranch in Hazard Valley and find out where Rochelle's husband was that faithful evening. Or if the old man wasn't the shooter, how about the son, Chad?"

At this point I could have added my anecdote about a revolver-packing Leroy Millman coming to my trailer door—with Chad Millman in tow—and my earlier run-in with him at the Four Star Hotel in Middleburg, and about my nearly getting killed just an hour before at Millman's ranch. But I wanted to keep my mouth shut.

"Look, Ray, just because a guy has a gun like Dave had and just because he might have offed somebody else who touched his kid awhile back...hey, I admit it sounds interesting, but it doesn't add up to a case. If you took that to the D.A.'s office here, with no confirmation of the first homicide, they'd laugh you out of the place."

The Turkish-style music got louder. I heard the crack of a whip at the other end of the house, followed by Kathy making some loud exclamations.

"Bad boy! Bad boy! BAAAAAD boy! You need to be taught a lesson. A lesson you'll never forget!" More cracking sounds.

"I just wish her bloody tits were bigger," Ray said, casting a glance toward the door to the kitchen. "I'm going to have to do something about that." He looked back at me. "So what do you think of my theory, mate?"

I reflected on it for a bit. "Millman would not be my first choice, Ray."

"Who then?"

"Dave was on the Benchley case, working for Ann Benchley. I assume from what you just told me about their break-up that they remained friendly enough for her to retain his services as an investigator."

"We haven't got to my other theory yet," Ray said. "I think Ann—"

"Save it," I said. "Sure, what happened to Dave looks like a suicide, but setting up something to look like a suicide isn't impossible. I don't know if the County Medical Examiner did a full-scale trace metal test on Dave's gun hand."

"That's to see if he fired a gun, right? Would that take that long?"

I could have told Ray about my seeing a deputy engaged in some sort of search up by Cramner Creek, but I decided to leave it off. "Who knows what else they're looking into?" I said, after a short amount of reflection. "There are a couple different trace metal tests they could do, depending on how thorough they wanted to go. But even if they determined Dave fired a gun, that doesn't prove he did the job himself. But it must have looked close to an actual suicide for Russ White to be so sure about it. That's one big point against your theory on Millman doing the job. According to you, Millman just took a gun, shot some kid and buried him on his ranch. In other words, his *modus operandi* is shoot, carry and bury—a spur-of-the-moment perpetrator. Whoever did this set Dave's body up to look like he killed himself, and they had to know enough about ballistics and crime scenes to make a good simulation of a suicide. If Millman did it, Dave would be underground somewhere."

"How about you offing him, Harvey?" Ray said. "You were a cop. You'd know how to do it, right?" He chuckled. I wasn't amused.

"I'm ruling myself out as a suspect for the time being," I replied coolly. "My money is on somebody putting Dave on ice because he was getting too close to what happened to Jack Benchley and the murder of Carolyn Mason. There's a little outfit in San Francisco I want to look into."

"But the murder took place 350 miles from San Francisco. Why not just kill him down there? Why wait until he's back in Oregon, then kill him?"

"So the cops think it was either a suicide, or, if that angle falls through, that Dave was murdered by some local. Somebody could have kidnapped him down in the Bay Area, transported him up here, motorcycle and all, then killed him a few miles from here to make the thing look like a suicide, and a local one at that. That's the main reason I'm going down to Frisco. I've got some time off, and I'm doing some back-tracking on where Dave went and whom he saw."

"So, you've pretty much ruled yourself out as a suspect. Have you ruled out the battered wife?"

This surprised me. I'd thought that, as friends, Ray would have left Wendy out as a suspect. But Ray was no sentimentalist.

"Battered wife is always a good suspect in a husband's murder," I said. "The trouble with that is that Monday evening Wendy was over in Klamath City. Her mother had another angina attack."

"Who says she was in Klamath City?" Ray said. "Her mother? Her Aunt? Ever hear of a somebody hatching a cover story? Let me run this by you. You know Ralph Bates, right?"

"I've met Mr. Bates," I said. "He's a security guy at the festival."

"He comes in to O'Leary's sometimes, usually during baseball season. You guys got into a argument one night, something to do with baseball."

"Oh, yeah," I said, suddenly remembering. "That jerk Bates is the one who thinks they should have the Designated Hitter Rule in the National League?"

"That's the guy," Ray said. "Anyway, a couple weeks ago he stops in for a couple beers when I'm on shift. I'm at the bar and Wendy's serving drinks. He looks at her going by and then tells me he saw her at the Middleburg Gun and Rifle Range the weekend that Dave was down in San Francisco. Says she was on one of the firing lines, target shooting."

"What?" I said, in total disbelief. "Wendy doesn't practice

with guns. Dave gave her a Golan one Christmas. He wanted her to carry it when she worked late at the bar. She told him to keep it so he used it as a back up weapon. Wendy's not a shooter. She's a pacifist."

"Oh, yeah, right," Ray said. "Well, according to Ralph he saw her firing away at targets. She was using a nine-millimeter pistol. Ralph's an ex-cop, he knows about guns."

"No," I said. "That wasn't Wendy."

"He said it was her. And I trust Ralph. He's a good mate."

"He's full of shit. Did you ask Wendy?"

"I asked her after Ralph left," Ray said. "She denied it, of course."

"Because she wasn't there, that's why. Dave tried to drag her to that range two or three times when the two of us went shooting. She's never shot a piece in her life. That stuck-up jerk Bates was mistaken."

"I'm not so sure," Ray said.

"C'mon, Ray, you know Wendy. You really believe she would shoot the father of her kid?"

Ray gave out that annoying chuckle again. "You only seen her as your friend Dave's wife. You probably think she's a goddamn saint. I've worked with her, and I know things she's told me about her and Dave that she wouldn't tell you because you guys grew up together. She put up with Dave, but I wouldn't be so surprised if she ended it."

"That's a bad take," I said. "Wendy's no killer. She just kicked Dave out once before. I'm just saying she's not about violence."

Ray ignored my remarks. "Wendy would have left Dave a long time ago, but she was afraid wherever she went Dave would track her down and use his connections in the courthouse to get custody of Jill."

"She said this to you?"

"In so many words," Ray replied with the sound of a cracking whip echoing behind us. "Dave would have been dead long ago, or hurt real bad, if he had married the other sister and fooled around on her. I knew Rochelle when she was an actress at the Festival. She's a bitch on skates when she wants to be. Plus, she told me once her first husband beat the crap out of her a couple times, like Dave did to Wendy. The third time Rochelle took an aluminum baseball bat to her hubby's kneecaps, then she walked out. I guess it was a couple months before her ex-old man did any walking."

He paused. "You know," Ray said in an absent-minded manner, "that Jennifer of yours had big tits. I guess you knew that, being her husband. Figure wasn't too bad. My ex-wife Susannah had an okay figure, but Jennifer was right tasty. I might have been able to do something with her. Of course, she was into accounting, wasn't she? No, I take that back. I don't see her whipping a guy into submission."

"Your respect for my soon-to-be ex-wife is truly touching," I said.

"So you don't like my Millman theory? Or even the possibility Wendy found some spine?"

"Ray, you're the same guy who says the FBI knocked off the Kennedy brothers and O.J. Simpson was framed."

Ray rolled his eyes. "Not the *whole* FBI, you stupid git! Just J. Edgar Hoover and a special assassination team of Russian-trained hitmen imported from Bulgaria. Just read your history. And as for that Simpson business—"

"No, Ray," I said, holding both hands out in front of me. "Let's not go there tonight." I checked my watch. It was going on midnight and I wanted to make a reasonably early start to the Bay Area the next morning. Ray's Ann Benchley theory could wait, I thought.

But before I left, my host handed me a book he said would be a "good introduction" to his theory.

Chapter Eleven

I made sure I checked the back seat this time before I got into my car.

After I got back to my trailer, I had a quick shower, took a couple of Tylenol to deal with the pain in my jaw and back, and then folded up some towels, socks and underwear I needed to put away from an earlier trip to a coin-operated laundry. Next I turned off the kitchen and living room lights and headed for the bedroom.

I opened the bedroom window behind the headboard to take advantage of the unusually cool breeze coming up from the west. Next I sat down at the computer desk which took up most of the room that the bed failed to cover. Jennifer took the computer so I now had plenty of desk space. I wrote out a list in my note book of some people and addresses I would need for my investigation. Then I checked all the locks on the windows and the doors again.

The digital clock on my nightstand said 12:08 when I finished my notes. I put my clothes on the hamper in the bathroom, pulled my socks off at the bed and threw the disheveled covers over me. I put my .38 under my pillow.

I spent the next few minutes reading a chapter from a book Ray had given me earlier. The paperback was called *Hollywood Unsolved* and featured a rehashing of several notorious episodes involving film and television moguls and stars. The book had chapters on the Fatty Arbuckle—Virginia Rappe Rape/Murder Trial, screen comedienne Thelma Todd's mob-related demise, the Errol Flynn rape case, Marilyn Monroe's liaison with John Kennedy, the Manson Family Tate-LaBianca murders, as well as some information and speculation on my newest employer. *The Shooting of Talbot Strunk: the Verdict and the Truth* was the objective, disinterested title of the chapter the author, a woman named Anita Shumpsky, chose. Then and there I checked to see what outfit published the book.

The Institute for Factual History.

I knew the basics of the story, pretty much what I had outlined with Dave on our last night at O'Leary's Pub. So did most everyone else in the United States and Canada if they were around in the early eighties and over the age of twelve. The article began like this:

"Ann Benchley, a raw-boned 25 year-old beauty, who had gone from magazine model to Oscar-winning actress with her first major movie role—as the Countess in her father Jack Benchley's *The American*—had eloped with Talbot Strunk, younger brother of present-day media baron Sherwood Strunk III.

"They had been wed in the Dominican Republic and had been honeymooning at the Forest of Arden, the private retreat of the Strunk brothers grandfather, Sherwood R. Strunk, founder of The Strunk Oil Company and father of the influential Truth Party. The sprawling 600-acre estate had been designed in the late 1920's in the Northern California Redwoods above the city of Santa Rosa. The estate was—and is—a living three-dimensional celebration of the old English Countryside and the works of William Shakespeare."

"Sometime around two in the morning on June 25, 1981, a 62 year-old grounds keeper named Fred Wyden was awakened by a shouting match between a man and a woman. The man looked out from his bedroom over a six-car garage to the main house. He testified that he saw Ann Benchley and her new husband engaged in a struggle down on the driveway. Ann appeared to be resisting efforts by the young man to wrest an object from her hand. The object, according to Wyden, appeared to be a gun. The bride broke away, according to the eyewitness, and ran into the wooded grove that adjoined the carport. The servant, a long-time retainer of the Strunk family, quickly dressed himself to try and catch up and, as he said, 'keep something bad from happening.'"

"He heard the first shot ring out as he descended the staircase to reach the carport. He heard a man make a 'terrible, short scream' and believed the man who screamed was Talbot Strunk He also heard a woman screaming and, about ten to fifteen seconds later, according to Wyden, a second shot rang out. The second shot was confirmed by Strunk's chauffeur, Jackson Sharpe, who had also been aroused from his near-by quarters by the disturbance."

"The two men, neither armed, cautiously entered the wooded glen to investigate. What they found, in the middle of the main aisle of an open-air amphitheater called the Globe Auditorium, was a sobbing, hysterical Ann Benchley. Her reddish hair had fresh blood all over it. She was on her knees, wailing over the lifeless body of her husband. He had taken a bullet from a Walther P5 nine millimeter automatic pistol. The shot had entered his skull at the right eye. Sharpe checked the body for signs of life and found none."

"Upon seeing Wyden and Sharpe, according to their official statements, Ann threw up her hands and ran screaming out of the theatre area and into the surrounding woods. Two Sonoma County deputy sheriffs found her two hours later, after a search was organized. She was cowering in a hollow log off the grounds of the estate, two miles from the scene of the tragedy."

"Ann Benchley got to tell her side of the story at the inquest, which was held in the eye of a media firestorm that ascended on the Sonoma County Courthouse. She testified that she had discovered that her husband intended to divorce her when she revealed she was not planning to allow him to keep seeing a woman, Claudia Desart, who apparently was distracting Strunk even on his honeymoon. Ann claimed that Strunk had snuck out of the family mansion about midnight to keep a tete-a-tete with Desart. The other woman was staying clandestinely at one of the guest cottages on the compound. When the newlywed returned, Ann Benchley met him in front of the carport. She told him she had overheard a recent conversation between him and Desart over an extension phone in the house library. Talbot Strunk denied that anything of a sordid nature took place, according to Ann, who went on to say that Strunk told her he was a good friend of Desart, she was also a friend of his sister, and that Ms. Desart would remain a close friend."

"Ms. Benchley admitted that it was after her husband made that last statement she drew her Walther P5 out from the pocket of her pink cashmere robe."

"Ann Benchley always claimed her intention was to kill herself in front of her husband unless he swore to kick Desart off the property and stop seeing her. An argument ensued. Talbot had struggled with her to retrieve the firearm. Ann broke away and ran to the amphitheater. According to her, Talbot managed to catch up and tackle his wife in front of the elevated mock-Elizabethan stage. Another struggle ensued. It was at this point in her testimony that the widow broke down on the stand. From somewhere in the courtroom, a clicking noise had been heard. Someone had snuck a camera into the inquest. A recess was called and the wily photographer placed under arrest. The camera he used was later somehow smuggled out of the police department and the developed shot later reproduced by every news outlet in the free world."

"The testimony resumed the next day. Ann said that her husband had pushed her down and climbed on top of her to force her to release the gun. In the struggle to possess the gun it had accidentally gone off. Hence the first shot Fred Wyden and Jackson Sharpe heard. That shot ended Talbot Strunk's life. The second shot, about a minute later, had apparently struck Ann Benchley on the tip of her left ear. This caused the bloody hair. Ann said she was trying to kill herself in despair over her husband. It was his finger on the trigger, she claimed, that had depressed hers and caused the gun to accidentally go off the first time, the bullet going right into his eye."

"Six months later, there was a trial. Ann Benchley never testified. She was acquitted, perhaps in large part to the efforts of a team of high-priced attorneys brought in and paid for by Jack Benchley. The trial was postponed midway for Ms. Benchley to give birth. The child was a seven-pound, eight ounce girl, christened Avalon Grace Strunk."

It was at this point that the article went off into speculations, all casting doubts on the verdict of the jury being correct. I had been at San Jose State University when the incidents above took place, studying Criminal Justice. I was always sympathetic to Ann Benchley because of the other-woman's angle. I felt if she had plugged her husband deliberately it would have been done at their first encounter at the carport. Now, reading the chapter, I was not so sure. It was laid out in such a way to throw maximum suspicion onto Ann Benchley without flat-out stating that she was a cold-blooded killer and not the hapless young bride her lawyers had made her out to be.

It didn't take a law degree to figure out why Ray had suddenly wanted me to read this chapter. A good number of thought patterns entered my mind, keeping me awake. Ray's message seemed to be that Ann Benchley had killed Dave because he was no longer seeking her attention. If I took my bartender friend at his word, there had been some sort of conversation between Dave and Ray relating that Ann Benchley suffered from a bi-polar mental disorder, manic-depression. From the screaming fit she threw at Bonnie Noel at the Ryskind Theater and her make-up lady's references to the star not taking her medication, you could certainly speculate that Ms. Benchley was not going to make *People Magazine's* Top Twenty-Five Mentally Balanced Celebrities.

Then there was his information on Leroy Millman: the fact that he bragged to Ray about murdering and disposing of some Mexican kid who was having a little bedroom aerobics with his daughter. Besides having his son hijack me this evening, Leroy had come right into my home with a loaded gun. He was a bold bastard who thought he was above the law. Before the incident at the ranch tonight, I doubted the veracity of Ray's story about the murdered farm worker. Now I didn't. From Leroy Millman's own lips I had heard his professed fearlessness—a frank arrogance—where local law enforcement was concerned. Why not brag about killing some poor kid to a disinterested bartender if you were in tight with the local police chiefs, the county sheriff and the local district attorney? Short of a blatant piece of evidence, they would never go after Millman or his son.

Could Dave have stopped somewhere on Interstate Five coming back from California, been bushwhacked by one or both Millmans, and then dumped by the creek where he was eventually found? If Dave had been off his guard...

Then there was Rochelle Millman. She was certainly a forceful person in a way that Wendy wasn't. They had different mothers and, from what Wendy had told me, Rochelle had more of her forceful father in her than she had inherited. But what was Rochelle's motive? She was the Other Woman, not Wendy. And then this business of Wendy actually sneaking over to the pistol range, firing the Golan handgun Dave gave her. Was it true? How could I know for sure? I could not just come out and ask her, no way.

And why was Ray trying so hard to implicate Ann Benchley or the Millmans in Dave's murder? A guy trying that hard might have something himself to hide. There was the certain fact I had, from Ray, that he had an affair with Wendy during one of the bad turns in her marriage to Dave. Wendy had told me she "had leaned on Ray" for a while after Dave had broken her nose in a drunken rage and she had kicked him out of the house. Might Ray have killed Dave to protect Wendy? The trouble was I had the impression that Ray, who, as I said before, had his share of brief sexual encounters over the years, always maintained that he had no use for love in the romantic sense and basically used women for play things. I had never seen anything in his behavior to contradict that.

That would seem to preclude Ray knocking off Dave. But, then again, I knew from personal experience that men might talk one way in regard to the effect feminine allure had on them but that the truth going on inside their heads and hearts was another matter. I wondered what Ray had been doing the afternoon that Dave had taken a bullet.

I let all this speculation roll around in my head. It depressed me. I got up in the middle of the night, sat in my chair in the living room and wrote all my speculations down. Then I tore up what I wrote. And then I worried some more about being caught bugging Trevor Warbeck's office.

I went back out to the living room and watched some of the old movie I was taping. *Dark Passage*, a movie I had seen before, was on and Humphrey Bogart was playing an escaped convict fresh out the San Quentin Prison above San Francisco. Lauren Bacall was playing a beautiful young woman who just happened to be driving around beautiful and monochromatic Marin County in an old Packard or a Desoto. She is a beautiful young woman with a soft spot for middle-aged convicted wife-murderers and picks him up. So now Bogart is hiding out in the back seat of this Packard or Desoto car and the two of them are stopped by a police dragnet near the Golden Gate

Bridge. The cops are looking for Bogart. Bacall does a reasonably good job of lying and Bogart lies real low under a blanket on the floorboards.

She says all she has under the blanket are her painting supplies. The cop doesn't look under the blanket. Okay, so it wasn't plausible, but nobody who breaks out of jail in an old movie is ever guilty of the crime and how can you find the real killer of your wife, or meet any attractive substitutes, sitting in jail?

While watching the movie, I picked up a three-day old Sunday Edition of the *San Francisco Chronicle/Examiner* I had stuffed under the coffee table. It was while scanning over the 'Arts' Section that I took note of an upcoming personal appearance of a fellow named Trevor Warbeck in the City-By-The-Bay.

Chapter Twelve

In the nightmare I had later that night I was in a plane. I hated planes and anything else that had the ability to go up to great heights. It was some damn old wood and canvass World War One biplane on top of that. I was in the rear cockpit and someone I couldn't see was in the front. We were crop dusting and after each pass over the long fields of green wavy cornstalks the plane would go in an almost vertical climb. I was scared out of my wits, hoping that each pass would be the last one. I kept my head down, just looking up enough to see a bit of the light blue sky and the streaks of clouds. At one point in the last of many ninety-degree climbs I looked out across one of the wings. Dave was there, strapped to the wing by some kind of harness. He wore grey pinstriped overalls, aviation goggles and a leather cap and he was laughing—his mouth wide, his arms stretched out at his sides, his body leaning backwards—as the plane climbed. The whirr of the engine noise stopped as we became directly vertical. Now we glided downwards, nose first. I saw the fields spinning about below us getting closer and closer. I looked back across the wing where Dave was and saw him undo the harness. He waved at me, then let go of the last harness strap and flew off the wing. A white puff of billowing silk opened up over his head. The man in the front cockpit had just disappeared. I got up in the cockpit as the plane plummeted and began to try and climb out. As I jumped I pulled a cord I had seen attached to a bulky harness. The parachute opened and engulfed me in it. I seemed to be tumbling downwards, free of the plane but not able to grab anything to control myself. I would float for a moment or two then fall like a rock for longer periods, knowing the ground awaited.

I woke up with a start, shaking, glad to be on the ground and in bed.

I got up around seven-thirty, shaved, dressed, and stopped off at a drive-thru coffee booth to get a breakfast muffin and a latte. I stopped by the side of the street where the local hospital was. There I checked my weapon I had in a shoulder holster. I also checked out the small electronic bugging device Bonnie Noel had given me.

I was a couple of stoplights from the Interstate Five on-ramp when I turned around and headed back into town. I decided to go back over to the McLoughlin Building, specifically to Dave's office. I knew the key he had given me would open up the closet he kept locked up. If I didn't get into Dave's locked closet and clean out the skin magazines and the hard booze from the closet, then Wendy would not have to see it all and deal with it. I could put it all in a box and drop it all into a dumpster behind the building. I figured it was the least I could do for Wendy since I wasn't entirely sure I would be back from California.

The office had not changed from a few days ago when I had checked Dave's messages. That was about twelve hours before I found out he was dead. I had not gone back to the office since then. It was just too hard to deal with the memories. The room was semi-dark because I had shut the venetian blinds tight on the window behind the desk. After I turned off the alarm system, I flicked on the overhead light and looked around the room. It was painful. The room reflected Dave's life in a way the apartment he had shared with Wendy and Jill never did.

I opened the closet and started to load up the magazines. Then I noticed a flashing light on top of Dave's phone message machine. According to the digital read-out, he had two new messages from the last time I had checked, a few hours before he died. The first was from an attorney for a local insurance company who had hired Dave to spy on some guy who the company suspected had faked a work-related back injury. I had notified the attorney that Dave was dead a couple days earlier. The second message was from a famous person I had just met.

"Dave, this is me. This is me. I need to see you. I want to talk to you. I've been acting like such an idiot, but I've got my shit together now. When you get back Tuesday night, meet me at our spot. I will be waiting for you there. I will be there by six o'clock, and I'll wait for you. Don't call the ranch. Just remember—I'm waiting for you. I love you, Dave. Be there. Don't let me down." I suddenly felt cold, cold enough to shiver. I knew who the second caller had been. So would a lot of other people.

The voice belonged to Ann Benchley. She must have called right after I left the office the day Dave was found dead.

I was totally distracted by what I had just heard, which was too bad. It would have been helpful if I had heard the door to the office opening behind my back. As it was, all I got in the way of warning was a smell. It was a musky, masculine smell. The lights went out, first from the toggle switch on the wall and secondly from a blow I took to the back of my head. I didn't know what hit me but I took it hard. Luckily, I have a hard head so when I hit the floor I was still awake.

I rolled over, reached under my coat for my gun and took out my .38. I thought I had a form above my head, a dark outline at least. But by the time I aimed and squeezed the trigger the form was gone. The door to the office opened and I caught a glimpse of a hooded, broad-shouldered man a couple inches over six feet making a quick getaway. Then I tried getting to my feet. I didn't make it. Things got dark fast.

I must have been out for a while. When I got my senses back I had a head full of throbbing pain and a goose egg on the back of my head. I heard a strange noise, like somebody had forgotten to hang up the phone. I got to my feet, wobbled around like a drunk and managed to grope to the toggle switch on the wall. I turned it on, and turned about to rest myself against the door. I looked around the room. Only one thing was missing: the phone message machine. It had apparently been ripped away from the phone on the desk because the phone itself was upside down and the receiver dangling off the edge. I put the receiver back on the cradle, stopping the jarring electronic noise that was doing no good to my head.

The next people I saw were two uniformed Rogue Falls Police Officers. I recognized one of them as Bill Folger, a beat cop I knew who had testified a couple times in severe evasion of child-support cases the D.A.'s office had handled. The furniture dealer downstairs had heard the shots and called 911. I gave them a deposition, but I couldn't describe the man who hit me other than his height and weight and that he wore a mask.

"Why would he just take the phone machine?" a female officer with big eyes and a heavy chin asked.

"I don't know," I said. "Maybe he thought it was something else. He probably would have ransacked the place, but I got a shot off."

There was a bullet hole in the stucco seam between the wall and the ceiling. The bump on my head and my general condition—barely able to stand—was enough to satisfy the cops. The furniture dealer told the cops he had heard the shot, but he had stayed in his office in the back of his store, so he was in no position to see anyone come down the stairs. He said he had heard a vehicle peel out of the gravel driveway in back of the building, but hadn't seen it.

I showed the two nice police persons my driver's license, my concealed weapons permit, and my investigator's license. I didn't mention what I had heard on the tape that was in the phone machine. What would have been the point? I had no evidence, only a bad feeling that my 'client' stood a good chance of being a prime suspect in my friend's death. Of course, the police had it as a suicide so, again, what was the point? I knew whoever had slugged me certainly wasn't Ann Benchley, but that didn't mean he wasn't a hired hand for her, as I was. The police woman asked me if I wanted to go to a hospital. I declined. I figured I would live. Besides, California beckoned and I had some Tylenol in the glove compartment of my truck.

"I'll just sit down for a little while," I said, doing so on the padded swivel chair Dave had in front of his desk for visitors.

"You sure you didn't see any features on the guy as he ran out of here?" Folger asked me.

"I just could tell you the height and the build of the guy," I said. "He had a mask on."

"Could you see his eye color? What he was wearing?" the lady cop asked.

"He had jeans on, I think."

"Were they blue? worn out? Brand new?"

I was frustrated because I knew I should have taken in more of a description but I hadn't.

"I think they were...no, hell, I can't be sure. I know he wore some kind of black pullover. Damn it, I can't think. If the bastard hadn't hit me..."

The cops finished their inquiry, then left. I stayed, nursing my head in the chair. After a while I felt good enough to stand up again. I got a drink of water from the sink in the little closet-sized bathroom Dave had just off from the desk. I put a wet cloth on the back of my head and headed for the door.

Before I could get there, there came a knock at that door. I reached for my .38. Then I put it away when I heard Wendy's voice.

"Harvey?" she asked in a small voice I could barely hear through the door.

I put the gun in my holster again and let her and her sister in. I told her the story. Apparently, she had gotten some of it already from the furniture dealer, who had told them about the excitement upstairs. Wendy seemed concerned. Rochelle, on the other hand, bore an expression that only conveyed polite sympathy.

"What did the asshole do to you?" Wendy asked.

"Caught me when I wasn't looking," I said.

Wendy gently touched the back of my head where, I strongly suspected, the large bump was still growing in size.

"Why did he break in?" Rochelle asked. Her heavy-lidded, large eyes scanned the room as she asked and settled a hostile gaze on the box of booze bottles and porno mags I had taken out of the closet.

"I have no idea," I said, feeling dizzy. "I think he had to have been following me around. He must have wanted in here bad and was spooked by the alarm system tag on the door. Whatever he was after, he forgot about it when I got off my shot."

I didn't mention the phone machine being gone. No point in that.

"Well, let's pick you out a new bed, kiddo," Rochelle said to her sister after her curiosity was satisfied.

"You go ahead, Rochelle," Wendy said. "I want to talk to

Harv. I'll be right down."

Rochelle looked perturbed at Wendy, but said nothing. She told her younger sister to hurry up and then walked out the door.

Wendy watched the door and listened for the sound of her sister's pointy heels going down the stairway. When she heard the heels descending, she looked back to me.

"Rochelle and Leroy aren't getting back together," she told me. "I guess Rochelle's had it. She says Leroy made too many demands on her, some of them quite degrading. You probably don't want to hear what she had to do for him."

"Things of a sexual nature?" I ventured.

Wendy nodded. "She went back last night to the ranch and got the rest of her stuff."

And more or less told her sociopathic husband I was the guy she met at the Four Star Hotel, I thought.

"Well, I guess she'll get a nice chunk out of the Millman Empire," I said. "He wants to get it done fast so it won't interfere with his campaign for Congress."

"She won't be doing that well," she said. "Leroy had her sign a pre-nuptial agreement before they got married. She would have had to stay with him a lot longer than she did to get any real money out of him. Rochelle got a good settlement before, when she and Jack Benchley divorced. But she spent a lot of that on trips and jewelry. She might have to go back to acting to support herself, or maybe get a regular job."

"Gee—that's tough," I said evenly.

"She'll get a little bit of money, not much by Rochelle's standards," Wendy remarked, the wry expression on her face telling me she caught my irony. "Rochelle does not want to work; she wants to shop. She's on a shopping spree now. I'm going to get a new bed out of it. I think I need a new bed. I think I need a new life."

"I'm sorry I haven't been around to see you in awhile."

"Forget it," Wendy said. "Rochelle has been taking up my time, as only Rochelle can do. Now tell me about what happened between you and Leroy. Rochelle says you told her Leroy threatened you at gunpoint. What was that about?"

My head hurt so bad I couldn't come up with any great story, so I settled for the truth flavored with a major lie. I told Wendy about meeting up with Millman at the Four Star Hotel in Middleburg last Friday night. I told her I had followed Rochelle from the Safeway in Rogue Falls out of curiosity since I knew she was supposed to be on the coast.

"I think she was sleeping around on our local cattle baron," I said. "She went into a room there with a bunch of groceries. I never saw him, but I heard his voice. Some big guy I think from the sound of him."

"Sounds like Rochelle," Wendy said. "Did you know who she was seeing?"

"Negative," I said. "I heard a man's voice greet her when she walked into the room, but I didn't recognize it. She wasn't at that swank retreat on the coast, that's for sure. Leroy must have been tipped off somehow. The guy got away, apparently, before he saw who it was. And, to top it off, because I was in the hotel visiting some friends from the Bay Area—"

"He thinks you're having an affair with Rochelle?" she said, then shook her head. She looked back up at me, cocked her head in a cute way that told me she was inquisitive.

"I'm not seeing Rochelle," I said.

Wendy folded her arms under her stomach, then smiled. "No, Harvey, I know you have more class than that." The spirit of the old Wendy was back for a moment. She looked back at the door, her eyes resting on the cardboard box. She could see the skin magazines and half-empty whiskey bottles.

"Those must be Dave's," she said.

"I was trying to get that crap out of here before you came in to clean up."

She looked back at me. "You didn't want to embarrass me. That's nice, Harv."

"You doing okay?"

She shrugged her shoulders. "Yeah...I'm okay. I got a couple things to take care of, then I think I'm going to take Jill and move on."

"You thinking about moving over to Klamath City?"

"Or maybe I'll stay here. I'm not sure. It's too early right now to make solid plans. I better get back downstairs. Are you sure you're okay?"

I rubbed my aching jaw and felt the back of my head. "I'll be fine," I said, even though I was beginning to wonder if I would. "I have to get down the road."

"Don't worry about me," Wendy said in a firm voice. "I'm

a survivor." She touched my shoulder and gave me a quick peck on the cheek. I patted her gently on the back.

She turned to leave.

"Wendy?" I said.

She turned around. The sunlight coming through the small window above the desk highlighted the bump on her nose that had come courtesy of Dave's right fist. She was beautiful anyway.

"What is it, Harv?"

"Dave was a great guy," I said.

Wendy's forehead wrinkled slightly in the middle. A slight grin formed on her face. For a second she was the Old Wendy, the Wendy who was her natural light-hearted self when things were going right with Dave, the Wendy that I always wished I had laid eyes on before Dave ever saw her.

"Well, that's not a question, Harvey," she replied. "Dave was Dave."

"That he was," I said. "I had a question for you—but let me ask you another time."

"That's cool," Wendy said. She turned, and opened the door to let herself out. "Take care, Harvey," she said. The door closed behind her.

I called a restaurant in San Francisco, Rock and Roll Hamburgers, where Jane Willey worked to see if she was back from her vacation. No luck, but I did find out she was due back in a couple days. I hung up, wondering what the fourth and final message on Dave's machine had been. I finished gathering junk out of the office for a minute or two, then proceeded down the two flights of stairs to the dumpster. As I walked out of the McLoughlin Building with the trash, I glanced in the large display window of the Midsummer Night's Dream Bedding and Futon Shop. Wendy and her sister were looking over a futon. Rochelle looked up and saw me. Her countenance did not convey cheer. I'm sure my face didn't either.

It was a six-and-one-half hour trip down to the Bay Area from Rogue Falls. I had a lot of time to think about the situation I was in. I had heard evidence that established Ann Benchley as desperately wanting to meet Dave at some 'spot' as soon as he got back near Rogue Falls. Ray Harrison had told me that Dave and the actress had had a long 'fling' and had only recently broke up. The 'spot' could have very well been Cramner Creek, near the town of Bowman.

Ann Benchley, my client, now supplanted Leroy Millman or even Trevor Warbeck in my mind as the prime suspect in Dave's murder. The problem was I had nothing solid on Millman and I was getting paid to go after Warbeck, not after my own client.

But someone had stolen the evidence I would have needed to prove my client's potential involvement: the audio tape with Ann Benchley's message. Someone who wanted it bad.

I stopped at a rest stop that afforded a nice vista of snow-capped Mount Shasta, took out my notebook and wrote down what I could remember Ann Benchley saying on the tape. I know it wasn't word for word—getting sapped on the head does not improve your short-term memory—but I wrote it down anyway even though it was useless as evidence.

I realized I had better watch my back. That concern for self-preservation had better include a weariness regarding Bonnie Noel, too. She might be setting me up. But who knew anything for sure after what I had experienced in the last twelve hours? I did know I was getting well-paid by my client/prime suspect.

I tried to concentrate on the Sherwood Strunk/Trevor Warbeck/Institute for Factual History angle on Dave's death and Benchley's disappearance. After all, maybe Ann Benchley had nothing to do with Dave's death.

And maybe I was doing some Olympic rationalizing.

Chapter Thirteen

Give Trevor Warbeck and the gang at the Institute for Factual History credit; they had a great neighborhood for their office.

The IFH was cocooned in a three-story blue-with-white-gingerbread trim Victorian townhouse in an up-up-upscale section of San Francisco known as Pacific Heights. There was even a park that looked down on the place so I could get out of my car and take up an inconspicuous position on a park bench that was sheltered from the hazy sun—and from anyone getting a good view of my high-ground position—by a stand of eucalyptus trees.

It was around noontime, the day after my trip started. I staked out the place from late afternoon yesterday until about 7:30 in the evening when a short, husky-looking Asian man wearing a dark suit had left the building and locked not only the front door but also locked the wrought iron gate that served as an entrance from the street. I had gotten his picture courtesy of the zoom lens on the Nikon camera I normally employed in my Family Support work, as well as several images of other folks going in and out of the place before the man closed things up. There was still no sign of Trevor Warbeck, but I had a feeling he would be making an appearance this afternoon because he was due in town for the *Tower of London* exhibit at the Museum of Western Art.

If you were to get up from the park bench where I was, and walk up to the crest of the hillside park away from the object of my study, you would find yourself taking in a good deal of scenic San Francisco. The top of the park sported a public tennis court and, if you looked beyond the playground of the elementary school just below the courts, you could see the Golden Gate Bridge on the far western horizon in all its International Orange splendor. Beyond the bridge rose the bare and jagged grassland hills that jutted out into the Pacific and made up the Marin Headlands across the Bay. Looking eastward from the bridge, there was a small flotilla of white sailboats in the choppy bay waters. They looked very tiny and vulnerable from such a distance, like any one of the boats could vanish into the swells of dark blue water.

Further into San Francisco Bay rose the undeveloped Angel Island, a spot whose chief historical distinction was that it had served as the Ellis Island of the West Coast for Asian immigrants a century or so earlier. (Until the 1900's, Chinese and Japanese kids had been segregated into Asian-only schools in the city.) Past Angel is the more developed and more infamous Alcatraz Island. The towers and the outline of the old prison compound on top of 'The Rock' made it look like a mothballed aircraft carrier waiting to be towed out to sea for bombing practice.

Looking in from the Bay through the wisps of fog swirling above Coit Tower, a viewer could take in Telegraph Hill with its clusters of attractive houses perched around the steep hillsides in defiance of Nature's periodic shifting of the earthquake-prone San Andreas Fault. Adjoining that was the landscape of high-rises that had long since made the downtown area no different than what a traveller would find in Dallas or, for that matter, Singapore or Frankfurt. In spite of the urban blight, it was a damn gorgeous city and, having grown up just south of the place, I had strong and pleasant memories walking up and down the hills, taking in the architectural and geographic uniqueness that one could find in the outlying parts of San Francisco. I sat on that bench wishing Dave was still alive and I could take the city in without having to be on a job.

And especially without having to worry about getting caught trying to bug an office in the townhouse I was focused on. Or wondering if my client was the one who killed Dave and her dad the one who really did strangle Carolyn Mason.

After the Asian man had closed up the IFH on that first night I had been in the city, I paid a visit to the address that

Jane Willey gave me. It was in the center of the city, a block or so above the main drag in Frisco, Market Street, at 1884-A DuBoce Avenue. It was a non-threatening if slightly rundown neighborhood of townhouses and old-fashioned corner groceries wedged tightly together with a couple postage-stamp sized parks to break up the monotony. DuBoce Avenue was situated between the predominantly poor and crime-ridden Western Addition of the city and the predominantly upper middle-class and Gay Castro District. It was raining hard when I found a parking space about a block up from the address. And I mean up literally, as the neighborhood was on one of the city's many steep hillsides. I got up the hill and parked the Celica, illegally, in a slot reserved for residents with a special sticker on their vehicles. In addition to the rain, there was a chilly blasts of wind coming in from the Bay. Perfect spring weather for Frisco, I thought. I turned the collar of my water-repellent green coat up, pulled my Australian-style bush hat down on my forehead, and walked into the sheets of diagonally-falling rain.

I knew that apartment three was where Jane Willey, the former roommate of Carolyn Mason, was supposed to be living. The last name Willey was even on the shiny metal directory, framed by little grecian-style plaisters, outside the entryway.

"Yeah, what the hell is it?" came an unfriendly feminine voice over the intercom. She sounded like she had had a libation or two that evening.

I pushed the intercom button. I introduced myself, and lied that I was Richard Thorpe, an investigator with DBS Investigations.

"Am I speaking to Jane Willey?"

"Yeah...what the hell do you want?" Her tone was sharper, her voice more slurred.

"I have a few questions for you regarding Miss Mason," I added.

There was a short pause, then my answer.

"Go away."

That was it. I buzzed again, and used the intercom. "My client is prepared to—"

"I'm calling the police," the woman's voice said. "You people are the one's who've been bothering me at work. I'm calling the police if you buzz me again."

As if to emphasize the threat, a black-and-white police cruiser went by on the street. The tires of the car made little waves in the rainwater on the street as the black-and-white rolled by at a leisurely pace. I got a nice stare from the officer on the passenger side.

I stood there a few more seconds, deciding if I should ring again or not, then gave it up. Reasoning with a drunk was usually futile unless you had police power, and I didn't. I walked back to my car, first crossing the street and turning about on the sidewalk to see if anybody was looking down on the street from the building. There was. I could make out the profile of a thin woman standing behind some narrowly-open venetian blinds. She was up on the second floor. Something was in her hand. It looked more like a tumbler glass than a phone receiver. I gave her a friendly wave and walked on. At least this time the rain wasn't blowing right in my face.

At ten o'clock that same night I had been where I told Bonnie Noel I would be. I was "crashing" in the spare bedroom of an apartment that a long-time friend, Arthur Nelson, and his wife, Patricia lived in.

The ten o'clock phone call had been right on time. The caller had an upper crust/BBC news reader accent and he did not mince words.

"Mr. Stoker?"

"Yes," I replied.

"Kipling here." When the voice said that I imagined a short, bald, portly English fellow in a pith helmet and khaki shorts sitting in a rattan chair with a bare-chested Rex Ingram—the genii from the *Thief of Baghdad*—billowing his sweaty forehead with a giant ostrich feather. "Are you alone?" the voice asked.

I was.

"I trust you know where the IFH is? At 7:30 tomorrow evening, I want you to be near the three telephones situated at the bus stop on the corner of Clay and Steiner Streets. You know where they are?"

"Half a block from the IFH," I said.

"Exactly. By all means, don't forget to bring the transmitter and wear gloves so as not to leave fingerprints. Tell no one of your plans. Do you need me to repeat these instructions?"

I said I did not. That terminated the conversation.

The next day, I divided my attention between the IFH building and an IFH publications I had brought along.

The book, *Shadow On the Crow*, was a recent publication. The author was listed as Trevor Warbeck, but since Warbeck's name appeared on almost everything that came out of IFH—the book with the chapter on Ann Benchley and Talbot Strunk had him down as an editor—I suspected Mr. Warbeck was more supervisor of underlings than lonely man at a word processor. The main thrust of the book's argument was the one Bonnie Noel had laid out for me back at the Shakespeare Festival: that William Devant, 15th Earl of Grantum (1542—1612) wrote the plays and poems of William Shakespeare. Shakespeare and Grantum were contemporaries in the England of Queen Elizabeth I and her successor, King James. Shakespeare had been a front for Grantum, the book alleged. Since nobility could not write for the '*trey declasse stage*,' as the book put it, Grantum had sought out "a rude commoner, recently come to London from Warwickshire," and fed him the completed works for presentation on the stage. When Grantum died in 1612 Shakespeare was forced to leave "play-writing" behind and return to Stratford-On-Avon, where four years later he also died. Warbeck called Shakespeare "an undoubtedly barely literate actor whose undeserved fame is the most insidious cover-up in the history of literature."

The book had a middle section showing a reproduction of the only existing painting of Grantum. He had been a corpulent fellow, bald on top with curly tufts of sandy blonde hair along the ears. One eye looked larger than the other; was the larger one a glass eye? His nose was long and slender. Had he been fifty pounds lighter he might have been handsome. But the doughy face only highlighted the sinister-looking little black eyes that gazed out at the viewer. He was dressed in a broad, multi-layered white ruff—the front of which was hidden by a thick tuft of beard—and a shimmering light blue doublet with a pattern of silvery triangles down his chest. The painting took him in from the waist up, so below the doublet one could only glimpse the hilt of a sword supported with a gold braid-like belt.

The face was familiar to me. Then it hit me. He looked somewhat like Trevor Warbeck. From the background of the book, I learned that the Earl had been a high-living guy who squandered the family fortune—from a licensed government monopoly on imported claret—on lavish parties to please the Queen when she visited his grand estate north of London near where Hampstead Park is today. Warbeck didn't come out and state it, but apparently the Earl's lovers were strictly of the boy-toy variety. That might explain why he spent so much time haunting the theatres around London since all female parts on the public stage at that time were played by adolescent males. He was especially fond of 'Paul's Boys,' a troupe of young actors who were quite popular in the late 1590's when they rivaled Shakespeare's theatrical troupe, the Lord Chamberlain's Men, and other officially-designated acting companies. It was this rivalry between the boy troupe and the adult troupe Shakespeare was in that, according to the book, soured the bond between Earl and commoner. The relationship had suffered earlier when Shakespeare staked out a new patron, The Earl of Southampton, and dedicated two major poetic works, *Venus and Adonis* and *The Rape of Lucrece*, to the younger nobleman. Warbeck admitted he wasn't sure who wrote the poems.

The Earl of Grantum had, according to Warbeck, kept a journal of his life from roughly 1591 to his death in 1612. Much was made of the printed copy of the journal Warbeck said he found in 1994 at the Strunk-owned Sobel House. According to Warbeck, he had found the printed journal "in a priest-hole tucked away under a decaying wooden post in what remains of the cellar of the old Grantum Manor."

The reference to a priest hole, it was explained, referred to a hiding place for Catholic clergy who had been smuggled about England from the time that Henry VIII broke away from the Roman Church in 1533 and on through his daughter Elizabeth's reign and beyond. William Devant had been a secret Catholic who outwardly observed the Act of Supremacy—giving the Anglican Church and, most importantly Queen Elizabeth, total political allegiance—but he also was a link in a sort of Catholic Underground Railroad for young English Jesuits who were smuggled back home after being trained in France and the Papal States.

A letter from the 17th and last Earl of Grantum, Charles Devant, was reprinted in the book:

"'It [the journal] has the most remarkable passages of wit of my grandfather's career as a man of Eliz.'s courte *(sic)*. There are details of many of his visits to the Tower to see Walter Raleigh, and his services to King James and commentaries he made on the writings of Sir Francis Bacon, Ben Jonson and Leonard Diggs, the last three being remembered in his Will and Testament. There exists also this startling revelation: the trove of plays contained in the folio that Shakespeare has been credited with is revealed in these volumes to have been the treasure of another William, namely my esteemed ancestor. A deception was fused 'tweenst my noble relation and this rude, prating mountebank *(sic)* from Stratford-On-Avon to spare the repute of the Devant family. There being no more need to maintain the guise, fate betakes me to bring the truth of these matters to the artful and learned men of our time. It is a token of what I and my late lamented father owe to him whose achievements have dwelled in secret 'lo these past years.'"

Warbeck acknowledges that Charles Devant was a debt-ridden gambler on the outs with the Restoration monarch, Charles II. But he maintains that the letters told of a genuine journal and were not, as Jack Benchley and Bonnie Noel thought, just laying the foundation for a literary hoax for Charles Devant to scare up some money in the 1660's and help save him for selling his estate.

To quote the book: "'Painstaking detective work on my [Warbeck's] part (and the fortune of having my good friend Mr. Strunk owing the estate where Grantum Hall stood) enabled me to make this wondrous find. The find restores William DeVant to his rightful place in letters. He, not the illiterate Stratford glove maker's son, is the rightful great master of the English language.'"

Throughout the book there were several "selections" from the DeVant Journal. I recognized a few of them because they had been cited in Jack Benchley's rebuttal article to *Shadow on the Crow* which appeared in the *San Francisco Chronicle* a month before the scheduled debate between Benchley and Warbeck at the Strunk family's Forest of Arden. The debate, of course, was canceled when Benchley vanished.

The article that Jack Benchley had written summarized the main thrust of Warbeck's book. Then Benchley outlined his own "discovery" that put another spin on the Shakespeare-DeVant relationship. According to Benchley's article, which I had a copy of with me, "Shakespeare had been a friend of the Earl of Grantum. But a sampling of poetry known to be in the Earl's own hand showed him, "to be, at best, a flickering spark of a talent as compared to the solar-sized intensity of Shakespeare's illumination of the mind and soul of existence." Benchley made much of the analysis of the handwriting and document experts from the Huntington Library who stated that the journal was forged by William Devant's grandson.

"Young Shakespeare of Stratford had come to London after a short career as an assistant schoolmaster," Benchley wrote in the article. "His early efforts at playwriting attracted him to another budding poet, the Earl of Grantum. Grantum befriended the younger man, giving him a place in his London household for a few years until Shakespeare had established himself. It was in Grantum's townhouse on the banks of the Thames that young William became acquainted with another Peer of the Realm: Henry Wriothesly, Earl of Southampton and Baron of Titchfield. It was the latter relationship, whether platonic or profane, that inspired Shakespeare to his mature works for which the poems *Venus and Adonis*, *The Rape of Lucrece* and the superb courtly comedy, *Love's Labor's Lost* belong. A transition took place in the author's life and Southampton became his chief patron. William DeVant, Earl of Grantum, had no rancor in his heart for Shakespeare or his new friend, despite the efforts of one modern psuedo-scholar to twist history into his own paranoid vision of all events as a series of unending conspiracies."

Benchley quoted from a copy of the original, handwritten William Devant Journal, the one he claimed was currently in the private possession of a Scottish barrister who wished to remain anonymous. The rest of the article went into detail on the literary investigations being done on the original journal at the Huntington Library.

My rumination into this controversy was interrupted by a group of kids who had taken over a section of the tennis courts behind me. Apparently, it was lunchtime at the local school and some teenagers were utilizing the park to get a few drags on their cigarettes. Seeing some of them with food and drink reminded me of my lunch and I set out for a delicatessen on the north edge of the park, opposite the IFH.

After getting my turkey-on-wheat with chips and a milk, plus a package of fig newtons, I pulled out my cell phone and placed a call to the Santa Rosa Republican newspaper. I had been trying to get a hold of Christy Mathewson ever since Dave had died. She had been out-of-town on a vacation and this was the first time she had been at her desk. She confirmed for me that Dave had no abrasions on his face when they had talked together about the Forest of Arden and Jack Benchley.

"You say he committed suicide?" Mathewson asked. Dave had been right: she did have a very sexy voice.

"I don't say that," I replied. "A cop up in Rogue County tells me that, but there hasn't been an official determination released. But this detective I know is betting on suicide."

"You know, for a guy who was a couple hours away from knocking himself off, he sure seemed cheerful."

"Why do you say that?"

Mathewson chuckled in a breathy, alluring tone. "Well, I'm not used to having a guy flirt with me ten minutes after we first meet. Especially when we were here in the office. I mean, I knew he was just a big flirt right away. We met about nine in the morning and he asked me if I was available to go to lunch with him after he got back from the City. I told him I was seeing somebody. He still flirted away."

"I'm not surprised," I said. "Did he happen to mention going to the Institute for Factual History?"

"Yes," she said. "Said he had an eleven o'clock meeting with Anita Shumpsky. Shumpsky is Trevor Warbeck's personal assistant at IFH. She's also his girlfriend. Warbeck himself is at the IFH offices over in London. He pretended he was applying for an office job there. Said he needed to stake out the inside of the place as much as he could."

I felt the blood start shooting through my temples. Could Dave have also been working to plant a listening device in that office? From Dave's last phone message, he had said he was trying to go undercover into IFH and see someone connected with Warbeck. He must not have planted the device or something had gone wrong with it. Some of Warbeck's minions might have caught him and the transmitter and then set him up for the 'suicide' up in Bowman. Or he could have just conducted the interview and got away and headed home. It was certain he didn't successfully plant a listening device otherwise I wouldn't be getting paid to do that later on. Could somebody have double-crossed him?

Mr. Kipling, for instance.

All these possibilities went through my mind as Christy Mathewson talked on about all the work that was on her desk and how she had to get back to it. I asked her if Dave had made any phone calls when she met with him."

"Yes, as a matter of fact," Ms. Mathewson said. "Just before he left here, he asked to borrow the phone. He wanted to check his office messages. He used his phone credit card, so I let him."

So Dave heard the message Ann Benchley had left him. Knowing that, he could have walked right into a trap.

"I take it there were quite a few political and economic insiders at the Forest of Arden Gathering," I said.

"I'll say," Ms. Mathewson said. "It's been going on for a dozen years. Supposedly it's just a friendly little long weekend where all these men—and it's men only—get together and talk shop about the economy and the country in general, then get to see a couple live performances of Shakespeare's plays at the theater the Strunk family has on the compound. Every year the V.I.P. list gets longer, and harder to confirm. We know the Vice-President was there this year, and Norville Hardy from the FBI, and several Senators and Congressmen. I've interviewed a good deal of the help for my articles and I can tell you there are some wilder things those guys get up to than just watching Shakespeare and hugging redwood trees."

"How wild can it get if there are no women allowed?" And, at that moment, I remembered Carolyn Mason's presence.

"Let's just say, as Shakespeare said in Hamlet, 'It is a custom more honored in the breach than in the observance.' Women are allowed if they aren't politicians, business executives or wives of the select."

"Bimbos only."

"Right," she said. Ms. Mathewson repeated to me about the amount of work on her desk and how she had to get back to it. There must have been a question in there somewhere, too, because it suddenly registered to me that she was saying, "Are you still there, Mr. Wells?"

"Yes," I said, like I had awakened from a light sleep. "You

were saying, Ms. Mathewson?"

"I wondered if you have anything to go on connected to your friend's death?"

I was about to give her a standard 'nothing conclusive, but the investigation is on-going' response, when I saw a tan-colored Rolls Royce with tinted side windows roll past the corner where I was standing, just before it vanished behind an electric orange-and-silver MUNI streetcar. I saw the right turn-signal go on. The Rolls was going to turn down the street where the IFH was located. It was time to hustle back to my post. I promised the lady on the phone that I would get back to her if there were news-worthy developments, then hung up. I dodged my way past the slow-moving Angelo's Sourdough Bread truck and hot-footed it across the street and back to the other side of the park.

I arrived at the bench to find it occupied by two young mothers who were taking up the seating to adjust their young kids in their respective strollers. I had left my camera and the books under some evergreen bushes just down from the eucalyptus tree in front of the bench. Retrieving the camera would have to wait.

But I got my first look at Trevor Warbeck, at least my first look of him outside of a movie or the newspapers. He was being pulled out of the Rolls Royce by a very tall white gentleman with a chauffeur's uniform on. I say pulled out because Warbeck must have weighed 300 pounds or more and the makers of that luxury vehicle had not made the backseat doorway quite wide enough to allow him an easy time getting out. He was a fat man with salt-and-pepper sideburns and wore what had to be a toupee on his scalp. He wore a charcoal grey three-piece business suit that was big enough for a four person tent. The most prominent feature on his face from the distance I saw him at was his jowls. They drooped down his face between that strong chin. The second chin under the first was the same color as the face, a grey pallor. The chauffeur was tugging away, gripping his passenger's out-stretched arms. It was quite a struggle, even though the driver looked to me to be built like a basketball power forward.

"Look at that," one of the mothers said. I turned about to see one of the women pointing down to the scene below. The other woman looked up from her diaper-changing duties. In a few seconds she had a response.

"Oh, hell, that's that fat son-of-a-bitch Terry Warbeck. He's always going in and out of there. My husband loves that jerk. Monte tapes all of his specials on our VCR. He's another one of those political nuts." The woman looked over at me for a moment, noting that I had glanced over at her. I gave her a quick smile that I hoped registered approval on my part to what she had just said. Then I turned away, keeping my eye on the continuing struggle to dislodge the celebrity from my vantage just to one side of a eucalyptus.

For a time I believed paramedics with special equipment would have to be summoned, but at last Warbeck was out of the car and on his feet. I smiled at the thought of the mother referring to Warbeck's Christian name as 'Terry.' There was nothing 'Terry' about him He stood for a moment in the street where the Rolls was double-parked. A small blue Honda had stopped just in front of him, but Warbeck held his ground and the driver of the car had to maneuver around him. The chauffeur pulled a couple suitcases and a large garment bag out of the trunk and then the two of them walked slowly toward the townhouse.

A woman came out of the Victorian and walked briskly down to the first step leading to the porch. She was a light-skinned African American lady with a short haircut and a long thin body. She wore dark Ray-Ban sunglasses and a red power suit. Even from a considerable distance I could tell she was pleased to see Warbeck and that Warbeck was doing good for himself. As Warbeck walked through the half-open wrought-iron gate, she came forward. With surprising agility for a fat man, Warbeck suddenly moved quickly toward her a few steps. There followed an embrace and a serious locking-together of lips. Warbeck even dipped her, and saw a broad smile on her face as her head tilted backward and he buried his face into the side of her neck. It seemed safe to assume, from the ardor of the embrace, that he was back from a long trip somewhere, probably London, as Christy Mathewson had earlier alluded to.

Once the bags were taken through the door, the chauffeur came back down the steps and walked briskly over to the double-parked vehicle. Warbeck and the lady stayed on the front stoop of the house, then the two of them slowly ascended the stairway arm in arm. Could this be Anita Shumpsky? Do African-Americans have Polish last names? Could she have had an upbringing in an African-American/ Polish-American household, maybe in Chicago? Was anything I was thinking at all relevant to my case?

After the mothers continued their stroll, I resumed my seat. My camera and books were in their hiding place, undisturbed. No more unusual activity happened out front of the IFH. I had my camera handy again, but the people who occasionally came in and out—like the husky fellow who last night had locked the place up—were people I had already photographed. I dutifully noted arrival and departure times of these familiars in my notebook.

The afternoon dragged on. I took my coat off as the afternoon sun broke through the wisps of fog that hung overhead. Occasionally I got up and walked around, always trying to keep the Victorian in sight, but myself out of sight.

Hours passed. At 5:32, I could see Warbeck through a second floor window at IFH. At 6:14, he emerged from the townhouse. Ms. Shumpsky was on his right arm. He was now decked out in a smart-looking black tuxedo. She was wearing a shimmery white cocktail dress with a matching jacket over her shoulders to ward off the twilight chill. The Rolls appeared in the front of the townhouse. Just as the pair reached the car, there was a figure emerging from the front of the townhouse. He was a tall, stocky man with a full head of chestnut-brown hair in contrast to a long reddish beard that had grown out several inches past the chin. He, too, was sporting a tux. I thought the guy must be a film or television actor, like I had seen him somewhere before. He looked about on the top stairway for what seemed a long time. "Haste!" came a cry from the Rolls. It was the deep, resonant voice of Warbeck. The man seemed to snap out of whatever trance he was in. He gave a final look in my direction, causing me to slowly turn away. When I looked back he was bounding down the steps like a kid. There followed two more people from the townhouse. One was the Asian-American man I had seen before. The other was a long-haired blonde man who wore a black pinstripe suit with a tieless shirt buttoned up to his neck. He looked to be in his twenties and his face bore an androgynous quality. He looked like a rock star yet I couldn't place him. As he came down the stairs I detected the strut of a fellow who was quite taken with himself. As he reached the limousine, the redbearded fellow gave the rock star a pat on the back. The tall chauffeur opened the backseat door and the pair went in, angling themselves as if they were taking up jumpseats just in front of the backseat itself. Presumably the backseats were occupied by Ms. Shumpsky and rotund Warbeck.

I checked my watch. It was 6:17. The Asian-American man was locking up the front gate. He then walked down the street, stopping at a bus stop with a covered awning. I waited a couple minutes until a bus came by and picked him up and the small group of commuters who also clustered about the stop. Then I got up.

I strolled down to the Pacific Medical Center a couple blocks away on Sacramento Street. The area offered a good section of non-resident parking and I had grabbed a space for my car earlier that morning. I put my camera, the books and the radio behind my front seat. I then went down Sacramento to an area which featured a spate of small markets with the names in both the Roman and Chinese alphabet. I found a small restaurant I had liked on my last visit and ordered some kung pao chicken and pork fried rice. During the middle of the meal I slipped into the Mens Room, *a la* Michael Corleone at the Sicilian Cafe in *The Godfather*. I was alone so I checked my .38 out to make sure all five chambers of the revolver were loaded, double-checked the hammer, then tucked the piece into the holster under my right armpit.

I finished my dinner, looking over the sports section of the San Francisco Examiner. I gave the news sections a glance, then checked my watch. 7:16. I had fourteen minutes to stroll back down Sacramento Street to the corner of Sacramento and Steiner, right below the park and half a block down and across the street from the IFH building. I stood near—but not right at—the public telephone and pretended to be waiting for a bus. I was actually waiting to hear from 'Mr. Kipling.'

Chapter Fourteen

Twilight had faded away to night by the time I got back to the park. It was 7:28 and I watched the 46 Muni Bus pull up and the passengers get out from the two swinging doors at the front and the middle of the orange and white bus. After the bus left, I pretended to be engrossed in reading a news headline in one of the coin-operated machines. Two couples talking in German passed by me. I gave them a look. Had to be tourists. Just then the phone booth at the corner of the park started to ring. The tourists took note of it, no doubt wondering what half-wit was going to answer a public phone.

The half-wit in this case was the incomparable Harvey G. Wells. The voice on the other end of the call was Mr. Kipling's. He was his usual terse self.

"Run your hand under the base below the phone, Stoker."

I did so. The aluminum shelf had a set of keys taped to the underside.

"I got them," I said. I glanced out of the corner of my eye. The tourists were headed down the street.

"Right," the voice said. "Now, looking past the IFH, to your right, you will see an apartment building. Using the key with a blue patch on the head, enter the building. Proceed to apartment 306, on the third floor. Enter that apartment with the key that has a red square on the head. Undo the top lock first. That's the deadbolt."

"What then?" I asked.

"You will find a cellular phone on the table near the side

window that faces out onto the IFH townhouse. Pick up the phone when you get in. I will call you there in two minutes." The next sound I heard was a click.

The apartment building in question was a three-story structure, with a Corinthian-style cornice across the front and rectangular windows and classic-style pediments jutting out a few feet from the main part of the building. I entered the place without a problem and took a winding red-carpeted stairwell up to the third floor. The interior of the hallway was lit by a series of lights shaped like upside-down crystal balls that were spaced out about ten feet apart on the ceiling. Right above the elevator there was a small glass chandelier on the ceiling and, next to the block control buttons on the console, one of those old-fashioned fire extinguisher outfits with a mass of cloth hose and a metal nozzle encased behind a glass and sheet metal door.

I recognized the Grateful Dead song, *I Will Survive*, drifting through the hallway. Jerry Garcia was doing the vocal. It got louder as I took up the trail to 306, which was shown to me via an arrow on the wall. I passed 302 and found it open. I took a quick look in. There was a middle-aged man with bushy hair strumming an electric guitar while perched on a barstool in the living room. He was following along with the music coming from the stereo in back of him. A younger pale brunette with soulful eyes and long stringy hair sat on the black leather sofa a few feet away. She gave me a stare of defiance as I passed, as if my looking in through the open door was an insult.

I undid the two locks and walked into the semi-dark Apartment 306. The place was stripped of all furnishings save for a table at the far end of the living room. I gave the place a quick once-over while I waited for the phone on the table to go off. When it did, right on schedule, the phone gave that funny buzzing ring that cellular phones emit. The window just above the table was shut and the blinds drawn.

"Nice place you got here," I said after I picked up the phone. "Is this unit under rent control?"

'Kipling' ignored my levity. "If you look across the way, Mr. Stoker, you will see that this apartment window looks out on a portion of the roof of the IFH building. The alleyway separating the building at this point is exactly 12 feet, 9 inches across. If you look below the table in front of you, you will find an extension ladder. Once it is extended to the maximum, the ladder will reach across from the window sill in front of you to the roof across the way."

My stomach started churning. As Kipling started explaining how to extend and lock the ladder, I twisted the plastic stick that was attached to the venetian blinds over the window. As I opened the blinds, I set the phone down on the table for a moment and turned off the table lamp that was providing the only illumination into the room. There was indeed a narrow alleyway between the two buildings. If the ladder was hoisted straight out the window, it would come to rest on a flat portion of the neighboring roof. Just to the left of that section was a triangular-shaped gable with steep slopes. The sloping side closest to where I could cross would hide any view of me from the street.

"Do you understand how to operate the ladder?" 'Kipling' asked.

There was no way I wanted to crawl across on that aluminum contraption. I pressed my nose against the window, and looked down to the alley. There was a bit of light from the street. I couldn't see much but the concrete below was probably forty feet down. Now add a dizziness in the head to my churning stomach. I might as well have been looking down at the Pacific Ocean from the deck of the Golden Gate Bridge.

"Do you understand how to secure the ladder?" 'Kipling's voice was insistent.

"Yeah," I said between gulps. "OK, I cross the alley to the roof. Then what?"

"Then you climb up from the flat part of the roof to your right. Hold on to the peak of the roof and work your way across sideways like a crab until you reach the end of the slope. From there you can jump down to another flat section of roof."

"Go sideways at a forty-five degree angle?" I nearly shouted. "Then swing around and jump? Then what, may I ask? A backflip off the gutters and a two-point landing forty feet below? Am I a goddamn trapeze flyer here?"

"Are you finished, Mr. Stoker?" The voice was patient, but firm.

I took a deep breath. "All right, the Flying Wallenda

touches down on this section over to my right."

'Kipling' continued. "You cannot see it from your vantage, but there is a skylight close to where you will land. There shouldn't be a lock on it. Simply lift up the rim of the skylight. And use the gloves that are placed before you on the table."

"I brought my own gloves."

"Use the gloves provided," the voice said, sounding perturbed. "They have special gripping enhancers on the fingers. Now, once you are through the skylight, you can jump down to the room below. That is the utility room. Place the phone you are holding in your coat pocket. Once you gain access to the utility room, do not move. Do not touch anything. Wait for me to call you. You have the audio device, I trust."

Burning a hole in my pocket right now." I replied.

"Good, Mr. Stoker. Now, do you feel up to carry out this phase of the plan I have laid out?"

I was developing a dislike for the snotty, emotionally-detached voice I was dealing with. "Yes, Mr. Runyard Frigging Kipling, I'm up for it. Just be warned I'm reporting you to the American Acrophobia Society. You got that?"

"Good show," 'Kipling' said, in a parody of his own voice. "I'll call you in a few minutes. Good luck." The line went dead.

I got the ladder out the window, and after a couple attempts got the far end of it to rest on the flat patch of roof across the way. Now came the fun part. I crawled out on the narrow sill of the window, then grabbed hold of the sides of the ladder to balance myself. The ladder jostled a bit as I put the rest of my body out onto the ladder. I dangled one leg over each side of the ladder, then pulled myself slowly to the other side by grabbing hold of one rung at a time and yanking myself along. I did not look down, but my memory of that first look was enough to make me almost turn back after that first pull. I felt for each rung and made sure I had a white-knuckle grip before going forward. I took a glance to my left, to see what kind of view from the street someone might have of my situation. Luckily, there were mature beech trees that obscured the view from the street.

I made it to the other side, then carefully placed one foot in the rain gutter and both on the horizontal section of the roof. My heart was pounding like a jackhammer as I pushed off from the ladder with my other foot and rolled onto the ledge. The ledge was just wide enough for two people my size. I wiped the sweat off the top of my forehead and then just laid there for a couple seconds, thinking up the safest way to stand up.

Once I was vertical, I leaned forward against the sloping roof. I used the small chimney that separated the ledge from the gable for further support. The best way I could see to mount the roof was to climb on all fours along the seam between the gable and the main roof. I did so. Even with the gloves, which had little rubberized ridges along the fingers and thumb line, it was hard to get hold of the shingles. I kept my center of gravity as low as possible. It was slow going. I had a flashback to when I was a kid at the beach in Santa Cruz and was climbing some bluffs at a state park. I had gone off the trail and suddenly found myself on a slope with a similarly precarious angle. I had made the mistake of not looking down as I climbed quickly to catch up with some friends. It was only after the sand became soft and slippery where I was climbing that I risked a dose of vertigo and looked down. I had gotten myself at a point where with one slip I could have rolled down to a cliff where my next move would have been a vertical drop of 150 feet to the beach below. I could still see the wisps of sand particles I had disturbed floating out over the cliff as I looked down. If I wasn't acrophobic after the ballpark incident, I was after that trip to the beach.

I got hold of the peak of the gable. I pulled myself up, then swung one leg over the peak so I now sat as if I was astride a horse. I glanced over my shoulder at the park across the street, which was illuminated by two lighting towers. A few kids were playing a pick-up basketball game on the court at the top of the hill. Nobody paid heed to my roof activity, so I got slowly to my feet. After balancing myself on the apex of the gable, I slowly removed my hands, then spread myself on the slope of the roof itself, with my arms reaching for the peak. I was short by a few inches so I grabbed hold of a heating vent with one hand and then pulled myself up to where my free hand got a grip on the peak.

Now came the "crab" part. I suppose 'Kipling' wanted me to simply hold on to the top of the roof with my gloved fingers to avoid someone seeing me. I made one effort to do it that way, then gave up and pulled myself up further to where my torso tottered out over one side of the roof and my feet remained on the other. Carefully, I got myself sitting up in the saddle position again. I tried keeping my eyes as low as possible in front of me. The less scenery I could see, the better. Once I felt balanced I did decide to look southward, which was the way I was facing. We were up on a hill, so the central part of the city looking down toward the Mission District stretched out before me. There were blocks and blocks of apartment buildings illuminated in little squares, a couple skyscraper-sized hotels, and dark patches of trees that must have been parkland.

The view in this direction wasn't as good as the one looking out over the Bay the other way, but I did see a landmark: the Sutro Tower, a giant television and radio transmitter on top at the apex of the steep hillside known as Twin Peaks. The tower actually was four separate towers joined diagonally by girders. It was lit up like a Christmas tree, festooned with airplane warning beacons that glowed through the layers of fog swirling about the top of Twin Peaks, on the western fringe of the horizon. If King Kong ever showed up in San Francisco, he'd grab a damsel and head right for it.

I worked myself over to the back end of the roof, trying to keep my body as low as possible to the roof. I felt at times like I was on display for the world. The pervading sounds of automobiles, trucks and airplanes was drowned out for a time by a police siren. I was relieved immeasurably when the siren noise started to grow faint and change direction.

Once at the end of the roof, I leaned over and saw my goal: a skylight just below where I was situated. There was a tar-papered horizontal section of roof about the size of a parking space around the skylight and some cover was provided by an adjacent heat pump unit. I slid off the roof and dropped the few feet to a spot near the skylight. I sat down, resting my back against the heat pump. I checked my coat pocket to make sure the bugging device was still on me. It was. I felt my chest. My heart was going like a male rabbit on top of a doe. I checked my watch. 7:48. Twelve minutes from now, Trevor Warbeck was due at the San Francisco Museum of Western Art. I was going to be late for that show.

The phone in my other coat pocket went off. "Captain Ahab's Seafood Shack," I whispered after opening the phone.

"How may I direct your call?"

"Are you in?" It was 'Kipling.'

"No, but I'm at the skylight. Hold on." I reached over with my free hand at a latch just below the clear plastic cover. It opened easily. Either security was sloppy at IFH or somebody inside was helping me—or us—out. I looked down the shaft into a tiny, semi-darkened room below. A neon light was on so I could see that I had about a ten to twelve foot drop in store for me. I informed 'Kipling' of this development. He instructed me on how to get to the office that was to be bugged.

"Go to the third door to the right once you open the closet door. Once you get inside, you will see a large desk at the far end of the room," the voice said. "On that desk is a large cigar humidor. Place the bug on the underside of the humidor. Peel off the adhesive cover on the back of the bug and attach it dead center. Also, push the small lever on the side of the microphone to the 'on' position. You'll see the indication mark if you hold the bug up to the light. Use the tip of a pen to adjust the lever. Touch only what you absolutely must. Once you are back in the utility room, you'll find a large step ladder hanging from the door. Use it to exit from the room via the skylight. Then retrace your route back to the apartment, return the ladder to the place you found it, then leave."

"Got it," I said.

"Thank you," Kipling said, "And good luck." The other line clicked off before I could finish snarling, "That's a real comfort, dude," into the phone.

I dropped down through the open shaft, being careful not to scrape myself on the sharp sheetmetal edges that ringed the opening. My feet hit the floor below with a noise I thought shook the townhouse. The neon light, now overhead, seemed much brighter now. As I heard nothing but the soft electric hum from the light, I concluded I was alone inside.

The utility room looked like what a normal office utility area should look like. There were shelves of computer paper, pens and pencils, ceramic coffee mugs with the IFH logo, a box of toilet paper, a plastic drum of disinfectant (with Carolina Pine Scent) and sundry other mundane items. I turned on a small flashlight I had in my pocket before I opened the door. I crept slowly out of the room and into the darkened hallway. It was then, flashing my light about, that I realized this was no ordinary office. The walls and doors along the hallway were paneled for one thing. And the decor was not cheap particle board stuff, but a rich, dark lacquered wood-paneling shaped into coffered squares. From the light coming from the open door of the utility room, and my flashlight, I could see a myriad of geometric patterns in the borders of the squares. All of it was inlaid and, although I was no expert, something about the designs made me think it had been done by hand. The floor also featured elaborate wooden parquetries, mostly in the shape of giant flowers. One thing for sure: this layout did not come from JC Penney®.

I went down the hallway to the third door on my right. That was my target. I scanned the office with my flashlight. I went in to find the decor of the office very much like the hallway. The major difference in the office was the furniture: wooden tables with bulky, circular-shaped legs; a large, intricately-carved fireplace with an arched facade and some sort of coat of arms situated above the fireplace itself; a display of old-fashioned firearms (wheelock muskets with septenine-shaped hammers and long barrels) that would have been out of date in George Washington's day; a huge dresser across the room from the fireplace with the same bulky legs as the small tables; and designs of scrolls covering the spaces between the drawers. On top of that dresser was a bust. It looked to be made from terra-cotta. It was a close likeness of Trevor Warbeck. I say close because the figure depicted on the bust looked serene, almost cheerful. From what I could remember of Warbeck's mug from movies and television interviews, he had a melancholy broodiness about him, an unpleasantness missing in this visage. The artist must have doped the fat guy up to get that cheerful an expression out of Warbeck.

I found the humidor on the right corner of the large desk. The desk actually looked modern, although the woodgrain matched the decor of the room perfectly. I put down the flashlight, turned on the downward-facing table lamp next to the humidor, did what I had to do, then set it back down as carefully as possible. The case looked expensive: the underside of it had an inscription that it was made in Havana, Cuba. Probably long before Castro took over, I reckoned. The desk itself looked to be made from mahogany and was clean of papers. A small laptop computer was dead center on the blotter. There was also one of those white, streamlined acoustic wave radios on the opposite end from the humidor. Pasted on top of the radio was an advertisement done in black lettering over a red, white and blue background. "COMING TO A RADIO NEAR YOU!" the bold lettering said. "Factual Radio! Up-to-the-minute news reports and lively call-in talk shows. A bastion of American Truth and Honesty coming from the Strunk Broadcasting Center at Number One, Battleship Plaza, in San Francisco. Radio that pulls no punches!"

There followed a long list of stations all over America that were going to carry the new radio network.

I paused to look at the display of photographs above the aforementioned dresser. Mostly they were photographs of Warbeck. Some were from his days as a slimmer film and theatrical actor. There were stills from *The House of the Dead*, the Benchley film for which Warbeck won an Academy Award as Dostoyevsky's autobiographical character, Alexander Petrovich. There was also a photo from *Love On Appeal*, a late Sixties film where Warbeck attempted to play a Cary Grant-type. His character is a young judge who begins a romance in the middle of a case with the spirited defense attorney, played by the late Sandy Dennis. It was a dud. One film critic said the film should have been called, *Love Without Appeal*. Another photo: Warbeck standing on the Golden Gate Bridge. Next to him is Sir Alfred Hitchcock. The Master of Suspense is pointing off into the distance, a pixy-like grin on his chubby face. Warbeck is paying no attention to Hitchcock or whatever the director is pointing at. The actor has his arms folded and looks glum. This picture had to be from the production of Hitchcock's next-to-last feature, *The Clock Strikes*. Faye Dunaway, the co-star, was to Warbeck's other side, laughing at something or someone off-camera. There were also photos from Warbeck's stage career in London and New York: Warbeck done up as *Richard III*, menacing some pretty Lady Anne and a theatrical program, featuring Warbeck, billed just below Peggy Ashcroft and Ralph Richardson, in the 'Old Vic production of Thomas Kyd's *The Spanish Tragedy*.' There was also a photograph showing what looked to be the entire cast of some English drawing room play. Warbeck, youthful and handsome and trim, is wearing a cardigan sweater and holding a cricket bat. There was one picture I thought was out of place. It was Warbeck and Jack Benchley. The actor had his hands tied behind his back with coils of strong rope. He was standing sideways with his head cocked to one side, glaring at Benchley. He was dressed in an open-necked black shirt and a dark pair of hose. Benchley was standing straight in front of him, a light meter dangling by a cord around his neck. The director had his mouth open like he was yelling. His arms were straight down at his sides and his hands were balled up into fists. Warbeck was glaring back at Benchley. It looked like the two men were close to coming to blows. Judging by the alarmed-looking background extras, dressed not unlike the Pope's Swiss Guard behind the two men I judged this still to be a production shot from *Essex and the Queen* the film for which Warbeck had been dismissed by Benchley after only three days of shooting and replaced by Charlton Heston. The still had to be from the set of the last scene in the film and the first one shot by Benchley: the Earl of Essex being executed at the Tower of London for leading a rebellion against Queen Elizabeth I.

Why the hell would Warbeck have this photo in his office? It had to be the biggest humiliation of his film career and, from what I had read, the project that began his slide into unbankableness as a film star, a declining status he always blamed on an insider smear campaign done by Jack Benchley before Benchley's own fortune's declined. Why have this to remind him of his failure?

Suddenly an overhead light went on in the office. I turned around to the door. At that moment I realized I could ask my question about the photograph to the man himself.

Chapter Fifteen

Trevor Warbeck stood in the center of the door frame. He was decked out in his tuxedo and looked like a mutant emperor penguin, at least from the folds of the flesh that passed for his neck down. His face was menacing to behold. His eyes were almost hidden under a heavy browline, his aquiline nose made his face look like it was chipped from marble. He had thin lips that almost seemed to recede into his mouth. Anyone who had not seen Warbeck in twenty years would have trouble recognizing him. It was not just that he was fatter. The added weight had made him look almost lifeless up close. He was something that belonged in one of those cheesy Wax Museum places; a hollowness to the man in spite of all the bulk.

If Warbeck was a fat, mute penguin, the fellow next to him was no life of the party, either. He was the chauffeur. He stepped in front of his boss, and I might have been tempted to go for my gun a few seconds previously were it not for the salient fact that Warbeck's minion had a gun, a luger to be exact, pointed at me. The chauffeur looked to be closer to seven feet tall than six. The minion had a swarthy skin tone, deep-set beady brown eyes that looked slightly cross-eyed, a long narrow nose that hung from his face like a disjointed outcropping from a cliff face, and a gash of a mouth surrounded by a thin line of dark whiskers about his jawline. The stare he gave out told me his IQ number was probably less than his height in inches.

"Good evening, Mr. Harvey Wells," Warbeck said in that

vibrant baritone voice he possessed. "I trust you find my office commodious?"

Before I could offer a rejoinder, the chauffeur was on top of me. I was spun around and searched. My gun was roughly removed from its place, then I was spun around again. The chauffeur said nothing to me; he let the onions on his breath do the talking. Up close to him, I noticed his left eye was skewed to look a bit sideways while the other eye was properly centered. Physically, he reminded me of a guy who had once played center for the Los Angeles Lakers. The difference with this guy and the athlete, however, was that screwy left eye and the weird way he stepped back from me, almost like he was walking in high heels. Still, he looked imposing enough to do a good deal of damage. The German automatic he had in his hairy mitt of a hand helped with that effect.

There was a third person in the vicinity, who cowered behind Warbeck. He was the guy I had seen lock up for the last two nights. He looked about as nervous as I felt.

Warbeck made a tsk-tsk noise with his tongue, then walked past myself and his driver to the mahogany desk where I had planted the listening device. His movements were wobbly, the jiggling of his gut rippling the red cummerbund he wore about his waist. He leaned over and ran his hands across the desk blotter and lifted up the laptop computer. I looked back over at the big guy, who was pointing a long-barreled Luger at me. He had a sneer on his face that made me think he had done this sort of thing before.

"Dromio," Warbeck intoned to the big guy. "The first order of business if you please."

The big guy turned that dopey expression away from me and walked over to his boss. He walked backward so his two guns—mine and his—covered me. He handed his Luger to Warbeck, then tucked my .38 into his pants. I noticed when he walked backwards he was pigeon-toed and seemed to have to stagger about to keep from falling. An awkward henchman. Therein was a chance for me to stay out of the morgue if I got an opening.

Warbeck trained his gun on me. He held it loosely in one hand, like it was a banana. I was ten feet away and was in no position to test his reflexes.

"Because we had to wait for you to break-in, you've

already made me late for the museum," Warbeck said to me. "We have the Senator and his wife there, and Mr. Strunk and his wife coming, plus the British Ambassador flew in from Washington. This is all most inconvenient." He turned to the man he called Dromio and said, in a voice one might use to ask a waiter for the wine list, "Would you deal with Mr. Park first. He is a traitor and has to be dispatched."

The fellow named Park tried to run for it, but Dromio grabbed him by the collar of the coat as the small, but husky man tried to make his getaway. A struggle ensued that, despite Park's apparent best efforts, concluded in the giant wrapping his hands about his neck, then lifting him off the ground. Park's legs kicked about in the air and his arms flailed about to reach his foe but it was all over. At one point the poor guy managed to pivot Dromio about a bit so they both faced me. I saw the smaller man stare at me with imploring eyes. I had seen that look before from a little girl whose life ended prematurely on a crummy half-paved county road. She died because, in the line of duty, I had run over her in my patrol car, by accident, but dead as if I had shot her deliberately. That memory blocked my immediate fear for a few moments, then the feeling of near-helplessness came back in an internal wave of nausea mixed with panic. Park dangled and danced in the air for a little while longer until the inevitable snapping sound. I looked over at Warbeck. He glanced at me with that same bored expression he had standing with Hitchcock on the Golden Gate Bridge in the photo behind him.

The body of what had been Mr. Park was thrown face down on the parquet floor. His limbs were still spasmodically twitching away. The whole thing was giving me the shakes. I took my left hand and gripped the right wrist to try not to show my fear.

Dromio stepped back from the body. He then retrieved my weapon from his pants and took aim again at me. He looked like a guy who had just finished the Breakfast Special at Denny's, and was ready for the day. I strongly suspected lunch was coming up soon and I was the entree.

"Where is the device, Mr. Wells?" Warbeck said. He glanced at his watch. It looked to be a gold Rolex or something similar. "Come now, I know that you are nothing but a hired bagboy of the Benchleys. I know all about you already except for the location of the bug you've planted."

"Know all about me, you say," I replied, trying to drag out the business to get an opening, trying not to show fear. "OK, pal, when did I graduate from high school?" I figured sarcasm might stall the situation a bit until something better came along.

"You graduated in 1978 from Prospect High School in, let's see, -yes, Prospect High School in Saratoga, California. You're a former policeman with a few years of college. While you were at the university, you also served in the Army Reserves, attaining the rank of an E-5. You left the Sutter City Police Department some time ago. You hold some job with the Rogue County District Attorney's Office. You are recently divorced. Papers were filed by your ex-wife in Parker County, Arizona. Irreconcilable Differences. Allow me to offer you my regrets. You have a concealed weapons permit and a private investigator's license with the Oregon authorities in Salem. No children, no property holdings. You see, Mr. Wells, you do not have to be an ex-cop to access public records."

"Or to bug an office," I said. "You must have had Jack Benchley's office bugged to find out when I might be stopping by here."

"Yes, I did have Benchley's office wired," Warbeck said. A smug grin crossed his kisser. "Ann Benchley had a good idea. Bug the office of her father's enemy to see if he knows about the old man's disappearance. If this were a chess game I was playing with her, it would have been a sterling move. Of course, I would have mated her king before she could have executed said move. There was another fellow who came before you. He tried to pass himself off as someone wanting to be a volunteer for the Truth Party in the coming state elections. A David McCreedy I believe was his real moniker. He was also a graduate of your high school. You were probably friends."

"You killed him," I said as if I had him in an interrogation room. "You killed him up on the Oregon border and made it look like a suicide."

"Oh, is David McCreedy deceased?" Warbeck said a mocking formality. "Oh, dear. Well, I would have you offer my condolences to his family, but I am afraid any long-terms tasks you may need to complete will be left—undone."

"I'll bet your little outfit has bugs all over that Shakespeare complex. Even if you kill me, you're screwed. McCreedy found out about Carolyn Mason. She worked for this IFH outfit through a temp agency. Sooner or later, somebody will find Jack Benchley, dead or alive. Ann Benchley has the material to tie Mason into you. The cops will be at your door sooner or later."

Warbeck smirked.

I looked to Dromio, but continued speaking to his boss. "Once you got hold of Benchley, you probably let Little Lennie here strangle her, then dumped her in Benchley's Mustang to make it look like the old man offed her, then took a powder for parts unknown. Stop me if you're bored by all this rehash, Warbeck."

Warbeck looked up at me again. A wolfish grin appeared on his face.

"For your short-term satisfaction, Mr. Wells, let me assure you David McCreedy received no harm from me. I knew his game, but I wanted to see him play it out. He was making a blind stab to gain information. He was no threat to my organization. You, on the other hand, have behaved in a manner that forfeits reasonable hospitality on my part."

Dromio stepped toward me. "Not a big man without a gun, eh?" the thug said in an accent I thought might have been Eastern European.

"Stay where you are, Dromio," Warbeck snapped. "You'll kill him when I say so. Show some patience, please." He glanced at his watch. "I'm sorry to cut your final moments of ego satisfaction short, Mr. Wells, but I have to be down south of Market Street shortly. I cannot let a vision like my Anita go unescorted amongst the wolves of this dark city." He walked toward the door. As he passed Dromio, he handed him the Luger. The big guy stuck it on the table behind him.

"Get this taken care of," Warbeck said, stepping over the body of Mr. Park. "Once you have finished with the other guest, you'll find an ample assortment of trash bags in the supply room. Be sure and replenish the supply before Monday rolls around." Warbeck shot a glance back at me, then went through the door.

I stared back at my remaining host. I've heard it's harder to shoot a man if he is staring right at you. Dromio leveled my own gun at me and walked slowly forward. The gun stayed on me as he leveled a backhand against my head. After a flash in front of my eyes, I found myself sliding across the floor. The desk stopped my head very effectively. I was stunned for a few seconds. I figured I would be attacked before I could get upright, but I was wrong. I shook my head and looked up. Dromio was looking at a small slip of paper that I recognized. It was a pocket baseball schedule, with two tickets inside. I recognized them. The papers must have come out of my coat.

"Those are baseball tickets," I said. "I got 'em for Opening Day tomorrow at Pacific Bell Park. We're talking lower reserved seating. Those are yours if you let me go. Those are good seats, right on the first base side. Barry Bonds is coming off that bad hamstring injury he had in Spring Training. Weather's supposed to be good, too, and I'm pretty sure Pat Boone is going to sing the National Anthem."

"Fuck your baseball," Dromio said. The next thing I knew I was being hoisted on my feet. "You piss me off," he said in guttural tones, ramming my gun into one of his coat pockets. "I'm going to make this slow because you're a smart ass." I tried to get him to break his grip on me by thrusting my arms up and smashing into his wrists. This only seemed to annoy him. I was flying backwards next, slamming into the black leather swivel chair on the other side of the desk. It broke my landing a bit, then both chair and detective went crashing to the floor.

Despite the stinging pain now shooting up my back, I jumped back to my feet. If I was not long for it, at least I could go out standing up. Dromio came at me from around the desk and swung a left hook at me. Fortunately he moved like an inebriated circus bear so I managed to duck the blow, and I then came up to land a left of my own into his stomach. He clutched his middle with his right hand, but it only slowed him up for a moment. I tried to hop over the desk for the door. He reached out and took hold of me by the coat.

Then the alarm went off. It was a high-pitched, screeching alarm coming from someplace downstairs. Dromio hesitated. Thoughts of the police were no doubt dancing in his head. There was an opening here, and I took it. I broke his hold with a quick left elbow smash to the throat, grabbed the humidor with both hands and brought it down hard on the side of his face. This seemed effective, so I did it again. My second effort was partially blocked by his hands. I delivered a cross chop as hard as I could to a point where I hoped the nerves around his clavicle were. I dropped the now fragmented humidor, rocked back on the desk, and kicked my legs out at him. The combined thrust from the heels of my shoes caught him just below his sternum. He fell back against a partially-closed cabinet. The impact of his fall brought a variety of books and ceramic knick-knacks down on his head.

I got off the desk and slammed the cabinet door against his reclining self as hard as I could. I saw the bulge of my gun in his coat pocket. I could slam the door again and retrieve my .38 while he was pressed into the cabinet. I promptly did so. My gun restored to me, I made a dash out of the office and headed toward what I hoped was a way out.

Getting back through the skylight would have been too much rigmarole, so I took off the opposite way down the hall. The alarm grew louder as I maneuvered around the receptionist area. I found a narrow stairway that seemed to lead downward so I took it. I descended the stairs two or three at a time. When I hit the foyer there was a trail of broken glass on the floor extending from the front entrance. A section of grey cinder block was also on the floor. The oval-shaped stained glass window had been smashed. I undid the deadbolt, made a quick glance to see if Dromio was after me, which he wasn't, then yanked the door open. I jammed my gun into my coat pocket, climbed over the ornamental iron gate and struck out in the general direction of my car. My flight was suddenly halted courtesy of a black, furry chow dog, her slender male owner and a leash.

I picked myself off the sidewalk, untangled myself from the leash and took a bite in the pants leg from the snapping black mouth of the yelping chow. The man was knocked over by the impact of my hasty departure. I never got a good look at him. "I'm sorry," I said to the sidewalk and took off down Sacramento Street. It was here that the noise of the alarm was eclipsed by the siren noise heading toward me. There were four or five townhouses to pass before the street corner and I resolved to hotfoot it there and make a fast turn. As I turned the corner a car caught the corner of my eye. It had shot out from the curb over the next block and taken the same turn I had. I decided to stay on the sidewalk, then dash across the street as soon as the car passed me. But that didn't happen. Instead the vehicle, a Ford Escort, jumped the downward-sloping curb in front of me, cutting off my escape unless I dodged onto the street.

The slope of the street made stopping and changing direction problematic. Maybe the great San Francisco 49'er receiver, Jerry Rice could have made the cut, but yours truly wound up putting his hands out and my body became the not-so-irresistible force colliding with a relatively immovable object.

I repelled off the hood of the Ford Escort as quickly as I could. The hood of the vehicle was only about a foot from the wall of the adjacent building, too tight for me to get around. As I turned to go around the vehicle, the driver's door flew open. Out stepped Bonnie Noel.

"Get your ass in here," she exclaimed. Considering the situation, I thought her idea had merit.

Chapter Sixteen

As soon as I got in, Bonnie directed me to occupy the backseat and get down. I did so. The Escort rolled backward, spun about, then came to a stop a short distance away. The siren noise indicated the responding squad car was perhaps a block away. In a moment it roared past the intersection. Bonnie shifted the car into drive and we pulled away down the hill.

I looked up from my position in the backseat. Bonnie was wearing more make-up than on our first meeting. I also saw she was wearing a crisp-looking black blazer, the kind one might wear to a job or a formal event.

"I think you can get up now," she said to me.

"If its all the same with you," I gasped between huffs for air, "I think I'll just stay down until I catch my breath." I proceeded to gasp, then I retrieved enough lung power to ask what she was doing down here.

"Your intended partner had to leave town," she said as the car seemed to be turning a corner. "I was monitoring the bug you put in with the receiver over here on the passenger seat. I was listening to your trouble with Warbeck and his stooge. I've got everything he said on tape with the receiver, including his admission of bugging Mr. Benchley's office."

"I take it you were the party that deposited the cinder block in the foyer."

"I figured you needed a diversion," she said as she executed a quick stop, then whipped around a corner. "I found the piece of cinder block on the sidewalk. I had to wait until

Warbeck drove off before I could throw it through the door."

"Thank you," I said. "I feel like I owe you my life, or at least dinner in a three-star restaurant."

"What happened to Cam Ho Park?" she asked.

"If you mean the Asian guy, he's dead. Warbeck's boy, Dromio, strangled him. I'll bet he's the scumbag who strangled Carolyn Mason, too."

"Shit," Bonnie said. Suddenly she must have slammed the breaks because I was thrown forward onto the floorboards of the vehicle.

"What is it?" I asked, fearing that we were cut off by the cops.

"Shit," Bonnie exclaimed again. "Why can't kids learn to cross the street at the crosswalk? Are you okay?"

"I should heal eventually."

"Please sit up," she said as the car surged forward.

"Point taken," I replied. "Being hunkered down in the back seat has it disadvantages."

I sat up. We were driving down Geary Street, past two long rows of parked cars in front of 1940's-era apartment buildings in various states of renovation. We were getting closer to the Van Ness Avenue intersection, where the high rise hotels and art deco-style restaurants began. There was an intersecting hoard of tourists on the street, some with name tags on their lapels identifying them as out-of-town conventioneers for the benefit of pickpockets and whores.

"Are you sure Mr. Park is dead?" Bonnie asked.

"If he isn't, he can now see behind him without turning around. Where are we headed, by the way?"

"The Museum of Western Art, just South of Market. We need to have a follow up with Trevor Warbeck, this time in public where we're safe. I feel bad about Mr. Park. Ann's bodyguard, Ralph Bates, recruited him from inside Warbeck's organization. Park was the guy who left the skylight open for us. He wouldn't try and plant the bug, though, because he said it was too risky. "Dave McCreedy was going to try to get in...." Bonnie paused there. "I think Warbeck had Dave killed."

"I agree on that point," I said. "That stooge Warbeck has is as strong as a gorilla." I rubbed my lower back where I landed hard. "What plan do you have for the museum appearance?"

"I want to see if I can trade the tape for Mr. Benchley's where-abouts."

"It's worth a try," I said.

"I don't think Dave McCreedy was a suicide considering what just transpired with you and Mr. Park. I'll have to tell Ann when I talk to her tonight. After all..." She was obviously going to say something about Ann and Dave, but changed her mind. "After all, she hired him and he was a good friend of her father."

And a pretty good friend of hers, too, I thought but did not state. I took in the rest of Bonnie's apparel from my position just behind the passenger seat, looking over the middle armrest to the driver's side. She had on a knee-length pleated black skirt with dark hose and black high heels. She looked fetching, of course. I leaned forward over the headrest of the passenger seat. There was a square-shaped hard-plastic cube a little bigger than a shoebox. The box had a long spiral antenna at the top, a lot of frequency-measuring gismos on the top and a set of headphones hung on one corner of the machine.

"I take it that's the receiver you used to pick up the audio from the office."

"Right," Bonnie said. "I was going to stake out here for a couple days, what with Warbeck back in town and see if they would disclose what happened to Mr. Benchley. All that's shot to hell now. What were you going to do, after the bugging job, I mean."

"Do what we're doing now, head for the museum, try and follow Warbeck around tonight. If he was staying in a house, try and case the place out to see if Jack Benchley might be in there."

"That second part is shot to hell now, too," she said, swinging the car around another corner behind a stream of vehicles.

As we continued down Geary Street, we crossed over into the theatre district. Bonnie pointed over at a Neoclassic building with a fancy awning and double-wide entry doors. "That's the American Conservatory Theatre," she said. "It's where I got my first professional job."

"That's right. You said you were an actress."

"Still am," she said. "This just pays the bills better right now. I was in rep here in 1985. My best part was in Moliere's,

The School for Wives. Annette Benning was the ingenue. That was a few years before she hit it big down in L.A."

"You kind of remind me of Annette Benning," I volunteered. "Especially around the eyes and nose."

"Funny nobody ever mistook the two of us before," she replied. "Certainly not the Internal Revenue Service."

We crossed Market Street, the great gap shown between the comfortable haves and the working class have-not's in the first century of the city's existence. The Museum of Western Art loomed ahead of us. It was a huge building, overlooking a terraced park. The distinguishing feature of the place was an enormous oval skylight that jutted out from the upper roof of the museum. The skylight was set at an angle, like a radio telescope. It looked like something out of a James Bond movie. The banner across the facade read, "*Secrets from the Tower of London, April 14-May 16.*" Bonnie found a spot to park at the underground lot below the promenade and fountains in the square that fronted the museum. When we got out of the car, I made a point to check the number on the ground so I could remember where we had parked.

"By the way," I asked as we walked, "how do we get in this place?"

Bonnie reached into her purse and handed me a small digital camera. "You're now a journalist. So am I."

My credentials were there for us in the lobby at the information booth. It was a formal affair, but we were excused from that dress code because we were 'observers.' Bonnie was a 'representative' from the Northwest Shakespeare Festival. I apparently was a staff photographer for the N.S.F.. We took an escalator up from the ballroom-sized ground floor to an exhibit area. (At Bonnie's request, I left my gun in the car.) I had not been in the museum before, and it struck me how much wall space was given over to a multi-storied blank white wall that started in the lobby and continued all the way up to the catwalks that connected all four floors of mezzanines on both ends of the museum.

My back was still hurting from the fall I had taken over the desk and my left palm was scraped up from my tripping incident with the dog and his leash. I hoped the owner got that chow his or her rabies shots. Other than that, my heart was still thumping too fast. At least I didn't feel guilty that I wasn't earning my money.

Bonnie showed her media credentials to a couple of coat-and-tie security people, then we went in. It didn't take long to find Trevor Warbeck. He was speaking from a podium on an elevated state at the far end of the gallery. We stood in the back of the place where the reporters and camera people were clustered. I saw a camera there labeled, '*Strunk—Culture Network*' and several more news cameras and their crews from local stations. The guests were seated at several dozen circular tables.

Warbeck spoke: "I don't wish to make this speech any longer than I have to, as I was unavoidably delayed in getting here, a circumstance for which I owe all of you an apology." His voice was quite resonant and he probably could have done without the microphone.

"I am grateful to Her Majesty's Government for allowing this collection of paintings, armor, jewels and other artifacts to temporarily leave the Tower," Warbeck intoned to the couple hundred guests seated about the gallery. "You will see things that have been on display in the Tower of London since it opened to the public. But you will also be the first modern viewers to glimpse works of art, weapons, devices of torture, jewels and sundry other relics not seen by the public. In some cases, you will come across *objects d' art* not glimpsed by the public in our lifetimes. Thank you all for coming to this benefit for the Restoration of Western Humanities Foundation, just one of the many enterprises Mr. Sherwood Strunk III and Strunk Communications are undertaking without any aid from government bureaucrats or the keepers of political correctness in the art world. Enjoy!"

There was a hearty round of applause as Warbeck sat back down at his front table. Seated next to him was the divine-looking Anita Shumpsky and, next to her, the two fellows who had entered the limousine with them that afternoon. The tall Redbeard was leaning back in his chair, taking in the gathering of swells like he was the guest of honor. Next to him was the flashy kid in the pinstripes who looked like a rock star. He was downing the contents of a champagne glass with one hand and summoning a waiter over for a refill with the other. There were two or three other people there I didn't recognize.

When the Strunk camera crew went down the main aisle, Bonnie followed right behind them. I followed her reluctantly. We dodged in and out of teams of waiters and waitresses who were unloading food and drink at the tables. We were almost at the Warbeck table when a blazer-clad rent-a-cop intercepted us.

"I'm sorry," said the middle-aged bruiser of a fellow, who had ex-cop written all over him. "Mr. Warbeck is only granting an interview to the Strunk television representatives. He will have a general statement for the media after the exhibit is over."

"Oh, my," Bonnie said, "there has been a most grievous misunderstanding." Her voice had changed. The sharp edge was gone, replaced by a flighty femininity: Scarlett O'Hara sans the drawl.

"I'm sorry," the man said. I could tell he was already buckling a bit. "I don't know who coordinated your requests, but—"

"I represent the Northwest Shakespeare Festival," Bonnie said, continuing her flighty tone. "I spoke to Mr. Warbeck directly just last night from London. He assured me.... Hold on just a moment." She dipped into her purse. Up from a side compartment came a flash of green in her hand: three pictures of Ben Franklin on rectangular green paper .

The old cop took a quick glance at the offering in Bonnie's hand. Then the transaction was made. His speed and precision were worthy of a Chicago public servant.

"I can't have you interviewing Mr. Warbeck until the Strunk crew is finished," he said. "And then only for a minute or two."

"That's all we need," Bonnie said. "We will wait patiently right here."

The man dropped away, giving us an unobstructed view of the gathering around the table. And those at the table had an unobstructed view of us. It didn't take long for Warbeck to see us out of the corner of his eye. His face took on an expression of cold contempt as he realized that the guy who was supposed to be in a garbage bag stashed away in his office closet was in his face again, back for more. I returned his gaze with a friendly wave and a smile. An endearing smile at that, I reckoned, but it didn't alter Warbeck's disposition.

It was a couple minutes before Warbeck got over to us, but get over to us he did. In the interval, he finished up his taped interview with the crew. He mentioned his *Shadow on the Crow* book a couple times and got in a plug for some documentary called, *The Real Shakespeare*. Then he got up, excused himself from his seatmates and walked over to us. Another tuxedoed gent stopped him and they exchanged pleasantries. When he finally made it over to us, a fixed smile was on his face. His attention was focused on Bonnie, and I might as well have been a potted plant.

"Good evening, Miss Noel," Warbeck said. His tone was about as polite as one could get while speaking through clenched teeth.

"A first-class presentation, sir," Bonnie replied. The edge was back in her voice. She was not overawed in the presence of a member of the *glitterati*. "I have something a keen collector like yourself may want. In exchange, I only ask the truth of a certain matter. Surely, the President of the Institute for Factual History knows the real truth behind most events. Events such as the disappearance of Mr. Jack Benchley, for instance?"

"I am charmed by you, Miss Noel," Warbeck said in a way that indicated he was anything but. The creases of his face twitched, particularly about the jawline. I noticed a trace of ruddy make-up to his cheeks that wasn't on his mug back at the office. He made a hacking noise to clear his throat, then looked back at his ladyfriend at the table. "Whatever you need to discuss, Miss Noel, this is not an ideal place for it. Perhaps we could step to a more discreet location."

"Perhaps we could," Bonnie said flatly, "But Mr. Wells and I would rather remain in the public eye."

Warbeck now looked at me for the first time since he had risen from the table. Seeing him without being in a state of anxiety revealed something I found disturbing. Those little dark eyes looked glassy and fixed, like those of a corpse. And the artificially grayed toupee on his dome did nothing to animate his overall look. No wonder he had been most successful in movies playing disturbed, remote characters. His gaze dropped down to the plastic tag I had on that identified me as a journalist. "The detective game didn't work out so well eh, Wells? I'm glad to see you have made a swift transition to a more intellectually stimulating line of work."

"I owe it all to you, Mr. Warbeck," I said.

"You realize, Mr. Wells, I should have you arrested right here and now for breaking into my office." His voice was soft, but still intimidating.

"Which you won't dare do," Bonnie replied. "I have a little recording that makes you an accessory to a burglary charge up in Rogue Falls, plus a little matter of what became of your security man, Cam Ho Park. And how is Dromio doing, by the way? Did he get the office cleaned up before the police arrived?"

Warbeck looked around. I was glad to see a look of worry cross his face. He looked back at his table and gave a little wave to Anita Shumpsky. The lady was mouthing something at him I couldn't pick up on. Warbeck turned back to Bonnie. "Do you have any objection to walking over to the entrance of the exhibit, Miss Noel? I will be serving as the docent for the evening's tour. I could listen to your presentation, as distressing as it might be on a nearly empty stomach, and practice my opening monologue with you two as my first visitors."

"I would be charmed," Bonnie said. "As would Mr. Wells."

"I would rather Mr. Wells remain here," Warbeck said, his teeth clenched again.

"That's too bad," Bonnie replied. "He's my escort for the evening."

Warbeck put a hand to his chin and rubbed his jawline. "Very well," he said. "Allow me to make excuses to the guests at my table."

After Warbeck came back from saying something quietly to Ms. Shumpsky and to the tall red bearded man, we followed behind him as he crossed from the dining area to an equally spacious but nearly empty room. A couple security men stood guard at the front entrance to what had to be the first exhibit of the tour. The walls were lined with portraits of men and women from the Renaissance. I recognized a portrait of Sir Thomas More and one of his rather exacting employer, Henry VIII. The rest of the portraits in the gallery looked like they had been important personages, but they were strangers to me. Warbeck told the men at the entryway to depart for five minutes, which they did.

"Perhaps we should talk in the Gunpowder Plot Exhibit,"

Warbeck said. "The room is smaller and sound is less likely to carry."

"Let's not stray too far," Bonnie said. I cut in front of her as Warbeck led us into a narrow hallway. It featured a wood paneling similar to what was in his office. The hallway was further narrowed by the presence of several large suits of armor. Warbeck took the opportunity to point out the personal armor of Henry VIII that was mounted on a pedestal at the end of the hallway. It was enclosed in a plexiglass case which was lit from below to enhance the size of the combat gear.

"Of course Henry VIII never wore this in battle," Warbeck said with a touch of cheerfulness to his voice. "It dates from 1540, when the monarch was in his early stages of dotage. Men aged quickly back then, especially if they were overindulgent in food and drink." Warbeck turned completely around to us, patted his belly a few times, and let loose an extended sigh. "How do you think my little belly pat will go over with the thongs, Miss Noel?"

"Your timing is still impeccable, Mr. Warbeck. I saw you in Los Angeles at the Mark Taper when you did Captain Boyle in *Juno and the Paycock* back in 1983. I was at UCLA studying the craft. You were an inspiration to me that night."

"Thank you," Warbeck said solemnly.

"It's too bad you went into politics," Bonnie added.

Warbeck smirked at this comment, then turned about and led us with a wave of his hand into the next room. This room was much darker than the preceding one. The only lighting came from what looked like torches hanging from the walls. The 'flames' from the top of the prop torches were actually lightbulbs with transparent reddish cells coating the exterior of the bulbs. The effect was suitably eerie.

In the center of the room was an elevated circular stage. On the stage were costumed mannequins representing men dressed in Renaissance garb: long robes, fur collars, doublets, puffy sleeves, ruffs, etc.. They were gathered around a torture rack, the kind designed to stretch people out and bust their joints. The central figure was some kind of high official with a long robe and a thick-linked chain about his neck. At each end of the torture rack were burly, ugly mannequins dressed in flat felt hats and leather aprons. They were positioned as if they were each turning a crank connected to a giant wooden spool which had a thick coil of ropes. The still-life depiction had the goons apparently turning the crank. The rope that was wrapped around it was taut and connected to the lower limbs of the victim. The upper arms of the model were tied to two separate stakes that stretched his arms well apart. The tortured dummy, dressed in rags and appearing to be sweating profusely, had his painted face fused into a countenance of agony.

Warbeck spoke after we had some time to take the display in. "This display symbolizes a man about to confess his participation in the great Gunpowder Plot of November, 1605. Disgruntled Catholic subjects living in England during the reign of the Protestant King James I decided to try and blow His Majesty back to Scotland from whence he had come. The King was to appear in Parliament. Kegs of gunpowder had been secreted under the building by Guy Fawkes and his confederates from a house in Westminster the group had rented nearby. They built an elaborate tunnel between the two structures and had the greater supply of the munitions in place before the plot was uncovered. The conspirators were rounded up and those who did not confess of their own free will were put to the tender mercies of Jacobean Justice."

"What about Carolyn Mason?" I asked Warbeck. "Didn't she work for you? Wasn't she at that Forest of Arden wingding the night before she was found strangled?"

Warbeck shot me an icy stare. "I don't know Carolyn Mason."

"She worked for you," I said.

"It must have been in a clerical capacity. Oh," he said, rubbing his forehead, "you must mean the late paramour of Jack Benchley, the noted fugitive. I did meet her at the Forest of Arden—briefly. She mentioned working for the IFH now that I recall. And I believe she mentioned that I introduced the two of them at the local film festival. It was a major moment in her life I suppose. It wasn't worth remembering in mine, and I have an excellent memory."

"You had your pal, Dromio, calling her at her apartment, trying to pump information out of her. I've got a witness to that."

Warbeck ignored my statement. "If you want to find the killer of that poor woman, ask your questions of Ann

Benchley's father. I'm sure the beauteous Ann knows where her father is lurking."

"Let me tell you this," Bonnie said to Warbeck. "We know your organization bugged the office of Mr. Benchley. We know you hated him. We know Strunk Enterprises not only sponsors IFH, but also the temp agency that Carolyn Mason worked out of."

Even, I hadn't known that, until then.

Bonnie continued, "We know her next assignment, after working at IFH, was as Mr. Benchley's personal assistant during the San Francisco Film Festival. We also know that, as Mr. Wells intimated, you had someone in your employ trying to contact her regularly via regular and unfriendly phone—"

Bonnie stopped speaking when Warbeck waved his hands in front of her face.

"None of which would be provable in court even if they were true, Miss Noel," Warbeck said as he reached inside his tux—which startled me—and pulled out a pile of 3x5 index cards. "Give me just another moment to run through this first part of the tour, if you please," he said. Out came a pair of light framed glasses. Warbeck moved his lips as he scanned over the notecards. The spectacles went back into a pocket in the lining of his tuxedo. He cleared his throat with a noise like a garbage disposal starting up, then continued.

"The discontented Catholic conspirators remained unrepentant for their terrorist actions. Ambrose Rookewood, one of the lay plotters, wrote from his cell in the tower these defiant words, 'Blessed are they that suffer persecution for righteousness.' And suffer Rookewood did, along with the most famous of the terrorists, Guido, or Guy, Fawkes. After being interrogated by means verbal and excruciatingly physical, the lay plotters were condemned to be taken from the Tower to the front of the Houses of Parliament. Here, in front of the very structure they had planned to demolish with the King and his nobility therein, the men were hanged, beheaded and quartered. The Jesuit Underground in England was also made to pay. Leaders sent from Rome to undermine James' government, like the Jesuit superior Henry Garnet, were also executed for complicity in the plot."

Warbeck glanced over at the grisly exhibit, then looked at me. "As a former policeman, Mr. Wells, I am sure you appreciate the need to extract the truth from lawless rogues. Institutional torture, employed sparingly for certain career criminals, would keep many a guilty man from inflicting greater harm to the community, don't you agree?"

"Also put many an innocent man in prison," I replied. "Sure, there's a lot of scum out there. You can't start breaking out the blowtorches just because someone won't incriminate himself. I probably have a lot more experience with criminals, low-life ones at least, than you, Mr. Warbeck. But torture isn't the answer to crime."

Warbeck shook his head. "Yes, the rights of the criminal must be protected. That is why crime is so rampant. It is pitiable to hear it from a former officer of the law. As the Bard, that is the Earl of Grantum, wrote 'What makes robbers bold but too much lenity?'"

I wanted to be spared of the philosophical chatter, and was about to say so, when someone else came into the room. It was the Redbeard. He came up to Warbeck and whispered something to him. Warbeck nodded, then the men shared a laugh. Then the younger man—I took him to be about thirty, allowing for the maturity the facial hair gave him—turned to Bonnie and I. He reached toward his coat pocket. I reached into my coat until I remembered that my gun was in the trunk of Bonnie's rental car. But Redbeard did not produce a weapon. Instead a small, rectangular object was pulled out and casually tossed to Bonnie. She caught it with both hands.

It was a micro cassette tape, except the tape had obviously been pulled out of the cartridge. Only a few inches of leader were hanging from it now. "You bastards broke into my car!" Bonnie yelled. "That tape is my property."

"Thank you, Robert," Warbeck said. "I will be joining you and Henry in a few moments."

The look of smug satisfaction on this Robert guy's face burned me up inside. He could have just walked back out, but not this guy. He went right up to Bonnie and stuck his hairy face against hers. "Stop trifling with your betters, pale gypsy," he said in some kind of weird accent that must pass for English somewhere on the planet. I stepped between them, and took a backhand slap from the guy. Having already got pushed about enough by Warbeck's hired help, I sent a left cross to his furry chin.

"Whoa-ho!" Robert said as he pulled his head back just in time. There was that smug look again. He was not taking my exertions with the seriousness I expected. I came back with a hard, straight right to his solar plexus. That took the smug look off his mug. We were ahold of each other's lapels when that old ex-cop who took the bribe from Bonnie showed up. He pulled us apart with some elbow action, quite adept I thought for an aged fellow. Bonnie put her arm across my chest to prevent me from restarting what I wanted to finish.

"This man struck Robert," Warbeck said, pointing to me.

"This clown started it," I replied, pointing to my opponent. In the next second, he was pushing the burly old man aside and getting the lapels of his tux torn in the process. His face reddened to match his facial hair.

"Insolent varlet!" Robert shouted at me as he kept up at working himself free. "I would not take such a vile offense from a peer of the—"

"Robert!" Warbeck thundered in a tone that probably echoed all the way back to the dining area. Warbeck put a hand to his friend's chest. Robert clammed up after that, contenting himself with sending out a belligerent glare in my direction.

"You two are leaving," the ex-cop said to Bonnie and me. At this point, Robert broke away from Warbeck. The only thing between him and me was the ex-cop and he moved his bulk between us. Robert pawed the atmosphere like he was trying to get to me. There was now a look in his eye that transcended anger. I had seen that look before from crack cocaine addicts who chose to resist arrest even if I had a gun and a nightstick and they were buck naked. I had seen it from a deadbeat dad who came after me once in a courtroom as I walked out of the witness box after giving my testimony. This was a look of temporary madness. It was a look that got people drilled, stabbed or bludgeoned when the demons inside some brain-addled punk were in full fury and a gun or a knife was in his hands. Frankly, unarmed and with Bonnie to worry about, I was just as glad to be ejected from the place.

On our 'escorted' way out, Bonnie stopped off at the admission table to deposit her credentials and pick up a color brochure on the exhibits.

"Please put that down, Miss," the ex-cop said gruffly. "You

two are lucky Mr. Warbeck didn't have his friend press charges."

"His redhaired pal was a lot more out of control than I was," I said. It was futile to reason the point, but I tried anyway. Bonnie tossed the program to the floor as we passed the table. We were led out through the lobby to the front entrance. Our escorts stopped following us once we were on the sidewalk. I turned around and saw the two of them standing in front of the glass doors. The old guy was standing with his legs spread apart military-style. The younger man was trying to emulate the stance.

Just past the sidewalk, a jet black stretch limousine was parked in the middle of the zebra-style crosswalk. Reporters and camera operators were crowded about the passenger side door as the driver came around to open it up. Two men wearing dark suits were positioned around the door already. They looked tall and burly enough to be bodyguards, but right now all they were doing was holding the cameras and reporters at bay. Bonnie and I stopped on the perimeter of the media crowd to see who was coming out. The first person to emerge from the passenger door was a stunning Supermodel-type blonde woman who was dressed in a skin-tight gold lame party dress with a slit up one side that only started to cover her legs at mid-thigh. She looked to be six feet tall and twenty-five, if that. The flashes of camera lights bathed her in micro bursts of white light. The next person out started the reporters chattering away with questions.

"Well, lookie what we got here," Bonnie said to me. What we got was a chubby man with a face only a plastic surgeon could love with thick horn-rim glasses and dark blue eyes, one of which was slightly crossed. He also wore what must have been a toupee because his hairline was too perfect. His face looked like he had been in a bad car accident at an earlier time: his mouth was off-center to one side and his cheeks had all sorts of extra indentations and lines extending from his nostrils to his ears. It was hard to get a good look at him with the crowd around but it seemed from the harsh glare of the camera lighting that one whole side of the face had an enormous patch of dark red skin.

I now recognized him. I had seen the face before in news magazines and the identification was made even easier by the media people shouting his name out.

"Mr. Strunk! Mr. Strunk! What are your chances in the California Governor's race?"

"Will the Truth Party endorse Congressman Randolph or Mayor Haskell if you decide to drop out of the race?"

"Several economists say you cannot roll property taxes back to 1993 rates without hurting the education system. Can you comment?"

"Look this way, Mr. Strunk! Mr. Strunk!"

Sherwood Strunk, the media baron who owned the Strunk Sports Network and the Strunk News Update Network and the Strunk Movie Network and the Strunk Cultural Cable Network as well as a couple dozen newspapers and a company that designed software for U.S. Armed Forces, ignored the questions thrown at him. He just smiled, took his lovely bride by the arm and followed the path that the two stoic-looking men made for him toward the sidewalk. "I'm not commenting," he said to the ground as he ducked under a swaying microphone boom. "This is my night off. I'm just here to see the treasures from the Tower of London."

"How does it feel to be married to the most powerful man on the West Coast?" a female reporter in a bright red power suit asked the wife. She had no comment, but she did smile and did look up at the questioners.

I felt someone poke me in the back. I turned to see the young rent-a-cop not a foot from me. He had been sent on an errand.

"You are still on museum property," he said. That was all he had to say. Bonnie and I dodged around the fringe of the frenzy and made our way toward the portion of the crosswalk unblocked by the limo.

"Did you catch the accent on the guy Warbeck called Robert?" I asked Bonnie as we walked down the ramp that led to the underground parking.

"Yes, I did," Bonnie replied. "He might be from New Zealand. I remember when I was a waitress down in Westwood I had a regular customer from Aukland who sounded like that, sort of. That was a while ago but I remember how he talked. Very peculiar."

When we returned to the rental car, we saw what had transpired while we were being led around by Trevor Warbeck.

The front passenger door of the Escort was unlocked now. I had locked it, of course. Someone had opened the door, probably with that flat metal device car thieves used, and stolen the electronic monitoring set Bonnie had tried to hide in the floorboards of the backseat. The only part of the component still left was the hard plastic cover for the cassette holder. It was lying on the gearshift box, cracked in half.

"Ann will not be happy. I put a lot of her money into tracking down and buying that thing."

"What now?"

Bonnie threw her purse into the backseat. "I'm hungry," she announced. "You nearly got killed and we both nearly got arrested. Plus, we struck out on blackmailing Warbeck. I think that calls for a meal with a high fat content Did you ever go to a Rock and Roll Hamburgers? They have a franchise over on Van Ness."

"No," I said. "I hear from my friend Arthur that the food is good, but the music is so loud your ears start to bleed. Besides, it's a nostalgia pit. Besides, theme restaurants are for the tourists."

"I agree," she said. "But Jane Wiley works there. I think we should pay her a visit."

"I went over to the apartment on DuBoce last night. She was there, but she wouldn't let me in. She sounded drunk, and scared. I think somebody got to her after she talked to Dave."

"Well, let me take a shot at her," Bonnie said.

"You think Warbeck might try something against her?"

"We know he killed Park," Bonnie said. "Or, rather, had this Dromio character do it. We're pretty certain he killed Carolyn Mason. You strongly suspect your friend died because of Warbeck or his pal Strunk. I'm afraid you made a mistake back there by letting Warbeck know we knew about his phone calls to Carolyn Mason. Jane Willey is the obvious leak for that information"

"I probably did, but she's scared enough to be on her guard," I said. "If you can get Jane Willey to go to the cops, it might take some of the heat off Jack Benchley."

"You think Jack Benchley is still alive?

The question surprised me. "You were the one who told me you had a feeling he was alive," I said. "What's all that talk

I've heard about the power of feminine intuition?"

"This is true," Bonnie said. "Just keep reminding me about that in the next couple days."

As we waited in line to pay the parking attendant, Bonnie filled me in on what she knew about Sherwood Strunk and his friendship with Trevor Warbeck. Apparently, Strunk was a big contributor to Warbeck's failed campaign for a U.S. Senate seat. Warbeck, naturally, was a fixture at the Forest of Arden event, including the one where Jack Benchley was with Carolyn Mason last month.

"How did Strunk get his face messed up?" I asked.

Bonnie handed her parking card to the young male attendant—who had the especially close-cropped hair, thin mustache and dainty movements indicative of a gay man—then she answered me. "I read where Sherwood Strunk was working on one of his father's oil platforms off the coast of Angola back in the early seventies. A group of guerrillas apparently planted some high explosives under the platform. Strunk's face was burned in the fire that resulted from the blast. After his father died, the eldest son sold the oil company and bought newspaper and television stations. Now, he wants to be Governor of California. He's got a good chance with all his money. Strunk just married that lady he was with, by the way. She's thirty years younger than him."

My cheek was still stinging from the slap I had taken from good old Robert. Add to that the dull ache in the middle of my backbone from the tussle with Dromio back at the office and I felt done for the evening. As we pulled out onto the street I got to see my first opponent for the evening. Dromio was standing on the sidewalk in front of the museum. He was talking animatedly with one of Strunk's bodyguards. The limousine Strunk had used was still parked at the crosswalk, but the mob had moved inside.

"That's Dromio," I said, pointing the giant out to Bonnie. "That's the guy who killed Park." Just as I pointed him out, Dromio noticed the vehicle and did a double take when he saw me. As the car passed I saw his beady eyes widen and his ugly face contort into a sneer.

"He looks like a killer," Bonnie remarked as we drove by.

Thus ended Phase One of Operation Benchley. So far this evening I had already been out on a steep roof, attacked by a man-mountain with intent to kill me, narrowly escaped capture by the police and still I found time to brawl with another big jerk in a public building. And, despite it all, I still wasn't really sure if I was on the right trail of Dave's killers or if I was simply aiding an accomplice in covering up the murder her boss committed.

Chapter Seventeen

We went to Rock and Roll Hamburgers, home of the famous Elvis Burger. The music was loud. The decor was festooned with movie posters from the King of Rock and Roll's checkered career in motion pictures, as well as cinematic efforts by The Beatles, Cliff Richard, The Dave Clark Five, The Who and The Rolling Stones. Above the bar and grill area, with green candy-striped tile on the wall, was a billboard-sized poster from the first big-studio rock film, Frank Tashlin's too campy *The Girl Can't Help It* from 1956, which advertised the ample proportions of Jayne Mansfield as well as specialty acts by Chuck Berry, Little Richard, Eddie Cochran and Fats Domino. There were also guitars hanging from the walls, proportedly from various famous musicians. The front of the restaurant featured a gaudy souvenir shop where key-chains, glossy photographs and sweat shirts featuring living and dead rock performers could be secured, along with the inevitable trinkets sporting the company logo, a hamburger with arms growing out of its sides, the better to strum an electric guitar with. Here was kitsch on a grand scale. The waitresses and cooks were young. The customers were mainly baby-boom middle-agers.

And the place was packed.

Bonnie and I sat at a small table too close to the kitchen, but at least it was a non-smoking area.

I ordered a quarter pound Buddy Holly Burger and a strawberry milkshake. Bonnie went with an Elvis Burger and fries, then asked our waitress if Jane Willey was around. She said she was on a break, and on the phone), but she would pass the word that someone wanted to see her. After our orders were taken, Bonnie excused herself to make a call to Ann Benchley up in Oregon. I engaged myself with a discarded *Chronicle* sports section left on an unbussed table. I got to read how my San Francisco Giants were spanked by the Cleveland Indians in their last pre-season game.

Bonnie arrived back about the time our food did. She looked perplexed as she sat down. I waited until the waitress departed before I asked what had transpired in the call.

"A very strange thing," Bonnie said as she unfolded her napkin and made ready to attack the Elvis Burger—with a pineapple slice and teriyaki sauce, the 'Blue Hawaii Special'—and fries. "Ann decided yesterday to move in to her dad's ranch on Pinecone Mountain. She feels safer there since her bodyguard changed jobs.

"Ralph Bates, the creepy bodyguard, packed it in?"

Bonnie nodded, then said, "Apparently he got a better job offer. Ann could hardly stand him, but at least he was protection.

"So what's strange?"

Bonnie ate a fry. "Ann was going through some of her dad's stuff in his editing room. Mr. Benchley still calls it an editing room but he hasn't done a film in over ten years. Well, Ann found a can of thirty-five millimeter film. It's some of the new film stock Kodak put out a couple years ago. So, she looks at some of it through the editing machine he has down in the basement there." Bonnie shook her head again.

"And?"

Bonnie ate a couple more fries. "There are a lot of old monuments and manor houses in the footage, which is to be expected because Mr. Benchley is into that. But there are other things on the film that...that...I guess they don't make sense. Ann says they don't make sense, anyway."

"The things on the film?" I asked.

Bonnie cupped her hands, resting her chin on the top of her intertwined fingers. "There are these weird people in some of the footage. People in boats. People riding horses. People carrying bundles on their backs. People pulling carts. People putting hay into stacks with pitchforks. And the thing of it is, all these people are in costume. They are dressed like extras in some period production."

"Where did he film these people?"

"Ann thinks it's somewhere either in England or Scotland. Mr. Benchley spends about a month in the U.K. every year, about half his time in London going to the live theatres and seeing plays. He also pays calls on old friends. I was with him a couple years ago for one trip. The last two weeks he goes off on a fishing holiday in Scotland with an old friend of his who lives in London."

"That would be Major Trubshawe," I said.

"You've read *The Rise and Fall of Me*, of course."

"Yes," I replied. "I have a pretty good idea that those two do more in Scotland than just fish. From the content of Jack Benchley's autobiography, I'd say they were quite a fun-loving pair."

"They are not as bad as they used to be, according to Ann. Ann has a distaste for Major Trubshawe. She thinks he's a bad influence on her father. Of course her dad is in his seventies now, but she still thinks they push the envelope on drinking and horsing around when they reunite."

"Anyway, what about these people? Is this footage from some kind of movie?" I asked.

Bonnie took a bite of her burger, chewed, then continued. "That's the thing: Ann believes the only plausible explanation is that the footage is left over from some second-unit work on Shakespeare. That's the movie Mr. Benchley made with Peter Sellers back in the seventies."

"The one that lost millions of dollars," I said, poking into my salad. "The one that helped make him *persona non grata* in Hollywood."

"Right," Bonnie remarked with a wry smile. "Mr. Benchley calls that film his contribution to the disaster-film genre. It did pretty well in Britain, of course, but the New York and Los Angeles critics panned it mercilessly. Critics generally liked Sellers as Shakespeare, but the film itself was another matter. Besides, that was the early seventies. Americans wanted to see movies about gangsters or talking apes, not a word-happy movie about some dead English writer. Anyway, Ann thinks that the footage might have been shot by a second unit for *Shakespeare*. The trouble is the costumes don't match what the extras wore in the film. And the film can isn't marked as footage from *Shakespeare*. Plus it is on film stock that wasn't even around in 1972 when Mr. Benchley shot the film."

A family of four sat across from us at the table where I had retrieved the newspaper. One of the children, a towheaded boy around five or six years old, was putting up quite a fuss. "I don't want any fish," the boy said over and over in that shrill, high-pitched tone children employ when they wish to draw the maximum amount of attention to themselves. The little girl, roughly the same age, was trying to distract the mother from all the attention she was giving to her brother in a so-far futile effort to calm the boy down. The father was trying to draw the boy's attention to the menu a waitress with bright orange high lights in her red hair had handed him. "Timothy, we are having baked fish," the father said. "This is Friday night and this is baked food night."

"I don't want dumb fish," the boy cried. His shrill voice carrying over John Lennon's vocal on *Back in the U.S.S.R.*

"You liked the baked potato chips you had at the ice show," the mother said. "You were a good boy all the way through the ice skating show tonight. Can you be a good boy just a little longer?" There was a jagged tone to her voice.

"She's at the end of her rope," Bonnie whispered to me. "The little guy reminds me of Tyler, Ann's little boy, when he gets tired and hungry."

"Did you tell Ann about what happened to us tonight?" I asked in between the exclamations against low-fat cod coming from the nearest table.

"Of course," Bonnie said, "and she's quite convinced we're on to something. And she's afraid for herself and for Tyler. She wants me back on the first morning flight. Apparently, she's been getting weird phone calls. The Benchley phone number is supposed to be unlisted. They never stay on very long. She thinks they are white supremacists or something because they use very vulgar, racist language. She's still on edge from the break-in that happened a couple weeks ago."

"The ranch was broken into?"

"Yes, the day after Mr. Benchley left for the Forest of Arden. The basement of the house was broken into. The caretaker didn't discover it until the next day. Somehow, the robbers had managed to beat the alarm system."

"What was stolen?" I asked.

"Nothing valuable, really," Bonnie said. "Just some big slabs of myrtlewood that Mr. Benchley had in his craft shop down there. His main hobby is woodworking right now. He makes animal sculptures. Life-sized bears and deer mostly. He's quite good. Several of the slabs are missing now, according to the caretaker. They must have broken in while he was asleep over in the cottage one night. It's funny. From the basement there's only a short flight of steps to the editing room. There are thousands of dollars of camera equipment and kleig lights right there. Plus the editing machine and a multi-track audio console. None of that was touched."

Our conversation, and eating, was interrupted by a petite brunette-haired woman with a pinched face, thick rouge on her cheeks, a small mouth, and her hair wrapped in a ponytail.

"You wanted to see me?" Jane Willey asked.

Bonnie introduced herself. "We want to ask you a few questions about Carolyn Mason. We were wondering—"

The waitress began to violently shake her head. "I'm sorry," she said. "I can't talk to you now — or ever." She looked around the immediate area, like a small dog hearing an unfamiliar noise. "You'll excuse me. I have to get to my station."

She departed in a rush. "Stay here," Bonnie said to me, then got up to follow her. She caught up to Jane Willey just in front of the ladies room. A brief conversation ensued with the waitress becoming more distraught as Bonnie put a hand on her arm to keep her from walking away. I couldn't hear the conversation because of the stereo system. The two ladies went into the rest room. Bonnie emerged about a minute later. When she sat down, my partner confirmed what I already had assumed.

"She's been threatened. She didn't come right out and say it, but that's what it is. I gave her my cellular number in case she changes her mind."

"She looks really scared," I said.

"Let me tell you how scared she is. She told me she's packed up and is planning to move back to Jamestown, North Dakota. She has her rent paid on her San Francisco apartment for two more months and she's quitting her job and heading for North Dakota. That's fear."

"One of Warbeck's people have got to her. I tried to talk to her yesterday. I didn't even get past the intercom in her building."

"I screwed up," Bonnie said. "I gave too much away to Warbeck at the museum."

I asked Bonnie if she would level with me on something, that something being the identity of 'Kipling.'

"It's Trubshawe, right?" I said. "He was the one on the phone when I was scrambling around on the roof, I'll bet. The voice sounded like an old English guy."

A smile broke across Bonnie's face. "You flatter me," she said.

"What do you mean?"

"Good evening, Mr. Stoker," she said in a voice that suddenly became husky and butch. "Are you ready for the next assignment."

"It was you," I blurted out, genuinely astonished.

"I told you I was an actress," she said. "I studied voice at UCLA. That mock-Britannic tone I employed is the voice I used to play Viola in *Twelfth Night*. She gets shipwrecked in Illyria and disguises herself as a young man. That was the highwater mark of my career at the Cape Cod Shakespeare Festival."

"How do you do that with your voice," I asked.

"Training," she said. "In '91, I went from the American Conservatory here in town to the Northwest Shakespeare Festival. That's when I got to know Mr. Benchley. I was in three shows every year for three years, all running consecutively. I usually had one major part—like one year I was Mrs. Stockman in An *Enemy of the People*—and two smaller roles. Mr. Benchley himself directed *King Lear* one year and I was his Regan. I love playing nasty bitches and that's one of the best. I wish I didn't have to die off-stage. I like doing death scenes. Anyway, I was in *Julius Caesar* that year, too. I was Calphurnia, the wife of Mr. Big Shot. I had a couple short scenes, the spurting blood from Ceasar's statue business, then I'm off-stage for the rest of the play. The year before I rotated as the Nurse in *Romeo and Juliet*, Emilia in *Othello* and a maid in Strindberg's *The Father*. That was Roger Rafferty's first production with us. I like Roger. I wish Ann did, too."

"When did you get to be Benchley's secretary?"

"That was in 1998, just before the season started up again. He was having problems with a personal computer that he had installed in his office. I had taken a few computer courses at UCLA, something to fall back on, I thought, just in case the acting career went south. Anyway, I got him over the computer jitters. He was doing his autobiography then, and his secretary had taken another job up in Portland—Mr. Benchley is a nice guy, but he's a little tight when it comes to payroll—so I took over that job. He liked the way I organized his files and all the office stuff. I was just going to help him part-time, and try and hold onto at least one role in a production, but Mr. Benchley needed a full timer. So, I figured, why not? I really want to become a director. I figured It might be a good move to be the right-hand of the Artistic Director for a few years. Then, after her dad talked my organizational skills up, Ann wanted me for her secretary and so here I am. I feel like I sidetracked myself, but at the time I took over as Ann's assistant, my Angie was living with me, so a full-time all-year job seemed like a good move. I helped Ann get herself up for performing Shakespeare. She had never done Shakespeare outside a few practice scenes at Stanford. Mastering the cadence and the verse gave her fits."

"I know Ann Benchley did a male voice in one of her plays. I saw her doing Rosaline in *As You Like It* a couple years ago."

"I taught her that voice," Bonnie said with a note of pride. "Worked with her day and night. We got to be friends. That's when I stopped being Mr. Benchley's secretary and started working for Ann."

"Well, I think your voice is more effectively masculine than hers," I responded.

"I'm not entirely sure that's a compliment," Bonnie replied, just before letting out a throaty, feminine, laugh.

"So you've been at the festival about ten years, right?"

Bonnie nodded. I silently admired her dark green eyes.

"You must have run across Rochelle Millman?"

Bonnie laughed again. "Yes, I did. Dear little Rochelle," she said in a tone of mockery. "She was Rochelle Watkins then, just off her second marriage. Then she met Mr. Benchley and made him her third husband. The old May-December romance angle. Lasted a couple years. She tried to run over me, figuratively speaking. She played Goneril to my Regan in *Lear*. She thought the play was supposed to be about her character, which I don't think was Shakespeare's intention, and certainly not Mr. Benchley's. I hated doing scenes with her because she was always playing tricks, trying to upstage me and step on my lines. And she had her husband for the director! I heard she retired and married Leroy Millman, that cattle baron who owns about all of Hazard Valley."

"That she did," I said. "I guess they're separated now. Rochelle is also the sister-in-law of Dave McCreedy. They had an affair going before Dave was killed."

"Hum," Bonnie said. "Rochelle stepping out with her sister's husband. Classy. Well, she's a strong-willed person. Rather pushy, but in an unfriendly sort of way. I can't say I'm surprised."

"You say she was strong-willed?"

I liked Bonnie's look, especially the bright gleam to her eyes that went with her laugh. Her less-than-perfect face—round about the cheeks, turning more opal-shaped when you took the whole outline from forehead to jawline—reflected a soft pinkish-beige shimmer from the lighting above the booth. My sight traced the line down one side of her neck from a dime-sized earlobe down to the point where her tender throat joined up with the lapel of her blazer and black top. I could see a portion of her narrow shoulder blades followed downward to a clear expanse of flesh, decorated with a circular gold amulet hanging from her neck. Then came the swell of her breasts as they moved slightly, rising and receding, under the sheer canopy of her clingy scoop-neck top. I had been with her for a couple hours, but this was the first time I really *looked* at her.

Trying to put my mind back to business, I asked her about the infamous Trubshawe. Apparently, he was not even in Frisco but in London. He was in contact with Ann Benchley regularly since the disappearance. Trubshawe had kept his eye on Warbeck's comings and goings from the IFH branch office in London.

"You have a phone call," the young girl said to Bonnie. "You can take it up by the register."

"Ann again," Bonnie said as she excused herself and got up to field the call. I went to use the restroom.

Alone and staring into the long bathroom mirror, I had an attack of acute ethics. Perhaps it stemmed from my close brush with death. I was going to tell Bonnie about the tape I had heard, and put all my cards on the table.

When I returned to our table, she was still on the phone and stayed there long enough for me to finish my meal, and listen to *West End Girls* by the Pet Shop Boys, *Stop In the Name of Love* by the Supremes and *Bossa Nova Baby* by Elvis himself. I watched the waitresses and busboys hustling about, trying to keep up with the endless demands for food and drink. Bonnie still had half her burger on the plate and it was on its way to becoming cold.

Bonnie finally hung up and returned to the table. As she came closer, she looked at me and shook her head before sitting down. “Ann has decided to move back into the house she’s renting in town where she was before. Her dad’s place is spooky, she says. I don’t blame her really. I just don’t know why she wanted to go up to the mountain in the first place.”

“Maybe she could feel closer to her dad up there,” I offered.

Again, Bonnie shook her head. “Ann says they weren’t really close until after her mom died. The problem is they both have big egos and they both want their way. As a little family unit, they’re great; as an artistic team they’re a disaster. That’s what Mr. Benchley told me and Ann basically confirmed it when I went to work for her.”

“I heard the two of them had some viscous shouting matches over in France when they were working together on *The American*.” I was dipping into tabloid lore here.

Bonnie nodded. “That’s true,” she replied. “Do you want some of my hamburger, by the way? I can cut it with a knife.”

I accepted the offer. Bonnie continued talking as she sawed the bread and meat. “Of course, I wasn’t with them in ‘82 when they shot that one. I was an unemployed white chick going to UCLA, trying to break into show business down in Hollywood. But even I heard about the yelling matches in the trade papers. They’re part of the Benchley family legend now. That Paris shoot was Mr. Benchley’s last feature film.” She added “so far” after a pause. “The major distributors wouldn’t pick it up even though he flogged it at every festival from Sundance to Cannes. He was trying to get Ann’s career going. That’s why he made it. He mortgaged the apartment he owned in San Francisco, the one he bought in the 1950’s. It was the apartment building he used in the Robert Mitchum film,

Telegraph Hill. It was the same apartment Carolyn Mason lived in. Benchley used to own the whole building. After he financed the movie, he sold it and signed a lease for the third-floor unit that was Faith Domerque's apartment in the film."

"That was a good film," I said.

"A classic," Bonnie said. "Almost as good as *City of Night* with pretty much the same cast. That scene where Mitchum finally recovers his memory and realizes that Faith Domerque's character was his wife before the war—"

"And he runs to the apartment and looks up at the high window from the sidewalk—"

"And sees her shooting that always-suave asshole George Sanders because he's blackmailing her," Bonnie said, finishing the scene.

"And Mitchum realizes she's the woman who killed John Ireland and set up Gloria Graham to take the fall. And he's the cop that has to solve the case or lose his stripes."

"Yes, indeedy," Bonnie said. "Well, Mr. Benchley owned that place until he needed the money for *The American*. He also sold off some undeveloped property in Ventura to finance the post- production work. Finally, an art-house distribution wing of United Artists bought it. Mr. Benchley never got a nickel back on the deal, however. That's why it was his last movie. He just had no clout left in Hollywood after that *Shakespeare* movie lost so much money, so his profit participation deal on *The American* guaranteed he would never make a dime even if it did boffo box-office wise. It did well, but not boffo. The only good that came out of it was Ann winning an Oscar. Not bad for only her third film and her first big part."

Bonnie drank some ice water then continued. "Problem was the studio bosses knew he wanted to make that movie very badly. Since he couldn't play the system like he had before—use his old 'I can take it or leave it' attitude when some producer wanted to get him to commit to a project—he was bound to make a bad deal. Hollywood is all about making deals, and God help you if you can't hang up or walk away from a bargaining session. I do know the entertainment biz, at least the fringes that a non-principal performer gets to see. It's very cut-throat. Loyalty is non-existent. The Benchleys are the exception to a lot of what you hear about Hollywood, especially Ann's father. Sometimes I wish Ann was more like her father. Oh, dear. Ann's been incredibly helpful to me and hear I'm being catty behind her back."

"I think you've been pretty helpful to her," I replied. "You went toe-to-toe with Trevor Warbeck back there, plus (I lowered my voice) you must have been the one that set up our little after-hours entry into the Institute. That's not normally part and parcel of being a private secretary."

Bonnie leaned over the table to me. "The set-up around IFH wasn't my doing. Ann's bodyguard, Ralph Bates, the one who just left her for a security job with Rockwell International, was the one who devised it. And Dave McCreedy was the one who actually cut open the latch on the skylight so you could get into Warbeck's office."

"This is news to me," I said.

"McCreedy was going to go ahead and do the break-in a few days ago with Bates doing the electronic monitoring. But they tested the bug and it was unreliable. Dave was on his way to pick up the spare bug he had left up with Ann when...well, then that thing happened to him. Bates came back to work as her bodyguard, then took off on Ann right when she needed him. No notice. Nothing. Which reminds me, what are you doing for the next few days?"

"I'm on vacation, technically," I said.

"Ann wants to know if you'd keep an eye on her and her son, Tyler," Bonnie said. "She called Jack Picasso and he told her the security agency he works with in Los Angeles is going to take a week to replace Bates. She needs somebody who can handle any trouble."

"All right," I said. I must have seemed somewhat hesitant because Bonnie sensed my anxiety.

"Usually guys who find out they get to be close to Ann are happier than that. Is what happened at IFH making you want to back off the job?"

"It's not that," I said. "It's something else."

"Tell me," she said.

I told her about what was bothering me: what had happened to me when I had checked Dave's office yesterday afternoon. I told her about the message I had heard on the phone machine, the woman's voice that implored Dave to come to a certain spot near Rogue Falls around six o'clock on the day he was due back into town. I told her that, as best I could tell, it was Ann Benchley's voice. I also mentioned being whacked on the head by a large male assailant who grabbed the phone machine and made a fast getaway.

"I had a reliable friend tell me Dave and your boss had an affair," I said. "What I heard on the tape confirms that. It also says she wanted to get together with him as soon as he got back and possibly at a place where he was later found dead."

Bonnie looked perplexed for several moments. She put her elbows on the table and rubbed her hands back and forth a couple times. Then she spoke.

"What did the voice say?"

I pulled out the notes I had of the monologue on the tape. Bonnie scanned over the entry in my notebook. Suddenly her eyebrows arched up.

"If these notes are close to verbatim of what you heard, then I think I know what this message is about. And it's not what you think it is."

"I know Ann Benchley's voice. So do a few million other people."

"That's Ann voice," she said, "but the words are put together from lines she has spoken in movies and plays. It's been edited together to create the illusion that she is speaking in one monologue, but, believe me, it's an editing job."

"Are you sure?"

Bonnie nodded vigorously. "I recognize two of the lines right off. When she says, 'I've been acting like an idiot but I've got my shit together now.' That's an important line from a movie she was in two years ago called *Nightmare Moon*. There's another part, referring to the ranch and 'our spot'; that's from the *Calamity Jane* thing she did for Home Box Office. There are some very sophisticated audio mixing devices out there. Somebody has looped some of her lines and individual lines from some of her recent movies and made a fake message. Somebody's trying to frame her for Dave McCreedy's death, and I don't think you need three guesses on who that might be."

"Are you sure these are lines from her movies?" I said, half-hoping, because I liked Bonnie, that her theory was the truth.

"I've been reading all her scripts closely for the last couple years," Bonnie said. "It's part of my job to run lines with

Ann because her memory is not the best. I think Warbeck is setting her up. Did you hear this message after your friend was found."

"Several days after. Yesterday."

"O.K., then," Bonnie said confidentially. "Ann is being set up because she was in an affair with Dave McCreedy. Just like Mr. Benchley's been set up for Carolyn Mason's death. It's Warbeck who's doing this, Warbeck and his network of scumbags. Don't worry, when we get back to Oregon, I'll show you the movies I'm talking about, specifically the point where Ann says these lines. Any halfway decent audio engineer can splice lines and individual words together. Stop worrying, you're on the right side."

I really wanted to believe that. But I needed more.

"Do you know where your boss was the Monday before this last one, between, say, five and eight that evening?"

Bonnie frowned. "You want to make sure Ann has an alibi?"

"If somebody's setting her up, she's going to need one."

Bonnie stroked her chin with her long right index finger, gazed upward at a back-lit poster of Chuck Berry across the room, then slowly shook her head.

"We've got a problem," she said flatly. "That Monday was a matinee day for Ann. We got back to the ranch about five in the afternoon. Ann's always drained and tense after a show. She has to get away from people. She went off on her Harley-Davidson. Whenever the weather's good up there, she likes to ride her motorcycle on the backroads. She ate a little something, then took off about five thirty. I didn't see her again until after seven when it got dark."

"Think she could have stopped for gasoline anywhere?"

"Mr. Benchley has his own gas pumps. Ann never goes into town if she can avoid it. The tourists try to crawl all over her. When Dave got killed, she was probably riding that big blue Hog of hers on some two-lane county road. She could have been anywhere. Damn. Somebody must have known her patterns."

"What did she do after she got back to the ranch? Did she seem tense?"

"No, she was relaxed, like she always is after a solitary ride. She and I went over some letters I was e-mailing for her, then she got on the phone and talked to Jack Picasso for about an hour."

That rang a bell in my head. "He's a film director, isn't he?"

"Some people think so," Bonnie said, a trace of bitterness in her voice. "A better description would be that he's a slick little hustler who's made a few movies. He's the son of Silvio Malatesta. The father was a talented and passionate man. From what I've seen of his son's movies, the son is all passion and no talent."

"What's he to your boss?"

"He wants to get into her pants, just like old times," Bonnie said. "They had a fling when they were young and he was an apprentice on one of Mr. Benchley's movies. Oh, there's the other reason he's wooing her. Jack Picasso is trying to worm his way into directing Ann's next movie, and he hopes to direct the *She Came to Europa* sequel. She owns the rights to those Belle Killroy novels, and has directorial approval from Cintricity Studios. He's had a couple flop pictures and needs a green-light project—badly. She wavered for awhile on doing this first movie—"

"It's a prison picture right? I understand that's his specialty."

"I'm afraid that's exactly what it is, another nasty Jack Picasso penitentiary film. It's called *Forget Me Not*. Ann is supposed to play a sexually frigid kleptomaniac. The warden of the prison tries to unfreeze her. They marry after his friend the governor of the state paroles her. But she's still frigid so..."

"Wait a minute," I said, holding my hand up. "Except for the prison angle, that sounds pretty close to that Alfred Hitchcock movie with Sean Connery and Tippi What's-Her-Name, the actress who got pecked up in *The Birds*."

"Tippi Hedren," Bonnie said. "Yes, basically, it's a remake of *Marnie*. I don't think anybody believes in sexually-frigid females anymore, except Jack Picasso. *Marnie* is Picasso's favorite Hitchcock movie, even though most people wouldn't even put it on Hitchcock's top dozen films. Cintricity is bargaining with Universal right now to buy the rights and keep everything out of court. We're waiting for a script from Picasso's writing team now. It will probably be a bad script but Ann will do it anyway. Jack knows how to play her."

A waitress came and asked if we wanted dessert. We both declined. When the server left, I decided to ask the big question.

"Do you think Ann was still stuck—?"

"On Dave McCreedy?" she said defensively. "As far as I know, she dumped him. I was with the two of them a few times, once down in L.A. when your friend was sneaking around on his wife. Ann's not exactly the most stable character I've ever worked with but she's no killer. Yeah, breaking up with Dave was hard on her, but Jack Picasso has, for better or worse, filled that void. She's being wooed all over again and that keeps Ann happy." She brushed a strand of frizzled hair off her ear, then looked me right in the eye. "No, Harvey, no matter what it looks like, there's no way she'd kill somebody. Now, do you believe me? Do you still want the job? Answer the first question first."

"I believe you," I said. Bonnie sounded, and acted, too honest not to believe her. Plus she had saved my life back at the IFH. If she was going to set me up, why would she had bothered?

"And I also want the job."

"Good," Bonnie said.

I sure hoped it really was.

Chapter Eighteen

Van Ness Avenue was still crowded with pedestrians at 10:15 when we left the restaurant. A few blocks down the street you could see four lanes of heavy vehicle traffic. A light rain was falling.

"Tell me more about this break-in two weeks ago at Jack Benchley's ranch," I asked Bonnie.

"Nobody was home at the time, but the caretaker's wife, Mrs. Kincaid, said the day before she saw a large man sitting in a pick-up truck up on a hillside road about 100 yards from the rear property line. That was two weeks ago. She told Ann they drove away fast. She's not sure what make the truck was but it was a big one."

"Did she get the license of the truck?" I asked, as we walked down the sidewalk to our cars.

"No luck," Bonnie replied. "She did say the truck looked very new. She thinks it was blue. At the time, she just assumed the guy was some tabloid paparazzi looking to see if he could get a picture of Ann. She didn't see the face but she thinks the man in the truck was tall."

"I wonder how tall this man in the truck was?"

"Think it might have been Dromio?"

"Could be," I said. "That guy probably was the robber. He also might have somehow planted the listening device in Jack Benchley's office. Warbeck knew we were coming to plant that bug. Benchley's office had to have been bugged. Somebody must have listened in to our talk in his office and relayed the information down to IFH."

"I assume nobody can just walk into Mr. Benchley's office and plant a bug. Who around the festival has free access to Benchley's office?"

"Just myself and Bea Ryskind. Bea is the Acting Artistic Director."

"Any relation to Morton?"

"She's the widow of Morton Ryskind, the founder of the Shakespeare Festival. She was the Dramaturge before Mr Benchley vanished. She would have the alarm code to the office and then Mr. Benchley and I. No one else."

"Morton Ryskind was a scientist or something, right?"

"He was an atomic physicist," Bonnie said. "He studied under J. Robert Oppenheimer at UC Berkeley in the late 1930's. Oppenheimer recruited him for the Manhattan Project. He started the Shakespeare Festival in the 1950's after he went back home to teach at Southern Oregon College. He wanted his hometown to be a cultural mecca. Thanks to Mr. Benchley devoting his energy to it, that's what happened. Professor Ryskind died about six-seven years ago."

"Dave told me Ryskind died in a boating accident when he and Mr. Benchley were on a trip to England."

"Yes," Bonnie said. "Their fishing boat sank in the North Sea. Mr Benchley was lucky to make it to shore. He blames himself for Mr. Ryskind's death. But it was just a sudden storm."

I shook my head. "Bad things happen sometimes," I said. "When I was a cop in Sutter City, I had to deal with a lot of traffic accidents. Sometimes somebody can die just by being in the wrong place."

"How long were you a cop?" Bonnie asked me.

"About nine years," I said.

"Why'd you quit?" she asked.

The enviable question.

"I didn't exactly quit," I said. "I started drinking pretty heavy. I more or less got fired, although the chief allowed me to officially be laid off due to budget cuts."

"What...I mean, did you always have a problem with alcohol?"

"Not until I got into police work." I was glad Bonnie didn't ask specifically why I left. I didn't want to tell her that my police career included accidentally running over an eight-year old girl in the high-speed pursuit of two bank robbers who had kidnapped a teller. The girl was in the wrong place at the wrong time. But I had years of self-blame to accept that I was not one-hundred percent at fault.

"The job just got to me," I said, trying to bring a coda to this part of my past. "An old sergeant told me to compartmentalize my life and keep it separate from my duties. Do your duty the best you can, don't fuck up, and forget about whatever went down at the end of the day. He always said that. I couldn't do it—not always. Things I saw and did had a bad effect on my work. Anyway, that's the story."

"For what it's worth, I think you handle yourself well," Bonnie said.

I nodded. "You too, Ms. Noel. I want to go back to that robbery in Benchley's basement. You say they just stole some slabs of wood when they could have taken expensive electronic equipment?"

"Weird, huh?"

"Quite weird," I said. "Drug addicts would have stolen everything that wasn't nailed down if they got that far. And you say nobody was home when the break-in occurred?"

"No one," Bonnie said. "Roy and Sharon Kincaid were in town on a shopping trip. They came back to find that someone had cut open the fencing under the barbed wire. We reported it to the sheriff's office, but they don't have any leads. Somebody at the festival must be working for Strunk and Warbeck. There has to be a spy working for them."

"I've got a roll of film I took yesterday outside the IFH," I said to Bonnie. "Might not hurt if you took the roll up to your boss tomorrow. We might have a possible tie-in with Warbeck and the theft. I have it at Arthur and Patricia's. They're the friends I'm staying with."

"You have photos of people going in to IFH?" Bonnie asked. "I would like to see that. Maybe I can recognize somebody who worked in the Festival. I can get it developed pretty fast at the theatre workshop when I fly back." Bonnie and I crossed the street, or half the street to be exact, stopping at a pedestrian island in the middle of four-lane Van Ness Avenue to allow a stream of traffic to shoot through the intersection. Bonnie tapped my shoulder. "Why don't you let me follow you back to your friends' apartment. I'll pick up the roll. That way

I'll have it on my flight back to Oregon. I can get it developed for Ann and I to look at tomorrow afternoon."

"Sounds good," I said. I looked about the intersection, keeping a wary eye out for Dromio or anybody else who might be following us. When the light changed again, we crossed the northbound lanes, passing a couple short-haired, leather-clad ladies who were holding hands as they walked around us.

It turned out that Bonnie had a very good idea as to where the apartment I was staying at was. As a girl, she had gone to a Catholic School just a block down from the building where my friends lived. On the drive over to my car, we shared our experiences with life in the Bay Area. She had grown up in the city, and moved over to Berkeley when her father took a job teaching Speech and Drama at one of the high schools. Her mother worked as a registered nurse at one of the Kaiser Hospitals. I had been a suburban kid down in San Jose, and so my urban experiences had been scant. We did share a fondness for seeing silent movie and early sound features at the old Avenue Theatre down toward the southeast end of the city. It had long ago been torn down to be reborn as a sterile first-run multiplex monstrosity.

"Do you remember the old guy who used to play the pipe organ there on Friday and Saturday nights?" Bonnie asked.

"Yeah, the guy with white sideburns and a jet-black toupee. What a funny-looking dweeb he was," I replied. "I often wondered what became of him when the VCR came in and people stopped going to revival houses for movies."

"He was my Uncle Pete," Bonnie said matter-of-factly. "And what happened to him was death. He's buried down in Colma. Actually, his ashes are in an urn."

A definite faux pas. "Oh, I'm sorry. I didn't mean..."

"Forget it," Bonnie said as her car climbed up the sloping section of Sacramento Street where my truck was. "You just went by his looks. I thought the hairpiece needed updating myself. Uncle Pete was part-owner of that theater. He used to get me in for free. I saw old movies there twice a week when my folks would let me. In many ways I was closer to my uncle than I was to my father. My father was always...well, let's say he was remote. When I was a kid, there was always this barrier between him and me. I had to see a shrink for a few years to deal with the fact that my father favored my little brother over me. I've forgiven him, as best I can. I've even tried to break through that barrier of his in the last couple years but it's still hard. My uncle was, emotionally at least, my father. Anyway, seeing movies at my uncle's theater and seeing live drama and musicals at the Curran and the ACT got me hooked on wanting to be in the business."

I was dropped off at my car. I actually followed Bonnie over to the apartment since she thought my own plan for reaching Church Street was too roundabout.

Patricia and Arthur lived on the top floor of a three-story walk-up. The building was in the Eureka Valley section of the city, a small neighborhood sandwiched between the predominately Gay Castro District (with its chichi boutiques, spendy bistros and a great old Art Deco movie palace) and the predominately Latino Mission District (with its collection of multiethnic restaurants, colorful Diego Rivera-type murals sprucing up the sides of businesses, and public parks that had more cement than grass). The oldest structure in the city, the adobe-walled Mission Dolores, stood just a block down from their building. It had been built in the 1770's by Native Americans under the direction of the Franciscan Friars. That place and a couple old buildings in the Presidio, at the entrance to San Francisco Bay, were about all there was left of pre-Gringo California. The Spanish soldiers and padres had come to the site of what one day would be a great city to 'Christianize' the Native Americans, i.e. make them do harsh manual labor for low pay, and keep the soldiers and clerics from the encroaching Russian Empire from setting up shop too close to New Spain, i.e. Mexico.

We found a place for our vehicles a block and a half away from the apartment in a perpendicular-parking section facing the Catholic School Bonnie was an alumnus of.

"You forgot to signal a left turn back on Church Street," she said to me as I stood waiting for her to lock up the Escort. "Consider yourself lucky to not be receiving a ticket."

She was right. Motorcycle cops in San Francisco are as numerous as parking spaces are scarce. I had been cited for a moving violation on my last visit to the city a year back. The fine was not greater than the amount of personal income tax I paid to the State of Oregon, but it was close.

I retrieved my gun from the trunk of her car and we

walked toward the apartments. This part of the city was still reasonably nice by modern urban standards, but we were still treated to the sight of an older woman walking toward us wearing a shabby cloth coat, bedroom slippers, and knee-length hose that were bagged around each ankle. She looked pathetic and used up. The only new article of clothing she wore was a bright orange wool cap that sat up in a peak on top of her head. I averted my eyes from her as we passed. After I took a few steps more, I noticed that Bonnie was no longer at my side. I looked back and saw her catching up with the old lady. Bonnie walked in front of her and appeared to ask her something. I couldn't hear the street lady's response either, but I noticed she had stopped looking down at the sidewalk. I heard Bonnie ask her what she had in the grey laundry bag she was trudging along with. The old woman said something. Then Bonnie took some money out of her purse and gave the old lady some bills.

"Feel better?" I asked when she came back.

"I will for awhile," Bonnie replied. "I spent three hundred to get to talk to a pig like Trevor Warbeck. I could only spare five dollars for her. I'll feel good until I see the next lost person and when I can't spare them any money I'll feel guilty again."

Half a block before the apartment Bonnie asked if we could stop at a nearby market. "I need some cigarettes," she said. "I'm suppose to be trying to quit, but after what's gone down tonight..."

Considering how my own nerves felt, her craving for nicotine seemed reasonable. The market was a small mom-and-pop grocery like a couple hundred others in the residential sections of the city. Narrow aisles were crammed together with shelves of overpriced foodstuffs. The perishable items like fruits and vegetables always looked close to perishing. At the check-out counter a small wizened Asian man sat on a captain's chair watching a small black-and-white television. His choice of viewing fare was some kind of cheesy soap opera with people dressed up like they were Peking Opera stars.

"This neighborhood hasn't changed," Bonnie said as we got the cigarettes and ourselves outside. "The last time I was here was with my Angela. That's my kid. I got married way too young and it was over before we both realized how immature he and I were. But I have a great kid at least. We were living a couple blocks from here when I was at the American Conservatory. She was just a little kid then. She's twenty now. I haven't seen her in a year. Her husband is stationed in Germany with the Army."

Bonnie tore open the pack of cigarettes she had purchased. For someone who was supposed to be trying to quit smoking, she had three disposable butane lighters in her purse. The third one worked and she drew a long drag from her smoke. "My first one in two weeks," she said.

We walked down the street to the apartment building. Arthur was at the first Giants' home game with a friend and Patricia was teaching a Renaissance Art class at San Francisco City College that evening so I used the spare key they gave me to let us past the wrought-iron security door and then the entry door to the complex.

We walked into the foyer of the building. As Bonnie told me more about her daughter, I heard voices up above us. There was an echo to the sounds as we climbed up the stairway. There seemed to be two men talking on the third floor landing, just outside my friends' apartment.

"She's in her second trimester," Bonnie said. "The doctors thought at first she might be having twins, but they did a procedure to—"

A hoarse, elderly male voice yelled out: "Who the hell are you!" The shout was from the third floor landing, one flight above us. We both stopped in our tracks. The question was repeated in the same tone. I thought at first it must be Arthur doing one of his voice impressions in order to throw me off. I poked my head over the handrail so I could look at the landing above.

I expected to see Arthur with a mischievous grin on his face. What I got instead was a tall, thick-waisted figure wearing a silver-and-black Oakland Raider ski-mask over his face. His build reminded me of the guy who had conked me back at Dave's office the day before. I caught a glimpse of another man—older, dressed in pajamas—facing him. The masked man was looking across the landing at someone at the doorway of a neighboring apartment. The door to my friends' place was half-opened.

The next moment Mr. Raider Fan caught sight of me. A flash of metal appeared in his hand from the pouch in the front of his black pullover sweatshirt. It had a barrel aimed down at me. I jumped back, swinging my extended left arm back to push Bonnie against the wall. I was reeling backward when I heard what sounded like an explosion. I caught a flash of intense light in front of me. The bullet must have missed because I looked down and I was not bleeding. My ears, however, were ringing from the blast as it echoed down the open stairwell. A man yelled. A door slammed. A second shot went off.

I looked over at Bonnie. She was also in a sitting position, but her upper body was reclining sideways. She was sitting two steps down from me. Her eyes were shut tight and by the expression on her face, she was in pain.

"Are you hit?" I asked her.

She shook her head, then rubbed the back of her scalp. "No," she replied after a couple seconds.

"Stay here. Stay down," I said, pulling out my gun. I looked up the stairs to make sure the gunman wasn't coming down. Then I looked back to Bonnie. Her eyes were wide open and she looked okay. I looked up the stairway. The guy in the mask was still not coming down—yet.

From upstairs I heard a woman yelling her head off. The sound was muffled by something, probably a door. I held my .38 at shoulder point, straight out in front of me, and crept up to the next flight of stairs, my back against the wall. I held still once I had reached a point on the spiraling stairwell where I was at the end of my cover.

"Stay down," I said to Bonnie. She had got to her feet and moved up from the stairs just below the second floor to one of the back corners of the landing. She was digging into her purse for something. I hoped she had something more lethal in there than eyebrow tweezers. I gave her about a second of my vision then looked back up to the underside of the landing above me.

"I'm a police officer," I said, lying. "We have back-up units on the way." No sound from the landing. The muffled cries of the woman had stopped. I talked louder. "Throw down your weapon and come down the stairs. Hands on top of your head. You will not be harmed." I looked over to Bonnie. She was using her cellular phone—the one she must have used when she directed me into IFH—to make a call. She was shaking and spoke rapidly into the receiver.

"Hello, hello," she said. "Yes, we have a situation here. Someone is shooting up an apartment. We're at—" She looked up at me.

"455 Church Street," I said. "Gunman on the third floor. People may be down already!" I repeated my masquerade as a cop to whoever was on the floor above, and again told the intruder to come down sans whatever toy cannon he was carrying. This time I heard a door bang shut and the sound of retreating footsteps. I took a couple steps across the landing between the second and third floors, pivoted as fast as I could and now was against the other side of the landing with a clear shot at the third floor walkway.

There was nobody there. The door to their apartment was wide open, however. I figured the gunman had slammed it on his retreat and it had reopened from the impact against the door frame. The next thing I knew I was up on the landing, my eyes and the barrel of my pistol trained on the open door. I was ready to fire at anything that passed for a tall human figure. But the only thing I could see was the hallway inside the front of the apartment, and beyond that about half of the living room. I could see an overturned easy chair and a litter of papers all over the carpet. A light from around the corner of the front hallway could let me see if anyone was moving around. But no one was.

And then a noise. It seemed to be coming from the spare bedroom, just to the left of the living room. Someone was messing around with the aluminum blinds that shielded the bedroom window. Then there came a sliding noise: metal brushing against metal. I knew it was the window for sure because I had opened it to get some fresh air last night and closed it in the morning. The guy was trying to get out that window.

I ran forward, positioning myself just to the side of the door frame. I held my .38 to my chest and took a glance over at the apartment door at the opposite end of the landing. There was a hole dead center in the door, surrounded by pieces of splintered wood dangling from the point of impact. From the size of the hole, the guy was shooting at least .44 slugs.

I heard the sound of the blinds being jostled again. I knew

there was no fire escape outside that window. I also knew someone cannot hang from a window sill and hold onto a gun. If I was going to catch this guy, the time was now.

I hurried down the entryway of the apartment, stopped at the corner just before the bedroom for a second, then stepped into the doorway of the bedroom gun first. The lighting behind me showed a trashed bedroom, my suitcase lying on the bed, ripped apart. There was nobody there. I did, however, see the tips of eight human fingers wrapped around the bottom of the window sill. I shouted "Freeze!" at the top of my lungs, then lunged forward to get to the window. Peering over the sill, I saw my quarry dangling from the three-story drop. Below him was an atrium that served as a common area for the tenants. My head was starting to spin from looking downward, which was going to be an impediment to keeping the shooter in my grasp. With my gun back in its holster, I grabbed onto the hood of the shooter's pullover with one hand and took hold of one of his forearms with the other.

"Give it up, man," I said. "You're under arrest." Once I had a good grip on him I closed my eyes to stop the spinning.

For a moment I thought somebody was actually taking my advice for a change. He seemed to be trying to push himself back up. When I reached down to try and grip him by his pants, I suddenly felt a meaty forearm being wrapped around my neck. The guy I was trying to rescue obviously had a separate agenda and that was to send me down first. I felt myself being pulled down over the ledge. I delivered some kidney punches to his back with my free fist (the other hand was being controlled by the shooter) but that did not seem to halt my progress of being pulled down as he was straining to pull himself up. Then I felt two slender arms wrapping themselves about my waist. I hoped that this was Bonnie because if the shooter had a skinny-limbed accomplice I was going to take a serious fall. Since I was being pulled backward I hoped for the best. The added support gave me the chance to get both arms free. I utilized the freedom to deliver some combination blows. This loosened my assailant's grip but also my own.

I found myself falling—backward, and into the room. As I lay sprawled on my back, I heard the shooter give out a yell, then the window rattled, then a second later came a noise like a giant beer can being popped open. Then there was another noise: a dull thud I knew was a heavy object hitting the alley below. There followed a metallic clanging sound.

I slowly got up and off of Bonnie (who was on her back under me) then helped her up. "Are you okay?" I asked. She nodded as she held one hand to her forehead. I turned back to the window, forcing myself to look down. The robber was lying on his stomach three floors down.

Amazingly, he got to his feet and started moving in a staggering manner, but only as fast as a snail, dragging a bad foot. Then he collapsed. I hoped he would stay where he was, but now he was starting to crawl. From the light filtering down from the adjoining apartments, I could see a sheet of metal lying next to him. It looked like a window awning. Apparently, he was hoping to drop down to the awning on the second floor after he jumped from the window. But instead of breaking his fall, the awning gave way. That was the popping sound I heard. The second impact was him hitting the ground, followed by the awning. I got too dizzy again and got my head back inside.

I turned back to tell Bonnie the guy was still moving. That's when I noticed she was starting to wobble. I rushed over and took her in my arms. It might have been taken for a romantic clinch by an uninformed observer, but my only concern at that moment was to steer her over to sit down on the bed before she fell down.

"Thank you," she said weakly as she sat down. "I think I hit my head when you knocked me back."

"Don't talk," I said, my mouth a few inches from her ear. "Just keep your head down and breathe slowly. Deep breaths." I put an open hand across her neck and gave her a few gentle pats. Then I took off out of the apartment and down the stairs.

The grey haired man was back on the landing, now armed with a hunting rifle. "Put that thing down and stay where you are!" I told him as I dashed past him on my way down the stairs. "Where is that crazy bastard?" he yelled at me. "The son-of-a-bitch took a shot at me and my wife!"

"Stay where you are," I yelled back. The last thing I needed was an angry, trigger-happy civilian firing away at my back.

When I reached the bottom of the stairway of the building I saw an "Emergency Only" door leading out to the side of the building where the guy was down. I hit the metal bar to open it. The screech of a fire alarm went off.

I didn't jump right out, not knowing if the guy was armed. I took a quick glance out the corner of the door and saw where he was. He was back on his feet, dragging his left foot that I guessed had to have been broken in the fall. The alleyway was blocked at both ends by tall cyclone fencing. At least one side had barbed wire at the top. It was a dead end.

"Don't move!" I ordered. "Get your hands up and turn slowly around! Do it!"

The burglar turned around and this time did exactly as he was told.

I grabbed the guy by the collar and threw him up against the wall of the building.

"Watch my leg, goddamn it! You're killing me," he said as I pushed him against the wall.

"Quit whining," I replied. I checked him for weapons and found no weapons, nothing more lethal than a pair of metal handcuffs. The .44 he used must have been left behind in the apartment. In addition to the fife alarm I now heard police sirens wailing, the noise coming up louder every second.

I grabbed him by the collar again and this time pushed him down on his stomach, being careful not to bend his left leg. I decided to put his handcuffs to good use and pulled his arms behind his back. It only took a couple seconds to slap the cuffs on him. I'd let the cops worry about finding the keys on him.

"Stop squirming around, asshole, you—" I said. And that was all I got to say. The next moment my eyes were assaulted by a harsh red light coming from the end of the narrow alley. Suddenly, about twenty feet away from where there had been nothing but a dead end, appeared a large wooden cube, maybe seven feet tall. It was covered in a shell-like lining on three sides. The cube was open on one side, the side facing me. There was a platform in the middle of the cube. And, from inside the apparition I saw a figure looking toward me. It took a moment for my mind to take in exactly who the figure was.

Ralph Bates, the festival security manager and Ann Benchley's bodyguard.

Bates was wearing a black outfit similar to the burglar. He looked as surprised to see me as I was to see him. In a brief instant the red ball of light overwhelmed his body and the figure and all I could see was light. The light seemed to grow and grow. And then I felt like a tidal wave had come out of nowhere and threw me off my feet.

❖ ❖ ❖ ❖ ❖

I woke up flat on my back, wondering where all the lights were coming from. Why were there so many people shining lights in my eyes?

"This one's coming around," a tall black lady wearing an ambulance uniform said. She had her hair in dark com rows and was looking down at me. I could see flashes of all colors of the rainbow going off in front of my eyes.

The lights began to fade. "Where's the shooter?" I asked.

"The guy that was cuffed? The cops got him," the paramedic replied.

I heard Bonnie's voice. "It's okay, Harvey," she said. Then I saw her face, above me, her copper-blonde hair and soft eyes assuring me she was okay and on her feet.

The lights in front of my face dimmed. I could see the area around me and could make out the faint clouds and pale moonlight in the night sky above the two apartment buildings.

When the medics allowed me to get to my feet, Bonnie lead me in to the foyer. I saw that the apartment entryway now looked like something out of Groucho Marx's shipboard stateroom from the movie *A Night At the Opera.* In addition to the two white male cops, we were joined by the landlord and his talkative bottle-blonde wife, and about a dozen other people. I saw that my friend Arthur and his wife Patricia were standing next to Bonnie.

"This is a crime scene," one of the cops said to everyone in general. "Nobody come any closer."

"I'm sorry," I said to Arthur and Patricia.

"What matters is you're okay," Patricia said in a tone that didn't convey much sympathy. Considering what had happened to the interior of her apartment I could not blame her.

"Take a look at this thing, sir," the first cop said to a man in a suit who had just arrived. I recognized him from his profile. He happened to be Detective Kayama, the fellow I had stonewalled on the Benchley case back outside O'Leary's Bar a couple days back.

As one of the cops started asking me to make a statement, I craned my neck over to see what Detective Kayama was doing at the end of the alleyway. He was shining a flashlight down on the ground, the same ground where the platform that Bates had been standing on had been situated. Another guy, probably a detective sergeant, brought himself over and, wearing a glove, leaned down and ran his hand over the ground, not touching it. He yanked his hand away almost as soon as he touched the ground.

"Damn it, that's like an oven," the detective sergeant said.

I had seen ground like that before. I had seen it back on the outskirts of Bowman, Oregon, along Cramner Creek in a spot near a ledge where my friend Dave McCreedy had been found dead.

"What happened here?" Detective Kayama asked me.

The ground next to the cyclone fence was charred. It was charred in the shape of a circle about six or seven feet in diameter.

"I saw the man who was standing there," Bonnie said. "He burned himself up. He must be dead. It was suicide."

"The guy, name was Ralph Bates, burned himself up," I reiterated. "I guess that's what happened."

Chapter Nineteen

Kayama questioned both Bonnie and myself. The landlord's side of the story stated we had only tried to protect ourselves and catch the burglar with a gun. There was no trace of whatever it was Bates had stood in to incinerate himself. Bonnie said she had seen Bates go up in a ball of light, a fact also confirmed by a couple tenants who were looking out their windows at the time of my altercation with him in the alley. Nobody connected with the investigation knew what to make of how so much light and heat had generated so quickly, nor the noise of the platform, nor anything else about the last part of the crime-in-progress, least of all me.

We were released into our own custody. After that I took Bonnie to get her head injury checked out at the emergency department of the nearest hospital, the University of San Francisco in the middle of the city. It turned out the back of her head was only bruised but some sharp pains she felt in her left arm turned out to be a a hairline fracture a couple inches above her left wrist. She was fitted with a soft velcro cast and released. By then it was just after midnight.

I then drove her back to where she was staying at The Holiday Inn on Van Ness Avenue. I insisted on going up to the room with her, not for the reason men usually want to get into a desirable woman's hotel room, but because I wanted to make sure there were no more nasty surprises. The room checked out fine, which made it the first thing that had gone right all evening. In addition to having a sore back from wrestling with the giant, Dromio, I could now add an annoying pain in my upper back from someone trying to make me part of his no-net acrobatic routine. Combine that with Bonnie's hairline fracture just below her right wrist and it all seemed to work against my making a pass.

I also had a feeling you didn't rush things with Bonnie Noel.

I went back to the apartment on Church Street. A few hours of sleep followed. The next morning, as I was helping Patricia and Arthur put their living room into some semblance of order, I received a call. It was from Bonnie, and from the grogginess of her voice I could tell she had had probably less sleep than I managed.

"I'm at the airport," she said. "My flight was delayed getting out of here so I just made a couple calls. I think you'll find this information useful to us."

"Fire away," I said between gulps of instant coffee.

"I had a hunch about Warbeck, so I called British Airways. He's confirmed on a 9:42 flight from SFO to Heathrow. It arrives at 6:36 Greenwich Mean Time in London. So, he's just blowing in and out of town."

"That tells me he's got a pressing commitment back in England," I said. "How'd you get this little tidbit?"

"I called British Airways and pretended to be Mr. Warbeck's secretary," Bonnie said. "I told the airline representative that Mr. Warbeck wanted a vegetarian meal on his flight. I got her to confirm the time and number of the flight. Mr. Warbeck is traveling with two other companions. They also will be eating veggies."

"Your concern for the good health of our nemesis is touching," I said. "I wish I had an enemy as nurturing as you."

"Call it my maternal instinct," Bonnie said. "I noticed the Warbeck party was having lobster thermidor at the museum gala last night. They need a break from all that rich wine sauce. Did you know the cholesterol content of lobster, by the way?"

"Try not to scare me, I just woke up," I said. "How's your wrist this morning?"

"Nothing a couple Tylenol can't help," she replied. "The nurse told me last night I should be playing the violin again in about six weeks. I didn't have the heart to tell her I gave up the violin at sixteen."

I enjoyed hearing the cheerfulness in her voice. "What was the other call you made?"

"I saved the best news for last. I called Ann last night and told her what happened. Well, what I could understand of it, not the last part where Ralph Bates destroyed himself and that thing he was standing on. I'm so glad you weren't burned or anything."

"I share your gladness, Ms. Noel."

"Anyway, Ann called Detective Kayama's office at San Francisco Homicide this morning. He wasn't in yet, but there was another detective there who was working on this same case. She asked the woman detective about this Bates character, then rang me on my cell phone at the airport with some good news. Turns out the guy you captured was a paroled felon named Charles Lindsay Aarons. According to Detective Lonergan his fingerprints match some fingerprints the police have from the trunk of Mr. Benchley's car."

"The car they found in Golden Gate Park, with Carolyn Mason's body in the trunk?"

"That's it. The cops lifted some prints they couldn't identify as belonging to Carolyn or Mr. Benchley off the trunk of the Mustang. They eliminated some fingerprints as belonging to a guy who was a valet at The Forest of Arden. A police forensic team matched some other prints up with our guy Aarons."

"Wow," I said.

"It gets better," Bonnie said. "The police got a warrant to search Aarons' hotel room over by Fisherman's Wharf. They found a diamond pendant Mr. Benchley gave Carolyn on her last birthday. He had it specially made. Plus, there were blood and tissue samples taken from under Mason's fingernails at the autopsy. They know the blood isn't the same type she had. It's 'O' type blood, the type that Mr. Benchley has. But Aarons has 'O' type blood, too. They're going to do further tests this afternoon on some fiber samples of clothing found on Mason's body. If they match up with fibers on some of Aarons clothing, and when they get a sample of Charley Aarons blood they can try to get a DNA match with the blood from the woman's fingernails."

"Then maybe Jack Benchley's in the clear," I said. "Probably take a few weeks before a laboratory can get DNA results. If we find your old boss before then, he'll still have to answer to the police."

"The important thing is that the police have a suspect other than Mr. Benchley. Ann sounds elated. I just hope we find her father. Alive, I mean." Bonnie's voice became sad. It was obvious he was more than a former employer to her.

"I wish I could be optimistic, Bonnie. Fact is that he's been missing going on two weeks. And from the way Warbeck had that Mr. Park fellow killed right in front of me...let's just say if Jack Benchley is still alive it's because he's holding out on something Trevor Warbeck needs. Has Ann Benchley got anyone over in London to put a tail on Warbeck?"

"Major Trubshawe is available," Bonnie said. "I'm sure Ann will have him go to Heathrow to follow the Warbeck party when they hit London." Over the telephone I heard a female voice in the background announce a boarding call. "Gotta go, Harvey. Remember, go to the Benchley Ranch as soon as you get back to Rogue Falls. You know the way?"

"Last house at the end of Pinecone Mountain Road," I said. "Have a nice flight. I'm real sorry about your wrist. I guess you knew that."

"You're not the first man to push me around," Bonnie said. "Not by a long shot. Get back to Rogue Falls as quick as you can, but observe the speed limits."

"Right," I said. "See you after."

After I hung up, I did some more clean-up around the apartment, then said goodbye to my friends. For some reason, Arthur seemed not altogether upset to see me go.

Driving back north, out of the Bay Area, my head was swimming with the new events. Ralph Bates had to have been a traitor to Jack Benchley. He must have gained access to Benchley's office and bugged it. He was working for Trevor Warbeck, that was certain. And he helped this guy Charles Aarons to burglarize Arthur and Patricia's apartment to find out what information I had on Warbeck.

But—and this was what was hard to wrap my brain around—how was it Bates just seemed to appear and then burn up in a ball of light? He must have been in the alley all along, even though I did not see him at first. Then, with the police on the way and trapped, he burned himself up.

But the charred ground was just like the blackened circle

near to where Dave's body was found. It was too much alike in size to be a coincidence. Could Dave's killer have just burned himself up, too? And who, outside of some wacko political martyr, does something like that?

The traffic going out of the Bay Area on Interstate 80 wasn't too bad. Of course this was a Saturday morning. Five and a half hours later I had traversed the Northern San Joaquin Valley crossed over the Siskiyou Pass (elevation 4000+ feet) and back into Oregon. I decided to stop off in Bowman again and pay a call on Wanda Truax of The Elegant Lady Beauty Shop. I hoped she could give me more details on the woman in the platinum blonde wig that she saw with Dave.

I took the first turnoff north of the California/Oregon border and descended in to Bowman. The Elegant Lady Beauty Salon was open and Wanda Truax was working on a style job for a silver-haired older woman wearing three strands of pearls over the plastic purple smock she was wearing. I made eye contact with Wanda as soon as I walked in.

"I need to talk to you," she said to me. That was encouraging. I sat down and leafed through a two month old copy of *Time* until the slender, stork-like older woman she was working on slowly got up, took seemingly forever to get some money out of her purse, exchanged some friendly chit-chat, then finally left.

"I tried to contact you," Wanda said to me as she finished jotting down something in what I took was an appointment book. I was standing across the counter from her. She was wearing a red sweater that made her grapefruit-sized breasts even more prominent than I remembered.

"Did you try and leave a message on the number I gave you?"

"Yes, but you never got back to me."

"I was called out of town," I said. "Do you remember something?"

She shook her head. "But I think I know someone who saw Mr. McCreedy the night he was found next to the creek. He says he saw him around five-thirty out in front of Herb and Bernice's convenience store. There was another person with him."

"Who is it?"

"Lawrence Webber," she said. "You know the guy I'm talking about? The guy they call Sheepman down in Rogue Falls? He's a homeless man. Hangs out in the county library."

"Yes, yes," I said, feeling a warm surge of excitement blow up like a balloon inside me. "I've talked to him before."

"He saw Dave McCreedy," Wanda Truax said. "Apparently they knew each other before this."

"Who was he with?"

"A woman," she said. "That's all he told me."

A woman.

"How about a description?" I asked.

"He wouldn't give me any description of her. He told me about Mr. McCreedy and a woman who were arguing in front of the Bowman Country Store. He was up here visiting a friend of his and he was on his way back to Rogue Falls on his bicycle when he passed the store. That's when he saw this couple going at it."

"They were fighting?"

"That right, apparently the woman was shouting. He said the lady was physically attacking him, shoving him hard and calling him filthy names. She slapped him in the face. Your friend then shoved her down, shoved her down on the gravel, got on his motorcycle, and drove away."

"Where was Sheep—I mean Lawrence—when all this happened?"

"He was across the street from the store, in front of the old Cascade Theater. He stopped the bike and watched it go on from behind the old ticket booth. He must have had a pretty good view. Lawrence said that after McCreedy left, the woman got into her car and turned her head down. He thought she might have been crying. Then, according to him, the lady started up the car and headed down the Cramner Creek Road, going the same way the man she was fighting with went."

"Did the woman see him? Did he say that?"

"He says the woman saw him just as she was pulling out. A couple minutes after the shoving she took, he decided to ride across the street and see if she was all right. But she only glanced at him and put her car into reverse." "She just got into her car and drove up the Cramner Creek Road in the direction your friend went."

"He's sure this was Dave McCreedy?"

"Yes," she said. "He told me your friend had given him

money several times in the last few months."

Dave had mentioned dropping a dollar or two to Sheepman. This sounded more generous than that.

"He said Dave gave him money, huh?"

"Apparently quite regularly," Wanda said. "Mr. McCreedy also told some fellow who bothered Lawrence down in Rogue Falls to lay off him. Threatened this guy with bodily harm if he hurt Lawrence. I think Lawrence said the guy's name was Sweeney or something."

Sweeney. The weasel who Ray had literally thrown out of O'Leary's when I was being interrogated by Russ White. Dave was helping a poor old street guy out, in ways above and beyond tossing some random change around. That in itself was startling.

"And this woman," I said, getting back to the subject, "she drove off after Dave after a couple minutes of crying in the car?"

"Yes."

"Heading down Cramner Creek Road, right after Dave on his motorcycle?"

"Yes."

"Didn't he say what this woman looked like? What make of car was she driving?"

"I didn't ask him right then. I should have. I made a bad mistake. Right in the middle of Lawrence telling me about this he mentioned your friend's name. That got me excited because I had the business card you gave me with his name on it. I told him about you, how you were this detective trying to find out about Mr. McCreedy, and how he was found dead. Lawrence doesn't read newspapers or watch television. He never knew about the body being found. I told him right after he mentioned this incident in front of Herb and Bernice's store. I managed to find out where the woman went after that, but he wouldn't say anything else. He doesn't want to get involved with the law. He's scared somebody might come after him."

"Christ," I said, gritting my teeth and swatting the counter top to the table. "The guy I needed to talk to walks right in after I leave. Do you have any idea where he might be now?"

"No," she said. "I imagine he's down in Rogue Falls. "This Sweeney guy beat him up a few days ago. He had a bad bruise over his right eye. This young hood took all the money he had.

I fixed him up as best I could and told him to go to the hospital down there. But Lawrence won't go to the hospital; he says he can't afford it. I'll bet it's also where his wife and child died after that car accident. I'm hoping you can talk to him—get him to go to the police—not just about this other business with your friend but with this Sweeney character who beat him up."

"I'll take a look down in town," I said. "Thanks for the information. Do I owe you anything?"

"Yes," Wanda said. "Help Lawrence. If he won't go to the police, tell him to get his butt up here," she said. "He's a stubborn old man and he doesn't like to rely on people, but he needs help."

"Did he mention any other possible witnesses, to the man and the woman having the argument up here I mean?"

"No," she said. As she said this, I heard a truck drive up to the curb in front of the shop. An old, frumpy woman in a tent-like dress gingerly exited the beat-up gunmetal-grey Ford truck from the passenger side. I recognized the person in the driver's seat. He was the old bald fellow in overalls who told me about how he had lost his brother at Bowman Lumber.

"That's Mrs. Helms," Wanda said. "She's here for a permanent."

I thanked her and left the shop.

It was easy enough to find Lawrence Webber, a.k.a. Sheepman. He was at the Rogue Falls Library, typing away on the old Olympic typewriter not far from the reference desk. He did not look happy to see me.

"Who beat you up?" I asked him as I looked at the large butterfly bandage that partially covered the crescent-shaped, puffy red bruise where his right eyebrow should have been.

"A rat named Sweeney and a pal of his. They're both a couple bums from eastern Washington. They saw that damn newspaper article and decided I must have a bit of money. Never should have talked to that reporter."

"Sweeney is a rat," I said. "A guy I knew had thrown him out of O'Leary's Bar three times. How'd you like me to get your money back for you, with interest?"

"Why the hell would you do that?" he said.

The librarian at the desk behind us made a shushing sound. I lowered my voice. "I had a friend—Dave McCreedy. I guess he helped you out."

"I knew Dave," the old man said.

"Mrs. Truax tells me you saw him up in Bowman about twelve days ago. He had some kind of altercation with a lady in front of the store out here, then he drove off toward the Cramner Creek Road. The lady followed him. And, later on, Dave was found dead."

"I told her not to tell anybody," Webber said.

"If you don't want to go to the cops on Sweeney and this other rat, I'll deal with him for you and get your money back."

"What's the catch?" he asked, his wizened eyes crinkling at the edges.

"Go with me to the cops and give them a description of the woman you saw Dave shove around up in Bowman."

"No," he said firmly. Then he cast his eyes down at the typewriter. He started to shiver. I thought he might just go back to typing but instead he put a hand up to the bandage on his face.

"What's the matter?"

"I'm damn hungry, mister," he said softly. "The rapacious wolves who bushwhacked me took all my money."

"Let's blow this place," I said. "I'll take you anywhere you want to go and get you some food."

"I'm not making any deals," the old man said firmly.

"I'm not asking you to," I said. "You said you were hungry, right?"

I drove Lawrence over to a restaurant on the edge of Rogue Falls. We put his bicycle in my trunk and I tied the half-open hood down with a spare piece of rope. His body odor was not much better than the last time we had been together. As I drove, I glanced over a couple times and saw some other bruises partially hidden by his beard. There was also a cut along his ear, not deep, but indicating a knife had been used in the attack. I asked him if he was in pain.

"No more than a couple days ago," the old man said through his heavy beard. "I'll live."

He wanted to go to the Happy Times Restaurant. He said he liked the food there. I got the impression it was a treat for him. Happy Times had a rustic, informal atmosphere with plastic red-and- white tablecloths on the tables, laminated menus featuring high-fat fare and a few salads, and arcade games for the kids on the side of the premises opposite the tables and booths. You'd have to be deaf not to hear the computer-generated sounds of mock electronic battle beyond the paneled facade that separated the serving area from the video arcade.

The restaurant had a cute blonde waitress, the same woman Webber was sitting with on the bench at Shakespeare Plaza a few nights earlier. She made a big to-do over his injuries and gave him enough sympathy to cover two good beatings. His haggard face beamed up at her, taking all the sympathy in. He next ordered a roast beef sandwich, a bowl of soup, garlic fries, a strawberry milkshake, and a green salad from her. He also asked Marsha—that was her name—for a big glass of water.

"How's your book coming, Larry?" Marsha asked.

"I was going to get it in shape for sending out to a publisher next week," the old man said in a tone of assurance that surprised me. "But Thursday night I got mugged by a couple young punks. They took my backpack. My manuscript was in there. I'm going to have to practically start over. I didn't type it on a fancy computer so I had no spare. The punks got all my money, too."

"I'm sorry, Larry," she said, sounding genuine. "I hope you told the police."

The old man nodded a lie and handed her back the menu.

As I waited for the food to arrive I heard about the book from Larry. As Wanda Truax told me, he was doing a history of Jedidiah Gasburg, the Confederate Colonel who was also founder of the town I lived in.

"I'm an authority on the Civil War," he said in a matter-of-fact way. "That and the Reconstruction Era was my main focus when I got my master's. I taught American History at Bowman High School for several years, until it closed up when the mill went belly up. I had to teach the whole great arc of American History, but my passion was always material on The Civil War and Reconstruction. I've read just about all I could find on those eras. I know I can't absorb it all—there's too much."

"I know a few details about the Civil War and Reconstruction," I said.

"What do you know about Jed Gasburg?"

"A colonel or something in the Confederacy, wasn't he? Then he came back here and got into politics, right?"

"He was a *general* in the Army of Northern Virginia," the old man said, correcting me. "Gasburg has never had a biography published about him. He deserves one and I'm trying to give him one. Takes me three years of effort and some punks..." He sighed, then went on. "Here's a man who fought from First Bull Run to the Siege of Petersburg; who went from a private soldier to a General in four years; who was wounded three times by Union musket balls at Malvern Hill and still stayed on the front lines to keep his company from breaking and running; who lost a leg outside Spotsylvania in May 1864, but he stayed with his troops. He stayed right until the end when Lee was boxed in by Grant and Sheridan, when what was left of his division fell back on Lynchburg in April of '65. Then of course he came back here."

"That he did," I said. What I knew about Gasburg would lead me to believe he was a firebrand racist who deserved every round of iron he ever took and then some. Still, he probably was a brave man, if wrongheaded. Sensing the old man's strong liking to the rebel commander, I steered the conversation to a discussion of the American Civil War in general, withholding my strong opinion that the Lost Cause was better off lost. This we engaged in until he finished his meal. When I tried to bring him around to the subject of what he saw out in front of the Bowman Country Store on the night of April Fourth, however, he was adamant.

"I'm not talking," he said after slurping up the last of his soup. "I'm not getting into it." Some of his soup stained his ratty-looking beard. I told him he had some calm chowder on his beard and he wiped it off, much to my relief.

"I'll get your money back from Sweeney," I said. "You just go to the sheriff's office—"

"I'm not doing nothing," the old man said. "The law is a joke. The law let the drunk who killed my wife and my little girl in his car walk away years ago with a slap on the wrist. I still see that butcher, the drunk who plowed into my Janet and my baby, driving around Rogue Falls like he owns the town. That old drunk is alive and free as a bird and my wife..." He stopped, bowed his head as if to collect himself, then looked back up at me with a trace of redness in the bags below his eyes.

"The law doesn't care about guys like me, and nothing I say will bring Dave back."

"You may have to talk," I said after a short interval to make sure he wasn't going to bust out crying. "You might have to talk— like it or not," I said. "I know enough from Mrs. Truax that you saw a woman follow Dave after he rode down the Cramner Creek Road."

"That's what you say," Lawrence said after biting into his sandwich. He chewed his bite slowly, then continued. "If you go to the cops, I'll deny I said anything to Mrs. Truax, or to you. You just have secondhand evidence—hearsay. I read up in the library about this business with Dave. He's down as a suicide. You're his friend, so I imagine they'll think you're making up a murder story to frame some enemy he had. Well," he lowered his voice, "you're out of luck. I know the law."

Lawrence Webber was not an ignorant man.

"What if I got your money back for you? What if I got that manuscript back?"

"Still no deal," Webber said.

I turned around and left Happy Times. I untied his bike from my car, left it where he could see it and pulled out in my Celica. I started to wonder again if Dave's murder and the Benchley kidnapping case were not actually related.

I saw no reason why Webber would lie about seeing a woman with Dave. He had volunteered it freely to Wanda Truax, so the question was, who was the woman? I couldn't rule out Ann Benchley. Even if Bonnie was straight with me about her boss leaving the ranch in a motorcycle, that could have been a ruse to fool Bonnie. She might have ditched the motorcycle and went up to Bowman in a car. I couldn't rule out Rochelle Millman, either. Or Wendy.

Or even Bonnie Noel.

Chapter Twenty

I was supposed to go right to the Benchley Ranch when I hit town, but I put that off a few minutes more and stopped in over at the McLoughlin Building. I parked on the curb next to the Bed and Futon Shop, next to the vacant lot behind the building and just below a faded red-and-white mural advertising Coca-Cola on one side of the brick exterior.

I walked around the corner of the building and discovered Wendy's car parked just below the entryway to the narrow flight of stairs. It was Saturday. They were moving Dave's stuff out one day earlier than expected, and without my help.

Wendy and her sister, Rochelle, were in the office. There were several cardboard boxes scattered about the floor, and the women were loading up papers and wrapping Dave's bowling trophies, pictures of ballplayers and the other useless objects a man leaves behind. I expected a greeting of sorts from Wendy once I made my presence known. But from the way she looked when she turned around to acknowledge me, I knew something had changed between us.

"What are you doing here?" Wendy said sharply. "I thought you weren't due back into town until Sunday."

I was taken aback by her response. I looked past Wendy and caught Rochelle shooting daggers at me with her eyes. I felt about as welcome there as a giant anthrax spore suddenly arriving at a cattleman's association breakfast.

"Well," I said. "I'm kind of in a hurry now, but I thought I'd just stop in and...I just thought I'd get a couple things I might have left in the file cabinet."

The optical daggers kept coming from Rochelle. She straightened up, placing her hands on her lower back. "There's something over on the desk for you," she said in an edgy tone I didn't appreciate. "Take it. Dave wanted you to have it. Oh, by the way, you needn't bother stopping by here tomorrow. Ray is helping us move the big stuff outta here, today and tomorrow."

Ray. It all became clear. He had told Wendy about his theory that Ann Benchley had murdered Dave and made it look like a suicide. This meant that Wendy and her sister also knew about Dave's affair with Ann. Which meant Wendy must assume that I knew all along about it and kept my mouth shut. And she also knew from Ray that I was working for Ann Benchley and, for all Wendy knew, I was busy covering my rich movie star client's tracks.

"Where's Ray?" I asked.

"He's getting us some take out food," Rochelle said flatly. "If you don't mind, why don't you leave the keys to this place with us. If you don't mind."

I took the two keys I had for the office off my chain, and let them drop a few inches from my fingers onto the desk.

"I guess I'll be going," I said sheepishly.

I received a lukewarm goodbye from Wendy. I probably could have just left with things as they stood—it would be better if I talked to Wendy alone—were it not for something that her sister said to me on my way out.

"So," Rochelle asked, "have you collected your big wad of money from Ann Benchley yet? You'd think a guy wouldn't work for the woman who had his friend murdered. But I'm sure Dave would understand. Money comes first with some people."

Now my blood was up. I turned around and looked Rochelle squarely in her icy baby blues. "Look, Dave McCreedy was my best friend. And I'm not working for the person who killed him. The one who did that is on a flight to London right now and I'm going to do my best to help get him back here to face the music."

"Money comes first with some people," Rochelle calmly repeated. "Wendy knows what the Benchley money has done to you."

"You're one to talk," I half-shouted. "You married Old Man Benchley, remember? I'm sure you fleeced him good when the divorce went down."

I looked over at Wendy. Her attention was on a trophy she was wrapping in newspaper, but I could see her cheeks getting red and her eyes becoming moist.

"Just go, Harvey," Wendy said softly. "Just go." She bowed her head and went on wrapping. I felt like blowing the secret of Rochelle's hotel romps with Dave to Wendy. But that feeling passed quickly. It would come off like I was making up a story to get back at Wendy's sister.

I left. But not before I told them that Ray Harrison had it all wrong. As I descended the semi-dark stairway to the bright light out on the street I resolved to call Wendy later.

As I walked back to my truck, I caught sight of an unmarked Rogue Falls police car. It had just turned a corner about a block away and was headed in my direction. I came to a stop on the sidewalk when the car pulled up next to me on the curb. There were two cops sitting up front: one was a uniformed officer, the other was Detective Russ White.

Russ White opened the passenger door and walked around the vehicle towards me. I noticed the backseat was occupied by two Hispanic kids, both maybe fourteen or fifteen, both wearing identical dark shirts with dark baseball caps positioned backwards on their heads. One of the kids shot me a look. He had a baby face coupled with a wispy goatee.

"Taking a couple orphans to the ballgame?" I asked Detective White.

"I caught those two on the way over here. They were spray painting on the back of the old Thrifty Drug Building." He looked up at the stairway I had just descended. "Have you just been in Dave's old office?"

"Not for long," I said.

"What's going on up there?" Russ asked, pointing up in the general direction of Dave's office.

"Wendy is moving things out. Her and her sister..."

I wouldn't have imagined Detective White could move as fast as he did, but he shot by me and bounded up the stairway. I decided to stay where I was. In a few minutes White descended the stairway. Rochelle and Wendy were right behind him. Wendy was crying, her face buried in her hands.

Her sister had her arm around her shoulder. I started to walk toward the two women but one hard look from Rochelle Millman changed my mind about that. The two women got into Rochelle's black Lexus and the elder sister, after getting Wendy some Kleenex, started the engine and drove away from the curb. I watched them drive off, knowing with almost absolute certainty what had made Wendy cry.

Detective White had stopped a few feet away from me. When I turned from watching the ladies driving he had a look on his face like he wanted to tell me something.

"I've got news," White said, reaching for a cigarette from his shirt pocket and breaking off the filter with his forefinger and thumb.

I knew but I started to ask anyway.

"Is it about...?"

"Dave McCreedy didn't kill himself. Somebody did it for him."

I heaved a sigh, and felt that ringing in my head, similar to when I first heard about Dave's death.

"Have they caught the woman who did it?" I asked.

Russ snickered. "The Sheriff's Department hasn't even got a gender on the perp, much less anybody in custody, and you already know it's a woman? You want to explain that to me, citizen?"

I told him about what I had learned from Wanda Truax and about my talk with Lawrence Webber. I felt relieved. Russ White could put the squeeze on Webber in ways I obviously could not.

"All it is now is hearsay if Webber won't talk," I added after I filled Russ in on what Webber told me.

"Not for long. I'll get an APB out on this Lawrence Webber. You say this is the guy the locals call Sheepman?"

"That's the guy," I said. "You broke it to Wendy I see."

"She didn't take it well," Russ said casually.

"Do you blame her?" I asked. "You just opened everything back up and made it worse."

"No, I don't blame her," Russ said, casting his eyes downward.

"How'd they determine it was homicide?"

"Our buddy was shot with a Golan nine millimeter, as you know. He owned a model for a back-up gun."

I nodded, and averted my face from the smoke coming out of the detective's nostrils.

"The day after the murder, when it still looked like suicide, Deputy Westphal was sent up to the creek to do some backtracking. Just a routine go-over to see if there was anything the crime unit they sent up there the night before had missed. Westphal was the one who called to run a check on you."

"Right," I said. "What was it she found?"

"Two nine-millimeter shell casings. That was a problem because we could only account for one bullet, the one that Dave shot into his skull. So they did a blanket search. The day after I talked to you with that Kayama guy they found something else. You know what lands and grooves on a slug are, right?"

I nodded. We both knew that 'lands' referred to ridges and scratches left on a bullet after it has been fired through the barrel of a pistol or a rifle. The marks left on the spent bullet differ depending on the type of weapon used. The more a handgun or a rifle is fired, the more identifiable it becomes from any other firearm, even one identical to it in make and design. Because of that, a firearm expert can usually tell what bullet belongs to what rifle, pistol or revolver.

Russ nodded. "Well, the county boys found the second bullet that went with that second shell casing."

"A nine millimeter slug, right? Not from somebody's hunting rifle?"

"Not from a hunting rifle," Russ replied. "A slug from a handgun. The same type of bullet: Remington cartridge, 115 grains, full metal jacket. And the lands on that second bullet don't match up with the remains of the slug they recovered from the scene, the one that was fired through Dave's head."

I waited for more detail. "Well?" I asked after a few seconds.

"The lab fired some test bullets from the gun they recovered from the scene. They sent the results up to State Forensics in Salem. They have an electron microscope at the lab up there. State Forensics studied all the ballistic evidence. The bullet that went through Dave's head was fired by a Golan that had to have been relatively unused. The barrel of Dave's Golan had extensive wear that showed on the test slugs. The gun we had at the site was registered to Dave."

"He and I used to hit the gun range on weekends. I know he liked to use that Golan, probably more than his Colt .38. So when did they find the second slug?"

"Funny you should ask that," Russ said, taking another drag on his smoke. "Yesterday. They beat the bushes around both sides of the creek for a couple days, and finally found the slug embedded in the trunk of a ponderosa pine a couple hundred feet away from the crime, on the opposite side of the bank. Except for the head, the bullet was in good shape. The lands on that second slug match up with the test slugs. They also found a nice fragment from the slug that killed Dave a couple days earlier. It had splintered off the major fragment when it hit Dave's left temporal bone. Whoever did shoot him got close enough to make it look like a self-inflicted headshot."

"Somebody either snuck up behind him or got right in his face."

Russ nodded. "You put the two fragments together and you got a fairly complete slug from a different gun. That makes the case a murder investigation. That's why I got Wendy and her sister out of Dave's office. I've got a warrant to search his office. I'm going to drop these two youngsters off at the station to be booked, then I'm headed back here with Officer Demaret over there to search the place. The women said they hadn't brought anything out yet."

I knew the one thing Russ could have used—the tape in the phone message machine—was already gone. Apparently, he hadn't read the report about the assault I had been on the receiving end of. I would have to answer about that.

Russ looked up at the mid-afternoon sun. His already squinted-up eyes squinted some more. "I also have to do some interrogation work on this," he said, looking back at me. "The chief wants us to help out the Sheriff's Department. You're on my list. I'll need to question you tomorrow or the next day. I trust you'll be in town?"

I nodded, then tried to analyze what Russ had told me about the ballistic evidence. I stared over at the dilapidated old railroad depot. I could almost imagine some of the loose clay tiles on top of the high gambrel roof crumbling before my eyes in the hot sun. After absorbing what Russ had told me, I stated my thoughts out loud.

"Somebody killed Dave with a Golan just like he had, then fired Dave's gun at the scene so whoever found him would know Dave's gun had recently been fired."

"Looks that way," Russ said. "They took the gun that actually did the deed with them. That one had a nearly virgin barrel judging by the lack of marks on the bullet."

"Anything else?" I asked, trying to be as nonchalant as Russ was.

"Nothing more I can tell you. Oh, you ought to thank Vernon Ritts when you get a chance. You know the guy who runs your trailer park?"

"Why?" I asked.

"Because you were playing pool in the recreation room with him between 5:45 and 7:15 on the evening that Dave bought it. I called over to your place to see if anyone might have seen you that night."

"Nice of you to put me so high up on your list of suspects, Detective White," I said.

"This is a homicide now, Wells," he said grimly. He finished the cigarette, tossed a half-finger width of rolled tobacco onto the gravel we were standing on, then stomped the smoking butt out with the heel of one of his freshly-polished black shoes. "Nobody who knew Dave or his wife is going to get a free pass until we get some more evidence. The county mounties will be interviewing anybody who lives around Bowman, trying to get some kind of line on anybody out of the ordinary who might have come around that area. Bowman isn't much of a town so a stranger would stick out."

"And you're going to interview Lawrence Webber, right?"

"From what you told me, I'll be very interested in what Mr. Webber has to say. I'll pass the information about Wanda Truax up to Middleburg so some deputy can get a deposition out of her. I told Wendy somebody will be dropping by her apartment tonight. Just routine, but it has to be done."

Russ broke the filter off another cigarette and lit it. He exhaled the first drag as if he was suddenly exhausted; his shoulders sagged and he let his arms fall limply to his sides.

"I never thought Dave killed himself," Russ added, contradicting what he had told me the night Dave was found dead.

"The hell you didn't think that," I said. "You had him offing himself before they even got him in the bag."

"I just thought it looked that way. That's what I said. You have a lousy memory, Wells."

I knew what I had heard. Russ told me Dave was dead and I remembered everything he said with a terrible vividness. But I let my end of the argument ride. Russ looked over my shoulder. I heard the hum of a well-tuned car engine coming up behind me.

Russ continued. "Oh, by the way, Wells, I hear you're working for Ann Benchley now, and working with some broad named Bonnie Somebody."

"The broad's name is Ms. Noel," I interjected.

"Right. Anyway, you two made a ruckus at a black-tie engagement Trevor Warbeck was appearing at. Frankly, I don't give a shit what you do outside this town. But you're a friend of McCreedy and McCreedy was a friend of mine. This is a little advice I'm going to repeat for your own good. Stay away from the Benchley Case. According to Chief Holden, who's been in contact with the police down in Frisco, Warbeck checks out. He checks out with the FBI, too. And as for that circumstantial bullshit you're trying to make into something—the professional rivalry between Warbeck and Jack Benchley—well, it's a dead end. Warbeck and that Truth Party outfit are clean in the Benchley matter. I suggest you take my earlier advice and stay on your own porch for awhile. I wouldn't be surprised if even Ann Benchley gets the once-over on this." He turned and walked away from me, toward the cruiser with the uniformed cop and the two suspects.

"Take a look at the San Francisco papers tonight," I called to Russ as he walked away. "There's a fellow named Charles Aarons. He's the new prime suspect down there, not Old Man Benchley. Tell that to your pal Holden."

White never turned around. The patrol car pulled away after he got in the passenger side. I was left standing in the hot sun, just like the mad dog in the old song.

Chapter Twenty-One

Jack Benchley's Scrub Oak Ranch was located at the top of a winding two-lane dirt road near the summit of Pinecone Mountain. From what Dave McCreedy had told me, the layout featured a spectacular, unobstructed vista of Rogue Falls and the surrounding valley from the second floor verandah at the front of the house and, on the backside, an equally impressive view of the Rogue River as it wound through the pine-encrusted Kit Carson Canyon on its way to the Pacific.

The only vehicle I passed going up Pinecone Mountain Road was a spanking new blue Buick four-door. Two men were in the front seat of the vehicle; both of them were wearing sunglasses and business suits. The driver gave me a return gaze as my truck and I sped past. From my rearview mirror, I saw an "official use only" tag on the back bumper of the car. The city cops drove Fords and the county sheriff's patrol cars were Chevys, so I knew Ann Benchley had just been visited by either the State Police or the FBI. I made a right turn onto a side road, following the trail of dust that the Buick had kicked up on its way down.

At the end of the side road was a long stretch of tall chain-link fencing topped with razor wire. The entrance to the estate featured thick spear-shaped iron spikes—designed like upside-down spades from a deck of playing cards—protruding along the top. On either side of the gate was a short tower, about twenty feet high, made from blocks of grey limestone and mortar. The top of each tower had miniature battlements, like a rook on a chessboard. The right tower had a video surveillance camera mounted on its apex. A sign on the tower to my left proclaimed: "Scrub Oak Ranch/No Trespassing/No Hunting/No Solicitors." The sign was just below a niche in the tower which featured a statue of a gargoyle with horns on its head and a long tongue protruding out from its hideous stone mug. The set-up would have discouraged anybody from feeling welcome, even a busload of Jehovah's Witnesses.

Another feature of the left tower was an intercom receiver embedded into one of the stone blocks. I pushed the button next to the speaker. A few seconds later, Bonnie's voice came over the speaker asking what my business was. I identified myself.

"Hi, Harvey," she said in a voice that sounded even more tired than the one I had spoken to from the airport that morning. "Is your back still bothering you?"

"Not really," I replied, lying. "How's your head? Does the back of it still feel like somebody gave you the jackhammer treatment?"

"Not really," Bonnie said blithely. "For some reason my thinking has actually improved. I can now do long division math problems without a calculator."

"I'm impressed," I said, trying to sound cheerful. The news about Dave being seen with a woman in Bowman shortly before his demise made me anything but.... A second later, an electric buzzing sound came out of the speaker. The portcullis in front of me began to slide to the right. I noticed a tractor wheel rolling along a metal groove just under the gate. In about half-a-minute, the driveway was clear and I drove onto the property.

The road turned into a circular driveway in front of the house. In the middle of the driveway was a golf putting area with a ring of taller grass around the green. The ring was sloped to allow for chipping practice. I parked just beyond the four-car garage. When I got out of my car, I took note of a perfectly circular artificial lake located downhill from the garage. A flock of wood ducks had taken up residence on the small cone-shaped grassy island in the middle of the lake. A golf flag stuck up in the middle of the island. I surmised that the island was used by Benchley to improve his approaches to the flag. On the opposite side of the lake, a skinny ginger-haired man in a pith helmet was riding about on a lawn tractor. This had to be the caretaker, Mr. Kincaid, the one who had discovered the slabs of myrtlewood missing from the basement. A frumpy-looking older lady was kneeling down in a flower bed, tending to a long row of blue and white hydrangeas. This had to be Mrs. Kirkland, the lady who saw the pick-up truck behind the house shortly before the break-in at Benchley's workshop was discovered.

A small dark-haired boy with startlingly large eyes and a high forehead stood in the front of the walkway leading to the porch. He looked to be around six or seven. I took him to be Tyler, one of Ann Benchley's two children and the one she had adopted after her father took him out of an orphanage in Romania. He had a large video camera—an older, bulky model—mounted on an aluminum tripod. The boy was looking through the viewfinder of the camera at me as I walked toward the porch.

"Don't look at the camera," the boy said to me in a sharp, high-pitched tone. "It's not good to ever look at the camera."

"Sorry," I said. "I didn't realize you were rolling."

"It's a broken camera," the boy announced. "But I didn't break it."

"Good for you," I remarked. "I didn't think you did."

"My grandpa let me borrow it. He's going to teach me how to be a cine...cinema-tographer person when he comes back. Are you the detective Miss Bonnie's been playing with?"

"Well, I wouldn't say we played together."

The child's attention returned to the viewfinder. "My mom wants to see you," the boy stated as he played with the automatic zoom buttons on the side of the camera. "Can I see your gun?"

"I really can't let you," I said, looking up at the front door and hoping someone would emerge to rescue me. "Your mommy wouldn't want me to. How did you know I carried a gun?"

"My mom says so. She's my mom, not my mommy. Have you ever shot a bad guy?"

"No," I said. "I've been lucky."

"Have you ever karated a bad guy? I know karate." Suddenly the boy jumped away from the camera and into a martial arts attack stance. "I'm a purple belt," he announced.

A small foot, clad in a basketball shoe, came at me. He had a good straight-leg kick. If he had advanced another six inches before making the attack, my groin would have taken the brunt of his demonstration.

"Tyler!" came an adult voice from the porch. It was Bonnie, and not a second too soon. "Leave Mr. Wells alone."

The boy darted back into his stance. "I'm showing him karate. We're going to karate together."

Bonnie came down off the porch. "Tyler why don't you let Mr. Wells pass? He has to talk to your mom right away. She has to go to work soon." Bonnie was wearing a white and green fern-pattern twill top and snug-fitting denim pants. She looked good.

"Okay," Tyler said discouragingly. "Miss Bonnie, can I play with Rufus for awhile? Please."

"No, Tyler," Bonnie said, emphatically. "Your mom needs a break from Rufus. Rufus has to stay in his cage. He can't run around the house all the time. Even a spider monkey needs rest. You can feed him with Mrs. Kirkland supervising in a little while." We left Tyler to his videocamera and I followed Bonnie up the red flagstone porch steps.

The Mock-Tudor manor house style outside gave way to an American Wild West decor inside. As we crossed from the foyer to the living room I felt I was walking into a saloon out of a painting by Charles Russell. There was a long wet bar with a metal footrest and a couple spittoons. The pictures behind the bar featured scenes of dusty Western streets from the last century, as well as theatrical bills for traveling dramatic troupes. Bonnie brought my attention to one framed poster advertising a performance of *Ben Hur* at the Virginia City Opera House in 1914. The role of Masala was listed as performed by Walter Benchley. She informed me that this was Jack Benchley's father in his first major professional role.

While she was looking over the old black-and-white poster, I said, "The Dave McCreedy case is being handled as a homicide."

Bonnie turned to me with a look of what I thought was genuine surprise. "So you were right then. Do the police have anybody in custody?"

I went over what Russ had told me. I didn't mention the business with Lawrence Webber. I wanted to gauge her reaction without the news of an eyewitness seeing Dave and an unidentified woman.

"Ann will want to know about this," Bonnie said evenly, "but we better not spring it on her just now. She's had a little jolt this afternoon already."

From Bonnie's reaction, I'd say she wasn't personally worried about Dave's case changing from suicide to a murder investigation. Her green eyes kept looking right at me and she didn't turn her head away from me: things I'd learned that people do when they start getting worried or begin to spin stories. Of course, I remembered. Bonnie was an actress.

We went through a hallway and came out to a large formal dining room, complete with high-backed chairs around the long rectangular wood table (probably solid oak and very old). Going through a door at the other end of the dining room, I followed Bonnie down a red-carpeted stairway to a short hallway which led into another room about the size of a master bedroom. Here we found Ann Benchley. She was sitting in an oval-shaped modern leather chair, with her feet up on a black ottoman. Behind her was a bay window which took in an unobstructed vista of the canyon and the Rogue River threading along the bottom of the two steep hillsides.

Ann Benchley was showing no traces of the gaudy Cleopatra look she had sported when I last saw her. She was wearing a sleeveless blue denim top, no make-up that I could detect, and her maroon-colored hair was tied up in a ponytail. One side of the room had built-in bookshelves stacked from floor to ceiling with books. After exchanging greetings with the actress, I gave the shelves a quick perusal. Jack Benchley had a great deal of material on Shakespeare—all kinds of editions of his plays, biographies of the playwright and books with titles like *Shakespeare and His Critics, Elizabethan Dramatists, A Survey and Hamlet and Oedipus*, et al—as well as books on theatre in general. There were books on American and European History, African and Oriental Art, a good number of 'literary' fiction titles and, on a set of high shelves nearest the floor, a large number of coffee-table sized painting and cinema books all in colorful dust jackets. The walls had no paintings, only theatrical masks and some exotic African tribal masks. There was also an old Remington bolt-action rifle and, mounted on an oval-shaped wooden plaque, the head of a wild beast I guessed was a water buffalo.

Despite the library-sized array of serious reading matter, Ms. Benchley was contenting herself with a glossy copy of *Handguns and Rifles* magazine. There was also a nine millimeter handgun within a comfortable reach on the table next to her. I recognized it as she moved her elbow. The pistol was either a SIG/Sauer P228 or P239 semi-automatic. Also assisting in her contentment was a bottle of Bailey's Irish Creme and a half-filled glass snifter. The portable television was on across the room, and the movie, *Breakfast at Tiffany's* was on, the volume down low. There was a scene on the tube I knew well: Audrey Hepburn surprises George Peppard by climbing, via a fire escape platform, into the bedroom of the apartment Patricia Neal has set him up in. Bonnie started to say something, but her boss put a finger to her lips and pointed toward the set.

The three of us watched as Hepburn/Holly Golightly asks the shirtless Peppard, who is sitting up in bed and pretending to look surprised that this woman he barely knows has snuck in on him. She glides into bed with him, child-like, somehow sexy and innocent all at once, and then she is out the door of the bedroom.

"Wow," Ms. Benchley said. "What a nice meet-cute scene. I wish I could have done a part like that when I was thirty."

"She's my favorite actress," I said, looking at the divine female image on the television.

"You have taste, Wells," she said. "And you like your women thin. Too thin if you ask me. Hepburn was the same height I am, but she could stay at one hundred-ten pounds. Disgusting! It should be against the law for any woman her size to fit into the outfits she could get into. Christ, she must have been a size six or something. I met her once at a American Film Institute gig my father made me go to. A bunch of photographers lined the two of us up. I saw a couple of the photos that made it into the magazines. I looked like a red taffeta zeppelin next to her. Hell, I was only a size ten and I was practically forced to live on rice cakes and diet coke!"

"By the way," Bonnie said. "The script for *Forget Me Not* arrived special-delivery from Jack Picasso's writing team, Rodney Ugarte and Ward Provolt."

The Beaumont and Fletcher of the San Fernando Valley?"

Ms. Benchley said in a rueful tone. "Have you done a full autopsy on it yet?"

"I scanned it," Bonnie said, "between the time I got back and just before the FBI men showed up. I don't want to worry you too much about it, but I just hope this is supposed to be a draft and not the shooting script. You're going to have to talk to Jack about a re-write. Suffice it to say the script needs polishing. Plus Jack better get the *Marnie* rights from Universal or I smell lawsuit."

"Is it that derivative?" Ms. Benchley asked.

"Yes," Bonnie replied. "And your character needs two more major scenes at least."

Ms. Benchley shook her head. "If it wasn't for Jack being involved, I'd walk away from it, right this second. I haven't even gone into fees and points and I'm already getting cold feet. Save the full critique, Bonnie, please. I'm almost feeling good." She took another sip of her drink. She looked up at me, her light green eyes wide and enchanting.

"How are you doing, Wells?" she asked. "Bonnie tells me we almost lost you a couple times down in San Francisco."

"I admit I was having doubts about seeing my next birthday, Ms. Benchley. What's brought the FBI into the case if I may ask?"

"The Bureau sent two agents down from Eugene. They told me they think my father might be in the hands of an interstate white supremacy group. I think they have another agenda they weren't telling me about. I'll let you in on that. Have a seat." Ms. Benchley pointed to a small cranberry-colored sofa. I sat down. As I did I noticed an interesting photograph on the small table situated under the bay window. Next to a large glass vase filled with fresh roses was a family portrait of the Benchleys that must have been taken a quarter of a century earlier. Jack Benchley was striking a genial pose. The teenaged Ann was leaning against her dad and beaming a smile that looked genuine, like the two of them had just shared a good joke. Standing above the two of them, with a hand on each of their shoulders, was Ann Benchley's mother, Maria. If anything she was more beautiful than her daughter grew up to be. I knew Ann was in her early forties, roughly the age of her mother when she died in a car accident in Costa Rica. That had been twenty-odd years ago.

Bonnie sat down on the sofa next to me. Ann Benchley turned down the volume of the television with the remote control. "First off, Bonnie, let's bring Mr. Wells up to speed on what the Federal Bureau of Investigation is trying to pass off on me. First, the good news. There is now another serious suspect in the murder of Carolyn Mason besides my dad. A Mr. Aarons from San Jose is now in custody. His blood type matches the traces of blood found under Mason's fingernails."

"Plus we might get a DNA match," Bonnie added. I looked over at her, enjoying the way the late afternoon sunlight illuminated the wisps of copper blonde hair that hung delicately over her forehead.

"Now, all we need is to tie this scumbag to the IFH and Trevor Warbeck," I said.

"And here's the bad news," Ms. Benchley said. "The FBI is still not going after Trevor Warbeck. Officially they want to link Charles Lindsay Aarons to a Neo-Nazi group. Apparently, Aarons has some relatives in Northern Idaho who belong to some pack of white power goons who play grabass with each other up in the woods on weekends. Two G-Men were just here, as you know. They tried to convince me that the best lead to work on is the Idaho Nazis angle. They said that weird letter I got just after dad disappeared was from some underground private militia group."

"Do you still have the letter?" I asked.

"The FBI has the original now," Ms. Benchley said. She took a sip from her drink. "I'll show you a copy if you think you can make head or tail of it." She set down her drink, got up gracefully, and went over to the bookshelves. She opened a book called The Great American West, opened it to the middle and handed me a single sheet of paper from between two pages. This is what was written on the paper:

> TO THE MONGREL BITCH WHORE OF HOLLYWOOD: REMOVE YOUR PLAGUE OF NIGGERS AND QUEERS WHO ASSAULT ARYAN CULTURE WITH THEIR PRIMPING AND HOWLING ON THE STAGE IN ROGUE FALLS. NO MORE MONGREL-I-ZATION OF THE NORTHWEST! MADAME, BECAUSE YOUR SIRE, JACK BENCHLEY, HAS POLLUTED THIS RESERVATION GOD BESTOWED ON THE ARYAN CHOSEN OF THE HUMAN

RACE HE HAS RECEIVED HIS JUST SENTENCE. TAKE YOUR ARTISTREE BACK TO WHERE YOU CAME OR YOUR COMEUPPANCE AWAITS YOU AND YOUR LITTER, INCLUDING YOUR SLUT AVALON IN ENGLAND. LEAVE!!!!!! YOU ARE NOT A RESPECTABLE FEMALE BUT A WHORE OF HOLLYWOOD JEWRY.

MOSBY'S RANGERS

I knew Mosby's Rangers had something to do with a Confederate officer and his band of Irregulars who raided the Shenandoah Valley during the Civil War. There were one or two small white-power hate groups in the area—one named in honor of Lawrence Webber's main guy, Jed Gasburg—but I had never heard of these clowns.

"Not the most laudatory fan letter I've ever received," Ann Benchley said. "I guess I'm supposed to be non-white because my mother was from Costa Rica." She made a huffing sound. "Shows you what those morons know about the world. Even if my mom had been African or Asian, what difference would that make? I've been around white people all my life, white supremacy is an oxymoron. Norville Hardy is trying to get me to think the FBI is on my side. I'm not buying that until they nail this guy Aarons for Carolyn's murder."

I looked over the letter again. "Have you had hate letters like this before—before your dad vanished?"

"Not lately. I told those Special Agents who were just here that we haven't had any problems from white supremacist groups in years. The Festival put on *Hamlet* a few years ago with an all- black cast and a play by an African-American author, Rita Dove, that won several international prizes. My dad got some angry letters and phone calls from anonymous idiots. There were a few Neanderthals who showed up in Shakespeare Plaza with home-made hate signs, but that's all died down. I told them about how you two confronted Warbeck at the museum and what happened afterward when you went back to that apartment."

"I hope you omitted our little after-hours' excursion to Warbeck's office," I said to Ms. Benchley. "What we tried to do there is usually something the Feds frown on."

"Unless it's the FBI itself who does the illegal wiretapping," she replied. "Don't worry, Mr. Wells. When I was born, my father was testifying as a hostile witness in front of the House Un-American Activities' Committee. Our phones were tapped for years at the express orders of a fellow named J. Edgar Hoover. That's not paranoia by the way. The records in my father's FBI file prove it. I've seen the reports myself, thanks to his lawyers and the Freedom of Information Act. I am a secretive person when it comes to most matters. I reward well those who follow my example."

"One of the people who worked for you was murdered, by the way," I said. "I just talked to Russ White. He's a city detective. He told me that Dave McCreedy's suicide was no suicide. I already figured that but the Sheriff's Department says it's official now. Somebody shot him with a gun similar to his and tried to make it look like it was his own gun. Somebody lured him to Cramner Creek and somehow got close enough to shoot him in the head."

I gave it to her as straight and cold as I could, to see what her reaction would be. She closed her eyes, her full lips bunched up tight. She shook her head, wrapped her arms around her stomach and drew a deep breath."

"Do they know who did it?" Ms. Benchley asked.

"No," I said. "I don't know if Bonnie told you, but somebody left a message on Dave's phone machine. The message had your voice on it. I only got to hear it once before somebody broke in on me in Dave's office. He cracked me on the head from behind and took the machine. It might have been this Aarons guy Bonnie and I dealt with last night. I can't be sure, though."

"I told Ann about the message," Bonnie said calmly. "I thought you'd like to see and hear the videotapes of the movies where the words that were spliced together came from."

Bonnie ejected *Breakfast at Tiffany's* from the VCR. For the next few minutes the three of us watched videotapes of short bits from four of Ann Benchley's past films. The lines she said were, as best I could remember, word for word what had been on Dave's phone message. Bonnie had stopped each tape at the point where her boss spoke the lines. After the short bits from the four movies were finished, it was Ann Benchley's turn to be cold and straight with me.

"Do you think I killed your friend, Mr.Wells?" she asked.

"No," I said, reserving some lingering doubts I had from being expressed until I had a better grip on the case. "I do think somebody wants to frame you for the job. Whoever did kill Dave knew you'd be out on your motorcycle late that afternoon—alone. Bonnie tells me you were out on the backroads on your Harley between five and seven on April the Fourth. That's pretty much the time window the Medical Examiner gave for Dave being shot. Did anyone see you at any time? Did you stop anywhere where other people could have seen you?"

"Are you saying Ann needs an alibi?" Bonnie asked.

"Not yet," I said. "But if, say, Warbeck had somebody kill Dave, he might make it real easy for the police to find that stolen tape with your voice on it. Then you'd need an alibi."

Ann Benchley took another sip from her drink, then spoke, "I don't remember the exact route I took that day but I try to stay clear of the public eye when I go out. Nobody saw me except for Ralph Bates, and Mr. Bates is an annoying man. I did the best I could to lose him, and I handle the roads around here a lot better than he can in the Kincaid's jeep."

"Kind of strange that a woman whose life had been threatened would try and ditch her bodyguard."

"Well, if your bodyguard is the incomparable Ralph Bates..." She stopped and took a drink. "I received the lout as a sort of present from my friend, Jack Picasso."

"What did he do to get on your bad side?"

"He made unwelcome references to my anatomy, told me I had a 'hot little bod'," Ann Benchley said, speaking the last three words in a derisive tone. "He said little remarks in a similar vein several times. I suppose he thought he was complimentary. I never felt threatened by him, but the effrontery of it was unbearable. Frankly, Ralph Bates wouldn't have stayed a minute under my employment after that first imprudent remark were it not for my father hiring him for the job. Apparently, they enjoy each other's company."

"You don't have to worry about Bates or Aarons," Bonnie said.

"Indeed," Ann Benchley said, "Bates, according to what Bonnie has told me, is apparently no more. He burned himself to death rather than be captured by the cops. Odd, don't you think."

"Very odd," I replied.

"He had to be working for Warbeck," Bonnie remarked. "He was the one who planted the bugs."

I turned and looked at Bonnie's boss.

"Where did you go on that motorcycle trip on April the fourth?" I asked.

"Nowhere near Bowman, if that's what you're thinking," the actress replied testily. Ann Benchley leaned back in her chair, folded her arms under her chest, and looked up at the ceiling. She looked like she had just spotted a large insect flying above her, but there was nothing there.

"I get up into the trails around the mountains," she said, before emitting a soft chuckle. "I go some places you're not even suppose to take a motorcycle. Usually I see somebody—backpackers or mountain bikers—but not often." She took another sip, more like a gulp, from the drink. She was starting to look upset.

"Ann," Bonnie said. "You have a show in a few hours."

"It's a very weak drink, Bonnie," Ann Benchley said. "Most of what's in here is chocolate milk. Honest."

"Ann," Bonnie said quietly but firmly, "you still have a show to do yet."

Without rebuttal, the actress slid the snifter away from easy reach on the table. She looked up at me. Her eyes bored into mine.

"I suppose you know that Dave and I saw a good deal of each other in the last few months. I suppose, since you were his friend, that he bragged a good deal about his being involved with me."

"He never mentioned it to me," I said. "I'm sure he knew I wouldn't think much of him for being involved with any woman other than Wendy."

"Oh, yes, Wendy," the actress said. "His wife, I presume?"

"Yes," I said. "I was also a friend of Dave's wife. Still am."

She gestured with her hand like the imaginary insect was still fluttering about her face. "But other people down there—his regular acquaintances in town—they must have known. One of them probably planted this nasty fake message on his machine."

"Were you and Dave ever in Bowman? Perhaps at the

local beauty salon up there?"

Ann Benchley's eyes bored into mine. "Perhaps... but not for months. What are you getting at, Wells?"

I told her about Wanda Truax and her story about Dave and a woman in a platinum blonde wig stopping at her shop.

"I sometimes go out in disguise," the actress said. "I remember Dave and I rode our motorcycles near Bowman back around Christmas. I think we did stop at a salon. I wanted him to get a hair trim and that was all that was open."

Ms. Benchley gulped hard, then stood up. For a second I noticed a trembling in her hands. She stopped the tremors by wrapping her arms against her ribcage. She looked disturbed. She drew a quick breath and started talking again.

"There was no real animosity between David and I when I broke it off. We had some fun here and down where I hang out in West L.A. David had found my son—my little man, the real man in my life—and I suppose that made me grateful to him. He treated me like a regular person. Not with the casual disrespect of a goon like Ralph Bates, and not like some Serene Highness, which I hate worse. Dave wasn't intimidated by me. It had been a long time since I found a man who was man enough to act that way. But we had our fun and I broke it off. The only reason he was back in my life was my hope that he could locate my father before the police did."

I spoke, "You didn't renew your...romance with Dave during this latest problem involving your father?"

"Is that any of your business, Mr. Wells?" Ann Benchley said tartly.

"No," I said. "But if that tape gets into the hands of the local cops, you'll have more to worry about from the law than the FBI trying to snow you on where they think your father is. I'm asking you these things so you can prepare yourself if the tape goes public."

Ann Benchley breathed deeply again, expelling the air from between clenched teeth.

"No," she said finally. "No, Dave and I didn't renew anything. He was an employee, just as you are. I hired him for his skill. I'm hoping some of that skill rubbed off on you. But Dave and I didn't get involved again. I've moved on to another relationship and Dave made it clear to me that he'd moved on, too."

Bonnie interjected, "Even if somebody turns the tape over to the police, that's not solid evidence. We can show that the tape is just bit and pieces from Ann's movies spliced together."

"Yes, but the case might still go to court," I said. "There's no telling about a jury. They might think you or Ann deliberately spliced the tape together yourselves to make it look like it was a frame-up. A good prosecutor might use that angle. The best defense against that tape would be someone who could put you away from Bowman during the timeline before and after Dave was killed. Don't forget that whoever killed Dave set it up to look like a suicide. They fired a bullet from Dave's gun into a tree down the creek not far from the crime scene. Why not fire Dave's gun into the air at a forty-five degree angle? Maybe the bullet would never be found. They didn't want it to go down that way. They wanted the police to find it sooner or later, run some ballistics tests, and disprove the suicide theory. That way it looks like a murder that some amateur tried to make look like a suicide."

"Bates," Ann Benchley said with the enthusiasm of someone who thinks she sees the light. "Ralph Bates, the jerk my father hired. Bates would have known I like to take long rides on my Harley after a Monday matinee."

Ann Benchley took another sip of her drink, then continued. "Now I've got this other thing hanging over my head, along with my father just vanishing." She tilted her head downward, rubbing her forehead with long slender fingers. Her eyelids suddenly shut tight, like a major headache was upon her. When she spoke again the tone was very near to being a shriek.

"All this hanging over my head and nobody can do a damn thing about it but blame me. God damn it! Goddamn all of you!"

Suddenly she lost control, her cursing rapidly becoming as rough as the English language would permit. She clenched her fists and started pounding a bookshelf—hard. Then the books started flying all over the room. They weren't directly aimed at either Bonnie or me but they were strewn by the dozens all around us in a very short time. Ann Benchley looked possessed. Her eyes were wild, her smooth brows now contorted, the skin creasing up on her, bulging up above the delicate bridge of her nose. Then came the full fury of the tantrum.

"Stupid damn bastards! The fucking Strunks are destroying me! I want somebody to do something about this. What the hell do I pay you people for?!"

More pounding against the shelves, like a spoiled child losing out on Christmas. Bonnie came over to Ann. With surprising swiftness, she grabbed her boss by the shoulders and shook her.

"Ann, don't do this," Bonnie said firmly. "This isn't going to help. Get control of yourself." Ann Benchley struggled free of Bonnie's grasp, turned her back on her assistant and stooped over one of the book shelves. She rested her head on the now empty shelf, both hands over her face. "I'm sorry," Ann Benchley said in a tone I could barely hear. I thought the actress would start to cry, but no tears came. After the meek apology, she slowly turned about and stood in the middle of the study. Her own arms wrapped back about her torso, she looked angry and lost. I looked at Bonnie. She had stepped back from her boss, a worried expression on her face. Ann Benchley breathed heavily, her eyes closed, her posture again stooped.

"So," I said, thinking it might be a good time to get back to the real world, "the gist is the FBI is either going to go chasing after a bunch of congenital morons up in Idaho or try and find your father in Mexico and, either way, come up with zilch while Warbeck flies off to London. What did the Feds say when you told them about Bonnie and I being attacked at the museum, and shot at by Aarons at the apartment?"

"Circumstantial evidence," Bonnie said, carrying on, as I was, as if Ms. Benchley's little tantrum was acceptable social behavior. "So far, the San Francisco field office says there is no link between Aarons and Warbeck, or Aarons and any associate with the IFH."

"Like they are really trying," Ms Benchley said bitterly, her eyes reddening. She turned around and reached for the Irish Coffee that was poised on the edge of the lamp table. She finished the drink in two gulps then slammed the glass down so hard I was afraid it would shatter in her hands. Bonnie said nothing.

"Warbeck and his bunch are in tight with the FBI Director," Ann Benchley fumed. "Warbeck has been going to that Forest of Arden V.I.P. campout for years, so has Norville Hardy. I begged my father to stay away from that place. It's an evil place. I lost my first husband there. I had to go through a terrible ordeal because I married into the Strunk family—the worst mistake of my life. I begged my father to stay away from the Strunks. Yet my bastard of a father goes anyway. 'Time to bury the hatchet', the old fool said." She looked up at the ceiling. The tears now came.

"Well, they b-b-buried the hatchet with you, Daddy," the actress sobbed. "Now the Strunks have set me up to face a murder charge. Does that make you happy, Daddy?" Both of her hands were balled into fists now and those fists were trembling. "And Daddy, you gullible bastard, they probably buried you along with it."

She threw her snifter across the room. It crashed into the books stored above the television set. "Bastards, lousy fucking bastards!" she shouted. The complexion of her face changed to beet-red. After the initial ranting subsided, she collapsed back into the chair and put her legs up, cradling herself and rocking like a child with too much energy and no place to go. It was frightening to see such a rapid and total loss of composure in an adult.

Ann Benchley kept her head down. She wasn't sobbing out loud anymore, but the trembling that had started in her hands was all over her body now. I looked to my associate to see what I should do.

"Give us a few minutes," Bonnie whispered, to my great relief. "There's a great view from the deck. Just go to your left and you'll see the French doors. I'll meet you there later."

I walked around the array of upended books on the floor of the study then turned left in the hallway and found my way to the redwood deck. I took a seat on an old-fashioned wooden patio chair with armrests as wide as a car bumper. The first thing I noticed was a large mound of earth that was piled up just across the lawn near the razor-wire fencing. Just in front of the mound was a metal pole shaped like a C-clamp. Hanging from the top end of the pole was a sheet of bullet-riddled plywood with the outline of a large man chalked on. There was a fresh piece of plywood laying on the lawn in front of the present target. The close grouping of nine millimeter bullet holes told me that Ann Benchley was a good target shooter.

To the left of the target line, here was a green sloping knoll in back of the house before the ground flattened out to what looked like a fire trail. Then the terrain rose again to a tree-covered hillside. The wind was kicking up and there was the smell of moss in the air. A large bird big enough to be a hawk swooped overhead in the air. The only noise that was man-made was the faint drone of a small aircraft flying somewhere beyond view. You wouldn't have even noticed it except for the surrounding quiet. I stood up and took in the vista of Kit Carson Canyon and the broad ribbon of dark blue-green water that flowed along below the steep tree-lined ridges. I could see where someone could get used to a place like this.

Off to the right of the main house, was a small tudor-style guest cottage.

From what Ray Harrison had told me when I visited him before leaving town, this was the little "sugar shack" where Dave and Ann Benchley got together. Dave probably came over when Wendy was staying with her mother in Klamath City.

After a few minutes Bonnie came out. She had a large circular metal can under one arm. Her eyes were shielded from the sun by a pair of aviator sunglasses. She first asked me if I wanted something to drink.

"No thanks," I said. "How's Ms. Benchley?"

"Better now," Bonnie said. "She hasn't been taking care of herself. I go away for a couple days and she stops taking her pills. She went to a local doctor last week for something to help her deal with her dad's disappearance. He told her to stop doing the play for a couple weeks. He doesn't know Ann would fall apart if she just sat around waiting. Now we dump this other thing on her. It's too much for her."

"Does she still want me for a bodyguard?"

"Most definitely," Bonnie said. "I know you have a regular job, but this will just be a few days duration until the security company down in Los Angeles can replace Ralph Bates." Bonnie licked her upper lip with her tongue. It was a pleasant sight.

"I called Zuma Oil, but there's nobody in the personnel department today," she said. "I'll try Monday morning. We'll find out if Mr. Bates was lying or not."

"Good idea," I said. "Can you fill me in on what a bodyguard is supposed to do for Ann Benchley?"

"Keep your eye on her and Tyler. There's a spare room for you just off the editing room. Mr. Benchley used to sleep there when he and his editor, Tony Harbeck, would do post-production. It's a little dusty now, but Mrs. Kirkland will give it a good once-over before we come back this evening." She glanced at her watch. "I guess I can take five," she said, taking a patio chair next to me. "Ann is lying down now."

"Think she's up for a performance tonight?"

"I hope so," Bonnie replied, gazing out toward the thick growth of pine trees on the hill opposite us. She pointed up at the crest of the hillside, at a clearing in the trees.

"That's where Mrs. Kirkland, the caretaker's wife, said she saw that big pick-up truck with the man in it. That was shortly before the break-in near the editing room."

"Too bad she didn't get a license plate on the truck," I said. "What exactly is it that's up there?"

"There is a fire trail up there. She said she could see a person sitting in the cab of the truck. That was about an hour before dusk. The next day the basement was broken into and the alarm system didn't go off. Like you said last night at dinner, whoever it was sitting in the truck probably had something to do with the break-in."

"She reported this to the sheriff's department, right?"

"Of course," Bonnie said. "They checked with the Bureau of Land Management people over there past the road. The rangers don't remember seeing a truck fitting that description. There are so many old lumber company roads in and out of these mountains that there's no way to catch someone who knows the area."

"Too bad she didn't get a license number," I said again for no good reason. The warm sun was slowly engulfed by a morass of pepper-colored rain clouds moving slowly up the river valley. Bonnie sat there watching the sight and I sat there watching Bonnie.

Bonnie drew a deep breath. "Beautiful little place, huh?" she said, watching the clouds floating over the river. A flight of a dozen Canadian Geese flew across the sky in a diagonal pattern. From the noise they made, it was easy to see why some people called them 'honkers.'

"It is very beautiful up here," I said. "Very peaceful. That looks like a reel of film you got there."

Bonnie nodded, tapping her fingers on the metal canister she had placed on an armrest. "This is the film footage Ann found down in her dad's editing room last night." She handed me the canister. It was about the size of a medium pizza, with a similar shape. There was a strip of masking tape across the top of the can with the words *First Viewing* written on the tape in black felt marker.

"First Viewing," Bonnie said, pushing her sunglasses slightly up the bridge of her nose. "Neither Ann nor I ever heard her dad mention that as the title for a project. Ann looked over the production stills from *Shakespeare and Essex and the Queen* this morning, by the way. None of the footage in this reel matches the sets or location work on that film."

I shook my head. "And you say that the film is film stock that's only a few years old?"

"For certain, Ann already gave one reel of the film to show Bea Ryskind. She's the Dramaturge of the Festival. She's also the acting Artistic Director."

"What is a Dramaturge?" I asked.

"Someone who's an expert on everything historical and cultural as it relates to theater," Bonnie said. "She helps out the directors on period details and historical background. One of Bea's specialties is European architecture. There's a small screening room that is used to show a brief film about the history of the Festival for tourists who go through the little museum there. It's down for renovation now. Bea's probably screening the footage right now. We can go over to the screening room and find out what Bea determined when we go to the festival."

"And what is Bea Ryskind supposed to determine?"

"Well, hopefully she can say where in the hell Mr. Benchley shot that footage. It has to be somewhere in Europe. Ann thinks maybe Ireland. Bea has prowled around Europe a good deal since her husband died. Maybe she can recognize where these places are. Let's hope so."

There was a pause.

"You really look...sharp in those sunglasses," I said impulsively.

Bonnie's elfin nose crinkled up. "Thank you," she said, favoring me with a smile.

I felt another impulse, an impulse to take Bonnie in my

arms. Her lips were looking soft and moist and I thought she wanted to be kissed.

Bonnie must have sensed my feelings. Our eyes locked together.

"Bonnie!" came a shrill cry. It was her mistress' voice.

Our eyes unlocked. "I need, ah, I need to check on Ann."

Chapter Twenty-Two

Ann Benchley recovered well enough, by Bonnie's estimations, to do her Cleopatra that evening. We left the ranch just after six o'clock.

The three of us reached the public parking area above the Shakespeare Plaza. I was behind the wheel in Mr. Kirkland's red Jeep Cherokee, with Bonnie in the passenger seat and Ann in the backseat, her loaded handgun—I had watched her load it— in her purse. I was half-expecting Russ White and a couple uniformed officers to be there, to take Ann Benchley into custody for questioning. I expected that Russ would catch up to Lawrence Webber and get out of him through good old fashioned police coercion ,what I couldn't get out of the old goat with food and money. I hoped Webber had seen the woman who probably killed Dave, but I hoped she wasn't either Ann Benchley, for financial reasons, or Wendy, for that matter.

But there were no police waiting in the gathering twilight when we arrived at the parking lot. Instead, a television news crew was waiting to ambush Ann Benchley. A petite Asian-American journalist and a slender pony-tailed white guy carrying a video camera approached the actress. Figuring this was the sort of intrusion my employer might not want, I got to her side as quickly as I could park the truck and get out.

"It's okay," Ms. Benchley told me when I got between her and the news crew as she exited the vehicle. Then she turned her attention to the reporter. "You're Annie Chou, aren't you?"

"Yes, Ms. Benchley, I'm with Channel Nine News," she replied.

"I watch you on the Noon News all the time," the actress said.

"Thank you," the reporter replied, somewhat thrown by a compliment from a celebrity she was supposed to ambush. Ms. Chou recovered quickly, however.

"Ms. Benchley, I want to get your reaction to the developments in San Francisco. We have a report that the police have a strong suspect in the death of Carolyn Mason, the woman seen with your father just before he vanished. In light of newspaper reports that your father was a suspect in her murder, how do you—"

"I can't comment, Annie," Ms. Benchley interjected. "The FBI is keeping me informed of all developments. Beyond that I can only repeat what I have previously stated publicly. If someone has information leading to the whereabouts of my father, there is a three-hundred-fifty-thousand-dollar reward the family is offering for his safe return. Did you get that?" She directed the last remark to the cameraman.

"Yes, ma'am," was his reply.

"Thank you," Bonnie said to the reporter. "Ms Benchley is late for an appointment." Ms. Chou tried another question, but Ms. Benchley moved quickly past the cameraman and headed at a deliberate pace, with Bonnie and I a step behind on either side of her, toward the set of concrete steps that led up to the Festival Offices.

I had pictured Bea Ryskind, the Dowager Empress of the Northwest Shakespeare Festival, to be a pale, bird-like woman with thick glasses and bad teeth. My expectations were off. She was short and busty, maybe in her seventies, with a rosy and robust glow about her. She had perfectly straight teeth (very white) warm brown eyes devoid of prescription eyewear, and a slight accent I placed as coming from New York City. She offered to shake my hand upon Bonnie formally presenting us. Her grip was strong, but it still harbored the velvet texture of a woman's skin. The four of us stood in a small circle between the imposing desk and the glass-enclosed display case.

"Have you heard anything more on Jack," Ms. Ryskind asked Ms. Benchley.

"We have a suspect in the Mason death, but no sign of my dad. Not yet at least."

The older woman emitted a deep sigh. "I pray to God he's

all right," she said.

"We all do," Ann Benchley replied. "Well, Bea, what do you think of the footage?"

"Well, indeed?" the older woman said. "I sat through the footage twice. I think I can give some idea where your father shot this work. I'm afraid it's hard to explain *how* he photographed it."

"I've only got a few minutes before I'm due in make-up," Ms. Benchley said, glancing at the digital watch on her wrist. "You've seen the film now, Bea. So what do you think?"

Ms. Ryskind walked over to the desk. On one corner was a pile of thick books. She pulled one of the books, a cloth-bound edition, out from the middle of the pile. As she came back to our group, she opened the book at a page that had been bookmarked. The tome was frayed at the corners and looked to have been repeatedly thumbed through.

"Here it is," she stated, setting the open book down on the display case. Her index finger directed our attention to a half-page illustration. It was a sketch of a combination castle and manor house. The castle part was a large keep, or tower, with two tiers of tooth shaped parapets at the top. It was probably 150 feet high if the scale of the drawing was correct. Surrounding this was the manor portion of the structure which seemed to have been built out from the tower. On each side was a structure about two-thirds as high as the tower. This looked newer, with windows, gables and a sloping roof that appeared to be tiled. On each end was a circular tower very close in design to the rook-like structures at the entrance to the Benchley Ranch. Several tall brick chimneys jutted out from various positions along the roof line. The foreground of the drawing featured a broad expanse of green field dotted with bushy fruit trees. In the extreme foreground was a body of water with a shoreline marked by more trees and a thick marsh. A man was pictured in the marsh holding an antique rifle or a fishing pole, I was not sure which. Two large dogs were also in the sketch, chasing about on the field between the water and the estate.

"I recognize this," Bonnie said. "This estate is featured a good deal in Mr. Benchley's footage. Matter of fact one of his longest takes is almost at this exact perspective. The person who did this sketch could have done this from a blow-up of a frame of film he shot."

"So, where is this place?" Ms. Benchley asked. "I thought maybe one of the converted Norman keeps in Wales or Ireland."

"No, this is in England," Ms. Ryskind replied, putting on a pair of wire-rimmed glasses. "Not very far from London. Rather close to Hampstead. But I'm being misleading. It is not a question of where this is. The correct pronoun is when, not where." She let that last statement sink in for a few moments, then continued.

"The sketch we are looking at is of an estate called Grantum Hall. It was built during the reign of Henry VIII. Actually, the central tower goes back to the late twelfth century and the reign of Henry II. Anyway, Henry VIII prosecuted and beheaded a certain Thomas Langston, Earl of Grantum, who made the mistake of paying undue attention to Henry's second wife, Anne Bolyen. Either that or he was framed by Henry's ministers because of the King's desire to change wives and plant a treason rap on poor Anne. Whatever it was, Henry confiscated all lands Langston had and gave them over to a land-poor hawking and jousting buddy of his, by the name of Mortimer Devant. Devant was made Earl of Grantum."

The phone on the desk rang. Bonnie responded to it. "Nina is ready for you in make-up," she told her employer.

"Bea, cut to the chase here," Ms. Benchley said.

"All right, Ann," Ms. Ryskind said. "This sketch was done by an artist named Wenceslaus Hollar. He did the famous panorama of London around 1647. This sketch is the only known representation of Grantum Hall. The only representation, period."

The two other ladies looked puzzled, and I felt puzzled. "So this is a sketch of an estate..." I stopped there.

"That doesn't exist," Bonnie added.

Ms. Ryskind nodded. "It did exist of course. Up until the late 1660's. In 1667 Mortimer DeVant's great-great grandson, Charles DeVant, the last Earl of Grantum, had to sell Grantum Hall because he was so deeply in debt. The estate was bought for a portion of its actual worth by King Charles II. Four years later he gave it to a friend of his. The friend, Sir Anthony Culvert, had it torn down and rebuilt by an Italian architect in the Palladian style. That place is called Sobel House."

"And is owned today by Sherwood Strunk," Bonnie added.

"I won't bore you with architectural history. Suffice to say the new estate bears no resemblance to the one in this sketch. None whatsoever. I would say this footage would have been impossible to photograph. Ordinarily that is."

Again, Bea Ryskind let her last statement sink in for a few moments.

Ann Benchley shook her head. "Bea, I love you almost as much as I loved my mother. But don't play games with me, darling. If you know something..."

"Ann," the older lady said, "it's time you knew something about your father and my late husband. But I must only tell you. Bonnie and this gentleman must leave the room."

Bonnie and I got up and went out of the office and into the hallway. But we both stayed close the door.

"Do you have a clue on this?" I asked.

"No," Bonnie said.

We couldn't hear anything through the door but Bea Ryskind saying something unintelligably soft, just above a whisper. Then Ann Benchley yelled something clear enough to be heard by anyone in the hallway who was not stone deaf.

"You have got to be fucking kidding me!" She repeated the phrase twice more, each time at a higher pitch.

"Somehow, I don't think Bea is fucking kidding her," Bonnie said quietly to me.

Chapter Twenty-Three

When Ann Benchley left Bea Ryskind's office after about ten minutes, she looked like she had seen a ghost. She turned to Bonnie, her eyes looking like those of a little girl lost in a shopping mall.

"Take me to my dressing room," she said to her assistant. "Wells, Bea needs you to do something for her in the office. Take care of that, then get over to my dressing room yourself."

It turned out that Bea Ryskind wanted me to draw the platform that Ralph Bates used to burn himself up on. As I drew the image on the blank sheet of paper she had, I told her about my being knocked to the ground by some sort of powerful force emulating from the platform and the intense light.

"And it left a large burn mark on the ground in the alley you say?"

"Yes," I told her.

"And no explosion, and you weren't burned?"

"Right," I said.

"Thank you, Mr. Wells," the older lady said. "You better get back to keeping an eye on Ann and Bonnie."

"How about letting me in on what all this is about, Mrs. Ryskind?"

She shook her head. "If Ann wants you to know, you'll find out. Good-bye Mr. Wells."

I closed the office door behind me and headed for the back stage.

There was a general make-up room in the hallway on the other side of Ann Benchley's private one. Nina, the frail-looking Asian make-up artist, shuttled back and forth between make-up rooms. She was apparently helping out in both places.

"She's a little better today," Nina whispered to me on one occasion as she exited the star's chamber. "Must be a bigger dose of Lithium," she whispered as she closed the door.

Lithium medication meant one thing to me: manic depression. Judging by Ann Benchley's wild mood swings...

My thought pattern about the strange film footage and all the other weird developments was interrupted by the appearance of a heavy-set white guy about my age and size—with two-tone light and dark blonde hair—who came right over to the door I was supposed to be guarding. He had light brown eyes, or at least they looked light thanks to the fluorescent lighting in the hallway. His eyes darted about, very alert to his surroundings, the look of somebody who could be wired. His face was pale, too pale, like he slept his days away in a coffin. There was a prominent nose, heavy on cartilage at the tip, to go with the darting eyes. To say he was dressed in an odd manner was to err on the side of understatement. He wore a black leather jacket that hung down to his knees, with a black belt loosely tied around his thick waist. The jacket had a set of large metal buttons down the middle—two of them undone at the top to display some chest hair and the crew neck of a dark purple t-shirt—and oversized zippers on the two sets of diagonal pockets at his midsection. His hair hung down to his shoulders, which made up for his receding forehead.

He was trying for that Young Thor look, but he was too old and thick about the waist to pull it off. I guess he would have been considered a tough-looking guy in some districts, but I knew the real tough ones didn't draw attention to themselves in dress or hairstyle. He was a show, not a threat.

And he was breezing right past me to the principal performer's door. Or trying to.

"Hello," I said, putting a stiff arm move on his shoulder. "I think you have the wrong door." The dude looked at my hand on his jacket like I had put a dripping paint brush on him.

"Do you know who I am?" the dude said.

"No," I said. "State your business."

"Who the fuck are you?"

"Name's Wells. Harvey Wells. Now, let me have the pleasure of knowing your name."

"I'm not telling you shit, little man," was the reply. He was an inch taller than I was, if that. He gave me a look I hadn't seen since I saw Anthony Hopkins behind bars in *Silence of the Lambs*. "I'm here to see Ann. You're in my way."

"Take a long walk elsewhere," I said. But my newest pal stayed right where he was, and still made with the Mad Ghoul look. "Step back," I said firmly.

"Fuck yourself," he retorted. He made a move to go by me. I stiff-armed him again. He suddenly felt an urge to try and push my hand off him. This was okay with me because I had another hand. I grabbed his outstretched arm, pulled him forward, dropped myself to one knee, and leveraged his off-balance legs over my bent knee. A second later he was flat on his back and I was ready to give him a quick chop to his larynx to chill him out. The thing that stopped me was Bonnie's voice from way down the hall.

"Stop," she cried. "Everybody stop right there!" Her exclamation brought out a passel of actors dressed in togas and scantily-clad harem outfits from the near-by dressing rooms. All of their eyes were on Bonnie and then turned to two grown men who were poised like two kids in a playground tussle.

"Hello, Jack," was Bonnie's reply to the leather-clad man sprawled across the floor. "We weren't expecting you. Harvey, would you help pick Jack Picasso up, please?"

I did so. So this was Jack Picasso, the film director and Ray Harrison's former colleague in porno movies. I had read and heard about him, of course, but I couldn't recall ever seeing him in a photograph. After I helped him up, he cast another nasty look at me in the way of thanks and turned his attention to Bonnie.

"Mr. Wells is an investigator," Bonnie said to Picasso. "Right now he's our security. Ann has received threats."

"I'm on my way to a prison up in Washington State to scout locations," Mr. Picasso replied. "I decided to forego the studio jet and drive it. I was going in to see Ann when this character..." He shot a glance at me that communicated excessive disgust.

"I'm just doing my job," I said. "Nobody told me to expect..."

The door behind me opened. Ann Benchley, clad in a fleecy white robe and wearing her brunette wig, appeared. Her expression was one of radiating pleasant surprise.

"Jack!" she exclaimed. "What are you doing here? I thought you were up in Tacoma." Jack repeated his story, then was permitted inside the room, but not before giving me yet another nasty look.

"I guess this is where I lose my job," I said to Bonnie once the door was closed.

"That's not likely," Bonnie said. "Maybe if you had just let him in, it would have been bad for you. Jack Picasso is a..." She lowered her voice. "He's a forty-something punk. At least he got rid of that razor blade earring he had down in L.A."

"He's got his own look," I said. "He looks like Howard Stern meets Dracula."

"Precisely," Bonnie said. She wiggled a couple of fingers at me, a signal for both of us to move away from the door. I followed her over to the opposite wall.

"That, for the moment, is Ann's designated swain." Shortly after Bonnie said this she rolled her eyes upward. The effect was cute, and told me all I needed to know about Jack Picasso.

After we went down the hallway, Bonnie continued: "Jack came up here to see Mr. Benchley and Ann, mostly to see Ann, about five months ago. That's when Mr. Picasso found out Ann was having an affair with your friend Dave. He wasn't happy about the competition, but Ann and Dave were a real item back then. Jack had left his wife and I think he wanted Ann to hive him some romantic attention."

From the hallway we could hear the sounds of Ann laughing. A couple seconds later Nina walked out. She shut the door. "She's done," Nina said.

"Indeed," I said quietly.

"She's not serious about him," Bonnie half-whispered to me. I caught a whiff of her perfume as she edged closer to me, her shoulder resting almost against mine. The proximity gave me a twinge of desire in my stomach and points south.

"So, why does she hang out with him, again? Something to do with her career?"

"He wants to do the sequel to *She Came to Europa*," Bonnie said. "Cintricity Studios has given him the green light, as long as he gets Ann for the lead. That's one project where she is considered a reliable box-office star. Something about Ann in a tight-fitting spacesuit cradling a snazzy-looking anti-matter blaster just draws in the male audience. Some women dig that butch stuff, too. Ann owns the movie rights to all the Belle Killroy books—she bought all six in the series from the lady who wrote the novels—and the only way Jack can get this project off the ground is with her."

"So this romance is all business then."

Bonnie frowned. "No, it's not that simple, nor that sordid. Ann and Jack have known each other since they were kids. Jack's father was Silvio Malatesta and he worked with Jack Benchley on a few projects. Of course, you know all this because you read Mr. Benchley's book. From what Ann told me, they had a little fling together in Spain when her dad and Mr. Malatesta were making *Essex and the Queen*. They were kids, of course, so it never got serious. They stayed in touch over the years though, and partied with the same crowd down in L.A. It is true that Jack needs a hit movie bad, and this *Europa II* or whatever they're calling it is almost pre-sold big box-office. And he wants her to do this other weird picture, *Forget Me Not*.

"The remake of *Marnie*," I said. "Where Ann Benchley gets to play a sexually-frigid office secretary who's a kleptomaniac."

"Yes," Bonnie said, sounding dismissive. "Maestro Picasso's contribution to the Cinema of Misogyny. The script is plain bad. I told you the basics: Ann's a mid-level corporate executive who gets sent to prison for stealing money from her company and this male prison warden marries her after she's pardoned and tries to thaw her out. The notion of a sexually-frigid woman is old-fashioned pop psychology garbage. Picasso wants to get Mel Gibson to play the warden. Somehow I don't think that's going to happen. He hasn't even obtained the rights from Universal yet. By the way, Harvey, do you have a valid passport?"

"Why?" I asked.

Before Bonnie could answer Ms. Benchley and her director came out of the dressing room.

"Good job, Mr. Wells," my employer said. "I'm glad you're not letting every lounge lizard in a leather coat gain access to my private chambers."

"Part of the job," I said. "I didn't know anyone would drop by." I noticed Jack Picasso only had eyes for his girlfriend, which was fine with me.

"C'mon, Jack," Ms. Benchley said provocatively. "I'll show you how the costume looks."

"Lead on," said the writer-director-punk.

Bonnie and I followed the pair to another room at the end of the hall. On the way we passed a contingent of men dressed in the sort of medieval battle garb I had seen on the tour. Loud metallic clanking echoed in the hallway. "Hi, Peter," Bonnie said to one fellows who was wearing an obviously false beard, a chainmail uniform and a helmet with a nose protector hanging down from the cone-shaped rim. Pete twirled his twin-edge battle-ax in reply.

"Dress rehearsals tonight for *Henry VI, Part One* Bonnie told me, sensing my curiosity. "That opens this season at the Elizabethan next month. We're rotating all three plays at The Lizzie this year."

While Ms. Benchley and Picasso did whatever they were doing in the fitting room, I was outside in the hall again. Bonnie asked again about passports.

"I think my old passport is valid for three more years. Am I going somewhere?"

"London," Bonnie said. "Ann hasn't told me much about what Bea said to her. But she wants me to get us on the next flight to San Francisco, then onto England. Ann wants to see Major Trubshawe right away. Are you game? She needs protection from Warbeck's goons and the media."

"Sure," I said. "I'm your guy."

Actually, the thought of flying across the Atlantic 36,000 feet in the air made my stomach churn. I had taken one aircraft flight in my life: a honeymoon excursion to Jamaica with my ex-wife. I almost tried to jump out of the 747 before take-off and vomited three times—twice going and once coming back—on the airplane. It did nothing to temper my fear of heights. I was still recovering psychologically from it seven years later.

Inspired by the photograph in Jack Benchley's study, I ventured a probing question. "Does Ann, that is Ms. Benchley, ever talk about what happened to her mother?"

"You mean the accident she was in in Costa Rica, the one

that killed Maria Benchley?"

I nodded.

"Never," Bonnie said. "The gutter press tried to make it sound like it was Ann's fault of course. I don't know if she or her mother was driving. I do know it was the rainy season at Maria's family *finca*—that's a cattle ranch in Spanish—up in the mountains. They were driving down the mountains to do some shopping in Cartago. A mud slide came down and washed the car right off the road. I don't know how Ann managed to get out of the vehicle. The family Maria came from kept the police from having a public inquest. Ann was only seventeen, on holiday from boarding school in England. Imagine what losing a mother at that age does to a girl."

"I can't," I said.

"I can't either—yet," Bonnie said. "Between that accident and what happened to her and her first husband, that Talbot Strunk guy, I wouldn't blame her for being terse with anybody from the media."

"Doesn't she have a daughter by Talbot Strunk?"

"You mean Avalon?" Bonnie said. "She's in England, at the Palmerston Prep School. That's the same one Ann attended before she went to Stanford. Truffie, that's Major Trubshawe, and his wife keep an eye on her. The Strunk family pays half her fees in exchange for her fraternal grandmother getting to see her a couple weeks a year. Ann has no contact with the Strunk family. Zero. The payments and the visits are all handled by her lawyer."

A young, full-figured woman clad in a long, clingy dress of maroon-colored velvety material passed us. She was wearing a silvery crown and was rubbing her hands together, headed in the same direction as the metal clad men. A distant look was in her eyes. As she went by I noticed her lips moving slightly. She looked like Marilyn Monroe on a crash diet.

"Looks like Queen Margaret is still getting her lines down," Bonnie said after the woman passed. "Say, I'm going to get a sandwich at the deli down the street. Can I get you anything?"

I gave her a five for a turkey sandwich and a bag of potato chips. When she returned a quarter of an hour later, Ann and Jack Picasso were still in the fitting room. Bonnie came back with a cardboard tray of food and a couple diet cokes.

She also had two newspapers under her arm. I brought over two chairs with attached desktops on one arm over from the near-by performers' lounge area. We sat beside one another classroom-style. As we ate, we shared the newspapers, *The San Francisco Examiner* and our own *Rogue Falls Daily News*, both afternoon papers.

The capture of Charles Lindsey Aarons and how it related to Jack Benchley's disappearance got a big article in the San Francisco Paper. San Francisco Homicide had a press leak, either deliberate or clandestine, which supplied the news organization with a source 'close to the investigation.' The unnamed source of the story tied Aarons to "unnamed white supremacist groups in the Pacific Northwest. This information is reportedly what Aarons himself told investigators."

"Maybe there is something to the Nazi-American angle," I said to Bonnie as we exchanged front sections of the newspapers. "I mean, we know IFH puts out books and newsletters sympathetic to the political extremes. Somebody in Warbeck's organization probably recruited members of some Far-Right fringe groups to go after Benchley. After all, his father was blacklisted in the late forties and fifties. And Jack Benchley has lent his name to civil rights groups and certain politicians who were anti-establishment types."

"He's lent more than his name," Bonnie said. "Don't forget he was Chief Media Consultant to Senator Barbara Wasserman, the woman who beat Warbeck for the Senate down there. I think you're half right. IFH probably did recruit some Nazi-geeks to do the dirty work on Carolyn Mason. But I'll bet Charles Lindsay Aarons sincerely believed he was working for some secret organization of white supremacists. He has no idea Warbeck is the guy providing payment for his dirty work. Warbeck would only deal indirectly with lowbrow racists through a go-between he could disavow, especially where murder is concerned."

A large brunette woman with a radio headset on came waddling down the hall. She rapped smartly on the fitting room door. "Five minutes to curtain, Ms. Benchley," the woman said. A couple seconds later, the Queen of the Nile came out of the room. Her real-life Mark Anthony followed. Bonnie stood up. As she did, she reached over, picked up the front section of the local paper off my desk and quickly folded it up.

"Is that *The Examiner?*" Ms. Benchley asked. Bonnie handed her boss the front section of the San Francisco paper. Cleopatra gave it a glance for thirty seconds or so, no doubt gleaming the main points about the break in the Mason murder.

"The *Daily News* story is pretty much a rehash of this," Bonnie said. "The gist of it all is the same line the FBI gave us. They think your dad is in the hands of some white hate group."

Ms. Benchley handed back the paper. "Figures," was her only remark on the news story.

She handed the section back to her assistant, then turned her attention to me.

"Wells, I have need of your services in London. Can you be ready by morning, passport and all?"

I nodded my head.

"Bonnie, I want you to take Jack here to a seat in the front row. And make sure it's the front row." She turned and cocked her slender neck back, shook the long and sensuous tresses of her brunette wig and batted her heavily-accentuated eyelids before speaking to me again.

"Wells, you follow me, please. I'll put you in the wings over by backstage right. Don't get in any of the performers' way, and don't step out onto the stage unless some clown from the audience attacks me or you decide you're a better Octavius Caesar than the mumbling amateur thespian dear, dear Roger selected for the part." She placed the tiara with the cobra design on the top of her forehead. That crown, her long brunette wig, and the form-fitting butternut leather costume she wore made her look every centimeter an image of a female erotic power.

"One more show tonight, and then we're off to England to bring back my father, come hell or highwater." She planted a quick kiss on Picasso's scruffy cheek. "See you after the show, lover. Bonnie, show my boy where he's sitting, will ya? You did get him a front row seat, right?"

"Right," Bonnie said. "The one the box office keeps in reserve until the last minute."

"Great," Cleopatra said. "And, Bonnie, call Mrs. Kincaid and see if she can look after Tyler for me for a few days. C'mon,

Wells, let's go. We're burning limelight."

Chapter Twenty-Four

Bonnie came backstage after escorting Jack Picasso to his seat. We watched the tragedy unfold together from the wings. Or, rather, I took in the travails of Tony and Cleo while Bonnie opened up her IBM laptop computer and, after securing a desk, tapped out some professional correspondence on behalf of her boss. While she did that, I dropped in a few personal questions between the short, formal paragraphs she was composing out of Ms. Benchley's scrawled notes to her agent, her publicity manager, financial consultants, legal representative, two producers, and a woman who ran the Famous Personalities Autographic Company in Newtown, Connecticut, who wanted her to part with any personal letters she might have from her father in exchange for generous remuneration. The latter request was politely declined.

I learned Bonnie had been married back in the early eighties to a fellow actor who looked a great deal like John Lennon, but it only lasted a few years. The actor, a guy named Paul Rhodes whom I had never heard of, was now playing a doctor on a daytime soap, *Restless Lives*, which was taped in New York. They had met during an audition for a Sam Shepherd play in New York. Neither got their respective parts, but they did get each other. That union had produced her daughter, Angie. Bonnie enjoyed the cosmopolitan milieu of New York City, where the couple lived before the divorce, but she always angled to get back to 'The Coast' because the weather in California was more to her liking. She met her second husband, a guy named Jim who was an engineer for the San Francisco Water District, while appearing with the American Conservatory Theater in that city. "He was a better father to Angie than the natural father was," she remarked.

"How does a lady from the fine arts meet up with a chemical engineer in the civil service?"

"The same place all great romances start," she replied. "We were stuck together in a glass elevator at the Pan-American Hotel. Jim, myself, and Peggy. She's a friend of mine from my wicked college days. The two of us were on our way to do lunch at the revolving restaurant on the 28th floor. Jim was our fellow prisoner for forty-five minutes while the guys from the building maintenance crew tried to get us out."

"I'm glad I wasn't along on that ride. The 28th floor is a little high for me."

"It was giving me the willies, too. My claustrophobia was getting to me. If that elevator hadn't been made of glass, I would have freaked. I never take elevators now if I can avoid them. Anyway, I got to talking with Jim. I was casually seeing some other guy, but that was going nowhere. Jim was good for me. He had a strong sense of self and a great sense of humor. Plus he was from Scotland, Glasgow, and had an accent that made me weak at the knees."

"You must be a big Sean Connery fan," I said.

"He's my second favorite movie actor," she said, putting the finishing touches on a letter. "Sean comes right after Basil Rathbone."

"Basil-?" I muttered. "You mean the dead guy who played Sherlock Holmes?"

Bonnie rolled her eyes. "Why does everyone think that's so weird? Yes, he's dead now, but he was alive and he's still in all those movies. I guess it is weird, but back to the elevator."

"Yes, the elevator."

"After we got out, I was ready to faint from being enclosed for so long. I was leaning against the hostess' podium at the restaurant. Jim was going to eat there—turned out he was on a blind lunch date—and when Peggy took off to throw herself at some other guy she'd met before, he asked for my number. I never just give out my number to a guy I've just met—not as a rule at least—but I was so weak and I liked his eyes and his voice and he had cracked some great jokes while we were stuck—"

"How long before the wedding?" I asked.

"Six months," she said. "Yes, I was insane. I swore off marriage after Paul and I broke up when I was back in New York. But I had eleven good years with Jim. The seventh year, when his drinking got the best of him, that was bad."

"Did he lose his job?"

"How did you know?" she asked.

"Lucky guess," I said.

During the play, when 'Anthony' was meeting with 'Octavian' in what was supposed to be Rome around 35 BC, Ms. Benchley was back in her dressing room. Bonnie went to join her so her boss could check over the letters. I followed them, and stood guard as before. A few minutes later Bonnie came out again. She walked up the stairway toward the stage entrance and, a few seconds later, walked back.

"Ann's worried," she said to me.

"I am too," I said, anticipating a trans-Atlantic flight. "Anything specific?"

"Jack," she said. "She noticed Jack isn't in his seat. She checked a few times during the scene. Jack never showed. I just checked from the wings. He's still not there."

"Probably in the latrine," I said.

"He doesn't take that long, according to Ann. She's worried about him. She doesn't want to go back on stage and not know where he is. She's afraid he's, uh, doing, ah..."

"Smoking a Havana cigar in the Plaza? Don't worry. I don't think the local cops are going to enforce the Cuban Embargo Act."

"All I know is that she's worried. She wants you to try and find him."

First I was a detective. Then a bodyguard. Now an errand boy?

"He did drugs for years," Bonnie said quietly. "Jack told Ann he was clean now, but that might not be the truth. Ann's afraid he's taking a hit somewhere."

"Do I bust him or try to get him into the Betty Ford Clinic?"

"Just find out where he is, what he's doing. I'd do it myself, but if he is in the Men's Room..."

"Keep the door locked until I get back," I said. I checked

to make sure nobody was in the corridor, then pulled out my revolver. I handed it to Bonnie.

"I can't guard Juliet and play hide-and-seek with Romeo all at once," I said. "Can you use this?"

"I don't know very much about these," she said. "I'm strictly a pepper-spray girl. Ann's the high-velocity shooter around here. I'll give it to her."

I went up the stairs, then down a corridor perpendicular to the one that led to the stage. Then I pushed open both of the double-wide emergency exits. I was now in the carpeted stairway that led to the spectator seating. It took me three seconds to track down Jack Picasso. He was shoved against the wall of the stairway just under an arch-shaped niche where a large copper bust of Shakespeare was situated.

The man pushing his back to the wall was his bigger relative, Ray Harrison. It didn't look like a tender reunion of artistic collaborators.

"Hey guys," I said lightly. "Need a referee?"

Ray relaxed the grip he had on Picasso's jacket. The smaller man dropped down from the wall a couple inches, straightened himself out and tried to get his composure back. His fear level reduced, he summoned up his haughty exterior.

"Did she send you looking for me?" Picasso asked with a sneer.

"Something like that," I said. "Well, I found you, so now I'm going to the can." I walked toward the lobby, descending the near-by stairway.

Picasso called after me. "Who's watching her?"

I turned around on the stairway. "I got my best woman on it. Might help Ms. Benchley's confidence if you got back to your seat. That's the message." I turned away.

When I returned from the lobby, Picasso was gone. Ray was still there, talking to a pretty young brunette with waist-length hair, an usher in black slacks and a white blouse. He was telling her he once worked for the Festival, and was waiting for his 'date' to come back from the 'powder room.' When I returned, the willowy, dark-haired vision then opened up one of the wide double doors that led to the theater. I caught a snatch of dialogue from the stage as she opened the doors: Marc Anthony was going to marry Octavian's sister, for all the good that would do The Second Triumvirate.

"Great body," Ray said to me just as the doors closed. I'd like to make a plaster bodycast out of her. And then add a little foam rubber molding."

Just the thing for those long winter nights," I said. "I take it your lady is with you."

"Kathy's here," Ray said. "We got here late. She went to the bathroom while we were waiting to be seated."

"Didn't know you and Picasso were so close," I said. "Why were you putting his back to the wall?"

"Because he called me a loser," Ray said. "Because I tried to introduce him to Kathy and he stiffed her. Because he was a wanker years ago and he's still a wanker. Christ, I showed him all the ropes when I directed that *Murders in the Rue Morgue* movie and now he comes on like he's Lucky Luciano to me. He's lucky you came along—I would have schooled him."

"Time passes," I said. "Best to let all that shit go. He's not worth an assault charge."

Ray nodded his head. I asked if he had contacted Wendy.

"Rochelle's over at Wendy's tonight. Older sister giving her support and all that. The news of Dave being murdered really blew apart the recovery she was starting to make."

"Too bad," I said. "I don't think Ann Benchley bumped Dave off. If I did I wouldn't be working for her."

"Tell that to Wendy," Ray said. "You better wait until Rochelle isn't around."

"Or you," I said.

Ray smirked. "I call it as I see it. I hope you're right and the big diva didn't pull the trigger, but she did something like it in her past. Which reminds me, if you're finished with the book on Hollywood scandals? I'd like to get it back pretty soon."

"To show Wendy?" I asked.

"To show Kathy," he said. "I'd appreciate it if you could get it back to me in the next couple days. And the videos you borrowed from my collection."

The movies I had borrowed from Ray—the original *Frankenstein* with Boris Karloff and David Lean's *Bridge Over the River Kwai*—had slipped my mind.

"By the way, I was hoping you could do me a favor, Harvey."

"I'll try."

"I did an audition video featuring Kathy. It's legitimate, there's no sex stuff. I'd like to get it to Ann Benchley. Picasso wouldn't help Kathy. I'd like to bypass that and get it to Ann. She'd love to have a small part in Ann's next Belle Killroy movie. Seeing that Kathy was a stand-in for Ann in a movie down at Universal, she can at least look at it."

"O.K." I said. "I'll get the tape to Bonnie Noel. ASAP."

"Thanks, Harvey. You're a regular mate. Make sure Ann Benchley sees it. I think she'll be very surprised."

"How's your dominatrix deal working?"

"Wanda the Warrior had her maiden client last night. Things went quite well. Got one customer up for tomorrow night," Ray said. "That lobbyist coming up from Sacramento. I normally wouldn't set foot at the Festival, not after what they did to me, but Kathy wanted to see Ann Benchley live and so I thought I'd give her the treat. I'm trying to keep Kathy happy. If I get enough clients, and I get the price I want for the house, it's good-bye Oregon and hello England."

I saw Kathy Quisted, alias the Turkish Dominatrix, heading toward us up the stairway. Her tall and slender form was adorned in a sensible purple top and black slacks, with a sweater tied in a loose knot about her neck.

After a quick hello, Ms. Quisted and her escort for the evening went back into the auditorium.

Chapter Twenty-Five

There was little sleep for the wicked, or anyone else in the Benchley orbit, that night at the Benchley Ranch. Ann and Bonnie were up getting prepared for the trip. I checked the perimeter of the ranch out, then headed for a bedroom, alone. I was up and around at 6:30 a.m, and drove bleary-eyed over to Gasburg to pack a few clothes and essentials in a gym bag and a couple suits in my plastic suit bag. Then I dug through all my drawers in the trailer until I found my seven-year old passport from the Jamaican honeymoon fiasco with Jennifer. I was headed for London. My official assignment was to guard the body of Ann Benchley and render all assistance, legal and otherwise, to rescuing her father from whatever lair Trevor Warbeck had him holed up in. Apparently Trubshawe told Ms. Benchley he had located her father, but he didn't actually have him free yet.

I had a message from Ray on my message machine. He was reminding me to bring back the book and his videotapes. Also, he mentioned again about me picking up the audition videotape of Kathy Quisted so Ann Benchley could see it. I packed up the movies and the IFH book on Hollywood scandals, along with my luggage and headed over to Ray's house around seven thirty that morning. I wanted to be early for the ten-fifteen flight to San Francisco, so I didn't plan to spend a lot of time there. I resolved not to tell him, or anybody else, about my impending flight to the U.K.

The first wrong thing I saw when I got up to the front

porch was that the front door was ajar. Things were pretty informal around Casa Harrison. Ray might have been out looking for his cat or he'd forgotten to shut the door when he went out to pick up the morning paper. I noticed Ray's new Cadillac wasn't in the driveway.

I walked into the front room, calling out Ray's name. No answer. I walked through the kitchen and the adjoining laundry room to the garage. The door to the garage was halfway open, and the television was on inside next to Ray's bed, but no one was there. I concluded he must be in the back yard. I turned around to open up the back door to go outside.

My hand froze a few inches from the brass knob.

There was a blood-stained impression of two fingers on top of the knob.

I took a second look at the kitchen. There were three small blood splatters, spaced out a few feet apart, each larger than the head of a thumbtack. They looked as if they had fallen vertically onto the kitchen floor. I walked around the splatters to the hallway. I touched nothing, keeping my eye down on the wooden flooring that led to the bedrooms. I saw more blood: a thumbprint on the stucco wall next to the thermostat. I remembered now I had left my .38 at home since they wouldn't allow it on the plane. I wished I had it.

I carefully looked around the corner of the L-shaped hallway. The door to the back bedroom was partially opened. I did not like what I could see through the opening.

Two legs resting in a horizontal position on the floor, one leg twisted over the other and the soles of the shoes facing the door.

I walked gingerly to the door and, squeezed in between the edge of the door and the frame. The legs on the floor belonged to Ray but he wouldn't be needing them anymore. I moved in closer. He had been shot at least three times in the head. Both eyes had been shot out and one slug had gone through his forehead. Oblique splotches of blood and brain matter had dripped down from the wall behind him—he had been shot standing up. Ray's head had dark rivulets of coagulated blood that covered both sides of his face, around each ear, and made two small lakes of blood on either side of his head. What had been his mouth was a small caldera of brown-red blood, the residue of which having seeped down past his cheeks. His face and body had all the life of a ragdoll.

He was in his Turkish harem garb: a collarless white silk shirt with red fringe around the cuffs and baggy red pants. A red fez was lying upside down a few feet away from the body.

I calculated from the way Ray's body was positioned that he turned around and saw the person who shot him just before the shots were fired. I scanned about the room and took in the thick red curtains and the plush red sofa with curved armrests that was on one side of the room. A long, coiled bull-whip was resting on a black tasseled throw pillow. Framed sepia-toned prints of mounted Turkish cavalry in funny cone-shaped helmets were mounted above the sofa. There were other pictures about the room: veiled women in some low-tech marketplace, and a painting of a sharp-eyed mustached man with heavy eyebrows and a high-crowned fur hat (Mustapha Kemal Ataturk, the picture Ray showed to me in his kitchen). In the center of the room, above Ray's body, was a leather body harness suspended by a thick steel-link chain attached to the ceiling. There was the odor of incense and strong tobacco—and the sickening stench of decaying flesh—about the room. A candle was burning on top of one table, with the wax burned down to where it half-covered the silvery, hourglass-shaped holder. In one corner of the room was a metal tripod with a compact video camera mounted on the top.

I went back out the bedroom door, and called the police from the kitchen phone. Then I called Bonnie and told her I might be a little late for check-in at the airport.

A few minutes later I was giving a deposition to a policewoman. Russ White was standing next to Ray's refrigerator. He was on the phone, trying to get a hold of the Medical Examiner. His left hand was twitching. I could tell he needed a smoke. A crime scene photographer was in front of him, on his knees, taking a photograph of one of the bloodstains on the kitchen floor.

I gave Officer Charlotte Graves the complete run-down of my movements from the front doorway to the garage entry to the back bedroom. Not long after we finished, the examiner arrived. He was a stork-like middle-aged chap with a fringe of dark hair that looked dyed between his ears and his bald scalp, a thin face, thick black eyelashes and a thick-lipped mouth that looked like it could break out in a smile any second.

"Where's the client, White?" the M.E., whose name was Forbes, asked. The detective pointed down the hallway and the two men disappeared. I was getting nervous I might miss the flight, but I knew I wasn't leaving until the M.E. had his look and something close to a time of death could be established.

"Looks like he bought it around midnight, give or take a two hour window," Russ said to me. "Body temperature readings are always erratic. Forbes will have a better idea when he cuts him open back at the lab and checks his stomach. What brought you to this neck of the woods so early?"

"I was up at the Benchley Ranch most of last night," I said. "When I got home, Ray had a message for me on the phone. He wanted back a tape and a couple books I had borrowed from him. I'm leaving town later this morning so I had to get here early."

"What's with the S&M set-up in the bedroom?"

I told Russ what I knew about Ray fixing Ms. Quisted up to be a dominatrix. I omitted telling him that it was a money-making proposition.

"You think Ray just wanted to get his rocks off with this Quisted chick?"

"That as far as I know," I said. "I was just here one night when he was fixing her up. I also know Ray belonged to some thing called the Society of Nature."

"A pack of sex perverts," Russ muttered. "The city police always have complaints about their carryings-on up above the park. A couple old sisters live near their little gathering place. They call once in a while when the fun gets too noisy. Trouble is, the little group always gets their clothes back on and stash their reefers before our people can get there. You don't smoke, do you?"

"Marijuana?" I replied as innocently as I could.

"No, moron. A cigarette."

"Sorry," I said. "Too bad about Ray."

Russ nodded. "Good bartender. Made excellent whiskey sours. Kept his ears open good, too. Body's pretty cold, so you'll be happy to know I don't think you just stopped by this beautiful morning and offed him. Want to tell me what you were doing between eleven and three o'clock last night?"

"Guarding Ann Benchley," I said. "I was up at the

Ryskind Theater until after eleven, then up at the Benchley Ranch after that. I got to bed around two o'clock."

"Guarding Ann Benchley's booty," Russ said with a smirk. "Sounds like you landed in clover, Wells."

"It's not as glamourous a job as it sounds," I said. Just then I heard the sound of something butting up against the threshold. Two paramedics were bringing in a collapsible metal gurney. Ray was on his way to the morgue.

By now I was over the surprise of seeing Ray dead. I remembered the little note of animosity between Ray and Jack Picasso. I was thinking of mentioning it to Russ when a young uniformed officer with a pudgy nose, a full face and a perfectly trimmed carrot-colored mustache came in and told Detective White about a couple in the house across the street. They had just come home from a party between one and two last night. They both said they saw a tall, thin woman leaving Ray's house and getting into a Cadillac parked in his driveway.

"Did you get a decent description of what the woman looked like?" Russ asked.

The officer referred to his notebook. "The husband said she was wearing what looked like a black one-piece bathing suit. She had long dark hair. The wife thinks she was wearing some kind of lingerie. There's no streetlights near here so they couldn't give a facial identification, but they're sure the woman was tall. The female witness says she might have seen a woman that looked like her over there before. She drove here in a small car. Either a GEO Metro or a Yugo, something like that. It was a battered-up little car for sure."

The gurney went by us, the paramedics taking out what was left of Ray.

I stepped to the window. As Ray was wheeled across the lawn, there was a small crowd of neighbors on the street outside the house: a couple old people I recognized as next-door neighbors of Ray's, a Latino man wearing a Los Angeles Dodger's baseball cap, and a couple blonde kids in baggy shirts and oversized pants holding onto their skateboards. A truck with two men and a gun rack in the cab slowed down to try and see what the police cars and the ambulance were doing in front of the house. Russ walked over to the window as well.

"First murder in town this year," Russ said. "This Kathy

Quisted, is she by any change tall and dark-haired."

I nodded and gave White a description of Ray's business partner.

"Do you know where she lives?"

"I don't know her. I've met her here once and I saw her last night for the second time. She was with Ray last night at the Ryskind Theater for the play they were running. That would have given them something to do until eleven."

Russ buried the tips of his fingers into the top of his forehead for a couple seconds. He was having first-class nicotine withdrawals.

"If these neighbors are right," White whispered, "then Kathy Quisted was here with Ray. Then these people see someone, a woman who happens to fit Quisted's description leaving sometime just before one in the morning. And you say she's tall?"

"About my size," I said. "And she's thin as a rake. And that get-up they described the woman leaving here wearing sounds pretty close to what I saw her in when Ray was dressing her up for her kitten-with-a-whip routine."

Russ nodded his head. "Did you touch anything in the house when you first came in?"

"The front door knob—and the telephone."

Russ scratched his nose, then glanced over my deposition again. "Okay, Wells," he said after a minute, "for the time being you're being officially classified as the dumb snook who found the body."

"That me," I said.

"You might as well go then. You'll be in town, right?"

"I'm flying out today. Ann Benchley's going to see her daughter," I said.

"Where?"

"London—England."

Russ snorted and shook his head. "And you get to go first-class and guard her pretty booty," Russ said. "What a lucky little boy you are. Wherever you're going, you'll be back right?"

"Oh, yeah," I said. "You think I was in on this?"

White looked behind him as the ambulance pulled away, then turned around and shook his head. "No," he said grimly. "I'd have the cuffs on you by now if I did."

"Anyway, I already had Graves over there call the Benchley Ranch. Your employer vouches for you. She says you were on the job and never left."

"Anything new developing on Dave's case?" I asked.

"I haven't heard," Russ said. "I guess a couple county dicks interviewed Wendy last night. I don't know what came of that. Probably routine stuff."

"Did you get hold of Lawrence Webber? I mean Sheepman?"

"Yeah, I talked to him over at Happy Times Restaurant. We had a nice discussion."

"You got him to describe the woman he saw with Dave over in Bowman on the Fourth?"

"I talked to Sheepman," Russ said in a jagged voice. "He's a scared old weasel. Some guy beat him up good. He won't say who."

"The guy's name is Sweeney," I said. "He's a cheap pool hustler. He puts the squeeze on easy targets like Webber when he needs extra money. That's the guy you should go after."

"Yeah, I know about Sweeney," Russ said. "He's done time for dope-dealing. He's on probation now. A guy like that should be in a cell but the jail in Middleburg is overcrowded and we had to let him go early. I can't do anything unless the old man wants to testify, and he doesn't. I had enough trouble getting him to talk about what he saw of Dave McCreedy up in Bowman."

"Did he identify the woman who was with Dave?"

Russ said. "I told him that clamming up on his own assault was one thing, but to stonewall the police on a murder case was unacceptable. I told him he needed to help us on Dave's murder or he'd be going downtown to a little cubicle for some real questioning. Suddenly he started getting informative."

"Did he describe the woman who was with Dave out in front of that store in Bowman?"

"He was informative," Russ said curtly. "The Sheepman speaketh. That's all you need to know. Everything right now is ongoing. Dave's case is with the Sheriff's Office now. I got my hands full now with this mess. Don't worry—you'll find out."

I started to say something else, but Russ held up his right hand in my face.

"Whatever it is, I don't know," he said. "It's up to Sparks, he's the county detective on the case. Just go ahead and get out of here."

Chapter Twenty-Six

I had turned my car around and was headed toward the airport. I had a lot on my mind: the deaths of two close friends coupled with a now rapidly-building fear of flying. I thought a couple times about turning back and dropping the news about the altercation between Ray and Jack Picasso at the theater the night before. But what would it prove? Everything pointed to Kathy Quisted. Picasso had been pretty much in my sights most of the evening, and in the company of Ann Benchley. According to Ray, his second cousin had been disdainful to him on their chance meeting. Quisted was the likely perpetrator. The question was what drove her to do it?

Russ White was wrong. I wouldn't be flying first-class to London. Bonnie and I were booked coach to SFO (San Francisco International), then coach again across the Atlantic via British Airways. Ann and Jack, "I'm going with ya, babe," Picasso would be up front of us in the first-class section. It was nine-thirty when I made it to the Middleburg-Rogue County Airport.

After standing in line with Bonnie to pick up the tickets, I called Wendy at a kiosk of telephones from the one terminal that the local airport boasted.

I managed to spit the bad news out to Wendy better than I had told her about Dave. I could tell she was shook up.

"Oh, migod, oh, migod," Wendy's first reaction. "Why, Harvey, why?"

"The police don't know why. They have a couple eyewitnesses who saw someone leaving around one last night. I can't say anything more than that."

Wendy spoke to me in a civil manner, not exactly friendly but better than I expected considering the anti-Benchley spin doctoring given to her by Ray and her sister.

"They'll catch the person who did this," I found myself saying as I had said time and time again to people when I was a cop.

"But Ray will still be dead," she said sadly.

At this point Bonnie came up to me in the terminal. She wore a lavender turtleneck sweater and matching slacks. She held out a cup of espresso to me. I thanked her. A flight announcement came over the intercom. Wendy asked where I was.

"I'm at the airport, Wendy. I can't talk about it now. I'll be back in town in a few days."

"You're still helping that Benchley woman, aren't you?" she said, her tone becoming harsh.

"Ann Benchley didn't kill Dave," I said, trying to sound more convinced than I really was. "Wait a few days until I get back and I'll prove it to you."

"Whatever you say, Harvey," she replied with a hard edge still in her voice. I didn't expect her to believe what I said about Ann Benchley. I still had doubts myself and I knew Wendy assumed my judgement could very well be clouded by any retainer money I had received from my client.

"The cops were at my place last night. I guess you know somebody killed him—that's certain."

Then there was the sound of Jill crying in the background.

"I'm your friend, Wendy," I said. "I'll always be your friend."

"I have to go, Harvey. Watch your back."

"Right," I said. "Wendy, I'll prove it to you."

A pause. "Goodbye, Harvey." She sounded remote.

"Goodbye, Wendy," I said. I put the phone down, feeling sick from a combination of the impending flight and the bad turn in my friendship with Wendy. Bonnie came back over to me.

"Ann should be out of the ladies' room any second," she said. "I think we've been lucky. No press or autograph hounds around so far. What's happened?"

"Ray Harrison," I said. "He was found dead. Shot three times in the head."

"Oh, dear. And did you—?"

"I was the lucky guy who found him."

Bonnie shook her head. "I'm sorry about what happened to Ray. He wasn't my kind of guy, but he did good work when he was at the Festival. Is that why you're sweating?"

"No," I said. "I've seen my share of stiffs. Of course it's been awhile. Yeah, I guess it bothers me somewhat, but what bothers me more is knowing I have to get on that plane out there. Do you remember I told you I have acrophobia?"

Bonnie nodded. "I think you said vertigo, but I got the idea."

"Well, I'm getting a head start on it here on the ground." I ran a hand across my forehead. It was sweaty.

Bonnie took a small red case out of her purse, and gave me a pill she said was for motion sickness. At that point I would have taken L.S.D. if it could relieve my anxiety over the flight.

It turned out that the fight to San Francisco was not as bumpy as I had heard tell it usually is. I had secured an aisle seat on the flight, and kept my nose buried in a *Sporting News* I picked up at the airport shop. Bonnie sat next to me, talking about various things and trying to keep my mind off of our flying through the air at a higher elevation than Mount McKinley. She also thankfully kept the shade to the window pulled down so I wouldn't catch a glimpse of how high we were. For a couple minutes when we left the ground, I could feel the urge inside me to run screaming down the aisle and bust into the cockpit to hijack the plane for a landing at the nearest runway. It was futile because a hijacker needs a serious weapon and since my five shot .38 revolver was back in my trailer, locked away in a cupboard over the dining table.... Thankfully, Bonnie asked me a bunch of questions about the rules of baseball—feigning an interest, I suspected—and I made it through the flight without having a psychotic episode.

When we got to San Francisco International, there was a VIP lounge courtesy of British Airways for first-class passengers. Bonnie, Picasso and Ann Benchley knew where it was and I dutifully followed the latter's directions, keeping a few feet in front of the rest of the party. Our film actress caught a second glance from several people milling about the restaurants and magazine stands that lined our way to the British Airways' terminals. We were held up by a line to get through the metal detectors. Ann Benchley was wearing sunglasses and a wide brimmed hat. She kept her head bowed slightly, but someone must have recognized her because I suddenly heard people murmuring Ann Benchley's name around me. One older man tried to pass an autograph book to me.

"It's for my granddaughter," the stooped-over, Birkenstock-wearing grandpa said. "She's seen the Belle Killroy movie four times. Can't wait for the sequel."

I relayed the information to Bonnie, who whispered to Ann. I saw the actress nod her head. I took the autograph book, and passed it to Bonnie, who passed it to Ann. Without turning around, Ann scrawled something.

"Her name is Carrie," the old man half-shouted. Ann nodded again, and scrawled something else into the book. It went back to Bonnie, back to me, and back to the old man. I gave him a quick smile to make up a bit for the lack of eye contact he received from the object of his attention.

The VIP lounge had long plush sofa sectionals, soft green colored wallpaper and an excellent view onto the tarmac where the air-leviathans from Boeing, Macdonnell-Douglas and Airbus jockeyed around for take-offs and positioning at the various accordion-shaped boarding ramps that jutted out from the terminals. From over the public address, Ann Benchley was paged to a white courtesy phone. Ann's reaction to this was to slam her purse down against the glass coffee table in front of her. She got quite a few stares from the other well-heeled folks waiting for their flight. Bonnie went over to the local white phone, then brought the cellular receiver to her boss.

"That last call was from Mr. Trubshawe," Bonnie told me after we had boarded the coach section of the 757. "He's had a British private investigator tailing Warbeck and his party since they landed at Heathrow. The Major figures that where ever Warbeck is, Ann's dad must be over there, too."

"Her dad is somewhere in London I take it. So, does Trubshawe know he's alive still, or is there a better chance—"

"I know what you're thinking," Bonnie said. "All Ann would tell me was that, yes, Mr. Trubshawe says he thinks he knows where Mr. Benchley is now, and he needs our help to get him out of wherever he is. He did also mention that Warbeck is traveling with his girlfriend and a very tall man."

"That would be my pal Dromio. He's the guy who strangled that Mr. Park fellow and tossed me around the office a couple times. A guy like that makes me wish I could come into England armed."

"Mr. Trubshawe, I suspect, will take care of all that. He's very resourceful according to Mr. Benchley."

"Have you ever met Trubshawe?"

"Two years ago," Bonnie said as she foraged into her purse. "Do you want some gum? It'll keep your ears from plugging up."

"It's not my ears I'm worried about. It's my head and my stomach."

"You did fine on the flight down here. This is just the same deal with a few extra hours added on. Don't think about it. Watch the movie or read a book. I'll be around, most of the time anyway. Ann might have me up to first class to go over her correspondence but that might not take long."

"I'm hoping you are around," I said with more emotion than I expected. "Tell me about the mysterious Major Trubshawe."

"He's a little guy, very out-going, probably in his early sixties. He's very agile for his age. Keeps himself in shape. He has to with all the drinking he does. When I saw him in person, he made me think of a...I don't know, a rugged Woody Allen maybe."

"I saw that picture Benchley has of him in his office," I said. "Hard to imagine a rugged Woody Allen, but from his picture I suppose it's possible."

"Mr. Benchley took me on one of his excursions over to Great Britain. He meets up with Truffie—that's what he calls him— for a week of fishing up in Scotland. I wasn't along on that leg of the trip. I was with him the first week when he was in London, auditioning actors for a movie he was planning to make."

"A movie? I thought he was done with movies." The 'Fasten Seat Belts' sign came on over our heads.

"Well, the movie was in pre-production. I don't know if he'll get the money for it. It's not a terribly commercial idea if you ask me. He already bombed doing the story of Shakespeare. Now his idea is to do a documentary-style, small scale account of Shakespeare's life. It's going to be a good deal more surreal than the Peter Sellers film."

"Interesting," I said. "Did he have a script?"

"He had some narration written out. He had a few dozen actors do readings for him at the Phoenix Theatre over in Charles Cross Road. That's part of what they call the West End. Trubshawe has a rare books and antique store near there. That's something. You ought to see the artifacts he's got in there. Anyway, that was my first trip to London. Mr. Benchley was invited there to receive an award for the Festival. I got to go with him to the Royal National Theatre. He introduced me to Vanessa Redgrave and Derek Jacobi and several other heavyweights."

"I thought this Major Trubshawe was in the British Army or something."

"Oh, he retired a long time ago. He might still be in what they call the Territorial Army. That's the British version of the National Guard. That and the antique store and his drinking keep him busy. He has a son who helps him run the store and another son in the Royal Marines. When the dad was active in the Army, he was in an air defense regiment. Flew helicopters. That's where he got the training to do the aerial camera work for Mr. Benchley's Battle of Britain film. The Major was a technical advisor on that film, *Operation Sea Lion.* Mr. Benchley and Trubshawe became friends and he taught him how to become a second-unit action director."

The captain came over the intercom, saying we were the next plane to take off. My stomach rumbled and the dizziness started.

"You'll make it," Bonnie said. "Take-offs are the worst part."

"No, quick unscheduled landings are the worst," I replied. I kept my head down and took deep breaths. "You know, I thought of something. It's kind of crazy, but this whole case is crazy."

"Tell me," Bonnie said. "It will keep your mind off things."

"OK, Trubshawe has a bead on Jack Benchley; thinks he's alive and being held by Warbeck. Now, factor into that scenario the strange footage that Ms. Benchley found. The film of a big manor house that hasn't been around for 330 years. The shots of people in costumes doing farm work in fields somewhere. You know what I think? I think the footage is part of a Trevor Warbeck movie that Sherwood Strunk is producing. Strunk wants Jack Benchley to direct the movie. I'll bet another director started it and Strunk fired him or he quit the production. Jack Benchley looked at the footage and decided not to do the film. So Benchley went to the Forest of Arden gig last month, and..." The plane started accelerating down the runway. I tensed up even more.

"He turned him down," I continued, "and so Strunk and Warbeck decided to kidnap him, frame him for the murder of that Carolyn Mason woman, and make him direct this movie. Trubshawe probably has found a secret location where the movie is being shot. I'll bet Warbeck needs Benchley to do the movie because he knows that Jack Benchley is the best director for the Renaissance Period material. If we don't rescue the old guy, Warbeck will knock him off as soon as the principal scenes are shot."

Bonnie laughed. "Wow," she said before laughing again. "That's a little ruthless even by Hollywood standards. But still..."

"It's far-fetched, I know, but it's a possibility," I said. The plane began to leave the ground. My legs started to tremble. I felt that awful feeling just at take-off when the belly of the aircraft seems to drop off the plane, along with your guts. Bonnie reached out and held my right hand with her Velcro-bandaged left. Her touch was soothing. After a minute or so I put my hand over hers, and gave her fingers a light squeeze.

"Take-offs make me nervous, too," Bonnie said, her green eyes and elfin nose making her look totally distracting.

The next thing I remember was leaning across the armrest between us. I kissed Bonnie full on the mouth. I felt some force of passion against my own mouth, and so we continued. Nothing in a long time tasted as good as the slight espresso-mocha taste on her tongue and the touch of her cheek as I lifted my left hand to its tender warm surface, the better to kiss her better.

The "fasten seat belts" sign went off, and so we stopped kissing and put up the armrest. Bonnie slid over and cuddled herself next to me. Time passed. I gently ran my fingers over her copper-blonde hair and nibbled once or twice on her ear-lobes. She returned the favor, then touched my belt.

"I wonder how large the restrooms are in first-class?" she whispered to me.

"Are you serious?"

She giggled, "No. It was a good idea, don't you think?"

"Yes."

We held each other a little bit longer, "What the hell took you so long?" she asked.

I was about to reply that we hardly had much free time in the last few days when a female flight attendant leaned over the seats.

"Excuse me, Mr. Wells," the lady, who was over six feet tall, trim and had two Union Jack earrings dangling from her ears said. "Ms. Benchley has a message for you."

I opened the note. It read as follows:

"Wells—

When you are finished seducing my personal secretary, could I borrow her for a time?

—A. Benchley"

"Oh shit," Bonnie said. She smoothed her top, and went down the aisle to the first-class section. I watched her walk, then leaned back in my chair.

I no longer felt any fear of flying. I actually started reading, then dozed off.

Bonnie came back about an hour or so later. I was just waking up. She noticed the book on my lap, my copy of *Henry V*.

"You have a literary bent I see."

I explained my self-imposed desire to wade through Shakespeare's works, a task that I gave myself before the Benchley case began.

"I figured since I live in a town whose biggest industry is the Shakespeare Festival, I might as well be conversant on the old boy."

"What's the best play of his you've read—in your opinion?"

"Coriolanus," I said.

"That's unusual," Bonnie said, adjusting her glasses. "Why *Coriolanus*?"

"He's a lot like a police sergeant who was my mentor back in Sutter City. He liked people as individuals but he had a poor opinion of them in groups. And, like *Coriolanus*, he wound up on the wrong side. Cynicism engulfed him."

"What's the worst play of Shakespeare—the worst you've read so far?"

"Want me to be honest?" I asked.

Bonnie smiled. "No, bullshit me if you think I'd be disappointed."

"I'd say *Romeo and Juliet*," I said. "Romeo is a sap. I mean, I know he's young but the guy has no perspective on himself. He gets his best friend killed then he kills himself over a girl he sees maybe two or three times. I understand it's a romantic tragedy, but that's a bit much."

Bonnie paused, then popped open her laptop computer and began typing. "That's my favorite Shakespeare play, Harvey," she said, shaking her head as she worked. "I've played Juliet and the Nurse and I loved doing them both. You knew I've played the Nurse at the Festival and I told you I liked the part."

"I should have bullshitted you," I said.

"I think so," she replied, repressing a smile at the left corner of her mouth.

Our meal arrived. Both Bonnie and I had 7-UP to go with our pressed fish and potatoes, with a salad the size of a cassette box. Bonnie sighed as she opened up the cellophane bag to get at the plastic cutlery.

"Anything wrong?" I asked.

"Oh, nothing. Its just that first class is getting sirloin tips, baby asparagus in hollandaise sauce, petit fours and champagne."

"Not so loud," I said. "What coach class doesn't know won't hurt them. We don't need a riot at 36,000 feet...I wish I hadn't reminded myself we're so high."

"You're fine," Bonnie said. "We are flying, but we are totally safe. We're just not eating very high on the food chain. Ask me a silly question to take your mind off flying."

"What's the deal with who wrote Shakespeare's plays? I mean, the guy existed, didn't he? And the Brits must have copies of the plays in his own writing somewhere or at least with his name on the title page, right?"

Bonnie finished a swallow of her potato and spoke up. "True, we have copies of plays published with Shakespeare's name out front. There were seventeen or eighteen plays published and registered in his lifetime. The problem is there's no written evidence in Shakespeare's hand that he wrote anything. There is not a copy of *Hamlet*, for instance, in his handwriting. There are 160 lines of a play about Sir Thomas More that some scholars think is in Shakespeare's hand, but that is controversial because it wasn't discovered until the 1870's. Plus the fact is we only have half-a-dozen scrawls of his signature to make any graphological match."

"Well, if he published his plays..."

"But he didn't," Bonnie replied, waving her fork at me for emphasis. "Back then, acting companies hardly ever published their plays. It would make it too easy for rival companies to steal them, plus the fact that plays were not considered serious literature, anyway. The only works William Shakespeare bothered to have printed were the major poems he dedicated to the Earl of Southampton."

"The guy who laid money on him after he left this Earl of Grantum character?"

"Right," Bonnie said. "Back in Elizabethan times there were no newspapers, certainly no show-biz magazines. Players were considered rude low lifes. A great number of people attended plays at the theaters or the inn-yards or the law courts, but very few bothered to record their experiences. There's not much of a record of William Shakespeare the man so revisionists like Warbeck can come along and play havoc with serious scholarship. Mr. Benchley was lucky to somehow locate the original copy of what's supposed to be William Devant's journal entries. He got experts to prove that it's more likely that the journal Warbeck uses for his *Shadow on the Crow* book is just his grandson's forgery. Warbeck only has the copy from 1666, the one that Richard Nelson's printshop put out just before the Great Fire in London."

"I remember: Devant's grandson wanted to have it widely distributed to scare up some money. That Earl of Grantum had blown the family wad and Charles II had stiffed him because his father had supported Oliver Cromwell and the Puritans."

"Right," Bonnie said. "That's the copy Warbeck somehow got ahold of in the cellar at Sobel House, the one Sherwood Strunk uses when he's in England. He deliberately falsified the text in parts to make it look as if Devant was feeding Shakespeare plays. Mr. Benchley was going to try and prove that during the Forest of Arden debate."

"So, somehow, Jack Benchley got ahold of the original copy of the journal."

"Right."

"Any idea who this Scottish lawyer is who gave Benchley the original journal?"

"No. It was on his last trip to England, but I didn't go with him on that one."

"So where is that copy?"

"It disappeared with Mr. Benchley, I'm afraid. He was going to show it to the assembled parties at the Strunk's Forest of Arden event. He was going to show the number of cuts and recent additions Warbeck had made. But now...now I don't know.... Let's just hope we can get him back and the hell with the documents."

After eating, Bonnie was called back into the first class cabin for some letters Ann Benchley needed to have E-mailed when we got to London. I made myself as comfortable as possible in the narrow confines and set my seat back to catch a few winks. I must have been dead tired because when I woke up again Bonnie was asleep next to me. Her laptop computer was in her lap and her glasses were perched on top of the keyboard. Her head was tilted back and she was lightly snoring. I wanted to kiss her again, but I didn't. I borrowed a paperback book she had turned open and placed upside down on the armrest. It happened to be a biography of Queen Elizabeth the First. I found a brief section of the book devoted to William Shakespeare. One sentence caught my eye.

"We know as much, if not more, about William Shakespeare as a purchaser of real estate and agricultural commodities than we know about the habits and practices of

Shakespeare the playwright."

I leafed through the book, then started to get sleepy. I nodded off, half-listening to a man across the aisle from me who was telling another man about the advantages of mutual funds over treasury bonds. That mundane monologue, coupled with the muffled sound of the jets doing their job outside, put me to sleep. It must have been awhile before I was conscious again, but when I came to the passengers around me were putting up their trays and straightening up. The 'Fasten Seat Belts' sign was on and it felt like we were descending. Bonnie was not at her seat.

She did return a few moments later, receiving a gentle admonishment from the flight attendant for not being buckled in. She had the Queen Elizabeth biography in her hand, and she seemed anxious.

"What's going on?" I asked as she passed in front of me to take her seat. Her face looked flushed.

"Remember that Robert guy?" she said as she buckled herself in. "Remember the guy with the red beard who took a swipe at you back in the Museum of Western Art?"

"Is he on the plane?"

"No," she replied, "but take a look at this picture in the book. I just got through showing it to Ann and Jack."

She opened the book to a picture. There was a small color reproduction of a man who looked just like Warbeck's pal, Robert the Redbeard. It was from a painting and the subject was wearing lace ruff around his neck along with a green sash by which a medallion of some sort was suspended above his glossy silk-like shirt at the chest.

"This is him," I said. "Who is he?"

Bonnie gulped before she spoke. "That is Robert Devereux, Earl of Essex. He was Queen Elizabeth's last boyfriend."

"The guy at the museum? He'd be dead by now. Unless you mean the Queen Elizabeth who's living in Buckingham Palace these days."

Bonnie shook her head. "I mean Queen Elizabeth the *First*! Either the guy we ran into, Warbeck's pal, is an absolute dead ringer for the Earl of Essex or you took a swing at a guy two days ago who was beheaded in 1601!"

Chapter Twenty-Seven

Hugh-Trevor "Truffie" Trubshawe, aged around sixty-five or so, had a handshake like a vise. I experienced it just past the Custom's Area at Heathrow Airport. I also experienced a cluster of men and women holding video cameras, portable cassette recorders and microphones. As Bonnie figured, the media had been tipped off that Ann Benchley was in London, trying to locate her missing/fugitive father. That explained why two officials from Scotland Yard—a dour-looking coat-and-tie man with ginger-colored hair, most of which was combed over what was left of his receding hairline, and an olive-complexioned Indian or Pakistani woman with a long sharp nose and a crop of butch-looking brunette hair—showed up to flash their badges in Ms. Benchley's face just as she finished hugging her daughter.

"Am I being arrested?" Ms. Benchley asked.

"Just a few routine questions, Ms. Benchley," the woman said. She identified herself as Inspector Desai. The male officer was named Bothwell. The actress, along with Bonnie, went into an office adjacent to the custom's area. With Trubshawe's help, and some slight assistance from Jack Picasso, I took the carry-on luggage over to the nearest waiting area.

Bonnie was not far off when she said that Trubshawe, face to face, had the facial features of a rugged Woody Allen. He couldn't have been much above five and one-half feet tall, but he was built like a fullback with less paunch than most men his age and body frame. His hair was reddish and thin, almost entirely white at the temples. He still had a good growth of hair on the crown of his head, which made me jealous. When you got close to him, there was the lingering odor of pipe tobacco. He wore those thick-rimmed, rectangular-shaped glasses that were popular in the Eighties and they went well with his wide, short nose—reddish in hue, with large pores about the nostrils—a close-cropped David Niven-style mustaches on an otherwise clean-shaven face and strong dimpled chin. He stood next to Avalon with his hands behind his back at a military parade-rest position.

Avalon Strunk's choice of dress was quite a contrast to my image of a young lady at an English Public School. She was wearing a faded denim jacket with a multi-colored tie-died t-shirt, tight red and black checkered knickers and high-laced black boots that would have barely allowed her to bend her knees. She was dressed retro, a child of the Sixties thirty years too late. She was tall and slender like her mother, but at that gawky middle-teen stage where teen-aged girls get all their height but still have to wait for their breasts and hips to develop fully. She had her mother's auburn shade of hair, which she wore to a length halfway down her back. Her face bore a dewy similarity to her mother. If there was any part of her face that betrayed the Strunk lineage, it was her eyes. They were large and dark blue. One of her eyes was slightly crossed, like her fraternal Uncle, Sherwood the Third. The teenager tugged a couple times at the sleeve of Major Trubshawe's crisp blue blazer to get his attention. They behaved like old friends.

"When are we going to find grandpa?" the girl asked her guardian in a soothing whisper of a voice.

"I'll bet your mum will be needing a spot of sleepy-bye before we can, luv," Trubshawe replied in a gruff, Cockney voice. He looked over at me. The look radiated skepticism. "Wells, is it? You're the bodyguard Ann hired, right?"

I admitted it.

"I see," Trubshawe said, stroking his chin and looking me over. I had the feeling I hadn't quite met his approval at first glance.

"I'm also a private investigator," I added.

"Good for you," the Major said dryly. He looked away from me toward the office Bonnie and Ann had gone into. Then he folded his arms and did a good job of looking impatient.

While this get-acquainted session was stalled, Jack Picasso was several yards away on one of the stiff-backed metal-framed chairs you find at airports and train stations. He was still wearing that knee-length black leather jacket that made him look like quite the punk. He had secured a copy of *The Economist* and was perusing it with the magazine pulled close to his face as if, as a semi-famous American film director, he was in serious danger of being recognized by the throngs of busy people trying to get out of the terminal to hook up with their next mode of transportation. After the terse greeting he gave to Trubshawe and Avalon, he had not exchanged a word with anyone other than his girlfriend since leaving the plane.

"So what's your professional background, Wells?" Trubshawe asked, as if he were interviewing me for a position I already had.

I gave him a brief rundown of my law enforcement background. He asked me about tactical weapons training and hand-to-hand combat, both of which I had as a cop.

"Any military experience?"

"Five years in the National Guard back in the 1980's. I was in a military police unit stationed out of the Oakland Army Base in Northern California."

One corner of Trubshawe's thin mouth drooped. "And when would be the last time you had refresher courses in personal combat?" he asked.

"About...a year and one half," I admitted, recalling my last workouts with Mr. Han's Karate *dojo* back in Rogue Falls.

"It's been awhile for you, then, has it?" Major Trubshawe said as dryly as he had spoken before.

"True," I said equally dry. "But I've had a few real-life encounters lately that have come out reasonably well." Trubshawe unfolded his arms and put his hands behind his back. "I hope you're up for what's ahead of you, Wells," the Major said.

"I think so, sir. I haven't had anything Warbeck's pack has thrown at me yet that I couldn't handle." That was a lie. I was plenty scared backed at Warbeck's office in San Francisco, when I almost wound up stuffed in a garbage bag at the hands of Dromio. Bonnie had helped me out a good deal during that crisis. He wasn't my client, but there was something about the demeanor of the solid old bantam rooster in front of me that made me want to impress him.

A dark-haired lady in a white trench coat who could have passed for a younger version of the actress Joan Collins if you squinted just right, came up to the three of us. She had a palm-sized cassette recorder in her hand. She stuck the device in Avalon Strunk's face.

"Are you Avalon?" the woman asked in a firm, strong voice as her potential target stepped back toward Trubshawe. "I was hoping you could answer some..."

"Take a walk, lady," Trubshawe growled. "This girl hasn't seen her mother since Christmas and your lot can't give them a moment's peace."

"I was just wanting to—"

"Take...a...walk!" Trubshawe spoke back crisply. "Speak English, do you?"

The woman backed away.

I heard a cacophony of clicking sounds behind me. The still photographers and video camera hounds were closing in on the frosted-glass door to the Customs Office. Bonnie emerged from the office. I hustled over, jostling my way through the crowd. Bonnie pulled me to her so we made up a small cordon between the Fourth Estate and Ann Benchley. The actress emerged from the office. I noticed Trubshawe stayed behind with Avalon, but he was watching me and probably grading my actions in his head.

There were shouts of Ms. Benchley's first and last name from the assembled press. Multiple camera flashes sent blinding white novas of light at us. The questions came flying as fast as the flashes, and as rude and direct.

"Is your father in Great Britain?"

"Is he in London?"

"Do you believe he murdered Carolyn Mason?"

"What did you tell the police?"

"Will you make a statement?"

There were other questions, along a similar line.

The male Detective Inspector, Bothwell, replied: "Scotland Yard has no comment on the search for Mr. Jack Benchley. Ms. Benchley has been cooperating in our investigations." Bothwell and Inspector Darsi next side-stepped the phalanx of reporters and camera people.

"I have a statement," Ann Benchley said quietly, her eyes downcast, her expression somber.

Someone shouted, "Quiet, she's speaking!" Another reporter shouted: "Move!" and a cameraman snapped back with, "Bugger yourself!" Similar oaths and requests filled the air. I was told by a bearded man with a zoom attachment to his camera that I was in his way. I didn't move. After about a quarter of a minute, the collective din died down enough for their object of scrutiny to speak. Ann Benchley clutched a slip of paper just above the strands of her small black purse. Her speech began in a halting manner, unlike the way she projected from the stage.

"I...I am here in England to visit...to visit my daughter. That is the main reason for my being here. Our family has been under great strain for the past two weeks. I am hopeful you will grant me time to be with my daughter without further invasions of our privacy. I am confident my father is both alive and innocent. I will have no more to say during this visit. I will only reiterate that a substantial reward is available for anyone who can give the FBI or the British authorities information leading to the safe return of my father. Please let myself and my party continue through the airport unimpeded. Thank you."

Ann moved forward, flanked by Bonnie and myself. I kept in front of the two women, projecting my arms out in front, until we reached the luggage carousel that was designated for our flight. It took a few minutes, while media people fired away further questions that went unanswered. "Welcome to the big time," Bonnie whispered to me as we watched the leather and synthetic bags plop out of the metal chute and onto the carousel.

I heard Ann Benchley ask Trubshawe about the whereabouts of her father. He told her he would elaborate when they got out of the airport. Trubshawe, Bonnie and, rather reluctantly, Picasso handled the luggage and loaded it onto metal carts. I grabbed up my suit coat, one of the large suitcases, and my gym bag. The other two men also made up a second moving barrier between ourselves and the back-pedaling press.

More hot flashes of light, more questions, more confusion. I pushed one photographer back faster than he wanted to go, and he let me know about it. I kept on a straight path, with Bonnie just behind me now, holding the end of my coat. Some of the reporters dropped away. The rest formed a retreating semi-circle around our group until we came to the entry to a moving sidewalk which, according to the illuminated black on yellow sign above us ,took us to either one of the Underground Stations or to the car parks, I wasn't sure which. I placed one hand on the black rubber handhold to retain my balance as I stepped onto one section of the treadmill-like walkway.

"Where is Dylan parked?" Ann Benchley asked Trubshawe, using her full voice.

"I'm not sure," Trubshawe said. "I wish you'd have let me fly you out of here in my helicopter."

"We're staying in Kensington," Ms. Benchley shot back. "You can't very well land a helicopter at the Kensington Gardens Hotel, can you?"

The walls on one side of the moving sidewalk featured painted silhouettes of Big Ben and the Houses of Parliament, the Tower of London, Stonehenge, etc. There were swarms of passengers in front of us, and this had the effect of squeezing us in closer to the remaining photographers. I noticed that there was a large woman standing at the off-ramp area ahead of us. She caught my eye because she was wearing a chauffeur's uniform (a green blazer with a matching green military-style cap). She was holding what looked like an artist's portfolio in her hand.

"There she is," Trubshawe pointed out. At that point one of the photographers, walking backwards too quickly, rammed into two lean Sikh men in full beards and turbans—bystanders—and the resulting collision knocked all three men over. The three men slid along on the moving sidewalk, trying to disentangle themselves. Bonnie and I waded in to assist, and all parties were on their feet and a proper apology was given out by the newsman by the time everyone was off the people-mover.

"I'm sorry, everybody," the woman in the uniform said. "I would have been here sooner, but the guy who drove the Duchess of Wigam to the Docklands last night didn't bother to clean or refuel the Rolls when he dropped it at the garage. There were champagne bottles—"

"Never mind, girl," Trubshawe said. "Where are you parked?"

"Car Park Three, Level Six, Section E," the chauffeur said. She had strawberry blonde hair, a light pinkish complexion, a round face and a figure that could generously be called 'big-boned.' "Hello, Ann," she said to Ms. Benchley in unexpected familiarity.

"Hello, Dylan," Ann Benchley said warmly. She went up and hugged the chauffeur. "How is my favorite erstwhile in-law?"

It turned out that 'Dylan' Jenkins was the niece of Tommy Jenkins, the actor turned Australian real estate agent who had been the second Mr. Ann Benchley. Her real first name had been something other than that, but she liked Dylan better. She always escorted the Benchleys about when they came to London. Her goal was to use her degree in Visual Arts to become a costume designer. Ms. Benchley had promised to look at a portfolio of sketches she had created at the University of London. If Ann Benchley liked her work, and felt the desire to practice a little favoritism, Dylan could be eligible for the Visiting Artists Program at the Northwest Shakespeare Festival. I learned all this vocational information from Bonnie as we shared the front passenger section of a jet-black Rolls Royce with the driver.

Before we had set out, Ms. Benchley, Picasso, and Trubshawe had held a quiet conversation together next to a concrete pillar in the catacomb-like car park while Bonnie and I loaded the luggage. I could hear none of it, but from Ann's expression of puzzlement it was clear Trubshawe was not answering her questions to her satisfaction.

Bonnie's boss and Picasso were in the spacious burgundy leather backseats and Avalon was in a matching swivel seat that was just in front of them. The teenager's long stringy legs were crossed on top of the miniature television set that stuck up on a stand from the floor. There was a small cabinet built near the television which housed a refrigerator, a CD player and a videocassette player. Trubshawe followed behind us along the roadway in a Red Range Rover.

Dylan maneuvered the Rolls on descending slopes of concrete ramp, spiraling down past signs that either warned, 'No Entry' or showed the proper exit from the maze with yellow back-lighted arrows and the succinct term, 'Way Out.' The glass barrier that separated the front interior from the spacious rear section of the luxury vehicle was open. Ann Benchley was on the limousine's cellular phone, trying to call someone in France and having to employ a halting, uncertain knowledge of the language with a French phone operator. After a few minutes, she was speaking her mother tongue with someone named Bebe. I assumed this was Bebe Dupont, a former wife of her missing father.

I was beginning to feel the effects of the dreaded jet lag. My body was telling me that it was late at night and I was exhausted, yet Greenwich Mean Time was around eight in the morning. Once past the airport, we got on an expressway called the A31 and headed east. Names like Hounslow West and Boston Manor beckoned to us from the signs in front of the off-ramps. There were long stretches of two-story townhouses beyond the expressway, occasionally broken up by the soccer field of a school or the business district of a township. This was my first exposure to driving on the left side of the road and I had an uneasy feeling that our driver was headed toward a head-on collision for the first few kilometers, a feeling lessened as I saw traffic progressing across the median, also headed on the 'wrong' side of the road.

We were all listening to the phone conversation, from Ann's side:

"You play the mother of the newlywed? Who's the girl who plays the part Jane Fonda had?...Never heard of her. English actress, huh? Well she could be another Emma Thompson for all I know. Well, I'm sure it's a good show."

Ann took the phone away from her face, shook her head like a dog trying to dry off, then went back for more.

"Yes, I think daddy is safe, Bebe. No, Truffie's not telling me exactly where he is.... He says that in order to get at him, we are going to have to do something arduous, and he wants me to rest up at the hotel before we get started...He says he is going to show me where he is, Bebe, but the first thing I need to do is rest.... No, I don't want to rest. I want my dad. Well, Truffie is a stubborn old bastard, isn't he? Well, you were married to Dad for ten years so you must have noticed what a stubborn old bastard Truffie is.... The authorities?! Forget the authorities on this one, Bebe. They just want to get dad and send him back to America and into jail.... Well, they have another suspect, some scumbag named Charles Aarons, but it's going to take a DNA test to clear my father and it's going to take a couple weeks to get that analyzed.... Yes, I'll keep you informed. (She grimaced as she listened to the other woman talking, which sounded like high-pitched static from my position and blended badly with the sedate whirring noise of the motor.) "Definitely. Oh, definitely, Bebe. You'll be the first person I call when we have him safe.... Yes, well, I'll tell him how much you care as soon as I see him.... Yes, you told me about doing *Barefoot in the Park* over at The Hyperion.... That's right, when all this is done, I'll call you to arrange the tickets. Yes, love to you too, Bebe. Bye-bye."

After waiting for a fraction of a second, she slammed the phone back into its cradle between the two leather seats she and her boyfriend were occupying.

"Fuck an A!" she exclaimed in full exasperation. "My dad—her ex-husband— is held hostage somewhere I don't even know, his best friend won't tell me where he is, and that stupid bitch wants me to bring him to some play she's in, some Neil Simon revival on the West End. Why does she think I could even think of something like that right now? Fuck that play! Fuck Bebe's career! Fuck her!"

She sat back against the backrest, squeezing her eyes shut. Vertical lines appeared on the center of her forehead, perhaps portending another attack of nerves.

"That does it," Jack said. "That cunt Bebe Dupont is out of my movie."

"Shut up, Jack," the actress snapped back. "My dad wanted her to play the assistant warden in our movie and, damn it, she is." She turned away from her companion and looked out onto the roadway going by. The harsh early morning sun suddenly made her look all of her forty-odd years. Previously, I had seen her bathed in a glow that must have been some act of mental cinematography. Now she looked to me like an ordinary, garden-variety being: a tired, middle-aged woman with mussed-up hair, blood shot eyes, and a slight but consistent case of the shakes.

"All this has got to be a dream," she added to no one in particular. She pressed a button near the console where the phone was. A thick pane of glass slid up and partitioned the back section off from Bonnie, Dylan and myself. The famous woman with blood-shot eyes leaned her head on her boyfriend's shoulder. I turned away and looked at Bonnie, and she returned back at me a half-smile that led me to believe that our first kiss had not slipped her mind.

The traffic on the roadway began to get heavier, like that in any big-city commute in the States, only the cars were usually smaller and, for some reason, the trucks (rather, lorries) were cleaner. London did not suddenly engulf you the way San Francisco did, by the dramatic act of crossing a lengthy multi-span bridge, or across the broad, single-span Golden Gate. London slowly absorbed you, like Los Angeles did, but with an architecture and a feel totally different from that of an irrigated sprawl of desert communities. There were the modern buildings, yes, but there were also Neo-Classic structures that, even with the probable restorations of the past, looked like they were older than the Grand Old Republic we had flown in from.

Slowly, after a few more merges, the vast city took us in. The cars began to be restricted on the street to narrow gaps between the bus lanes. The sidewalks had long rows of iron fencing with little gaps for the disgorging of bus passengers; the crosswalks were laid out with diagonal markings instead of parallel lines; post office boxes looked like oversized fire hydrants and street signs designating avenues were mounted on the sides of buildings instead of poles at sidewalk corners.

The tortoise-like London cabs you always see in movies were great in abundance as were the clusters of pedestrians dressed in long coats and sweaters to ward off what looked like a poor excuse for Spring.

"First time in London?" Dylan asked me.

I told her it was.

"I love London," Bonnie, who sat between us, said. Then she yawned. I followed suit.

"I hope the cops didn't give Ann too bad a time back there," Dylan asked Bonnie.

"They just wanted to know if she knew where her father was," Bonnie replied. "She said she didn't, that she was just here to see Avalon and to recover from the press scrutiny. It's the truth, really; I don't think Truffie has told her anything specific yet."

Dylan shook her head. "I hope he knows where the hell Ann's dad is. And I hope this is over with quickly, for her sake."

Dylan Jenkins was correct on the first of her hopes, and quite incorrect on the second.

Chapter Twenty-Eight

The Kensington Gardens Hotel looked like a combination of Hearst Castle and some Moorish palace. It had a dozen stories of red brick with long colonnaded terraces, conical peaks spaced out between sections of the ski-jump sloped roof, a huge Spanish Renaissance bell tower in the center and elaborate Art Deco figures in the Grecian style—long muscular bodies, little clothes—adorning the main archway. The flags of four nations, including Canada's Maple Leaf and the Union Jack, flew from over the impressive cathedral-style entry.

Our two-vehicle convoy was met by a doorman dressed like a general's adjutant from the Boer War, assisted by two bellmen equally out of fashion. We also had a bearded, flak-jacketed man with the build of a rugby player right on top of us, focusing his still camera on Ms. Benchley. He was a member of the *paparazzi*, active as a puppy, clicking away as she emerged from the limousine. Jack Picasso tried to snatch the camera from his hand and a scuffle ensued. I was not involved because I was busy keeping another man, who bore an uncanny resemblance to Anthony Perkins (dark-haired, lanky, an overage-juvenile sort of face) from intruding on Ann and Bonnie's private space. He was clean-shaven with a pointy chin, dark eyes and a missionary zeal to somehow make eye contact with Ann Benchley. He wore a tattered green U.S. Army jacket, grungy jeans, well-worn sneakers and a look of desperate longing.

"I have something important to convey to Ann," the neo-

Norman Bates said in a Brit accent. "I must speak to her."

"Convey yourself out of here," I said. "She's not available." I glanced from the man I was intercepting to see about the fracas between Picasso and the photographer. The scuffle had degenerated into a child-like pushing and tugging match, each man with a death grip on the expensive-looking still camera. Although smaller, the director had the other man pressed against a concrete pillar halfway up the stairway to the glass doors leading inside. Two men in blue blazers came through those doors. They had blue blazers on with monograms that featured a capital 'H' and 'K' intertwined.

The struggle for the camera continued. "Let go, you bloody Mohican!" the photographer shouted to Picasso. The other two men arrived and tried to pull the struggling men apart, each taking one combatant from behind and trying to pinion the flailing arms of the battling pair.

Ann Benchley and her daughter slipped into the hotel, having the door opened for them by the doorman.

"It's only a minute of her time," the young man implored to me. "I have a personal statement to confide in her."

Bonnie came up to my side. "Hello, Brian," she said in a surprisingly soft, empathic tone. "Why are you here?"

"I have a statement," Brian said. "I've waited over a year to give it to Ann personally." I noticed then that his teeth were crooked and he was missing one of his canines. His military coat didn't have any conspicuous bulges so I assumed he could at best be armed with a knife. Which, since I was unarmed since leaving the States, was a possibility that kept me alert.

Ann Benchley reappeared and came down the steps toward the melee. "Ann! Ann!" Brian called out, waving his hands over his head to draw her attention. The actress caught sight of the scarecrow-like admirer and looked away in two quick motions of her head.

Finally the two hotel security people put together enough force and pulled Picasso and the photographer away from one another. The cameraman regained his camera, shook off the man who held him from behind, and took off running down the street.

Bonnie told Brian, nicely but firmly, to go home. After giving her a folded up envelope, he turned and crossed the street toward the vast tree-lined park that faced the hotel. I found out in the lobby, as we were sorting the bags and Trubshawe was checking us in, that Brian was a rabid fan who tried to meet Ann Benchley or her father every time one of them visited London. Bonnie had first met the young man when he crashed an event at the South Bank Center she had attended with Jack Benchley. Brian was obsessed with the actress and frequently wrote to her agent's office in Los Angeles with romantic sonnets and pledges of eternal love. Sometimes the agent would forward the letters to Bonnie, especially those that said Brian was preparing to visit the States and meet with his beloved. Bonnie had alerted the Los Angeles Police Department on one occasion, but Brian apparently was content with ambushes on his native soil.

The lobby was swank, of course, with an indoor fountain in full gush, loads of healthy live ferns in decorative ruddy terra cotta pots, marble, or certainly marble-like plaisters depicting ionic columns on the fringes of the front desk area and the entrances to the stairways and elevators, and dark, glossy wood paneling around the entrances to the meeting rooms and the restaurants. To top it off a man in a tuxedo was tinkling out George Gershwin's, *The Man I Love* in a roped off section next to the fountain.

This was no Motel Six.

A manager was summoned to speed up the check-in for our VIP party. I accompanied Ann and Picasso on one of the elevators, a 'lift' reserved for those who had rooms on the twelfth floor of the establishment. Two bellmen stood in the elevator in front of us, holding the luggage. Bonnie and Trubshawe stayed behind in the lobby, settling the room charges. Avalon bypassed the elevator, going to the designated floor via the stairwell. "She's trying to lose weight, if you can believe it," Ann said to us.

"I think it would be better if you and your daughter stayed together," I said. "There's no telling what Warbeck might have planned."

Ann Benchley nodded, then turned an interested gaze at Picasso. "Damn vulture, I should have belted him harder," the director said between pants for breath. His chest was heaving up and down and he was in a sweat, all from a rather brief altercation. I was surprised he could put up that kind of fuss after a Transatlantic flight.

We got out on the twelfth floor, the decor of which matched the lobby. There was an expensive looking Grecian vase in a small glass-enclosed niche built into one side of the hallway. The vase was about a yard high with an hourglass shape. The background was black. The horses, chariots and charioteers were painted in an adobe-red between the elaborate border design running across the middle of the piece.

"An obvious reproduction," Picasso said with a sniff as we passed the niche. "I saw the original in the British Museum last year, along with the Elgin Marbles."

"Ah, yes, the Elgin Marbles," Ms. Benchley said happily putting her slender arm around Picasso's shoulders. "I wonder if the Athenians won't send their fleet up the Thames someday and try and take them back."

We got to a door marked Suite A. Jack Picasso swiped a card in a narrow gap between two shiny metallic boxes situated a few inches above the door knob. A few small lights on one of the boxes switched from red to green. Ms. Benchley turned the knob and the door opened.

The room was spacious, with two large, plush sofas in the middle of the room. Between the sofas was a large marble topped table with a large bouquet of fresh red tulips. A fireplace with an elaborate mantle was just past the furniture. Avalon entered the hardwood foyer into the suite just as the bellmen, loaded down with luggage, disappeared into what looked like an adjoining bedroom. The actress followed them into the room, and told them to take some of the luggage and put it into another room which was on the other side of the living room area. I recognized these two pieces of luggage as what Avalon had already stowed away in Trubshawe's Range Rover. After the bellmen returned from the second bedroom, Ms. Benchley took out her purse and handed each young man a few large bills, which they took with gracious displays of thanks.

"Jack, Avalon, and I are going to retire to rest up," Ann Benchley said to me. "Bonnie has made arrangements for you to take the servant's quarters adjoining my suite. There is a connecting door. If I need you for any reason, I will contact you."

I took this as my cue to go into the hallway and wait for

Bonnie, which I did. I only had to wait a minute or so for Bonnie to emerge from the elevator. Trubshawe was right behind her, and behind him was another bellman carrying some stray bags, a couple of which were mine. I took the gym bag and the suit coat from the bellman. Bonnie took out two room cards from her purse, and handed one to me.

"Your room is just to the right here, adjoining Ann's suite," she said. "There's an adjoining door to her suite, so if she needs you-"

"Got it."

"I'll be occupying the second bedroom. If Avalon stays over, I'll probably be on a couch."

"You will definitely be on a couch," I said.

Bonnie sighed, then she pulled a small envelope out of her purse and handed it to me. "Here's an advance on your services. The check is in dollars. You'll also find some money for expenses here. The folding money is in English Pounds. You'll find they pass for real money over here."

Trubshawe had gone into the suite for a few moments, then came back out. He put his stubby, thin-skinned hands gently on Bonnie shoulders. "I never thought I'd see it: Little Annie actually organized." He took a swift glance back at the closed door to the suite. Can't say I can say much for the bloke she's with—bit of a nutter that one." He gave her a peck on her cheek. "Dear Bonnie, what a paratrooper you would have made. You would never have jumped out without packing your parachute would you?"

"I don't jump out of planes, Major Trubshawe. And we're not as organized as we look. I have a backlog of mail I've got to get to that I brought over on the plane. By the way, when are we going to find out about what the plan is on getting Mr. Benchley back?"

He glanced at his watch. "It's coming up around nine. Judging by the red in your eyes and those of Ann's, I'd say you need at least a few hours sleep before you get your Intelligence Briefing. I'll be back about four o'clock then. Trust me, luv, you'll all need some rest for what we're getting into."

The bellman came out of the suite, and asked if there would be anything else. Bonnie handed him some money and he departed for the elevator. Trubshawe gave us both a good-bye—mine more terse than the one Bonnie received—then he followed the bellman into the 'lift.' Now Bonnie and I were alone in the hallway.

Bonnie gave me that puckish, cute little grin of hers. There were a few moments of awkwardness, then we headed for our respective room assignments. I found my room to be a cramped affair, slightly bigger than a two person cell in the Sutter County Jail. This must have been some type of servant's quarters for the visiting VIP's domestic staff. Suddenly, I wasn't as sleepy as I had been in the limousine. Perhaps dealing with Ms. Benchley's stalker had put my body on some reserve of energy.

I sat down on the twin-sized bed and rested against the nightstand that was built into the wall next to it. The bellman had left the window slightly open and the curtain pulled about halfway back. I had no balcony and the window faced out in the opposite direction from Kensington Gardens. The view I had was of a few white townhouses in the distance, a forest of brownstone apartment buildings, and an old-fashioned red-brick smokestack that stuck up from the residential area like it was left as a reminder of the Industrial Age.

I did not know whether to lay down and rest or stay up and wait for the feeling of sheer exhaustion I had just had. I started monkeying with the built-in radio console. I listened to a song called, *My Baby Just Cares for Me* sung by Nina Simone. I had heard it before and liked the tempo. I went to hang up my extra coat and pants in the chifforobe located next to the bathroom door.

There was a knock at the door. It was Bonnie.

"Ann wants you to stand out in the hall for an hour or so," she said. "She's afraid that our boy Brian is coming back. The hotel staff has been alerted but she's not feeling secure."

"That's doable," I said. I picked up my entry card off the night table and vacated the room. Bonnie and I were alone in the hallway.

"I know it's a pain," she said, "but it will put Ann's mind at ease."

"She's paying the freight around here," I said. "What was her reaction when you showed her the picture of the Essex guy in your book?"

"She can't make heads or tais of it, either," Bonnie remarked. "It's probably just some weird coincidence. Maybe this Robert guy is some distant relation to Essex. That's the only logical conclusion unless Warbeck has found a way to bring people back from the dead."

"And sew their heads back on," I added.

"Yuck," Bonnie said, making a face. "Don't be so Gothic."

"Sorry," I said. "Do you feel tired?"

"I'm beat," she said. "I hardly slept on the flight. I never do, really. Ann is even worse. She's laying down in her suite right now. Avalon is reading a paperback of Sophocles' plays on the sofa in the French room. It's for school, apparently. She's also watching a tennis match on the tube with the volume off."

"What about the C.B. DeMille of prison flicks?"

"Young John Ford is preparing to crash his butt in the main bedroom with Ann," Bonnie said. "I'm crashing on the settee. You should see the layout in the suite. There's a great four poster bed. You could film a Jane Austen novel in there."

I looked over at the sound of a door on the other side of the hall. A tall, frizzy-haired, bottle-blonde woman in a white robe and a shorter gentleman with a a heavy set of love handles, a full-moon face, bulging eyes and no clothing other than a pair of Speedo trunks, emerged from the door opposite the entrance of the Benchley suite. We both gave friendly nods to the couple on their way to the elevator.

"Could be a Swedish couple," Bonnie said. "Or Germans. There are a lot of great amenities in this flophouse. They have an indoor pool and several sauna booths, plus a tennis court. Do you play tennis?"

"Shoot," I said, snapping my fingers, "I left my racket back at the country club. I thought this was going to be all-business and no pleasure."

"Well, we can be optimistic," Bonnie said in a tone I found provocative. "After we get Mr. Benchley, there may be some time."

"I'd like to take you to dinner while we're here," I said, trying to build on our furtive romantic encounter back at the ranch. "Maybe you and I could see the Tower of London. Or how about a play or two?"

"Yeah, sure," she replied shyly. "There's the South Bank Center or the Garrick Theater maybe. We'll have to find out what's playing. I'd really like to go to the Haymarket over near

Piccadilly Circus. Just the exterior of the place is worth the price of admission, not that what I just said makes any sense. Then there's Kew Gardens, of course. Or Harrod's. That place has a great food court." She paused, and glanced up and down the empty corridor. "Or how about this?" she said, taking a step closer to me. She brought her face up close to mine, her shimmering lips slightly parted, her eyes closed. I obliged her. We made contact.

She broke off the joining of our lips after a couple seconds. I initiating another contact. I placed my hands upon her hips, and lightly squeezed her soft flanks. I'd wanted to do that.

We were both breathing a little hard. Bonnie gave out that little throaty laugh, then fixed my eyes with a provocative look that made me forget how tired I was. She could tell I was thinking: what with Avalon helping herself to her designated resting place...

"I'm going back to the suite," she said, taking a deep breath. "Umm, I'm tired and you're tired."

"We are tired," I said. "But other than that, what are you doing in the next hour or so? Do you have anything to do? I imagine that suite probably is crowded. I get off in an hour and..."

"I've got some luggage in there and all I'd need is...." My turn to make a move. We kissed again, a nice wet kiss. I got to explore the gentle curve of her back and the warm contours of her lower body that were covered in those lavender slacks.

"I'm going to the suite, but I think I'll be changing rooms here real soon. Real soon. You going to be around awhile? You'll still be here in the next few minutes?"

"Count on it," I said in a voice that barely concealed how inflamed I felt inside. She turned around and went to the suite. A few minutes later she left the suite with her luggage and went into my—now our— room. While I guarded the hallway I heard her taking a shower in my room.

I did my hour in the hallway. No Brian appeared, nor any other Stalkers of the Rich and Famous. I felt amazingly tired toward the end of the hour and my back hurt. Bonnie gave me a back rub using some body cream she had warmed up in the kitchen of the suite. After that, we made love with the exuberant ferocity of two people who were discovering one another for the first time. The bed we used was small but workable. The experience made me feel like I had been missing a vital part of being alive for too long.

In all the James Bond movies I had ever seen, Agent 007 invariably awakens from a sexual tryst before his glamourous Bond-girl conquest. He sneaks off to continue saving the ruins of the British Empire and other selected patches of the Free World while the Bond-girl wakes up later all alone in a tangle of mussed sheets. I, on the other hand, woke up to the tangle of sheets in the narrow bed. I was alone and the only signs of Bonnie there was the bathrobe she greeted me in after I got back into the room. Now she was gone and the damn phone was ringing.

Someone had set the tone on the ringer loud enough to wake the dead. I grasped the receiver and suppressed an urge to slam it back down in case it was an alert from Bonnie.

"Is this Harvey Wells?" came a vaguely familiar male voice that responded to my groggy hello.

He identified himself as Richard Allen, the news editor of my hometown paper, *The Rogue Falls Daily News*. The name and the voice rang a bell. I had played pool a couple times casually with him at O'Leary's Bar. He had also interviewed me a few months earlier about the county Family Support Division.

"I'm Wells," I murmured after taking a second or so to recognize the voice. "How'd you find out where I am?"

"Good investigatory journalism, utilizing the resources of the telecommunications revolution," he said. "Truth is, the lady who's taking care of Jack Benchley's grandson told me where your client stays in when she's in London. Were you asleep or something?"

"No, I was painting my toenails a nice shade of teal," I said.

"Sorry to disturb you, Harvey. I really wanted to speak to Ms. Benchley or her representative. But this was the only number I got from the front desk."

"O.K., I'm no longer in deep REM. Now what do you want, Richard?"

"Ever hear of Mosby's Rangers?"

"Civil War Trivia time?" I said, checking my watch. I had slept a couple hours at least. "O.K., let's see...John S. Mosby, nicknamed The Grey Ghost. A Confederate type, I believe. He gave the Union Army fits with nasty little guerrilla operations in the Shenandoah. His gang and Phil Sheridan's boys didn't get along so well. Now what do I win?"

"I'm talking about the white supremacist group that has sent threatening letters to Ann Benchley. The paper got a letter from them. No return address, of course. They say they have concrete proof Jack Benchley knocked off his girlfriend. Besides the racist rants, they also said they had something bad on Ann Benchley they may release. Do you think your client would like to make a statement reacting to any of that?"

"When did I become European correspondent for the *Rogue Falls Daily News*?"

"She made a pretty tepid statement at Heathrow, according to the Associated Press wire," Richard stated. "Do you think she didn't knock your friend off? C'mon, level with me."

Through the hotel room wall I heard a shrill feminine voice. It was Ann Benchley, shouting at someone. She was definitely upset. Then I heard Jack Picasso's voice shouting, too. I couldn't understand either one of them.

"Still there?" Richard asked.

"Yeah," I said. "I can't go into anything on that, Richard. I'm Ann Benchley's bodyguard not her press secretary. You media guys never let go of somebody once you get a hook in them, do you?"

I expected Richard's ire to be roused by my remarks. Instead, his voice remained calm and reserved, like something was bothering him.

"I'm sorry," Richard replied, sounding almost contrite. "I got some more news for you. It's about the death of Ray Harrison. He was a friend of mine, too."

"What's the news."

"The cops caught up to Kathy Quisted."

"Where was she?"

"State Police nailed her about twelve hours ago about a hundred miles north of here, above Roseburg," Richard said. "She had her kids with her, and about everything she owned. Got her on a county road so she was at least smart enough to stay off the Interstate. Probably headed for Canada or someplace like that to hide. I found out some interesting facts from my source at the police department."

"Such as?"

"Considering the way you're stonewalling me, I shouldn't tell you. But since Ray was your friend, I guess you deserve to know. Quisted was questioned. My source in the department tells me she's got quite a weird little story she's passing off for an alibi. Seems she told Russ White and my source that she came home with Ray after seeing Ann Benchley's play. They were going to spiff up their little bondage room for some clients they were expecting in a few days. Ray wanted her to do a dress rehearsal of her Wanda the Warrior number. While Ray was setting things up in the room she went out into the kitchen and was making coffee for both of them. That's when she supposedly was grabbed from behind by an intruder."

"Did she see this supposed intruder?"

"For a second. She says it was a big guy. She claims a big guy jumps her and then something smacks her from behind and the lights go out. The next thing she knows she's waking up in the back bedroom of the house. And she's got a gun in her right hand and her right arm's covered in blood. And guess what Ray Harrison is doing?"

"What?"

"Nothing. He's lying next to our heroine, dead and all bloody. So Quisted thinks she's been set up to take the fall. I'd say that was a good deduction on her part. So she freaks out, goes home, tells her kids she has to take a quick trip, then makes a run for it. She left Ray's place and goes out the front door, dripping blood from her hands. Ray's blood. The prints on the back door match her fingerprints."

That explained Ray's neighbors across the street seeing a scantily-clad woman leaving his house late that night.

"And what about the gun? What did she do with that?"

"She says she threw it out going down the highway. The cops haven't found it yet. She told the cops where it was, but so far it hasn't been located."

"Anything in the house indicate another intruder?"

"Funny you should mention that. The window into Ray's bedroom had been forced open from the outside. Maybe Kathy Quisted set it up that way, my source said."

"Doesn't look good for Kathy Quisted does it?"

"I agree," Richard said dryly. "The cops also tested her for drugs because they found several ounces of methamphetamine in Ray's bathroom. Ms. Quisted also tested positive for meth in her system. Of course, she says she's been clean, says she must have been given the junk by her attacker after she got bonked on the head. You have the signs of entry through a window, but you also have a lot of evidence against Ms. Quisted, including her finger prints in blood on the hallway leading to the back bedroom. If this lady is set-up, she's in for a regular Franz Kafka nightmare. I feel sorry for her kids."

"What about Dave's murder? Anything on that?"

There was a pause on the other end of the line.

"Richard?"

He said a few words, words spoken softly and close together. I couldn't make out what he said and asked him to repeat it.

"I said the cops picked up Wendy McCreedy," Richard said.

"What are you talking about?" I asked. "They picked her up for what? You talking about Dave's murder?"

"Cops got a search warrant this afternoon. They searched their apartment. They searched their car. Harvey, they found the gun under the driver's seat—a Golan semi-automatic—the gun that drilled Dave."

I pounded my right fist into the night stand. "You are kidding me?!" I shouted over the phone. "C'mon, Richard, I don't need this garbage."

"It's true," Richard said. "Remember that guy they call Sheepman? Well, he identified Wendy as the woman who slapped Dave and got pushed down in front of some little store up in Bowman. A couple deputies drove him up there and he showed them where he had seen them. You match what time it was Dave and Wendy were yelling at each other in beautiful downtown Bowman with what the Medical Examiner determined was Dave's approximate time of death, then you have a close match. That's the line we're running in the paper tomorrow, along with the gun-in-the-car angle. It fits, Harvey: Dave pushes her down, then rides off on his bike and, a couple minutes later, according to Lawrence Webber, Wendy drives off in the same direction. It fits."

My head was spinning. I was no longer groggy—I was bewildered.

"Wendy wouldn't even touch a gun," I said, trying to convince myself more than Richard.

"Harvey," Richard said calmly, "she just got pushed too far. Dave was probably off seeing Ann Benchley or something and she found out about it. Then they get into a fight and he goes off to see her or some other chick...hell, do I have to fill it all in for you?"

"They found a gun," I said. "How do they know it's the same gun that killed Dave. Have they done tests?"

"My source says yes," Richard said. "Crime Lab fired a round off into the water tank this evening. My source called me an hour ago. That gun was the instrument, Harvey. It looks like Wendy killed him."

More theatrically-trained shouting came through the walls.

Thoughts raced through my mind as I listened to the dull hum of static over the phone. Why the hell didn't Wendy just leave? Just pack up Jill and run for it? Because Dave was a good detective and he'd track her down. Why didn't she go to the courthouse and get a restraining order against him? Right, Wells. How many times had I heard about women getting restraining orders against a guy and the guy still comes around to beat the crap out of them or steal the kids—or both.

Maybe Richard was right. Wendy did just finally snap. Sheepman saw them together, saw them both drive one after the other in separate vehicles, to the murder scene. And then solid evidence—the gun. Now all there was needed was a confession; I imagined Wendy saying she didn't mean to shoot him but she just lost it. She doesn't even remember what happened after she got out of the car and walked down to the creek, but the next thing she knows she's driving like a bat out of hell down the old highway, which was the point that Lawrence Webber last saw her. She just snapped. It had happened in battered spouse and child-abuse cases before.

Except that it wasn't in Wendy's nature to even carry a gun in the first place.

"Harvey?" I heard Richard say.

"Yeah," I said.

"You think Wendy really did it?"

Richard started to reiterate what the evidence seemed to point to. Then there was more shouting from the other side of the wall. I wanted to get off the line and find out what was up over in the suite.

"I have to go, Richard."

After I hung up, my phone rang again. This time it was Rochelle Millman.

"Who is this? Who is this? I need to speak to Jack Benchley right now," was her greeting.

"Hello, Rochelle. This is Harvey. Mr. Benchley's not here. Don't tell me. You wanted the Benchley suite but the front desk gave you this number instead."

"Is that you, Harvey?" she said. "I need to speak to Jack Benchley. Wendy has been arrested for murder. I know he's hiding out in London. I want you to get him for me and have him shell out for getting my sister a first-rate legal team."

She rattled on hysterically for about a minute about how she had been married to Jack Benchley for a whopping twenty-five months, two years, and how she had given up her acting career for him in the last year of their two year marriage and so on and so on.

"Ah...Rochelle, why don't you get your husband Leroy to help you on this one."

"We're separated! You knew that. Stop stalling with me, Wells. Get me-"

"Look, Rochelle, I don't know where your ex-husband is. I'm trying to find out. You need to take care of Wendy right now, Benchley can't. And I can't help you either... not right now."

The hotel operator broke in on the line. There was an important message for me from Ann Benchley's suite. I gave Rochelle a brisk goodbye and hung the phone up. It rang almost immediately. Bonnie was on the line now.

"I think you should come over here," she said, sounding dazed. "Mr. Trubshawe has something he's showing us right now. It's a shade beyond incredible."

"Give me a couple minutes and I'm there," I replied.

I put myself together, all the time mulling over the news, especially what had happened to Wendy. I remembered Ray Harrison telling me about Ralph Bates seeing Wendy down at the gun range in Middleburg a few days before Dave bought it. I had found that implausible hearsay. Bates was in a league with Warbeck after all. But, with this other evidence, who could say now if it wasn't true?

When I got to the suite, Avalon answered the door and I followed her to the spacious living room area. Bonnie was seated at an antique desk on the periphery of the room. The desk was a large roll-top type, probably mahogany. There was a laptop computer on the desk, but Bonnie was ignoring her device. She was looking across the room, watching a large television that was framed in intricately-carved hardwood console built right into the wall. Avalon plopped herself supine on one of the sofas, one skinny leg dangling over the thick upholstery of an armrest. Both ladies were now intently watching the screen like high-stakes gamblers watching the final round of a boxing match.

"Take a look," Bonnie told me as she pointed to the television.

I looked. The picture was a stationary shot featuring a Gothic-like tower maybe a hundred feet high that was the center of a town square. The shadow of the monument was long, indicating it was videotaped or filmed either at daybreak or twilight. A stone statue of a woman, decked out like an angel or an empress, stood out from the side of the monument. It was a tri-level structure, with a large cross at the apex. There were low-lying buildings around the square, all of them made of brick or wood. The ground looked like a mixture of dirt and clay. There were no people in the shot. To me, it looked like a film set or some section of a Renaissance Era theme park. There was music on the soundtrack: the fife, drum and horn music you got before a Shakespeare production at Benchley's festival. The effect was haunting.

I looked back at Bonnie and shrugged my shoulders. "What is this?" I asked. "Vacation tapes from Euro-Disney?"

"St. Eleanor's Cross," Bonnie said to me without taking her eyes off the screen. "It was situated on West Cheapside, near the Guildhall, in the middle of London."

"Huh," I said, not quite sure what to make of her last remark. I looked back. Now there was a cluster of people entering the frame of the shot from both sides. They were dressed in costumes similar to what I had seen in plays and production stills from the Northwest Shakespeare Festival.

"I'm going to speed this up," Avalon said, picking up a remote control device from the table.

"Go ahead," Bonnie said. She sounded a little miffed at

the teenager's impatience.

"I want to see some more people," Avalon said. She fast-forwarded the video. In about thirty seconds the light in the shot became brighter, like a cloud had passed across the sun.

"Stop," Bonnie said. Avalon touched a button on the remote. The screen jiggled a bit, then the shot returned to a natural pace. Now there were more people in the shot. The foreground in front of the monument was a sea of men pushing carts and women carrying sacks on their backs. The pedestrians seemed oblivious to the camera. Those who passed a few feet in front of the camera had a look about them that was distinct from participants in stage productions. There were all dirty-looking, many with flies swarming about their faces. There was something about their faces, a look of strain and wear in the faces, a look of real dirt and real sweat on their faces that just cuts above fake. Some people were moving idly, some rapidly jostling around the idlers. The movements did not seem choreographed.

There was a woman standing a few feet from the camera. She was selling some kind of fruit from a cart. She was chewing on something and spitting every so often. She was shy all of her front teeth, and they weren't blacked out because you could see the crooked line of her jaw as if she had long ago compensated for a lack of a normal bite. Flies buzzed about her wares and she did nothing to shoo them away. And people bought them, and stuck them right into their mouths without so much as rubbing them against their blouses or jerkins to clean them off.

"Where is this?" I asked Bonnie.

"Better to say, 'Where was this?'" she said gravely. "This is London, circa 1597, A.D. The London of Shakespeare and Sir Walter Raleigh. What you are seeing doesn't exist anymore. You are seeing a video transfer of a film made 300 years before the movie camera was invented."

I shook my head. From somewhere in an adjoining bedroom I heard Ann Benchley barking. "But it's preposterous!" she shouted.

I heard Trubshawe say, "But it's real, Annie. I'm sorry, but that's what you have to believe."

Trubshawe's Cockney tones were followed by Picasso spouting off with a bit of Hands-Across-The-Sea diplomacy.

"Bullshit! This crazy Limey's full of bullshit!"

Looking back at the screen, I saw two horses enter the foreground of the shot. They were so close to the camera they blocked our view of the people milling about the square. Both horses were harnessed to something. They went a few paces further and I could see the team was pulling a coach with large wooden wheels that stuck out from the main frame of the coach. A man was seated on a buckboard at the top of the vehicle. He wore a broad-brimmed dark hat, a musketeer-style red-with-white-trim jacket, and a high collar that looked like an enormous coffee filter that I found out later was called a ruff. We got a close look at him as he descended to the ground.

"He's wearing a mandilion jacket," Bonnie said. "Also short breeches and hose. See how the breeches end at the knee. The aristocracy wore their breeches shorter at that time."

"He's got weird little shoes," Avalon said. "They look like slippers."

The coachman on the screen reached into a pouch hanging from his waist. He was wearing tan-colored gloves that covered half of his forearm. He pulled an amber-colored ball from the pouch and held it up to his nose.

"Is that what they called snuff?" Avalon asked.

"More likely a pomander ball," Bonnie remarked. "People used them to spare their nostrils from the smells around them. Sanitation was incredibly primitive at this time. They also thought it prevented infections. Boy, this is thrilling. I can't wait to go."

I shuddered. "*Go!*" I said, louder than I would have liked. "Go there? You're kidding, right?"

Bonnie gave me a fragile smile. "You don't have to...I'd like you to come though."

I looked back to the screen. Now a well-dressed woman entered the scene. Both ladies gasped when they saw her. The woman wore an hourglass-shaped bodice that was cut straight across her upper chest, and extended down her waist. From the waist down she wore a long, billowing skirt, elaborately embroidered with floral patterns of green fern. Her dress made her look unnaturally broad in the hips. The fern style of her skirt matched the design on her long sleeves, which were trimmed at her wrists with a pattern made from what looked like lace. Her face seemed young, but as she smiled at least two of her front teeth on the upper bridge were either decayed or missing. Her hair was a very light tint of blonde and it was piled up on her head, and a strand of jewelry dangled somehow from her hairline and across her forehead. A string of large tear-drop shaped pearls hung from her neck. She looked off-screen to her right, appearing to speak to someone. With the music, it was like watching a colorized silent movie. I kept waiting for the title cards to insert so I could find out what she was saying.

"That bodice that tapers down her waist is called a stomacher," Bonnie announced. "I wore one of those when I was in *Twelfth Night* at Berkeley. I was Viola and had to tape down my bosom with a couple ACE bandages. It was like a two-hour long mammogram every night." She groped herself. "Jeez, just thinking about that hurts. This girl looks luckier than me, figure-wise. Oh, look at that!"

The woman we were watching flicked open a fan and began to flutter it in her face. The fan was quite long as she opened it with the dexterity of a magician.

"Bonnie, did you just say we're *going* there?" I asked. The whole concept was escaping my mental grasp.

Another man entered the picture. He bore a light complexion and wore a hat with a high crown and a narrow brim. His lean face sported a sharp-edged black goatee. He was wearing a high ruff that completely covered his neck and brushed up right at the earring on his right earlobe. The man wore a dark blue doublet with diagonal slashes across both sides of his torso and white puffy sleeves as long as the woman's, but with a trim not so lacy at the wrists. He offered his arm to the lady and they walked out of the picture. There was a slow fade-out and then we saw a pastoral scene: a long shot of a cleared field amongst a setting of gently rolling, treeless hills. Rudely dressed men and women were cutting wheat with scythes, them gathering it up and piling the harvest onto multiple rows of haystacks.

The bedroom door swiftly opened. Ann Benchley emerged, dressed in a pair of jeans and a plain grey t-shirt. I noticed she was going braless. Jack Picasso followed, wearing what looked like a samurai outfit. He was stocky, but didn't have the build to make anyone forget Tirshiro Mufune.

Ms. Benchley had a look expressing confusion on her face, a look I could really relate to. She looked at me for a moment then sat down next to Avalon on the coach. Jack Picasso sat down next to his girlfriend, crossing his legs so no one would have to see what was under that oversized kimono. He kept shaking his head like his ear canals were full of water. He ran his right hand over the stock of two-toned hair like he had acute dandruff. I looked back over to the bedroom door. Trubshawe was standing there, dressed in a blue turtleneck with some sort of military emblem on the left pocket. He strolled over to the television set and addressed me.

"I don't imagine you've ever seen any footage like that, eh?" He gave me a devilish wink, with a corner of his centipede-sized mustache twitched upwards.

"Frankly, no," I said. "Bonnie tells me this is a blast from the past, filmed back in 1594 or so."

"1597, to be exact, Wells," Trubshawe said.

"You can't go back in time," I said firmly. "I'm no scientist, but I know enough to know it's not possible."

"I'm no scientist myself and it is possible. What's more, Jack Benchley and I have done it several times. Morton Ryskind built three time machines, and we used one once a year for the last six years. And we'll need to use the last one we still have again if we ever want to get Jack Benchley back."

"Gotta be bullshit," Picasso muttered.

Chapter Twenty-Nine

"I need a drink," Ann Benchley said.

"Coming up, luv," Trubshawe said, lowering the volume on the television set. He pressed a button on the wall next to the television set. A large rectangular panel slid open, revealing a well-stocked bar. He turned back to Ann. "What's your pleasure," he asked her.

"Irish coffee," Ms. Benchley said.

Bonnie asked for a Tom Collins. Picasso said he would make his own drink. I declined the offer of a beverage but, after the twin shocks of hearing about Wendy in police custody and this videotape, every fiber of my being called out for a tall Long Island Iced Tea. Hugh-Trevor Trubshawe mixed the drinks and filled me in on this time travel business, not that I was really buying a word of it at this point.

"I'll give you the bare-bones of it," Trubshawe said stolidly. "What you have just seen is a copy of some footage for a documentary old Jack called *First Viewing*. That was just a working title, of course. Every year we pretended to go up to Scotland fishing when we actually took a trip into the past via one of Ryskind's time machines. We stay about one week, renew old acquaintances and try to get some hidden camera footage for the documentary. We also pick up odd knick-knacks from the shops along Cheapside and a few quartos from around the book stalls at St. Paul's. Old St. Paul's, that is. That's how we started the bookstore and collectible shop my son manages up in Hampstead."

"You're not in the West End anymore?" Bonnie asked.

"Moved six months ago," the Major said. "Up to Hampstead. Got a better lease."

I tried to steer the conversation back on track. "So, this Ryskind fellow built a time machine?" I asked.

"Three time machines, actually," Trubshawe said. "He and old Jack grew up in Rogue Falls. Well, Mortie was actually a few years older than Jack. Mortie was class of 1942. Jack went into Stanford in 1943, then he was inducted into the Army a year later. Jack's father spent as much time as his Hollywood contract would let him in Oregon. They both went to Stanford University. Mortie later transferred to Berkeley. He was a whiz kid in physics. He was one of J. Robert Oppenheimer's bright boys. Oppenheimer was a nuclear physicist who was in charge of the Los Alamos—"

"I know about the Manhattan Project and all that," I said.

"Very well then," Trubshawe said, stirring up the Tom Collins drink with a crystal swizzle stick. "Well, Mortie was recruited by Oppenheimer to work at Los Alamos. After the war, Mortie went back to Berkeley and the Lawrence-Livermore Lab. Then comes that period you Yanks call the Red Scare. Around 1954, Mortie had his security clearance revoked because of his association with Oppenheimer and some other people the FBI thought were a bit pinko, as they used to say in the States."

"He was blacklisted," Ann Benchley added. "The same thing that happened to my grandfather in the movie business, and almost happened to my dad." Trubshawe brought her an Irish coffee and Bonnie her drink. Both ladies thanked him.

I wondered what Trubshawe's tale had to do with the weird tape and the business about time traveling.

"I'm missing something here," I said, wondering where the hell all this was going.

Ann Benchley picked up the story. "So Mortie goes back to Rogue Falls and takes over the Physics Department at Southern Oregon University. Eventually, the Cold War hysteria dies down after a few decades or so and the Johnson Administration gives the university a contract to experiment with high-energy particle beam technology. It's super-secret stuff. The government builds him a small atomic collider up on the south face of Pinecone Mountain, not far from my dad's ranch. When dad had a bellyful of Hollywood, he went back to Rogue Falls, too. He and Mortie renewed their friendship. Mortie's family had money, so he helped bankroll the Ryskind Theater and the expansion of the Elizabethan playhouse. Mortie was a great theatrical angel. He loved the notion of all the best young actors coming to the boondocks in Oregon and packing tourists in for Shakespeare."

"Okay," I said, lost more than ever.

"Cut to the chase, kid," Picasso said to his girlfriend.

"Right," Ms. Benchley said. She uncrossed her legs, put them together, and leaned forward in her chair, toward me. "Now we come to 1981. My fellow Screen Actors' Guild member Ronald Reagan is elected President. We are back to the era of Joseph Mc Carthy and the Witch hunters, at least as far as national security is concerned. The Department of Defense cancels the contract they have on particle beam development with Mortie and the University. But Mortie uses his own money to keep the experiments going. He cuts the staff down to himself and his younger daughter, Judith. The Feds let them use the old collider unit. It was obsolete anyway. So now Mortie has carte blanche and he turns the particle experiments to new directions. Don't ask me, or Truffie I presume, but he develops a way to take matter and propel it beyond the time-space continuum and place the matter into another time period. He confided his discovery with my father and they used the first time machine, after some safety tests, to travel back in time. Now, where do you suppose two Shakespeare buffs would like to go if they could go backwards in time?"

"Okay," I said, throwing up my hands. "This is about as reasonable a development as we've had in this case so far. We got a couple guys traveling back in time, taking pictures of people who've been dead for a few dozen decades. I'll buy that, maybe. So, now you're saying your father is in the 16th Century or something?"

"We think around 1599," Bonnie said calmly. "So, really, it's more like the 17th Century."

"Good point," I said. "Let's remember to be precise. Tell me this, Ms. Benchley: how long have you known your father and this friend of his were time-tripping?"

"Not until this afternoon when Truffie told me," she

replied. "Neither did Bonnie. But that's the only way to explain this film we uncovered at the ranch. The video was made from it. My dad didn't have money to build sets like this footage shows for his Elizabethan pictures. The stuff is beyond Hollywood."

Trubshawe said, "The only person Old Jack ever told about this was me. Annie is a bit of a talker, no offense, luv, and so he kept mum about it with her."

"That and a whole lot of the other things," I heard Ann Benchley murmur under her breath.

Jack Picasso got up and poured himself a thick finger of Scotch.

"So how does Warbeck fit into this whole picture?" I asked.

"Warbeck's been wanting to get back at Jack since he got fired from *Essex and the Queen*," Trubshawe said, taking a seat on the sofa opposite Ms. Benchley and her daughter. "Somehow he found out about the STUMPs, at least one of them. How he managed that I'm not sure."

"Did you say STUMPs?"

"Yes," Trubshawe said, before lifting a shot glass to his lips and taking contents in one gulp. "STUMP is an acronym for Subatomic Transference Utilization Machine. Mortie Ryskind added the 'P' at the end for a giggle. Jack had one at his ranch in Oregon. That's one that was stolen. There's one at a flat Jack owns in San Francisco. That's turned up missing as well. Warbeck must have it, too. I have the last STUMP at a location only myself and my family know about."

"That's what the break-in of the basement of the ranch house was about," Bonnie said. "The thing that was supposed to be just a giant stump of myrtlewood. Only it wasn't organic matter at all. Mr. Ryskind had combine synthetic resins that simulate wood and inside the thing was a...a..."

"Wait a minute," I said. "Bea Ryskind wanted me to draw a picture of that wooden platform Ralph Bates stepped on before he burned himself up. Was that wooden contraption a Stump?"

"Yes," Trubshawe said.

"So Ralph Bates isn't dead?"

"No," Bonnie said. "Bates is back in 1599. With Trevor Warbeck and his crew of cut throats. Thanks to a time machine."

"A time machine," Picasso said, his tone of voice telling me he wasn't buying a word of it.

"You think Warbeck stole machines and took Mr. Benchley back in time?" I asked.

"I'm sure of it," Trubshawe replied, pounding a fist into an open palm. "I took Bonnie's tip that Warbeck and his pack we're headed back to London. I'll say this for the fat old toff, he travels about first class. He had a Bentley pick him, his lady friend, and a tall chap up at Heathrow. They went into town, made a stop at the IFH headquarters on Oxford Street, then headed up Finchley Road, stopping off at Hampstead. That's not too far from my shop. Warbeck had a swank Georgian house on the west edge of Holly Hill, near the park. They nestled in about seven last night, just about nightfall. I hired a detective to follow them, then I took over after he tracked them to the house. I parked my rig down the hill and trooped up a couple hundred yards to the backyard area; had to drop some doped-up ground beef to quiet the two blasted rottweilers that barked up a fuss. After they dropped off for a nappy, I hopped over into the yard."

"That's pretty bold," Bonnie said.

"I had my Auto-Ordnance Thompson on my belt holster for comfort," Trubshawe said in a wry tone. "I wasn't hidden up in the bushes back there thirty minutes until I saw what I needed to see."

"Which was?" I asked immediately.

"The intense light," Trubshawe replied. He took a sip of his drink, finishing it off. "It was coming from the ground floor window. There were closed Venetian blinds over the window, but the glow came through the slits like the inside of the place was on fire. That's the high intensity light you see once the STUMP is activated. That told me somebody inside was time-traveling. I was ready to go after that, but this pigeon-toed chap—the same bugger who flew in with Warbeck and his woman— came out into the backyard to feed the dogs.

That chap had to be my old friend Dromio.

"He sees the mutts lying down with their tongues hanging out. Fortunately, he was a slow-moving lout. While he was scouting about I stole up behind him and gave him this—(he demonstrated a karate chop, displaying good agility for a man in his sixties.)—to give him a little nappy, too. I have no qualms about killing a man, but I avoid it if I don't have to. My best guess is that they have Jack back in time. Since the time coordinates on the machines were pre-set by Mortie Ryskind, he's back in the 1590's the England of 1599 I would reckon."

Picasso let out an audible sigh. "Bullshit," he stated loudly.

"What do you mean, Jack?" Ms. Benchley asked.

"A friggin' time machine?" Picasso said, standing up. "We're a bunch of grown people talking about time traveling." He gestured at Trubshawe with his drink in his hand. "This guy is a loon."

He looked to his girlfriend. "Look, Ann, I know this is tough for you, but you need to face this: your dad is dead. He's been gone two weeks. Warbeck hated him. He's dead."

"Fuck you," she said, her lips curling into a snarl.

"Fuck me?" Picasso said, thumping the hairless expense of his chest that showed through the front of his kimono. "Fuck me, you say? You don't want to believe me because I'm making a reasonable deduction." He gestured at Major Trubshawe. "You would rather believe Lord Alzheimer here with this irrational drivel about going back in time? Oh, that makes much more sense, doesn't it?"

Trubshawe pointed to the television screen, which was now showing a shot of the combination castle/manor house that Bea Ryskind had identified as the no longer extant Grantum Hall. His voice rose to a high timbre.

"Explain to me then, Sonny, how I can shoot motion pictures of buildings that were torn over three centuries ago. I have photographic evidence of Old St. Paul's on this tape. Old St. Paul's! It burned to the ground in September of 1666. Do you think Jack and I rebuilt the bloody thing?"

Picasso was quick with a response. "You used effects: bluescreens and computer-generated imaging. You can't fool a professional. You're a lying old bastard, playing mind games with Ann for God knows what reason. Do us all a favor and stop the crapola."

I saw Trubshawe's hand clench into fists, his body turn rigid. He took two steps toward the younger man. They were within striking distance of each other. Don't let the pot belly and the white hair fool you, you little twit. I'll take you out to the terrace and dust the—"

Trubshawe stopped talking when a harsh rotary noise filled the air. It was a sudden avalanche of harsh mechanical sound coming from outside through the glass doors to the terrace.

It was a helicopter. The markings on the side door indicated it was the property of the London Record. The whirling blades made a vibrant chop-chop sound. The wind generated by the rotors was blowing the patio table and chairs about like the ground below us was experiencing a massive earth quake. Through the windows I could see a tall man aiming a camera lens at us through the open hatch in the belly of the craft.

A very tall man.

By the time I realized who it was Picasso had thrown open the sliding glass door. He had pushed his way past Trubshawe and stormed unto the terrace, waving his arms and shouting profanities at the person he must have thought was a newsman intruding on Ann Benchley's privacy. The artificial gale blew open his kimono, revealing his magenta-colored boxers. He threw his glass at the side of the helicopter.

Then I saw the camera get thrown back into the belly of the helicopter. Dromio now grabbed another instrument.

"Get down!" I shouted out to Picasso.

Dromio picked up what looked like an AR-15 automatic rifle. Picasso, who did not get down at first, now hit the terrace like a seasoned infantryman. A split second later there was a flash from the barrel, followed by glass shattering inside the room.

"Hit the ground," Trubshawe shouted out. Bonnie did so. Ann Benchley screamed, frozen in a sitting position on the sofa. I dropped to my knees, intending to crawl over and drag her down below the line of fire. Above the din of the rotors, sharp popping noises registered in my head. Avalon jumped to her feet, screaming, trying to run out of the room. I lunged forward to stop her, but she was in full flight and I missed her legs. I looked up to see her take a round in her right arm, the light-colored sleeve over the arm taking on a darker hue at the point of entry. Her mother now walked over the top of me trying to get to her. I could feel the vibrations of bullets zinging above my head. I didn't see how the mother wouldn't be hit. Staying low on the rug, I crawled toward Bonnie to pull her down. She was coming toward me on all fours. We collided heads. I grabbed her by the shoulders and pushed her down unto the rug. I found a spot to bury my nose into the carpet.

"Stay down!" I heard Trubshawe shouting. Ann Benchley was still screaming, banshee-like, across the room from us. "No! No! No!" she let out in a voice broken by sobs. "Don't die, baby, don't die," she moaned.

Suddenly the air, which had seemed to be exploding, was calm. The vacuum was filled by Ann Benchley's plaintive wails. I looked over at Bonnie, sitting up to see if she was still moving. She had a dazed wild-eyed expression that probably matched my own.

She lifted her head up. I half expected her to be shot, but the next thing I knew she had turned to me. Seeing I was breathing and my eyes were open, she gestured to a point behind me. I looked over my shoulder. A telephone was on the table next to the fireplace.

"Get somebody up here!" she shouted at me, then staggered over to see about the other two women.

I got to my feet. The room had been shot to hell. The painting of a cathedral on the wall was splattered with bullet holes and a large flower-filled vase on a table hutch below the painting was now no bigger than an ashtray, with jagged shards strewn about. I pushed away some of the shards that had covered the phone, picked up the receiver, pressed 'O,' and flinched at the sound of bullets being fired off at a rapid clip from behind me. I turned about to see Trubshawe, standing over Picasso's shaking, prostrate body, firing his Thompson pistol into the air at what I assumed was the retreating helicopter. The front desk answered my call and I implored them in an addled tone to summon help.

As I knelt next to Bonnie, I could see that Avalon's condition was bad, but not fatal. She had been turned over on her back. Her eyes were showing the effects of shock. Her lips were trembling but no sound was coming out of them. Bonnie had ripped a sleeve off her blouse and had twisted it up for a tourniquet for her arm. A nasty exit wound had torn through the muscle, skin and bone of her biceps. Blood was all over her shoulder and neck as well. Ann Benchley was on her knees next to Bonnie, her hands to her face, sobbing uncontrollably.

I got up and went to the terrace. Picasso was now up and moving. He looked dazed, a sensible reaction for someone who thought he was only dealing with pesky photographers and, instead, almost got his head shot off. He held onto the iron-work barrier of the terrace like he was on a ship in a storm.

"Bloody gutless bastards!" Trubshawe growled, staring at the receding helicopter. He ejected the empty clip from his gun, then threw it to the ground in disgust.

The police came in about two minutes later, one uniformed officer cradling an assault rifle I could have used five minutes earlier. Then followed the paramedics. One of them took over for Bonnie on administering to Avalon. She went out on a collapsible gurney, a blanket over her slender body, an oxygen mask over her face and her mother holding her hand. She looked bad, but the bleeding had been stopped. Picasso kept insisting he was all right, although nobody was asking him otherwise. He and Bonnie followed the Benchleys and the medical team out of the hotel room.

"We believe this is the work of a militant strain of the Irish Republican Army," said Chief Inspector Clement Dunston, a tall middle-aged fellow with sharp blue-grey eyes, thinning-greyish blonde hair and a passing resemblance to Michael Caine. He was talking to Trubshawe and myself. We were the only witnesses to the attack left in the suite. Bonnie had followed Ann and Picasso, telling me she couldn't leave her boss alone. That left the two of us to give our statements to the police. Bothwell, who had greeted our party at Heathrow, had arrived about twenty minutes after the ordeal. There was another man there, a Deputy Inspector named Rivers from the Kensington Division and sundry uniformed police with their black-and-white checkered hats. The Chief Inspector was standing just outside on the terrace, with his back to the vista of Kensington Gardens. He had just finished a cellular phone call to his headquarters and while he spoke to us, scanned a notebook used by a uniformed officer to take our statements.

The two of us were standing just inside the suite, side by side. Trubshawe had his arms crossed and a lit brier pipe dangling from his mouth. I was leaning against the glass door, trying to keep my left leg from shaking. Behind us a crime team was marking the bullet holes and probing the holes in the walls for the errant slugs that had sprayed the room.

At the mention of the IRA, I looked over at 'Truffie.' He removed the pipe from his mouth and asked Dunston how Scotland Yard had arrived at such a conclusion.

Bothwell explained, "London Channel Six reported one of their traffic-spotting helicopters had been stolen from Gatwick Airport. Apparently, the pilot was overpowered about an hour ago as he walked into the hangar to check the craft before a flight. He's in the hospital now with a major concussion. A phone call went into the London Sun a few minutes ago, stating the copter had been hijacked and the attack made on the hotel by a subgroup of the IRA called the Londonderry Watch. The male voice on the phone claimed the attack on your party was made to show that pro-British American artists were not safe in London. I understand Ms. Benchley and her father are an integral part of a Shakespearian theatrical company in Oregon."

He pronounced the last word, 'O-re-gone' instead of the proper, 'O-re-gun.'

"Anyone could be a target of the IRA," Dunston replied smugly. "There may be a link between your Yank skinhead group and..."

"Bloody nonsense," Trubshawe interjected. "I know a little something about the lads of Shin Fein. I was in charge of an army barracks outside Armagh back in the Seventies. Those IRA buggers don't fly around in helicopters. They make bombs with cute little timers on them and set them to go off at bus stops or in pubs or police stations. The don't fly about in bloody aircraft! Besides, Ann Benchley has never said a bloody word in public about the IRA one way or another. So you tell me these terrorists are going to make an attack by air in broad daylight just to scare off the silly tourists?"

"What do you think then, Major Trubshawe," Inspector Bothwell asked?

"I'm not sure, Inspector, except that I'm looking at two of Scotland Yard's best who don't know the IRA from a pack of boy scouts."

That pretty much terminated the productive part of the interview. Dunston said he would consider "the Major's experiences and consult with him later." The way the Chief Inspector said those last four words told me he had a strong dislike for Trubshawe and they were not about to be consulting together anytime soon. And I was not high on his list for a darts partner in a corner pub, either, judging by the way Dunston told a uniformed black female sergeant to "take down Mr. Wells' statement, but wrap it up quickly."

Trubshawe called his wife to let her know he was all right, and for her to get to Cromwell Hospital double quick to see after "poor Annie." I was unscathed, but still, poor Harvey could have used a little comforting right then as well. After the call, Trubshawe and I left the hotel in the Range Rover for the drive over to the hospital. The trip took us south of Kensington Gardens and Hyde Park, on a four-lane road, passing such American transplants as Pizza Hut Restaurants, Safeway Supermarkets, and Arby's Roast Beef franchises. Looking down the side streets afforded glimpses of swank townhouses with Neo-Classic facades on one-way streets—called such-and-such 'mews' or whatever 'gardens' or whatever 'place', anything but 'street'—bristling with "NO PARKING" or "NO ENTRY" signs to keep non-residents in their rightful place.

When we got to the hospital there was a phalanx of reporters and cameramen gathered around the emergency room area. There also a cordon of police about to keep the emergency area from being clogged by those looking for a story instead of medical treatment. It took some explaining from Major Trubshawe and the intervention of Bonnie to get us into the place.

I spent a couple hours with Bonnie in the Emergency Waiting room at Cromwell watching the continual parade of wary nurses, anxious would-be patients, bored orderlies in white outfits pushing empty stretcher carts and the occasional doctor walking past in haste with a distracted look on his or her face.

I told Bonnie about Wendy being arrested for Dave's murder a few hours earlier.

"How did you find out?"

"Rochelle Millman called me. The front desk must have given her my number in the room."

"That's too bad. Well, thank God it wasn't Ann being arrested. I'm sorry for your friend, Harvey, I really am."

"Me too," I said, still not believing that Wendy was capable of killing anyone.

There was a television mounted on a wall above the visiting area. A soccer game was on. The announcers kept going on about some sort of championship cup. Then there was a newsbreak. An announcer did a story on the attack at the Kensington Gardens Hotel. He said there were "unconfirmed reports Ann Benchley had been wounded in the assault." That wasn't true, of course.

What had happened to Ann Benchley was a nervous collapse stemming from her daughter being wounded. The mother had been admitted to the hospital herself. Jack Picasso was somewhere else, probably as close as he could be to his girlfriend.

Trubshawe, who made forays to the information desk and buttonholed one of the doctors, told us that Avalon was in surgery and that Ann was resting comfortably after being heavily sedated and placed in a private room on the top floor. Mrs. Trubshawe, whom I gathered was a sort-of substitute mother for Ann Benchley since her mother's tragic accident, was in the hospital room with her.

"Did she ask for me?" Bonnie queried Trubshawe.

"She's asleep, or close to it," Trubshawe replied. "Jo was looking in on her, and that nutter of a boyfriend. Then the nurse sent them out. The best thing is to let the sedatives do their work and pray for poor little Avalon." He sat down on the hard plastic chair next to Bonnie. "Soon as I find out about Avalon's arm, I'm going back. And when I say 'going back', I don't mean to Kensington. Wells, you're welcome to come along but if you want to stay I won't talk you into it. I'm getting my man Jack back from Warbeck, alone or with help, and that's the end of it. I'd take my eldest boy, Stephen, but his mother has put a halt to that. She only wants to lose one family member at a throw—can't blame her there. My younger boy, Malcolm, is a Second Lieutenant. He's in Labrador on a training exercise. We could use that lad."

"I'm with you, Truffie," Bonnie said.

"Count me in," I replied, with less enthusiasm.

Chapter Thirty

Trubshawe and Sons, Books and Curiosities was located in the middle of a quaint, high-rent alley called Flask Walk in the burg of Hampstead, just north of London proper. The shop was on the first floor of a three story red stone brick affair and the environs outside were teeming with art galleries, chic clothing boutiques, old fashioned pubs with names like *The Horse and Groom*, and restaurants with well-dressed people waiting patiently in a mass at the entrances for tables to be freed up. It was creeping Bohemia in the best tradition of similar tony villages in California, like Sausalito and Laguna Beach, I had briefly visited years before.

The store was crammed with all sorts of antiques ranging from fully intact brass cannons (with a stack of grapefruit sized cannonballs next to the caisson), a display of old-fashioned four poster beds, and myriad examples of matchlock and flint-lock riffles from the 16th through the early 19th centuries. There were also a few strategically placed portrait paintings, sewing tables, a virginal, a few multi-colored coats-of arms with family crests painted on the front, several racks of hardbound books, and even a few manuscripts of old English Bibles and pirated 'quarto' editions of plays by William Shakespeare and his contemporaries. The latter manuscripts were in glass-enclosed display cases, and a sign in antique calligraphy at the base of the central case proclaimed the manuscript section: "One of the finest private holdings of rare British literary specimens." Now that I knew about the thing

Trubshawe called "The STUMP," I didn't need to ask a lot of questions as to how they secured most of the 'rare' finds.

"Dad got 'em right in front of St. Paul's most of them," Trubshawe's son, the thirtyish Stephen, said to me. "Back in the 1590's, of course. We gave the really valuable stuff to one of the big auction houses. With the money we get for the sales, we buy more contemporary stock to boost the inventory."

Stephen Trubshawe was a good deal taller then his dad, about six foot one or two, with a clean-shaven face, clean cut reddish-brown hair, and owlish eyes that I assumed must have come from his mother's end of the family, although I had not seen Jo Trubshawe yet. He was dressed in a charcoal grey suit with s pale red vest and a checkered red-and-black tie. I judged from his get-up and the visible stock that his customers were of the high end on the economic scale. Stephen stood at the sales counter, adding up the credit card receipts for the day. It was about eight in the evening, the shop was closed, and the heavy red curtains were drawn over the high-arched display window and front door. This was good for me because I would rather not have passers-by seeing how I was dressed. It was my first time wearing an Elizabethan-style jacket, or doublet, made from a stiff, heavy fabric called buckram. I also had a puffy-sleeved shirt, pants-like breeches that barely covered my thighs and, covering the rest of my legs, a pair of sheer dark brown hose. Add to that my curious long-brimmed hat with a feather sticking upward from the brim and the whole outfit gave me the willies. There was a radio on behind Stephen and, in low volume, there was the Vienna Philharmonic Orchestra playing what I recognized as a sad movement from Beethoven's Seventh Symphony.

"The bastards used a helicopter, did they?" Stephen growled. "I hope Avalon will come through surgery all right. I'd like a piece of those bastards for what they did."

I nodded, more worried about whatever it was that lay ahead for Bonnie and me, and the Beethoven in the background was not helping.

"Have you ever been on one of these—time trips?" I asked.

"Yes," Stephen said. "I got to go three years ago. It will blow your mind. History laid out right before your eyes. It's amazing. Beats the hell out of a week in the Lake District, I'll tell you. Even Gibraltar. I envy you, Wells."

I was still not sure the whole thing wasn't a colossal gag, but if I was being played for a sucker a lot of people had been going to an awful lot of trouble just to do it. Having picked up some fish-and-chips on the way over to the shop, and put on the only Elizabethan duds that would fit me in the back storage room, all I was waiting for now was Bonnie to get her costume on and for Trubshawe to put up or shut up on this time machine business.

"Damn," Stephen said. "I forgot about Nottingham Forest." He smacked his forehead with an open palm, turned off the music and switched to the radio. Now we had two jovial commentators doing coverage on a soccer, or European Football, game.

"Football," my host said. "Liverpool versus Nottingham Forest. The winner plays West Ham at Wembley next week in the Final. He talked about seeing some American football games broadcast late Sunday nights on some station. He thought American football was, "quaint, with all the padding and the silly penalties." I did not argue on behalf of America's most popular sport; I wasn't feeling too macho in my brown hose.

Above the desk where the boom box sat was an oak-paneled wall which sported photographs, plaques and framed certificates of a military nature. The other man noticed my interest in the display and filled me in.

"The pictures are mostly of my dad," he said, casually looking over his shoulder. "The one on the upper left is dad getting a Distinguished Service Cross from some general for some mopping- up mission his platoon did in Malaya back in the Fifties. He was a subaltern then. The one next to it is Dad in front of his first copter, the Westland Dragonfly. The color snap below is my younger brother, Malcolm. He's the chip off dad's block in this outfit. He's doing his bit in a training operation in Labrador as we speak. Just got promoted last month. That one just next to it is dad and Mr. Benchley when they were doing *Operation Sealion* over on the Isle of Guernsey. And that last one to the left of it is me at an evacuation hospital on South Georgia Island."

"You were in the Falklands war?"

Stephen nodded. "And it was no bloody holiday camp, let me say. Argie batteries hit us on a reconnaissance run over

Darwin. I had to pitch it into a cove. Three of my boys got out, two didn't. We held out on some high ground—fortunately the Argies weren't too aggressive—until the Paras landed and the place was secure enough for evacuating the wounded. I was on my back for a couple months, then I had a couple months of rehabilitation. Endless fun, that was."

"Are you still in the Army?"

"Sort of," Stephen shook his head. "Territorial Army, like what you'd call the National Guard in the States. I might have stayed active, but the gamy leg I got would've meant I'd been a desk-bound paper shuffler until I retired. Dad needed somebody to run this shop when he and Mr. Benchley got started. Mum's health isn't good, so here I am."

"Was your dad in the Falklands?"

"No, he couldn't get in it. He was Territorial Army back then and his unit was left home because somebody would have to help deal with the Russians. Or deal with the IRA, as the case may be. Anyway, he tried to get some strings pulled, but it was a no go. Too old, the CO at Aldershot said. It pissed him off something royal to miss it, too."

Trubshawe himself came out from a back room behind the counter. Like myself, he looked rather anachronistic in his chosen outfit. It was Renaissance Ready-To-Wear, similar to my dress, but with a shiny herringbone-style grey-and-black doublet with a black cape that fell to the small of his back. Over his reddish-grey locks was a derby-like, almost brimless hat, with a gold-colored braid around the crown. On his hip was a long red velvet scabbard with the decorative hilt of the sword sticking up from the top. He also wore butternut-colored leather gloves.

"What kind of gun do you prefer, Wells?" Major Trubshawe asked.

"Anything that fires bullets," I said, "and preferably a firearm from the 20th Century rather than one of those black powder contraptions you have on the wall."

"Try this," Trubshawe said, unlocking a drawer on the counter. He pulled out a pistol and handed it across to me. It was a long-barreled nine-millimeter Beretta with a plastic stock. The next thing he handed me was a full ammo clip.

"There's more clips that come with it," he said. "I'm putting the rest of the supply in the ordnance box we're taking, along with the grenades and such. The Beretta there can fire off ten rounds to a magazine. I take it you Americans enjoy getting off as many rounds as you can."

"I'm more the revolver type," I said, ignoring the negative inference. I checked out the feel of the firearm in my hand, checked the safety to make sure I wasn't going to shoot my foot off, then loaded the magazine. I pulled open my breeches on the left hip and put the gun into the belt holster I had brought along from home. "You say we're taking grenades along?" I asked the senior Trubshawe.

"Yes, some lethal types my unit confiscated from the more zealous Unionists over in Ulster. Also, a couple dozen M84 stun grenades. The British Special Air Service uses them. You might know of them as concussion grenades. You said you were a policeman, Wells. How much experience have you had with explosives."

"Not much," I said. "Drug dealers in California usually don't go in for grenades. I've confiscated some AK-47's from some brown heroin retailers, but nobody ever lobbed a grenade at me."

Trubshawe nodded, apparently not overly impressed by my law enforcement background. The next thing he handed me over the counter was a short, thick leather scabbard. It contained a sword, which I pulled out a few inches. My cutting implement was thicker than Trubshawe's, but his was longer.

"We didn't go in much for swordplay back in Sutter City, either," I said. "What do you want me to do with this turkey slicer?"

"Hopefully, you'll just need it for show. You're coming into Merrie Old England posing as my servant. Servants were expected to be armed to help protect their masters—and themselves. You'll carry a sword. I'll be packing my Bilbo blade rapier. I'll also have a wheelock pistol for local color. Keep that Beretta out of sight unless we're in a tight spot. And, I'll thank you not to call that sword and scabbard I handed you a bloody bird slicer from now on. That's good English craftsmanship you got in your mitts. I got that, and the rapier, from the finest sword smith in London, a Huguenot chap named Jacques Gabin, who had a fencing school in one of the townhouses on London Bridge, back when there was only one London Bridge. He did fine work for a lad in a time before they had precision equipment and fancy machines."

"I stand corrected," I said humbly, giving the portion of the sword I had pulled out a second look.

I next saw the attention of both Trubshawes go upwards to the stairway leading to the mezzanine that made up the second floor. Bonnie was descending the stairway, and she was quite a vision. For starters, she was wearing a style of dress similar to the lady in the *First Viewing* video who was standing next to the coach fluttering her fan. She wore a dark forest-green cut away coat over her shoulders that matched the design on her stomacher—green with thin concentric circles of purple embossed over the main color scheme—and also went very well with her dark green eyes. Below the stomacher, the underskirt, which only showed at the very front, was decorated in a floral pattern of green fern. The skirt she wore above it was made of a thicker material, green again, and billowed out at the hips. Bonnie later told me the skirt was called a farthingale. The hem of her skirt, which extended to her ankles, was a purple fringe. Instead of the high, wide ruff the lady in the video wore, Bonnie had a shorter neck piece that flared outwards a couple inches above her collar and accentuated the delicate lines of her neck. Her hat was shaped like a garrison cap with a white plume sticking up from the short upcurved brim. Her hair was now braided in the back. Her shoes were almost invisible under her skirt but, as she walked down the steps, I caught a couple glimpses of some medium heel pumps that were secured to her feet by what looked like ribbons.

"You have quite a selection of garments up there," Bonnie said to our host. "Did they come from the Shakespeare Festival or from Tudor London?"

"The real stuff, mostly," Trubshawe said. "The things we know are rare we sell to Soterby's to be auctioned. The proceeds from those, and the books and artifacts we've brought back, have financed this shop. The more recent artifacts we got from other dealers either in cash or barter."

"You look spiffy," I said.

"Thank you," Bonnie said. She executed a full pirouette, obviously pleased with her fashion choices. "I'm excited," she said. "I'm also scared."

I could concur with that, especially the latter feeling.

"Don't worry, luv," 'Truffie' Trubshawe said. "I've seen you act Shakespeare. You can pull this off. Just help Wells here pass for an Elizabethan. Right, then. We're ready for the shots and the STUMP. Picasso is supposed to be joining us. If he's not here, we go without him."

After I bowed to Bonnie, we went through the Dutch door behind the counter and followed the Trubshawes into the stock area, which was filled with wooden shelves of books mixed with some sculptures and paintings. I took note of Stephen Trubshawe's severe limp in his right leg. It was 'gamy' to be sure.

We turned a corner in the stock area, just past some tall metal three-tier shelving and came up to what looked like a decaying myrtlewood tree stump, about seven feet high and completely open at one side so it had the shape of an enormous upright seashell.

It was almost an exact replica of the cube-like device I saw in San Francisco. There were a couple of knotholes on the inside of the 'bark' and there was about a foot-high platform of wood that constituted the bottom of the STUMP. Trubshawe stood next to it, looked it over, then spoke to the three of us.

"I had this stored away in a commercial hangar, along with my old Westland, over at Heathrow. I figured that was the best place I could keep my eye on it. After I found out Warbeck had the other STUMP, I transferred it over here in the company lorry. Stephen or I have been here around the clock since to make sure none of Warbeck's boys try and pinch it."

Opposite the STUMP was a large metal shed surrounded by sand bags. I gathered this was where bystanders went into when the time machine was in use.

Next to the STUMP, on a table covered with a white cloth, was a set of hypodermic syringes surrounded by a cluster of small bottles with medical labels on the sides. Trubshawe told us we had to all take three shots. It was necessary to ward off a variety of diseases we would come into contact with when we traveled back in time. Something I was still not quite convinced we were going to do.

"I won't need them but you and Wells will have to have them. 16th Century London is as bad for diseases as parts of West Africa or New Guinea are today. I know neither of you are keen on it, but it has to be done. We already lost one of our fellow travelers because we didn't take along the right vaccine for what he came down with."

"Who was that?" I asked.

"Mortie Ryskind," Trubshawe replied somberly. "God bless the poor bugger."

"Couldn't you get him back to modern times to be treated?" Bonnie asked.

"Circumstances wouldn't allow it," he replied. "I'll explain that later. Right now time is running short. Every minute—"

There came the sound of a jingling bell from somewhere inside the sales area of the shop. The Senior Trubshawe cast a withering glance at his son.

"Stephen, you sot, did you forget to lock the front door?"

"You're late, Mr. Picasso," Trubshawe said as the director came into the room.

"I was still at the hospital," Picasso said. "I waited to see if Avalon came through so I could tell Ann some news."

"Did they save the arm?" Bonnie asked.

"Yeah," Picasso said. "She might not be able to do much with it for awhile, but the docs saved it. Ann is still zonked out from the drugs the docs put in her. Your wife is at the hospital, Major Trubshawe. She said she'd let Ann know about her kid when she woke up."

"Good," the Major said. He then pointed to a rack of clothes. "Get in a get-up, and we'll give you a shot or two."

"You know I don't believe in any of this time travel stuff," Picasso said.

"Then keep your arse out of the way," Trubshawe replied. "We're going and you can hide and watch."

Picasso murmured something under his breath and walked over to the wardrobe rack.

I took my shots in my right arm and Bonnie took hers in her left. Picasso finally did grab a doublet, jerkin and some other accessories and retired into the bathroom. Then I helped Stephen place two heavily-laden saddlebags on top of the platform of the STUMP. The contraption might not have been real wood, but it certainly felt like it. I noticed Bonnie was now trying to light a cigarette, only the second one I had seen her take out since I'd been around her. She went through three of her butane lighters before she found one that worked.

"Are you sure you don't want a pistol?" the senior

Trubshawe asked Bonnie.

"Positive," Bonnie said. "I'm nervous enough without worrying about accidentally shooting you or Harvey."

"As you wish," he replied. "Just remember to stay close to me if things get dicey. There is food and drink in the saddlebags to get us through. The only thing we'll need to pick up back there are horses. We can get them in Old Hampstead. Fellow Jack and I know keeps a stable there."

Horses! Christ, I couldn't ride a horse. I said as much to Bonnie when both Trubshawes left us alone to set the security alarm and phone up Jo Trubshawe at the hospital.

"Have you ever been on any type of riding animal?" she asked.

"I took a mule ride down into the Grand Canyon a few years ago."

"Nothing to worry about; we'll get you a mule then. They're easier to handle than a horse."

"The mule I rode was not a well-motivated animal. I hear they have their own agenda sometime. Will I be able to keep up with you guys without breaking my neck?"

Bonnie rolled her eyes. "Don't worry about it. I'll give you a crash course. You'll just be riding, not show jumping," Bonnie said, sensing my weariness. "If they don't have mules, we'll get you a Dartmoor Pony. Whatever you ride, all you have to remember is that you're in charge and not the animal."

My stomach began to develop a case of the butterflies worse than when I got on the plane back to San Francisco. I looked up at the glowing neon-tube fixture above us and wondered what the hell I had gotten myself into. We were past the stage where this could go down as a joke. Could this big block of synthetic 'wood' actually go into the past? How could this be accomplished? Would we be pulverized into atomic particles and restructured into some fourth-dimensional void like some poor saps in a rerun of *Star Trek*?

Was the surly Jack Picasso right? Was Jack Benchley long dead and this a fool's errand?

My right shoulder started to ache from that little session with the hypodermics. I leaned against the vertical posts of one of the book shelves, next to Bonnie. I could tell she was nervous. She had started on her second cigarette.

"I thought they went fishing up in Scotland for a couple

weeks every year," she said between drags. "The time I went with Mr. Benchley to London, he and Truffie were supposed to be fishing up above Inverness. I heard that Morton Ryskind died when there was a boating accident in the North Sea five or six years ago. Supposedly, the body was never found. If any of this time travel stuff is to be believed, then all this fishing business was just a smokescreen for—"

Bonnie broke off when Jack Picasso emerged from the bathroom. He was dressed in a shiny slate-blue doublet, jerkin, breeches that covered him from the waist to his knees, pointy shoes and hose. Far from looking self-conscious, he looked at home in the garb. He eyed the table where the hypodermic needles and bottles of vaccine were set.

"I'm not taking any shots until I see how this time-tree crap works," the director said defiantly.

Trubshawe and his son reappeared. "Anyway, Avalon is out of surgery, thank God," the father said. "I don't think Annie could've survived anything happening to her." He rubbed his gloved hands together. "Well, let's get to it, then." He took Bonnie by the hand and the two of them climbed up to the base of the STUMP.

Bonnie looked pale, like she was ready for a good faint.

Stephen and I loaded up a pair of saddlebags that we set at the feet of Bonnie and Trubshawe. The one I carried was full of bulky items and weighed a ton. When I turned around from that chore, I saw Trubshawe again. This time he was carrying what I first took for a 12 Gauge shotgun.

"A Ruger," he said, patting the wooden stock. "Mini-30 Carbine. Gives us a little extra firepower. Wish I had one for you, Wells, but the gun laws here are a bit tighter than in the States." He slipped the rifle into a leather case that looked a lot older than the inception of semi-automatic rifles.

"Here," Bonnie said, handing me what was left of her cigarette as I stepped away from the platform. The tip was still emitting smoke. "Hold onto it for me. It'll be something to remember me by."

"I'll save it for you," I said. "You get a few more drags on it when we—well, wherever we're going."

Trubshawe patted her on the hand. "Don't worry, luv," he said heartily. "It's easier than taking the Underground line to South Kensington Station." He looked at me. "You follow us,

Wells," he said. "You won't have long to wait."

My left leg started to shake. Stephen, Picasso and myself went into the metal shed. We watched Bonnie and her escort through a multi-paneled window.

Trubshawe set the rifle case against the inside of the STUMP, then positioned Bonnie into a crouch, putting one arm lightly on her shoulders. With the other arm he opened a small panel on the side on the interior of the 'bark.' Inside the panel, which was impossible to detect previously, was a series of vertically arranged buttons marked in blue and red above a rectangular-shaped digital read-out. Trubshawe punched one button and the whole panel lit up. He punched more numbers with fast and efficient dexterity. The digital read-out displayed a series of electronically calibrated numbers. There were about a dozen and a half numbers displayed, something like 6870338.... Whatever it meant it made no sense to me;the sequence was certainly was not an ordinary calender date.

A few seconds later, as I watched Bonnie's face and she looked back at me with her lower lip trembling, a vivid red cloud engulfed the entire STUMP and a circular patch about the perimeter of the machine and the voyagers on the platform. A blast of artificial wind rattled the shed.

Then, suddenly, the reddish cloud was gone and Bonnie and Trubshawe were somewhere else. The three of us stepped out of the shed.

Nothing occupied that space now but the bare concrete floor. But there was a large darkened circular ring on the concrete, similar in shape to the spot where Dave was found dead back in Bowman. No sound could be heard as the people and objects vanished before us. The dark circle was emitting smoke and the room felt hotter.

I gulped, tried to say something, felt my mouth dry, my optic nerves being disbelieved by my brain.

Picasso was more demonstrative in his reactions. He backed away from where he was standing, his face looking like he had suddenly happened on a full-sized grizzly bear while taking a nature hike.

"Fuck this," he said. He then turned around, grabbed his pants that were laying on the table and ran out of the stockroom. From the sound of the bell, and the alarm going off, he had left the premises. Stephen went to override the alarm.

After it was shut off, I heard the sound of a car driving away. The intrepid director had taken off, leaving most of his wardrobe behind.

Stephen walked back into the stockroom, shaking his head.

"No guts," was his reaction to Picasso's sudden dash. Suddenly there was that bright red light again and the STUMP reappeared at the exact spot it was before, sans Bonnie and Trubshawe. The equipment and the saddlebags had not made the return trip either. The control panel on the STUMP was still open, the digital numbers flashing.

"Mum doesn't like to see dad vanish like that," Stephen said to me. "It's just as well they said their good-byes over the phone. O.K., Harvey, Dad has it set for automatic return. Jump up on there, man."

I did what I was told, quickly, before I let myself have any time to think about it. I crouched down on the platform, as Bonnie had. I could feel the adrenaline flowing to my extremities.

"Your watch," Stephen said, pointing to my arm. "You don't want that showing. Put it away."

"I will," I said, undoing the hook then ripping the timepiece off my wrist and tossing it at Stephen. "What else do I have to do?"

"Just stay where you are," he said, folding his arms. "Dad has it set automatically." He checked his own wristwatch. "You have eleven seconds before you evaporate." He ducked into the shed.

I didn't like that last word. I felt a tingling sensation in my stomach growing to an intensity I could hardly bear. Those next few seconds took a long time to elapse. And then a brief flash of red seem to engulf the whole room. I heard nothing. I felt nothing. I saw no form, just a blob of primary color.

And then the red about me vanished. I was no longer in the stockroom. I was outside. It was daylight and I found myself in either a park or a forest. The first sound I heard was the trilling of a bird. I saw Bonnie and Trubshawe a few yards away from me, watching me, shoulder to shoulder, near a line of sturdy oak trees with thick trunks and gnarled branches thick with flat brown leaves. Bonnie had a smile on her face, which I took as a sign we had made it to wherever we were supposed to be.

I stepped slowly off the platform. My two companions were silent, allowing me to take in my surroundings. We were surrounded by tall trees in a narrow enclosure that afforded no view beyond the circle of trees.

"Where?" I asked. I felt short of breath, nauseated and not up to making complete sentences.

Trubshawe spoke: "If my calculations are correct, this is September 27th. This is the year of Our Lord, 1599."

Bonnie reached out for her cigarette. I gave it to her. She took a quick, long drag. At that moment, I envied her habit.

Chapter Thirty-One

A minute after I stepped off the platform of the time machine, I sank down to my knees. My head was swimming. I felt a numbing sensation in my jaw which, joined with the upset stomach, to made me think I was due to vomit. The suspense was short-lived. I began to retch. There followed the remains of my dinner coming up and finding a new home on the rocky, leaf-strewn earth.

"One of the side effects," I heard Trubshawe say from above after my heaves ceased. "My boy Stephen had the same reaction when he went through the device."

Bonnie crouched down to one knee in front of me. "Can you sit up?" she asked me in a gentle tone. I tried to answer but my ribs ached, and I was preoccupied with cleaning my face off as best I could with my hand. She handed me a much-needed handkerchief which I used about my mouth and nose. Then slowly I rose up. I still felt wobbly, so I followed Bonnie's lead to a weathered tree stump a few paces to our left. Judging by the small band of curled up centipedes I had to wipe off before I sat down, I was now dealing with real wood. As I sat down, the STUMP glowed red again and faded from view as abruptly as before.

"I gave Stephen instructions to be back here in fifteen hours," Trubshawe said. "That, hopefully, will be enough time to do what we've come to do."

"Where are we exactly?" I asked after collecting myself.

"We are at the same place we were back in our own time. We are no longer in Hampstead, however. The old Hampstead is to the west of us. It's just a village. The shopping district where my collectible establishment is won't be developed for another 250 years. We have traveled back in time 401 years. You can bet if Warbeck had us followed, then his thugs have traveled back into time as well, to warn their boss of our coming. It will take them some time to get across to the west section of Hempstead Heath, where Warbeck's probably waiting at his house, but not that long. They'll have the dogs after us soon enough, but by then we'll have cleared out of here. That will give us some time to secure transportation and reconnoiter out target."

"But would the other STUMP machine go back to the very same time we're at now?" Bonnie asked.

"The exact same time," Trubshawe replied. "All three machines were designed by Mortie Ryskind to work in synch in case we ever took a large party back into time with us. They are synchronized and intended to be used together. That is why Warbeck wanted to get his fat mitts on all of the STUMPs. When synchronized, in a triangular formation, they create a high-energy particle field capable of transporting large groups of travelers—or large amounts of equipment. I know it works because the first time I went with Jack and Mortie we used all the STUMPs together and took three horses and a pack mule along with us so we would all have a beast to ride when we got back to the past. After that, Jack and Mortie decided to keep one STUMP in a separate hemisphere to prevent some nutter from getting his hands on all three at the same time in case something went wrong. And now, kids, something has gone very wrong."

"Can I get some water?" I asked.

Bonnie opened up one of the saddlebags nearby and handed me a plastic water jug. I pushed up the plastic spout and took a long drink.

"Don't drink too much," Trubshawe warned. He took a seat on the large smooth rock opposite where I was seated. "We only have four gallons of water. After that, we'd have to set up to boil the local stuff or risk dysentery."

I replaced the spout and leaned back, propping myself up with the palms of my hands. "So what's so important about having all three of these time machines? Once you have one, wouldn't that be enough?"

"Not for your boy, Trevor Warbeck," Trubshawe replied with a shake of his derby-topped head. He paused to pick up a twig, then took to scraping off a specimen of dung that was squashed and stuck under his boot. (I had on slipper-like footwear, slightly too-large. I guessed it was what servants wore, but I wasn't looking forward to walking a great distance in them.)

"No," the Major said, still scraping away, "Your boy Warbeck must have bigger plans than just soaking up a little Elizabethan civilization for the odd holiday. The STUMPs synchronized together can send heavy equipment back into time—say a tank or a helicopter. That's what he needs all our STUMPs for."

"Why?" I asked, afraid I already knew the answer.

Trubshawe looked behind himself with quick glances over his shoulder, first to the left then to his right. From out of a pocket in his doublet came his brier pipe. He then leaned over to one of the saddlebags, procured a pouch of tobacco, and spoke as he loaded his pipe. "It would seem, Wells, from what Miss Bonnie here has told me and shown me in her book, that Fatso Warbeck has already traveled at least once back into this time and made himself two new friends. One is a fellow named Robert Devereux, Earl of Essex. That was the red-bearded chap you had the altercation with in San Francisco. I'll bet ten pounds that the other chap, the younger long-haired one, is a fellow named Henry Wroithesley. He's the Earl of Southampton. Both those toffs might be nancy-boys, but I wouldn't wish to cross swords with either one in a dark alley. They are both excellent swordsmen, brave as the blue-bloods usually are in a pinch, and both are now desperate men, especially if Warbeck has filled them in on what the future holds for each of 'em."

I recalled the story of the Earl of Essex and his rebellion against Queen Elizabeth I from a couple films I had seen—including one written and directed by Jack Benchley—plus bits and pieces from a couple history courses in school. The Earl of Essex was a hotshot at Elizabeth's court, who wooed her for his political and economic advantages. The Queen had about forty years on him, age-wise.

When Essex led an English Army into Ireland in the 1590's to pacify an indigenous rebellion, she was outfoxed by the Irish Chieftain, Tyrone, and he returned to London in disgrace. The Queen, angry that he had concluded a worthless peace treaty then booked it back to her court, started turning the screws on him, figuratively at least. She yanked some monopoly on imported wines he held, which effectively bankrupted him. That move, coupled with his being prosecuted for some related offenses and his loss of status in court, pissed him off.

Some months after these bad turns in his fortunes, he and a couple hundred of his closest friends (including, if I remembered right, this Southampton guy) launched an abortive revolt against the Queen. It failed, and shortly after that Essex and the ringleaders took up residence in the Tower of London. His head hit the basket shortly after that. As I recalled this, Bonnie must have recalled her knowledge of this little ignoble chapter in British history, because she came up with a question for Trubshawe.

"Well, if Warbeck told Essex and Southampton about their failed rebellion, which comes about in roughly eighteen months if this is September of 1599, then obviously the two Earls are going to alter their plans, right?"

"You can count on that, milady," Trubshawe said ruefully. He packed his pipe with the dexterity of a long-time smoker. "I'll bet Warbeck has not only filled them in on their personal future, but I'm sure he gave them a good look at our modern world when the three of them went to London and San Francisco. Warbeck may have decided to throw in his lot with these gentlemen, and bring along a little 20th Century technology back here to make the rebellion go off sooner and better."

"If Warbeck wants to upset the path of history, he has the finances of the Strunk Empire backing him up," Bonnie said. "That means unleashing all kinds of modern weaponry on people back here who couldn't even fathom what they'd be up against."

I was starting to feel a few fathoms over my head, too. "Are we supposed to do something about this other business?" I asked.

"I'm only interested in getting Old Jack out of here alive," Trubshawe said as he put a match to his pipe. "We have a few nasty little weapons from modern times ourselves, but this is phase one of a rescue operation. If things are really as bad here as we think, then Good Queen Bess will have to protect her own bum from getting blasted off the throne." He took several puffs, producing alternate exhibits of flame and smoke from the pipe, then I watched as he sat back and looked up at the trees over our heads. A strong wind had just started up, rustling the branches. I looked up as well. I didn't want to believe we were back in time, but I had noticed something strange. When we were in what I was sure was modern England, the trees were beginning to sprout leaves. Now that we were here, wherever and whatever 'here' was, the leaves were turning brown and were falling to the ground. If nothing else, there was an undeniable change of season.

"Must be around 4:00 or 5:00 in the day judging by the position of the sun," Trubshawe said. "We are about a mile from the village of Hampstead. We can walk to Harry Tunsdale's Stables and secure some mounts. After that, it's a short ride to Grantum Hall. We'll start looking for Jack there. My guess is, since Grantum was pals with Essex and Southampton, then the whole lot could be there now. If not there, we'll go west of London and check out Essex House on the Strand."

"How will we be able to tell if they have Mr. Benchley inside one of those estates?" Bonnie asked as she lifted up a small portion of her long skirt to get in a scratch at one of her calves.

Trubshawe reached back into the saddlebag nearest to him. After removing a pair of binoculars, a plastic bag with two rolls of while toilet paper, and a small plastic bowl with a lid, he brought out a black box the size of a television remote clicker with an aerial protruding a couple inches from the top.

"This will tell us," Trubshawe said, holding the device in one hand. "This will pick up a signal the stolen STUMP admits within 1,000 yards. It was designed by Mortie Ryskind to help someone find the Stump if they forget where they left it. The time machine has a small transmitter embedded inside it. It activates automatically after use and stays on for three months if needed."

"How did you know we would wind up in the cover of trees?" I asked. "I mean we might have wound up in someone's bathtub, right?"

"More likely a dungpile then a bathtub, mate," Trubshawe said with a snicker. "I'm afraid this age you're in does not put much faith in soap and water. To answer your question: I knew this was a safe place to transport because I transported to this spot the morning before I picked you two up at Heathrow. Before that, Jack and I made annual trips back in time from my shop to this forest. This is a very secluded spot, a good quarter mile from any trail. I rented the shop space on Flask Walk precisely because 400 years earlier, even 350 years earlier according to surviving maps, it was a grove a good mile from any habitations."

"Why make the time machine look like a tree stump?" Bonnie asked.

"Camouflage," Trubshawe said. "In case we ever left the STUMP at our point of arrival. It's just an old tree stump to any shepherd or wayfarer who happens by, and not many would happen by in this part of the forest." The major took another toke of tobacco, then smoke exhaled from his thick nostrils before he spoke again.

"I timed our transference so we'd arrive in mid-afternoon. By the time we reach Grantum Hall it will be dark. If we can get a hostage from Warbeck's party, we can swap him or her for Jack. That's a best case scenario."

"What do we do if Warbeck tries to make hostages of us?" Bonnie asked.

"Then we hold them off with a little bit of fantasy and a dash of reality," Trubshawe said. "Inside those saddlebags, along with the ammo and the grenades, I've got some special strobe-lights that simulate gunfire for movie work. I also have a little noisemaker for some audio distraction—make anybody coming at us think twice as to estimating our actual numbers and firepower. And, in this little kit"—he pointed to the rectangular box— "we have a couple extra concussion grenades and a couple Claymore M18A1 fragmentation mines. The noise and light fool 'em; the Claymores stop them."

"Can you be sure they won't accidentally go off?" Bonnie asked.

"I've trained men to use 'em in my past duties," he said. "They're inert now. Just let me handle 'em."

"That answers my questions," Bonnie replied. "When do we set out?"

"If you two feel up to it, right now," Trubshawe replied, standing up with just a flexing of his legs. "Wells, I'll have you carry one of these saddlebags, the one with the food and medicine. I'll carry the one with the pyrotechnics. Bonnie, have you done any studies into Elizabethan dialects?"

"Bits and pieces," she replied, as she stood up and stretched. "Mostly things I've picked up from college lectures and a couple directories at the Shakespeare Festival in Rogue Falls and the one at the Globe in San Diego. The problem is I can only recall snatches of phases— 'God Save the Mark'; 'Alack the day'; 'All health unto my gracious sovereign'; 'What news from France?'" I could recite Portia's 'Quality of Mercy' speech from *The Merchant* or Rosalind's epilogue from *As You Like It*, but the thing of it is those lines might be a little hard to work into ordinary conversation."

"When we go into town, let me do the talking then. You've probably done enough Shakespeare and Ben Johnson plays so you know some of the slang, but don't speak at all until you're comfortable and don't use words like 'computer' or 'electricity' or...."

"Computer!" Bonnie exclaimed, slapping her forehead. "Shit, I was going to e-mail Ann's correspondence from the hotel. Not that it matters, considering the state she's in right now, but still it's my job."

"Your job now is to save her old dad," Trubshawe said. "As for you Harvey, you should remain mute. I think we'll pass you off as my mute servant. Bonnie can be my daughter."

"Excuse me," I said, holding my hand up. "I don't mean to rain on your parade here, Major, but how are we going to rescue Jack Benchley? With light arms and a couple landmines?"

"We're the advance party," Trubshawe said. "What we are going to do first is locate old Jack and try and ascertain if he's alive. If we can grab somebody in Warbeck's bunch wandering outside the castle, then we snatch him or her and swap 'em for Jack. But I'm not counting on that. I just want to get his exact location. O.K., that's Phase One. Phase Two will be me convincing certain parties as to his whereabouts—senior military officers, men I trust—and convincing them of the STUMPs' workings and then have them give me a company of soldiers to rescue Jack. In exchange, I'll turn over the STUMPs to the

British Army and let them have what they can make of them. Jack won't like it—he didn't want any government to have time-travel technology—but that's probably the way it will have to be. As for that bit of it, don't get your knickers in a twist about that. I will go to Whitehall and secure the troops I need for the actual rescue. You two just have to help me pinpoint Jack and make sure he's alive."

"Sounds easy enough," Bonnie said uneasily. She turned back and looked at me, probably to gauge my reaction. I tried to look stoic enough for the plan the Major laid out, but inside...

I liked what the farthingale did for Bonnie's figure. The stomacher, the V-shaped piece that started at her bosom and came down to the middle of her waist, looked nice on her, too but I could imagine it was uncomfortable.

Trubshawe and I each took up a saddle bag, and walking single file with Bonnie in the middle, we emerged from the grove. Luckily, Trubshawe had been on the path toward the nearest town before. It was a warm late afternoon as we followed him up a narrow path surrounded by thick brush. Our leader commented that we were in one of the thickest parts of the original Hampstead Heath, and that in our time the original forest and heath was all but gone. There was no other foot traffic on the road and my mind started entertaining the notion that it was all a practical joke after all.

"Look at that," Bonnie said to me, turning about suddenly and pointing to a pocket of windflowers coming up from some leafy bushes along the roadside. I peered through the bush and saw a small mammal with a long snout and a thick layer of short quills covering its back. The little creature gave me a quick look, then scampered back into the undergrowth.

"Porcupine?" I asked.

"A little hedgehog," Bonnie said softly. "They don't have them in the Americas. There were two of them in there. I'll bet they were a couple."

Trubshawe had turned around to see what Bonnie was pointing out to me. When I caught his eye, he said, "I'm going into brush here for a minute to see a man about a horse. Will you wait for me?"

"Of course," Bonnie said to him. She smiled back at me. We both knew he was heeding to a call of nature and not checking out horseflesh. Bonnie leaned forward, putting her hands to her knees, and took in the tender buds of the wind-flowers and their aroma. "Primroses," she remarked dreamily. "Go ahead and take a whiff."

I did, not all that taken by the experience. It was a pleasant aroma, but I was still shaky inside from tossing my cookies. "Very nice," I stated, trying to muster some enthusiasm for my friend's sake. She put two fingers gently up to her lips, and gazed upward for a moment, then closed her eyes and began to recite a poem:

> "'Witness this primrose bank whereon I lie!
> These forceless flowers like sturdy trees support me;
> Two strengthless doves will draw me through the sky,
> From morn till night, even where I list to sport me:
> Is love so light, sweet boy, and may it be
> That thou shouldst think it heavy unto thee?'"

"That's very nice, too," I said. "Shakespeare, I presume?"

Bonnie opened her eyes, "Yes, it is. From *Venus and Adonis*. It's a work he dedicated to the Earl of Southampton."

I saw Trubshawe reemerge from the clearing. He reached down and put his saddlebag back on his right shoulder. He waved us forward.

"When you say Southampton," I said to Bonnie as I lifted the other set of saddlebags to my shoulder, "you mean the same Southampton that we saw with the red bearded guy at the Museum of Western Art?"

"Yes," Bonnie said as she removed her plumed hat and ran her fingers over her pinned up hair. That's the one. The guy who looked like a rock singer. It has to be him. Southampton was Shakespeare's patron after he split from William Devant, the Earl of Grantum."

"So, if we're headed to Grantum Hall to find Benchley, I presume that this Grantum guy is in on the Essex Rebellion as well."

"Unfortunately, yes," Bonnie said. We were now walking

side by side since the path widened. "The only reason Grantum did not suffer the same fate as Essex after the rebellion is that he warned the Queen's Privy Council the night before the attempted coup that his friend meant to storm Whitehall Palace and seize the Queen. He must have had a change of heart for the old Queen."

"Or he chickened out," Trubshawe said from a few paces in front of us. "Or he liked the odds better with the Crown. William Devant did keep a journal. It's nothing like the printed copy his grandson forged up to make it look like his grandfather wrote Shakespeare's plays. I've also read some of his private papers. He used to translate Horace, just like the Queen. It was a passion they shared, translating old Roman poets that is."

"What do you know about William Devant?" Bonnie asked as we walked along single-file through the narrow path that cut through a dense thicket of brush.

"I met him—briefly. Been to Grantum Hall. That boy was a shrewd customer. He went to Cambridge with Sir Francis Bacon. They were good friends and I'm sure Grantum was sharp enough to absorb some of Bacon's political savvy."

"Bacon turned against Essex as well, didn't he?" Bonnie asked.

"Indeed," Trubshawe said. "Bacon saw that Essex had lost his wits the year before the rebellion. It took Grantum a little longer. Of course, now that all these men know the future and how it all played out..."

Trubshawe did not finish his thought. He did not have to. I was not as up as my fellow travelers on the details of English history, but it sounded like we were up against some heavy hitters. I had a financial interest in seeing this through, but I began to seriously wonder if the odds on us pinpointing Jack Benchley and packing him back to the STUMP for a hasty exit were getting too long for any comfort.

The sight that convinced me the STUMP really did what was advertised came when we reached the summit of a gently-sloping hill about a mile from the grove we had set out from. The older man was leading us through a dense section of bramble when we came out on a clearing. Trubshawe set his load down (with more visible relief on his face than before) and walked over to an outcropping of rocks. I unburdened myself and followed Bonnie over to him.

Trubshawe was looking at a town that seemed to be several miles distant over the broad stretch of rolling grasslands that separated us from the town. He took off his derby hat and wiped the sweat from the top of his brow with a sleeve. Then he put the derby back on with a quick tug.

"Is that London?" Bonnie asked.

"Yes," Trubshawe said quietly. He put his hand on the crown of his hat to keep a gust of wind from blowing it off. "That is London, Miss Bonnie. That massive tower in the middle is Old St. Paul's. The steeple to the right is St. Andrew's. The smaller towers with battlements on top are either private homes or warehouses. God, look at all the chimneys on the houses in front of Paul's now. There's a good deal more of 'em than our visit last year even. Little London is coming up in the world."

There was indeed a great cluster of sloping roofs with chimneys situated about the large Gothic structure Trubshawe said was St. Paul's Cathedral.

"I thought St. Paul's had a great dome like the Vatican," I remarked.

"It does, Wells," Trubshawe remarked. "but that's Christopher Wren's St. Paul's that comes along after the Great Fire of 1666. All that you see before you is long gone by the time we come along. You're seeing a vista no living man could ever see until Mortie Ryskind came along. I'll fetch the binoculars so you can have a better look."

Through the binoculars I could make out a herd of sheep on the outskirts of the town, and a massive gate area where rustic wooden carts were lined up to go into London. It was real and unreal at the same time, like looking at a moving painting. We were too far away to see much detail. The horizon of the city itself was so far away that just seeing the buildings would have been impossible except that it was a clear day. I moved the binoculars to some closer terrain and saw my first human figure. He was maybe a mile away: a man in baggy clothes and a wide-brimmed hat standing near a herd of sheep. He was walking with a long shepherd's crook with two long haired medium-sized black dogs close to his heels. I panned upward from the shepherd and his dogs to a large windmill perched on a hillside. The oblique sails of the wooden structure were slowing turning about, although we seemed to be getting a fair amount of wind where we were. The windmill reminded me of the mock windmill used in the first sound version of *Frankenstein*, with Boris Karloff, where the monster throws his scientist-creator (Colin Clive, or rather, a dummy) from the loft and the body is caught in one of the moving sails for a couple seconds, before dropping to the angry torch-and-pitchfork wielding villagers below.

The reality of this being the past suddenly caught up to me. I felt out of place, very out of place, like I had walked out of my trailer back in Oregon and I found myself in front of the Taj Mahal. A feeling of danger came over me. I had not experienced these feelings since my first months as a peace officer. I wished I was back home.

At her urging, I handed the binoculars to Bonnie. “Incredible,” she stated as she scanned the panorama for half-a-minute. She seemed to be trying to catch her breath as she took it all in. “We really are here, you know,” she said as she returned the binoculars to me then cupped her hands around the back of her neck. “Doesn’t it make you tingle inside?”

“Yeah, I’m tingling,” I said. “I’m tingling all over, Bonnie. But it’s not a good tingling.”

From behind us I heard a burst of static. Trubshawe had taken a small multi-band radio receiver out of one of the saddle pouches. He looked around to double-check that we were alone, then yanked the antenna upward.

“My guess is that Warbeck has the dogs out on us,” Trubshawe said. “If Dromio is back in time by now, then he knows we survived the helicopter attack. I’ll see if he and his lot are sending messages to each other over a short wave band.”

“While you gents are checking things out, I shall retire to yon powder room,” Bonnie said. She walked over to a saddle bag, pulled a roll of toilet paper from a plastic bag, then retreated to the near-by trees and bushes. I crouched down next to Trubshawe and watched him fiddle with the dials. This being 1599 A.D., the choices for audio entertainment were somewhat limited. All he was getting was static for awhile and then there was a buzz, a fluttering noise, and then a human voice. The voice was vaguely familiar.

“No sign near Hampstead Church,” the rather high-pitched young male voice said. “Do we continue? Over.” I had heard that voice before, but I couldn’t match it to anyone.

“Search the area east of the sector,” Trevor Warbeck said. “Trubshawe has an antique shop that would be about a mile into the forest at this point in time. Bring them to me. Over.”

“Jesus,” I said,” It’s Radio Free Warbeck.” Trubshawe and I looked at each other. I could see he was fretting.

“Well, we know their plans,” the older man said as he carefully lowered the antenna, then slowly stood up. “Fat lot of good that will do the three of us if we don’t have horses and they do.”

“Too bad we couldn’t bring the horses with us,” I said.

“We have to get horses in Hampstead,” Trubshawe said. “You can’t get a horse into a single STUMP machine. The energy field is too bloody small.”

“Where do you think Warbeck is broadcasting from?” I asked.

“The signal was strong on that younger chap, but Warbeck’s voice was a good deal weaker. I’d make book he’s either in London or across Hampstead where Grantum Hall is. I’d say we try and reach the Hall first. That’s a bit closer.” Trubshawe waved away a bee that was darting about his face. “Sure as hell we have to get moving. If we can get Miss Bonnie to stop malingering in the forest there we can make some distance bet—”

“Stand!”

The voice that interrupted Trubshawe belonged to a moon-faced masked man carrying a long musket. He was a bulky, pot-bellied man in a leather butternut-colored jerkin with shoelace-sized drawstrings in front, long dark sleeves with patches on the elbows, and a hat that sported a long V-shaped visor that jutted out from above his forehead. The hat was metallic, with a high circular crown that made him look like a conquistador from a history book. But this guy was not history.

I reached for my handgun, which I had secured by means of a leather holster hidden under my breeches and supported by my belt, but Trubshawe told me to freeze. This was because there was another soldier, younger and thinner with a similar uniform. He was also masked and held the business end of a wooden crossbow to my partner’s back.

"Hands high," the paunchy man said. (From the direction of the ambush, they must have snuck up on us from the opposite side of the rock outcroppings.) "If either of you gentlemen move to even scratch at a louse on your person, you'll be blown to hell by my hagbut or you'll catch my cuz's crossbow. Either way you'll lose the scarlet of your cheeks and become food for flies."

"Who's your commander, lance-knight?" Trubshawe asked the paunchy one as the latter moved toward us.

"We were soldiers, lately of Her Majesty's forces In Ireland," the soldier said in a gravelly voice. "We'll have your goods, sir, and not the benefit of your questions."

"You are renegades," Trubshawe said as calmly as if he was striking up a conversation with someone at a bus stop. "Masterless men of arms. That's a tough position to be in these uncertain times. If it's money you need, I'll give you some willingly."

"You will give us *all* your money," the fat one said, "and, if you can still your bold tongue, you and your knave might live to see the sunrise. Otherwise—"

The younger, beardless man, having seen me make a move for something at my hip, spun me around and removed my sidearm from the belt holster I had just under my breeches. (It was becoming ridiculous for me to even bother carrying a gun. I would just lose the damn thing as soon as I stepped out anywhere.)

The only faintly good points in this ambush was that Bonnie was hidden away somewhere and they seemed to be intent on robbing us rather than working as scouts trying to track us down, as the men on the radio seemed to be up to.

Other than that, it looked about as bad as it could get.

Chapter Thirty-Two

The paunchy soldier, who smelled as bad as if he had recently rolled in dog crap, relieved Trubshawe of his rapier and the antique pistol he was carrying on his waist. He also found his serious firepower, the nine-millimeter automatic, and then helped himself to my sword. The younger man kept the drop on us with the cross-bow. He had the handgun he had lifted off me stuck down the front of his breeches.

"What manner of pistols are these?" the lance-knight asked Trubshawe, glancing at the pistol.

"Petronels," Trubshawe said calmly. "A new style of arms from the Continent. I acquired them for myself and my servant in Bristol."

Old Moon-Face took the weapon and fumbled with it. I saw him undo the safety. Now if he could only point it at himself or his pal and squeeze the trigger, it might be a whole new ball game. Instead he put the modern gun down and went back to his musket. I could see a small plume of smoke rising up from the snake-shaped hammer. The tip of the hammer was alight. I figured it was lit to permit firing.

"Search the old man," he barked to the younger man. The man with the crossbow complied, holding his weapon in one hand while he searched Trubshawe's breeches, until he pulled out a leather pouch with a string tied about the top. The little bag made a jingling noise as he snatched it up.

"Hand that to me, sirrah," Moon-Face said. The younger man walked carefully around Trubshawe and then delivered the goods to his partner. I noticed that both their uniforms were frayed and tattered. The younger man's hose was ready to fall apart. He had multiple runs in his stockings and they were caked with dirt. The older man had a more intact set of hose and his boots actually looked fairly new. I wondered if he had taken them off a dead soldier—or perhaps the last man the pair robbed.

Both their faces were caked with dust. The clean streaks here and there on their cheeks were flushed red with sunburn.

The older soldier shot a glance down on the radio. From his expression I could tell he didn't know what to make of the contraption. Static was coming out of the speaker.

"This is the devil's work here," he said.

I looked at Trubshawe. I could see his eyes darting back and forth at the faces and the weapons of the two men. He said nothing. I said nothing.

"We saw you from a distance back," the younger man said. "You had a woman with you. What has become of her?"

We said nothing.

"No matter," the younger man said. "Gilbert and I will find her and make sport of the wench. I will woo her first, in my own—" He was interrupted with a smack upside the head by his colleague, whose gun tipped downward for a second. I was too far from him to capitalize on the move. Trubshawe was a couple steps closer, but he only flinched.

"God's Wounds, to be saddled with such a clod," Moon-Face (a.k.a. Gilbert) said. "You used my given name in the presence of these gentlemen. You know I am a marked man, and can ill afford my name bandied about. Now we must kill these men. I will have the cloak of the master there, Clement and, mark me, you shall bury their carcasses as recompense of your stupidity."

"Must we kill them?" Clement asked pitifully.

"'Tween us, we have killed a score of men in the bogs of Muenster. Before you were pressed into service, I'd killed a score of men myself in the Azores under Raleigh. What of it?"

"Those were Irish kern and Spanish heretics," Clement said. "These men are our own countrymen. My father would say that such a blood-letting was sinful in the eyes of God. Can we not simply—"

Gilbert landed a second clot, with the fist of his free hand. Trubshawe must have anticipated it, because he sprang forward, and grabbed hold of the barrel of the musket, tilting it upward. The gun fired in a blaze of fire and smoke but the shot went up into the air. I was moving, but not fast enough to keep the younger soldier from firing his crossbow, but he was too anxious and the arrow whizzed into the ground. He then lunged toward me, swinging the crossbow over one shoulder with both hands. The blow he gave to me landed on my back, just below my ruff. It hurt, but probably not as bad as my opponent felt when I gripped his forearms and e-mailed my kneecap to his crotch. The howl from his gaping mouth told me we were a couple centuries shy from the invention of the jockstrap. His head came down in reflex, and I met his chin coming upward with my left fist. I then grabbed his right wrist and brought his offending arm behind his back, ramming his forearm and elbow against my body. I wrapped my free arm around his neck and tugged his pinned arm upwards into an unnatural position.

I turned about to see how Trubshawe was doing. He was on his back, not in any position to defend himself. Blood was coursing out of his shirtsleeve; his right biceps had sustained a wound. The paunchy soldier was on top of him, getting ready to stab him-again with a short dagger. Being too far away, and somewhat engaged, I couldn't stop him.

But Bonnie could.

She darted out, grabbed the fat soldier's weapon hand by the wrist with both her hands, pulled him off-balance and downwards, then delivered a strong dancer-style kick to his head. The knife flew out of his hand, and he rolled over Trubshawe, landing next to him. Bonnie was right on top of him, her legs spread across his torso, administering a viscous downward blow to his solar plexus with her two hands joined together. The fat robber made a simpering "uhhh" sound. She sent another blow down in the same area. The same sound emitted from the soldier, this time in a weaker tone. He was done. Trubshawe's Baretta lay on the ground next to her foe. She alertly picked it up. That's when I noticed my own foe begin to squirm. I ripped his helmet off his head and hit him as hard as I could on the back of his neck, just below his skull. He dropped forward like a sack of bricks. I then recovered my weapon and stepped on Clement's back a couple times on my way to help Bonnie.

I needn't have bothered. She was standing over her opponent, in a good firing crouch, her right arm extended perfectly, the left bent at the elbow just like she was modeling for an FBI training manual.

"Don't move, asshole!" she told fat old Gilbert, who looked in no hurry to move anywhere. She handled the firearm so beautifully, it made me wonder why she had been reluctant to carry a weapon in the first place.

All in all, we seemed to have come out on top and okay. At least I thought so until I saw what had happened to Trubshawe.

He was sitting up now, his left hand grasping his right arm. His normally stoic face was a study in pain. He had obviously sustained a deep wound.

❖ ❖ ❖ ❖ ❖

"That's the best I can do," Bonnie said, as she finished bandaging up Trubshawe's arm. We were away from the clearing now, having found a spot in the woods where he had cover. While Bonnie was bent over at our leader's feet, putting the finishing touches on the gauze and bandages she had wrapped about the middle of his right biceps, I was cinching up the ropes on our would-be killers. They were tied to a large oak tree, each man facing in the opposite direction. We had marched them deep into the woods, then, after hog-tying Gilbert, I had Clement remove his uniform. His body didn't smell any better without clothes on than when he had them on. I repeated the process, this time getting the shabby, smelly uniform off Gilbert. I next tied both of them, one at a time, to a tree. Lance-knight Gilbert cursed me in a strange kind of accent. I had heard a similar dialect out of the Warbeck's 'guests' at the museum back in San Francisco. It didn't sound like what I'd call an English accent. The words were vaguely familiar but the inflections and pronunciations were strange to my ears.

I left their masks on, because, this being England after all, it would have been 'unsporting' to leave them totally naked.

We also had acquired the two horses which belonged to

the robbers and the saddle and tack that went with them. One was a sturdy chestnut mount. The other a smaller beast, a mare, with a generally white coat, a thick white mane down her neck and a few black patches of hair around her nose, forehead and haunches.

After the men were tied up and gagged, Bonnie unhitched the horses and I threw our saddlebags across their backs. It was decided, since the gelding was bigger, that I would ride with Bonnie on him, and Trubshawe would take the smaller mare, which Bonnie said was a pony.

Trubshawe lightly patted Bonnie's hands then got up. He walked, poised, over to the tree I had secured the men to and confronted Gilbert. He employed an accent similar to the ones the soldiers used.

"All right, lance-knight," Trubshawe said, "let me appraise you of the situation as it stands, lest you be too pig-headed to appreciate it. The pair of you are tied to a tree without so much as a codpiece over your naughty parts. You are desperate, unscrupulous men, you especially, Gilbert. Your vile intention was to at the least rob us, and at the most murder us, then hunt down our lady friend here and accost and kill her. Then you would have stripped our corpses and sold our clothes and weapons for wenching and drink. Even by the standards of a couple of Royal Marines let loose from their base on a three day furlough, your behavior is shocking."

He got right into the fat soldier's face.

"I need information. If you give it to me, I will reward you well. I will also kick in a few coins of the realm for the horses and clothing we are borrowing from you. You give me the information quickly and without fuss and you'll be the better for this whole bloody-minded affair."

Gilbert took in a deep breath that puffed out his hairy chest. I could see his torso had been scarred by sharp objects on two occasions, but they were only scars now. "What would thou art know, good gentleman?" he said in a friendly tone.

"You say you were soldiers of the Queen, sent under the command of Lord Deputy Essex to deal with the recent unrest in Ireland," Trubshawe said. "Judging by your uniforms I'd say you were under the command of the Master of the Horse. That would make you part of Southampton's cavalry in other words. That means you were in the advance body that recently left Ireland. I need to know the whereabouts of these noblemen, and the strength of their retinue."

"Exactly how much will I receive for these remembrances of mine?" Gilbert asked.

Trubshawe chortled. "Tied naked to a tree and he wants to open negotiations?" He drew out his rapier with some effort, and held the tip aloft a few inches from the soldier's face. "You will not negotiate with me, fellow? Your cutting of my arm has put me in a foul humor, Old Sport. I may still slit your gizzard if you try my patience any longer."

Gilbert gulped. "The captains of our force gave us our release in Maidenhead. We were deprived of our fair measure of pay by the officers, of course."

From the other side of the tree, Clement spoke up: "What we got you gamed away at the nearest tavern, throwing what Edward coins we had away at the shovelboard game."

"Blast thee to hell, oaf!" Gilbert shouted in response.

"Where is Essex?" Trubshawe asked, drawing the rapier back to its scabbard. "Where did you last see him?"

Gilbert continued: "That was in the village of Maidenhead. The Lord Deputy and the Master of the Horse were met there by the Earl of Grantum."

Trubshawe nodded, looking satisfied. "Go on."

"Grantum had come up from his manor to meet the Lord Deputy. His son was Captain of our regiment; a better, braver lad never drew breath. The noblemen retired to the private house of some fat alderman for a conference. They were in conference the full of the day. The scuttlebutt around camp was that we were to accompany Essex south to London, then beyond to Nonesuch Palace for a meeting with the Queen. Instead, we were mustered out in the village, at only a portion of our due wages. We hung about a bit at the Goatherd Tavern, then left the burg for the Great North Road. Last I heard Essex and his guard were still at that house. That was a bit over a week ago."

Trubshawe nodded. He took out the leather pouch that Clement had lifted off him at gunpoint. He opened the pouch and out came several coins with the embossed profile of a woman in a headdress on one side. He dropped a few of the coins on the ground.

"Those are gold angels for you, lance-knight. Some for the

beasts we are taking and some for your knowledge, inadequate though it is."

"Am I to be untrussed, good gentleman?" Gilbert asked as sweetly as I think he could.

"Getting to the coinage before some other bandits come along is your problem," was the good gentleman's reply. "I judge a couple hours of struggling will afford you freedom."

"I have information to better the lance-knight, good sir," Clement called out.

"Tell him nothing more," Gilbert shouted. "I won't be hunted down like Wat the rabbit for your loose tongue."

"I know exactly where Essex is right now, good sir," Clement said.

Gilbert's face reddened. "God grant that I live to smote your head—" His threat was interrupted by a hard slap to the face.

"Tame that noise, you," Trubshawe said, his accent slipping back to modern Cockney. "Hang on, private. I'll have a word with you."

The gist of Clement's story was this: he and Gilbert were with Essex and Southampton's forces only two days before, and not in Maidenhead, but at Grantum Hall. They had bivouacked outside the house and made up a rotating guard of men. They had deserted two days before, when they heard volleys of shot from inside the courtyard of the manor. Both men feared executions of enlisted men were taking place as a way to mask the total failure of the Irish expedition. Taking what pay they had received, they slipped out of camp. Essex had apparently never left the manor to ride to this place called Nonesuch Palace to see the Queen, as was his supposed intention upon leaving Ireland. Once more, they had gone through Hampstead after deserting from Grantum Hall. And, at the tavern where Gilbert stopped to gamble, they heard some interesting things about the Earl of Grantum.

"Grantum is a fat fellow, is he not?" Trubshawe asked Clement.

"Fat as the player who delivers Sir John Falstaff on the stage," the young man replied. "The villagers say he has suddenly grown even stouter in the short period since he left Hampstead for Maidenhead, and whence he returned a few cockcrow's later."

"Did he have a tall man with him. Dark-complexion, beady eyes?"

"Aye," Clement said. "A very gargantua! He was accompanied by other men as well, men the villagers had never seen before. The Earl was normally a cheery fellow, stopping to exchange words with the townsfolk. But this time he only nodded to acknowledge their greeting. This was according to the old waterman I was in company with at the tavern. Said the Earl would not even look at him as he rode by the conduit where the gray beard was drawing water. The old fellow had brought clean water to Grantum Hall for two score years while Grantum's father had held the estate. He knew the Young Earl, who had never failed to greet the old dog with a familiar 'what say ye, Johnny?' But this last time Grantum only stared at him with eyes what looked stolen from a dead man. 'Twas strange,' the old man said. 'Twas most strange'."

"Interesting," Trubshawe said. I thought back to what I had read in the *Shadow On the Crow* book put out by the Institute for Factual History. One of the picture plates in the middle of the book, a painting of William Devant, bore a fair resemblance to Trevor Warbeck. I articulated as much to Bonnie. We both looked at each other, knowing we each thought the same thing.

"How long were you in Ireland, lad?" Trubshawe asked Clement.

"Long enough to curse the endless, stinking bogs more times than I could count. I saw friends in my troop drop like flies from the swamp-sickness. I was, by the grace of God, spared from such a nameless grave as befell my cousin Peter. He and I had been herded up with the rest of our men in the village—all but the very young and the toothless—and pressed into the Queen's service. We chased Tyrone and his kerns up and down those pestilent bogs, to no good end. I curse the day I was mustered into the service under a posturing pack of silk-legged officers and strutting gentlemen. I saw hundreds of honest men's lives wasted to save a patch of swamp that's not our homeland to begin with."

"Not that you be an honest man," Gilbert guffawed.

"Please loosen my bonds," Clement pleaded. "For our stealing away, we are marked men. Some of our troop were in the manor. Judging from the volleys we heard inside the manor, they are now resting in a grave."

"Are you sure there were executions at the Manor?" Trubshawe asked.

"Marry, sir, firing squads they were sure as night follows day. I know the noises a brace of matchlocks make when they discharge their powder and shoot. I saw enough captured deserters shot by lines of soldiers back in Ireland. There may be men out after us now. If we're caught—"

Trubshawe had me slightly loosen the ropes around the younger man. "This way, you'll work your way out before your friend Gilbert," he explained. "You can take his money and scatter to the wind or stick with the wretch, that's up to you. We're going to gag the both of you so you won't draw any attention to yourselves before you can get free. I'll leave your money on the ground in front of you. That's a damn sight more mercy than you two would have shown us."

"I was never for killing you, sir," Clement said.

"If you're not for killing, then get yourself free of this Gilbert Fatfellow," Trubshawe said. "He's been branded on the hand by the authorities for being a felon. He's another pinch away from a hanging on Tyburn Hill. Heed me, lad." He stepped away then motioned me forward.

I gagged both men, taking note of the large reddish-black 'T' mark on Gilbert's hand. He was marked alright, on a fleshy part of his hand. It looked like he had been branded. We left the duo tied to a tree and went to the horses.

"Where did you learn that karate kick you gave old Gilbert?" I asked Bonnie as we walked back to our mounts.

"Karate class," she answered. "I lived in New York, remember?"

"And that shooting stance?"

"I played a patrolwoman on one episode of *Beverly Hills P.D.*," she said. "Not a big part or anything, but it let me keep my Screen Actors' Guild card. Stunt woman taught me the stance."

"Remind me not to try and steal your purse."

"I don't have my purse. Or make-up. All I have is this little coin purse," she said, rustling the small chain that attached the purse about her waist. "Plus, I'm out of cigarettes and I could really use one now...badly."

"How does your wrist feel," I said, pointing to the one that was now bandaged in white cloth instead of a modern pressure bandage.

"Better," she said.

Bonnie made sure the saddle and tack was squared up before she mounted the left side of the chestnut horse. I provided a handhold for her left leg as she gripped a tuft of the gelding's mane and she propelled her right leg over the animal, settling herself into the saddle. She made some clicking noises with her mouth as she put the horse through some paces. The saddle she had to use was not designed for riding sidesaddle, so her dress and petticoat was bunched upward, revealing a bit more leg and thigh than the dress was designed for. She pulled down her hemlines as best she could while maintaining the horse on a straight path.

I looked over to check Trubshawe's progress in mounting the pony. The wound to his arm did not deter him from mounting, but I could see he was in some pain from the way he winced when he had to put weight on the arm to settle into the saddle.

Bonnie brought the horse about, back toward me. "When did you say you were last on a real horse?" she asked.

"About eleven. On my cousin's ranch up by Mount Hood. I just rode an old nag around the corral. Before that was the mule trip down the Grand Canyon with my parents."

She extended her hand. "I'll ride up front then," she stated. "You can get behind me and take notes." She extended her right hand across her body and I hoisted up on the back edge of the saddle. We followed Trubshawe and his horse onto a narrow pathway through the trees.

After I got situated, Bonnie asked me: "Do you believe anything of what's happened in the last...what has it been, an hour?"

"I'm not sure about the time," I said. "I left my watch with Stephen. But, no, I don't believe it. I mean, that looked like some town way back in the past and those bandits seemed to be real enough. But part of me still wants this to be a great big practical joke."

"I wish it was, too," Bonnie said. "but I'm afraid we're back in time, like it or not."

❖ ❖ ❖ ❖ ❖

"Are we anywhere near Grantum Hall?" I asked Major Trubshawe, who was about twenty feet ahead of us on his own horse.

"I've been using the compass and the locator." (He held up the remote-sized device.) "The signal from this little gizmo is getting stronger. We're moving to the Northwest. The trick is to skirt past Hampstead Village so we don't ride into an ambush."

"Any idea as to how we make sure Benchley is even *at* Grantum Hall."

"We'll reconnoiter when we get to the bloody place," Trubshawe said. "I haven't totally given up on springing Jack without getting the paper-shufflers at Whehall involved."

Great, I thought. I'm 400 years out of my time, lightly armed in a platoon numbering all of three, and the leader of the trio is talking like we can crack a veritable castle.

"The manor is a couple miles north of the township," Trubshawe added. "Like I said, I've been to Grantum Hall. Jack and I went last year, as a matter of fact, with the Lord Chamberlain's Men. I think I can remember the landmarks, but I need to get to a roadway above Hampstead. I hope I can get us above Hampstead before nightfall."

Bonnie held up a hand, then spoke: "Did you say you and Mr. Benchley went somewhere with the Lord Chamberlain's Men. That was William Shakespeare's company, right?"

Trubshawe nodded, guiding his mount around with the reins to face us. "He's got ten percent in it, yes. He also writes the plays and acts a bit. Yes, he and Old Jack are mates now. Have been so for a few years. That's what all this time-travel is about, to see what Will of Stratford and his mates are all about, for Jack to fill in the gaps on a few things about Will Shakespeare. I was never much into reading Shakespeare. Or seeing the plays, really, but it enthuses Jack to no end. Give me a good Tom Clancy thriller or an Alistair MacLean—"

"You know Shakespeare?" Bonnie asked.

"And Dick Burbage. And Will Kempe. And Augustine Phillips. I know the lot. I've got pissed with them a couple times at 'The Mermaid' tavern over in Cheapside. Shakespeare's the only one who knows who we really are. The others think Jack and I are a couple blokes from Bristol who's an old friend of Will's. Not Kempe, I mean, but Shakespeare."

"Of course," Bonnie said, clearly dazzled. "You've seen them perform?"

Trubshawe nodded. "And I'm proud to say the last time I saw one of Shakespeare's plays, I stayed awake all the way through. The last time Jack and I were with those boys was at Grantum Hall. That was a few months ago. Francis Bacon wrangled us an invite to meet the Earl of Grantum at this party he was throwing. Clever chap, as I said before. I had to sit through *The Merchant of Venice*. Bit of a ramble, that was. No pretty girls in the pretty girl parts. Just some skinny, pimple-faced boys. Suppose to be a comedy. Damned if it's very funny to me, especially if you got nothing against Jews. They have this Jew, Shylock, and he loans out some gold pieces or ducats to—"

"I know the story," Bonnie said impatiently. "You've seen Shakespeare and his company perform?"

"Yes, many times," he replied as if she asked him if he ever went to a pub.

"When you went to Grantum Hall, did you—?"

"That's where we got a portion of the real journal of the 15th Earl of Grantum, yes," Trubshawe said, anticipating the rest of the question. "That's after Warbeck published his book, *Shadow on the Crow*, and claimed that this chubby toff William Devant wrote Shakespeare's plays. Jack wanted to get his hands on the real journal to refute the phony one Warbeck had located, the one written by the grandson of the one who's alive now. While Devant was showing Jack and Bacon around his estate, I slipped into the host's study, looked about, found the journal under an hourglass on the toff's desk, pinched the bloody thing, then slipped back into the Great Hall where the play was running along, and—"

Bonnie broke in with a harsh whisper: "You mean you actually stole—" That was as far as she got. There came the sound of hoofbeats and breaking branches from somewhere around a bend in the trail.

"Get into the trees," Trubshawe said. "Be quick about it."

We did so, with Bonnie and I leading the horses into the woods. In a minute, it was apparent what was coming our way, what we were hiding from. It was a horse-pulled cart with wooden wheels. A man and a woman dressed in plain clothes in the buckboard up front, and a passel of dirty-faced children sitting on a large stack of hay piled on the tumbrel-sized cart. A pitchfork was affixed by a rope to the side of the cart. They passed without noticing the three people lurking in the brush.

It was down to the water to refresh the horses, and to dig into the provisions of food that Trubshawe had brought along with him, after our close non-encounter with the farm family. I ate a granola bar and had some orange juice. The foliage on both sides of the stream was very thick, so we had good concealment. While the horses drank greedily from the stream, Trubshawe tried the shortwave radio again.

Again came that high-pitched voice we had heard over the radio the first time: "Moving Northeast out of Hampstead," the voice said. "No sign of the party. I'll draw water at the falls, then we'll head back to HQ. Over."

"Message received," came the voice of Trevor Warbeck.

"Falls," Trubshawe said, taking a quick gulp over the plastic container of orange juice he had selected from the saddlebag. He stood up, extending his arms, palms downward.

"Hear that," he said, looking to me and then Bonnie.

There were unusual sounds, coming from upstream. It was a flow of water, not the steady rippling sound of water flowing down a nearly-level stream bed, but a cataract.

"That guy on the radio said something about stopping near the falls," I said. "Do you think what we're hearing—"

"Indeed," Trubshawe said, rubbing an index finger across one side of his thin mustache. "And I got an idea who that voice belongs to now, the one other than Mr. Warbeck's. Might be just the place they're stopping. It's worth looking into, I say." He wet the tip of that index finger and cast it up over his head.

"What breeze we have is coming down from the north, upstream. That means we can got on top of anybody near the falls without their horses getting a whiff of ours. "Shall we do some reconnoitering, kids?"

"Lead on, Stonewall," I said.

Trubshawe caught the Civil War reference. "I'd rather you call me General Sherman, Wells," Trubshawe said. "I always prefer being on the winning side."

After proceeding north along the creek a couple hundred yards, we tied the horses up to a fallen log that stretched over the now swiftly-moving stream, then proceeded ahead. The sound of the falls was now a roar of water, and we could scramble up the rocky cliff on our side without too much concern about being heard. Trubshawe trailed us, his arm wound keeping him from making quick progress. Bonnie was right behind me as I led us between the rocks. At the summit of the cliff, next to where the falls began its twelve to fifteen foot drop, I poked my head up to see what was ahead of us.

What was ahead, past the falls and on the same side of the water as ourselves, was a horse. The beast was drinking water from a clearing along the embankment. Behind him was a sheer cliff face of huge rocks, situated in an upright position like the objects were waiting for the bus to Stonehenge. The bank was only a few yards from where the flowing water cascaded from the drop, so I had to lean forward over the rock to get a look at the beast. The tack and saddle that the animal wore had a fancy embroidered look, the grey blanket draped down past the horse's stomach providing a background for the crest that could be seen behind one of the stirrups. The design was a yellow cross cutting through the middle of what looked like a shield, with side views of four gulls in each of the four segments. The horse itself was tall and majestic, like a thoroughbred, with a uniform black sheen to its coat.

A young man now entered the same clearing, causing me to duck down. I came slowly back up, making sure he was looking away from the falls. He had long dark hair that came down to his shoulders in long braids. He wore a uniform, but it was unlike the military garb our last two adversaries wore. This kid, maybe sixteen or seventeen, had a blue doublet and breeches and a flat, mushroom-shaped blue cap. On one of his shoulders was a crest of the same design as that on the horse's blanket.

Another figure emerged from out of the woods. I recognized him right off. We had met briefly a few days earlier back in San Francisco. (I should say a few centuries forward.) The Earl of Southampton was wearing a light-green doublet with short breeches in a variety of vibrant-colored stripes, including a matching green. The doublet was further accentuated by a darker green cape. He had long hair like his manservant, but this fellow had his dark blonde locks spread out and perfectly tapered. He looked like a rock star back in San Francisco and he had changed nicely into a first class Renaissance dude in every detail, except for that rather unusual accessory he had slung about his shoulders and cradled in his hands.

It was an AK-47 assault rifle complete with the telltale banana-shaped clip and a laser mount. I couldn't get a great look at it from my position, but I knew that much. In the wrong hands, it would make a nice 'street-sweeper' for mowing down the unarmed or the under-armed. Our little group was in the latter category. I climbed down and reported my sightings to Bonnie and Trubshawe.

"Are you sure it's an assault riffle?" Trubshawe asked, a look of worry on his face.

"Definitely," I said. "I don't know how much training he's had on it, but if you want to take him out, we better open up on the two of them right now, where we got 'em. We won't get him or his man alive with what he's packing."

"No," Trubshawe whispered back. "I have to have that inbred little shit alive. He's our ticket to getting Jack sprung. Let me have a look at the situation."

I boosted him up as best I could, allowing for his injured right arm. When he signaled me, I helped him back down to where Bonnie was standing.

"I've got a plan," he informed us. "I've got something in my bag of tricks for this. Mind you, Wells, you're the young buck here. It will be up to you to get around and prevent either of them from escaping if the concussion grenades don't completely do the trick. You've got to make like a Red Indian and get about them. Think you're up to it?"

He laid out his plan. If it worked, great. If not, I'd be, like truth in war, the first casualty.

Chapter Thirty-Three

In order for Trubshawe's plan to take effect, it was necessary that I position myself downstream from our intended targets. The hardest aspect was to get down from the rocks on the opposite side of the falls, then, risking exposure for a few seconds, move rapidly across the slick stone outcroppings to the cover of brush. In the spirit of Major Trubshawe's reference to Native Americans, I had left my shoes behind so as to make as little noise as possible. Apart from the bearable pain I took while stepping on jagged stones and sharp briars, I was constantly worried about being seen. Once past the steep sides that made up the falls, I crawled on my stomach across the apex of a bluff. Just below the bluff was a cliff face about thirty feet above the clearing. I had some cover, courtesy of some young trees that had taken root out of the rock-strewn bluff. I had circled all the way around the targets and now was perched nearly opposite the falls. In order to block the escape of Southampton—if the concussion grenade Trubshawe planned to lob over the rocks was off the mark—I had to be able to set up to get the drop on him if he or his servant tried to take off.

To my left was a trail Southampton and his servant must have used to reach the creek. A steeple-like outcropping blocked my view directly below. There was a very steep fissure between that outcropping and a flatter one on the side opposite the creek. If I had to get down fast, this was probably the way to go but, from my position, I couldn't see where the sixty-degree angle of rock ended and met the flat trail. I would have to take the chance.

I could remain concealed as long as I kept myself crouched down. On the other side of the steeple rock, I could see the targets through another v-shaped gap between two stones. I could also see a saddled mule from my new vantage. The servant, having watered the master's horse, was now bringing his beast up for refreshment. Southampton was talking into the handset of a cellular phone, another anachronism under normal circumstances. The servant had his cap off, and was combing his hair with his fingers. Trubshawe had given me three minutes, by his stopwatch, to get into place. It seemed like a very long three minutes.

I heard a noise. It was the wrong noise, coming from the wrong place. From about a hundred yards away a horse was coming over a hill and down the trail, carrying a young man with a barrel-like chest in a broad-brimmed hat (which obscured most of his face) and cape. The rider had the horse in a steady gait. My first instinct—to use the pistol I had just drawn—was a bad risk since Southampton, with his AK-47, would spot me and open up rapid fire on my position.

Before I could summon up a second idea, an explosion went off near where Southampton had been standing. The grenade must have hit water because a plume of it rose above the rocks and water splattered on my back. The explosion was followed by the neighing of the horse and mule. The horse reared up in surprise. My attention was drawn down the trail, back to the new interloper. The sound of the explosion caused his horse to rear up, almost dislodging him from the saddle. The young man whirled the horse around and, seeing me, galloped off. I fired two shots off, but he was already over the other side of the hill before I had a bead on him with the Beretta. I might as well have thrown a couple rocks.

I scrambled down the ledge a few feet. I soon realized why I couldn't see where the fissure met the trail. It didn't meet. The fissure just went vertical. I had to jump the last dozen feet to the trail below. I landed on my legs, trying to keep my knee joints as relaxed as possible, and pitched forward on my stomach.

I scrambled to my feet, then fell to one knee. My right knee, the one I had landed on, was sending a sharp, undeniable pain through my nervous system. I planted myself down on my one good knee, drew my sidearm, and aimed toward the creek side. I heard Trubshawe yell out something and then came the sound of gunfire. It wasn't the rapid metallic burping of an AK, but the steady fire of Trubshawe's Ruger Carbine. Because of the rocks, I couldn't see what was happening. Then the mule galloped down the trail, riderless. I threw myself to the side as best as I could. A few yards behind the mule, running on foot, came the servant.

I was in the middle of the road, on one knee, directly in his path. He let out a yell as he saw me, and pulled a fat wide-bore pistol out, aiming the thing at me while still on the run.

I squeezed off two shots. He took one round to the stomach, the other to the chest. His gun hit the ground before he did, but not by much. I hobbled over, favoring the bad knee as I knelt beside him. He was lying up at me, his eyes fixed directly upward. I felt for a pulse, but I knew already from the eyes that he was gone.

Added to the girl I had accidentally run over, this made the second person I had killed. It left me shaky, but at least this time the other person had aimed a weapon at me.

It took me some effort to get back up. When I did, I put my hands on my knees like a baseball outfielder, and tried to get the adrenaline slowed and my limbs to stop shaking. The sound of heavy footsteps coming up the trail brought me up again, gun drawn. Luckily, it was only Trubshawe. He came around the corner where the servant had just run from. He seemed to be limping, but I figured he had stumbled on some rocks as I had.

"Are you hit?" he asked me.

I shook my head, too out of breath to speak.

He looked down and saw the servant lying motionless. He stepped away from me and hopped down to the inanimate figure. I watched him check the pulse of the man by his neck. He stood up, shrugging his shoulders. I could have saved him the trouble, but I was still in need of air.

"He's dead," Major Trubshawe told me.

"Where's Bonnie?" I asked.

"Back at the creek, tying up his earlship. The grenade stunned him, but the lad here was a bit out of range. We got the horse, too. His tack was tied to a tree back there." He reached down and picked up the pistol that was lying next to the corpse. A strong smell of gunpowder entered my nostrils as he brought it up.

"Wheel lock," he said, showing me the weapon as he cradled it in both hands. "Pretty good pistol, really. Probably made in one of the Italian states. Trouble is, you only get one shot at a time with one of these things. He took his shot at me. Missed." He slung the carbine over his back as winced in pain from the exertion on his wounded right biceps.

"Hurts like the very devil now," he said through clenched teeth. "Anyway, you got the lad so he can't run off and warn them."

"There was another one coming up this way over that hill. He turned tail when the explosion went off. He saw me. I got a couple shots off, but I couldn't hit him before he got back over the ridge."

"Could it have been that Dromio ape?"

"Too short," I said. "Had to be another guy. He was wearing a floppy hat so I didn't get a good look at him."

"One of Southampton's subalterns, I'll wager. He's probably double timing it to Grantum Hall right now."

"You need to get that thing re-dressed," I said, pointing at the knife wound in his right arm that had reopened in the scramble down to the creek."

"We have more bandages," Trubshawe said, just before he sucked air through his teeth, a sure sign the pain was getting to him. "Never caught so much as a scratch in the service, in training or in combat. Now I get knifed by some loafer and twist up my leg—all in one day. What bloody next?"

"What do I do now?" I asked.

"You can be a help by dragging that poor bugger into the bushes over there. No sense leaving the poor bastard in the middle of the trail. Just be quick about it." He turned and limped back to the creek.

I dragged my victim off. The kid I had shot was probably no more a bad guy than I was. He had already made his one shot and he was bluffing me. I didn't need to use lethal force, but it was too late to know that now. He deserved a burial and a marked grave and, hell, a little something out of the Bible for good measure. What he got was a dumping in the weeds. I dragged him on his stomach so I wouldn't have to look at those glassy, wide-open eyes of his. I walked away from the dumping ground as quickly as I could.

Southampton was prostrate and unconscious when I first got a close look at him. His arms and legs were bound tightly with rope. Bonnie had Trubshawe sitting on a rock. She was redressing Major Trubshawe's wound. Leaning on the stone nearby was the AK-47.

"That knife blade may have cut into your humerus bone," she said, tightly bandaging the exposed arm. "That's probably why it's hurting so bad."

"You sound like a nurse," Trubshawe said.

"Just played one once on a soap opera when I was in New York," Bonnie replied. "I got a slapdash course in medical terminology from an associate producer. My character was killed in a balloon crash with her fiancée, one of those romantic interludes that go tragic. They never found our bodies. The writers made it look like an ex-girlfriend did us in, but she beat the rap. All I'm sure of was my character got written out and I got unemployed. But I did get the slapdash course." She stood up after the bandage was tied. "That's all I can do. You might even have a hairline fracture there. You need a visit to the hospital, a modern hospital that is."

"It will have to wait until tomorrow, when Stephen comes back to get us," Major Trubshawe said. I had fetched our guide a flask of whiskey from the kit, and he was taking sips from it to help deaden the pain in his arm. I hoped he knew when to stop.

A couple minutes after Bonnie had finished the first-aid, Southampton started to stir, and his limbs began to strain at the ropes. Trubshawe had me lift him up by the collar of his cape and pull him to his feet. After that, I sat the Earl down on the large flat rock where Bonnie had tended the major's wound.

The effects of the concussion grenade was wearing off of the nobleman now. Even with his dazed countenance, a strong haughtiness beamed from his face. It was a lean face, with a curled upper lip, a sharp nose, high cheekbones, and large dark eyes. There were streaks of sandy blonde in his hair, which curled down past his shoulders. All in all, his features were androgynous. He looked very much in the mold of a rock star, as I had first pegged him. I felt a twinge of jealousy just looking at him. This was the type who always had his pick of the best women even if he had nothing to offer them beyond looks and a bad attitude.

He first focused his gaze on me, shot a surly gaze at Trubshawe, then looked over to Bonnie. He recognized us, then redoubled his efforts in a futile attempt to break his bindings and the grip I had on the back of his cape to prevent him from toppling over.

"Unbind me, sirrahs!" Southampton spat out.

Trubshawe stood over the earl, his arms folded over his doublet—pocked with damp patches from scrambling over the water-soaked rocks near the falls—and looked down on his captive with a tight-lipped smirk.

"My humblest apologies, Right Honorable Earl of Southampton, and Baron of Titchfield," Trubshawe in a voice dripping in irony, "but you are now our prisoner."

"Unbind me, swine," the earl growled.

"Begging your pardon, your Right Honorableness," Trubshawe continued as he reached over and picked up the assault rifle that was leaning against another rock, "but if you want to live to see anything more than peach fuzz on that mug of yours, then you'll keep your mouth shut and do what I say."

"And who might you be, rogue?"

"Major Trubshawe, late of 'C' Company, 15th Para Brigade. I come from the same time frame as your friend, Trevor Warbeck. He was a British subject, but I'm sorry to say he's gone over to the Americans—for the money it would appear. I was an active soldier of Her Majesty Queen Elizabeth II, who was named for your most gracious and renown sovereign. I am now in the Territorial Army. Unlike yourself, I am a loyal subject, not a plotter of treason like you or your friend Essex."

"Call me disloyal?" Southampton said, turning his head up and cocking it like he was posing for a painting. "I am a gentleman of noble birth, a peer of the realm. And you, dog, are a common mongrel whose ancestors bowed and scraped when one of my ilk deigned to acknowledge their presence."

"There's never been a bloody war Britain had to fight without men like myself or my old dad in the midst of it," Trubshawe said firmly.

"Oh, yes, Major Trubshawe, the common herd will fight—if they be rounded up and given no choice. My bloodline is made up from men who fought willingly, risking their lives willingly and outfitting lesser men for battle from their hard-earned treasure, and leading them into fiery battle at great risk to their noble persons. My forebears created this kingdom, wrestling it from the Saxons, drubbing the Scottish invaders, putting sword and blood-soaked lance to the rebellious Welsh, charging headlong into columns of desperate French pikemen at Poitiers and Agincourt and every battle in that great span known as the War of a Hundred Years. My own generation hath rained fire and cannonshot on the heavy galleons of the Spanish Heretics who coveted Albion for their miserable King and his lackey, the Pope. I have braved the wiles of the Irish savages for my land and kingdom. Call me disloyal? Here, upstart, receive thy pay for such impudence." He spit upward, aiming at Trubshawe's face and hitting his doublet.

Trubshawe struck the young man hard to the side of his head with a swipe from his right hand. A second blow knocked Southampton to the ground. Then Trubshawe raised him back up and planted him roughly back down on the rock. The interrogator turned away, and wiped off the spit with one quick swipe of his hand.

"Wells," he said to me in a commanding voice, "take the uniforms we acquired from the other men and hide them someplace. We won't need any masquerade to complete our job, not while we have this dandy in our hands." He looked to Bonnie. "Did you search our prisoner?"

Bonnie shook her head.

"Right," Trubshawe said. "I'll do so. Wells, get ready to use your pistol." I drew my weapon. "Hold this on our guest here," he said. I undid the safety and took aim at Southampton's head. The young man sneered at me, as if I was only pointing an index finger at him. It struck me he either wasn't afraid, or wasn't about to show a trace of what fear the situation had on him.

"If he so much as scratches his nose, shoot him," Trubshawe told me. Then he started to search the prisoner.

In addition to the anachronism of a 16th Century nobleman packing an assault weapon with laser scope and retractable stock, Trubshawe found two other items anachronistic to Merrie Old England. One, tucked into an inside pocket of the Earl's breeches, was the cellular phone. In another pocket, he came up with a scroll of paper. The scroll had lettering on it that looked as if it had come off an ink-jet printer, not some old-fashioned printing press. He pocketed the scroll.

"All right, Wells, if you would, heave this dandy over your shoulder and let's get him on his horse. I'll tie him down over the animal's back. C'mon, let's be quick about it."

Chapter Thirty-Four

It began to rain, a drizzling late afternoon rain that turns the skies darker than they would have been in a cloudless twilight. Rumbles of thunder, such as you would expect from a late Summer shower, could be heard. I brought up the rear of our group, riding the mule I had inherited by shooting the owner. We had caught up to the beast on the trail. I found him slow but manageable—and better than walking. Bonnie was on the pony. In between us, on his black mount, was Southampton. The Earl was gagged, bound and bundled up in blankets so he would look to a passing stranger to be ordinary wares or a corpse on the way for burial. Trubshawe was riding on the other horse, up front.

The rain was good in one way: the weather and the gloom seemed to be keeping people off the rutted, narrow poor-man's-excuse for a road we were on. After running into the two ex-soldiers turned highwaymen in broad daylight, I doubted too much traffic passed between townships toward nightfall. Bonnie and I said nothing, the better to pick up any oncoming hoofbeats from a rescue party for Southampton which might be headed our way. Our mounts had just finished splashing through a small ford in the trail when Trubshawe lifted a hand. Bonnie pulled up on the reins, then we came up parallel to him.

Trubshawe pointed down a trail that ran perpendicular down a steep hillside, then came out onto what looked, in the ebbing light, to be a broad stretch of road.

"That's gotta be the main road north out of Hampstead,"

Trubshawe said. "We'll walk the horses and the mule down this path here. From there we need to find a marker for East Heath Road. That will take us directly toward Grantum Hall. We'll even go to the trouble of announcing ourselves."

I dismounted, helped Bonnie off her mount, and then we followed Trubshawe to the shelter of a tree. The rumble of thunder seemed far enough away not to fear lightning strikes. With that, Trubshawe took the cellular phone out, and pulled the aerial up. He punched the redial button. In a few seconds, he was talking to someone.

"Never mind who this is, sonnie," Trubshawe said, almost cheerfully, into the receiver. "I want to speak to your boss, Trevor Warbeck." There followed a pause for about a minute.

"Yes, Mr. Warbeck, good evening to you, sir. Hope I'm not interrupting your supper...you guessed right, sir, or should I say your Earlship, this is Hugh Trubshawe. Friends call me Truffie, but you needn't bother."

Even standing a yard or so away from the phone, I could hear the low-register drone of Warbeck's voice. What he was saying, however, was unclear to me.

"You know about Southampton, then? Good for you. I like a fellow who can build a staff to keep him on top of things. Here's the deal, Warbeck: I have Goldilocks here, you have Jack there. We meet somewhere out in the open like, and we swap 'em." Another long pause, then a droning noise. Trubshawe pushed the mute button on the phone, then spoke to Bonnie.

"Poor fellow's daft. He wants us to throw in the third and last STUMP, along with Southampton, before he lets Jack go." He went back to the call. "That was a stinking bad deal before you shot up the hotel suite back in 2001 and it stinks worse now. You know Southampton is mates with Essex. You can't afford to get Essex mad at you, so you take the first deal and Jack and us go on our merry way...right.... Nah, pull the other one, Warbeck. We're talking straight swap, man for man, and that's all we're talking.... Do the exchange inside the manor is it now?.... Oh, you are a nutter, Warbeck!" He chortled, then continued:

"Here's how it will really work: I want the Earl of Essex for my guarantee. Essex escorts Jack out while my man escorts Southampton to you. We'll meet at that little bridge over the lake, assuming it's still there from six months ago.... Right, then.... It's so nice we trust each other. Well, we're still a ways off...right out the front way of your new house in about ninety minutes. I'll be out to meet you.... We're all clear, then."

Trubshawe signed off. I had a sick feeling in my gut that I was Trubshawe's 'man,' the one who would be escorting Southampton up towards Grantum Hall.

❂ ❂ ❂ ❂ ❂

Through the lenses of Trubshawe's night-vision binoculars, Grantum Hall looked almost exactly like the sketch that Bea Ryskind had shown us back at the Shakespeare Festival: the medieval castle tower, or keep, with two tiers of parapets, the last set rising at least fifty feet above the surrounding newer manor house. The outlying complex featured gables, sloping shingled roofs, and large oriel windows that exuded a glowing yellow light, magnified in intensity by the binoculars. On each corner of the manor house were one of four rook-like towers with conical-shaped pinnacles rising above the circular parapets of each. Chimneys were in profusion, at least two on each tower and several jutting above the sloping roof.

We had been waiting in a cover of trees about a hundred yards from the front entrance to the castle. There was a small lake exactly halfway between ourselves and the manor house. It was the body of water that the artist, the guy named Hollar, had depicted in his sketch. The water glistened from the light of the full moon above us. A narrow wooden bridge crossed the lake, putting one on a straight course for the concrete steps and the arched double doors that made up the main entrance. I handed the binoculars over to Bonnie.

"That lake is part of what was once a moat," Trubshawe said after Bonnie told him about the similarities between the sketch and what we were seeing. "If it was light, you could see remnants of the outer bailey of the castle complex just past the lake there. It's a beauty inside, but you won't have to go past the bridge there, Wells, to do your job."

That sealed it. I was going to the bridge. It had to be that way. Trubshawe was hurt bad in the arm and I had more agility than the older man.

We were also reducing the risk for our retreat. While Trubshawe supervised our movements, Bonnie and I laid out an elaborate and, I hoped, effective trap in case Warbeck planned to launch an attack on our retreat after Jack Benchley was secured. The ingredients for covering our retreat were in three basic components, a mixture of special effects devices designed for film production and real-life anti-personnel booby traps.

Component Number One: a dozen or so small battery-operated strobe lights that could be attached into the ground by means of a hardened stake. (I also attached a couple into the fork of some nearby trees.) The lighting equipment had been designed by a special effects whiz who worked on some of the films Benchley had been second-unit and assistant director on in the past.

Component Number Two complimented the first: two acoustic speakers, small in size but, according to Trubshawe, capable of producing eardrum-popping noise if tuned to full volume, which, assisted by a flashlight I made sure they were. Trubshawe had a stereo receiver, again operating on direct current, which would play the sounds of a pre-recorded battle featuring bullets, mortars and bombs. The bellicose noises were courtesy of a sound library of battle sounds created for the war films Trubshawe had worked on, and used again and again if another project arose.

The third component was the real thing: two Claymore steel fragmentation mines, along with about a dozen of the flashlight-sized M84 concussion grenades, the ones favored by the British counter-terrorism unit, the SAS. Bonnie and I spaced the Claymores out, making sure the metallic green little death machines had their 'Front Toward Enemy' emblems facing toward Grantum Hall. Trubshawe could activate the first two components of the plan as we were leaving the cover of trees. The Claymores would be set off by a trip wire attached between each mine and the trunk of a tree. I fixed the M84 "flashpoint" grenades to some tree trunks, using wire to hold them tight. Trubshawe himself, thankfully, activated the mines once we had them in place. He crept slowly and methodically along, still limping on his wounded foot, and using a flashlight cupped in his hands carefully to give off just enough light for him to do his work without being seen from the manor. He put in the trip wires that would set off the M84s if we were pursued. There was a yard-wide open space between the two lethal booby traps, a cordon we had to traverse to get to the horses and one that an advancing enemy hopefully would not be able to find before one of this soldiers/executioners set off a mine.

"We might not need this set-up at all," Trubshawe said as he finished the job and joined both of us in front of the cordon between the trees. "Of course, we'd be bloody idiots if we didn't expect the worst out of 'em."

Bonnie asked Trubshawe where he had secured the special effects equipment.

"An Italian-American friend of mine," he replied, talking to us while scanning the grounds around the estate with the night-vision binoculars. "Fellow named Silvio Malatesta. He was Jack Benchley's good friend. Old Silvio made me his second-unit director of *The Last Caesar*, his little revenge on Benito Mussolini. That was made in '75, the year before Silvio died. Did you happen to see it, Wells?"

"Yes, I did," I said, recalling the superb anti-war, anti-Fascist film, the plot which centered around Mussolini's brutal and senseless conquest of Ethiopia in 1936. I quickly recalled a bit of information from Benchley's autobiography, which mentioned his friend Malatesta's last film. "You were in charge of all the battle scenes, weren't you? And all the aerial combat sequences?"

"Pretty much," Trubshawe said with a crooked smile. "We filmed the thing in Morocco. I had a hell of a time rounding up and renovating all the old biplanes we needed to reenact the bombings. My training in handling helicopters came in handy there, let me tell you. Helicopters were the only way to film the biplanes in the air because they were so damn slow."

"I heard Mr. Malatesta almost collapsed during the shoot," Bonnie said.

"He did collapse," Trubshawe said. "I practically directed the main unit myself in the last couple weeks of the shoot because Silvio came down with dysentery. I actually got to direct Richard Burton, which was a bit of a kick. Poor old Silvio—he had to wait twenty years to make that movie, thanks to the blacklist in the States. At one point in the Sixties he asked Jack to direct it, but Jack wouldn't touch it. It was Silvio's baby. Malatesta was the one who took time off from directing films in America to go to Spain during their civil war.

He made a pro-Republican documentary to try and raise money in America against Franco and his Fascist pals. After the documentary played out in America, he even went back in '38 or early '39 and enlisted in one of the International Brigades. He did sabotage operations behind the lines, practically suicide missions. He told me he probably killed a lot of his own countrymen in Spain—and a few Germans, and the odd Spaniard. He even lost a brother in an ambush outside Barcelona. That was just before the Fascists took the city and the bloody war ended. No, that was Señor Malatesta's film to make."

As Bonnie handed the binoculars back to me, we heard a woman's voice cry out: a desperate screech of a cry. There followed the sound of gunshots. The gunfire, sounding like several modern assault rifles going off at once, came from Grantum Hall. We all looked at each other.

"One of those robbers mentioned firing squads, didn't he?" Bonnie said nervously.

About a minute later, a second volley of guns went off, then silence.

A few minutes later, from around one of the rooks, came a large cart being pulled by two draft horses. (I could see all this through Major Trubshawe's night scope binoculars.) There was an escort of soldiers marching with the cart and one soldier standing up in the front of the vehicle controlling the reins on the horses.

The cart was filled with men, women and children. They were apparently dead, all piled up on each other in diagonal and horizontal positions. The collection of bodies probably contained three dozen people at the least, a small hill of human beings reduced to blood-smeared ragdolls, their heads and limbs bobbing as the thick wooden wheels of the cart rolled over the lawn.

"What is it?" Trubshawe asked.

I gave him the binoculars.

"Bloody bastards," the major said, shaking his head and dropping the glasses. Bonnie asked to look.

"You don't want to look at this," Trubshawe said.

But Bonnie said she did. The major sighed and she took the glasses, scanning the area until she saw the creaking cart that had brought forth the work of the firing squads from

Grantum Hall. It was impossible to see anything more than the outline of the cart from the moonlight but I knew the exact moment Bonnie had focused onto the cart. She made a gasping sound, like somebody had just hit her from behind. The binoculars came down and Bonnie unfolded out of her crouching position and sat down on the brush. She put a hand to her forehead and began to tremble. I was sure she was going to vomit then when she started making choking noises. Trubshawe muffled her involuntary sounds by pressing her face against his chest. In a few seconds, however, Bonnie put her hands to his forearms and gently pushed him away. She was breathing a little rough, her head was down, but she was in control of herself.

"I hate this place," she said between gulps for air.

I put a hand to her shoulder. She brought her right hand up to cover mine.

"I'm okay," she said.

"How can we trust these people?" I asked Trubshawe. "They're goddamn Nazis."

"We're not trusting them," Trubshawe said stoically. "Nobody's going anywhere, Wells, until the Right Honorable Lord Essex himself comes out of that manor and parks himself on that bridge. And I'll have a bloody good look at the bugger to make sure it's him. Otherwise, if there's any tricks, Goldilocks back there will take a bullet in a strategic place."

Goldilocks (a.k.a. Southampton) was still securely bound and propped up against a tree. Other than Bonnie feeding him some orange juice and part of a cut-up apple, the gag had stayed on his mouth. My Baretta had been aimed at him to discourage any yelling out between bites.

"Have you ever seen this Essex character—alive and in three dimensions, I mean."

"Saw him about three years ago at the Globe," Trubshawe said. "Strutted himself through the groundlings like a peacock just before the play opened, then went up to the upper chambers to take in the play with the other nobs. He's very popular with the common herd these days. Don't ask me why. Charisma, I guess. Shakespeare introduced us to him formally the evening Jack and I went to a little banquet Southampton gave for him at some fancy house on The Strand. As far as he and Southampton were concerned, we were friends of Shakespeare's—merchants from Warwickshire. That toff Essex's got a smell about him, must use some cologne like it was water. Wait a minute—what's all this, then?"

A couple balls of light emerged from the front entry of the manor. They had to be torches. Trubshawe took the night-vision binoculars out of my hands and got himself a close-up look. From what I could see without the binoculars, it looked like three people were emerging from the open doorway. One of the number stayed behind, judging by the fact one torch remained on the steps of the entry and what looked like two figures walked slowly to the bridge in front of us.

"Looks to be Essex," Trubshawe said, as the figures got closer. "There's another fellow with him. Can't tell who he is. Wait a bit. Wait a bit, here.... It's Jack! There's something on his face. What the hell is it? What have the buggers done to him?" He put down the binoculars, and looked to me. "Get our lad on his feet. The two of you will meet that pair on the bridge. When you get down to the bridge, stick the flashlight from the saddlebag in his face so I can get a good look at Jack."

I cut Southampton's bindings, all but the rope joining his wrists, and we set out. I had some comfort in the fact that I had a hostage about two feet in front of me. No gunman from the castle could take me out without nailing an earl or two in the process. It was a short walk to the bridge. I had my handgun concealed in the belt holster, and a long watchman's flashlight—what Trubshawe called a torch—in my left hand. My left knee was still smarting, but I could put some weight on it and propel myself forward as long as I favored the injured joint.

"Don't get too ahead of me," I advised Southampton.

"I'll see you hanged, dog," was his seething reply. Evidently, he didn't like canines.

The party of two that came out from the manor stopped halfway across the bridge as we were just walking (or in my case, hopping) onto the far side of the wooden, railed structure. There was suddenly a dramatic stench in the air, like a truckload of fertilizer spilling onto a highway. My nasal passages almost stung from it.

We stopped a few feet in front of the other pair. Essex

looked a little different from the way he had looked back at the Museum of Western Art, facially at least: still the bold dark eyes, slightly crooked nose, a dark auburn head of hair accentuated by a long wispy orange-red beard. Only now he was dressed for his own time with a glistening doublet that looked to be of silk. It was lime green in color, speckled with the widest ruff I had yet seen. He had a cape, of course, and a thin velvet scabbard with the hilt of a rapier sticking out from the top.

He looked a good deal more formidable in this costume than in his tux back in San Francisco. He had a cold sneer on his face, an expression I had seen before and was sure someday I would see again in a bad dream.

"God's Lids," Essex exclaimed, looking me in the face. "They sent the rabbit who trifled with me in San Francisco. He touched his hand to the hilt of his weapon. For a second I thought it was going to be bad, but he only lightly brushed the hilt with his gloved fingers. "What say you, Harvey Wells? Do you care to test your fortune with me?"

"Next time you're on the West Coast, Robbie, look me up," I said. "I'm in the phone book. Don't be a stranger." I don't know what possessed me to call him Robbie.

"You wish you were in the Antipodes if we cross paths beyond this place," Essex said. "Mark me, varlet."

Who did this guy think he was? Leroy Millman?

As Trubshawe asked, I turned on the flashlight and lifted it toward the face of the second man.

It was the second time I had laid eyes on Jack Benchley in the flesh. The first time, at a bookstore signing, I had seen a robust looking, natty-dressed older gentlemen who looked like he had his share of sun and exercise. Now I was looking at a gaunt man with sunken cheeks and a pallor that was ghostly white from the artificial illumination I cast on it. Benchley seemed to have aged ten years in the year or so since I had seen him. His face, even as a young man, had been craggy and thin. Now it seemed almost like someone had grafted a pasty excuse for skin on a skull. He was stoop-shouldered—something I don't remember him being in person or when he'd been interviewed on television—and there was a slackness to his lower jaw that made me think he had been mistreated. He had about two week's growth of white beard that made up for the thinning hairline which you could barely see at the crest of his high forehead. His left eye had deep bags of skin underneath it, one area quite puffy and red—the only red on his face. I couldn't say the same for his right eye. I couldn't see his right eye. There was a black patch over it, held there by a leather band that went around his head above both ears.

"Are you with Truffie?" Jack Benchley asked me. His voice had a surprisingly strong resonant tone that told me there was still a hearty, if battered, spirit in the man.

"Yes," I said. "We're going to get out of here right now, Mr. Benchley."

"Hello, Henry," Benchley said to Southampton.

"Hello to you, Squire Benchley," Southampton replied in a tone that was almost cordial.

The transfer took place. Essex immediately cut the ropes that held Southampton's wrists behind his back, then lightly punched his younger friend on the arm. Essex whispered something to his friend, then he turned him about and let him walk ahead of him. Essex himself walked backwards, keeping an eye on me. I walked backwards, keeping an eye on him.

It was clear Benchley had trouble walking; his gait was an old man's shuffle. At first I thought I might have to hold him up under an arm, but he held his arms out toward me in a gesture that clearly rebuffed physical aid. I made sure Benchley stayed in front of me as we headed off the bridge.

I could see Essex and Southampton starting to run back toward the manor. This gave me a bad feeling. That feeling changed to flat-out fear when I saw several shadowy figures emerge from the front entry of the manor. A few moments later we were under attack. The sound of bullets, coming in a rapid clip, drove me to the ground. I reached both hands upward to drop Benchley but, to my relief I found he had hit the ground just behind me. There was nothing to do but crawl the last few yards to the cover of the trees and hope the shooters had not perfected shooting with the infra-red laser mounts they must have been using. I crawled into the cover of the trees and brush. Bonnie came out and helped pull Benchley into cover. She tossed me the Ruger rifle and I laid down a few shots at the dark forms around the castle myself. Trubshawe also came out, rapidly firing from the captured AK-47 to give us more cover. At one point I heard him exclaim loudly. It was later that I found out that one of the shooters back in the manor had wounded him.

I stopped firing when we were all in cover. Using the flashlight we all ran, hopped or limped our way to the horses.

"Are you up to riding, Jack?" Trubshawe asked his friend as he escorted him through narrow safety cordon.

"Hell, yes," was the freed man's reply.

I boosted Benchley onto Southampton's black horse, then joined Bonnie on the back of our horse. It had been decided to leave the mule behind for us to get out of there faster. Trubshawe managed to mount his pony unaided, although he gave an agonizing groan as he fixed his wounded foot into the stirrup. For a moment there was silence, followed by the not-so-distant shouts of men yelling and horses whinnying. Bonnie turned about in the saddle, alert as I was to the distinct possibility a posse was after us.

Trubshawe must have hit the electronic remote control device, because the next thing that happened the forest was ablaze in light and sound. From my perspective, receding on the back of a horse, the staccato noises and gunnery-like sounds would have been very convincing to an advancing platoon that were up against some ferocious concentrated opposition.

A few minutes later, we briefly crossed back to the main road. It was then that, above the waning noise from Trubshawe's special effects equipment, we heard a louder explosion. One of the Claymores had detonated. Several of the M84s went off seconds later.

"They'll have to check the area for more mines. That'll slow the buggers," he called back to us over the splashing sound of galloping hooves on the wet road.

A few minutes later, Bonnie and I got off the horse to search for the narrow trail that we had first joined the main road on. (Trubshawe had estimated the distance we had traveled from the stone signpost marking the East Heath Road.) While I cast the flashlight around the perimeter of the wood, Bonnie went over and helped Jack Benchley off the horse. Then she went over to Trubshawe who remained in the saddle. I glanced over and, from the flashlight Bonnie was using, I could see she was examining the boot on his left foot.

"Is Trubshawe—?" I whispered to Bonnie.

"He's been hit," Bonnie said. "It looks bad. The bullet might still be in the leg. He's lucky it didn't hit an artery. He needs a doctor and a hospital, but he thinks he can hold out until Stephen shows up."

We came up empty on the first try, but at the second stop we recognized the first leg of the trail we needed to get on to reach the site where, hopefully, the STUMP would reappear the next morning.

Chapter Thirty-Five

The bullet that Trubshawe had taken in our retreat from Grantum Hall had smashed into his foot and stayed there. Despite the pain, Trubshawe had kept riding until we were far enough down the trail we had taken to a point that we and Benchley felt safe enough for us to stop. It was now too dark to ride although the small flashlight Bonnie was carrying helped us somewhat. After we halted, we led the horses down to a creek we discovered by the sound of flowing water. We let the horses drink and fed them some apples and granola we had in the saddlebags. Bonnie looked to Trubshawe's left foot after we removed the boot for him. She treated the wound with a triangular-style bandaging job, but it would take surgery and doctors to deal with the bullet that had torn through some tendons just above his heel.

I supported Trubshawe into a grove of trees we thought would make good cover until daylight. He called for a fifth of whiskey that was in the first-aid kit and he preceded to down it in quick gulps to ease the pain.

We were well enough off the trail, far enough we hoped to escape detection by the scouting parties sent out by Warbeck and Company. (There was no telling how much damage we had done to their forces by the remote-control explosion of the Claymore.) We hitched the horses up to some low-lying branches just a few yards from where we made camp. It was a mildly warm night, with a bit of wind, which was fortunate because we could not risk the smell of smoke or the inordinate amount of light that a fire could give off. There was no moon out, thanks to a layer of overcast. We all sat together in a semi-circle and ate some granola bars and fruit and drank orange juice from plastic cups. I could hear crickets chirping and the wind rustling around the canopy of branches and leaves a few feet above our heads. The ground was wet, but we spread out blankets from the saddlebags around the crest of the knoll and made the best of it.

"How bad is the pain?" Bonnie asked Trubshawe.

"It's bearable," Trubshawe said between clenched teeth. I noticed by the light of a horizontally-positioned flashlight we were using for light that Trubshawe's face had winced a few times while we were eating. He needed to be evacuated to a modern hospital, but we would have to wait until his son returned with the STUMP. I hoped we were near the spot where the time transfer had taken place but it was too dark to know for sure.

"Do you know about Carolyn Mason?" Bonnie asked her old boss.

"She's dead, I know that," Benchley replied somberly. He possessed a deep voice, not unlike Gregory Peck, but it gradually became more reedy and halting as he talked about his relationship with the young woman.

"We met at the San Francisco Film Festival. I was a judge. The festival hosts had assigned her to me as a secretary and gofer. She knew my career quite well, said she had tried very hard to get the assignment. She seemed amenable to seeing me after the festival ended. I only got to know her a few months, but it was the first time since my wife Maria died that I felt truly simpatico with someone. She reminded me of my first wife, the one I should have held onto instead of being so footloose after the war."

"She was a soul mate for you," Bonnie said in her delicate way.

"Yes, she was," Benchley said. He seemed to choke up for a moment then continued. "The first time she met me was at the Roxy Theatre in the Mission District. Some rich kid from Switzerland had made an appalling little pseudo-comedy with his parents' money: a real dud. No way was that going to win anything. Anyway, Carolyn asked me to autograph something I had written. Not that autobiography everybody asks me to autograph, but a copy of a little monograph on fencing I wrote for the Stanford University Monthly Magazine back in my college days. Imagine someone her age going out and finding a copy of that? Well, I suppose some would say our romance was nothing but a May-December fling. But I loved her, and when we were together the age difference never seemed important. It only bothered me when I was alone and had time to reflect on it. I wish you could have seen her, Truffie. Beautiful violet eyes, hair soft and full and fluffy, a wry wit, a walk like a dancer. She was like a young Mary Astor. I could have made her an actress, I could have given her so much to absorb that I could never get through to Ann. She was lover and daughter to me, scorn that multiple designation if you must."

"No," Bonnie said. "We understand."

"Thank you Bonnie," Benchley said weakly. "How is your Angela, by the way?"

"She fine. The baby's fine. She and her hubby are still over in Germany. She's pregnant. I'd show you a picture of her sonogram, but I left my purse back in the twentieth century."

Benchley managed a smile, drank some more juice, then resumed: "After Warbeck and his goons kidnaped me, it was a couple days before I was conscious. He told me the machinations he had used on Carolyn and I. Seems she had happened to go to work for him at The Institute for Factual History. Warbeck should really have called the damn thing The Institute for Fatuous Hyperbole. She was just a secretary from a temp agency, but she got in to see Warbeck and asked a number of questions about me. Unfortunately, she assumed Warbeck and I were friends because we had done the Dostoyevsky film together. Warbeck took advantage of her naivete. He arranged to have her become my assistant during the film festival. Strunk Enterprises was a major underwriter for the festival that year because Sherwood was trying to score points for his Senate campaign. After our relationship developed, she told me that Warbeck had been phoning her and trying to get dirt on me through her. She realized his intentions, quit the position and went back to her old job as a waitress at the Cliff House over on Ocean Beach. I went down to see her as much as I could get time away from pre-planning on my Shakespeare Festival duties. And I got her a better apartment. She had a friend of hers over a lot when I wasn't there because she didn't want to be alone while I was away. It turns out that roommate who befriended her, Jane Willey, was bought off by Warbeck to keep an eye on us. While she pretended to be Carolyn's friend, she kept Warbeck informed of our movements."

"I talked to Jane Willey recently," I said. "Or I should say I tried to. She behaved like she was scared shitless. She was afraid that Warbeck was going to hurt her."

Bonnie confirmed what I had just said.

"She bullshitted you, boy," Benchley said tersely. "Jane Willey was Warbeck's contact. He told me so, laughed about it. He sent her to that restaurant to get a job and ingratiate herself with Carolyn. She was a long way from home and needed a good female friend. The worst of it was that she spied on my girl from right inside my own apartment. He also told me how Carolyn had died. He and Strunk were in on the plot. I trusted that Strunk bastard and he...he..."

Even in the fading light I could see him shudder from the memory. "That was part of my torture: telling me over and over how my girl died, how I was going to be charged with her death in the frame-up he had masterminded." There followed a fit of coughing. "I'm not in good health to begin with and they only gave me some of my medication. God, poor Carolyn." He put his hands over his face. Bonnie got up from her spot next to mine and put her hand gently on one of his shoulders. He flinched at the initial touch, then righted himself. "I'm all right, Bonnie. Thank you." Bonnie returned back to her place in the circle.

"What do you remember about your abduction," I asked.

Benchley shook his head. "I don't remember anything past trying to leave that VIP wingding at the Forest of Arden. God, was I stupid." He rubbed the growth of beard on his face with a bony, wrinkled trowel of a hand. "This is what happened: I went through with a camera rehearsal for the debate, along with Warbeck. That started an impromptu debate about the authorship of Shakespeare's Plays. I showed him photocopies of the original journal of William Devant, the 15th Earl of Grantum the fellow that Warbeck and his anti-Stratfordian cranks say is the learned nobleman who actually wrote all of Shakespeare's plays and poems. I had the original copy, not the forgery the grandson, Charles Devant, cooked up and Warbeck tried to pass off as the real thing. He was thrown for a loss to say the least, especially when I showed him documents in Devant's recognized handwriting that practically proved that he or someone else had doctored the original text. A couple of his supporters even expressed concerns they had been hoodwinked by the IFH. Warbeck was furious. He threw a tantrum, had the camera crew leave, screamed profanity at me, claimed that I was deliberately trying to ruin him. A very Nixonian performance. Sherwood Strunk was upset, too. I didn't like the feeling of being in the compound. Once the camera crews were gone, I felt like there might be trouble. It was then that Carolyn and I tried to leave the place—quickly. It was late at night. After we left the compound that evening, this was after midnight sometime because we had to pack first, a black Mercedes cut me off on the road to Highway 101. Two men in ski masks got out. I tried to roll the windows up but it was too late. I was overpowered and injected with something. Carolyn tried to run away but—" He stopped speaking, gulped, then recovered.

"The next thing I remembered was being flat on a stretcher of some kind and being loaded up into a hatchway by two men. I heard jet engine noises. Before I could get my eyes focused, I felt a prick to my arm. I blacked out. When I woke up, Warbeck was standing over me, his mistress, that Anita woman, close by. I found out later I had been flown to London and was a captive." Suddenly, Benchley took a good look at me, as if for the first time.

"Who are you?" he asked.

"Harvey Wells," I responded. "I'm a detective. Your daughter and Bonnie hired me. Needless to say, I didn't know anything about this little time travel package you have going. I take it Trevor Warbeck kidnaped you to get access to two of these STUMP machines?"

"At first I wouldn't talk," Benchley said. "They knew I probably had them up at my ranch or on Shakespeare Festival property, but Warbeck was afraid someone would get caught if they just kept trying to break in places and find it. As far as I was concerned he could screw himself." He shook his head, the sagging skin on the lower part of his neck quivering, then continued.

"I was stupid to agree to debate Warbeck on Strunk's own turf. I actually believed that Sherwood Strunk wanted to make amends for that unfortunate circumstance that occurred just after Ann and his brother married. He even said he was going to make a substantial endowment to the Shakespeare Festival if I just went to the trouble of appearing on stage and debating Warbeck so he could show it on one of his satellite networks." He paused and looked up at the canopy of tree branches one could barely make out above us. "It's nice to see the stars again," he continued. I've been cooped up for two weeks."

"How did you lose your eye, Jack?" Trubshawe asked.

"Warbeck needed to know where the STUMP was. He found out about Mortie Ryskind's time travel machines. I'm convinced he knew about them before Carolyn and I showed up at the debate. And I know who told him."

"Ralph Bates," Bonnie said.

The old man shook his head. "Bates wasn't the guy. He couldn't be—didn't have any idea about the time machines. Couldn't have. No, I don't think Ann's bodyguard was in on it." Benchley coughed some more. "Ann said she felt safe with Dave McCreedy around." He emitted a sardonic snort of a laugh.

This was Jack Benchley's first mention of Dave, his supposed friend, and it was not positive.

"What about your eye, Jack?" Trubshawe again asked, rubbing one side of his pencil-thin mustache with a forefinger. He took another quaff from his whiskey bottle. At the rate he was going, he'd be stoned in no time.

"I refused to tell them where the two STUMPs were. This was after I came to and found out I had been flown to England. I wouldn't tell Warbeck so he had his henchman Dromio put out this eye with his big smelly fingers."

"The bloody pigs!" Trubshawe exclaimed.

Bonnie, sitting next to me, shuddered audibly. Despite seeing my share of messy gunshot and multiple-stabbing victims, the idea of eye-gouging a helpless man startled me as well.

"Bonnie," Benchley said, after finishing his cup of orange juice, "you were in my production of *King Lear* back in '94, weren't you?"

"For a couple months," Bonnie said. "I was your daughter. That was when you offered me the job as your assistant.

Melanie Armbrister took over as your daughter after July."

"That right, I did play Lear," Benchley said, mustering a chuckle. "That was the last time I'll do any acting, that's for sure. Lear's taxing on an old guy, and if you're directing the blasted thing at the same time... Bonnie, was it you or Melanie who flubbed that line at the end of Act Two?"

"It was me, I'm afraid," Bonnie said. "Regan's line was supposed to be: 'For his particular, I'll receive him gladly.' Only, for some reason..." Her mouth curled in a smile and she hid her face in one hand. "For some reason, I said: 'For his testicular, I'll receive him.' Oh, damn, did the audience howl."

"It wasn't as bad as all that," Benchley said soothingly. "I've directed *Lear* five times and that was the best laugh Regan ever got from an audience. It was a better delivery than anything our Fool ever came off with." Benchley suddenly looked at me, as if for the first time.

"Who are you again?" the old man asked.

"Wells. Harvey Wells," I said.

"Right. Forgive me, Wells. I'm usually better with names. Anyway, there's a scene somewhere in Act Three of *King Lear* where the villainous Duke of Cornwall and Lear's bitch of a daughter, Regan, has Glouster bound hand and foot to a chair. Warbeck, not surprisingly, played Cornwall in the Bristol Rep sometime in the early Sixties. I'm afraid he knows the part well—too well for my tastes. The only change in the text was that he had his hired goon dig out my eye instead of having the balls to do it himself. Warbeck wanted my other eye, too, but Harry—that is, the Earl of Southampton—came into my cell and told Warbeck to stop his barbarity. Harry is a good young man but he's fallen into bad company. Losing one eye was bad enough. I haven't felt so much pain since I caught a bullet from a Japanese Zero in my younger days with the 49th Bombing Squadron. That was over Hokkaido back in 1945, Wells, so you see I'm quite a fossil."

"That Dromio was the same dirty bugger who fired on us from a helicopter outside Annie's suite at the Kensington Garden," Trubshawe said. "He shot Avalon in the arm."

"Avalon has been shot?" Benchley exclaimed. Now his face reddened deeply. "Where is she? She's not going to—"

"She came through the operation as good as could be expected," Trubshawe said. "They hope she'll be able to recover use of the arm, but it's too soon to tell."

"Goddamn!" Benchley thundered, a surprising huskiness rising from some reserve in his body. "I'll see that pigeon-toed gorilla dead, and hang the law! How the devil did they get at Avalon and the rest of you?"

Benchley's friend touched him on the shoulder. "Easy, Jack. One thing at a time. It was a helicopter, old sport. The buggers made off with a helicopter from Gatwick. This stupid git from London Metropolitan thinks it was the IRA. But by the build of him, I'd say he was this Dromio chap. I don't know who the pilot was. I just know it wasn't *modus operandi* for the Shin Fein crowd."

Benchley's head sank down. He murmured, almost to himself. "Carolyn. First Carolyn has to die, now they try and kill my little girl's baby." He looked up. "What about Ann? Don't keep anything from me, Truffie?"

Trubshawe looked over at Bonnie, his eyes imploring her to take up the rest of the telling.

"Physically, she's fine, Mr. Benchley," Bonnie stated soothingly. "It's just that—well, with her condition and all—"

"She's in the hospital, isn't she?" the old man asked.

Bonnie nodded. "Ann is in bad shape. She lost control in the emergency room of the hospital. It's like the spells she's gone through before. She had a similar thing when we found out Dave was dead, but now this is—this is—"

"A full-blown psychotic episode?" Benchley said.

"I wouldn't go that far, Mr. Benchley."

"Her mother had something like it, God rest her," Benchley said. "The doctors called them psychotic episodes back then. At that time, we didn't even have the right drugs to give her. She was misdiagnosed. It started with Ann only a few years ago. The lithium controls it still, doesn't it?"

"When she takes it," Bonnie said. "I've been down in San Francisco twice since you were kidnaped. Ann had me working on bugging Warbeck's office. Harvey here was in on that. When I left town, Ann stopped taking the medication. The stress of losing you like that, not knowing what became of you... I'm sorry I didn't do more for—"

"She's a grown-up," Benchley said firmly. "She knew she had to take her medicine. Damn it, why can't she take care of herself? Why does she have to be manic-depressive? What have I brought on another soul to deserve this curse on my family?"

Nobody could answer that. Bonnie was sharp enough to come up with some good news.

"At least one part of Warbeck's plan fell through. As far as the police are concerned, and the public, you aren't the main suspect in the murder of Carolyn anymore. The guy who did it is a fellow named Charles Lindsey Aarons. He's an ex-felon, with a long criminal record. The FBI matched his fingerprints being on the trunk of the Ford Mustang you drove to Sherwood Strunk's Forest of Arden. And they found the diamond pendant you gave her, the one that was specially made. They also have some blood samples of the attacker from under Carolyn's... uh, her fingernails. They're doing DNA testing right now to see if it matches up with this guy."

"That's some solace," Benchley said. "Warbeck kept me abreast of the news that I was a wanted man. If what you say pans out, at least I may be able to continue my life after all this is over."

"It was Harvey here who caught the guy," Bonnie said.

"With your assistance," I added. "And a bit from the San Francisco Police. It was Dave McCreedy who did the legwork on the IFH connection."

"Where is Dave McCreedy now?" Benchley said. His deep voice was hoarse from the effects of the coughing.

"He's dead," I said. "Somebody murdered him."

Benchley drew in some breath. He seemed to be puzzled for a moment, then he spoke:

"Maybe there is some justice in the world."

That took me back. Way back.

"I don't understand," I said. "I thought Dave was your friend."

"He's was my friend, but he betrayed me," Benchley replied testily. "He was in with Warbeck on the plot. I'm convinced of that. Dave had been up to Scrub Oak Ranch several times in the last year at my invitation. He found my grandson, the most important person in my life, and he didn't try to rip me off with his fees and expenses. He was a man's man, and there aren't many of those left. Ann fell hard for him, too. I couldn't approve of her being involved with a married man, but that was her business. She had him up to the ranch when she stayed there. He was up there for hours and hours when I wasn't around. He knew where all the keys were. That would have given him access to my basement office and to the safe. He must have discovered my private journals, the ones I kept on the time travels back to this era. After that, it was just a matter of time for him to discover where the STUMP actually was. He couldn't pull that off, but Warbeck finished that part off by torturing me."

"Wait a minute, wait a minute," I said, holding up one hand and trying very hard to keep from speaking too loudly. "Look, Mr. Benchley, Dave was the guy who went back to your daughter to help her find you in the first place. He was the guy who put the finger on Trevor Warbeck and the IFH. Why would he do that? Why would he do that if he worked for Warbeck? The obvious thing to do—"

"The obvious thing to do is to lead you all into a trap," Benchley said. "What happened down in San Francisco when you actually got on Warbeck's trail? Bonnie, what happened?"

Bonnie recounted the events of the last few days: how she had tried first to install an electronic bug in Warbeck's office and how Dave said the bug wouldn't work; how I had tried to plant a bug and was ambushed; and how it was apparent from Warbeck's knowledge of when we hit his office that he must have bugged Benchley's office at the Shakespeare Festival.

"You see," Benchley said. "We've all been led into traps. Warbeck wouldn't tell me who the fellow was that he had inside my house and offices. To me, it's awful damn interesting that Dave fights with Ann and they split up right when Warbeck and Strunk's plans for me go into effect. Awful damn interesting."

"But I saw Ralph Bates in San Francisco, using one of the time machines," I said. "He was helping your girlfriend's killer break into an apartment I was staying at."

Benchley shook his head. "McCreedy and Bates then. They were both working against me."

My head was swimming. It was hard for me to see Dave as being that duplicitous, that treacherous. Then I remembered that it was only a few days earlier that I had caught him shacked up in a Middleburg hotel with Wendy's sister. Adultery was one thing, but setting friends up to be kidnaped and possibly killed—myself included—was the difference between being unethical and being evil.

"Wait a minute," I said, trying to establish some measure of doubt in Benchley's mind. "You told us there was another person who had access to your office. Who was that?"

"Besides Bonnie, there's only one other person," he said. "I've known him all my life and I know he wouldn't do anything like that to me." His voice regained its strong Gregory Peck baritone.

"Who is it?" I asked.

"Jack Picasso," Benchley said. "He's not an ideal fellow, and he's hooked up in the past with some hoods, but I know he'd never do anything to gunnybag me—not after all I did for his father. Besides, he and Ann were renewing their relationship. They were going to make a film together. No, it has to be Dave McCreedy."

I still felt defensive about Dave, and carried on: "Are you certain it was Dave who was in with Warbeck? Can you really be sure?"

"Hell, yes!" Benchley said, fuming with anger. "He's the only likely..." He was so upset it triggered another coughing spasm. I waited until he finished.

"Did Warbeck tell you Dave was in with him?"

Benchley stopped hacking. "He didn't come out and say it, said he had to protect the identity of the man and all that, but McCreedy was the man. He had to be by process of elimination. You can't tell me Bonnie betrayed me."

I couldn't tell him that. But I couldn't accept the fact that Dave had led his sponsor and friend into a trap. For what reason? A spiteful action to somehow get back at Ann Benchley for breaking off their affair? Or to collect money from Trevor Warbeck in exchange for information he got stumbling onto knowledge of the time machines? Could Dave, my best friend, have been capable of that grandiose and immoral a sell-out, in effect selling out another person's life for a fat wad of money?

"What's going on inside Grantum Hall?" Bonnie asked. "We saw a wagon of dead bodies—" Bonnie stopped, perhaps not wanting to fully recapture the image in her mind.

"Mass executions. Firing squads," Benchley said. "Warbeck and Essex seized Grantum Manor by treachery. Now they're killing all the servants in the manor so Warbeck can pass himself off as The Earl. Slaughtered 'em, almost everyone. Including children. Their soldiers made sport of the female servants before they shot them. They were shot in the courtyard of the castle. Just the way the Nazi SS would mow down their prisoners."

"Why kill servants? Why kill children?" Bonnie asked.

"Because the servants and their families know who the real Earl of Grantum was," Benchley said, anger rising again in his voice. The old man sat up, planted both hands on his lower back, and emitted a groan. "Warbeck told me personally he extracted what information he needed to know about Grantum's habits and then had them all put to death. The Earl of Grantum himself was a prisoner in the same cell I was in. Who knows how much longer he has to live."

"A lousy butcher," Trubshawe said. His speech was slurred. The whiskey was starting to take effect.

Benchley continued: "Once Warbeck got hold of the time machine, he traveled back into time, taking advantage of the fact that the machine put him within a couple days of The Earl of Essex's hasty return from Ireland. As history happened the first time around, Essex rode to Nonsuch Palace, and burst in on the Queen in her private chamber one morning, ranting about his enemies at court stabbing him in the back. She had already heard of the so-called peace treaty he had agreed to with Tyrone. She wanted the Irish defeated, not toyed with. Essex lost her favor, and gradually he became a pariah to her. Well, Warbeck intercepted Essex and his party of personal guard, including Southampton, at a town called Maidenhead, just north of Middlesex County. He must have brought books or documents from the present to show Essex and Southampton what their future was, and offered them a remedy to change it. It involved Trevor Warbeck assuming the identity of William Devant, the Earl of Grantum. In exchange for helping Warbeck assume that identity, our fat friend offered them the modern armaments they would need to defeat the Queen's larger forces."

"We happened upon a couple soldiers who deserted from Essex's guard," Trubshawe said. "Had a bit of trouble with them at first, but no matter. One of them said they were bivouacked around Grantum Hall. They fled from fear of the firing squads."

"I heard the last of the domestics killed off just before my release," Benchley said. "It was a piteous sight. From my prison in the *donjon*, I saw a group of them lined up. I watched it once and that was enough. Once outside the castle, they take the dead bodies somewhere close to be burned—God, what a stench—then mix the bone fragments and ashes in with the manure buckets. What's left of those poor people is residing in some crude attempt at a cesspool the real William Devant had built to dispose of human waste."

That explained the awful smell I had gotten a whiff of when I brought Southampton up to be exchanged on the bridge, the smell of open sewage mixed with the stench of the dead.

"Jesus H. Christ," Trubshawe said, his speech betraying the effects of drink. "Lousy murdering bastards!"

Benchley continued: "Essex stormed Grantum Hall with his troops, took his friend Devant by surprise and turned the place into a fortress. Then Warbeck went back into the future and dragged me back with him."

The whole adventure sounded grisly and rapacious. I had no doubt Warbeck would have been up to his part in it. The real shock for me, however, was dealing with the old man's certainty that Dave was mixed up with Warbeck. If Benchley could be believed, my friend fooled me as badly as he had fooled poor Wendy with his affairs.

"Wait a minute," Benchley said, again staring at me like I had just walked into his line of sight.

"You name is Harvey Wells, right?"

"That's right," I said. "I'm Dave McCreedy's former friend, at your service."

Benchley's eye widened. "Yes, I remember you now. You were my bodyguard on the book tour in Seattle."

"And, with all due respect, sir," I said, "I don't believe my friend Dave had anything to do with Trevor Warbeck."

"I wish I could believe you, Wells," Benchley said sadly.

Benchley looked totally exhausted. His shoulders sagged, and he actually began to snore while still in an upright position.

"I think Mr. Benchley needs to rest," Bonnie said, reaching over to pull a blanket over the elderly man's shoulders.

In the muted light, I saw Benchley stir, then nod. "I...I need to rest. Truffie, will you take the first watch tonight? I need a couple hours rest before I can—"

"Wells and I can take the watches, Jack," Trubshawe said, sounding hammered. "You just stay bundled up and rest. That's an order, staff sergeant."

"Yes sir, Major Trubshawe," Benchley said weakly. He slowly laid himself down on another blanket that had been spread out for him. "Thank you, Bonnie dear," he said as she lifted up his head gently and placed a rolled up towel between his head and the blanketed ground. He was snoring again in less than two minutes.

"His hands are cold," Bonnie said as she tucked another blanket over Benchley's supine form. "I wish we could light a fire here."

"Too risky, Bonnie my luv," Trubshawe slurred. "Damn my bloody luck. Gone into combat in the Malay jungles and never a scratch. Jumped out of planes dozens of times and never a scratch. Did some risky business in Ulster and never a scratch. Now I'm a bloody mess." He stood up awkwardly, the way a drunken man does, then the effects of the whiskey planted him down on his rump. He fumbled in his doublet until he found his pocket watch, then flashed a penlight on the face of the clock. "I would say we have 'bout six hours until daybreak, mate. Two three-hour watches should do it. You want to start off on the watch, Wells, or should I?"

Chapter Thirty-Six

"Why did they do such a horrible thing?" Ann Benchley asked between choking sobs as she clung to her father. Benchley stood there with her, next to the STUMP in the middle of the clearing. The old man's liver-spotted hand gently stroked the back of his daughter's head. The rest of us—Bonnie, myself, a headache-racked Trubshawe, and Stephen—stood in a semi-circle around them in the early morning gloom.

When I had last seen Ann Benchley, she was emotionally overwhelmed by what had happened to her boyfriend and her daughter during the helicopter attack. She seemed to be in reasonable control of her faculties, all things considered, but there was no doubt she was devastated by all this, especially the mayhem that had been done to her father.

"Don't sweat it, kid," Benchley said. "The bastards only got my bad eye. How about my grandchildren?"

"Avalon is in Cromwell Hospital, Daddy. She's gone through surgery and she's going to be all right. She lost some muscle in her arm, but she's going to be all right."

"We know who the bastard is who shot her, kid. He'll pay in full. Nothing's happened to Tyler, I pray."

"Tyler is back with the Kirklands, at the ranch," Ms. Benchley said as she dried her eyes with the sleeve of her off-white Stanford University sweatshirt. "I talked to him a couple hours ago. He misses his grandpa. God, he'll be so happy to see you. Daddy, I'm so afraid for Jack."

"What about Jack?" Benchley said, his voice betraying a

dip in enthusiasm.

"He disappeared. I haven't heard from him since he visited me in the hospital. I'm afraid he's been kidnaped." She choked up. The tears came. She leaned against her father.

"I'm sorry, kid," Benchley said.

"I know...you never liked him," the daughter said between sobs.

"Not true," Benchley said. "I liked him. God knows I've helped him enough in the business. Anyway, since when have you cared what I think?"

"You're wrong, Daddy. Oh God, you're so wrong." There was a strain in his daughter's voice that told him she was far from being mentally on an even keel.

"I have something else I need to tell you, Annie. It's about your old boyfriend, Dave McCreedy. He was in on the plot to kidnap me and kill Carolyn. It was him and Ralph Bates. They sold me out to Trevor Warbeck."

Ann Benchley gasped. "I don't believe you." Her reaction was pretty close to mine.

Benchley explained the same theory on Dave he had given me last night.

"He couldn't do that!" she shouted. "Not Dave. Not Dave! He WOULDN'T do that!"

"Quiet, girl," Trubshawe hissed. "Warbeck's bunch could be out looking for us right now."

Ann Benchley turned away from her father and looked over to Bonnie. Her face, normally light, almost pale, was crimson red. She drew heavy breaths, like she was hyperventilating. I felt sorry for her. Bonnie said nothing. What was there to say?

"What's wrong with your foot, Dad?" Stephen asked his father.

Trubshawe, who was supporting himself using a tree branch for a makeshift crutch, looked down at his bandaged leg, then spoke: "Caught a bit of lead down by the heel, son. And my right arm has seen better days, too."

"Which is why Stephen is going to take you to a hospital, Truffie," Benchley said flatly. He looked at his daughter. "And you, kid, are going back as well. I can see you're in no shape for what's ahead here. Your place is with that beautiful little girl of yours, and Major Trubshawe has to get to a real hospital before gangrene sets in and they have to take his whole damn foot off. Stephen, you'll see to that. I'm staying on for a bit."

"Yes, sir," Stephen said. The way the younger man spoke I almost expected him to salute.

"What about your eye, Mr. Benchley?" Bonnie asked.

"I'm fine, Bonnie," the old man said. "Henry, that is Southampton, saw to it I was treated for my injury. They're not all monsters at Grantum Hall, you know, but there are monsters enough."

"Daddy," Ms. Benchley said forcefully, "you are coming home. Now."

Benchley spoke just as forcefully: "*You* are going home, Annie. I can see you are in a fragile state of mind. I'm not leaving here until I deal out some payback and you can't be a part of that."

"Don't you feed me lines from those silly old movies of yours," the daughter said angrily.

"Those silly old movies paid for your boarding schools and your orthodontic work," Benchley said. "I'll steal my own dialogue whenever and wherever I feel like it. That boyfriend of yours didn't mind stealing a few of my good lines for his last movie, so why can't I rip myself off now and then?"

I whispered to Bonnie, who was standing next to me: "What is the deal here? I thought this was just going to be a rescue job at the most?"

Bonnie threw up her hands. Considering the unfolding circumstances, that was as good a reaction as any.

Ann Benchley shook her head. "What do you need to do here that's so important it's worth your life?" she asked.

Benchley paused, put his hands together, sighed, then spoke to Trubshawe's son: "Stephen, I want you to take your dad and Ann back to modern London. Pronto. I want you to return with a suitable wardrobe for me to blend in around here. There is also a cedar chest your father has locked in his office safe. He knows which one that is. I want that, too. Then you will wait exactly forty-eight hours and return the STUMP to this exact spot. Bonnie, it would be wise if you and Wells took your leave from this time frame as well."

"I'll follow you, sir," Stephen said. He was dressed in Renaissance English garb so he was prepared to go.

"You will not follow, son," Benchley said firmly. "I promised your dear mother not to take you on any more of these excursions. She almost lost you in the Falklands, and I couldn't face her if anything bad happened to you on this business. Your main task is to take care of your bloody reckless father just as Ann's place is with her little girl."

"What is so *important* here!" Ann Benchley said, the word 'important' coming out in a screech. Her voice became calmer. "Is all this about Avalon? She wants you alive, not to have you die—"

Benchley interrupted: "Yes, kid, one part of this is revenge. Warbeck and his little group need a lesson, and that's reason enough for me to throw in against them with what friends I have here. But there's something else: it was my carelessness that gave Warbeck the technology to interfere with history in the first place. I spent two weeks locked up with the real Earl of Grantum. He's a good man, and I owe him something. If there's a chance to set him free, I'll do it. Plus, there's the matter of the blueprints that Truffie showed me this morning."

Benchley reached into his pocket and unfurled a large piece of white paper. It was the same paper that Trubshawe had taken off Southampton back at the falls. Benchley showed it to his daughter. From my angle to it, the paper looked like a blueprint, featuring what looked like designs for pavilions and carefully planned open spaces. There was small writing in some of the octagons, squares, and rectangles on the paper. I could make out words and numbers in the designs, which were laid out like the plan of a shopping mall complex. The only thing I could make out clearly was the heading at the top of the page.

'FOREST OF ARDEN' was the heading.

"Trubshawe and I believe Warbeck's sponsor, Sherwood Strunk, want to take over this kingdom. They're going to do it with the help of the Earl of Essex and his few dozen followers. Many of them are already supplied with modern weapons; assault rifles, grenade launchers, semi-automatic pistols, the small ordnance that can go through one STUMP. They mean to depose Queen Elizabeth in a bloody coup, put Essex on the throne and, after the legitimate powers here are squelched, Strunk means to erect this abomination somewhere near

London. This is Sherwood Strunk's second 'Forest of Arden,' a second private theme park for himself and his wealthy friends."

Ann Benchley took a bit of time to absorb the information. Finally, she folded her hands, sighed, and shook her head.

"Why?" the daughter asked.

"Why do you need ask?" the father replied. "You know Sherwood Strunk is ga-ga over Shakespeare and the whole Elizabethan Age. He knows the history of this time we're in probably almost as well as I do. Imagine the monkey wrench he's throwing into the time-line of Western History. Instead of Strunk having a simulated Elizabethan Theater and a few mock-Tudor buildings around his estate, why, he'll have this incredible theme park right smack dab in the middle of the real age! He'll probably keep it a secret from the modern public, just something for his chosen circle to enjoy, like the Forest of Arden in California is now. All he needs is all three of the STUMPs and he can bring in the men and equipment he needs to build it. And he won't stop at just this little jewel, not the Sherwood Strunk I know. Inside a year, this whole island will be in his hands. Oh, sure, he will let King Robert of Essex and his followers look like they run the show, but Strunk will be in charge, him or the new Earl of Grantum, Trevor Warbeck. And something else, Annie: with Warbeck back here, and the general public not knowing about the infraction of time that's taking place, he can create documentation that the Earl of Grantum did write Shakespeare's plays! He can hide the documentation back here, retrieve it in the modern world, and show the planted evidence to the world. And it will be impossible for scientists or scholars to refute. William Shakespeare will be stripped of his rightful legacy. He'll be put down as a semi-literate actor who served as a front for an Oxford-educated nobleman. And Warbeck's Institute for Factual History will get the credit for these great finds, and he can always come back here and be a bloody Earl! Now, for God's sake, Annie, tell me you understand."

Ms. Benchley buried her head in her hands.

"Wait a bit," Stephen said. "How is Warbeck or Strunk going to build this great park without everyone finding out? I mean, they'll need engineers, architects, heavy-equipment operators—"

"All they need is a few highly-skilled men and women," Trubshawe said to his son. "The rest of the workers he can get from the population here: train 'em on the spot like we do in the military."

"And those few skilled people he gets from the modern world, he can swear to secrecy," Benchley added. "Or just have them killed after their work is done, like the Egyptian priests did to the poor slaves who buried the Pharaoh in some secret tomb. Warbeck had no compunctions about killing the domestic staff at Grantum Hall. He'll be able to do it all over England, to any group that rises up against the new King. He and Strunk will own this realm."

Bonnie spoke: "So, all of London, all the townships, all the cathedrals, all the manor houses, all the castles, all these woodlands—"

"All England will just be a subsidiary of Strunk, Incorporated," Benchley said, nodding. He folded up the paper.

"I'm coming with you," Ann Benchley told her father.

"No, Annie," Benchley said softly. "What did I say before?"

"This is crazy, Daddy. You're mad if you think you can do anything about this. This is beyond your control. Isn't there a police force or something back here to handle this?"

Benchley laughed. "What police? The Sheriff of Middlesex? The Bailiff of Hampstead? The old fogies who do the night watch in Clerkenwell? There are no police here as we know it. And I suppose next you'll tell me to go back to New Scotland Yard and have them bring some Bobbies around to look into this. I'm going to do everything I can to stop this without getting any government involved. Besides, if Truffie and I did go to the authorities, who says they would even bother to let us demonstrate the STUMP. We might be locked up as a couple loonies."

"You are loony," his daughter replied.

"And you are a fine one to judge mental stability," Benchley said harshly. "All I need now is a manic-depressive case following me around, ready to fly off the handle—"

Jack Benchley recoiled from the hard slap his daughter gave him on the left cheek. Instantly, the old man's hand went up like he would return the favor. He wavered, however, and this gave his daughter a chance to cover her face with her hands.

"Oh, no!" Bonnie exclaimed as she moved to get between the Benchleys. "You two stop this right now," she said like a mother. "Stop it right now!"

The tearful reunion of father and child had turned ugly. This was the dark side of the father-daughter relationship that Bonnie had alluded to and that I had read about taking place on the set of *The American*. I could just imagine the French camera crew and all the extras standing about with gaping mouths, watching these two go at it. Bonnie was between them, luckily, but it was not over.

"You son-of-a-bitch," Ann Benchley yelled out at her father while Bonnie stayed between them. The actress's voice was at a theatrical pitch again. "How dare you throw up my illness at me like it's a character flaw! I'll tell you what a character flaw is, Daddy dearest. How about a man who insists on being a philanderer, chasing after young women, then lying about it to his wife and family? How about a big shot director who gives small parts to lousy actresses because they will sleep with him? I know what you were doing while my Mother and I were down in Costa Rica visiting my grandparents. You were unfaithful to my mother to the day she died! Bastard! Cold-blooded bastard! I hate you and your stinking lies..." The tears came again, along with the shaking. Ann Benchley sank down to her knees and squatted into a ball with her hands over her head like a little schoolgirl practicing a Cold War Era Duck-and-Cover drill under her desk. After some time passed, Bonnie gently got her onto her feet and led her away. The denim pants the actress had on were caked at the knees with moist brown dirt from the ground.

Stephen took his father and Ann Benchley forward in time, the red light of the STUMP flaring up and absorbing them on the perimeter of the device, then leaving no sign they were even there.

Shortly after that, I heard a buzzing sound above my head. Then I saw what made the sound—an arrow in flight—hit a near-by tree.

Bonnie and I took cover, along with Benchley. The arrow had flown over our heads and embedded itself in the trunk of a willow tree across the clearing. We hustled to the opposite edge of the clearing, behind a line of oak trees, leading the animals behind us by their bridles. It was not long before we heard the sound of footsteps coming through the woods off to our right. Trubshawe had wisely left Benchley his Baretta pistol. I had mine out, ready for a scouting party from Grantum Hall. If scouts were in the area, and they had trouble finding us before, the noise from the Benchley family reunion would have given them a sure fix.

But they were not scouts. They were boys. Two of them, to be exact, both light-skinned and slender and close enough to be almost twins, dressed up in smaller versions of the doublet and breeches that adults at this time were wearing. Both had little derby hats with feathers in them, and their hose and shoes were streaked with mud.

"There it be," one of the boys said. He had a bow and a quill of arrows. The other one was unarmed, but had a lifeless rabbit dangling by the feet from a rope attached to a stick he held, hobo- style, over his shoulder.

"A hunting party," Benchley whispered quietly to Bonnie.

It was the pony that gave us away, letting out a loud snorting noise despite the fact that I was stroking its muzzle at Bonnie's behest. My two companions were doing the same to quiet the horses. The boys looked right over in our direction.

"Who lurks there?" the young lad with the rabbit asked. His voice was of a high timbre, not yet ready to crack from puberty.

There was nothing to do but to show ourselves and hope a bluff worked. I thought of something and, since Benchley wasn't dressed for the season, Bonnie and I came out. She led the horse out, and I followed, leading the smaller beast. We figured Stephen would be back any minute, and if the kids saw the STUMP materialize we'd have a mess on our hands.

We approached the kids like we owned this neck of the forest, which is what Bonnie and I hoped to put across.

"What calls you here, my ruddy lambs?" Bonnie said in an accent. "Know you not that you commit trespass?"

The boys seemed to flinch at this pronouncement.

"Know you who holds the title of this land, boy," she asked the one with the bow.

The boy gulped, looked down from Bonnie's gaze, and kept his eyes aimed at her waist, or maybe just above.

"No, good madam," he said. "We thought this was part of the common land."

"Bah," she said, warming to the role. "Think'st thou that the whole great heath is yours for shooting arrows about? You nearly pierced the doublet of my servant with your errant shaft. This is land given over to the one John Benchley, newly located here from Bristol town. He is a kinsman to the Earl of Grantum. Surely, even two young sprigs such as yourself know of His Right Honorable Self."

The boy shook. "Pardon, good madam, we knew not—"

"My husband is Squire Benchley, and not a man given to little scamps who think the wide world is their free target to rain deadly arrows hither and yon. Flee this place, or my coarse servant will constrain both you saucy little buckram-clad schoolboys, and turn you over to the undersheriff."

The boys looked at me. I gave them what I hoped was the menacing stare of a coarse servant.

"Please, milady," the boy with the rabbit stammered. "Let us depart freely. We shall not trespass again."

"Get thee gone, then. 'Tis the morn, is it not? Why do you dwell in the forest like Robin Goodfellow? It is Sunday is it not? Obey the Queen's Law! Get thee to Church."

"Good lady," the boy with the dead rabbit said, "it is Monday."

"To Grammar School then!" Bonnie shot back. "Take thee both to thy heels and seek deliverance for your trespass the next Sunday. Be gone."

It was a close call. Less than a minute after the boys vanished over a knoll, the STUMP returned.

It was then, after Stephen returned with the clothes—a black cape, matching silk doublet, and black and white striped breeches as well as boots nice enough to befit a gentleman—that Bonnie volunteered herself to play a female Sancho Panza to Benchley's Don Quixote. I had no choice, for Bonnie's sake, to throw in myself in the package as well.

Chapter Thirty-Seven

"Believe me, I'd rather be at Fortmun and Mason or Harrods right now, or, better yet, jumping on a Chunnel Train out of Waterloo Station and doing some serious siteseeing over in Paris," Bonnie said to me at one point as we traversed down a broad dirt road which featured a few other travelers on horseback, foot or homemade-looking wooden carts. She told me this on one of those rare occasions when I managed to get my pony at the same pace as Bonnie's horse.

"That's right, give her a little slack," she said. The pony sputtered and shook his head as I got closer to Bonnie's mount. "That's better," she said. "Just keep in charge, keep up the routine." Benchley was several lengths ahead of us, riding perfectly erect like some cavalry officer.

"You were saying you'd rather be elsewhere," I said. "I can relate to that."

The terrain was level for the most part, with a few knolls to surmount now and then. We were headed toward London, which was barely visible at the top of the knolls as a cluster of spires, keeps and the broad roof of what I knew to be St. Paul's. Along the edge of the road were patches of farming plots, separated from one another by thick hedgerows. One could glimpse a farmhouse through the trees and hedges now and then. It was a cool morning, and smoke from the nearby houses hovered through the air, giving off the smell of burning wood. Actual trees were few and far between. We saw shepherds and dogs herding flocks of sheep in the rolling meadows. There were few people on the road. I figured it was either some sort of holiday or there were just fewer people around—period.

We passed a wooden signpost at a crossroads. If we went left, we were headed for a place called Kentish Town. Right would take us to a place called Kilburn. Straight ahead was 'London—Camden Town.' We headed straight.

A priest, or at least he looked like a priest, passed us going in the opposite direction. He had a crucifix on a leather strap about his neck that hung over his loose-fitting grey cassock. He was carrying a large black book under one arm, pushing himself along with a wooden staff. A small black dog with a short muzzle and skinny legs followed at his heels. He was wearing sandals that looked in serious need of repair. When he passed, I asked Bonnie what denomination he was.

"Anglican," Bonnie said. "Definitely not a Catholic. They don't allow priests around here these days. No Masses, either. There might be a few priests hiding in some nook here and there, but they wouldn't be out on a public road unless they wanted to go out as a martyr. The cells of the Tower of London are filled with captured priests. Jesuits get the worst of it. Everybody goes to Church, of course. If you don't you either get arrested or, if you're rich, you pay a big fine. Some Catholic sympathizers do that. They still can't practice Catholicism, but the Queen won't mess with them if they fatten her treasury and don't hide priests. The Church you attend has to be an Anglican or sanctified Nonconformist Church like the Puritans have for it to count, but it has to be a Church that will bow to the Queen's will."

"Well, that policy certainly helps the indecisive types," I said. "Unless you're rich, you hit the pews on Sunday. It's coercive, but it makes up for that with simplicity."

"It's damnable intolerance is what it is," Benchley said. I suspected he turned about to let us know he could hear what we said even from about thirty feet off. He had damned acute hearing for an old fogy.

The terrain got flatter and more cultivated as we rode further. There was still the occasional hill, with patches of heath and oak trees cropping up now and then. There was a greyness to the grasslands, but, as ominous dark clouds were coming up from the south, I suspected we were in for a strong dose of rain such as last night. I hoped not to be around here long enough to see the grasslands attain their Fall greenery.

We stopped off at one cluster of oaks up on the peak of a hillside. Benchley said his back was killing him, and I secretly emphasized. My lower back hurt worse than just after my first encounter with Dromio back at the IFH office, thanks in large part to the butt-jarring I had received in my fall from the pony. Now the motion of the beast as her hooves clumped along the road was aggravating the pain. I was in dire need for some sort of equestrian shock absorber.

Benchley said he liked the rest spot for its commanding 360 degree vista it provided. "We don't need to be ambushed by any highwaymen, not after what you two have already had to deal with," he said.

In addition to the roofs and spires of the city on the horizon, one could now see the system of stone walls and high gates that enclosed London off from the outside. The metropolis was still well in the distance. About a mile away, down the hillside, was a cluster of timber-framed two and three story buildings with whitewashed sides and steep-sloped roofs. A bell could be heard ringing in the distance, the faint sound probably emulating from the bell tower which stood up from the center of the village.

I got out the drinking supplies, which Bonnie had transferred from our plastic jugs to some time-appropriate leather bags with horn-shaped drinking stems that Stephen had brought for our use. Benchley slowly sat down by leaning his long, stooped-shouldered torso against the tree and edging down to the base of the tree using his back. Bonnie and I sat on rocks, our feet resting on a blanket of green and brown oak leaves that were strewn over the ground. Bonnie took off her green jacket and folded it over her lap. The sun came out from the clouds and gave us some direct warmth. We ate apples and drank from the bags of water and orange juice.

"There are a good number of highwaymen in this part of Middlesex," Benchley observed. His good eye squinted up to the sunlight, the warming rays seeming to energize him. "Fortunately, I think we're well-supplied with weaponry. Wells has a sword and I have a rapier. I fenced for Stanford as a young man. Plus our authentic handgun—the petronel. And I made sure Stephen brought a matchlock rifle back with him.

I have it tied in a leather case on my saddle. Interesting process to get the rifle to fire. I'll show you."

He pulled out one of Bonnie's butane lighters from a small pouch that was dangling from the holster that held the pistol. He took out a small piece of what looked like rope, then lit up one end of it and blew on it to get it burning. It burned slowly like a candle wick.

"Get the rifle," he told me.

I went to Benchley's horse and undid the leather strings that held the musket and its leather case to the saddle. (The AK-47 went back with Stephen and Major Trubshawe, Benchley having decided the handguns were enough for our defense.) The musket was nearly as long as I was tall. Attached to the long barrel of the weapon was a metal rod. After I handed the musket to him, Benchley took hold of it and put the butt of the weapon on the ground. He took a pouch and poured what looked, and smelled, like gunpowder into the top of the barrel. Then he used the rod to push down the measure of powder. Next he took a lead ball out of another pouch and rammed that down the barrel. He put the gun upright and rested the long barrel on the stump of what had been an elm tree. He showed me a small metal notch just above a curved metal protrusion that looked like a spring and was situated a few inches above the long backward-L shaped trigger. He added more powder, this time in a small compartment on top of the stock. Benchley had Bonnie check and see if anyone was coming up or down the road. Assured no one was, he cut the wick with a knife and attached the lit end to the small clamp at the end of the spring.

Benchley pulled the trigger. The spring came backward, the lit end struck the point on the stock where he had placed the last measure of powder, and the musket went off in a blaze of smoke and sparks. It was loud and I had no idea if Benchley hit whatever it was he was aiming at.

"Damn primitive but it works," the old man said. "I'm hoping just the sight of the musket, and our rapiers, will be adequate for our travels. Plus I have the wheel lock pistol Truffie took off that fellow you shot. That's easier to use."

"Don't forget the Berettas," I said. "I like the idea of getting off eight or nine shots while the other guy has to reload after his one shot."

"Let's not go to the modern pistols unless it's a real emergency, Wells," Benchley said as he handed me the matchlock. "Once we pull out those babies, the jig is really up. Anybody seeing you fire off multiple rounds with a firearm in these times will have you pegged as a warlock. They hang witches and warlocks in these times and you don't get a court-appointed attorney. We can't afford to let anyone think we don't belong in this time frame. It will screw up the whole plan if we give ourselves away. Now, if you please, put the rifle back on my saddle."

"What exactly is it that we have to pull off?" I asked Benchley after I returned from my duties and Bonnie handed me another apple. "Where we going exactly and what is the plan?"

"Good question," Benchley said. "What we do is simply forewarn a certain individual. That fellow is a templar at Grey's Inn by the name of Francis Bacon. You probably know him as Sir Francis Bacon, or Lord Chancellor Francis Bacon, but he's none of that yet at this stage. Bacon is one of the two men I've entrusted with my real identity. On my previous trips I've confided in Bacon some of the historic events to come in his own life and in the course of this kingdom and the world. He is a keen student of the future, which is understandable because he is one of the greatest minds of the age." Benchley bit into his apple, chewed, swallowed, then continued.

"Bacon, and his brother Anthony, are nominally aligned with the Essex faction at Elizabeth's Court. The party of Sir Walter Raleigh makes up the other main faction, and the two camps are always competing for the favor of the Queen. Since Bacon knows about the rebellion Essex was to lead in February, 1601, he has naturally begun to distance himself from the man. Essex is an egomaniacal hot-head. He can barely control himself in the face of criticism, even from the Queen herself. Essex would be considered a mentally-ill man by modern standards, but he is also a master courtier and a very intelligent, well-educated man. Bacon is personally fond of him, but he recognizes that the mental instability that seizes him in times of great stress will be his downfall. He told me he would have distanced himself from Essex even without my warnings, and history has shown that he did so. My intervention has allowed him the knowledge to know exactly when to go to the Queen and inform her well ahead of time that Essex is headed toward open treason. She would then have time to squelch the rebellion before it even started, thus saving her the ignominious necessity of sending her current favorite to the Tower and, shortly afterward, signing his death warrant."

"But that would change history," Bonnie said.

"It would also keep Essex and several other men alive. It would also keep William Shakespeare's friend, Henry, the Earl of Southampton, from being imprisoned in the Tower. It would give a dying old monarch a way to preserve the last of her suitors, false though he may be in his supposed attraction to her, and give her some peace and happiness before she faces death. Yes, Bonnie, it would change history, but it would change it for the better. All avoidance of bloodshed and woe was possible, until Warbeck and his minions tipped the balance of power to Essex's favor."

"Okay," I said. "You tell Bacon to get a move on and warn the Queen to call out her army, or whatever. If Essex's forces are armed with advanced weapons, what good can the Queen's soldiers do with single-load pistols and muskets that take over a minute to get off a shot?"

"The Queen's side can still gain advantage using a strong force of musketeers and heavy cannon, an overwhelming force to offset those Essex loyalists who have been just recently versed in using assault weapons. Without that third STUMP, Warbeck can't bring in tanks or helicopters." Benchley swallowed, then continued.

"It takes all three STUMPs lined up in a triangle formation and working in synchonicity to create a large enough matter transference field."

"The key is for Bacon to dispatch himself quickly to Nonsuch Palace and gain audience with the Queen. As an advisor to Her Majesty, albeit not a close one, he could persuade her to take action now and pin Warbeck and Essex inside Grantum Hall. If Bacon can persuade her, and we can keep the third STUMP out of our enemy's hands, then we should be able to thwart the rebels."

"Why does it matter?" I said, passing some apple slices I had cut over to Bonnie. "I mean, this is the past, right? It can't directly effect anything that is going on in modern times."

"It matters," Benchley snapped, "because my friend Morton Ryskind and I made a pact not to exploit these times. We aimed to simply observe and, in rare instances like the Essex affair, better it. Before he died, Mortie Ryskind made me promise to destroy the machines he created because he feared they would fall into the hands of men like Warbeck and Strunk. I didn't do that and now look what's happened. If such technology were made known to private developers and the military-intelligence communities of the major powers, then there's no end to what misuses could occur. I need to right my mistake. I have spent the greater part of my adult life profiting from the presentation of the plays of William Shakespeare, and I will not see his works stolen to gratify the ego of a mountebank like Trevor Warbeck. Somehow, someway, I have to retrieve those two STUMPs from his clutches. I don't expect you two to do that, but I will do it somehow. If I have to sacrifice what's left of my life to keep him from popping in and out of time and making a hash of history, then so be it."

"Is this the only time period that the STUMP machines can travel back to?" Bonnie asked.

"No," Benchley replied. "There is only one other time period available. Mortie invented the STUMPs as an outgrowth of his experiments in quantum psychics. He could tune the machine to travel backwards 150 and 398 years into the past. Don't ask me why there are these two particular openings in the span of time. It just works. The first time Morton Ryskind and I went back into time was near San Francisco. We went from 1988 to 1838. We visited the San Francisco when it was still the Mexican Village of Yueba Buena. A most amazing sight: this enormous San Francisco Bay with no big steel bridges and damn little human habitation. We got to see an Ohlone Indian village where my alma mater, Stanford University, is today. Saw a bullfight out in front of Mission Dolores. I speak some Spanish so I asked a lot of questions around the settlement—too many, actually."

"What happened?" Bonnie asked just after swallowing some apple.

"We almost got thrown in jail because the local *alcalde* thought we were spying on Mexican territorial defenses for the U.S. government. He notified the Governor. We were tipped off at the last minute by a priest we had befriended at the

Mission. We beat it out of there. Luckily we made it across to the eastern side of San Francisco Bay in a boat and got up into the hills. We reached a ranchero owned by a respected Yankee named Doctor John Marsh. He hid us from the authorities until the heat was off and the soldiers went looking elsewhere. We had transported from a spot near the peak of Mount Diablo, on that same side of the Bay Area, so getting back to the present was fairly easy, after the soldiers went looking for us elsewhere. Needless to say, we've never been back to Old California."

"But how does time travel work," Bonnie said. "I'm no science buff, but everything I've ever read says going into the past—or the future—is impossible."

Benchley threw up his hands. "Mortie couldn't explain it to me although he tried more than once. It has something to do with concentrating molecular objects into such an infinitely small, concentrated mass, that they become susceptible to pass through negative energy fields. Somehow, Ryskind discovered a loophole, as it were, in Einstein's theories on time-space. Turns out time can flow backwards as well as forwards, you just have to put somebody or something in a high-energy, compressed state to catch hold of the parallel flow that can pull everything backwards through a negative energy field. Were it not for the fact that the pull into the future, the positive energy, is a little stronger then the opposite flow, time as we know wouldn't be able to function. Ryskind knew how to reverse that flow from his experiments in quantum physics. After our government canceled funding for his atomic research center, Mortie devoted years to experimenting with various time-space theorems, and he had the money—and his brilliant daughters, Judith and Susanna—to see that time travel was a reality. If you want to know the details of how they did it, Bonnie, then we'll have to go to the University of New Mexico in Albuquerque and ask Judith when this is over. She is a full professor there. Susanna is Mortie's other daughter. She was the drama queen of the family, a fine actress. I directed her in *All's Well That Ends Well*. Last I heard, she was teaching drama at a school in Vancouver."

"Susanna, sadly, has bad judgement where men are concerned," Benchley continued. "She was married to an English chap named Ray Harrison. He was head Costume Designer at the festival. The fellow was making porno films on company property, behind my back. Had to fire him—I hated to do that."

"Ray Harrison died recently," Bonnie said.

"A very talented man," Benchley said softly.

"He made a body cast of Annie for her role as Queen Hermione in *The Winter's Tale.* Made the famous scene of the statue of her coming to life very effective."

Benchley got his wind back and we set off down the hillside toward the town. The sun was staying out, and the clouds that had threatened rain stayed in the distance over London. At one point on the road, a group of men and women came toward us on horseback. There were about a dozen of them, their numbers roughly even in gender. They all looked prosperous, the men in silk doublets and cutaway jackets of multicolored cloth. All the men had rapiers dangling from their waists across the left edges of their saddles, and most wore the high-crowned derby hats similar to the one that Benchley wore. The ladies were dressed similar to Bonnie, only the shoulders on their jackets were heavily padded at the shoulders. Otherwise, the jackets they wore were form-fitting, at least from the waist up. If anything, their outfits were less colorful than the men. All the women rode sidesaddle, with hats that were broad-brimmed in front, presumably to keep their complexions from taking in too much sunlight. They rode expertly, too, their feet completely covered by their flowing layers of ruffled skirts, some trimmed at the hem with rings of bright colors. Behind them, on donkeys, were young boys dressed like the men—sans capes and swords—and behind them, on foot, were other boys dressed in drab colors and carrying baskets and large jugs. Behind them, bringing up the rear of the train, were the dogs. Some were greyhounds. Some were shaggy and large like wolfhounds.

I noticed one of the men utilizing one arm and gloved hand to deal with the reins of his horse and had the other arm cocked at the elbow for a perch to carry a large hawk, its head covered with a hood. I soon saw two or three other men also riding with birds of prey on their forearms.

"Good day to you all," Benchley called out to the group as they came toward us. One of the gentlemen, a slender fellow in a black goatee, who bore a resemblance to Basil Rathbone—Bonnie, I am sure, took note appeared to be the leader of the group, and acknowledged Benchley and asked him where we were bound.

"Grey's Inn," Benchley said. "We have been on the road for many days. We heard a rumor in Oxford that Essex has returned from Ireland. Have you any news of the Lord Deputy?"

"Were that I had not heard it," the man said. "All London has heard of his flight from the Earl of Tyrone and his deplorable lack of progress in subduing the rebels. There is fear of Spanish ships raiding unprotected Irish ports, and giving aid and courage to our enemies. Even Cornwall or Devonshire may not be safe. There have been mustering of troops to Mitre End for dispatch to the Cinque Ports in case a plague of Philip's ships strike the Kentish Coast. The able men in the villages about here are being rounded up by sergeants for duty with the pike and the musket."

"What is the feeling of the people in London toward the Lord Deputy?" Benchley asked.

Basil Rathbone shook his head. "To the common folk, he is still their shining white boy," he said. "The uneducated mob is always swayed by a silk-tongued, snuff-snorting pretty boy. To gentlemen of learning in the affairs of the world, Essex appears as he is: an overreaching scoundrel, not without valor but devoid of good reason for all his advantages of birth and favor from our Gracious Queen. I fear he will not set until he has brought the factions about the court to fire and tong 'gainst each of the other."

"T'will be the battles of the Lancasters and the Yorks all again," a young man said, his hawk perfectly still on his leather-covered forearm. "This is what comes from God cursing us with a monarch who never took a husband and brought forth a prince to follow her."

A hefty, puffy-faced woman draped over the horse next to the lad, made a huffing noise. She next extended her arm out and swatted the youngster in the ear, knocking off his feathered hat.

"Fresh from seeing the Queen on progress and yet you speak like a drunken rogue," the chubby woman scolded.

"You do me offense, sister," he replied, putting a hand to his smitten ear.

"I'll do you worse if you forget your degree and speak

afoul of our sovereign," she replied hotly.

There was a flurry of 'yeas' from the group. The boy's face turned red.

Basil Rathbone's double continued conversing with Benchley: "The Queen has sent her soldiers from the Tower out to locate him. There are rumors which trace him everywhere from East Anglica to Surrey. Wherever he is, the Queen wants to bring him to account."

A bright-eyed and slim-hipped woman with a small chin, her honey-blonde hair swept back over her forehead into a tight mane, spoke out: "My husband is quick to skewer the Lord Deputy based on a few tattles gained from the alehouses. You would never guess he was one of those cheering lustily for Essex and his ranks when they left London to do battle with the wild kerns of Ulster. The Lord Deputy has many enemies. I will only believe these reports until these supposed reverses are officially proclaimed. Were it not for Essex and his like, the Spanish dogs would be choking off this island. The man alighted King Phillip's ships at Cadiz, did he not? Did he not lead the attack on the heretics and bring fire and shot to their doorstep? They call women fickle. Bah!"

"Bah indeed," a pumpkin-faced man behind them said. "The weather favors hawking and hawking is what I'm bound to do. If you wish to waste the day, let those who seek sport pass."

The rest of the party put in their preference for hawking above gossip. I maneuvered the pony to the shoulder of the roadway and the group passed around us.

"A bloody sport, hawking," Benchley said, turning his horse about to watch the mob of swells and their servants and dogs go forth. "Quite a favorable pastime these days. I went with Bacon and his brother on a sort of combination hunt and picnic. Some hunters used hagbuts—long muskets—but hawking was the big thing. A bird is nearly starved until it becomes tame, then they are trained to bring down smaller birds. For those who can afford meat and fowl from the shops, like that group there, it serves no necessary purpose. But I suppose it's no different from our modern hunting enthusiasts going out and hunting cougars and bears with dogs or trying to fool a duck with a wooden decoy. In some ways it's cruel of man; in some ways it is as natural to us as breathing. Do you hunt, Wells?"

"Never hunted," I said. "Not law-abiding animals anyway. My dad and I fish. I have nothing against folks who—"

"You should try it," Benchley said. "Preferably when we get back to where we belong first, of course. There's nothing like the experience of it. I was always against the notion of killing animals then I went elk hunting with John Huston and Hemingway up in Idaho. That opened my eyes a bit, as they say." He turned his horse about and continued down the road, no anecdotes about the aforementioned creative legends provided.

I told Bonnie I had to heed the call to nature before again starting toward the town. When I returned from the bushes, I mounted the pony (whom I named Jennifer after my ex-wife) and caught up with the other travelers. When I got Jennifer abreast of my fellow riders, Bonnie and Benchley were engaged in a disturbing conversation on expansion of the mission.

"Suppose we could get at the STUMPs Warbeck already has," Bonnie was saying. "You say you'd give your other eye to get it. How hard would it be?"

"Very hard," Benchley said, before taking a short drink from one of the leather canteens. "The STUMPs that Warbeck and Essex have are on the top floor of that medieval keep in the center of Grantum Hall. Warbeck brought electrical generators back with him on one of his trips. I was dragged up to the 'electric room' a few times. Warbeck brought a television with him through time and I had to endure watching that fatuous documentary of his that makes the case for the Earl of Grantum using Shakespeare as a literary front. He made the real Grantum watch the travesty, too. God knows what will happen to the real Devant. Essex and Devant are friends, but my boy Trevor might not like having the man he impersonates staying alive. No, Bonnie, Truffie and I will retake that STUMP. We may have to let many more people know our secret, but we'll get it back."

The sky still threatened rain, but now the early morning sun came out from a break in the sky and made things warm for a bit. I had no watch, but the gathering heat told me it was mid-morning, maybe nine or nine-thirty. I noticed Benchley turning his head upward, straightening his turkey neck to draw in some of those warming rays. He also ran a hand over his thin and wispy white locks that made up what was left of his hair. The hair was silvery and seemed to glisten in the sun. The crown of his scalp was bare skin, the bright sun revealing a pinkish tone to the top of his head. He scratched vigorously at the beard.

"I hate these damn farthingales," Bonnie said, adjusting the front of her dress. She was riding next to myself and Jennifer and, because the pony was smaller, I had to look up at her. The sun brought out the lighter blonde coloring in her hair and seemed to add a glow to her complexion. She looked beautiful in the welcome light. But plainly she was awkward as well, having to ride and continuously tug at her skirt.

"Is there any chance we could get a proper ladies' sidesaddle when we reach Camden Town?" she asked.

Before Benchley could answer, we heard the sound of horns. The noises came from the town, which looked about a half-mile ahead. It was an eerie sound, like an ancient call to arms. Shortly after this, there came a clattering of hoofbeats that seemed to rattle the ground. From out of the village ahead came a column of mounted soldiers, two long lines of them, coming at us full bore down the road. The most conspicuous item in the advancing phalanx of men and beasts was a large white flag, adorned with a red cross, that fluttered above the pack.

Benchley reached into the saddlebags and gave the advancing forces a quick visual check with a pair of binoculars. Back went the binoculars after a few seconds.

"It's not Essex, thank God," Benchley said. "Judging by the insignias on the uniforms and the bunting, they are a unit of the Queen's Guard."

We took to a knoll adjoining the roadway and watched the cavalry unit pass. Thankfully, they galloped by us, two rows of cavalry riding in unison. I counted about forty men in all. They wore armour plating over their torsos and sported the morion-style visor helmets Bonnie and I had previously seen on the deserters who attacked us the afternoon before. Some of the men carried pikes, others had long muskets slung across their backs with leather slings. Those riding at the side of the columns blew crescent shaped horns as they passed us. The force was at full gallop; they were in a hurry to get somewhere.

A thin-lipped smile creased Benchley's face. "I think I know where those chaps are bound for."

"Grantum Hall?" Bonnie said, articulating what I hoped was their destination.

"Indeed," Benchley said. "The real William Devant, Grantum that is, is known as a friend of Essex. Essex threw that friendship away when he treacherously took him prisoner in his own manor, of course. But Elizabeth believes they are friends. He almost went in on the Rebellion of 1601 with him. I figured the Queen would send a force to Grantum Hall when they ran out of other places to look for him. Poor bastards don't know what they are really in for."

"What do we do now?" I asked.

"Stay the course," Benchley said. "We get to Grey's Inn, Francis Bacon, and relative sanctuary."

I was not satisfied. "How do we know Bacon hasn't thrown in with this Essex character?"

"Because he doesn't need Essex," Benchley replied. "I know Francis and he knows his future. He will have everything he desires, including the Lord Chancellorship, in the coming reign of King James. James will reach the throne of England in little more than three years. Francis and I have already discussed how to deal with Essex when the time comes. The time has to be a bit sooner, that's all."

Chapter Thirty-Eight

Back on the road, we passed through farmlands, barns and cottages on the fringe of the town ahead. Men, women and children were in the fields, cutting long rows of wheat with scythes and then pitching them up into haystacks. An old farm woman in a straw hat with a scarf over her mouth and nose (did she have hay fever?) stopped her work momentarily and waved to us. It seemed if people here did not intend to flat-out rob you, they were rather friendly.

The closer we got into town, the more pungent the odor of manure was in the air. I put this down to a herd of cattle that was at the small creek we had to cross (via a short wooden bridge) before reaching Camden Town. As we crossed the bridge I noticed the water was brackish and smelled badly. I supposed this meant the local water source must also double as the sewer.

"Must not be much rain this season," was Benchley's only comment on the stench.

I resolved to drink only the water we had brought with us, and lobby for it to be used sparingly.

We entered the limits of the town, the three of us riding abreast with Bonnie and her gelding in the middle. There appeared to be only the one main road, running North-South. I could see an assembly of people in a cluster a hundred yards or so into the town. I had no idea yet as to what they were doing.

The main building in town was the most stately singlespired church. It had a broad horseshoe-shaped archway in the front that stood at the top of a long ranking of stone steps. I had the feeling that it had stood there for at least a century before we showed up. I wondered if the Gothic edifice had withstood the centuries into our own time. Given the threat of fire—the church was surrounded by multi-gabled buildings, all made of wood—and the changing tastes in architecture, I thought not.

Other than the group off in the distance, there were only a few pedestrians about. Directly in front of us was a thin man in a dirty apron. He was oblivious to our approach, his concerns being with clutching and straining at the bridle of a broken-colored donkey packed with heavy bundles. He was apparently trying to yank the donkey along down a side alley, but the animal was stubborn against it.

"God's Lids, I curse you, foul beast," the jug-eared man said. He took a leather crop to the donkey's flanks. That elicited a bit of movement and a good deal of braying. Past him, on the opposite end of the dirt street, was a blacksmith working at pounding a bar of metal into the shape of a horseshoe. A cluster of finished shoes was on the ground next to his anvil. He stood just outside his barn-like shop. The glow from his forge could be seen behind him. At the edge of the shop was a space of open ground. Three boys in mud-splattered knickers were playfully scuffling with one another to ride a fat black and white pig. There was a smell from the field: piles of organic garbage were situated around a greater pile that looked like an enormous anthill. A man was busily piling more filth upon the mountain of waste from a fresh supply he had in his wheelbarrow.

We passed shops with large signs that hung out from iron poles over the cobblestone footpath that passed for the sidewalk. The signs—'Langrum Bakery,' 'Chipps and Son—Milliners'; 'Norton Brew House'; 'Camden Market', etc— came in all shapes and all swung slightly in the light wind blowing up into our faces from London. The buildings on both sides of the street were generally two-sided affairs, the second story hanging a bit outward from the first and buttressed by a crossbeam of thick timber, and usually adorned with some flowing wave-like designs. Where there was a third floor it was a steep gable, usually joined with one of two others, like a

Victorian house back in San Francisco. Multi-pane windows, most of them open to take in the mid-morning breeze, had either rectangular or triangular-shaped panes.

From out of one building came two women, both lean and scrawny, with matching small pug noses that indicated to me they were closely related. Using a long pole that was put under the handholds, they were carrying a large wicker basket that was almost overflowing with shirts and stockings. Unlike the ruff that Bonnie had on, these ladies wore flat peter-pan type collars. Their dresses were brown and rather plain compared to the gentlewomen we had seen so far. There was a grim, determined look to their faces, as if they were marching off for battle. One of the women gave us a look-over as we passed them. I could see the sight of Benchley in his finery elicited disapproval by the way the woman's eyes narrowed and her mouth curled down at one side.

"A couple Puritans," Benchley said to us after we passed the women. "As a general rule, those people work themselves to the bone to try and prosper so they can find out if they are some of the few to escape the curse of predestination."

"They're not exactly party hounds, then," Bonnie said quietly to her former boss.

"No, not exactly—not in any public way at least. If the Puritans ever have their way, and they will eventually, all the playhouses and other places of public amusement will be closed tight. If it happened now, Will Shakespeare and The Lord Chamberlain's Men and all the other theatrical companies would have to go underground to put on their works. Either that or flee to Scotland. I can't say much for King James' statecraft, but, God bless him, he loved masques and plays."

We came to the widest part of the street, and I got a close-up look at what the people I had seen earlier from a distance were doing. It was a large water conduit, set up on a small stone pedestal. The small crowd was spread out in a semi-circle. Each person had a large bucket or container the size of a fire hydrant with a stein on the top. One woman was pumping away at the device and getting scant reward for her efforts.

Beyond the water conduit was a wide, four-story building with a sign, 'Turtledove Inn', swinging in the light breeze from the metal rod that held the wooden sign to the crossbeam above the entrance. There was a crude rendering of a dove above the lettering on the sign. I looked in and saw an enclosed yard with horse stalls marked out. Just outside the inn yard, on a narrow patch of closely mowed grass, a dozen or so men in leather jerkins and floppy hats were engaged in something that closely resembled bowling. Some of the men were sitting on large barrels, others leaning against the wall of the inn. All were holding tankards and I had the feeling they were not drinking iced tea. At Benchley's bidding, we dismounted and I led my pony toward the entrance to the courtyard.

The man bowling rolled his ball toward the flat turf, the ball bringing up a tiny wake of settled water as it passed. The ball, smaller than what you'd see at a modern bowling alley, managed to knock nine of the pins, leaving one pin wobbling. Despite a moment of wobbling, and some swift body contortions of the bowler, the pin remained unbowed. The other men either laughed or groaned.

"I am ashamed to take your money, sir," one man sitting on a barrel said, "for this is not your usual court. But thou wilt surrender the wager, lest thou would take up a new game at double the wager."

"It is my turn, Gilmore," an older man (in a baggy doublet he must have bought off the rack or out of a pile) said. "Let our traveler from Rutland pay up, and let a new knight take up the challenge 'gainst you." The men seemed to stiffen up a bit as the three of us approached. Benchley, his long and lean frame less stooped than before, stood out in size and scale of dress from the men about him.

"I have need of a postal cart bound for London," he said to the men. "Is there one expected?"

One man told us that the next postal wagon bound for London should be arriving, "At the next hour, give or take."

"I would not stake much on that estimation, squire," the man who was called Gilmore told Benchley. "The roads through Hampstead are none too good. Many's the time I have glimpsed the noontime post arrive with the setting sun."

"Indeed, they are notorious for slowness where I hale from as well," Benchley said. He looked on up the road. He looked to Bonnie. "Daughter, we will just have to send a note to your brother after we reach our evening's lodgings."

"As you wish, father," Bonnie said in an accent similar to the one Benchley was employing. "I have no desire to speak to my brother, anyway. He is probably locked up in the Marshalsea Prison, awaiting a branding for stealing some lady's snuffbox. Trouble yourself not with him, Father. He has 'shamed you with his debauched wenching and love of strong drink."

A couple of the men laughed at Bonnie's remarks.

"'Tis true, good daughter," Benchley said, seeming to enjoy the challenge of extending the ruse in front of the natives. "Come, let us not tarry for his concern."

We walked on through town, giving the horses a bit of rest by leading them rather than walking. Benchley, his back worn quickly out again by what riding we had undertaken since the last stop, urged us to stay on foot. He and his mount walked a few paces ahead of us. There were no locals nearby, so the mute servant could talk.

"You do that accent well," I said to Bonnie. "It sounds like an English accent in a way, and then it's different. How'd you learn how to talk like that so quickly? I mean, Trubshawe could do it, but he's been on a few of these—trips. And the actors back at the Shakespeare Festival don't really speak dialogue the way these locals talk."

"I was Mr. Benchley's secretary, though," Bonnie said. "I never knew about his time travels, but I got a great deal of informal lecturing on what Elizabethan speech might, and he always said 'might', have sounded like. When we directed *King Lear,* he taught the actors variations on these speech patterns, but we went away from it because we tested it out a few scenes in front of a preview audience, and a lot of people at the discussion afterwards said they had trouble understanding us. Language experts and Elizabethan scholars know something about pronunciations. They varied by region of course but Mr. Benchley was always telling me that even the experts could be wrong. Now I know why he didn't think so much of the experts."

"Squire Benchley!" a voice cried out from a building, the only one made of brick in the town. Benchley turned about, befuddled, no doubt, by hearing his name called out. The owner of the husky voice cried out again.

"Squire Benchley! God be praised! It is Rainesford, sir,

your faithful servant." The voice was coming from a small window situated at street level. The window was not made from wood and glass; iron bars, set only a couple inches apart, had been substituted instead.

Benchley moved closer to the window. He strained his eyes for a moment, then his countenance changed from befuddlement to recognition.

"Rainesford?" Benchley said. "It is you, my good fellow?"

There was a place to tie up horses, a horizontal wooden pole held up by two posts, in front of what turned out to be the local jail. Benchley threw his tack over the pole and advanced toward the barred window. Bonnie and I did the same.

"Rainesford, what in heaven's name are you doing in there?" Benchley asked.

The man was alone in the cell, which couldn't have been more than eight feet long and perhaps six feet wide. He had deep, long creases of skin between his cheeks and nose. His hair and whiskers, however, were colored a rich brown and betrayed no greyness so he appeared prematurely aged. His face was pocked in patches and a shiny silver earring dangled from one ear. His deep-set large brown eyes gave him an intelligent look. He had a small flat nose and a lantern jaw, covered with the bristle of a few days' growth of beard. When he put his right hand up to grip one of the bars, I saw that the letter 'T' had been branded on his right hand, between thumb and forefinger; this was the same mark that we had seen on Gilbert the soldier and highwayman.

The prisoner was wearing only a collarless shirt, fit to be a rag. Flies buzzed about his person and the whole enclosure. The foul odors coming from the cell testified to a lack of plumbing for the ill-clad man. He held his arms across his chest and shivered despite the warmth in the air.

"Alas, good sir, I am a masterless man," the man said meekly. "Since I left the Chamberlain's Men, work as a player has been hard for me to come by. My wife died last year. The sweating sickness took her away in less than an afternoon."

"Oh, I'm deeply sorry, man," Benchley said. "Your Julia was barely a score and ten." Benchley turned to us. "Rainesford was my guide on my past trip to London. He is a former player with the Chamberlain's Men." He looked back at the prisoner. "What has become of your son?"

"He has been sent to the pillory," Rainesford cried out pitifully. "He is to be put on display to suit the humor of the Justice of the Peace. Tomorrow, he will be whipped and driven out of town. He has no place to go, Squire Benchley. After the Law has done with me, he will be an orphan."

Benchley looked down and shook his head.

"I could not get work after I was dismissed from the company," Rainesford said. "I took to my poor father's trade. A rat catcher I became, armed with dog and club. I had a good terrier but he took sick. His mouth foamed and I had to take my club to him lest he bite some honest man. By the time I found a substitute, the Bailiff of Camden Town had hired another man. My son was hungry, sir. I could no longer endure his plaintive cries for bread. I was a desperate man. When the parish took no pity on me, I crept into the bakery during the wee hours. The night watch seized me coming out the window. Have no pity on me, sir. You are a good man, a man of means. Do what you can for my son."

"Where is the boy?" Benchley asked.

Rainesford pointed in the direction we were headed. "The stocks are on the edge of town," the prisoner said. "The constable of this village, Catsby, is a vile man, but he treads lightly about his betters. You are a good gentleman, sir. Perhaps you could do something. For the lad's sake, good sir, not mine."

We took to our mounts and rode to the edge of town. There we caught up to what looked like the local law enforcement: a stocky man in a black porkpie hat, dressed in a bright red coat with some sort of patch on his sleeve. He was pushing ahead of him a small boy who was no better dressed than Rainesford. One of the constable's meaty hands carried a coiled whip, the other a truncheon with a knob on the end. Every time the boy would hesitate in taking a step, he would be shoved forward a couple paces with the whip hand or given a quick rap to the head with the club. They walked toward a wooden scaffold about six feet off the ground.

The 'peace officer' grabbed the boy under one of his armpits, dragging him up a side stairway. By the time the three of us had dismounted and reached the area in front of the platform, the boy's head and hands had been placed into the bottom half of the wooden pillory and the top half had been slammed down on his wrists and neck. (There was a second pillory on the platform, one that was designed for the full-sized lawbreaker.) Despite the wooden block the boy was standing on, he was still on tiptoe because of the precarious position the pillory put his head in. The constable latched down the top of the pillory and stepped away from the boy with the look of a craftsman having decided he had carried out a job well done.

"I beseech you, good constable," the imprisoned boy said. "As you are a good Christian, permit me a taste of water before you leave me here."

The whip was brought down hard on the lad's bare back, resulting in a high-pitched cry from the helpless child.

"Damn," Bonnie said, accent distinctly American.

The stocky man had a smooth reddish face, a dark beard carefully cut so the upper lip was free of hair and the two sides of beard did not quite meet at the end of his dimpled chin. His nose was bulbous and redder than the rest of his face. When he opened his mouth I saw he was shy three or four front teeth from the upper bridge of his mouth. His jowls were prominent enough to make me speculate he was storing walnuts between his inner cheeks and his jawbone. His thick, protruding lips curled back over what few teeth he possessed as he spoke.

"You are here for punishment, not refreshment, boy," he said gruffly. "You'll receive water when water is scheduled for you to receive, and not before. If it rains, you can catch water from God's mercy by cocking your head to the heavens. Another impudence will land the whip upon you again."

Benchley approached the edge of the platform and glared at the constable. "Tell me, brave officer," he said in a sharp and sarcastic tone, "what this lad has done that warrants these acts of savagery?"

"He is a beggar, sir, if it be any interest of yours," the man said back. "His father turned to thievery. This lad is a masterless boy. We have no need of apprentices in this town. He was sent to a workhouse but he has returned to our town to beg at the doors of honest folk."

"The keepers beat me most rigorous," the boy said. "I only asked for bread because the jailer would not feed my father. My father is sick. He needs—"

The constable raised the whip again.

"Stop!" Bonnie cried out.

"Cease!" Benchley's deep voice rang out, loudly and with emotion. The constable stopped.

"Mark me, you swag-bellied lout!" Benchley exclaimed. "I'll see you summoned to stand before the High Sheriff to answer for any more blows to that child."

The constable brought down the whip and looked Benchley over carefully for a few seconds, no doubt taking in the old man's cape, sword and other accessories of fine dress. He surely wondered how much trouble Benchley might make for him.

The lawman walked off the platform then headed up to Benchley. Benchley would not back up a single step. The two men went nose to nose.

"Who might you be, sir?" the lawman said in a tone of barely-contained rancor. "I have never seen you in this township. What business is it of yours—"

"I am Jack Benchley, Squire of Bristol. I am a man of business, and my business has made me well acquainted with the law. I can recognize the fair judgement of the Queen's Law from this miscarriage of authority."

"He has been judged by the Justice of the Peace," the officer said. "The verdict will stand. He is to be pilloried until tomorrow at dawn, given a measure of food and drink, then whipped to prevent him from becoming the cur that his father has become, and sent away."

"You would send a boy from his father?"

"There is no need for him to wait upon his father, Squire Benchley. The criminal Rainesford has stolen before. He now has a date with the hangman three days hence."

Benchley took a step backward and drew a deep breath. "You say he is a masterless boy, constable. Well, he is one no longer. I have need for a lad. I will take him into my service. Release him. I will take him away from the tender mercies of this township."

"Not until he has paid the penalty for being a vagabond," the constable said, "as is the will of the Justice of the Peace. He will be pilloried until nightfall, then given the lash. So says the law, sir."

"I will have words with the Justice, then," Benchley said.

"He is not in the town," the constable said smugly. "He is

on the circuit. He will not be this way again for a month."

A crowd of townspeople gathered around the altercation. A skeleton of a man, an old codger with a dirty matted beard, slits for eyes, and breath reeking of onions, came right up to my back. I looked back at him, then over at an equally old and equally slender woman with an overbite that gave her a horsey look. Both of her pale blue eyes were clouded by a coating of white—untreated cataracts, I thought. The old man had a hold of her trowel-like hand. She probably could not see two feet in front of her. The old man glanced at me for a second, then his attention went to the two antagonists.

"He is a *boy*!" Benchley hissed. "You abused him far beyond what a fair judgement of the Queen's Law would ever have intended."

The stocky officer glanced at the youngster on the platform, then made a grunting noise like a hog with a pan of slops under his snout. "A beggar remains a beggar whatever his stature. The rat catcher's boy remains a prisoner, sir. Now hear what I say to you: I will give you a pisseth of time to take yourself and your clan from this parish or the trio of you will be thrown in a cell for disturbing the peace. Away with you, Bristol man." He reached out, trying to take Benchley by the arm.

Benchley shook his arm off. "Unhand me, insolent beadle! I have a close friend at Grey's. He is a lawyer to the Queen herself and a member of Parliament for this county. Think upon that, then lay your muddy trotters on me again! It will be yourself in a pillory or the stocks before the affair is concluded."

Constable Catsby stepped backward, anger in his eyes, his face red enough for spontaneous combustion.

Benchley stepped back as well. For a few seconds they just stared at each other. The silence was broken by a bellowing from some spot past the cluster of interested locals.

"Free the boy!" the gruff male voice shouted out. I turned around to see Trevor Warbeck, mounted on a white horse with an elaborate intertwined golden tack. His voice was different, part of the acting job he had undertaken, no doubt. He wore a beard now, which allowed his face to match the picture I had seen in the IFH book depicting the rightful Earl of Grantum. Dromio was on a roan-colored mule on his boss' left. Another man I had seen before was mounted on a dappled grey horse—slightly larger than my pony—to his right.

That other man was none other than Jack Picasso. He looked as chummy with Warbeck as father and son.

"Ohmigod," Bonnie said, taking in the same sight I was. She shook her head. "I should have known. I should have known."

All three men were dressed to blend in well for the period, with long swords at their sides and fat petronel-style pistols in holsters on the hips opposite where the swords were. I could only imagine what nasty late Twentieth Century weapons they had concealed on their persons. They made no effort to utilize their weapons so I just kept my hand to the semi-automatic concealed in my breeches, undoing the safety to be ready.

"That's right, sirrah," Warbeck repeated. "I said free the boy. So says William Devant, Earl of Grantum and Baron of Thomasfield, a Knight of the Queen's Noble Order of the Garter and, may it please you to know, a cousin of Her Most Gracious Majesty."

The constable's jaw dropped. Then his whole body shivered. "Yo—Your Right Lordship, uh, Right Honorable and Noble sir. I am Constable Cats—"

"I care not for your titles, varlet, nor the locale of the dunghill from whence you were hatched into the world. Simply free the boy and try my patience no further."

The constable bowed. "I am at your bidding." He hurried up to the platform and the boy was released— pronto.

Chapter Thirty-Nine

Again, you had to hand it to Trevor Warbeck. He was decked out like a first-class swell, like an earl, or a fake earl with the rightful earl locked away in a cell of his own castle, should look. His jerkin and the sleeves of his doublet both appeared to be made from shimmering silk. The jerkin was a cobalt blue that gleamed in the small measure of sunlight, the sleeves of the doublet were white with black striping. He wore a thick, spotless ruff that made his head look like it was devoid of a neck and just planted there on top of his bulk. His fat legs were covered in some type of fancy embroidered breeches. His calves bulged from under sheer hose the same color as the jerkin. The capstone of the ensemble was a heavy-looking gold medallion that dangled from his neck underneath his trim, pointy beard.

Picasso and Dromio were on either side of Warbeck dressed as ordinary men of the time. They had feathers in their bonnets and a crest on one shoulder that were similar to that worn by the young man I had shot back at the falls. Jack Picasso had a smug expression—as always—as he looked down on the three of us. Part of his two-tone blonde hair was done up in a ponytail that extended down his back and was secured by two of three leather bands.

"Thou hast played a nice little game with us, haven't you, Jack?" Benchley said in a somber tone.

Picasso was equal to an approximation of the local accent. "You did play a nice little game with my father for a quarter century, Benchley," he said with bitter invective in his voice.

Some of the locals in the crowd surged forward to greet the man they thought was the Earl of Grantum. The ruse seemed to be working well for him.He was a hit with the crowd, especially when he started to throw down large brown coins at the children gathered about their parents. While all this John D. Rockefeller-type goodwill was being carried out, the constable went back and retrieved the ragged jerkin and doublet that the boy must have originally been wearing. Once that was done, the obsequious policeman pushed his way through the crowd and asked if there were, "any further tasks your most honorable and excellent lord wishes me to fulfill?"

"Indeed, hound," Warbeck said. "I expect you to muster up at least two dozen able-bodied men for me to inspect. The Queen is in need of men to travel to Tilbury and prepare for a potential landing of Spanish invaders. This burg will send forth its share of good men and wastrels to provide a wall of flame and lead against the heretics." He waved a limp hand at the constable. "Now, make my orders thus: do your duty, sirrah!"

After a few minutes of accepting compliments from the crowd, Warbeck said, "I bade you subjects to please go about your business and let me take my leave for some refreshment." The locals finally left the scene, leaving just the six of us along with the freed boy.

"Your name, child?" Warbeck asked.

The boy, named Christopher, blessed Warbeck a good seven or eight times, then begged the 'Earl' to do something to help his father. Warbeck promised he would "take an accounting" of the prisoner, Samuel Rainesford, and then the boy ran off to tell his father of the hopeful news. That left just the six of us, all six being aliens who had no business there, each playing a part. Warbeck and Benchley eyed each other like two old roosters in the same henhouse.

"Congratulations on attaining your freedom," Warbeck said to Benchley, looking down on him from his horse. "In the confusion of last evening, what with all the details to tie up, I didn't have the proper chance to see you off with your friends."

"No need to be apologetic, Most Noble Lord," Benchley said in a tone that was anything but reverential. "I know killing defenseless kitchen maids, houseboys, the odd gamekeeper or two is all very taxing for you, I'm sure. Have you had a chance to kill any of Grantum's relatives, the better to secure your imposture?"

Warbeck sighed. "Alas, the old Earl's last wife, his second, died in childbirth two years ago. The child was stillborn. His only offspring, young William, is a Captain of Horse and still in Ireland. Essex left him at Dublin Castle. The Earl was a lonely old man. He has a few friends but recent reports have him unable to receive visitors. He only has time for his peers, the Earl of Essex and young Southampton."

"How good for you," Benchley said. "I have word you and your tall lackey there were responsible for wounding my granddaughter." The old man took two steps backward, and drew his sword. "Be so good as to climb down from your mount. I have some business to dispense with you."

I kept myself ready for the intervention of gunplay. I planned to take Warbeck out first, then drill Picasso or Dromio, depending on who moved faster. Both men looked at me, surely thinking along the same lines.

Warbeck laughed, his belly shaking like a tub of gelatin and his shoulders and head arching backward. "Good God, man, you have gone native," he said after a final deep, rumbling chortle. "A sword fight in the street at high noon would hardly set a good example to the commoners and serve neither of our causes."

"I taught you how to fence properly for the Essex film," Benchley said. "You attacked my family and put out one of my eyes. I would say that calls for a new lesson in the foils."

Warbeck snorted. "I have matters to discuss. I will do it in a civilized manner or not at all. You need to hear what I have to say, old boy. You really do."

Benchley brought the rapier up, his arm extended, his legs positioned for a forward advance. With a surprising amount of dexterity he whipped the foil about, then returned it to his scabbard.

"All right, Warbeck," Benchley said. "Dismount yourself from that horse. Tell me what you need to tell. Keep your lackeys mounted and keep their arms in front of them. I'll have Bonnie and Wells do the same."

"Very well, then," Warbeck said. "but I must be brief. I will have to inspect the local rabble for pikemen and harquebusiers. There won't be a decent man among them, just the typical scum a village scrapes up to fill the quota. The ugly rabble, the 'food for powder' as Falstaff says in *Henry the Fourth, Part Two.*"

"Those lines are in the first Bolingbroke play," Benchley said. "Act Four, Scene Two. Falstaff speaks to Prince Hal, the man who will turn against Sir John Falstaff without pity at a later stage." Benchley looked disapprovingly at Picasso. Benchley licked his thin lips, then cleared his throat before speaking.

"'Tut, tut,' Falstaff says to Hal, 'good enough to toss; food for powder, food for powder. They'll fill a pit as well as better. Tush, man, mortal men, mortal men.' That's from the first play, Warbeck, not the sequel."

"Bother your pedantry," Warbeck said, waving his hand at Benchley as if he could erase him. He next turned to his henchman. "Dromio, get over here and help me off this beast."

The tall pigeon-toed man dismounted, then came over to help his boss get to the ground. It was a struggle, as getting Warbeck out of the limousine had been days before. Finally, the boss was planted on the ground.

"Keep your hands where I can see them," I said. There was no one around us so there was no need for my muteness.

"The same for you," Dromio said back in his thick drone of a voice.

"Come now," Warbeck said, "this is folly. We should do this as becomes gentlemen of the realm. Your horses look tired and ours have ridden all the way from Grantum Hall this morning. I say we walk the beasts over to the Turtledove Inn, and have a bit of drink or a mid-morning repast. It's still early for what the locals would call their supper but food should be available."

"We've eaten," Bonnie said sharply.

"A bit of sheerisack or ale will not poison you, milady. Come, Benchley, you've lost an eye but gained your freedom. I have the STUMP machines, two of them at least. Our enmity should take respite. To 'The Turtledove' then. What do you say?"

"I don't like it," Benchley said. "I have places to go."

"Running off to Francis Bacon's house near Grey's Inn, are you?" Warbeck said. "If you think that queer little man will help you, good luck. He has been your friend in your past voyages to this time, that is true. But keep in mind that Essex despises him, says he will kill Bacon on sight the next time they meet. The Earl has made it known to the latter man through an emissary."

"Southampton was the messenger," Benchley said.

Warbeck nodded. "Because you told Bacon of Essex's future, he has slowly and cunningly turned away from the Lord Deputy's camp. Now Essex knows that Bacon will turn against him down the road, after the Queen humbles Essex and bankrupts him by withdrawing his monopoly on taxes for sweet wines."

"Bacon is a brilliant man," Benchley said.

"Without doubt," Warbeck quickly added. "But now Essex knows who will remain loyal to him during his trials and loss of power and finance. I suspect, Benchley, your plan is to use the little philosopher to tattle on our plans before the Queen. It will not work. The Queen is not and never will be infatuated with Bacon. She withholds office from him no matter how much he begs and cajoles her and her ministers for a real place at her table. No matter how cunning Bacon tries to be, she will remain in her heart infatuated with Essex. She certainly will not believe in the notion of men from the future coming to depose her. The more truthful Bacon is about the real situation, the more likely it is that Secretary Cecil will think him mad. And he fears Essex. I would be surprised if you will get him to leave his chambers at Grey's. Bacon fears Essex and with good reason. The Man of Books is no match for the Man of Sword. If your trump card is Bacon, it is futile for you to waste your energy going to Grey's."

Picasso spoke: "Basically, Jack Benchley, you're screwed. You're screwed almost as badly as the way you screwed my father."

Benchley, his expression a study in pain, stared up at the younger man. "What lies has Warbeck told you, Jack? Your father was blacklisted by Joe McCarthy in the 1950's. I did everything I could to help your father. I got him jobs when he came back from Europe. Your father was a broken man and I helped him. I tried to reunite him with your mother. I've done my best to help you, more from his memory than any gratitude you've ever shown me. Whatever lies this fat bastard has told you, they are just that—lies. Who helped your father, son? Who got you into the Director's Guild, introduced you to influential men at the studios. Who tutored you in—"

"Oh, shut up!" Picasso said. Realizing he might be overheard by the villagers, his voice toned down. "You find out soon enough. You can't go home because of the murder rap over your head and you can't last long here because there's changes coming to this little island. You're right where you should be, old man."

Benchley looked down at the road and shook his head

"Dromio," Warbeck said, turning about to face the giant. "Go out and scout up Mr. Bates. I want his whereabouts known to me."

Dromio grunted, remounted, then put his horse into motion. I moved my hand away from my concealed Baretta. Warbeck spoke to us as the tall, swarthy-complexioned man rode off.

"Dromio's real first name is a Lithuanian one I find offensive and unpronounceable," he said. "I renamed him as a condition of his employment. He was sent to the United States by a certain private syndicate in Moscow that makes sure that successful Russian-American businessmen do not forget their fellow countrymen at home."

"You mean he extorts hard currency from them," Benchley said ruefully, "otherwise the family members back in Russia are killed by some branch of their local Mafia."

Warbeck snorted. "We can't all be artists, old man. I lured him away from his former employers with a better employment package. He is good at his work."

While the two men spoke, I kept my eyes on Jack Picasso. He looked me over as well. I was sure from the telltale bulge that he had a pistol under his jerkin as well. A fast move by either one of us would turn this quaint, smelly English village into a temperate-zone Tombstone, Arizona.

"There, Benchley," Warbeck said. "Now you have only Jack and I. Your forces outnumber mine. Is sending Dromio away not proof that my plans no longer include violence? I have some information to reveal to you and, if you are receptive, perhaps a proposition. Let us go to the tavern of 'The Turtledove'. I have need of breakfast."

After entering the inn yard, strewn with straw and

smelling very much like a place to keep horses, several boys in blue livery-style uniforms came up and relieved us of our mounts. Benchley paid to have the two horses and my pony unsaddled, watered and fed. I held onto the bags with the supplies of modern food and ammo, taking those with me into the tavern.

There was a layer of cobblestones in the rectangular-shaped inn yard. Between the stones were deposits of mud and straw. Clusters of large barrels were set about, some still on carts. Human voices echoed about along with the neighs and whinnies of the equestrian livestock in the stalls. I could see from the rear entrance that there were two long rows of stalls, one row facing the other. The stalls were about two-thirds full. It was a parking lot for the pre-Industrial Age.

The entrances and exits to the inn were made up of thick rough-hewn wood in a simple post and lintel style. Above the yard were two flights of balconies that could be reached by staircases at either end of the yard. I could see the narrow-framed wooden doors on the second floor, separated by only a few feet, as you would expect in a motel. The difference was that the whole look of the place was rickety and wooden, except for the foundation of square stone blocks that made up the first floor. It was a world without building codes, I thought, or at least no safety inspectors.

I looked into a doorway and saw two women, each hurriedly kneading a separate large mass of white dough on a table. Both women had aprons on over loose-fitting dresses, tied about the waist by strands of unadorned rope. I could see waves of heavy perspiration stains that had soaked into both of the ladies' blouses. Flour dust filled the air inside the room, as did the intense heat from a large oven where loaves of baking bread were being taken in and out, apparently to be checked by a small boy wearing a brimless, floppy hat like mine and sporting an apron. The smell of bread was nice the first pleasant smell I had experienced since we had ridden over the bridge.

The innkeeper, a florid-faced bald man named Oswald Morley, acted flat-out honored about having "The Most Esteemed Earl of Grantum" on his premises.

"Will you be needing rooms, Noble Lord?" Innkeeper Morley asked as he wiped his hands off on his flour-smeared cloth apron.

"I generally sleep at night, and in my own household," Warbeck replied in the accent he used to pass as Grantum. "I require a bit of fortification 'tweenst breakfast and supper. Conduct us to the tavern. We require a measure of privacy and attentive tapsters to see to our thirsts."

The tavern itself was well-lit, thanks to a large window with diamond-shaped panes on one end of the establishment and, at the other end, an ornate brick fireplace decorated with stone pilasters on each end and a stone deer head in profile over the mantle. The fireplace itself was big enough to drive a small car into. There were thick logs piled up in the fire grate and they were smoldering away. It was hot and stuffy in the place, additional heat being provided by a large number of patrons, mostly vociferous bearded men being served by young men and girls who scooted about from table to table with trays of food—heavy on chicken and pork judging by the warm scents in the room—and pitchers of brewed drink. The customers were seated about around several large oaken refectory-style tables situated in the middle of the room. The tables all had bulky legs and sported fancy molding at the corners. Greyish-red tablecloths covered the tables. The chairs were high-backed and looked sturdy.

On one side of the fireplace there were a trio of young musicians, all men and all seated in a half-circle. One played what looked like a mandolin, the second a bass fiddle, and the third young man a long-stemmed flute with a sweet sound that Bonnie told me was actually a precursor of the modern flute known as a recorder. The musicians wore identical hats, doublets and short breeches. The bass player wore a long peacock feather in his high-crowned hat. The harmonies emitted from the trio were soft, slow-tempo, lilting and decidedly 'unplugged.'

There were tapestries that hung about the walls, all with a threadbare look about the sides and bottoms, depicting hunting scenes. There were also deer heads, some with amazingly large antlers, mounted between the faded tapestries. Save for the differences in clothing and the lack of electric appliances, the atmosphere was not unlike O'Leary's Sports Pub back home. I checked back and forth between Warbeck and Picasso. The director was a step behind us. Warbeck and

Morley the Innkeeper, the latter walking sideways, were in front of the three of us. The innkeeper was directing the 'Earl' toward, "a table affording the best in comfort and privacy for those men of stature who frequent our hostelry." The table was situated in an alcove.

As Warbeck walked between the tables, several of the seated men stood up and doffed their hats to him, addressing him as 'Right Honorable,' 'Most Worthy Grantum,' etc. He acknowledged the gentlemen with a brief nod of his head and nothing more. Nothing more seemed to be expected. The locals were buying the ruse hook, line and sinker.

About the only patrons in the place who weren't taking notice of Warbeck were six men standing around what looked like a shuffleboard game elevated on a table. The men had their drinking mugs positioned on the raised edges of the game board. The game area itself was about twelve feet long—with long boards joined together across the top—and maybe a yard wide. One man was sprinkling sand on the wooden table-top with a small glass cup. Another fellow, smoking a clay pipe, watched the sprinkling process, then spread the sand about the table with his gloved hand. The pipe smoker had what looked like an artificial nose. It had a metallic bronze color. At one end of the table a short man with a pointy chin and stringy red hair falling over his eyes was pushing a large coin back and forth on the table. As we passed, he slid the coin down the table with a good amount of force. The coin stopped on a wedge-shaped space that was part of a triangle painted at the opposite end of the table.

"Shovelboard," Benchley said to Bonnie when he noticed her interest in the contest. "A quick and efficient way to kill time and lose hard earned money to friends and acquaintances."

"What happened to that one man's nose," Bonnie whispered.

"Probably lost it dueling," Benchley said. "Or maybe he had a bad case of smallpox and decided to have it cut off. There's a lot of poxes going 'round these days, young lady, along with a bit of plague now and again."

The five of us were seated at a rectangular table in an alcove just off to the side of the fireplace. Sitting down for me was not a treat. My butt was sore from the pony ride, and the knee I had hurt falling off the rock yesterday bent only with a sharp pain.

Long-stem pewter drinking glasses had already been set out on the table. Two young men in uniforms arrived and asked if we wanted 'shecrisack and sugar' or 'small beer'. It sounded like strong stuff for what amounted to breakfast but orange juice probably wasn't on the menu. Picasso and Warbeck, on one side of the table, opted for the sack and had their glasses filled, along with a small bowl filled with plain paper sugar packets. Benchley asked for a small beer. Bonnie—told by Benchley that it was lightweight stuff and, since it was brewed, safe to drink—ordered one. I declined, alcohol in any form being taboo for me.

"I would like a serving of baked apples," Warbeck said to a woman who dropped by to lay napkins on the table, "and a slice of sweetmeat pie. My good fellow beside me will have the same." He looked to Benchley. "Do you wish something beyond drink, Squire Benchley?"

"No," Benchley said, firmly. Bonnie also declined, as did I.

The young lady, probably a relation of the Innkeeper judging by her face, did a low curtsy to the 'nobleman'. "As you wish, Honorable Lord," she said. "Your meals come anon. Do not trouble yourself or your party with the reckoning. My father has told me to inform thee that your mere presence is payment for anything you desire."

After she left, closing a curtain that separated us from the main dining area, Benchley spoke up.

"I saw a detachment of mounted soldiers heading northward toward Hampstead. It could be the Queen has discovered where her Lord Deputy is hiding."

Warbeck chuckled. "The Queen has an excellent intelligence service, thanks to the groundwork laid by the late Sir Francis Walsingham. Essex has his own friends in court and independent sources for intelligence. Yes, the detachment from the Tower is bound for Grantum Hall. They will be cordially received at my manor. They will not, however, find Essex or Southampton. Those two worthies, with some trusted followers, have been taken to the countryside. They will camp out like Robin Hood and his Merry Men until the time is right to strike. They also have all the AK-47s and other modern weapons with them, so even if the Queen's detachment wants to search the manor, they will find nothing. And I doubt if the Captain of the Guard has the *carte blanche* to order a search."

"What about all the electronic equipment you have up in the keep?" Benchley asked.

"It is all secreted away in one or two priest-holes—hiding places I mean—left over from the time that the original Earl of Grantum was beheaded for clandestinely supporting the Church in Rome over Good King Harry." Warbeck smiled then lowered his voice. "I feel sorry for King Harry's daughter. Her reign is coming to an early end. She barely has a few days."

"That's it then," Benchley said. "Have Essex hide out, then attack London in full force. Is that the plan, Warbeck?"

Warbeck snorted, then sat back and closed his eyelids over his cold slate-grey eyes. He looked blissful and quite at home in his doublet and ruff.

"Essex will make his presence known soon enough, Benchley," Warbeck said, eyes still shut. He took a sip from his mug, then pivoted his large head and looked at me. "Ah, Wells, we meet yet again. I would have thought you would have abandoned the Benchley Crusade by now."

"I just have a weakness for your type, Mr. Warbeck," I said. "Ever since I was a kid, I've been drawn to fat, power-hungry sociopaths. Mr. Picasso here must have the same disease."

Jack Picasso gave me a nasty look, which I returned with a fixed gaze.

"It was all a put-on, wasn't it, Picasso?" I said. "You knew we were going to be attacked back at the hotel in Kensington. You made a big deal out of running out to the terrace, then you hit the deck just before the shooting started. Then you pretended to be scared shitless by seeing the time machine working. It was all acting, wasn't it?"

Picasso maintained a stoic countenance.

"You knew Ann could have been killed, Jack," Bonnie said. "We all could have been killed. Do you realize that Avalon was seriously wounded, that Ann, who you supposedly cared so deeply about, is at the end of her rope with worry? What's all this for, Jack?"

"Nobody was supposed to get shot," Picasso said. He directed a cold sneer at Warbeck. "That was Strunk's arrangement with fat boy here. I have no vendetta against Ann. Yeah, I led her on. I led all of you on and you all fell for it. I'm not doing any films with Ann. That relationship is over. I can't have a relationship with her, not after finding out what I know now about her old man."

Warbeck snorted. "Mr. Picasso, it was necessary to make it appear to be a terrorist attack. Someone had to be hurt. Dromio knows his business. Avalon Benchley simply took a wound. It wasn't life threatening. You asked that Ann Benchley not be hurt. I've kept that bargain. Were it not for your pleading, Ann Benchley would have met her death—as she deserves. Ann Benchley is a killer. She murdered Talbot Strunk fifteen years ago."

"Bullshit," Benchley said.

Warbeck ignored the remark and turned to Picasso. "You are a most ungrateful young man, Jack. You have a lock-solid three picture deal with Strunk Films for three theatrical features. All you had to do was practice a bit of deception and perhaps deal with one troublesome fellow, a small-time mediocrity we might have had eliminated for a few thousand dollars. You are most ungrateful, Jack. Sherwood has tried to clear legal rights to the *Marnie* project you wanted from Universal. If Strunk enterprises offers the right amount of money, your little homage to Hitchcock is going to be a reality. You've been compensated. Your soft spot for Ann Benchley has been respected...." Warbeck droned on some more, but I paid little attention to what he said. I was now stuck on his reference to "one troublesome fellow."

Could it have been Ray Harrison? Jack Picasso had been manhandled by Ray back at the Rysking Theater. Picasso could not have shot Ray himself. He was with Ann Benchley all night. But he could have ordered someone else to.

"You won't come near my daughter," Benchley said forcefully to Picasso. "When I get back to..."

Warbeck interrupted. "That's just it, old man. Jack doesn't have, or want, to go near your daughter ever again. He simply means no harm to her. Of course, there is one small matter about your daughter you should know about. But I'll save that for now."

"Who was your inside man at the Shakespeare Festival?" Benchley said demandingly. "Was it Dave McCreedy? I'm right aren't I?"

Warbeck chuckled. "As for David McCreedy, he stuck his nose into places it should never have been. The fellow actually got into the IFH office, pretended to be a researcher interested in doing an article on my organization. He was probably in charge of the pathetic attempt to electronically bug my office. He made a traitor of Mr. Park, who was betraying me. Mr. Park has paid for that miscalculation."

"So Dave McCreedy wasn't working for you?" Benchley asked.

Warbeck chuckled. "Was that what you feared, old man? You were worried about the wrong man. It was Mr. Bates who found the material in your safe. He had access to the whole ranch house, thanks to his employ as your daughter's bodyguard. I had Bates as my fifth columnist inside the Benchley camp watching Ann Benchley, so what did I need McCreedy for?"

"Why would you betray me, Jack?" Benchley asked the younger man.

Picasso said nothing, did not even look at the old man.

Warbeck provided an answer. "Because I have shown him some documents—documents that reveal the real Jack Benchley."

"You murdered all those people at Grantum Hall," Benchley said to Warbeck in an excited voice. "You probably killed the real Earl of Grantum by now."

Warbeck put an index finger to his lips. He voice changed to a low growl. "Come, Benchley, remember I am an earl in this kingdom and you are merely a wandering squire." He leaned back into the chair, his head supported by a cushion. "True, many died at Grantum Hall. But their loss is minimal because, like most people, they contributed little to the path of progress. I certainly dispute your charge that I have killed Grantum, a Peer of the Realm. I'm not a barbarian, Benchley. William Devant will be freed from his cell once things have stabilized in this kingdom. And, since we are on the subject of laying waste to human resources, your friends here set up a landmine that dispatched three of Essex's soldiers and grievously wounded two others. I had to send one of my aides back to modern London for one of Mr. Strunk's personal physicians and a large supply of morphine. I'd say nobody should be taking the moral high ground at this table."

"You started this," Benchley growled to Warbeck. "You were the first to bring heavy weapons from our time to this." He paused, then spoke again: "You mean to tell me that Dave McCreedy was loyal to me?"

"Yes, yes, yes," Warbeck said testily. "For what it was worth, this McCreedy fellow was puppy-dog loyal to you. Bates was the man you should have watched. What Ralph Bates found one day, using the keys you carelessly left on top of a file cabinet, was the documentation of your time travels: your journals, your still photographs, your videotapes. You kept Morton Ryskind's wonderful invention all to yourself, Benchley." Warbeck's voice next changed to that of a scolding kindergarten teacher.

"How selfish, old man. How mean-spirited. How could you hide such a marvelous technology from the Outer World? What if the man who found the Dead Sea Scrolls had just left them undisturbed? What if Jean-Francois Champollion had kept his understanding of the Egyptian hieroglyphs on the Rosetta Stone to himself? How could you, Benchley?"

"Because of men like you," Benchley said, staring straight at Warbeck. "But how did Ralph Bates know what to look for?"

"A certain, shall we say, close friend told him about the time machines."

"Who?" Benchley demanded.

Warbeck grinned. "I'm sure you'll find out...one day." Warbeck rubbed the whiskers on his chin with two fingers. "I feel sorry for you, Benchley. I really do. What is to become of you? You did not actually kill Carolyn Mason, of course, but who will believe you? She was found strangled in the trunk of your car. She was last seen in your company at the Forest of Arden. And you simply disappeared from public view for weeks." Warbeck smiled. "You will someday have to return to the modern world. Your health will demand it. You will be found and arrested. The press will destroy your family. The world will readily believe an old man killing his young girlfriend. Most will put it down to your impotence, a case of misdirected rage at the loss of your virility. Perhaps Ms. Mason laughed at you once too often, or felt sorry for you. Poor old Benchley. You wanted a blood-gorged phallic erection, not the pity of a woman young enough to be your daughter. Your precious Shakespeare Festival will be torn away from you. Soon they will have to call it the William Devant Festival, anyway. This is the end of you, old boy. The bitter and ever so just end!"

Jack Benchley clasped one hand over another at the table to try and still his trembling hands. He looked beaten. He did not even bring up the matter of a better suspect in the Mason murder. That was left to Bonnie.

"The San Francisco Police have a man in custody for the murder of Carolyn Mason. A man named Charles Lloyd Aarons. He was found with a specially-made diamond pendant Mr. Benchley gave to Carolyn in his apartment. There are also clothing fiber tests that I'm sure will show he had contact with Carolyn Mason. Plus there is a DNA test being done on blood samples from under her fingernails."

Warbeck looked confused for a moment. He shot a glance at Jack Picasso. The younger man had a poker face.

"They have another suspect, eh?" Warbeck said, rubbing his bearded chin. "Well, the police may have a suspect, but—" For once, Warbeck was at a loss for words.

"You had Aarons kill Carolyn Mason," I said.

Warbeck shook his head. "This is fantasy. I never heard of Charles Lindsey Aarons."

"What did you say, Mr. Warbeck?" Bonnie asked.

Warbeck huffed. "Are you deaf, woman? I said I have never heard of Charles Lindsey Aarons."

Suddenly, Warbeck's lips pursed. He now realized what Bonnie had done.

"Oh," Bonnie said, "I'm terribly sorry, Mr. Warbeck. I meant to say Charles *Lindsey* Aarons instead of Charles *Lloyd* Aarons. Thank you for correcting me." Our meal was served.

Chapter Forty

For a couple minutes, Bonnie and I, along with Jack Benchley, sat at the table and watched Warbeck and Picasso chow down. Benchley's countenance, at first registering pale shock, slowly changed to reddening anger. I waited for Benchley to make a move. It was his show. For now, he just sat there simmering and I kept my main focus on the casual eaters, Picasso and Warbeck. Between bites, they looked at us. The atmosphere, thick with the musky odors of bodies and the smoke and heat from the fireplace, did nothing to ease the tension. Only the music was a mild sedative, for my nerves at least. It was like an old movie, some cozy so-civilized English drawing room mystery; all the suspects, total strangers to one another, sitting on edge. Soon another body would be found, the upstairs maid stuffed into the dumbwaiter.

"Why did you turn against me, Jack?" Benchley asked Picasso.

"Tell him, lad," Warbeck said, sticking a fork into his pie, the portion covered in spices and heat steaming upwards from his plate. His inadvertent admission of having knowledge of Charles Aarons had taken some of the haughtiness out of his general tone.

Picasso's reply to Benchley's question was to remove his hat. Out came two pieces of letter-sized photo-copied paper. He handed the sheet to Benchley.

"I don't have my glasses," Benchley said. "And I have only one eye at that. Can't you just tell me what it says?"

Picasso leaned across the table and snatched the paper out of the old man's hand. He cleared his throat, then, in harsh tones, began to speak.

"This is a document from a secret hearing that took place in April, 1953, at the Cannon House Office Building in Washington, D.C. The hearing was part of an investigation by the Senate Internal Security Committee. It was conducted by three members of the United States Senate Permanent Committee for Internal Security, one Senator and two staffers. You remember that committee don't you, Mr. Benchley?"

"Joe McCarthy's Committee," Benchley said. His face seemed pale again, his tone betrayed unease. "What has that to do with me? I never—"

Picasso interrupted him and continued to read from the paper: "'Senator McCarthy was present at the meeting. Also present were Roy Cohn, Chief Investigator for the Committee and Robert F. Kennedy, Associate Investigator. And there was a witness, only one witness at that hearing: a man named John W. Benchley, accompanied by counsel Thomas A. Scherzinger, a private attorney from Los Angeles, California.'" Picasso looked up from the paper right at Benchley. A smile lit the corners of his mouth. His dark eyebrows flashed upward, then he continued reading.

"'The witness testified under oath that he was born on August 29, 1925 in Rogue Falls, Oregon. He gave his occupation as a writer and director, employed at Warner Brothers Studios in Burbank, California.'"

"Jack," Benchley said, "you realize that this is a forgery."

Picasso ignored him. He read on.

"I will speak verbatim from the transcript itself. Mr. Cohn asks Mr. Benchley the following question: 'Do you know or have you ever been a member of the Communist Party?' Mr. Benchley replies that he is not now nor has he ever been a member. Senator McCarthy: 'Why, therefore, were you, along with your father, a member of the pro-Soviet, pro-Stalinist Hollywood clique known as 'Artists Against Fascism', of which your father, Walter Benchley, was a founding member and served on the Executive Committee?'"

"'Mr. Benchley: Senator, the organization known as 'Artists Against Fascism' had a variety of members, many with differing political persuasions.'"

"'Senator McCarthy: You are aware that you and your father were members of the AAF from January, 1939, until July of 1941, when the committee merged into another pro-Soviet group, The Aid to Russia Committee, from 1941 to 1945?'"

Picasso looked up at Benchley again. "I'll skip some of your testimony, the parts where you squirm around and try not to admit knowing who was behind that organization. Then, after several questions from Mr. Cohn and Senator McCarthy, that you, in Cohn's words, 'were a stalwart member of pro-Red groups up until your induction into the United States Army Air Corps in March, 1944.'" Picasso took a sip of his drink, then eyed Benchley with a haughty stare.

"Rivo!"

There came a husky chorus from the dining hall area. I peeked through the curtain. Men were standing up at both sides of one long table across from us, and turning their mugs bottoms up. The men at the Shovelboard table did the same trick with their beverages. One of the bearded gentlemen at the board cried out, "Bring us another round, tapster!"

"Anon, sir, anon," a young male servant cried out, obviously harried by all the other diners. From the other end of the room, I saw Dromio enter. I opened the curtain wider. He looked about until he saw me, then headed for our table in his pigeon-toed style. And then, right behind him, came a muscle-bound man a few inches shorter than him, a man who looked like the horse backed fellow I had shot at back at the falls. As he got closer, I felt I had seen him earlier as well. Something told me that, despite his Renaissance clothing, he was a time traveler as well.

If I had to pick one thing that gave him away, I think it would be the sunglasses he was wearing. "Big Boy's headed this way, and he's got company," I said to Bonnie, then threw open the curtain. I stood up, positioning myself in the aisle, ready to see what Dromio and this fellow—who I now recognized as Ann Benchley's ex-bodyguard and buff Bruce Springsteen clone, Ralph Bates—were bringing to the table.

Oddly, when the company arrived, the first person Bates acknowledged was Bonnie.

"Hello, babe," the stranger said in a raspy voice. Bonnie didn't return his salutation and the smirk on his mug told me it was the effect he wanted anyway. He smirked like a shallow punk. This second betrayer of the Benchleys wasn't as formidable as Dromio, but tall and rugged enough to present a problem. He had forsaken the two-day's stubble around the chin he had back at the Northwest Shakespeare Festival for a fuller growth of facial hair, trimmed sharply to accentuate his heavy jawline.

Dromio looked at me with a glum expression, then went over to Warbeck and leaned down to whisper something in his boss' ear.

"You have the material then," Warbeck said.

"Yes," Dromio said.

"Bates," Warbeck said. "Come here."

Bates obliged.

Warbeck wiggled a chubby index finger, the one with the ring on it, in Bates' face. "Lean over, please."

Bates complied. Warbeck reached out, snatched the expensive-looking sunglasses off his face and then broke the pair in half at the nose bridge.

"We'll have no more of that," Warbeck said. "You attract unnecessary attention with such adornments, Bates."

Bates recoiled from the reprimand by folding his arms and grunting.

"I have a query for you, Mr. Bates," Warbeck said, wiping his hands on a cloth napkin. "It concerns a man named Charles Lindsey Aarons. You told me the man was reliable, Bates. It appears I've been kept in the dark about your friend's progress. Is it true he is in the custody of the San Francisco Police?"

Bates appeared uncomfortable at the mention of Aarons. He sighed deeply. "I was going to tell you, Mr, Warbeck. I was going to tell you."

"Were you also going to tell me that Aarons was unreliable? That after he dispatched Carolyn Mason, he stole an item of jewelry off her body? A very identifiable item!"

A local came up to the table. He was a slender, silver-haired old man who smelled of alcohol and dried sweat, even from a few feet away. He had his hat in his hand, twisting the brim. His shoes had strips of leather dangling from the sides, and his toes, with fraying hose, were exposed. He waited until Warbeck asked him what he wanted.

"If you would, Noble Lord," the old man said. "A word, if you please. It concerns my grandson. He is being mustered for the defense of the coast. I have already lost a son in the Netherlands fighting the Spanish. This boy is my only living male relation. Could you not spare..."

"Away, whoreson cur!" Warbeck shouted out in his affected accent. He bellowed loud enough to stop the general commotion in the tavern.

"I have given my only son to the Queen's service against the Irish savages! I have risked him who is the heir of my lands and title. I have only one word for you supplicate. 'Denied', yeoman, that is the word. Have your grandson in front of the church with the rest of those on the rolls or I will have the High Sheriff seek him out. Away, dog."

The old man trembled, his mouth stammering but no words coming out. Finally, some did. "Call me a dog, Noble Lord? I was in your father's service. As a youth, you called me friend. I taught you to ride your first horse when the master was away fighting the Scots. I accompanied you on your first hawking in nearby wood. Do you not remember this face? I am John Mulligan. Your father, a good and just nobleman, gave me a modest stipend when I was too old—"

"Try me no more, old man!" Warbeck exclaimed, saliva spurting from his mouth. "Your smell and your dress bespeak of a palliard, simpering for a handout. I know you not. Begone!"

The old man backed away. For a moment the music stopped, and everyone in the room took in the elderly gentleman's humiliation. It was certain no one else would bother the 'Earl' for the rest of his meal. After a few seconds, the music, talking, drinking, dice playing and coin-shoveling went on.

"Aarons doesn't know you, Mr. Warbeck," Bates said when things got back to normal. "He just knows me. You're safe, Mr. Warbeck. Charlie won't talk, anyway. He's a good kid. We grew up together in Idaho. He won't rat on me."

"Just off-hand," I said to Bates, "did you gents make up that little white power note that was delivered to Ann Benchley? You spelled some words wrong so the note would look like it was written by racist morons."

"Who was your partner, Bates?" I asked. "Who told you about the time machines? Who gave you the information?"

"Fuck you," Bates said to me.

"Did you kill Ray Harrison, Bates?"

The same two words came out of his mouth.

"Go wait outside, Bates," Warbeck snapped. "Dromio will join you in a moment." Bates gave me a silent snarl and stalked off.

Dromio walked away, but not before handing his boss a rolled-up piece of legal-sized paper. Warbeck set it aside. Warbeck turned to Picasso and said, "So, let's wrap up. Please continue reading the transcript, Mr. Picasso. You're almost at my favorite part, the part involving Benchley's old friend, the late Senator Robert Kennedy."

"Yeah, right," Picasso said. He slipped the first page behind the second.

"Mr. Kennedy asks, 'In light of your father's conviction for Contempt of Congress in 1948 and the subsegment testimony of several witnesses against your father, could you not name one individual in your association who was affiliated with the Communist Party at that time?' Benchley does some more hemming and hawing and then, after McCarthy starts to lose patience with you, you say, 'I believe I can state categorically that the only man my father mentioned from the AAF meetings he attended who stated his allegiance to any Communist organization was Silvio Malatesta. He had fought in Spain with a pro-Trotskyite group of Italian patriots. He was a brave man, but misguided,' etcetera, etcetera. You go on to say that, 'I'm afraid his judgement was clouded by the way his family was persecuted by Mussolini in the 1920's for their socialist affiliations and by the effect the Spanish Civil War, and the loss of his brothers, had on his psyche.' Mr Cohn asks you if you have any reservations in stating that Mr. Malatesta was a Communist? You reply, 'No, I do not, Mr. Cohn. I believe, as I said before, that, although Silvio is a talented artist, a good man and—' At that point you are dismissed by the Senator. End of transcript." Picasso shoved the paper into his hat, laid the hat back down on the table, then spoke directly to Benchley.

"So what you did was sell my father out to the witch-hunters. All these years I thought you were the best friend my father had. He even named me after you, the poor ignorant schmuck. You sold him out because you were jealous of his talent and you knew he was a better man than you'd ever be. At least your father had guts. He kept his mouth shut in front of HUAC in '48 and went to jail. He didn't work in a Hollywood movie again. He died doing dinner theater in Omaha, Nebraska."

"I know all this," Benchley said grimly.

"I know what you knew!" Picasso said, pounding the table with his fist. "The point is you lied to my father. You lied to me. You lied to everyone in that stinking book of yours and all the interviews you gave. You were one of the squealing rat finks and you passed yourself off as a hero."

"Jack," Warbeck said to Picasso, "since you cannot remember to use the accent for this time and place, kindly refrain from raising your voice."

We all sat there without speaking, listening to the trio play in the background and to Warbeck chomping down on a singed, tan-colored apple.

"You're a phony, Benchley," Picasso said, his voice lowered. "All these years you told how you joined the Committee for the First Amendment and all those other liberal groups, how you supposedly fought the studio bosses to get guys like my dad off the blacklist. You were just another scared rabbit trying to save his fancy house and his fancy car and keep his kept women in diamonds and furs. I hate your chicken-shit guts."

"That document is a forgery," Benchley said calmly. "Jack, haven't I told you about the Institute for Factual History? They fabricate and tailor records to suit the Strunk family's political persuasions. Warbeck is just a tool looking to fool others. Don't you see that?"

The young waitress opened the curtain and asked if anyone "wanted for something." Warbeck asked for more wine and more pie. The girl bowed and, moments later, a boy in a serving apron came and filled up Warbeck's mug. He did the same for Picasso. Bonnie and Benchley declined a refill.

Warbeck took a long quaff from his mug, then smiled at Benchley as if they were old friends. "Here's some history for you, Benchley old man," he said. Long ago, or in the distant future if you prefer, came the year 1948. A young Congressman from Massachusetts came out to Hollywood. He wanted to meet and bed some female starlets. This Trolius, the son of an Irish-Catholic Priam who wanted him to be President someday, needed a Pandarus. He chose a certain young war veteran and screen writer who was under contract for Universal at the time. The young and striving would-be director and the young politician had met briefly in Washington near the end of the war. They both shared the curse of bright, handsome and driven men: licentiousness."

I looked to Benchley. He sat impassively, his eyes focused down at the table.

Warbeck continued: "A certain starlet at the studio was dating the screenwriter, but he was not interested in serious relationships then, so he allowed the Congressman to have at her. Soon he was giving young John Kennedy the phone numbers of several of his nubile cast-offs. The future American President had a friend. I can almost imagine young JFK, in that famous accent of his, saying to you, 'Look, sport, if there's ever anything I can do for you' and so on and so on. Am I getting the story right so far, Jack?"

"John Kennedy was a friend of mine," Benchley said flatly. "You seem to like making up these stories, Warbeck, so get it all off your gut."

Warbeck licked his lips. Not a pretty sight. "Okay, Jack, let's move ahead to 1953. Your friend, the frenetic fornicator, is now a United States Senator. He is also a friend of a Republican Senator named Joseph McCarthy. McCarthy is a powerful man, capable of destroying the careers of men and women in the public or private sector by pinning the badge of Communist on them. Sometimes he is correct, sometimes he goes a bit too far. No matter. Senator McCarthy knows that Walter Benchley is a former Communist and so the junior Senator from Wisconsin believes the acorn has not fallen far from the family tree."

Picasso took up the story: "John Kennedy wanted to protect you from McCarthy. So, instead of letting the McCarthy Committee eat you alive in public, he asks his fellow Senator to let you testify in a secret session—it was not unprecedented—and allow you the chance to throw somebody else to the lions. If you gave McCarthy a big enough name, you were off the hook. So, you gave him my father's name. My father was a big name in Hollywood, bigger than yours."

Warbeck broke in: "It so happens that Robert Kennedy is

a counsel on the Internal Security Committee, along with the zealous Roy Cohn and a few other young men grasping for the brass ring of political power. After you give your secret testimony, the records of the *sub rosa* session, kept by young Robert, mysteriously disappear after Robert leaves the committee later in 1953. So, you think, after both Kennedy brothers and McCarthy die, no one of prominence will ever know about your betrayal. So now your secret is safe with Robert Kennedy. But, thanks to my research staff at the IFH, I have retrieved some documents courtesy of the Freedom of Information Act. Apparently, Mr. Cohn retained a copy of your testimony, a copy that Robert Kennedy missed. Sometime before 1972, Cohn turned the documentation over to Director J. Edgar Hoover of the FBI. I didn't need to tamper with anything, Benchley. It was all there. The researchers at IFH just had to look in the right place."

"Forgery," Benchley said. "A damned forgery."

"The damned truth," Warbeck countered, the lids around his blackish-grey eyes narrowing. "Your pandering for JFK helped you greatly later on. Later, you did the same favors for his younger brother. Whenever one brother or the other visited Southern California, you made certain that both the Liberal Libertines from Hyannisport were well supplied with show business pulchritude. Do you remember 456 Ocean Avenue? That's the address of the bungalow you kept in Santa Monica for your own extra-marital carnal pleasures, as well as those of your political friends. Once, when you had your own adulterous engagement and your dear wife was out of town, you even allowed John Kennedy to have a sexual tryst with a certain well-proportioned actress in poor Maria Benchley's own bedroom. The date was July 14, 1960. The Democrats had their Convention in L.A. and John Kennedy needed a momentary diversion from his fight for the nomination."

"He never used my wife's bedroom—our bedroom," Benchley said, his voice trailing off at the last two words.

Warbeck continued. "Maria Benchley tried to take her life once. You remember that, Jack? Perhaps you've forgotten. She was all alone in the Beverly Hills house in the middle of the night and you were on a borrowed yacht off Catalina Island with Janet Cummings, the girl you tried to make into a star. You were supposed to be scouting locations in Mexico. That was the alibi. If little Ann hadn't found her mother right after she took the overdose, you would have paid dearly for your promiscuity. You didn't even find out about the suicide until your wife had been locked up in a psychiatric hospital for observation. You were incommunicado with the busty Miss Cummings. She had the same physical dimensions as Marilyn Monroe, didn't she? But after nature bestowed such ample dimensions on Miss Cummings, the Life Force neglected to give her any artistic talent. She was a terrible actress, but you gave her pivotal parts in two of your films. Perhaps she was good in bed, eh, Jack? Was she better in sating your carnal desires than your wife, Maria? Could Janet do more interesting contortions than your wife? Was she more seaworthy?"

"Don't talk about my wife." Benchley said menacingly.

Warbeck paid no heed. "Maria was too good for you, Jack. She was a good woman, a fine actress, and a good mother. Too bad you just threw her away. Of course, like most men, you did not take kindly to her having her own affairs. So, you struck back at those who sought to comfort her."

Benchley huffed, then his deep voice became cold and steely. "And, finally, there we have it: the reason for all this dredging up of the past, the reason for those lies you've given Jack here to poison his mind against me. You still think you were fired from *Essex and the Queen* because of your little fling with my wife. You can't let that go, can you?"

Warbeck leaned forward toward Benchley, his voice dropping almost to a whisper. "In my office back in San Francisco, on my wall, there is a selection of photographs. Many of them highlight my acting career and my subsequent forays into the realm of politics and journalism. There is one photo I keep in the dead center of the display. The dead center. It was taken on June 12, 1970. It is of you and I, Benchley. I am playing the Earl of Essex, about to be beheaded on the scaffold at the Tower of London. That was the day that, somehow, you found out about my relationship with your neglected wife. After you fired me, you campaigned around Hollywood, telling every powerful person you knew that I was uncooperative, unprofessional, and that I was a drug addict."

All the time Warbeck took to say that, and he said it slowly, his stone-colored eyes just stared, unwavering, hardly even blinking.

Benchley shook his head. “You fool. You know the truth. You were without doubt the most obstreperous individual in the business back then. Everyone knew that. Good Lord, man, you were a walking terror! I never worked with an actor as egomaniacal as you, and I worked with some real male divas. But none of them rivaled your behavior on a sound stage. Those men were humble as Trappist Monks compared to you. Do you want to hear the real reasons I fired you from the Essex picture? For starters, you were writing your own lines and refusing to speak the ones in the finished script. You said you didn't bother even to memorize the lines. It didn't help you throwing tantrums on the set every hour on the hour then skulking off to your trailer. I had a few days of it. I realized you were a star now and being a star takes some getting used to. But I was the director and I had to complete the picture at budget and on time. So I told you to snap out of it, and you responded by calling the boss at Paramount and demanding that I be fired! I had nothing to do with those drug rumors. I didn't care if you were taking opium as long as you showed up, hit your marks, and said the lines as written. Yes, I fired you—in self-defense. It was you or me, pal. But, it had nothing—nothing—to do with Maria, and that little affair you and she had.”

Warbeck's dark eyes rolled upwards. “I've read your fantastic autobiography, Benchley. You made up so much and left so much out.” As Warbeck went on about a few points he disputed as being truthful in Benchley's autobiography, he undid the scroll of paper that Dromio had handed him and began to read from it.

“...regarding your father, for instance,” Warbeck said. “The man was a member of the Communist Party. He collected money to be sent to Spain to help the Russians suppress the Spanish people.”

“Where did you learn your history, Warbeck?” Benchley said. “Spain was a democracy. Franco and his Fascist scum in the military tried to overthrow—”

He was interrupted by Warbeck waving his hand at him and laughing sardonically. “Spare me, old man. Do, please spare me. Your father was a commie. You were a commie, and a rat fink who told on a friend to save your skin. That makes you a double traitor, to your country and your manhood.”

Benchley exploded: “You cock sucker! Maybe you can lie

to that gullible young prick, but don't think you can foist that on me. If your stinking publishing house ever prints that, I'll sue you down to your dirty underwear. I fought for my country. You dodged your National Service duty with some phony doctor's report about your bad lungs. That's a real fact, you fat slob. You're a coward. A fat-assed coward!" Benchley's face was deep red. I was afraid he was about to have a stroke, and still he went on.

"Just try and say I caved in to McCarthy and Cohn and those witch hunters. Go on and try!"

The music stopped again. The curtain opened up. It was Constable Catsby. There was a look of alarm on his face. He shot a glance to our side of the table, then to Warbeck.

"Is there anything wrong, mi'lord?" Catsby asked. "I heard talk of witches. If there are any in our township, I will raise the hue and cry against the crones and they will be dealt with—"

Warbeck laughed. "No, constable. Nothing wrong, no witches. The old fellow here was just upset about some past action that he would rather not be reminded of. I trust, constable, you have the required number of men assembled for mustering."

"I do, Noble Lord," Catsby said.

"I will review them then," Warbeck replied. He struggled to get to his feet, his bulk almost knocking the table against us. Picasso helped him up, which allowed me to take my eyes off him and what he might be doing with his gun hand. The constable offered an arm to 'Grantum.' The three men then walked through the center aisle of the tavern.

"Oh, I almost forgot," Warbeck said. "You see that little leather pouch I left on the table? There is a (his voice dropped a bit) eight millimeter video tape on it. It concerns your daughter, Ann. You should look at it at your earliest opportunity."

Again, the 'Earl' briefly acknowledged the good wishes of several patrons. The three of us stood at the table, Bonnie and I waiting to see what Benchley wanted to do. But he did not say anything. He just sat, looking at the paper that Warbeck had thrown at us. He held it close to his face again, moving his lips slightly as he reread the article. Then he violently crumpled up the paper.

I looked closely at Benchley. The old man had been

through an ordeal, and it showed on his sweaty forehead and shaking limbs. He stood up. I did too, as did Bonnie.

The old man put his arm to my chest, indicating I should let him through. I stepped back. He moved past me, his pace around me I would have thought impossible for a man in his condition.

"What are you doing, Mr. Benchley?" Bonnie called out. Benchley ignored her.

What Benchley did was walk as briskly as his stiff legs would allow him toward the other side of the tavern. He tossed his hat away and put his right hand to the hilt of his sword.

Bonnie and I looked at each other. I think we both realized at that moment that Benchley had lost his grip. He was going after Warbeck, or Bates, or any of that group who stood in his way.

"Don't let him do this," Bonnie said to me. "We have to stop him."

We managed to stop Benchley. He was angry, but he was also weak and tired.

❖ ❖ ❖ ❖ ❖

Our threesome set out down the road again, heading south toward London. The walls of the city were now visible from the long, flat advantage our approach afforded. We continued a little ways further until we came to a cluster of oak trees. It was there that Benchley and Bonnie dismounted (I was on foot) and we went behind the largest of the trees. It was raining hard—hard enough to stop play in a baseball game—and Benchley wanted to get under some cover.

Once in the trees, I took off my floppy hat and rang the water out of it. "I always figured England was cold and rainy," I said to both of them.

While he rested, Benchley leaned an elbow against a tree. He looked at me with his one sad, weary eye.

"Who killed Dave?" he asked me. His tone was sympathetic.

"The cops think his wife did it," I said. "They were seen together up in Bowman an hour or so before Dave was found dead."

"That would be his wife, the woman called Cindy or something?"

"Wendy," I said.

"Do you think his wife could have done it?" Benchley asked me.

Bonnie looked at me as she brushed the dampness out of her hair with a thick, old-fashioned comb.

"McCreedy did beat his wife," Bonnie said when I paused before answering.

"True," I said. "It's possible Wendy might have killed him. The problem is she just wasn't into guns or killing anybody or anything. Anything's possible, I suppose." I looked down at the leaves and dirt about my feet. "I believe anything is most definitely possible now, especially after what's happened to me in the last 36 hours. If you'd told me I'd be standing under a tree in some smelly English town in the year 1599 two days ago...I just don't know what to think until I can talk to her."

"Be that as it may, I was wrong about our friend David," the old man said. "Dave McCreedy was a good man, and loyal to me. I hope, wherever he is, he'll forgive me for what I thought about him, and what I said last night. I'm so glad it wasn't Ann who's in jail."

That statement surprised me, and by the look on her face, surprised Bonnie as well.

"Ann is a... Ann has her bad moments, as you saw back in the clearing this morning," Benchley said. "I think even after she decided to stop seeing Dave and take up again with Jack Picasso she must have had moments of regret. If only Dave wasn't already married. I think he was a better man than any of the louts she married." The old man looked upward at the tree, the grey sky and the falling rain. Standing against a tree, he cursed against the pain to his backside from the riding (I could empathize) then put his hands on his knees. The next statement he made was directed to the ground, in a tone just above a whisper.

"There were even times I've had doubts about Ann being innocent in Talbot Strunk's death fifteen years ago."

Bonnie's face took on a pained expression. "But she was acquitted, Mr. Benchley. The jury—"

"But I had the three best lawyers on the West Coast defending her," Benchley said. "What's the worst you've ever seen Ann? The worst mental state you've ever seen her in? Was it similar to that little display of hers this morning? That was nothing. I've seen her smash a glass table with her bare fists. I saw her take Avalon, when she was maybe six years old, and throw her against a wall. I've seen her yank her little Tyler up by one arm and spank his butt with a wirehair brush so hard I had to put a stop to it."

"I've never seen her hurt Tyler," Bonnie said. "Ann has a temper, and she has spanked Tyler, but nothing like—"

"You don't know everything about Ann or about my family," Benchley said harshly. Then he paused and exhaled, his shoulders sagging, his crinkled eyelids shutting tight.

"I'm sorry, Bonnie," the old man said. "I just wish I could have as much faith in my daughter as you do. I'm especially upset about what Warbeck said about my testifying before Joe McCarthy's Committee. That's all bullshit, of course. He made up that transcript from his propaganda mill at The Institute for Factual History just to fool Jack Picasso. You realize that?" The old man said the last part with emphasis.

"Of course," Bonnie said. "You don't have to convince us that Trevor Warbeck is a pathological liar."

Benchley looked relieved. "We have enough trouble now for just the three of us. This is 1599. We have forty hours to stop Warbeck and Essex. So let's get to Grey's Inn and get my friend Bacon up to speed on what he needs to do."

"Do you have the tape, Mr Benchley?" I asked.

Benchley reached into his doublet and extracted the small videotape microcassette. "It will be interesting to see and hear what's on this tape. Warbeck said it had something to do with Ann. It could be nothing, of course." He put the tape back inside his doublet, then wrapped his cloak closer around his stooped shoulders. A wind had started to kick up, worsening the effect of the rain but, I hoped, making the shower pass by more quickly.

The rain abated after a few minutes and we then mounted up and continued the journey.

Chapter Forty-One

Francis Bacon was a dead ringer for Claude Rains, the actor who is best remembered by posterity for playing Louis Renault, the Vichy French police captain in *Casablanca.* I knew this because there was a painting of the guy in his study, where the three of us were seated in comfortable high-backed chairs. The study featured an entire wall of leather-bound books, a large wall map proporting a show of the world—all of California was depicted as a giant peninsula, which I assumed was ignorance rather than sloppy cartography—several terra-cotta busts of stern-looking people on a ledge above the ornate whitewashed stone fireplace, and above the busts was a second painting in the room: a portrait of Queen Elizabeth the First, dressed to the hilt and done in profile. I briefly scanned the library. Most of the titles on the thick spines were in either French or Latin. The best thing about the study to me was the fireplace and the hearty, crackling fire that was expelling prodigious heat throughout the room.

To get to this room and this large house, we had ridden a few miles beyond Camden Town and arrived at a complex of brownstone and high steepled buildings Benchley told us made up Grey's Inn, one of the four Inns of Court on the outskirts of London. The foremost building was a castle-like edifice three stories high with tall, narrow windows and pear-shaped towers jutting up from the main structure. The roof of the building abounded with chimneys laid out haphazardly on flat portions of the roof. While Bonnie and I waited with the horses, Benchley climbed the stairs into the building. While we waited, lots of young men in flat hats and dark robes walked by chattering to one another in the courtyard, many speaking in what I took to be Latin.

Benchley returned from the building looking weary but not as somber as before.

"I saw Bacon briefly," Benchley said. "He's in a meeting. He said we should go on to his house."

The house was across from an elaborately landscaped park. The greenspace had a variety of arbors, terraces, walk-ways covered by trellis-supported vines, beds of flowers, and manicured bushes. It sat on the boundary of the park opposite the law school: a large two-story wood-framed house, whitewashed with black horizontal and vertical support beams topped with a sloping roof not unlike a chalet. A short man named Geoffrey—who recognized Benchley and greeted him with a manner of near elation—met us at the main door to the estate, which was situated across a stone bridge over a small lily-strewn creek.

"Mr. Bacon will be most pleased you have arrived, Squire Benchley," the servant said. He had wispy ginger-colored strands of hair circling his bald pate. He had a long-crooked nose, beady hazel eyes, a chest that extended unnaturally far out from the rest of his torso, and the short limbs and loping peculiar stride that characterizes a dwarf. He wore a flat collar, tight-fitting doublet, and the knicker-like 'venetians' that came down below his knee. After he and Benchley exchanged greetings, our 'master' introduced us to Geoffrey.

Bonnie and I went to a small stable around the back of the house. There we helped the stable groom—a small boy with crooked teeth and a shy disposition—place the horses in an empty pair of stalls. Using three trips, I removed the saddle bags (including our matchlock rifle) from both horses and from Jennifer and brought them over the bridge into the manor. We were directed down an oak-paneled corridor and then up a flight of stairs with an elegantly carved and polished oak banister to an adjoining pair of rooms. Both rooms had large beds which took up most of the available space. There were also two stools in each room, one of which looked like a portable toilet contraption, and a rectangular-shaped window. The window looked out on a graveled pathway below and, beyond that, a large garden of green bushy hedges and arbors which adjoined the Inn of Court. The tall hedges we saw riding to the house now looked, from the upper vantage, to be part of a maze of hedges a dozen large squares and narrow pathways deep.

"Look at the marquetry here," Bonnie said excitedly, pointing to the patterns of flowers and the inlaid geometric patterns which covered the front of the drawers in the room that she was to use. I kept quiet, as I was still getting the accent registered in my head by following Bonnie's speech tones. After her initial reluctance, she seemed quite comfortable employing it.

"Tell me, Geoffrey," she asked in that strange accent, "how did your master know we were to arrive today?"

"Master Bacon told me yesterday to expect you, madam," Geoffrey said in his high-pitched voice. "I assume he must have received a letter from your worthy father sometime recently. I trust your journey from Bristol was without hazardous incident."

"It was trying at times but travel always is," Bonnie replied. "We were set upon by brigands, but my father and his worthy servant, Harry, drove them off with the vigor of their swordsmanship." Bonnie snuck a wink at me over the servant's head when she said this.

Geofrey turned to face me. "By St. George!" the little fellow exclaimed, "You must be an adept swordsman. I hope you and I will have time to do a bit of fencing if you have free time. I am but a moth of a figure, I grant you, but I enjoy exchanging thrusts with a good swordsman. Tell me, servant, are you a practitioner of the rapier and dagger? I noticed you have a rapier at your side, and you seem to have dagger hidden on your person."

That bulge between my doublet and breeches was my Baretta. I nodded to the dwarf.

"Excellent," Geoffrey said, bouncing up on the toes of his pointy-shoes and intertwining his child-sized stubby hands together over his chest. "May I see your foil?"

I withdrew the cutlery from my scabbard and handed it to him. As he looked it over, I took the opportunity to give Bonnie what I hoped was a withering glance. Why the hell did she have to mention swordplay? I hadn't been around long, but I knew from our experience back at the inn that waving sharp objects about was a big-time vice around here. The little guy would probably dice me to ribbons. I wanted to keep all six quarts of my blood in my body.

"It is a Bilbo blade," Geoffrcy announced. "I prefer the Toledo. Are you a practitioner of the Italian or the Spanish school?"

"Oh, Spanish, I suppose," I sheepishly answered. I didn't know what the hell he was talking about.

"Ah," the little guy said with a smile. He took up the blade and began to execute some moves with the rapier. His target was some imaginary opponent just a few feet in front of me. He handled the sword like it was a baton and he was a concertmaster. "The *pararla*," he stated whipping the blade uncomfortably close to my mid-section. "And next the *stoccata*...and now the *passado*, now the *punto reverso*." At the announcement of each unfamiliar designation, he thrust the sword about with an alarming dexterity. And then he flipped the sword about and handed it back to me, hilt first.

"We must put tips on our blades and do a bit of fencing in the garden if our masters will afford us the time," Geoffrey said. "Being of equal station as servants, we can have our own duel could we not?"

"Really?" I stated with zero enthusiasm.

"Oh, yes," Geoffrey said. "A mock-duel, however. One utilizing tips on our blades to prevent harm. What better sport could there be?"

I could think of several.

"Would that I could," I said, employing the local accent as best I could. "But I cannot give you a fencing match. I accidentally, uh, I accidentally killed my brother-in-law last Christmas day. It was a dispute regarding the cutting of the turkey. We had tips on the rapiers, but mine—whoops—fell off. I swore to my local vicar I would only draw my blade against heretics, infidels and uncouth bandits. Forgive me, fellow underling." I bowed.

"Of course," Geoffrey said. He turned and returned my bow. "I will go forth to the stables and make sure that our young groom is set about his work. Please excuse me, good mistress." Bonnie nodded and the little fellow went on his way.

"Thank you for telling that guy I was some kind of hotshot fencer," I said to Bonnie as we ascended the stairway.

"I was trying to make our journey sound authentic," Bonnie replied. "You won't have time to be fencing anyway. The part about infidels and heretics wasn't bad, but I don't think people do the *Grand Duelleo* on Christmas Day. And turkeys are American birds, not European. The Pilgrims aren't expected to hit Plymouth Rock for another twenty years."

"I apologize for bringing turkeys up before their time," I said, as we exited the bed chamber and headed back down the staircase.

We found Benchley in the large study, and that's where I noticed Francis Bacon's portrait and his shelves of books. I sat down on one of the hardwood, cushionless chairs that were situated around the room. Bonnie stood at the window, looking at the landscaping. Benchley was standing next to the fire, reading from one of the books. The old man had taken his wet cloak and draped it over a chair. Bonnie took her coat off, put it on a hatrack, and sat herself gracefully on an oak chest situated in front of the window. Benchley already had his hat on the wooden hatrack that looked like—a regular hatrack. I put my hat on a peg next to his and slouched back into a chair. It was just the three of us.

I looked up at the ceiling. It was the same rich brown as the rest of the wooden decor of the study, from the peak of the slightly vaulted ceiling (held up by three sets of thick wooden beams) down the wooden paneling to the wainscoting that met the floor. I looked at Benchley, reading with his one remaining eye by holding the book up close to his face.

"I know you and Francis Bacon have this 'Stop Essex' thing worked out," I said to the old man. "but I'd like to know a little more about all this business."

Benchley looked up. "Such as?"

"What is there left to do, for instance? And what have you done on these previous, ah, trips back here?"

"Certainly," Benchley said. The old man put the book down on a table, walked over to the hearth, and warmed his backside against the fire. "It's best to start from the beginning. It's all rather simple, really. I have made annual visits to this time frame for the past seven years. My first two trips were with Morton Ryskind. Then he died of tragic consequences on the second trip. I resumed my annual explorations with

Truffie, Major Trubshawe that is. We took his younger son once, his mother objected, and that much you know. During my first journey I made contact with William Shakespeare. The time hole that the STUMP took us through is set at approximately 399 years and some months. Our first trip was in 1994, so that put us in the Fall of 1593."

"How did you meet Shakespeare?" Bonnie asked.

"At a tavern near the Bear Garden on the Bankside," Benchley said, stretching his arms out and then nursing his lower back with both hands. "1593 was a plague year in London. We arrived in late September and the theatres were closed by the civil authorities."

"Because of the Puritans?" Bonnie asked.

"Because of the plague," Benchley said. "The plague closed all places of public amusement for most of 1592 and '93. The civil authorities knew nothing about modern vaccinations or effective sanitation so the pestilence carried off thousands. So, I met William Shakespeare at one of the first places I looked: The Roan Bull Tavern, near the Liberty of the Clink, where he resided at that time. In Modern London, the remains of that tavern is probably buried under where the Southbank Complex is today. William was sitting alone at a table near a window, nursing along a mug of ale and writing with a quill some of his lines for the long poem he dedicated to Southampton, *The Rape of Lucrece*. It was fortunate that I found him that day. He was to go his company into Kent the next day and tour the provinces with as an actor in two plays, one of which was *The Comedy of Errors* and the other play...I can't remember the title...written by the poor reprobate Robert Greene, the university man who called young Shakespeare 'an upstart crow'."

"Did you tell him you were from the future?" I asked.

Benchley chuckled, then shook his head. "Decidedly not, Harvey. I offered myself as a gentlemen from Bristol who was asking a seasoned city-dweller about news of the plague and what entertainments could be had if London was ever again free from the Black Death. In other words, I struck up a conversation. As Ben Jonson said in his eulogy for him, the man had, or has, a sweet and gentle disposition. He told me about the nearby archery fields, about the best taverns, about the bear-baiting in the nearby amphitheater and, most importantly, about the theatres in London. I found out in our first talk that John Aubrey, one of the Bard's first biographers, was right: Shakespeare *had* been a schoolmaster in a small village for a time. But he had a wife and three children to support, so he came to London because teaching offered little pay. He regretted the fact he did not have the means to undertake a university education, but he chose the theater precisely because it was a trade unencumbered by guilds or academic hoops to jump through. 'Circumstance,' the young man said, 'has enrolled me into the most rigorous college mankind can devise: the hurly-burly of London'. That is what he told me. I praised his *Venus and Adonis* poem, a copy of which I had purchased earlier at a bookstall just outside St. Paul's."

Bonnie turned around from viewing the garden. "Is that the signed quarto edition you supposedly found? The one with Shakespeare's signature on it?"

"Yes," Benchley said, his eyes twinkling. "I'm afraid Trevor Warbeck is not the first guilty party to exploit the past. I asked William, as he was getting back to his work and I took my leave, to sign the title-leaf of my copy of his great poem. Once back in our present, I put my autographed copy up for auction at Soterby's Auction House and the prize fetched half-a-million dollars. I gave some of the proceeds to Truffie to start his antique shop. We've brought back furniture and knick-knacks from the 1590's that we've sold as antiques. Most of the earnings go to support the Shakespeare Festival and the rest to Truffie's family and business interests. And he has earned it. Without his support, I couldn't have done the invaluable camera work I've done here."

Geoffrey appeared in the study, asking if we wanted food or drink. Benchley asked for some wine, which Geoffrey brought in a glass carafe with two green-tinted glasses.

"Mr. Bacon expresses his apologies through his humble servant, and says he will be with his client further than anticipated," Geoffrey said.

"Where is the other Mr. Bacon, Geoffrey?" Benchley asked.

"Mr. Anthony Bacon is currently in Bath, taking the waters," the servant said. The top log in the chimney fell to ashes in a brief torrent of sparks. Geoffrey then reached over toward the fireplace. I thought at first he was going to throw another log on the fire. Instead, he reached behind the small triangular pile of logs and produced what looked like a fat guitar.

"I am an adept player of the lute," Geoffrey said. "If you would like, I will favor you with divers ballads while you wait. I am told I have perfect pitch and a sweet tone of voice. I would know any ballad the young lady would care to hear." The way he said that last remark made me think Geoffrey had a crush on Bonnie.

"No," Benchley said, "you have brought us enough pleasure as it is, Geoffrey. Leave us for a time. You have presented yourself well. I will commend you to your worthy master."

Geoffrey bowed then left the room. Benchley's narrative resumed.

"On the second trip I was bolder. My friend Morton, who was an avid reader of Elizabethan history as well as a great physicist, wanted to forewarn a certain Dr. Rodrigo Lopez, Queen Elizabeth's personal doctor. He was going to be accused of trying to poison the Queen by the troublesome Earl of Essex. He was a Portuguese, and a former Jew, and both those factors was used by Essex to pester the Queen to have him imprisoned and executed on what, in history's judgment, was a thumped-up charge. And that, indirectly, led to the tragic end of my best friend." Benchley stopped, rubbed a hand across his face, took a sip of the drink he poured for himself, then resumed.

"We made a mistake," he said. "A terrible mistake. We arrived on what we thought was the day before the arrest of Dr. Lopez—May 14, 1594. Ryskind's plan was to warn him, and give him money to get to France. There was also the matter of a proper-looking passport. The passport we had was a forgery, of course, a computer designed replica similar to an Elizabethan artifact at the Stanford Rare Books Center. It had a facsimile of the Official Seal of William Cecil, Lord Burghley, and that would have assured Doctor Lopez safe passage out of England. After we transported back in time, we secured horses and rode to the good doctor's townhouse near Whitehall Palace. We convinced Lopez to let us into his chamber, and told him of the plot, without telling him we were time travelers, of course, but simply well-wishing men with ears within the Earl of Essex's circle."

Benchley had a coughing fit, then resumed.

"Lopez was not a foolish man. He was making his own preparations to depart England and was glad of our help. But Essex must have had spies watching his house, because as Morton was in the process of aiding Lopez in packing the Queen's Lord Lieutenant of the Tower, a man named Waad, came in force to arrest him. They took Lopez away, and my friend was also seized as a suspected accomplice. I was spared simply because I had gone to the Strand to procure fresh horses for the trip to Dover. When I came back, I saw my friend being taken away in an open wagon, a wagon reserved for—" He paused, drew a deep breath, then continued.

"There were chains on Morton's arms and legs. A crowd of apprentices and ragged layabouts had gathered and were throwing rocks and rotting vegetables at them. My friend was now caught up as an accomplice to a man considered an enemy of the realm. I was seized with rage. I had a modern weapon: an automatic pistol with two extra clips of ammo. I would have shot the troopers and made a desperate bid to free my friend, but Morton saw me and shook his head violently at me. I guess he wanted me—" Benchley stopped again. He shuddered.

Benchley's face flushed with emotion. "I had to help him. I went to Francis Bacon, showed him the guns and devices we had brought from the future, showed him the STUMP, where it was hidden and how it worked. I thought, with his devotion to science and the advancement of learning, that he was the one man from this time who could properly assimilate what gains in technology the future had wrought. I was right. Bacon went to his patron, Essex, and tried to stop him from pestering the Queen to have Lopez and Morton executed. Essex refused. His honor could only be satisfied with Dr. Lopez's death, and that included any accomplices as well. Francis certainly tried, but there was nothing he could do if the Queen's favorite feared for his honor.

"Bacon did attend the Start Chamber treason trial, but strictly as an observer. It was held in the Guildhall in London. Dr. Lopez insisted Morton had no connection to him other than as an acquaintance, but the good judges of the Star Chamber wanted blood and, besides, they had found Morton's Star of David which he always wore under his shirt. That alone was enough to seal his fate, no matter what the connection to Lopez. My friend was a Jew and that was crime enough here."

"What do you mean?" I said, "I know Jews were persecuted in Spain and in places like that, but in England as well?"

"Very much in England, Harvey," Benchley said, gasping out. He put a hand across his remaining eye, the lid of which was red and damp. He looked distressed. Bonnie came over to him, got him to sit down in a chair near the fire and stroked the top of his pinkish, bald head. In that moment their relationship became clear to me. According to what she had told me back in San Francisco, Bonnie's father had been distant, unable to accept or return affection. Jack Benchley was the affectionate father she had never had. And Bonnie was the emotionally stable daughter he never had.

"Very much in England," Benchley repeated after regaining his composure. "Jews were forbidden to come to this island unless they were converted. They have been so since the days of the Planetgents and will continue to be barred until Oliver Cromwell usurps control fifty years hence. They are considered infidels. It is hard enough to be a subject of Elizabeth the First and be, say, a Catholic. Many men are tied to a stake and burned for distributing Papal propaganda or even harboring a Jesuit priest in these times. Catholics can only find toleration by going to Anglican Mass or paying serious fines for not doing so. And they have to swear allegiance to the sovereign of the island and renounce the Church in Rome. Of course, Catholic princes were not kind to their Protestant subjects across the Channel, either."

"Take Catherine D'Medici and the St. Bartholomew's Day Massacre in Paris," Bonnie said. "Or the delightful Spanish Inquisition."

"Indeed," Benchley said.

"Did Mr. Ryskind tell the authorities about his real identity?" I asked.

"No," Benchley said. "He would have been scoffed at as a necromancer had he broached this subject of time travel. Bacon and I managed to visit him the night before his execution. He was in a grimy, rat-infested cell at the Tower of London. We also brought his beautiful daughters, Judith and Susanna. They had to see their father one last time. The pretext was Bacon's attempt to convert him to the Anglican Faith before his death, to supposedly spare his soul. Morton never denied his Jewish faith. He explained his strange accent by saying he was a Jew from Spanish America who had snuck into England to warn Lopez. He even claimed to be a former convert to Christianity who had returned to his Judiac roots. That was very much like Morton. Back in the 1950's, he defied the men in Washington who revoked his security clearance with the Atomic Energy Committee, and he defied the Star Chamber of Tudor England. The only thing Morton asked of me was to return to my own time and never return to this one. I should destroy the STUMPs and the plans for time travel. 'The past is not worth saving from itself,' he told me. He breathed in and out quickly,as if catching his breath."

"Morton died a few days later, of dysentery, in the Tower. He was my best friend. At least God spared him an Elizabethan execution."

"I could not destroy the time machines," he said after a pause. "I don't know if mankind can handle time-travel technology, but it is here. There has to be some reason, some greater design, for my friend to invent such a machine to probe the past."

Benchley suddenly stopped. His lined forehead suddenly squeezed tight as if he had a headache. He put a hand to his forehead then stood up as if shocked. "I remember now, the Tower of London, when I took Judith and Susanna to see their condemned father...there was someone else there. Susanna insisted that she needed him to come with her for support."

"Who, Mr. Benchley?" Bonnie asked.

"Ray Harrison!" he exclaimed. "That blasted pornographer! He was married to Susanna back then. Her mother couldn't come because she was recovering from an operation, so Harrison came along. Years later, when I fired him, he swore he'd tell the world about the STUMPs. I discounted that. He had no proof."

"But he didn't need to tell the world," I said. "All he had to do was tell your Security Manager, Ralph Bates."

"And Bates could've broken into your offices," Bonnie added. "And taken your notes and documents about time travel."

"And then told his former employer, Jack Picasso,"

Benchley continued, "and Jack, thinking I'd betrayed his father..."

"Told Trevor Warbeck and Sherwood Strunk all they needed to know," I said. "And that's why they set a trap for you down at Strunk's complex."

There was nothing more to say.

We all just sat still, listening to the dollops of rain plop-plop against the window. The spell was broken as the door to the hallway opened. Our host had arrived.

"Benchley, thank the heavens you have arrived safely," Francis Bacon said as he also removed his wet cape. "I prayed somehow you would escape the clutches of that fiend, Warbeck. What the dickens has become of your eye?"

Benchley explained the mayhem, then introduced us to the short dark-haired man, and then introduced Bonnie and I not in our aliases, but using our modern names and professions.

For the first time on the trip, I felt relieved to be in a stranger's company.

Chapter Forty-Two

For those who are not old movie buffs (i.e., those with whom the name Claude Rains does not register) I will describe Francis Bacon: a short man with active, piercing dark eyes, a sharp beak of a nose, bushy dark hair that completely covered his ear, and a well-groomed goatee and mustache. He looked younger than I imagined he would be, maybe thirty or so, with a wide ruff that made his head look like it was tilted upward on a plate. He also wore immaculate white gloves with laced trim. Give credit to the guy. He looked like an Earl with his knee-length cape, a silk lime-green doublet with black-piping running along the v-shaped hem where his slight pot belly protruded out from his trunk. His breeches were multi-colored and padded out, stopping just below the knee. The knees themselves were criss-crossed with garters, scarlet-hued, and his short feet were encased in some type of cork-heeled slipper with slits on top of the shoe so the hose could show through. I was surprised to find out from Bonnie later that our host was not an Earl, or a Baron, or even a Sir, but just a lawyer and counsel to the Queen. No titles had been bestowed on Bacon at this juncture in time, but he looked as if by his choice of fashion that he expected advancement shortly. He reeked of some type of cologne which smothered all but the more pleasant scent of burning wood in the room.

After removing his cape, Bacon slung it over an empty chair just as Benchley had. He half-sat on a wooden chair a few feet from the hearth, moving it about until he faced

Benchley.

"Inform me, Benchley," Bacon said, as he daintily took off his gloves and laid them on the table. "Who is this marauder that claims to be my old friend Devant? Apparently he has kindled a marked (he pronounced it mark-ed) haste in Lord Essex to carry forth with his hare-brained plans for open sedition."

"Yes, Francis," Benchley said. "I am afraid that a fellow named Ray Harrison, an ex-son-in-law of Morton Ryskind, and a security manager named Ralph Bates, have proved to be most untrustworthy. They gave this man Warbeck, through another foul fellow, the secret journal I was keeping on my travels through time. He's got his hands on both of the STUMPs. I told him what the machine was and where I kept it, but not before giving up my right eye. This Trevor Warbeck is a Machiavel. He has already killed a young woman I had great affection for, plus he has tried to kill my two companions here back in San Francisco. There was also a cowardly terrorist attack on a hotel in Kensington that left my granddaughter with near-mortal injuries."

"Oh, I am sorry Benchley," Bacon said, sounding genuinely sympathetic. "The imposter came a few days ago to my home," Bacon continued, somberly. "The fat one and Southampton, plus a tall man I would not let cross my threshold. He pretended to be Grantum. I, of course, knew he was an imposter within a few snatches of conversation with him. His Latin is abominable for one thing. He quoted a pair of epigrams attributed to Martial, and maimed the verse most grievously. Plus this fat man of your century displayed a countenance that betrayed the man had he not opened his mouth. He has the same casualness endemic in men of the twentieth century. It would not surprise me that he was some sort of player in one of those image-capturing plays such as delight the common herd in your time."

"Mr. Bacon has been to the future, as you might have surmised," Benchley said to Bonnie and myself. "He has been a keen observer and reader of what lies ahead for mankind beyond this age, and also, alas, a keen critic."

"So you've been to our time, Mr. Bacon?" Bonnie exclaimed.

Bacon curtly nodded to her, then returned his attention to Benchley.

Benchley continued his summation of the deeds of Trevor Warbeck, going back to his first contact with the man in the 1960's. "You were wise to label him a player of the theatrical sense, Francis," Benchley declared, "for that is essentially what he is. And a good actor, let there be no doubt. But as for the other avenues he has pursued—politics, agitation-propaganda, directing films and documentaries—he is a mountebank. He has a powerful patron in this corporate prince, Sherwood Strunk, and you already what sort of a loose cannon your Lord Essex is."

"Have you eaten?" Bacon asked.

Benchley nodded. "We had the remote pleasure of an early supper with Trevor Warbeck and his retinue," Benchley said with a sigh that revealed his exhaustion. "My friend Bonnie here and Mr. Wells think Warbeck was behind the death of a close friend of mine and my daughter. You met him when you visited Rogue Falls under your assumed identity as a 20th Century professor from Oxford. His name was Dave McCreedy."

Bacon furled his brow then said, "Mr. David McCreedy... was he the man who rescued Will Shakespeare's bastard—the one your daughter named Tyler— from some hovel in that desert state called Nevada? Was he the man who played about with those donkey-like internal combustion things, the Hogs he called them?"

"Yes, they are called motorcycles," Benchley said uncomfortably. I glanced at Bonnie. She looked surprised. Bacon had just let a cat out of a bag that Benchley wanted left in. So, Tyler wasn't a little Romanian orphan after all.

"Carolyn Mason was killed by Warbeck's henchmen." Benchley added. "You hadn't met her, but she was a charming woman. I almost felt I could have trusted her with this secret of time travel, even though we only knew each other for a few months."

Bacon made a snorting sound. "I would say enough of your countrymen already have been privy to the modes of time traveling. Southampton told me he and Essex now have magnificent weapons at their disposal, with potential to mow down rows of pikemen and bowmen and musket shooters. The Queen's forces have nothing to match this ordnance, save for the cannon in the Tower."

"Where is the Queen?" Benchley asked.

"The Queen has recently moved from Nonsuch to Greenwich Palace," Bacon stated. "She has to make a progress in three days which troubles me dearly. She will leave her Greenwich to bring her court to, of all places, Grantum Hall."

"She can't do that!" Bonnie burst out. "That is right where Essex wants her."

Bacon shot a glance at Bonnie, like she was creating a disturbance rather than adding to the conversation. He brought his attention back to Benchley's side of the table.

"The false Earl of Grantum is to be married to one of the Queen's former ladies-in-waiting."

"Married?" Benchley exclaimed. "He has only assumed Grantum's guise less than two weeks ago and he has already found a match?"

"The marriage has been arranged for months," Bacon said. "The true Earl wooed Lady Margaret Winwood when the Court was at Windsor last September, when Grantum had the title Order of the Garter bestowed on him by the Queen. His first wife has been dead for a year—died from the sweating sickness."

"I do recall you mentioning that," Benchley said.

"The Queen approved of the match, of course. Poor Lady Winwood knows nothing of the ruse, and is in transit with her family from their manor near Cambridge. She has only been in the company of William DeVant three times—the courtship was brief—so I doubt she will discover she is marrying an imposter until after the ceremony."

"And the Queen has to attend the wedding?" Benchley asked.

"Of course," Bacon said. "Her Majesty is Grantum's cousin, and the godmother of his only male heir. It is customary for her to grace such a ceremony with her royal personage."

I wondered if Warbeck's modern-age girlfriend, Anita Shumpsky, knew about her boyfriend's impending nuptials?

"The Queen is walking into a trap," Benchley said. "If she goes to Grantum Hall with a light escort of Gentlemen Pensioners, she's doomed. Bacon, you must get to Greenwich as soon as possible. Tell Her Majesty everything. Tell her the real story: that there is a time machine, that Essex knows of the future and that he is destined for the Tower and the ax. Tell her the real Earl of Grantum is a hostage in his own keep. She needs to know all this to save her kingdom."

Bacon shook his head. "Are you asking me to ascend to the highest sphere of this kingdom, the *primum mobile* of government, and deliver my reputation to Her Majesty based on fantastic sciences that even in your own time are beyond belief? If I went to Greenwich and informed the Queen and her Privy Council of my time travel experiences, I would be bound hand and foot and thrown into a dark room until my supposed madness eased. To spout forth the truth would be pure folly." Our host chuckled. "I'm sure my conniving hunchbacked cousin, Robert Cecil, would dearly enjoy my spinning such a tale before Her Majesty. The Principal Secretary would say I was as unstable as Essex himself, and not fit for further counsel to the Queen."

"Does that matter?" Benchley said. "You already know that James of Scotland will ascend the throne in less than four years. You already know great advancement is coming to you. You will process the title of Lord High Chancellor and Baron Verulam, plus all the intermediary great offices."

"Which is why I will have nothing to do with Lord Essex," Bacon said, "despite the fact that my brother and myself enjoyed his patronage for years, and despite his supporting me for Attorney General and Soliticitor General of this kingdom. I turned away from those favors. They did not bear fruit but the Earl did not make my case before the Queen with light intent. Why, I even turned down his gift of a great estate at Twickenham, an estate I would have accepted if my knowledge of later events had not been foretold. Instead, I have sufficed myself with sharing this house Essex gave to my brother Anthony. Do you realize, because of your errors, that Essex now knows that I will turn against him at his trial for treason eighteen months hence? He already knows that! Southampton told me as much in his visit with this Warbeck fellow. I was even offered forgiveness for my support of the Queen in Essex's treason trial. I was told my nimble mind and good counsel would have a place of high degree if the rebellion succeeded."

"And what did you decide?" Benchley asked. "Are you still loyal to your Queen?"

Bacon paused, got up from the chair and went over to his fireplace. He placed a couple logs on the diminishing fire, poked at the underlying logs with an iron tong, then looked back atBenchley. From what I saw of our host's expression, he enjoyed the suspense he was creating in the three of us.

"I turned Southampton down, of course," Bacon said offhandedly. "Now, *vis a vi* the forces at Essex's disposal, I am in a position of peril."

"Are you saying you won't try and stop this calamity?" Benchley asked.

Bacon shook his head. "I will do my best to stop this usurpation, this advancement of unworthy persons. But in order to do this, I must still pursue the course that God hath given me to take. I must, therefore, not develop the reputation of a man possessed by demons. Word of that would not sit well with the ministers of King James and would bar me from high office."

"You're right," Benchley said sadly. "But you do have the Queen's ear. Is there not some way to keep her away from the Grantum Wedding?" I noticed Benchley was gritting his teeth as he spoke, as if he were in pain.

"I do plan to take the boat from London Bridge to Greenwich this afternoon," Bacon said. "I will do so at three this afternoon. I have the honor to dine with the Queen in her chambers. Ostensibly, we will be discussing Essex and his faction, specifically their whereabouts. This matter troubles the Queen greatly."

"We saw the Queen's soldiers headed toward Hampstead," Bonnie said. "Warbeck told us Southampton and Essex will be hiding out from the soldiers. But even if the two are caught, they know from history she will be lenient on him this time. The worst they'll draw is house arrest."

Bacon did not look toward Bonnie but simply stared at his parquet floor and nodded. "Essex has the advantage of foresight, which makes up for his mental unsteadiness. The Queen, I'm afraid, will be too lenient. That is why I must employ falsehood to achieve a good deed. I plan to have the Queen's private astrologer, Doctor John Dee, meet me at London Bridge. He will accompany me by waterferry to Greenwich. In the course of the dinner, he will tell the Queen that the position of the planets and the stars proclaim ill fortune for Her Majesty if she leaves the palace. He will urge her to maintain her court at Greenwich until next week. The Queen trusts Dee. As a young heir apparent, the Queen was advised by him on the date of her coronation and sundry other events. Doctor Dee knows nothing of the greater peril, only that I will pay him well to read the heavens to the Queen's disadvantage. This ploy is our best hope."

"Did you arrange the dinner?" Benchley asked.

"The Queen ordered it," Bacon said, sitting back down. He then repositioned his chair toward the strengthening fire, lifting his feet up to get the most of the ensuing heat. "A herald arrived for me this morning with a letter bearing her seal. In so many formal phrases, she tells me in her letter that I am being brought in for consultation on what support Essex has among certain of the nobility in the North and the Midlands. Being a Parliamentarian, and a former follower of Essex, she values my knowledge of those who grow restless at her refusal to name a successor. Sadly, I cannot simply come out and say what a robust threat Essex is to her very throne. She won't see him that way as yet. The woman, the Queen that is, seems to have a capacity to see positive traits in the Lord Deputy that most of his peers see not."

"Does the Queen love Essex?" Bonnie asked.

Again, Bacon looked perturbed at Bonnie. This time he at least maintained eye contact with her. "One does not speak of such trivialities as love when dealing with monarchs," Bacon said to her in a chilly, disdainful tone. "Great personages, ancient and recent, are not transported to the mad degree of love, which shows that great spirits tending to great business keep out this weak passion."

"What about Marc Anthony?" Bonnie asked. "He held the Eastern Half of the Roman Empire in his hands but that didn't stop him from loving Cleopatra, did it?"

Bacon's unlined brow wrinkled up. He sighed, rubbed the tip of his goatee, then met Bonnie's challenge in a condescending tone.

"A woman is always prone to overestimate how greatly love and feminine wiles can affect the course of history. Wisdom, not the passion called love, is what is needed to attend to the great enterprises that buttress the pillars of government and business. Women are not suited for these undertakings because of their preoccupation with romantic and courtly love. It is said that it is impossible to love and to be wise."

"Is not your sovereign a woman?" Bonnie retorted, obviously a little perturbed herself. "And has she not lasted on the throne of a kingdom that has known great civil unrest in the reigns of her predecessors? And has she kept the peace in England without spilling copious amounts of her subjects' blood? Do you deny this woman intelligence? Do you deny her good judgement? Boldness? Determination of purpose without resort to fanaticism? Forty years surrounded by men grasping and jockeying for power and Elizabeth has held onto power while the male monarchs before her frittered away or grossly abused that power. You think because a woman might love she cannot utilize all her abilities? You counsel the Queen, one of the great monarchs in history, and yet you cannot appreciate her abilities?"

Bacon rubbed his forehead like he was having a migraine, then exhaled.

"The Queen is an exception," Bacon said after a few seconds. "She herself has overcome the weaknesses of a feminine nature to become a worthy prince, but she would be an even greater prince were she a King. Was Cleopatra the better sovereign for her love of Marcus Antonius, or did that love destroy both of their judgements to the injury of their powers of statecraft? The same threat hovers over the Queen because, in spite of her cunning and keen intelligence, she is nonetheless a woman and, ergo, susceptible to flattery by young fair-faced courtiers with sinewy limbs who profess to admire her beauty. Essex has charmed her in the throne room and her Private Chambers, and her feminine vanity renders her blind to his egregious faults and bouts of lunacy."

"Uh huh," Bonnie said, sounding unconvinced. "But Elizabeth had Essex sent to the Tower and beheaded after his rebellion. She wasn't blind to his ambitions even if she did once love him."

"But the Queen saw the rebellion coming in late 1600," Bacon said. "This is the Year of Our Lord 1599 and Essex has not yet used up her favors towards him. Essex is most excellent in flattery. He plays the courtier well. Besides being handsome, he is bold and treats Her Majesty in the familiar manner that must remind her of her closest male friend, Robert Dudley."

"The Earl of Leister," Benchley said. "The Queen's Master of the Horse and Essex's step-father."

"Alas, Dudley is dead these dozen years past," Bacon replied. "The Queen wants to see Lord Dudley in this step-son, and so recover her youth in the mirror of his eyes. A male prince would not have tolerated the fits of pique Essex has displayed in his debates with the other men of the Privy Council. He has put the Queen's councillors to bitter division. He detests Walter Raleigh and his followers and is ever testing the power of the Principal Secretary, Robert Cecil. In the latter case, he has a measure of my sympathy since Cecil's father, the late Lord Burghley, did little for me at court despite my obvious qualifications. As to Essex, he possesses a most unnatural choler. It has undone much of the good his military acumen has done in taking fire and sword to the Spanish in the Azores and at Cadiz. God knows I tried to steer my young former patron to a course less rash and, ultimately, fatal to his person and his co-horts. I have done so with vigor, that vigor increased when you came and told me of events yet to unfold. Alas, all for nought. You remember, Benchley, the event I spoke of last year?"

"When he almost pulled his sword on the Queen?" the old man replied.

"Indeed," Bacon replied. "It was during a meeting of the Privy Council. He fell into an argument and so lost possession of his wits that he actually turned his back on Her Majesty. And when she rebuked him, the scoundrel laid a hand to the hilt of his sword whilst standing in front of her. Saner men restrained him, thank God. For that offense alone, a male prince would have sent Essex to the Tower then and there. Instead, the Queen forgives him in quick time and grants him his fondest wish: to be proclaimed Lord Deputy and sent to Ireland. The templars at Grey's still talk of the day he rode out of London with his thousands of mustered troops and horses, marching through Cheapside to the acclaim of the London multitudes. I saw him pass myself whilst I was enclosed in a throng. The crowd exuded jubilation, as befitting a Coronation. I remember the wild cheering, the rush to touch his cloak or his hand, the starry-eyed women showering flowers on him from every high window. He became to Londoners what Alcibiades was to the Athenians and Scipio Africanus to the Romans. Songs were written for him. He was celebrated in the playhouses. Even our mutual friend, Shakespeare did not resist pandering to the public mood in his play about Henry the Fifth."

Benchley nodded, then spoke in graceful, theatrical tones.

"'Were now the General of our gracious Empress, as in good time he may, from Ireland coming, bring rebellion broached on his sword.'"

"Robert Deuvereux is no Henry of Monmouth," Bacon said, "save in his own mind, and in the mind of the common people, at least that portion of the herd who have not yet heard of the debacle in Ireland. There is also a collection of impressionable peers like Southampton who have grasped Fortune's Wheel at the same station as Essex."

My back was starting to bother me. I stood up, excused myself, and after walking toward the window, reached down and touched my toes with my finger tips while keeping my legs straight. It eased the pain, but, from his squint and furrowed brow, made me appear strange to our host. Small pill-sized clumps of hail started hitting the diamond-shaped window panes.

"Tyrone and the Irish kerns gave him a pasting," Bacon said, losing interest in my calisthenics. "By concluding a worthless truce with Tyrone, Essex has left the backdoor to Her Majesty's kingdom open to invasion from the bogs of that troublesome island. Alas, Ireland always seems to be the graveyard of English reputations. In your own century, of course, these 'troubles', as they are called, still —"

I spoke up: "What if you can't convince the Queen to stay away from Grantum Hall? Have you gentlemen thought up a backup plan?"

Bacon cocked his head in my direction. He gave me a look of reproach (I suppose for interrupting him) then let out another of those long sighs. "If Doctor Dee cannot convince her," Bacon said, "there is a second phase to the plan. This was planned by Benchley and me with the assistance of Master Shakespeare when the three of us met in this room a few months ago. According to history, Essex and his party plan to utilize the Lord Chamberlain's Men to perform one of the older plays in their repertoire. The play is *The Tragedy of Richard II*. Essex himself has a fondness for the play, because it contains a deposition sequence where the rightful king is imprisoned and forced to surrender his throne to a cousin. He hopes to stage the play to rally the apprentices, yeoman, and gentlemen who attend these little follies on the Bankside. It will serve as a propaganda for his plans and a signal to the disgruntled that a rebellion is at hand."

"Has anyone from Essex's group asked Shakespeare's company to stage the play?" Benchley asked.

Bacon nodded. "That play is set for performance on the afternoon before the wedding at Grantum Hall. A man named Sir Gilley Merrick, representing Essex, has requested the play and paid the company forty schillings to forge the bargain. This is all the more reason to believe Essex will stage the *coup de tat* the following night at Grantum Hall sometime during the wedding festivities. As it happens, Shakespeare's company has a long-standing commitment with the real Earl of Grantum to perform a play featuring Sir John Falstaff at the wedding. The character of Falstaff is a particular favorite of the Queen, and for the false Grantum to cancel the company's performance would arouse suspicion and risk the Queen's ire."

"So, what's the plan?" I asked.

For the first time, Bacon smiled. It was a cold smile, like a dead fish on display at a seafood market.

"Mr. Shakespeare wrote a new prologue to the King Richard play a year ago. The players have been secretly rehearsing it, along with the original work. The man who served as Essex's agent requires that the deposition scene in the play, previously banned by the Master of the Revels, be presented especially for the special performance. To undertake the deposition scene is in itself enough to jeopardize the legal status of the Lord Chamberlain's Players, but as mere players the troupe can hardly refuse the requests of a gentleman representing the Lord Deputy. Hence the need for a prologue to counterbalance the offending depiction. The prologue will extol the virtues of Queen Elizabeth, and come out with great vigor against the depositions of lawful sovereigns, even more so than in the final scene of the play where Henry of

Bolingbroke banishes the assassins of Richard from England. It will serve as a signal to Essex's forces that their plans have been detected and the Queen is prepared. Even if I cannot shake her of her attachment to this deranged nobleman, the prologue will make it appear so to his followers. But even this contingency plan will be futile if reports of these modern weapons Warbeck has given Essex are true. What do you estimate is the peril of the armaments at their disposal?"

Benchley stopped rubbing his hand, then sat back and took a deep breath before speaking. "Warbeck has Russian-made AK-47 assault rifles. I also saw various makes of AR-15's. We're talking about automatic weapons, capable of firing accurately at roughly one third of a mile. They also have grenade launchers. Since Warbeck only has access to two of the STUMPs, his firepower is relatively limited—for now. Still, these weapons could mow down anything the Queen's forces could put up against them if they have enough men who could use them. Since assault weapons of my time are easier to load and fire than a matchlock, I don't think training willing soldiers to use the rifles will be a major problem. The grenade launchers are light and maneuverable, unlike the heavy cannon that the Queen's forces could muster from the Tower. We can't have Essex and his forces break out from Hampstead and get into London. The only chance we have is to mobilize as much of the native forces as we can around Grantum Hall and lay siege to the manor with heavy cannon. That will neutralize the maneuverability of the advanced weaponry. Bottle Essex and Warbeck up, and the Queen's forces might have a chance if they came in overwhelming strength. Otherwise, this island, in time, will be enslaved."

"I must convince the Queen this evening," Bacon said, stroking his perfectly-trimmed beard. "Hopefully my years of training in the law will not fail me."

I noticed Benchley's left hand was starting to tremble. He looked to be gasping for air, then began to stand up, then sat back down.

"What's wrong, Mr. Benchley?" Bonnie asked.

"It's nothing," Benchley said defensively. "Just my damn asthma kicking in. It always gets worse in this wet climate."

It looked to me, from the paleness of his face, like something worse than 'nothing.' I could see from the concern on

Bonnie's face that she was aware her former boss was understating his condition. I could see his breathing was labored.

"Perhaps we could rent a coach," Benchley said between gasps for breath. "I don't know if I could mount a horse right now." He gasped for breath. "What do you think, Francis? Does a coach still draw outlaws in these environs?"

"Alas, Middlesex is peppered with outlaws," Bacon sighed. "I was relieved of my purse at a narrow pathway near Gad's Hill a few months ago. I was returning from the Court of Wards in Westminster on my horse when I was set upon. The fellow had a loaded musket with the wick alit and only a thumb's length above the powder pan. Had he been armed simply with a sword..."

"There was nothing you could do but give the guy your wallet or purse," I said in a a practiced way I always talked to crime victims back home. "You can replace money, but you can't replace your life."

"I was not afraid for my life," Bacon said in an aloof tone. "Thanks to Benchley, I knew in advance that I am due to live into my seventh decade. I hope to stretch that mark. I have read many biographies of myself, thanks to Benchley, but none told me of this ambush in advance. Had my biographers done a more thorough job, I would have avoided Gad's Hill the way I hope to avoid the mistakes and penalties of my latter years stemming from my...my misjudgements in the post of Lord Chancellor. I have chosen to know all I can about my future career, as well as the centuries my natural life span will miss, in order to improve my philosophy, health and powers of statecraft."

"By the way," Benchley said, still wheezing. "How did the chemical fertilizer I bought you last year do on your roses?"

"Quite well," Bacon replied. "You must see my garden, or rather the garden I designed for my fellow templars at Grey's. I have added an aviary to it this year."

"I would love to," Benchley said. "But do we have time? I want to be sure and reach The Globe this afternoon. We must alert Shakespeare..." He paused to take a breath, his frail torso shaking as he struggled to take in oxygen. "...to these new developments. Otherwise, the Lord Chamberlains's Men..." He stopped talking again and braced himself on the table.

"Then we will suspend the tour of the garden for now," Bacon said, with concern in his voice. "How long do you plan to be of this time?"

"Only until the day after tomorrow," Benchley said, between gasps. "Major Trubshawe will return to pick us up at a designated area in Middlesex Forest. By then, Shakespeare will be warned and, with your efforts, the Queen will have cancelled her appearance at the wedding." Benchley started gasping for breath again. Bonnie started to get up from her chair across the table to help him. Benchley motioned for her to resume her seat.

"It will pass," he said weakly to her, then turned to Bacon. "Tell me, Francis, there is some threat from Spain looming, is there not? I believe Spain has yet another Armada moving up the English Channel prepared to take advantage of the Irish situation across the channel."

"Yes," Bacon said. "Philip the Third has assembled a fleet for an invasion. It is a pale force compared to the great Armada that menaced our island ten and one years ago. Knowing the future as I do, I know the threat will meet with no success. The Spanish will have enough on their hands this season dealing with the Dutch fleet, who are poised to raid the Canaries and thus draw the Armada from the Channel. Nevertheless, our Lord Admiral Thomas Howard and Essex's arch enemy at court, Sir Walter Raleigh, have assembled ships and mustered soldiers about Plymouth and other coastal points. I could spare them the trouble, but I follow the course you have set for not interfering in the events of the future despite foreknowledge."

"Troops mustered at the coast..." Benchley said. He shook his head. "It would be better to have some here handy about London when Essex makes his move."

"There are some companies of recently mustered men drilling at Mile-End Green just outside the city gates," Bacon added. "I trust the Queen is savvy enough to leave them in place until she has Essex in her power. But against 20th Century weapons, those green troops will be so many pins bowled over."

Benchley started coughing.

"Benchley, would you like some madeira?" Bacon asked. "You look most pale."

"No, thank you," Benchley said.

Bacon asked the other two guests if we wanted madeira. It was probably alcohol, I reasoned, so I declined. Bonnie did, too.

"Well, I shall abide with a clear conscience then," our host said. He got up from the high-back chair he was sitting in and moved to a large, bulky bureau-like piece of furniture with elaborate carvings on the framework and the drawers. From the top of the bureau he lifted up a section of the countertop and produced a glass decanter with an 's'-shaped stem and broad oval-shaped base. He also brought up from the compartment a long-stemmed glass goblet, then poured himself an amber-colored drink.

It was after I watched the libation being poured, then put to our host's lips, that I noticed Benchley's struggles becoming worse. He had a hand to his upper chest. His shortness of breath had now exacerbated into a struggle for air. Clearly, it was a full-blown asthma attack.

Between myself, Bonnie and Bacon we managed to keep Benchley upright on a cushioned settee at the far end of the room. I went upstairs, retrieved the first-aid kit, and brought it to Bonnie. While I held Benchley upright, she got him to put his lips over the mouthpiece of an atomizer with a bronchial medication. After a couple puffs of the medication, he seemed to have less trouble breathing, but his inhalations sounded like a donkey braying. We set the old man back on the settee, propping his upper body up against the armrest with some pillows Bacon provided.

"I can't give him any more epinephrine right now, or he'll get sick," Bonnie said. She felt Benchley's forehead. "He probably hasn't been getting the tablets he takes to keep these attacks from coming. I think he'll be all right, given time and some steady doses of medicine."

"My servants know nothing of the medications of the future," Bacon said. "I told Geoffrey not to disturb us. Will he be well enough to travel to Southwark?"

"He's not going anywhere for a couple hours," Bonnie said. "I wish we had a vaporizer."

Benchley tried to speak, then indicated that he wanted to write something. Bacon went to a small desk and returned with a writing tablet, a sheet of paper, and a quill.

"I'll need to go upstairs to my study for an inkwell," he told Bonnie.

"Not necessary," Bonnie said. She reached into the first-aid kit and took out a ball-point pen.

The note Benchley wrote out read as follows:

"Leave me here. Go to the Globe. Warn Shakespeare."

After Bonnie and I had read it, we passed it to Bacon. He nodded, then tore the paper up and placed it in an oval dish on the table. He took a red-tipped match from his pocket, stuck it on the wood to light it, then held the lit end over the torn papers until they were alight.

"Why did you do that?" I asked.

"Why do I burn writing from a ball-point pen?" Bacon said after a sardonic snicker. "Perhaps it is because I do not wish to be hanged as a warlock. There are no self-inking writing devices in this time. Why, just to possess this friction match to start a fire would be enough for men to speak of me as some kind of Faustus in league with Mephistopheles. I only carry one of your convenient matches at a time from the supply Benchley here has given me. I would love to have an electric generator so I could process electric lamplight and heaters and have a machine to watch images on tape or what you call laserdiscs. Benchley has shown me many of his films over the years, but only when I have followed him in to the future. I dare not risk trying to explain a device like a television—something men of your time take for granted—to the authorities."

In a few minutes Benchley had recovered his voice. He reiterated the desire to get to Shakespeare and warn him. Bonnie offered to stay behind and nurse him.

"Young lady, I've had more asthma attacks than you've had hot dinners," he said before drawing the deepest breath he could manage. "William needs to be warned. Bacon, will you escort my friends through London and get them to Southwark?"

I was about to see the London of 1599—the one tourists hardly ever get to see anymore.

Chapter Forty-Three

Even if I was blind I would have known we were closing in on London from the stench that wafted into my nostrils. I first noticed the rancid smells as the three of us rode toward a knoll that, besides the wide and heavily traveled dirt road that bisected it, was dotted with slender willow trees set amid patches of brown grassland. It was a foul odor the strength of which I had never experienced before, even as a policemen coming across the occasional human corpse or, in one case, a woman who had befriended dozens of cats and was trying to keep them all in her one-bedroom house that was short of kitty litter. (The scent was noxious enough to arouse her neighbors. One whiff at the front screendoor of the woman's house was enough for me. I cited the woman and turned the case over to the Animal Control Department.)

Both Bacon and Bonnie were riding mature palomino horses. I was coping with a mule a few lengths behind them.

Once at the crest of the knoll, we were within a hundred yards of so or a low-lying wooden bridge spanning a steep-banked creek of water. Bacon, riding between us, identified the landmark for us.

"The Fleet Ditch," he said as Bonnie put a handkerchief over her nose. "We are in the environs of London now. Distressful scents await; here is but a commencement."

As we crossed over the bridge, jostling our animals between other equestrians with elegant leather satchels behind their saddles or stoop-shouldered pedestrians bearing up with heavy burdens (usually bundles of wood or bulging sacks coated with streaks of flour) I got a look over the railings at what was causing the stench. The waterway was choked with filth, the outstanding feature of which were the corpses of dead and decaying animals—horses, dogs, and pigs— floating in the stagnant stream. Despite the wretched sanitation, I actually saw some young boys swimming along a flat ridge of shoreline.

The city itself opened up to us as we passed under a high horseshoe-shaped arch with heavy blocks of stonework supporting the span. So far the mule and myself were getting along fairly well. I had sharply swatted the animal's rump with a crop a couple times when he started to lag behind the horses of my companions, but the mule was a better ride than Jennifer the pony. Bonnie had given me the mule to ride because it had, unlike a horse, peripheral vision, and I at least had a modicum of experience with such a creature from my past trip down the Grand Canyon. As we rode into the city, the ground changed to a cobblestoned street. The street was in need of repair: several times the hooves of our animals stepped down into a pothole, either of dry ground or filled with brackish liquid. Men pulling wheelbarrows, women pulling small carts or lugging burdens balanced on poles set across their shoulders, roaming packs of mangy-coated dogs, and wagons pulled by oxen were all moving obstacles to get about going into the city. The houses inside the high stone walls were mainly brick or timber affairs with red-tile roofs or, in some cases, thatches of straw supported by unfinished beams which protruded from the ledges of the houses.

A man I took to be some sort of criminal, naked from the waist up, was being led through the street at the end of a tumbril-style wooden cart. Two lengths of rope were attached from the wooden ribs of the cart to the wrists of the prisoner. One redcoated under-sheriff or constable sat in the cart, spurring on a large hairy draft horse. Another officer walked quickly behind the captive, spurring his pace by laying a short whip to his naked back, a back already pocked with welts from previous blows. The officer with the whip walloped the man with his instrument twice within our sight, drawing a piteous whelp from his charge. The man in front of the cart was going at a pace that was rather hard for the fellow tied to the back end to maintain. At one point the prisoner lost his footing in a pile of horse dung and then got dragged through the streets to the amusement of the stationary and scampering onlookers.

"And I thought people in our time were cruel," Bonnie said to me.

We next passed a line of folk outside a shack where a man in a dirty apron was selling freshly plucked chickens. The fowl on display were either hanging upside down from a horizontal pole over the counter or getting the rotisserie treatment on a revolving, hand-cranked spit operated by a woman behind the man collecting coins for the birds. The shack had a brick chimney, at the apex of the sharply angled peek of the roof, where the smoke escaped.

As we passed a row of crude wooden booths (that made up some type of shopping arcade—two or three men in aprons trotted alongside holding up clothing and, in one case, a large pie. "What do you lack? What do you lack, good sir?" one man, without any wares on his person, called out. Bacon did not answer him. At one point the salesman touched Bacon on one of his knees, and instantly received a shot with the crop that the lawyer was carrying in his right hand.

"You are too bold, yeoman," Bacon said. "Peddle your foul spirits and fouler doxies elsewhere." I found out later that doxies was slang term for whores. And the demimonde was well represented in the broad daylight of London. Whenever we passed what looked like a tavern there would be a covey of women wearing tight bodices that just barely covered the tops of the nipples and skirts without the farthingale, usually just a chemise sticking out from the openings of their dresses, obviously with little or nothing to get in a male customer's way for a back-alley quickie. In between the sordid spots were structures housing wares for those disinterested in vice. The wooden signs jutting out over the doors— "Symthe Shoemakers," "Thom. Middleton—Glovemaker," "Harris and Sons, Gunsmiths" and "Newgate Milliners"—had to compete for attention from dirty-faced men selling everything from harnesses and tack to small-time grocers hawking cabbages and apples, much of which looked well past their prime.

Tucked away on the edge of one side street was a small stage, fringed with curtains, where young women and small children were gathered about watching a Punch-and-Judy type show. I asked Bacon, this being a weekday, why so many kids were out of school. He held up his horse. I could take advantage of a gap in the traffic for myself and the mule to get alongside, then he answered my question without fear of eves-droppers.

"There are no state-sponsored schools for ordinary children," he said. "The children of skilled craftsmen and petty officials can usually afford at least a grammar school education for their spawn. The rest are home-taught the basics of common knowledge until they are apprenticed into a trade about the age of eleven or twelve."

"In other words, as soon as a boy's voice cracks, he goes to work?" Bonnie, on the other side of Bacon and his palomino, asked in a tone of incredulity.

Bacon nodded.

Suddenly all those hours I spent in the detention center at Prospect High School back in San Jose did not seem so bad.

"What about young girls?" Bonnie asked. "What can they become in your society?"

"Wives," Bacon replied, as we rode along together. "Granted, some are educated at home, enough to write or read a bit. Of course, ladies of the nobility can often speak Latin or French as well as their native tongue. The Queen can speak every language in Europe, save that of the princes of Muscovy. The only reason to educate a woman is to make her mentally fit to stimulate her husband in matters of the mind."

"But I see women working everywhere around here," Bonnie said. "They're not just keeping house."

Bacon chuckled. "The common folk, you mean. That stock will see no school, male or female. Most of these drabs you see on the street are serving wenches, laundresses, knitters, nursemaids, domestics. And the more brazen drabs you see loitering the streets are wanton daughters of Cressida. To be blunt, they are pox-infested whores, or punks, or harlots, doxies, saucy minions, Westminster geese. There are no end of terms for these bitches who serve the baser needs of men."

"Is anything done to get these hookers off the streets?" I asked. "Is there some form of rehabilitation."

"There are Poor Laws," Bacon said. "A parish will help a widow if she loses her mate. But this society around you is not like yours; we do not waste money trying to root out all means in inequality. Some must suffer; that is their fate."

"Is it a women's fate to be a prostitute all of her life because no one will educate her?" Bonnie asked, with an icy edge to her voice.

Bacon guffawed. "Ah, yes, the education of women. One of the festering ills of that which you call democracy. I do not expect you to understand the proper order of a body politic. You come from a civilization that lets the unruly stock of humanity control the fate of the nation. Rule derived from the common herd did not work for the Athenians against Philip of Macedonia. Republicanism failed in Rome even before the rise of Ceasar and Pompey. Democracy alters laws and customs, promotes the advancement of unworthy persons, promotes idleness, nay, rewards it, and steers the weaker vessels of humanity from their natural duties."

"And what, pray tell sir, is a woman's natural duties," Bonnie asked. I could see she was ticked off.

Bacon shook his head. "Methought you would at least know the natural female duties, milady. They are but four: birthing, nurturing the household, comforting the man with their soft natures, and taking care of their husbands and widowed fathers when they grow old. What else could their duties be?"

Bacon's horse made a huffing sound and Bonnie imitated it. "But, Mr. Bacon, with all due respect, a woman can do—-." She was interrupted by the sudden appearance of two boys who came rushing pell-mell from a narrow alleyway, chasing after a leather ball. I jerked back on the reins to draw my mule up from his trot. One boy stopped the ball right in front of my animal's forelegs. There followed a half-a-dozen more boys dressed in simple knee-length bluecoats with some sort of insignia on the sleeves. They piled on one another, fist flying, and legs dangling and kicking. My mule did not find this close-up horseplay enjoyable and backed up a few steps, then reared up and tossed me off the saddle and onto the muddy street. I landed sideways in the wet mud, not hurt, other than a scuffed elbow, but covered and getting some more shooting pains to my lower back.

The game the young men played was some type of football. The object, which I calculated from the prone position I found myself in, was to possess a round leather ball. On closer examination, it appeared there were two sets of teams, judging by the different insignias on their sleeves. One boy, sporting a black eye, emerged from the pile of wiggling, flailing bodies and limbs and dashed pell-mell down the street we were progressing on. He was pushed by another lad into a passing human-powered rickshaw-like cart loaded with apples and pears. Then followed the spillage of a considerable portion of the produce into the street. The burly man operating the cart added a new dimension to the game by whacking away at a couple of the players with the business end of a wooden club. Shouts and howls filled the air until one boy managed to take hold of the ball and dash down the street. All the other boys ran after the lead fellow, either to try and bring him down or to avoid the fruit-peddler's club. They dashed away and the man went back to salvage his produce. As he unrighted his cart, the peddler took sight of us. "Did you see what those vile apprentices did?" he called out to Bacon. "There are some shoemakers in Newgate who will see me a new crop of fruit or I will make it a matter for the Under-Sheriff."

"Good for you, sir," Bacon remarked.

I got up slowly, then determined that I still had a functioning body. After Bonnie helped me brush off, I remounted the skittish beast and we continued along.

I could see why Benchley and Trubshawe had risked giving themselves away to the native authorities by clandestinely photographing the streets. This was London, but, nothing like the modern city. It was like a Renaissance Fair run amok, or a great movie set with the budget going into the stratosphere instead of the lead actors' pockets. But there was a smell, rather a variety of odors mixed together, about the streets that undid any illusion that this was a film set. Dung, human and animal, was the prevailing odor. The physical fact of excrement was everywhere, from horsedroppings lining the road to heaps of dung mixed with straw that were set in buckets outside houses. Of course, there was also the nauseating, acidic taint of urine in the air. Horses seemed to be the main culprits, but there were also men casually pissing in alleyways and women in sweat-stained bonnets throwing yellowish liquids from doorways into the empty portions of the streets.

"What a God awful stench," Bonnie said, bringing out her handkerchief. "What happens to all the waste?" she asked

Bacon. It was so bad I covered my nose, with one hand, to lessen the stinging effect of the stench on my nasal passages.

Bacon, who seemed unperturbed by the aromas, answered her. "Some of it is picked up by the nightsoil crews that are paid by innkeepers and householders to remove that which emits from the bowels. The rest, such as urine, will wash down the street in the next good rain and become mixed with the pools you can see at low-lying parts of the city."

"What do the, ah, solid waste people do once they collect the stuff?" I asked.

"Fertilizers, of course," Bacon said casually. "Or the muck is thrown directly into the Thames to flow into the Channel and furnish the French a measure of our affection for them. I did an experiment recently to see how much heat can be retained if dung is buried into the earth for a period of time. I used a thermometer that Benchley brought me. An amazing instrument. I cannot share the implement with my colleagues, of course, but it makes my calculations more exact. It's truly amazing how much heat can be retained in organic waste by prompt burial. I originally did the experiment in the future as part of my *Novum Organum*. I have attempted to disengage science from the stagnation of reliance on Aristotle and Pliny. I've already read all the scientific works I will publish in the future. I no longer need to write them because of Benchley. Now I can devote myself more to matters of policy."

"So," I said, trying to make polite conversation, "you're sort of into science, the law, politics, gardening and, uh, you wrote some essays, right?"

Bacon shot me a withering glance, looking down his long nose on me like I had called his mother a rhino. "Did I write some essays, Wells? You sound if you have doubt on the matter. Surely in your period of education you were exposed to my collections of essays, my maxims on the common law, my *Advancement of Learning*?"

"Oh sure," I said, hoping that would make an end to the topic. A man dressed in a loose-fitting brown jerkin (the material of which resembled burlap) and billowy breeches was blocking the flow of traffic. He was trying to drive a herd of fattened pigs across the road. A man in a horse and cart was stopped on the other side of the road, blocked by the pig parade. The cart was loaded with a pyramid of stacked barrels with a rope pulled over the highest barrel and tied to both sides of the cart. Apparently, the men knew each other. They struck up a conversation, the man on the ground swatting his pigs on the rump if they strayed out of line. They called each other 'whoreson rascals' and seemed quite glad to be meeting. The herd of swine, now left to their own devices, began to break ranks and root around in the mud for food and pigs of the opposite sex. A good deal of grunting and squealing was going on and we were at an impasse.

Bacon watched the spectacle, looked perturbed.

"Recite something I wrote," Bacon said to me. "You needn't try to speak it in Latin. I know the deplorable state that great language has fallen into. Just give a few phrases in English. Benchley told me that in his day he had to recite great portions of noble works, ancient and modern, to receive a degree."

I couldn't think of anything right off, other than the fact that I had read some of the essays a good while ago.

"Well," Bacon said, his hands crossed and his eyes focused on the men blocking our way.

"'Too much study is sloth,'" I said, finally remembering one fragment. "'And something about chewing on books.'"

Bacon sighed. "And I suspect that is the sum of your recollections."

I confirmed his suspicion.

"In your case, I'm sure you were not a victim of any maladies caused by too much study," Bacon said, then barked at the men in front of us.

"Spartan dogs!" he shouted. "Mean you to glog the road forever? Cease your discourse! Get these beasts off the road. If you have need of discourse, get thee to the taverns or the stews of lewd women and go over your sordid feats of the past. You interfere with one of the Queen's agents. I am Francis Bacon, Council Extraordinaire to Her Most Gracious Majesty."

One pork wrangler, a stout fellow with a broad red nose, bushy Elvis-style sideburns bordered with a few days worth of beard stubble, turned around to face us. He crossed his mud-splattered arms, spit on the ground in front of Bacon's horse, and issued a reply.

"Sir, I care not if you are Phillip of Spain, leading your pox-ridden army to be enthroned at Westminster Abbey. I am a free man, not a vassal. Take your train around us, silk-clad fop. With that he turned around, bent over, pulled down his breeches, and ripped out a long, audible fart.

We went around the pigs, our animals getting into the deep mud that was on the edges of the walkways near the shops.

"A taste of my rapier would have settled him," I heard Bacon grumbling to Bonnie as we got back on better footing after the detour. The expression on Bacon's face was red anger.

"It pains me to contain my wrath," Bacon said, "when my very sinews entreat me to lay physical force upon such men."

He didn't sound too convincing.

At one point there was a break in the line of houses on one side of the street, and a park came into view. A group of men in bright orange costumes and high-crowned, plumed hats were dancing about in some kind of jig, in the middle of the expanse of lawn which stretched out over several acres. A group of musicians formed a a semi-circle near them, playing on instruments similar to what Bonnie and I had seen back at the Turtledove Inn. Well-dressed folk caroused about in small groups while dogs chased little children (and vice versa) about the fringes of the gathering. A row of tables were set up near the line of elm trees in the back of the park, where food was being laid out by women in black dresses and plain white bonnets.

"What is this?" Bonnie asked Bacon.

"A marriage feast," Bacon said to her. We had stopped to let him survey the landscape. "The couple being betrothed are no doubt too young for matrimony but, hopefully, a good business arrangement has been made between the families. I particularly like this park. It is well-maintained. Too bad so many common folk are traversing it. There is nothing more pleasant to the eye than green grass kept finely shorn. Do you not agree, Wells?"

"Yes," I said, "especially if someone else has to mow it." My mule brushed his snout against his horse.

"Turn that unsteady creature!" Bacon barked at me. "Can you not control your beast?"

"I'm a lot better with a five speed Toyota," was my reply.

Bacon could be an annoying guy to be with, I could see

that. Yet, once we got started back down the street, and my mule was no longer making undue advances on his horse, he began talking in more temperate tones, pointing out the features and names of a couple stately churches we passed, one of which looked like a small castle with a multiangular tower and great arch-shaped windows along the sides of the basilica that was attached to it. In front of the basilica was a series of water pumps with women, men and some small boys lined up as in a supermarket, most carrying long poles over their shoulders with large buckets or oversized tankards. Seeing the water being feverishly pumped out made me thirsty.

"Feast your eyes," Bacon said a few blocks later, turning about in the saddle to address us. He pointed up over the sloping rooftops on one side of the street. I took notice of a great edifice that had to be at least two modern city blocks long. Pinnacles dotted the side of the building, elaborate crosses poked up from their peaks. The place was a great Gothic pile with rows of gables and two sets of massive arches stacked up toward a great peaked roof that made the buildings around it look insignificant. I could hear the rumble of a large crowd ahead of us. Judging by the brown sootiness of the exterior, most of the church had to have been standing for centuries.

This was St. Paul's Cathedral. From a distance, through binoculars, as I had first seen it with Trubshawe and Bonnie, it was imposing. Up close, it was overwhelming, big enough for a professional basketball arena in Chicago or Los Angeles. Had it really been a basketball arena, this would have been Game Seven of a playoff series, judging from the swarms of people that were milling about the place. Above the swarm of humanity were enormous stained-glass windows and graceful buttressing that held the eye on the grandeur of the facade. The churchyard, just in front of the wide entryway, was a chock-a-block with stalls, like a food arcade in a shopping mall. There was food on display, and also stalls set up similar to big-city newspaper stands with displays of small chalk-white publications that looked like magazines. The stalls were all about the same size, but the signs above the counters provided distinction: 'The Green Dragon' (a huge green sign shaped like a monstrous lizard, with some calligraphy under the painted, two-dimensional beast), another stall, surrounded by ladies was named 'Cytherea's Closet"; another

'Absalom's Nook'. Crowds of people, from very well-dressed ladies in great hoop skirts and men in multi-layered ruffs with gleaming doublets and capes mingled with people who looked like they were down to their last ragged set of clothes. The stalls swarmed with perusers, all under the watchful eyes of the proprietors, mostly bearded men who perched themselves on high stools (perhaps the best position for stopping shoplifters).

"Bit of a crowd," Bacon said, alighting from his horse. "Wells, could you hold my mount? I wish to peruse the stalls for a copy of Virgil's *Pastoral Poems*. I shan't be long, then we will resume the journey."

Bonnie stayed mounted. I held Bacon's horse and my mule. There was a large trough of water a few yards away. Some horses were drinking from it already so I led the two animals to it for some refreshment. Near the trough, lined up in front of a long-handled water pump, were a group of women and men in shabby, well-worn clothes. The latter were "cobs," according to Bonnie: men who were hired to bring water to private homes.

Around me were the sort of people a modern person would find trying to draw attention to themselves in a place like San Francisco's Fisherman's Wharf. There was a fellow dressed in a color-clashing outfit befitting a clown who was juggling things like bowling pins. He had a hat at his feet, partially filled with coins. There were people selling apples out of carts, men carrying sandwich-board signs about their necks, advertising themselves as servants. There was a woman who approached me with a lantern-shaped bucket in her hand.

"Spare something for the poor wretches at Spitalfield's Hospital, good yeoman?" It sounded like a good cause, so I gave her a coin from the portion Bonnie had given me before we left for town. I had no idea how much I had given her, but she gave me a little curtsy before she left to hawk up the next sponsor.

There came a procession of about two dozen mounted soldiers coming our way, headed southwards on the street that ran perpendicular to the one we were on. They looked very much like the soldiers we saw headed up toward Hampstead that morning, but something was different about them. Some of them had tattered, dirty tunics and there were no banners flying. The horses had elaborately embroidered tack and long, tassel-fringed blankets under the saddles that almost touched the ground. Other people noticed the procession and began to point it out to others who had their noses in one of the books on display or were picking through a small hill of apples or pears for a ripe choice.

"Oh, shit," Bonnie said in the way that I learned meant trouble. She pointed out one of the horsemen: the Earl of Southampton. He was riding one of the horses, his chin propped upward, his gaze straight ahead. He was dressed in a black cape, and was wearing the same boots and hose that he wore back at the bridge in front of Grantum Hall. Unlike what Warbeck had said, Essex and Southampton were not hiding out in some local forest like Robin Hood's clique. Instead, there were here right in the middle of London in the busiest area I had seen so far.

Essex was riding a couple lengths behind Southampton, well insulated from the crowd by a group of mounted minions that rode near him like a mounted version of the Swiss Guard. Some in the crowd cheered, calling out Essex's name. He acknowledged them with a brief wave.

"Essex! Essex! The Lord Deputy is back!" shouted a thin young man with a pasty-white face and deep pock marks around his jawline. The crowd surged around me, one boy even trying to balance himself on the edge of the trough and hold onto the side of my mule to steady himself. I was taller than most of those around me (a new experience in my case) so I could still see the red-bearded wonder-boy as he rode up the same street we had just been down. It was Essex, all right, dressed in a snazzy silk outfit with broad epaulettes and wearing a hat festooned with six or seven ostrich feathers. He reined up his horse (the horsemen about him following his lead) and acknowledged the cheering crowd with a politician-sized smile and a wave.

And then his smile changed suddenly to a scowl.

"Foul toad of a man!" Essex shouted out at the top of his lungs. "I have sought you and now I have you. Hold your place, Francis Bacon. We have a quarrel to settle." In a flash, he was off his horse, diving into the pressing crowd. He ignored the back-patters and well-wishers, plunging toward the stalls where I had last seen Bacon. Essex drew his rapier.

I heard the sound of steel against steel, then a collective buzz from the crowd as the hot-blooded man disappeared into the throng.

“Oh, shit,” Bonnie repeated.

This did not look good.

Chapter Forty-Four

By the time I tugged and pushed my way through the crowd, Bacon and Essex were going at it. Or, rather, Essex was going at Bacon and the latter was falling back, his own weapon still undrawn. The crowd about the churchyard seemed to be enjoying the spectacle. The soldiers tried to break through the cordon of spectators by riding into the crowd. The horses reared up and down and clubs were swung by the soldiers in an attempt to get at the struggle in the middle of the circle. But there were too many layers of people to disperse without causing a panic and this is what quickly became of the crowd-control efforts. I grabbed hold of Bonnie as people surged forward between us. People fell forward about us as the horses came forward. Snorting horses reared up, swords swung about, men in helmets barked commands, men on the ground raised wooden clubs with thick knobs on the end to ward off the slashing strokes of steel. General panic, with the screams and wild flailing that becomes a great number of imperiled people in an enclosed space. Our only recourse was to try and stay in front of the crowd. I pulled and pushed myself and my companion forward into the vortex of the chaos, which gave us a close-up view of the predicament that Bacon now found himself in.

As Essex circled around his prey, I could see a fire in his eyes that reminded me of a guy doped up on methamphetamines. "Foul traitor!" he shouted at Bacon. "You seek to turn against me? I gave your brother a great estate. I am the man who lent you support to attain great office. What did I strive in your behalf for? To be rewarded with treachery?"

Bacon did not draw his sword. Instead of a defense he staggered backward, looking for an escape through the crowd. Sporadically he looked over my head, and the heads of the throng, hoping for salvation from somewhere. The rest of his attention he devoted to his attacker. Essex directed his blade in a fast, merciless, and skillful fashion. The blade of the rapier gave off quick silvery flashes in reflection from the sun overhead. Any other sword-play I had ever seen in a movie was slow-motion compared to Essex's parrying and thrusting.

I had two choices. I could stand there with a hangdog look on my kisser and watch Bacon get killed, or I could pop out my Baretta M92, undo the safety and pump a couple slugs into Essex. The former course would lose us a valuable ally, the latter course would get me torn limb from limb and/or hanged. I had an extra magazine to ward off capture, but I couldn't see myself getting off the shots, scooping up Bonnie and escaping by horse like some cartoon hero.

Bacon drew his sword. It took Essex less time to send it flying from the lawyer's hand then it took Bacon to draw it from his scabbard. It looked like little Frankie was going down.

Essex slashed open Bacon's doublet with a diagonal stroke that cut the smaller man's clothing from the left shoulder down toward the right hip. Bacon staggered backward, and fell into a section of the crowd peppered with dismounted soldiers from Essex's bodyguard. The civilians about watched in a jovial humor as the soldiers pushed Bacon up to his feet to continue the display, but he twisted his way out of their grasp and tried to duck into the crowd. One burly man regripped him under the arms, lifted him about, and thrust him into the impromptu ring. All Essex would have had to do was stick out his weapon and lance Bacon. Instead, he stepped aside and let Bacon fall to his feet. Bacon, wisely I thought, did not try and get up.

"Gain thy footing!" Essex said in a commanding tone. "We shall finish with this now." The Earl was still wild-eyed, his face florid, veins bulging on his neck and forehead. He looked the way he had when he and I traded jabs back in San Francisco. The exertions he had put into cornering Bacon had skewed the gold medallion about his neck to where it now dangled by its green sash down his back.

Bacon didn't move. Essex hovered over him, his rapier posed to strike.

"If it's a coward's death you want," Essex seethed, "then let it come to pass." He raised the hilt of the rapier over his head with both hands. Essex hesitated only a second, long enough for Southampton to pull himself through the crowd and lay restraining hands on him.

"My Lord Deputy," Southampton said, "waste not your honored blade on a timid worm."

Essex let himself be relieved of his sword by the younger man. Southampton put a gloved hand on the taller man's shoulders and led him out of the man-made circle.

There rose a mixture of booing and some scattered cheers now that the match was over—or seemingly over. Bacon now gained his footing and picked up the sword Essex had swatted from his hand. Aiming the business end of the cutlery at his receding foe, he lunged at his former tormentor. Essex had his back to him. Several in the crowd shouted a warning. The two Earls spun around but their movements were restricted by the throng around them. I had now jumped into the circle, hoping to reach Bacon before he rendered himself useless to our cause, but knowing I would be too late. Essex spun about, ready to skewer the smaller man. But before the men collided, a man came up and laid a tackle on Bacon worthy of a defensive lineman sacking a quarterback. He hit Bacon from the right side and the forward momentum of the blow hit me as I rushed to the spot. Bacon, the stranger, and myself wound up entangled together on the cobblestones.

The man who had the same idea I had was lying on top of me for several seconds. Then he got up, allowing me to recover my footing.

"Foul interlopers," Bacon cried out as he too managed to get to his feet. He made another lunge for Essex. The stranger once again grabbed Bacon. The other man was thirtyish, had a medium build, and wore a broad-brimmed dark-green felt hat (that went askew and fell off in the scuffle). His dress consisted of a pleated brown and tan doublet with a white peter-pan collar, a thin chestnut brown beard, a receded hairline revealing a broad, dome-like forehead, and a gold earring on the skinny lobe of one ear. Bacon tried to fight the larger man off, but the man had a bear-hug on him, a situation which drew laughs from the crowd as the smaller man struggled away. I took the opportunity to remove Bacon's sword from his hand, then the other man let Bacon loose.

Bacon turned around to confront the man who restrained him. It was then, with his hat off and his whole face revealed, that I recognized who this man was.

"What business is it for you to intercede in my affairs," Bacon said, his chest heaving from exertion.

"A spleen filled with choler ill serves a man," William Shakespeare said. "I reserve the right to intervene on behalf of any friend whose wits have flown from their master."

"A timely intercession, Master Shakespeare," came a familiar, high-pitched male voice from just behind me. I turned to find myself a few feet from Southampton. I turned about and stepped back, expecting trouble. But his eyes were only on Shakespeare, not myself.

I could see Shakespeare's large brown eyes dance with delight on seeing the young Earl a few feet in front of him. "It has been too long, Right Honorable Henry, since you have graced the nooks and shadows of this fair city. What I have taken for rumor I can now rejoice in as fact: you have come through the scourge of war with youthful sap still abundant on your fair cheeks. God be praised!"

Southampton came toward the playwright. There was an awkward moment, and then the two men quickly embraced, Southampton patting the older man on the shoulders as they physically parted. "Where do you go?" Shakespeare asked the younger man.

"To Greenwich," Southampton told his friend. "The Lord Deputy has been the victim of calumny from his allies. We are going forth to face the Queen and present the truth of the Irish matter."

Bonnie was next to me. I could tell from her rapt gaze that she, too, had recognized the fellow who tackled Bacon. The rest of the crowd, however, was focused on Essex, who, released from the grip of his escorts, now swaggered our way. Bacon had slipped into the crowd somehow, nowhere to be seen. Essex came up, took a brief glance toward Bonnie and I, and did a double-take worthy of a silent film comedian.

There was no immediate confrontation between us, despite what Essex had promised me on the bridge in front of

Grantum Hall. He gave me a grim stare but we were separated from one another by a crush of admirers who clustered about the tall nobleman. Somebody fixed the position of the medallion that hung from his neck, a clubfooted man brought him his cape, and an old woman presented him with his hat, the plume still intact. Others just wanted to be near him, putting a hand to his glossy doublet or trying to draw his attention with verbal praises. Essex ignored all but those bearing his accessories, and came over to Southampton and his friend.

"Greetings, good player," Essex said to Shakespeare. "I trust you have been visited by my messenger, Sir Gilley Merrick?"

"That I have, Milford," Shakespeare said, giving the Lord Deputy a slight bow. "The arrangements have been made for the presentation of *The Tragedy of Richard the Second* at *The Globe* two days hence."

"Good then," Essex said heartily. "I trust you will give my friends a good rendering of that most timely play."

Shakespeare nodded. "We are well rehearsed, Milford. The play is a bit worn from the telling. I have taken license to add a few new renderings on selected scenes, the better to make the play even more relevant to these times."

Essex frowned. "I have great appreciation of your skills, Master Shakespeare. I want no excises or additions from your original play. The original Richard, as you first rendered it, will serve my purpose. I hope you understand my meaning, sir," the voice dropping to a sinister growl on the last words.

Shakespeare bowed again, deeper this time, then spoke "My gracious lord, I tender you my service, such as it is which elder days shall ripen and confirm to more approved service and desert."

The Lord Deputy, now smiling, drew himself up right next to the writer. "I have great appreciation of your skills, Master Shakespeare. Do not let me down."

Shakespeare nodded. "Yes, my Right Honorable Lord."

"You need not fear Master Shakespeare's efforts," Southampton said, roughly patting his fellow earl on the shoulder. "If my servant Will made any additions to his tragedy it was no doubt in the spirit of his play celebrating the triumphs of Henry of Monmouth. He showed me the lines of the glowing tribute paid to your generalship by his Chorus. He compared you to a great king, Robert. What more can one ask from a man who has the ears of thousands? What greatter tribute can there be than comparison to Good King Harry, and his brave companies at Agincourt?"

"Dare you compare the battle of Agincourt to your unworthy campaign," called out a shrill, elderly feminine voice from the crowd. "The Lord Deputy a Worthy in the same sphere as King Henry the Fifth? Bah! We know of your great failure in Ireland, Lord Deputy. You were to bring Tyrone back in a cage, not bandy with him for a worthless peace. Your place is in Ireland, sir, at the head of your soldiers. Instead your hurry to fawn yourself at Her Majesty's Court to flaunt—" The shrill voice was drowned out by a chorus of other voices, hostile to her judgement. Most of the catcalls were made up of hisses and inarticulate guttural moans.

"To the pillory with the hag!" a male voice shouted.

"She's a witch, doubtless," came another voice.

"Seize her, bring her forth!" a woman behind Bonnie cried.

"She speaks the truth," came another voice, more timid than the others. This led to more rustling and shouting in the crowd, which was beginning to look more like a mob about to turn ugly.

The woman was dragged forward by some of the male spectators. She was a crippled, skinny old woman with black teeth and thinning waves of ginger-grey hair. Around her neck was a threadbare scarf. One of her spotted, trowel-like hands held a crude y-shaped crutch that she must have used to drag herself along. She was dressed in a ragged farthingale with a bodice that was several sizes too large for her. She also had an ugly wart on her face the size of a quarter. Far from being frightened, she looked stern and unrepentant. She was roughly dragged forward toward Essex, who looked at a loss to deal with the situation.

A gunshot went off behind us. A soldier, wearing a morion helmet and sporting epaulettes on his sleeves that indicated some rank, had fired his wheelock pistol, the barrel of which was now smoking.

"My Lord Deputy," the soldier said. "I see the banners of the Queen's Horse Guards making their way down no less than a half-mile down the thoroughfare. This is an unlawful assembly and we cannot yet submit to—"

"Aye, Captain Hope," Essex said. The Lord Deputy raised his voice to the crowd: "Good people, I must take my leave of you. My enemies in court wish to detain me and bring me before Her Majesty in a compromised position. There are already enemies within the chambers of power who shall be dealt with in good time." He negotiated a few paces through the crowd and stood on a small pillar that afforded the outlying crowd a look at the celebrated warrior.

"My victory in Ireland would have been more sweeping were it not for the plots laid against me from certain courtiers. These fair-haired boys plied the ears of our Most Gracious Majesty in her privy chamber whilst I fought against the wild kerns of Ulster, far away from even base comforts. I am the victim of envy and scorn for what I did against superior forces at Cadiz."

Shouts of approval. The Cadiz gig must have come off well. Essex continued.

"When the misunderstandings are cleared, I mean to once again rejoin my forces in Ireland and plant the flag of St. George on every castle and atop the highest roof of every township. This I promise on pain of my breaking my sword and leaving this kingdom as unworthy of my offices and my lineage. That is my vow, good people. Is there a man among you who doubts me?"

Cheers followed. Essex was getting ready to speak again, but the captain of the guard spoke up first.

"Lord Deputy, we have tarried enough at this place. The other force grows near. Remount, Milord, and let us leave this place."

Essex followed the request. A path cleared for him, the only obstruction being the old woman that had been dragged forth previously. She positioned herself directly in front of the Earl. Essex stopped and spoke to her.

"Know your place, woman," he growled low enough so only those in the inner circle could hear.

The old woman craned her neck up and looked the aristocrat right in the eyes. "Know your place, Lord Essex," she said in a hoarse voice. "I was a maiden, young and fresh, when our Empress came to the throne two score and more years ago. She navigated England and kept the peace in this factious realm long before you were even a pup. You wish to be the king or be a kingmaker at the least. You aim beyond your birth, your humor, and your ability. Know *your* place, my Lord Essex." Essex's face flushed red. He bent down to the woman and spoke in a harsh whisper.

"Like another woman I detest, you've a mind as crooked as your carcass." Essex gave the old woman a quick brush of his hand on her bony shoulder as he walked past her. This upset her footing, but Bonnie was standing close enough to catch her. A tall, bushy-bearded man came forward and also helped the crone maintain her balance. As he passed me, Essex shot a glance at me that radiated hate. I responded with a curt bow and a smile. The Earl then stopped in front of Shakespeare who was standing next to me.

"Beware, player," Essex said quietly but sharply. "I will not brook your changing the message and import of your original play. I will have the play as it was printed in the quarto I possess in my library, the one that Merrick gave your friend Richard Burbage as a guide. Remember there is one near and dear to you in this city, and he is within my reach." He turned away from Shakespeare, the latter looking quite intimidated by the threat. Southampton, who also was close enough to hear the threat, gave the playwright a sympathetic look without his fellow peer seeing him. Then he joined his leader in working their way through the crowd.

"Thank you, good lady," the old woman said to Bonnie.

As the group of soldiers rode away, I could see in the midst of the riders the plumage from Essex's elaborate hat, bobbing up and down from the unjulations of his horse. The force receded down the street. Someone brushed up against me in the crowd whose members were individuals again, jostling about and getting on with original business. Without even turning around, just from the smell of his cologne, I knew Francis Bacon had come out of hiding.

"Yonder goes Icarus," Bacon said to no one in particular. "He goes mounted on a winged horse, straight toward disaster. We need a fiery sun to bring him to earth, yet I fear there will only be a waxing and waning moon to confront the presumptuous rogue."

Bonnie gave Shakespeare a low curtsy when Bacon formally introduced him to her. I got a firm handshake. All Bacon needed to say was that we were "in the service of Jack Benchley." The expression on the playwright's face told me he understood our true situation.

"Are you Master Shakespeare, a sharer in The Chamberlain's Men?" the old woman asked.

"Indeed, good lady," Shakespeare said, tactfully bending down a bit and looking the woman in the eyes. "I have the honor to be a writer and actor for that company which enjoys the patronage of the Lord Hunston, Her Gracious Majesty's Lord Chamberlain."

"And your players have performed many times for the Queen?" the woman asked.

"Many a time, good lady. We are always ready to perform at the pleasure of Her Majesty. She especially craves our modest artisty during the feasts at Christmas time."

"Just so," the old woman said. "Just so. Why are you not at The Globe presently? Is there not a performance today?"

"There is a play," Shakespeare said. "One that I must be present for. I am winding up business at this moment, then I am bound by waterman for Southwark."

"Is it to be one of your works?" she asked.

Shakespeare shook his head. "One of Ben Jonson's humor plays, a triumph from last year, now returning by demand. My *Tragedy of Julius Ceasar* will be performed tomorrow. If you have read your Plutarch, I trust you will appreciate my telling."

"I think I shall see that," the decrepit woman said. "Not tomorrow, though. Things to do tomorrow. I take my leave. Just so, just so." The woman hobbled away. I noticed the tall, dark man taking her under the arm and leading her up the steps of the cathedral.

The mounted soldiers that Essex's captain had seen finally made it through the long boulevard to the cathedral. There were about as many armed soldiers in this company as had been in the group that had hastily departed.

The young scrawny officer in charge of the company, dressed in a crisp uniform with an armor breastplate, spoke in a high tenor.

"Fellow subjects! We have reports that Lord Essex is in this district. In the name of the Queen, I ask you to tell me whereabouts he and his are? What street did they take to withdraw from Paul's Walk?"

Men and women pointed in all different directions, and gave out testimony as to which way Essex and his pack had gone. Some directions were honest; some were misleading. Most people ignored him. I could see the leader of these horse guards could not make head or tail of the conflicting verbal directions. It was a wash. I had been in situations similar to the young man. A crime would occur and by the time we arrived potential witnesses either didn't talk or they tried to bullshit you because the perpetrators might come back and do them a dirty deed. The young Official implored again. It was futile.

The four of us walked up the stairway into the cathedral. Not surprisingly, the interior was enormous. The supports for the building consisted of two sets of massive stone columns, thick as mature Sequoia trees, which held up large horseshoe-shaped archways. There were no services taking place, but portions of several pews were occupied. Some people were on their knees praying but most were carrying on conversations in small groups. Laughter and the occasional shout of a visitor testing the acoustics of the place made me think activity in the church on weekdays were of a less than pious nature.

Above the archways was a second tier of arches supported by slender Corinthian-style columns and then a similar tier above that. Light entered the cathedral through large stained-glass windows in rows symmetrical to the archways. The roof itself was long and barrel-vaulted. All the light in the place came from some of the stained glass portals. All of the glass artwork depicted constipated-looking crowned men in long robes with crowned ladies looking serene. Above the altar were fading frescos of toga-clad, bearded men with disapproving looks on their mugs.

We sat in a pew well away from any other visitors. Bacon quietly filled Shakespeare in on the details of Benchley's release and the machinations of Trevor Warbeck, the Earl of Essex and the Strunk Corporation. Shakespeare bit the middle knuckle of his index finger, shaking his head slowly as Bacon laid out the situation.

"It is certain Essex and this fiend Warbeck will attempt to seize the Queen at the coming wedding at Grantum Hall,"

Shakespeare said. "Our company is to perform a play after the ceremony, one of my Falstaff plays, at the Queen's behest."

"Can you cancel your company's performance?" Bonnie asked.

"Alas not, milady," Shakespeare said. "It would be without pardon for the Chamberlain's Men not to appear anywhere Her Majesty wills us. She requested me to write the very play that we are to perform, and she will have it or there will be the devil to pay in consequence."

"Have you a horse, William?" Bacon asked after the recounting.

"Nay," Shakespeare said. "I took a waterman's craft from Southwark to Three Cranes Dock, then walked to Paul's. I had heard from a printer friend of mine that my company's Jew play was being sold here in the stalls. I was going to try to buy up all the available copies to keep the work from falling into the hands of the Lord Admiral's Men or any lesser troupe."

"Would that be *The Merchant of Venice*?" Bonnie asked.

"The very one, good lady," Shakespeare responded, before turning to Bacon. "Is Benchley in good health? What stays him from coming to London?"

"He has an asthma," Bacon said. "The important thing is to set our original plan in motion. I will do my part by taking dinner with the Queen. I will meet Doctor Dee at the other end of the bridge. We will take to the river for Greenwich Palace."

"Stay wide of Essex," Shakespeare said. "His eyes betray that the Furies are after him."

"Fear not," Bacon said wearily. "I have tasted enough wrath for one day."

"I fear the threat made by Essex concerns my brother, Edmund," Shakespeare said. "The Earl may have dark plans to bring him harm if I include the prologue praising the Queen. I cannot allow anything to happen to my brother. In his life I place a higher value than my own."

"It may be all up to me to blunt Essex's ambitions, then," Bacon said sadly. "I have access to the Queen and know her prejudices. I will use that knowledge to the utmost for the sake of the kingdom."

"Tell me again, Francis," Shakespeare said. "What of these strange weapons you speak of. Grenadine launchers, you say?"

"Grenade launchers," Bacon said. "And guns that fire torrents of bullets to mow down men in great numbers. You have heard Benchley and Trubshawe speak of these things in the past. They are weapons similar to the ones that buried half of Europe in the Great Wars of the 20th Century."

"So I have read from th books Benchley has presented us," Shakespeare said.

"Has the company rehearsed the *Richard the Second* play? Is it ready for presentation?" Bacon asked.

"Aye," Shakespeare said. "It may lead to trouble from our censor, the Master of the Revels. The deposition scene is not for public display by his express orders. But I have spared no positive virtue in describing our Queen in the prologue. The question is whether the mere fact that the Queen will seem aware of Essex's plans be enough to stay his hand."

"That is the question," Bacon said. "We must hope Essex will hold himself up at the news of the substituted play. With time, tangible evidence could be brought to Her Majesty of the planned treasons of Essex and your boon friend, Southampton."

"Alas, poor Harry," Shakespeare said. "Surely he will not face the block."

"He was to be spared, thanks to the pleas of his mother," Bacon said. "But that outcome was only certain before time was breached."

Again, Shakespeare bit his knuckle, his thumb brushing against the wispy hairs that grew above his chin. "I can tarry here no longer," he said. "I have to make sure my brother is safe. Plus, I act today. I must to The Globe."

I looked up at the sound of footsteps coming toward us. A curious group of men—some dressed in bright blue doublets with bright-handled swords and others dressed as club-carrying workmen—came down the aisle and stopped where we where sitting. Leading the group was a tall, dark bearded man. Just behind him was the talkative old lady who had spoken to Shakespeare and heckled Essex.

Bacon stood up, the expression on his face indicating that he recognized one of the party.

"Sir Hubert Carey," Bacon said. "What brings you to Paul's?"

"Duty," said the slender man, who looked about forty or

forty- five. I recognized two of the other men as the ones who had brought the old woman up before Essex. From his position in front of the others, he seemed to be the leader of the ten or so men who had approached us, even though he was dressed in plain clothes.

"Francis Bacon, you and your group are to accompany us to the Bishop's Chambers. Let there be no discussion of the matter. This is the business of the realm. Follow."

We went through a door to the side of the altar. That led us into a large office suffused with light from three large windows. The first thing I noticed was a little shrine about the size of a dresser and a hutch with a gold cross in the center of it. In a corner of the room was a coat rack. On the rack were some clothes. A woman in a long dress of heavy fabric was taking the clothes off the rack and carefully folding them as if they were going to be stored away. The funny thing was that the clothes looked very ragged and soiled. It was a few seconds before I realized they were the same clothes that the old crippled woman wore.

The man Bacon identified as Sir Hubert looked Bonnie and I over like we were a couple skunks, then turned to one of the men in a shiny doublet and sword.

"Take these two and lead them to the vestibule. Keep them under guard until—"

He stopped talking when a side door opened. Immediately all of the men turned to the door and bowed. I felt a hand to the back of my head, pushing me down.

"Bow, you damn fool," one of our escorts said to me as he tried to bend my neck.

I bowed. Bonnie, without prompting, curtsied. No one spoke. Everything seemed to freeze. I heard the footsteps of someone entering the room and the shuffling of a dress. I next heard a woman's voice. It was a reedy, high-pitched voice, but it had an underlying tone of strength.

"Master Bacon of Grey's Inn, and Master Shakespeare of the Chamberlain's Players," the voice said. "My time here is short and we have much to discuss."

"Holy shit," Bonnie whispered. I peeked at her as she shot a glance at the woman addressing us.

"My most Gracious Majesty," Bacon said, "I am flattered that you have asked me into your presence. Little did I know when I was invited to dine with your eminence that I would be graced with an earlier audience. I am blessed beyond—"

"Still the flattery, Bacon," Queen Elizabeth the First said. (I had looked up myself now and glanced at the monarch.) "You fawn at me not because you delight in my company, but because your fondest desire is a grant of high office. I have no worthy office for you—not as yet. Save your silked tongue for a formal audience in my Presence Chamber at Greenwich this evening. I have things to discuss with you, but the precedent of my queries will go to Mister Shakespeare. Now, the lot of you, stand upwards," she snapped. "William Shakespeare, come forward."

I stood up, getting my first good look at the Queen. She had deep set dark brown eyes, a nose that curved outward in the middle of the bridge, and a thin, puckered mouth that was devoid of sensuality. Her chin was strong, her skin pale about the eyes giving way to splotchy hues of pink and light brown around the cheeks and jawline. Her dress was jet-black, spangled with pearls and fringed with ermine. Her gold-colored ruff completely hid her neck. She wore rings with fat jewels on three of her fingers, and jewels on the band around her thin reddish hair. She had a wide gold locket about her neck, studded with pearls that were framed by the goldwork. She carried a gold-colored fan in one hand and a pair of black gloves in the other. She reminded me of a late-stage Joan Crawford.

Shakespeare as he came forward to her, bowed, and gave her outstretched hand a brief peck with his lips. "I am at your command, Gracious Majesty," he said.

"Just so, just so," the Queen said, in a cackle that reminded me of the old woman. I then realized she was that old woman who had heckled Essex. I also realized that her front teeth were almost uniformly black, with only a few traces of white enamel showing.

"What say you to my performance, playwright?" the Queen asked coyly. "Did I not play the part of the aged hag to satisfaction? Did I not only fool you yourself who has entertained numerous times at my court, but did I not fool my Lords Southampton and Essex? What say you to my masque?" Her posture, a bit stooped, seemed to straighten. She grew with every word of self-praise.

Shakespeare stood up. "Most impressive, Majesty. I had

no idea the crippled unfortunate before me was my empress. May I be so bold as to ask the reason for your sojourn by stealth amongst your subjects?"

"You may, man of Warwickshire," the Queen said. "I got the idea from your play concerning the campaign of Henry the Fifth. On the eve of the Battle of Agincourt, you had Harry go amongst his troops in the guise of an ordinary soul to discover their true feelings about their sovereign. I have since, on selected occasions, gone forth into the environs of Paul's and other places about the city to discern the opinions of my subjects as to various measures and acts I have undertaken. You have improved my statecraft, Mister Shakespeare. This is a feat I would not have thought possible in a man of humble background as yourself. Then, you are a wonder to more than just your Queen. I have heard scholars of renown speak highly of your verse. The critic Francis Meres sees you as a combination Platus and Seneca. Your sonnets excite the admiration of many in my orbit, and no knight or lord or lady in my orbit is without a generous muse and a prize wit. Most impressive for the son of a rural hamlet who has only graced Oxford and Cambridge as a wandering player."

"Your Majesty does me too much credit," Shakespeare said.

"Indeed I probably do," Elizabeth said, her tones suddenly turning cold. "For why would a man of such intelligence allow one of his plays to be preformed in order to incite rebellion against his sovereign."

"I—I—" Shakespeare stammered. "I know not what is meant by—"

"The play *Richard the Second* is what is meant," she said, quietly yet ominously. "A man named Gilly Merick approached Mr. Burbage and yourself, asking you to perform that dated play. Your company agreed to do it. Yet you know such a play contains a deposition scene and our realm is under threat from a possible Spanish attack and from certain..." She paused and drew breath. "Certain misguided members of the nobility who have gathered about the Lord Essex and poisoned his young mind."

"Your Majesty, I am but a commoner," the playwright said. "Sir Merick is a member of the nobility, and a boon companion of Lord Essex. The Lord Essex is a Knight of the Garter.

He is your Lord Deputy. I and the players in the company can only practice our craft under the sponsorship of men like our own patron, Lord Hunsdon. Otherwise we would be deemed masterless men, and put to the workhouses or the prisons. We must bow to our betters. How could we refuse a Lord?"

"Indeed you shouldn't," Elizabeth said harshly. "But you should have informed my Master of the Revels of this performance. Lord Essex has fled the field in Ulster after making a mock peace with the Earl of Tyrone. His place is before me, answering my questions. Know you not that your play contains a deposition scene, a scene banned by my censor? Do you not see the parallel between the deposition of Richard Planetgenet and the ambitions many in this kingdom have to depose me? I am Richard the Second, Mister Shakespeare."

"The play will not be presented, Majesty," Shakespeare said.

"A play *will* be presented!" Elizabeth shouted, then lowered her voice. "The play will go on and you will perform it. But you will present the Falstaff play about the wives of Windsor instead of the Richard play. That way you can perform it the better for me that same evening when I attend the Earl of Grantum's wedding. I enjoyed the play last year, and I mean to do so again. And I mean for any disgruntled subjects to enjoy it that afternoon as well. Do you understand, Warwickshireman?"

"Yes, your Majesty," Shakespeare said. He bowed.

The Queen shifted her gaze. "Bacon, you have much to tell me of Lord Essex, do you not?"

"Yes, your Majesty," Bacon said. "Much. I believe I know where he and his band took flight to after that-uh, disagreeable activity outside the cathedral."

"I'll expect you tonight at Greenwich then," Elizabeth said. "Take the river route. The tide is right. And be prompt, Bacon."

"As always, Majesty," Bacon said, bowing.

The Queen turned to the man in the workman's outfit. "I must have Essex brought to me, Carey. I must have him, alive and before me and away from the fools who prey upon his mind with unworthy advice. Come, Carey, the Bishop awaits his audience." The Queen turned and headed for the door she came in. One of the swordsmen opened the door for her.

Everyone bowed again.

After we were allowed to leave, we walked under the wide, high-peaked archway and down the wide stone steps of St. Paul's. Bacon spoke to me as we headed down the steps.

"Wells, you and Miss Noel have a choice: accompany me to London Bridge if you like, then cross over on the bridge to Southwark, or stable your mounts near The Three Cranes and accompany Mr. Shakespeare directly to The Globe. Which is it?"

Bonnie chose the latter course. I began to contemplate seasickness.

"Very well, " Bacon said brusquely as he pulled up his gloves. "I will rendezvous with you two late this evening when I return to Grey's."

"You will see me as well," Shakespeare said. "If I can invite myself to your home, I'd like to reacquaint myself with Jack this evening. I have to be at Lincoln's Inn tomorrow morning to confer with the Masters there on a presentation of *Ceasar* for tomorrow evening. As I will be in the neighborhood—"

"Of course," Bacon said. "Lincoln's is a stone's throw from my abode. You may have to share a bed, but you will be welcome as my guest."

Back out in front of St. Paul's, near the trough where we had tied the horses, Bacon got on his horse, wished us a hearty 'godspeed' then brought his mount about 180 degrees and headed off in a gallop. His back to the great cathedral, he held the reins with one hand and his derby with the other, giving us a quick wave before riding around a crowd and then out of sight.

Chapter Forty-Five

Bonnie and Shakespeare shared her palomino, the playwright riding up front and Bonnie behind him on the saddle holding onto his waist. I was more than a bit jealous. The reason for this doubling up was that Shakespeare was in a hurry to see about the safety of his brother, and to make it in time to hit the stage at The Globe. To accomplish this the horse he and Bonnie rode was put to a gallop. My mule was hard pressed to keep up, since it was clear to me the animal was not inclined to gallop under any circumstances short of fleeing the scene of a raging fire. It was only the throngs of horses and carts that congested the intersections of this strange, muddy, putrid- smelling metropolis that allowed me to keep my companions in sight. Bonnie would look over her shoulder at me from time to time to make sure I had not fallen off again and was still in sight.

A couple times she waved to me. I would signal back and put the crop to the beast's rump to prod her along.

Crossing the intersections of the street we were on, many carts were piled high with dead fish, and the swarms of flies that hovered about each pile gave each collection of dead gill-breathers the appearance of a hive for large black bees. Fish now replaced the reek of feces and rotting cattle guts as the pervading smell. There was also a scent of fresh air that would occasionally envelope me as I navigated the roadway. The air had a humidity to it that told me we were near water. I looked down the street and saw we were headed into a blanket of off-white fog that hung close to the ground and obscured the view past a hundred yards or so.

The private houses were getting bigger now and more ornate. There were still shops as well. Some of the timbers that supported the shops had beautiful, elaborate patterns engraved into the horizontal beams that separated one floor from the other. Some doorways to the shops were obviously the work of skilled woodworkers. Other doors were basic: three of four sections of wide planks of wood held together by iron crossbars nailed into the planks. Passing a shop, the sign above the door stating 'Decker and Sons, Bakers,' I noticed a good-sized grey rat scurry out between a gap between two planks in the entryway. The vermin was bigger than its small legs were intended to carry it. It waddled down the stone threshold, then, at the approach of human pedestrians, scurried into a narrow alley that separated the bakery from a silversmith's shop. The pedestrians, including a woman carrying a basket into the bakery, clearly saw the fat rodent come into close range of their feet but paid the creature no more heed than if it had been a stray cocker spaniel.

Towers and huge gables were atop many of the moss-covered, red-shingled roofs. There were also shops and storehouses. At times, if you overlooked the garbage in the streets and some of the more ill-kempt denizens who stood about in the midst of the activity of the street you could almost feel yourself in some kind of great theme park. A pretty young blonde woman cried out for donations to 'Whitefriars Almshouse'; a group of men unloaded barrels from a horse-drawn wagon and carried them on their backs up a wooden ramp into a storehouse; further down the street, men loaded a wagon with what looked at first like cotton but looked more like wool as I got closer. I saw a group of men dressed in fur overcoats with cone-shaped hats bantering and sharing a laugh with a covey of street ladies who wore their bodices like they were advertising themselves. One of the men had a large green parrot on his shoulders. Were these sailors?

Just as the mule and I passed the men in cone hats, I heard someone call out Shakespeare's name from down the street. He called out the surname again and I got a bead on where the stranger was. He was a short, thick-set fellow with a stock of bright red hair that could be seen even through the enclosing mists of fog. As I got closer, I noticed he had an egg-sized goiter at the base of his thin neck, to one side of an already-prominent adam's apple. He wore a doublet that was buttoned up to the middle of his neck and unbuttoned at the stomach area to allow a little extra room for his paunch. He was standing on the street in front of a shop designated by its large swaying wooden sign to be 'The Maypole Musick Shoppe.' A small white terrier was at his feet, a thin rope attached to his collar. The dog barked as the horse drew near. When Shakespeare alighted, the man let the dog go and he bounded up to him as dogs will to anyone who has paid them the least attention in the past. Bonnie stayed on the horse. The waylaying allowed me to catch up to them.

"I cannot tarry, Thomas," Shakespeare said as he finished petting and stroking the excited dog. "Lo, I would appreciate the conversation otherwise, yet—"

"I know, Master Shakespeare," the freckle-faced man said handing him a piece of paper. "My German clock struck one only a pisseth of time ago." He looked up to Bonnie, then bit his tongue. "My pardon mistress," he said.

"No offense taken, good gentleman," Bonnie said. "You face neither a cloistered maiden or a prudish Puritan damsel." I was beginning to prefer the sensuous phrasing of her Elizabethan speech to her regular voice.

"Seeing that you are due in the playhouse, I would not have called out for you were it not a matter of business," the fellow said.

I got off my mule, happy to be able to rest my backside. Looking into the window of the shop, I saw strange instruments displayed near the window. Some of the string instruments looked fairly familiar, like those back at the tavern we had stopped in that morning. Others looked like they were the proto-designs for automobile mufflers.

I was now close enough to Shakespeare to see what it was he was reading. I could see it, but I could not decipher it. There were certainly Roman-style numerals and letters on the unlined legal-sized paper, but I couldn't have read it to save my life.

Shakespeare shook his head, then folded the paper into quarters and thrust it inside his doublet.

"When did Edmund stop by?" he asked the man with the goiter.

"This morn'," the man said, swatting a large black fly that buzzed about his clean-shaven face. "He purchased a book of the latest madrigals and a crumhorn."

"And left this reckoning for his dear brother to deal with," Shakespeare said testily. He dug down into a purse he pulled out of the front of his breeches, which was attached to his belt, and gave the man several coins. "I will pay you the balance the next time I pass near Blackfriars, Thomas, be assured of that. Deny my brother any further credit in the while. My young brother is new to London. I fear he is already in love with a tavern wench and may well present her with a virginal of the finest marquetry if this pattern is not checked."

"You will be by next week, then?" Thomas asked.

"Aye, next Monday," the playwright said. "You will have your money before noon or I will buy that fine Munich clock from the wall of your shop and annoit my brother's empty head with it."

The shopkeeper chuckled. "I have heard Edmund tell of the wench," he said. "She is Priscilla, barmaid at Sinbad's down near Puddle Wharf. It is a haunt I myself go to pass a lonely evening. She is not a drab, but nor is she one who has never piled her wiles on young men 'sides your Edmund. If this wench can play the virginals, it would have been a talent she acquired as a very, very young girl." This brought another chuckle from the shopkeeper that his customer did not share.

"Good day, Thomas," Shakespeare said after he remounted the horse in front of Bonnie. I reluctantly returned to the bony back of my mule and tried to keep up.

❖ ❖ ❖ ❖ ❖

"Is Tyler Benchley your natural son?" Bonnie asked our latest acquaintance. I thought it remarkably blunt of her but, having been around Bonnie and seen her in action, I wasn't surprised.

"Indeed," Shakespeare said as the narrow wooden boat we were in bobbed in the swift current of the wide river. "Tyler, as you call him, is not my son in the way that the Official Church would sanctify, but he is my flesh as surely as my dear departed son Hamnet was."

Our horse and mule were stabled near the dock. The three of us were huddled together on planks in the bow of the boat. At the stern, two men in thick buckram coats, with wool stuffing sticking out of the armholes, were rowing alongside each other. There were no other passengers in the craft. The fog on the water was so thick one could not see our destination. I sat next to Shakespeare on one plank. Bonnie sat on the plank nearest the tip of the bow, the better to allow for the extra room needed for her dress. There were other boats, some with spinnaker sails billowing in the breeze. There were also long and wide barges pulled by oarsman, some as many as a dozen plying the water with long paddles. The cargos on the barges were covered over with large wooden shells that took up most of the boat's deck space. They moved in and out of our sight in the fog. Our rowers shouted out, "Ho!" or, "Mark there! Look to your starboard, men!" whenever the boats came too close. If it was a barge crossing our intended course, our rowers would lay up their oars and let up to give the freight-hauler the right of way. Judging by the nervous look on his face, this caused the time-conscious Shakespeare some measure of anxiety.

Bonnie leaned over to the playwright. "I have a picture of Tyler," she whispered. "Would you like to see it?"

We looked back to make sure the watermen were not paying attention to us. When the coast was clear, she reached into her small leather purse and pulled out the small snapshot of the boy in a soccer uniform. Shakespeare cupped his hands over the picture. He looked it over carefully, as did I. There was a definite resemblence in the eyes and in the prominence of the forehead. The outstanding difference between the two was that Tyler's facial coloring was darker.

"Marry, but he has grown a good deal since Jack showed me his image last," he said. "Could you allow me to keep this?"

"Of course," Bonnie said cheerfully. "Tyler's a great kid, by the way. A bit obstreperous at times, but most six and seven year-olds are that way."

"What is that word you say?" Shakespeare said. "The rather long one I mean."

"You mean obstreperous?" Bonnie said. "It means, uh, it means unruly, defiant. He's not that way all the time, though."

"His mother was defiant," Shakespeare replied glumly. "And she could be as unruly as Medea, for that I vouchsafe. The mother was a beauteous creature, could dance a galliard like no other. There I have done it again, spoken of her in the past tense. It is wrong for me to do so, but I find it comes natural in my discourse."

We listened to the rocking of the boat, the oars striking the water, the screeching of some sea bird not visible in the fog but surely flying over our heads.

"A tavern wench she was," Shakespeare said. "I met her in Dover in '92. That was a plague year and the theaters were shut in London. Only the outlying counties would admit players through the town walls if the contagion was not raging anywhere nearby. I was with another troupe then, one that relied on the works of Kit Marlowe. Alas, he is six years gone, the victim of a great reckoning in a little public house in Deptford. An obsteperous sort himself, but one whose gifts with quill and paper should have earned him a greater span of time on Earth. But to the wench. When she and I met I was beginning my serious poetry and making my way as a non-sharer in this company. I was bewitched by her. I would have swam the Hellespont a thousand times for her, for she was Hero to me and I her Leander. I wooed her and won her. I brought her to London. I improved her wit by schooling her in Ovid and Homer—in translation, of course. She improved my spirit with her beauty and her way with music. She birthed a boy, my son, my only living son. But, owing to my state of previous matrimony, she sought her own to betroth. She found that man, a Gentleman Pensioner of the Queen's Guard. They met in the Summer of '93. The plague was on in London again and I was with a new company. We were received at Southampton House by the Young Earl. This was about the first time I met Jack Benchley, though he was still in the guise of a trademan of Bristol. But to Harry of Southampton, the verses of my *Venus and Adonis* had pleased him and he allowed me to dedicate the work to him. On the occasion of this humid July evening, Harry asked that I present a comedy for the enjoyment of the Queen, who was on a progress, and the many retainers who sought refuge with Her Majesty from the terrors of Death's scythe. I also had my graceful, dark-haired mistress with me."

"Did your company present *Love's Labor's Lost* by chance?" Bonnie said softly in her natural accent.

"Indeed," Shakespeare said. "Prey, has Jack told you my

story before?"

"No," Bonnie said. "We knew nothing of all this" (she raised her hands out wide) not even three days ago."

"It was the play *Love's Labor's Lost*, Mistress Bonnie. A bit of irony, what?" he said bitterly. "I lost my dark-hued lady whilst I prodded on the hurridly-erected stage in the great room of the manor. While Pygmalion pranced and sang by the torchlight for the pleasure of the Queen, his Galatea mingled with the Pensioners—mingling with one in particular with all of her particulars at his disposal. The plague was finally quenched by the Grace of God, but not the fire kindled by Mistress Mary for a certain Captain Jaggers. Secretive meetings 'tweenst the two followed, methinks, and then one day I returned to our rooms at the Liberty of the Clink—I had been paying a brief visit home to Warwickshire—and found she had departed with all her dresses, linens and baggage. The son—we named him Henry after my patron, the Earl—was left behind to the care of Mary's sister in Moorfields. I was frantic to claim the boy, but when I did I had not the time or the nature to raise the child myself. And as for taking my bastard back to my good wife in Stratford? Oh, the folly of that!" He shook his head. "This is what comes of antic passions unchecked by reason."

"Why didn't she take the baby with her?" Bonnie asked.

"Good lady," Shakespeare said in seeming disbelief. "A gentleman of fine station would not provide for another man's bastard, especially the bastard spawn of a mere player. It is true, if Benchley's reports are truthful and I have no reason to doubt him, that I am an exalted personage in your age for my turn of phrase and the stenuous exercise of my wit. I thought my verse would live on, but not to the extent that—"

He shifted in his place, rocking the boat slightly, then turned up his hands again to peek at Tyler's photograph once more before putting it somewhere in the inner lining of his doublet.

"So, you gave the child to Jack Benchley," I said.

Shakespeare nodded at me, causing a few raindrops that had formed on his hat to flow off the brim. "He told me he had a daughter in Bristol who could not become heavy with child. I offered Harry. I could see he was a kind man and I hoped it would be a loving home for the sprig. It was a year later, after the Jew Ryskind lost his life in the Doctor Lopez business, that I discovered Benchley had dropped in this world from another time. My friend, Mr. Bacon, showed me the machine and demonstrated it."

"Have you been to the future?" I asked in a low voice.

"Nay," Shakespeare said, as if I had just sprayed him in the face with bug spray. "I have enough material to draw on for my work in this time. Naturally, I have a keen interest in the progress of the drama through the centuries. I am also glad to be of assistance in helping Benchley create authentic stagings for my plays. In return, he has brought me books and articles on how work is received. I have also seen some films made of my works. I do not view or read anything to do with work I am yet to write, nor do I want the texts of my future efforts brought to me. I have seen film versions of my *Midsummer Night's Dream*, *The Taming of the Shrew* and of the Lord Olivier's, *Richard III*—marry, imagine a monarch giving a lordship to a player—and some taped productions done at Benchley's festival in Oregon. I have not seen my *Julius Caesar*, for instance, which my company will stage tomorrow. The only exception I made was to see Benchley's version of Thomas Lodge's *Rosalynd*, a play adaption I am now laboring on."

"That would be *As You Like It*, sir," Bonnie said, getting a wet strand of dark blonde hair out of her face with a flop of her hand, only to have it fly right back across her eyes.

"Yes," Shakespeare said with a bemused grin. "I cannot say that I recommend seeing a work performed before one begins work upon it. Most disconcerting, really. But I thought it polite since Benchley himself filmed it. I understand it made little money but won a few estreemed awards."

"Yes," I replied. "Mr. Benchley always said it was flawed, really. He wanted to do more with the material but he ran out of money and had to leave out some of his best ideas."

"It is still a beautiful moving picture," Shakespeare said. "The fellow who played Jacques, the fat fellow, Welles, he did a very good Falstaff in one of his own pictures. Benchley showed me something called, oh what was it? *Chimes at Midnight*, yes. Quite an interesting blend of my earlier work, with the added device of creating moving images with nature herself as a backdrop. I would love to work in such a craft as film, but I am told by Benchley that writers fare none too well in that place called Hollywood."

"Nor do actors, for the most part," Bonnie said. "Nor anyone except the caterers and the producers, and the few actors who are stars."

"Such as that dark-hued woman?" the playwright asked. Our boat rolled up and then down from crossing the considerable wake of a good-sized wooden sloop, its triangular sail billowing in the wind.

"Dark-hued woman?" Bonnie asked in reply. "Was she in one of the plays from the Northwest Festival that Mr. Benchley videotaped?"

"No, I believe this was what Benchley called an A-picture. It was an imaging of the *Shrew* play I did years ago."

"Oh," Bonnie said after the clue. "You mean a movie. Was it filmed in black-and-white or color?"

"The moving images beheld a munificence of hues," he remarked wistfully. "It was the play as I imagined it in my mind's eye, without the contraints of the stage."

"That dark-hued woman is an actress named Elizabeth Taylor," Bonnie said. "And she was definitely a star, and quite beautiful too."

"Most beautiful," the playwright said, a note of wistfulness in his strong, resonant voice. "Now I remember Benchley telling me her name. O', to have a vision such as she to prance upon the boards. We would sell out The Globe all season to let the lords and common folk see her heavenly form and graceful movements."

Bill Shakespeare was stuck on the young Liz Taylor.

"But you can't have actresses on the public stage, right?" Bonnie asked.

"Alas," Shakespeare said in a forlorn tone. "The Master of the Revels forbids it. If we put actresses on the stage, we would be closed for lewdness."

"Why?" Bonnie asked.

"It is just not done," Shakespeare replied. "A woman might appear in a masque for private performance, but never, *never* in public. The Puritans would protest vigorously. They see themselves as God's chosen instruments trying to save all those Fallen from Grace."

"The fallen defined as anyone who isn't a Puritan," Bonnie

said.

"Indeed," Shakespeare said engagingly to Bonnie. "If the Puritans could, they would close up the theaters, The Bear Garden, any church with a gilded cross, any public assembly of men and women laughing and carousing in one another's company, anything that smacked of red-bloodedness and vitality..." Then he lowered his voice, and shot a glance back at the boatman. "I know they will win. They will make civil war upon the kingdom and later close the theaters. I hope sincerely I am in my tomb before I have to see it. But to lighter matters. Benchley mentioned on his last visitation of a lady named Bonnie, his assistant."

"At your service," Bonnie said.

"And that you were once an actress," he said.

"A once and future actress, yes," Bonnie replied with the alluring smile of hers.

"Then perhaps you can tell me of this Elizabeth Taylor," that playwright said.

Bonnie laughed. "I'm sorry. I'm not laughing at you. It's just that a lot of women in the Western World are actresses, and I don't know Liz, that is, Elizabeth Taylor. I've heard things about her."

This seemed encouraging to the Bard. "What can you tell me about her?" he asked. Benchley was reticent on details of her. I think he wanted to exchange information on this woman for my participation in one of his moving-image plays. There are supposedly a lot of people who wish to know every detail of my life. I cannot say I care to reveal all that much, and certainly not in a commercial form. But to the lady in question. Perhaps, good lady, you will afford me a better bargain."

"What do you want to know?" she asked.

"Doth the lady still live?" Shakespeare asked. "And is she still...."

"Beautiful?" Bonnie added.

"I was going to ask if she were still the thrice-crowed Diana, Queen of the Night," Shakespeare replied. "But your one word has a pith I approve of."

"Thank you," Bonnie said.

Gulls swooped low over the boat. The oarsman was eating something that looked like chicken. He was not about to share it with his feathered friends. My stomach started to feel rocky. It felt like the combination of the rocking boat and the stress of the new enviroment was catching up to my insides.

Bonnie went into the whole wild and famous Liz Taylor saga for Shakespeare's benefit. The marriages. The weight fluctuations. The career nose-dive in the mid-Seventies. The sojourn at the Betty Ford Clinic. (Shakespeare had been told about 20th century drug and alcohol abuse, but was ignorant of a treatment center named for the wife of an obscure U.S. President.) She mentioned the two marriages to Richard Burton.

"Burton played Petruchio," Bonnie said. "He was a noted interpeter of your plays. He was considered one of the great Hamlets of the 20th Century." She put her hand to her mouth. "Oh, I'm sorry. Do you know you're going to write a play about the Hamlet story?"

"Yes, I will," Shakespeare said. "You commit no fault, good lady. Jack has already told me of that work. Only spare me any of the dialogue you know of. I do not want the final form of the work to influence me in its creation."

"Phew," Bonnie said, with a sigh of relief, "Well, I think Elizabeth Taylor is very beautiful, but you have to understand that it has been thirty years, in our time, since she made that film."

Shakespeare sighed, the recited something:

> "Crabbed age and youth
> Cannot live together;
> Youth is full of pleasure,
> Age is full of care:
> Youth like summer morn
> Age like winter weather."

"That's nice," Bonnie said. "Is it from one of your plays?"

"No, good lady. A sonnet. I read the whole piece last night at The Mermaid for some of my friends. Ben Jonson also had a piece to read, as a compliment to my poem. Mine was judged the better by the gathering, so my victuals were on his bill. I have been bettered by him in the past, so he always brings my wits to a sharp edge. He is a keen-witted young man, as you will see if you tarry the two hours needed to hear his *Every Man in His Humor* this afternoon. You shall be my guests and be seated in the upper galley near the stage, the better to hear his lines above the clamour furnished by the more spirited of the groundlings."

"Thank you," Bonnie said. "Thank you very much. It is an honor to be here in your presense, sir," Bonnie said. "I would not trade being in this boat with you now to be the most successful actress in my time."

Shakespeare blushed, then he took Bonnie's hand and gently kissed it. It was the good lady's turn to blush. I saw her eyes sparkle and, yes, felt more than a little jealous.

"Look at that," I said, pointing to the east. The cloudiness and swirls of fog had lifted from the horizon for a moment. What had been a shrouded, almost undefinable span on the edge of our sight came into view.

London Bridge.

The bridge itself looked like a madman's idea of a condomimium development. From our vantage, it hardly looked like it would be passable for foot or hoof traffic but our guide told me theer were archways through each of the large buildings for crossing the span. It was more a housing project than a bridge, with block-long townhouses sporting peaked roofs and onion-shaped domes that rose several floors above the span. I imagined you had to be a swell to live there. Shakespeare pointed out some of the buildings, supplying names to each—Nonsuch House, St. Thomas' Church, names of the various taverns, goldsmiths, silversmiths, 'chandler' and 'milliner' shops, (one selling tallow candles and soap, the other women's finery according to Bonnie) plus grocers and such-and-such fencing school—all of these outfits doing business right on the bridge.

The foundation of the bridge was a series of stone arches, with wooden docks jutting out from each massive support. The current flowing through each of the arches looked close to white-water swiftness. I could see now why Bacon wanted to start his journey to Greenwich Palace from the other side of the structure.

I was feeling nauseous and was getting anxious to reach the shore. The fog engulfed us again, then it turned to wisps, enabling me to see the opposite shore and the ordinary wooden dock we were bound for. The brief rain had passed. Shakespeare took off his hat. He craned his neck to the port side of the small craft. Soon he started waving his hat over his head. I could see someone—a well-dressed young man with a derby-style hat similar to Bacon's—standing at the end of the dock. The man doffed his hat and waved back at us. I could now see he was a younger man who bore a resemblance to Shakespeare. The man held something in his non-waving hand: a long clarinet-like instrument.

"It is Edmund," Shakespeare said cheerfully. "Thank God the rascal is safe. And damn him for running up bills on my credit."

Above the young man waving from the jutting pier, above the row of gabled wooden houses that were set a few yards from the bankside, you could see an arena-type building made from wooden timbers with a small house mounted at one side of the not quite square structure. From this house a large white flag flew from the roof, with the figure of a man holding up a large ball.

"The Globe," Bonnie said to me. "That's The Globe."

Chapter Forty-Six

The elder brother was so glad to see his younger sibling that he only lightly slapped him upside the head, knocking his hat off. This happened the moment he got up from the ladder on the dock and got within arm's reach of the younger man.

"Have I a spendthrift for a brother?" William asked. "Did I bring you here to drive me to the Malshalsea Prison for debt? Were you spawned by our good parents to drive your brother to penury and ruin?"

There was no sense of strong anger in the elder Shakespeare's voice. There was firmness, however. As I stepped off from the swaying boat, then helped Bonnie out onto the pier, we watched the encounter. On firm footing again, my stomach started settling down, much to my relief.

"You were detained by the owner of the music shop in Blackfriars," Edmund Shakespeare said meekly, his large brown eyes downcast. He was a beardless youth, maybe twenty-something, wearing a floppy, brimless cap similar to mine with a blue and white doublet, a flat white collar for which only the sleeves and collar showed, and short breeches which showed his stockings from mid-thigh down. He had a wiry frame compared to his brother, who was stout in stomach and chest but had a weaker chin. The large brown eyes and prominent forehead marked him as a fairer-haired replica of his brother.

"You may keep the music book and the crumhorn," the elder brother said. "It will do you well to learn the ways of

Orpheus, for there is much call from the groundlings and the galleries and Lord's Rooms above them for a fair strain of melody. But mind you learn this instrument well before you pursue another. I will stake you to no more than your living needs for the next weeks."

"Will, good brother—" Edmund began.

"You are low-man in the company, a veritable apprentice in the theater as I was ten years past. You cannot afford to be a spendthrift nor a tavern wit-snapper. I have heard disturbing reports of your carousings during the hours best kept only by wanton idlers and the nightwatch."

"Our good parents did not rear a brace of monks, Will," Edmund replied. "My affairs outside the workday are my own."

"Your affairs are mine when I am to pay the reckoning," the elder brother said, a trace of anger flaring. He checked himself. "Come, brother, let us spare our visitors anymore of this family mussing."

We were introduced to the younger brother as Bonnie Benchley of Bristol and Harold Wells, manservant of Master James Benchley of Bristol. It was clear that Edmund was not in on the fantastic nature of our visit.

"I must to the Globe," Shakespeare said, "and don the apparel of the elderly gentleman I am to portray in this afternoon's diversion."

"I would dearly love to see the inside of the playhouse," Bonnie said.

"And so you shall, good lady," Shakespeare said. "Edmund how long until the play commences."

"One half of the hour," the brother replied.

Shakespeare turned to Bonnie. "Might I suggest, good lady, that you stroll about this green bank of festivities before entering the playhouse. Enjoy the flavor of the environs. After the performance, I will have time to acquaint you with inner parts of The Globe." Then he reached into his doublet and withdrew two small pieces of paper.

"These are two special passes, given to me for disposal," he said. "They will afford you good seats in the upper gallery above the stage. After the performance, come backstage with these passes and one of our men will take you to me."

Both Bonnie and I expressed our thanks. "How will we be sure when the play starts?"

"Listen for the trumpets," Shakespeare said. "They can be heard from any point 'twinst here and the Bear Garden. Present the tickets to the usher at the door with Perseus holding the head of the Medusa painted above the post. He will know where to seat you."

"What part are you playing this afternoon, Edmund?" Bonnie asked.

Edmund's face brightened at the attention. "I am to take on the countenance of a woman, specifically the wife of Oliver Cob, the comic water-bearer. Tomorrow I am to portray a servant to Cassius as well as Cinna in my brother's, *Julius Ceasar.*"

"He does not impersonate Cinna, the Roman Senator, allied with the Marcus Brutus," the elder brother added. "He is merely in a brief scene as Cinna the Poet, an unfortunate innocent murdered by the Roman mob after they are aroused by Anthony's oration."

"It is a small part," Edmund said. "But I will make much of it."

"You will show restraint and play the role as I instructed you," Shakespeare said coldly. "If you dare play your role out of proportion to the measure I intended it, you will return to carrying the signs that indicate change of scene."

Edmund shrugged his shoulders. "Sometimes I feel I should have stayed in the country with my brother Gilbert and learned to be an honest yeoman."

"Merry brother," Shakespeare said with a bit more joviality than before, "you may still get your London boots in the mud and muck of Warwickshire yet. For the present, confine your time to learning to speak the speech of the stage properly, in rehearsal and in quiet contemplation, and rub shoulders no more with the wenches of Sinbad's Tavern, or any other haunt of drunkards and punks. I have made a name here lo' these dozen years in London; its standing and credit are not to be abused."

"Come, come, elder brother," Edmund said, putting his hat back on. "You are too young in this."

Shakespeare again knocked the hat off his brother's head again. "Young lout," he said as his face seemed to be supressing a smile. "Dare you quote lines from my newest play to argue against me? Off with you then. Back to the playhouse and announce that I am coming forth as well."

Edmund left, but not before a smile and a bow to Bonnie, who returned the young man's courtesies with her own bright smile.

Shakespeare turned to us. "The lad is safe. If Bacon succeeds in his business with the Queen and Doctor Dee at Greenwich Palace, chaos will be averted—at least for the present. I must to the tiring house to prepare. When you next see me it will be in the guise of a ancient and bearded man, trodding the boards. Remember to listen for the trumpets." He turned and walked briskly off the pier and down a narrow alleyway between two houses. Ahead of the houses was a small park and, beyond that, the curved roof of the building Bonnie had identified as The Globe.

The passes Shakespeare had handed Bonnie were about three by five inches in length with the initals 'W.S' in large curiously-slanted script. In the middle of each pass was an ink sketch of the earth being held up by a large, brawny man (Atlas? Hercules?) braced under his load like a weightlifter just before the final jerk of the burden into the air. Below the man, in a semi-circle, was written the following: 'Globe: Bearer Granted Admittance to Porticus.'

When we reached the alleyway, we had to dodge a passel of horsebacked riders and pedestrians, mostly headed in the direction of the theatre. One pedestrian in particular caught my attention. An older fellow with a bony, aristocratic-looking face and a salt and pepper beard was coming at us with a big used car-salesman smile. Despite the tony features, he wore a tattered-looking brownish-white ruff, a doublet with sleeves that barely passed his scrawny biceps, and puffy artichoke-green breeches that looked as well-worn as the jacket. His hose also looked like a spent article.

"How now, good folk," he said, addressing us in familiarity. "It is good to see fellow townspeople in this tempest of humanity. Tell me, dear lady, how of your dear father. Is his business prospering?"

Bonnie paused for a second, took in the effrontery, then let forth.

"How now yourself, cony-catcher," Bonnie said in her accent. "Give way to me before my servant clears me a path. Trouble some gullible soul with your games."

"Do you not recognize a fellow-townsman, good lady," the man said, appearing genuine in his puzzlement. "It was not six months ago that I beheld you on the steps of our fair church, congratulating the vicar on his able sermon."

"Were it your attempt at swindle were as good as your imagined vicar's address to his flock," Bonnie retorted sharply. "I have no money for your imaginary widowed mother or your imagined crippled brother, bed-ridden since his return from defending the faith in the Netherlands. Get thee gone from my way. There are laws of necessity to rid the streets of scavengers like yourself. Do not make me—"

The man's face went from friendly to guarded. "I beseech your pardon, good lady," he said with a quick, cursory bow. "I will trouble you no further." He walked on, mumbling something to himself.

As we walked on, Bonnie told me that 'cony-catcher' was a slang term for conmen who prayed on gullible people, especially those newly arrived in London.

"I read about them in one of the books Mr. Benchley loaned me. Robert Greene, the fellow who called Shakespeare an upstart-crow, wrote about them in one of his pamplets."

"That's where Warbeck got the idea for the title of his book, *Shadow On the Crow*?"

"Precisely," she said.

The walkway opened up to a small courtyard with a cluster of quaint-looking one-story shops facing us. Bonnie picked one (Carrington Cosmetics and Perfumes) and we went inside. The establishment featured a long counter on one side of the room, with the table space occupied by a variety of vessels and jars. In between the niches behind the counter—also filled, like a medicine chest, with various glass and pewter containers—were narrow retangular-shaped tapestries depicting ladies and gentlemen looking fashionable for the times.

A young woman, with a pale-complexion wearing a ruff that fanned out behind her head, supporting her tightly coiffed hair, waited on Bonnie. The woman's neckwear was open at her throat and she wore a large teardrop shaped ornament that glistened in the light coming from the windows. I had some trouble taking my eyes off her throat, which was smooth and milky, as well as her eyes which rivaled Bonnie's for allure.

Bonnie tried some of the cosmetics, found them too thick for her taste, and settled on a small cloth bag that smelled strongly of cinnamon and other spices. She also bought a mask because the shoplady asked if she was attending the play this afternoon, and expressed what seemed like genuine concern that "a woman such as yourself, obviously of gentle breeding, should know it is not done to show your face unmasked in a public theatre where men of lewd disposition gather."

"Oh, dear," Bonnie said. "I am from the country and have never attended a public spectacle. Can you furnish me with the proper adornment?"

"I will show you an assortment of guises, milady, if you will wait anon." The saleswoman disapeared behind a curtain that must have led to the stockroom.

"You gave her a pretty good look-over there, sailor," Bonnie said impishly as soon as the other woman appeared out of earshot.

"My apologies, milady," I said, stooping over in a deep bow. "It was never my intention to offend." While I was close, I figured I'd reach over and kiss the soft knuckles on one of her hands.

"Mr. Shakespeare was a far better hand-kisser than you, my good knave," Bonnie said.

I gave her a second kiss, this time on the underside of her wrist.

"Are we not getting a trifle above our station here, sirrah," Bonnie said in the local dialect. "A good servant knows thy place."

"Thou art a harsh mistress, milady," I said.

Bonnie nodded, then spoke in a snooty fashion: "Degree and decorum must be maintained—at least in the daylight hours."

The counterperson returned. Bonnie selected a mask and paid for it, along with the small cloth bag that she reminded me was called a pomander, which ladies commonly held up to their noises to cover up the noxious odors abounding in public places, and also as a quack device to ward off infections.

We walked past a row of houses and then out into a park-like greenway, filled with numerous arbors and hedges cut in precise, cone-shaped patterns. There was a three story round wooden ampitheater just beyond the park, which was about the size of a basketball court. In the foreground, a pole supporting various arrow-shaped signs told us that we were standing before 'The Bear Garden'. A group of men were in a circle in the center of the park. One could see the thick plumes of smoke rising up from the crowd, courtesy of the pipesmokers. We could hear an inhuman growling noise coming from the epicenter of the crowd.

"I'll bet there's a bear in that crowd," I said.

"I don't need to see any bears right now," Bonnie said. "My nerves are on edge enough just now, thank you."

"No bears then."

We took advantage of a simple backless wooden bench in the park and sat down. Bonnie put her nose slightly upward, slightly craning her neck.

"I smell tobacco," she said. "Good tobacco."

"You left your cigarettes back in the future," I said.

"I saved a couple," she said. "I've got them at the bottom of what is passing for my purse. I also have one of my lighters."

"Do women get to smoke in Elizabethan times?"

"Probably not," Bonnie said with a sigh. "Probably get stoned as a witch if I do it in public. Damn, why did Mr. Benchley have to go so far back in time? If this were the 1930's or something, at least I could take a shower and have a smoke. Please, do something to take my mind off smoking."

"Such as...?"

"Try talking to me," Bonnie said, her teeth almost clenched. "Stimulate my mind."

I watched a few brown sparrows hop about in the brush, searching for food as I thought up topics of mental stimulation. A chorus of barking dogs could be heard every now and then, coming from the direction of the arena.

"Okay," I said. "This guy Shakespeare. Do you think this woman he had the kid with—Tyler Benchley, that is—do you think she is the Dark Lady of the Sonnets that all the writers and history buffs are always on about?"

"I'll bet she is," Bonnie said.

"What is the deal on the whole 'Dark Lady' thing?"

"How much do you know already?"

"Not much. I was studying to go to a police academy and be a cop. I spent a lot more semester hours at school learning about rights of suspects, 'just cause' provisions and protecting the chain of evidence than on old English plays. I've read some Shakespeare recently, but—"

We both kept quiet as two young women dressed in low-cut, bosom-projecting, tight green bodices passed. Their skirts were narrow, almost like pants, and not at all like Bonnie's more demure, formal skirt which exaggerated the hips but didn't seem provocative. One woman was fair, one was brunette. Both wore their hair long and both swayed in a certain way I learned from patrols to associate with prostitutes. Certainly the way they headed quickly toward the crowd of men indicated the strut of working girls. I made a point not to stare.

"Okay," Bonnie said after the pair passed by. "There is a portion of Shakespeare's sonnets that speak of a dark lady who has black hair, dun-colored breasts, whose complexion is nothing like the sun and all that. Tyler has dark features, as you know. Plus, it was pretty obvious that Mr. Shakespeare was smitten by Liz Taylor when Mr. Benchley showed him her *Taming of the Shrew*. Historians have speculated for a long time on her identity. George Bernard Shaw wrote a terrific little one-act play about it, with a certain Mistress Mary Fitton being the lady. Mary Fitton was also a lady-in-waiting to Queen Elizabeth. Trouble was, somebody found a portrait of her and the lady doesn't have dark features. I've read a lot of different studies on the 'Dark Lady' theory. Nothing about some barmaid in Dover. I wonder if Mr. Benchley knows that information."

"Sounds like Bill Shakespeare doesn't want to get the Barbara Walters treatment for the benefit of posterity."

"No it doesn't. Must be frustrating to Mr. Benchley if he wants to do that film. In a way, I'm disappointed that the dark lady wasn't some Baroness or Lady-in-Waiting. It takes the element of danger out of the romance."

"I take it the Queen doesn't like her women at court hanging out with the performing arts types."

"It was a good way to wind up in the Tower of London for a Lady-In-Waiting to marry anybody without getting the Queen's favor. Sir Walter Raleigh, who was the big guy at court before Essex came along, wound up in the Tower for a good stretch for running off with one of the Queen's attendants. So did his beloved, Mistress Throckmorton."

The growling erupted again from somewhere inside the circle of smoke-exhaling men. One didn't have to be a subscriber to National Geographic to know there was definitely a bear somewhere inside the crowd. Now Bonnie wanted to see the bear, perhaps to take her mind off the need for a cigarette.

"Step up, step up, good sirs," a pasty, pock-faced fat man in the center of the crowd said. He was holding a thick chain attached to a fully alert, adult black bear. Bonnie and I squeezed our way into the crowd to glimpse the spectacle. A man in the crowd was holding a long stick in his hand just a few feet from the bear. The business end of the pole had been stripped of all its bark and bore some nasty-looking claw marks. A few ladies were about in the crowd, most staying very close to their male companions.

"Step up, step up," the barker repeated. "Take a turn with the branch, if ye dare. Only half a crown to tempt this young bruin sired by the mighty Sackerson."

A clean-cut boy in a blue appentice outfit dropped a coin into the outreached hand of the barker, took up the stick, and poked at the poor beast. The bruin took some poking, then roused up on his hindquarters, slapped the pole from the boy's hand with a devastating swat from one paw, then sprang forward at the lad. Only the hard jerk of the handler held him back. Back toward the ampitheater, one could hear the husky barks of the dogs responding to the growls of the aroused bear.

"Where are all those animal rights types when you need them?" I whispered to Bonnie.

"It's not civilized," Bonnie whispered back. "I've read what this is about. Inside that place in front of us there's a pit. Inside it they chain a bear to a stake and let a pack of large dogs, mastiffs, attack the bear. Either the dogs you hear barking get mauled to death or they tear away at the bear with their fangs until the animal is dead."

"Delightful," I said, dispiritedly.

"It is brutal and uncivilized. But how civilized is bullfighting? Or boxing? Or good old American football? We're not that far from this in our own time."

"How does a guy get a face like that?" I asked, pointing at the barker, who was continuing his spiel and looking away from us.

"Smallpox," Bonnie said. "Not everybody survives a dose of it. The lucky ones get to look like junior league lepers for the rest of their lives. That's one of the reasons Truffie had us take those shots before we got on the STUMP."

"Let's head for The Globe," Bonnie added.

We walked over the knoll and got our first close-up view of The Globe, from about a hundred years away. It was as I had remembered seeing it in pictures in high school and college textbooks, and in the model on display at the Northwest Shakespeare Museum back in Rogue Falls: a large multi-sided structure about the same size as the Bear Garden, with the sides slanting slightly inwards as the structure met the sloping roof, which appeared to be open at the top. There was also a small building, similar to a treehouse, above the wooden planks and bundles of straw that made up the rim of the auditorium. On the roof of the house a flag was flying, the emblem of which was similar to the one on our passes. A large crowd was milling about the park-like front of the theater grounds.

Let it be said that Bonnie Noel, the first modern actress to gaze upon the sight of that great landmark in the theater of the Western World, offered this exclamation upon surveying the legendary, erstwhile edifice:

"God, I could really use a cigarette."

We retired into a remote part of the park, well away from both ampitheaters. Bonnie decided on the thick cover of some elm trees, where, after making sure we were alone, my traveling partner emancipated herself from the conventions of the times and lit up one of her two remaining smokes. After shaking up her one remaining disposable lighter, and finally getting a bit of flame, she took a good, long drag on the pre-rolled tobacco, then exhaled it through her mouth and nostrils. Immediately her shoulders sagged a bit and her voice retained the calmness that had been missing for awhile. I liked the way she supported the elbow of her right arm with the slender fingers of her left. I liked the way she delictely held the cancer stick between her gloved index finger and forefinger, the way her face softened and relaxed as the next drag was taken and the smoke diffused from her mouth.

"I don't think you weaker vessels were allowed to smoke in this age," I said in a stuffy, mock academic tone.

"Whose side are you on, anyway?" she said. "So, my presumptuous servant, do I still remind you of a reasonably attactive hybrid of a younger Jane Wyman and Annette Bening? Or do the Renaissance duds add a few centuries to my looks?"

I scrutinized her, tilting my head back and forth so she could catch that I was scrutinizing her. "Not anymore," I said. "With that Virginia Slims in your hand, you have crossed over into that *femme fatale* catagory of actress. I'd say more like Kathleen Turner in *Body Heat* or Bette Davis in *The Letter*."

"I'll accept that," Bonnie said. "I wish I had the figure of the first lady you mentioned and talent the latter had. Well, I can always improve on the second catagory. But if comparisons are made to Bette Davis, I'd rather be the catapillar-turned-butterfly Bette Davis of *Now, Voyager* than the homocidal Miss Davis on that plantation in Malaysia. That's my favorite movie of hers. I like my leading ladies—even the bad girls— to survive past the last reel if at all possible."

"No matter what they might be trying to get away with?"

Bonnie waved her cigarette in the air and said in a mock Bette Davis style: "No mat-ter WHAT they may have done!" Then, in her own voice: "Short of murder, of course."

I moved forward and gave her a deep, long kiss. This did for me what the smoking did for her. Trumpets sounded, not inappropriately as far as I was concerned. We smiled at each other, then headed out of the grove. As soon as we made it to the narrow trail that abutted a stone wall, we had to make way for a party of sporty-looking men and women who were riding toward the theater. As we got back on the trail, we encountered a thick tree which had a hand-carved niche in the trunk. Affixed inside the niche was a poster which, in heavy black lettering, told us what we already knew, that *Every Man In His Humor* was the play of the day. Below that, another poster told us that, on the following day:

The Lord Chamberlain's Men will present

Mr. William Shakespeare's Newest Tragedy

Julius Caesar

with Mr. Richard Burbarge in the role of

Marcus Brutus

as to be enacted before the Inns of Court

and

For the pleasure of Her Majesty's Court

"I wonder how much that paper would be worth in the present time?" I asked.

"I was wondering the same thing. But we'd have to hide it someplace where it would be undisturbed for 400 years to let it look properly aged to pass the scrutiny of experts. Let's leave it where it is. We'll see what souvenirs they have at the show."

We passed a group of musicians walking in the opposite direction. The smiling men, carrying flutes and drums, were going to make way for Bonnie and I (for a change), when I heard the rapid gallop of horses coming closer to us, horses as yet unseen from the bend in the trail in front of us.

"Make way! Make way!" the first horseman that appeared announced. He was in uniform. A few paces behind him came two more mounted men. I immediately recognized one of the latter horsemen.

Dromio.

The horseman next to Dromio was not in charge of his mount. He was slung over the saddle lengthwise, his head and legs bobbing up and down as his mount galloped along. There was a rope attached between Dromio's horse and the saddle-horn of the animal that was transporting the prisoner. Most of the musicians scattered into the brush. A couple jumped over the stone wall. We took the former route. The lead horseman was a husky-looking dark-haired man with a pointy black beard and a gruesome face that belonged in the Dark Ages to some Visagoth with hemmoroids.

The man who was tied to the saddle was Edmund Shakespeare. He looked up and saw us as he passed, and I caught a look of stark fear in his eyes. I also looked at Dromio, who looked right back. I could tell the moment he recognized us: a slight, thin-lipped smirk cropped up on his large, ugly, bead-eyed mug.

Essex had made good on the threat he had made to Shakespeare in front of St. Paul's.

I looked at Bonnie. She had a stricken look on her face as the fast-moving procession flew by us.

"His brother needs to know," she said. Bonnie lifted up her skirts and ran down the trail. I was right behind her.

Chapter Forty-Seven

It must have been close to showtime at The Globe because we soon had to dodge our way through a throng of spectators. First there was a crowd of men dressed up with colorful duds and peacocks feathers in their hats, with a sprinkling of ladies in those hoop-skirts called farthingales. Most of the ladies in this crowd wore bodices cut low to give their bosoms good exposure. Boys in leather jerkins were busy holding horses for the new arrivals. I almost ran into one kid, who was selling what looked like hazelnuts, unshelled, out of a tray that was rigged up with a leather strap about his neck like a ballpark vendor.

It was Bonnie's idea to go to the opposite end of the three-story octagonal edifice from where the crowds were mulling. There, she figured, would be the stage entrance and she figured right. What she didn't figure on was a burly, sandy-haired young hulk with clown-wide eyebrows and large ice blue orbs set in deep eyesockets, carrying a stick of hickory big enough for a baseball bat. He was standing guard at the narrow doorway on the far side of the theater. And he wasn't there to let anybody in.

"Get thee gone," were his exact words to our attempts to implore him to let us in. He said this several times, like he said it a lot and was proud of memorizing it. I figured his I.Q. was about 80, but you don't have to be a Rhodes Scholar to be a security guard.

We showed him the tickets with 'W.S.' imprinted on them. "Those are good for the Medusa Entrance to the galleries, but not here," he replied.

"But they're signed by William Shakespeare," Bonnie said. "He is a sharer in this company."

"I know not what these marks mean," the big fellow said. "You could say they were Master Burbage himself that made such marks and I would be a fool. 'Slid, you shall not enter."

He was illiterate. What a stroke of luck.

"Can you get a message to him then?" I asked.

"And leave my post?" the guard responded. "I am no mark for a cony-catcher. Go to the Medusa entrance." He raised the hickory stick up across his chest.

Enough already, I thought. I took hold of his stick. He contested the issue. I delivered a swift front kick to his well-upholstered mid-section. He relinquished the weapon. I threw it aside. He lunged at me, leading with his right arm. I side-stepped, grabbed his wrist with one hand and with the other hand took hold of him by the stubby-haired chin. After that, I just dropped my right knee to the ground and leveraged him over my upper left leg. Once I had him on his back, I came down with my elbow to his chest. That took enough wind out of him for me to get my foot planted on his chest and both hands on his right arm, one at the elbow joint.

"Just lie there," I said, "or I'll break your fucking arm." I looked over to Bonnie. She was already across the threshold and up the stairway directly past the landing.

The guard coughed a bit. Shy of his stick, his manners had improved considerably.

Bonnie returned with the elder Shakespeare and a large man with a long mustache, who, for a split second, made me think of Trevor Warbeck in disguise. But this fellow had lively, darting eyes and a lot more hair on his head which, in this case, happened to be red.

I let the guard up. He coughed and spit for awhile and probably would have taken another shot at me, but Shakespeare told him Bonnie and I were friends of his, with an urgent message. He picked up his bat and resumed his station. I followed the other three up the stairs.

William Shakespeare already knew about his brother being abducted.

He explained to us what happened in a small, crowded room cluttered with costumes. Men's streetclothes hung on pegs sticking from the wooden planks that made up the walls. It smelled like a men's gym locker, but the collective muskiness of dried male sweat was mixed with odors of paint and glue. The lighting was provided by a couple small lanterns and a few candles. On the little wooden tables, there were paint pots with dirty brushes and wigs. All types of shoes, from elegant boots to leather sandals were piled up in one corner. This was the 'tiring house', where the actors outfitted themselves for the performance. There were about eight to ten men in the room besides Shakespeare and myself. Many were only half-dressed. Bonnie stayed in the hallway, owing to propriety.

"A giant comes right into the place," Shakespeare stated to me, wringing his hands as he spoke. "This gargantua states he is the mustering officer for the Liberty of the Clink, and summons Edmund to follow him outside. There my brother is put in irons and thrown upon a horse. This is hard behavior, even for a Queen's officer mustering men. I protest, I offer him money as a substitute for my brother being dragooned. He refuses all my beseeching, and hands me a letter." He held a small brownish paper out to me. I read the short message that had been scratched out on the envelope. It was in modern script, but written with a quill, not a ballpoint.

"W.S.—Read the letter within."

> 'After the play, you will be required at the Anchor Tavern, in the Lord's Room.
>
> Come alone. You will be able to answer directly to our conditions.'
>
> Grantum

The man with a long mustache glanced over my shoulder as I read the paper. "Was that what the soldier left you when he took Edmund?"

"I fear he was no real soldier," Shakespeare said. "I think Edmund has been abducted. There are certain plotters among us who mean ill for the kingdom. The wedding at Grantum Hall is obviously a key to their plans. Edmund has been abducted as a surety of my not revealing certain facts to the authorities."

"Are these the same men who wish us to perform your old

play on Richard Planetgenet two days hence?" the redhaired man asked.

"Aye, Will," Shakespeare said. "They are in league with Essex. And the Earl of Grantum. And sadly, with good Harry of Southhampton, my friend and patron."

"Then it will do no good to inform the sheriff," the other Will said.

Shakespeare shook his head. "We are dealing with gentlemen of the realm. They pay no heed to constables and watchmen."

The other Will looked puzzled. "I thought that Grantum was your sponsor from years past. Why would he kidnap your brother?"

"Because he is not really Grantum," Shakespeare said. Then he stopped, obviously not wanting to get into the whole Grantum-as-Warbeck business. "What I mean is that he is a friend of the Earl of Essex. Grantum has become infected with the latter gentleman's hubris, as it has infected young Southhampton."

Another man came into our group. He had piercing blue eyes, bushy reddish blonde hair perfectly combed, a neat Van Dyke beard, prominent cheekbones, an aquiline nose and a scowl on his lips. Behind him I could see Bonnie in the doorway, looking in on us.

"Will," the handsome man said in an abrupt, unfriendly manner to the playwright, "is that a jade I see outside our dressing area?"

"Dare you call me a jade?" Bonnie said in a tone of indignation. "I'll mind you to hold your tongue, player, from any slanders when you address me." She stepped into the dressing area, propriety now lost due to insult, and got into the bearded man's face.

"I am here because I am conducting business with Mr. Shakespeare— through my servant," she said in a no-bullshit tone.

Burbage cast a burning look in my direction. "Best make it quick business," he said to me dryly. "After the opening dance, the first scene commences. Shareholder or no shareholder, William, you have ample time to deal in personal affairs outside our theater. Your place is in the wings, waiting for your prompting. Where is your wig and beard? You are playing Master Lorenzo Senior, are you not? He is an aged man, is he not?"

Shakespeare sighed. "I have received distressing news, Richard. My brother has been seized by men masquerading as captains mustering troops. I fear he is in grave danger. There—"

Burbage threw up his hands. "Edmund has been mustered into the army! Fie! Fie! Fie! Who will play Cob's Wife? We begin the play within a pisseth and no wife for our comic. We need a Tib by scene four."

"Field can play the part," Shakespeare said, pointing to a young man in the opposite corner of the room. He was a skinny youth, adjusting a reddish fright wig on his head. He already had on an unbecoming dress that looked like a housecoat.

Burbage threw up his hands then cried out. "A boy with even less time than Edmund in the company supporting Kempe! Kempe, know you your lines at last?"

"I do," the other Will said with a smirk. "Know you your lines, young Dick?"

"I am not in this production," Burbage said. "The jailbird Master Shakespeare engaged for us as a playwright wrote no part worthy of my trodding the boards this day."

"I meant are you ready to play Brutus tomorrow," Kempe said. "I saw you wenching at the Mermaid last evening. I did not realize memory could be shapened by wooing other men's wives."

"Bah!" Burbage said, as he turned away and strode out of the room. He gave Bonnie a wide berth, as she was still looking indignant over the 'jade' remark. She gave a wink to me after the handsome actor passed.

Anothor man rushed into the dressing room. He was a burly fellow: another soldier, I thought, armed with rapier and pistol. My heart sank.

But this was no real soldier. It was another actor. A bright red sash hung diagonally across his tunic. The thick trunk of his body gave him the look of a boxer or a football player, as did his face. He had acrooked nose indicating a past break and a long scar across his right cheek. He had a reddish nose on his young unlined face, but that face was sickly pale.

"I feel most unwell, Will," the burly man said.

"Thou looks like a whey-faced loon, Ben," Shakespeare said.

"I fear the play will be ill-received," the man continued. "The groundlings clamour like geese. The honey in my lines will turn sour from the overbearing hemlock of their babble. Word of mouth will turn against my work; my moiety from the ticket box will suffer. I need money for my debts lest I return to the cursed task of laying bricks."

I noticed the man, who I later learned was Ben Jonson, was sweating profusely. He was clean-shaven and the perspiration was running over the layer of make-up on his face like satellite photos of a river delta.

"I cannot afford to have this play fare poorly," Jonson said. "It will not bode well for the sequel. Could we not issue a pronouncement to still the tongues of those beggars and vagabonds who befoul the pit?" He was wringing his hands as he spoke.

"You know our policies," Shakespeare said firmly. "Be a spectator, a beggar or gentleman, they have paid for their two hours of diversion."

"Dammed rabble," Jonson said. "Their tumult plays upon my nerves. A pox on the whoreson louts! My stomach churns! My words need the favor of those with sensitive ears and minds bathed in the classics. I am not trained to despoil my talents to the raffed multitudes. There is one pimp in the yard who howls like a fishwife. I would run the cur through for a groat!" As he said this, Jonson ran his hand over the hilt of his sword.

Shakespeare did not speak to this sweating, hand-wringing fellow actor/writer about the episode with Edmund. Jonson looked like he had troubles of his own in spades.

"Ben," Shakespeare said, "you have nothing but stage fright." He patted his nervous colleague on the back. "Sadly, you are twice cursed from being both a player and the writer of the text. You have been away from the stage these many months, owing to that unfortunate duel with the late Mr. Spencer. Put that behind you. You are a worthy writer. The text bespeaks your wit and flair. You are a worthy player. I saw you act splendidly for the Lord Admiral's Men. Fear nothing, Ben. Tonight, you shall be a champion at The Mermaid, toasted by scholar and buffoon alike.

Jonson's breathing stopped. His jaw quivered. I knew exactly what he was going through. It was vomit time. He ran out of the room, a thick, hairy hand over his mouth, and stumbled down the same staircase we had entered. I heard the door at the bottom opening, followed by violent retching noises echoing up the stairway.

"He will be better soon," Shakespeare said. "Were it possible I could so purge my woes and be done with them. Mr. Kempe, will you excuse us for a moment? I need to conclude my business with this good lady and her servant."

William Kempe, whom I found out later was the actor tapped to play Sir John Falstaff in *The Merry Wives of Windsor* at the Grantum wedding, bowed to Bonnie and exited. The rest of the actors in the room had left for the wings.

"There is more writing on the other side of the missive," Shakespeare said. "I will tell you the gist of that part. It is from Grantum. He means to take credit for all past and future plays I write. At his upcoming betrothal, I am to declare to the Queen and her court that I am a mere strutting player and Grantum has been feeding me plays lo' these many years since I begat my career."

"But that's not Grantum," Bonnie said. "It's Warbeck."

Shakespeare nodded. "I am also to present him with a written copy of the declaration I am to give at the end of the Falstaff play. I have two days to compose it. Before I speak my speech, I am to hand the copy over to him. I fear he will take the copy to the future. Being in my very hand, he can use it as solid proof that he is the author of my plays."

"He could do that," Bonnie said. "He could hide the paper in a safe location, go ahead through time, retrieve the paper after it has aged, then show it to the world as a great find."

"If he gets a letter in your hand," I added, "he can sell a ton a copies of that *Shadow on the Crow* he's written. You'll be giving him perfect documentation to support his cockeyed theories."

"And," Shakespeare said, "with one of Benchley's time machines at his disposal, he can come back here and enjoy being a literary lion in this age. All he does is assume Grantum's life, kill or keep imprisoned the real Grantum, and he has both worlds to revel in.."

"And when Essex gains power," Bonnie stated, "Essex will

become a puppet of Sherwood Strunk Enterprises. They will come here with 20th Century technology and turn this kingdom upside down."

"Angels and ministers of grace protect us," Shakespeare said. He put a hand to his forehead. I noted a broad gold ring on his third finger.

From somewhere above us, the trumpets sounded again, followed by the strain of flutes and beating of drums. Shakespeare quickly donned a steel-grey wig that looked like it came from a horse's tail, adjusted it on his head, quickly marked up the upper part of his cheekbones with three dark half-circles under each eye, then looked himself over carefully in the mirror, utilizing the lit candlestick on the desk.

A young, pale-faced boy, the one called Nathan, opened the door. He was dressed as a woman, with a bodice and skirt, and a face painted up in the thick make-up of the day. He had some padding in the breast area, but he looked no more like a woman close up than a dragqueen in a low-rent gay bar.

"Mr. William, the crowd is clapping for —"

"Yes, yes," Shakerspeare said. "I am coming. Nathan, you are not on stage for three scenes yet, so get my two friends here two stools and seat them on the stage." Then he turned to us. "Take heart. Bacon is by now near Greenwich. Pray Jove he can persuade the Queen not to—" He broke off, took a deep breath, then went out the door in the direction of the tumult from the hasty clapping of impatient spectators.

Chapter Forty-Eight

Bonnie and I parked ourselves right on the stage which was a long-square-shaped platform with a pillar at each side. The pillars held up the large awning known as the 'Heavens', which, according to Bonnie, kept the stage dry in case of rain.

The wooden stage was damp but it was not raining. The sun was finally out, and the two of us were seated on stools which had been provided by the boy actor. We were roughly situated at the upper right portion of the stage along with a dozen men and women, all dressed like they sorely wanted to draw attention to themselves. The ladies on the platform with us were both wearing masks to cover their faces, and they cast cold looks at Bonnie, perhaps for her more fetching adornment and her being fashionably late.

There were two doors situated on the back stage wall. Above the doors was a second stage which, Bonnie informed me in a whisper, was called 'The Inner Above.' This is where the musicians were and where the trumpets must had sounded from.

There were about a dozen people seated on stools on the upper left hand portion of the stage. I did not pay attention to them at first. I was trying to take in the interior of the theater which was very much like the Elizabethan Theatre back in Rogue Falls. The stage jutted out into the orchestra area and three tiers of arena-style seating circled above and all around us. The top tier of the theatre was divided into loges with red curtains fringed with gold-colored designs. The people inside these top 'skyboxes' were, by their dress, the cream of the patrons. In contrast, just below us, were the representatives of the Great Unwashed. There were hundreds of people in the 'pit' area (the 'groundlings' Bonnie called them) and they were without seats and clustered in bunches around the stage, which was only about five feet above them. The stench of urine and feces wafted up from the crowd which, for the most part, was composed of rauchy-looking men in sweat-stained shirts and ragged aprons, and women who were, if young, wearing their bodices and blouses with an emphasis of decolletage. Some women wore filmy, shear blouses under their bodices that all but exposed their bosoms to the public.

"Whores," Bonnie whispered to me as she saw me take notice of certain ladies. "The dress codes around here are a bit lax. Oh, and by the way, heed this advice: keep your eyes on either me or the play."

"I shall, good mistress," I quickly added. "Look at the roof up there," I said pointing to the thatched straw which covered the curved rim that circled the theatre. There were hazy swirls of tobacco smoke wafting upward courtesy of the numerous pipe-smokers. I counted my blessings that I wasn't up in those 'skyboxes' above the stage for that looked about 100 feet off the ground. Such a view would have brought on an attack of acrophobia.

A fellow in fancy clothes, with a high ruff and long tassels hanging down the front of his gown, was the first actor on the stage. His appearance settled the crowd below us somewhat.

"This is the prologue," Bonnie said, her attention now rapt at the actor about to speak.

But he didn't speak. At least not yet. One of the well-dressed gents on our side of the stage got off his stool and walked to the center stage. Unlike the swells decked out for fashion statements, this character was wearing a plain brown doublet, unadorned hat with a high crown, plain buckram breeches and high boots which showed no portion of his legs. He spread his arms out in front of the actor and presented a vocal harangue suitable for a Baptist tent revival.

"Stop!" the man cried out. "Turn away from this idolotry of men dressed as women and rogues and vagabonds strutting in the apparel of kings and nobility. It is a sin in the eyes of God for such a profane display to be made public. The teaching—"

"Sit down, Calvinist meddler!" a thin, hatchet-faced man in the first tier of galleries shouted out. Others followed his example, hurling vocal invectives against the pilgrim-like fellow.

"You are headed for dammation, all of you!" the unscheduled speaker called out to his hecklers. "You turn away from God's message. Your very attendance here shows you are most deservedly bound to the inner circles of the underworld. Turn away now or your spirits will dwell forever within the firey gates of hell!"

"Remove the whoreson cur!" someone shouted. A chorus of similar oaths rose from all about the pit. Hisses and boos came from the galleries. The man was confronted by the hulk/bouncer from the rear entrance. The big guy made a grab for the speaker but he jumped off the stage into the pit. He did some vocalizing with the hostile groundlings in the pit before the bouncer caught up to him and escorted him roughly out the wide front entrance.

A man sitting next to me gave me a nudge in the ribs. He was a dark bearded fellow with dark eyes. His face was like that of a young Bela Lugosi, with a carefully groomed inch-wide growth of black beard that covered the outline of his face from ear to chin. I also noticed he wore an odd cape, emblazoned with five-pointed stars and crescent moons.

"When we all reach Damnation," the fellow said to me in a cheery voice, "you won't be able to count all the Puritans who have made their home in that parish." He chortled at his own joke.

I smiled. The group around Bonnie and me overhearing the remark, laughed as well, but it was an uneasy, nervous chorus of laughter.

There followed the prologue and then the play itself. Several times I could have used modern translations of antiquated words that the actors spoke, but I left Bonnie, looking transfixed by the show, alone to soak in the substance of the play. The actors were playing rather broadly for the most part, and this gave the play an in-your-face quality from our close viewership. Shakespeare played a father who was in London checking up on his son, a college kid who did more carousing about the taverns and stews (i.e. brothels) than studying. The playwright, Ben Jonson played the braggart soldier, Captain Bodadill. It was clear that Jonson wrote the most crowd-pleasing lines for himself, bellowing out strings of profanity—'Lord of the dunghills!,' 'Lowly black and meloncholic worm,' 'Lumpish whoremaster, I fart at thee,' etc—for his character.

Shakespeare, as the old man, seemed more restrained in his performance in contrast to his fellow players. He projected himself well. He did not flail his arms or walk directly to the front of the stage to deliver his asides, but rather seemed more natural than, for example, Shakespeare's fat friend from the dresssing room, William Kempe, who played the comic character, Cob, a 'tankard-bearer,' i.e. water delivery man. The fairhaired actor had several long speeches which he delivered at a pitch of hysterical indignation, to the delight of the groundlings. When he first appeared, the theater seemed to rock with cheers and shouts of "Kempe! Kempe! Kempe!" or "Falstaff! Falstaff!, look you this way!" Kempe acknowledged the crowd as popular actors like, well, Ann Benchley in *Anthony and Cleopatra,* by pausing after their entrance to allow the exhortations to run their course. Kempe and Jonson took turns trying to steal the show.

"What did Shakespeare mean about Ben Jonson being locked up," I asked Bonnie, during a brief lull between scenes.

Bonnie explained: "He fought a duel with an actor from another company, Gabriel Spenser, and killed him. He was sentenced to die but he escaped the sentence by being able to read and write. That was called by 'benefit of clergy'. It's an old medieval loophole they still had or have back here. He's going to jail a couple more times in his career. The next one, I believe, is when he collaborates on a play which King James is going to find insulting to his court."

"Maybe we better tell him to lay off writing that one," I said.

"I'll leave that up to Mr. Benchley," she replied. It was at this point, her head tilted back to talk to me, that she seem to notice someone. Her expression indicated alarm.

"What is it?" I asked, noting her sudden change of expression.

"Don't look now—" she began.

"Who is it now?" I asked. "Warbeck? Queen Elizabeth? Pricess Diana? The Dave Clark Five?"

"Try Sherwood Strunk III," Bonnie said. "He's standing up in that loge above the groundlings' access."

That he was. It was hard to see the occupants of the loges on the third tier. But there was a fellow standing on the railing decked out in a cape. That face, a potato with eyes, could only be Sherwood Strunk, the fellow running for Governor of California whom we had last seen way back at the Museum of Western Art in San Francisco. Apparently, he was taking a break from the campaign. Strunk stood there, looking around the place like he was at the Grand Canyon, which, for a Shakespeare enthusiast, was probably a similar experience. A young lady in a dazzling outfit and a mask came into view next to him. She probably was Mrs. Sherwood Strunk. I recognized her by her height and supermodel figure. She was wearing a silky bodice with a multi-layered ruff and dangling below the ruff was, a necklace that sparkled from the radiant late-afternoon sun.

I spoke in a whisper: "Mark my words: this place is going to be crawling with Strunk and his Jet Trash real soon. They'll set up some syndicate of goons to run this place so Strunk can have his themepark."

"Like he doesn't have enough mansions and condos or places to play in already," Bonnie muttered angrily under her breath. "Can't Strunk and his pack just screw up the future and leave the past alone?"

"You speak of the future, madam?"

We had been overheard. It was the fellow with the strange beard who had made the remark about Puritans. He was eavesdropping.

"Oh, yes," Bonnie said in her accent. The play had resumed so she kept her voice low. "I was telling my father's faithful servant I am anxious to know the state of my impending wedding. I am a widow from Bristol. My husband died lo' these many years ago. I am contemplating accepting the proposal of a wool merchant, but I fear, inspite of his invention at trade, he will prove to be a poor provider for myself and my children."

The man in the strange cape nodded. "Fear you that he might squander the widow's portion of your late husband's estate?"

"Precisely, good sir," Bonnie said.

"You speak of condos, good lady," the man said, inching himself and his stool over toward her. "I know not what objects they be."

"Condos?" Bonnie said. "Oh, condos are—uh, they are..." She looked at me for help. I strained to give us some cover.

"Condos are cows," I said. "They are wild cows that thrive in the New World. Around Florida or Virginia, someplace."

From the look on Bonnie's face, she was clearly hoping I would've come up with a better whopper than that.

"Wild cows?" the man said. "Strange, I have read translations of Spanish tracts documenting flora and fauna in the New World. I have read Thomas Harriot's account of the beasts of Virginia. But nowhere have I read or heard mention of wild cattle. Are they man-eaters?"

I looked at Bonnie for help with a plausible explanation. I could see from the smirk on her face and the disapproving look in her soft green eyes that I was on my own.

"Well, good sir," I said. "Surely you have heard of the lamentable tragedy of the Lost Colony of Roanoake?"

The man nodded. A masked lady leaned over her shoulder. "Husband, you are disturbing my hearing of the play."

"The play be damned," the caped Lugosi-clone said. "This man speaks of man-eating cattle. Are you saying that flesh-eating bovines wiped out that lost plantation Walter Raleigh sponsored?"

"Yes," I said, nodding my head. "Condos roam about the Virginia area, generally. At least that's what I heard from my friend, Archie Leech, a humble sailor back in Bristol. He almost got eaten by a cow after a shipwreck. He killed the creature, skinned it, and brought the hide back to our port. The hide of the beast is woolly, like a ram or a sheep. My master wants to make a big killing (I wasn't sure that was a good word for 1599, but I was in too deep to worry about details) by importing a bunch of the cows' hides to England. That is why my mistress is concerned about the future. She might lose all her money getting her groom a ship's crew for sailing to America." Good, I thought. I'll stop there.

"Marry," the man said, loud enough to be shushed by several playgoers near us. "Marry," he repeated, softer, "but this is fantastic if it be true." He looked to Bonnie. "I may be able to help you out in your concern for the future of your intended's fortunes. I am a cunning man, my name is Simon Forman, and I deal in the art of astrology. This is my good wife."

We both acknowledged the good wife. From the downward curve of her mouth (the rest of her face hidden by the black velvet mask she wore) I could tell she was annoyed at us, and only managed the briefest of nods in our direction.

"My establishment is located not far from the theatre, milady," Forman said. "Perhaps we could make an appointment following the conclusion of the play?"

Bonnie smiled. "I'm sure you are indeed a cunning man *par excellance*, good sir, but I have several appointments today. Do you know the Queen's astrologer, Dr. John Dee? He is to meet our party later this evening."

I caught a glance at the front entrance of the pit. There was a disturbance taking place there. People were backing away from the door, someone was shouting out "Disperse!" over and over again.

"Doctor Dee, the Queen's astrologer?" Foreman said in a tone of surprise.

"Indeed, Sir," Bonnie said.

"That is strange," the astrologer said. "I had heard Doctor Dee was across the Channel in Calais this week, delving into the report of a certain French alchemist named Linder. Linder has reportedly found the Philosopher's Stone, an element that will turn base metals into gold."

"Good for him," Bonnie said, sounding only slightly ironic.

"He's trying to interest our loving sovereign into sponsoring his experients on behalf of the English treasury. The good Doctor was going to ascertain the validity of the process on behalf of the Queen."

"We heard that Doctor Dee is in London," Bonnie said. "He goes to meet the Queen tonight with the lawyer, Francis Bacon."

I glanced away from the conversation to see how the disturbance in the pit area was going. A fight had broken out between two men, one wielding a type of club with a round knot on the end of it, similar to what the fruit vendor used on the football-playing kids. The sparing partners were being broken up by two redcoats who had come through the entrance.

The men were subdued without anyone getting their heads broken and both were escorted out of the theater. The groundlings turned their attention back from the fight (some had booed when the combatants were taken away) and back to the play.

A couple minutes later, between scenes, Bonnie whispered to me.

"This Mr. Forman knows John Dee. He says it's hard to believe that Dee made it back from France already. Usually it takes longer to get to France and back, but he could be wrong."

It turned out Forman was right.

Chapter Forty-Nine

Anybody who entered London from Southwark knew they were headed into a tough town, if for no other reason than all those severed human heads sticking out on long poles above the grand gateway to London Bridge.

Bonnie and I caught a look at this hideous display as we walked up Gracechurch Street—or Dover Road, depending on which sign you saw—with Shakespeare. We were on our way to the Anchor Tavern for the meeting with Grantum, a.k.a. Trevor Warbeck. It was getting darker now, the shadows from the buildings to our left growing, and the only artificial light came from the torches on the rampart of the gate to illuminate the severed heads, and a few candles that were perched in the windows of shops and private homes. The effect was errie and I was looking forward to getting to some halfway-decent and well-lit interior.

As we walked down the cobblestone street, we dodged grimy peddlers who grabbed at Shakespeare and turned on some spiel until he shook them off, rickety donkey-drawn carts with rustic men hitching the reins, and resplendent horse-drawn carriages with weary-looking men in livery hanging about platforms near the wheels. Bonnie, not comfortable with looking at the hideous sight on the gate above us, asked Shakespeare about the latest play he was working on. *As You Like It* was the play, the play that Benchley had made into a film back in the 1960s. Bonnie had played Celia, Rosalind's friend, in a version of the play for the American Conservatory

Company. They talked about the characters. Shakespeare seemed to appreciate Bonnie distracting him momentarily from the situation with his brother and the potential loss of credit for his lifetime of work.

"From what Jack has told me," the playwright said, "the film he made of my biography did not—how do I say it?—did not go over big at the box office. The film lost his investors a goodly sum of money."

"But don't take that personally," Bonnie added before exclaiming, "Shit!" A wave of mud from a fast-moving carriage managed to spot her dress with road muck as we crossed the street. When we got to the cobblestones on the other side of the road, she continued.

"Your movie, your life story I mean, came out in the Seventies. That was a very uptight time, particularly in the United States. I was just in college then, and people were concentrating on current events, mainly the protests over the Vietnam War, you know, with the secret bombings in Cambodia. We had Nixon in China, the Russians in Cuba, Jane Fonda in Hanoi. I'm sorry. You probably don't know what I'm talking about."

"I know of this man Nixon," Shakespeare said to Bonnie as we formed into single file to avoid oncoming foot traffic. I was behind Bonnie so I didn't hear what the Bard said of the 37th American President until the crowd passed us and we spread out side-by-side again. Then I heard Shakespeare say that Richard Nixon was, "a head case, as Benchley put it."

"Well, yes," Bonnie said a bit defensively. "He was probably referring to the Watergate scandals and all the negative stuff the Democrats and the media had on Nixon thanks to him bugging himself in his own office."

"Bugging?" Shakespeare asked.

"Audio tapes," Bonnie said. "He was a brillant man, but he wanted to hold on to power so badly it destroyed his good works."

"Powerful man felled by envious men grasping for his cloak, driven to near-madness by hubris and fear of downfall. This man Nixon, though not a King, would make a good subject for a play."

"And I'm sure Mr. Benchley gave you his Liberal Democratic perspective on him," Bonnie said, giving me a wry grin out of the corner of her eye.

"Why did this leader of yours, Nixon, go to Cathay?" He asked. "Benchley compared him to Plutarch's Coriolanus, seeking sanctuary from the wrath of the plebian multitudes. He said he went to Cathay even though he would have condemmed any other leader of his nation for doing so. Benchley also said Nixon gave way to choler when any of his mistakes were brought to light."

Bonnie shook her head. "I see Mr. Benchley hasn't explained the 1970's very well to you. You have to understand those were troubled times and there are a variety of opinions on those events he talked about. If your life story were coming out in the times we just came from, it would probably do much better. Hollywood and the studios in England have made quite a few features from your works in the past few years. There were film adaptations of *Henry V* and *Romeo and Juliet* fairly recently and both were financially successful."

"Perhaps I should visit the future after all," Shakespeare said, "and collect some of these points and percentages that Jack has spoken of in his visits. Alas, I would likely be thought mad for claiming a dead man's portion."

"Very likely," Bonnie said.

The Anchor Tavern was located on the edge of the street just before the bridge. It was a lively place inside, much more than the village inn we had been at that morning. This place had the bustle you would expect from a bar in a big city in the early evening. It was a bright room, at least as far as the first floor was concerned, thanks to a large ornamental fireplace crackling away and a group of lanterns hanging from the bottom of the wooden mezzanine that came about a third of the way out from the back of the room. The patrons were well-dressed ladies and gentleman, mostly gentlemen, who seemed to have taken up every table in the place. There was some standing room at the bar, which had a series of lion heads carved into the panels that made up the side facing the customers. Male and female 'tapsters' moved in and around the tables and the patrons. Some balanced pitchers and pewter glasses with one hand and a shoulder, sloshing the contained drink slightly as they worked their way around the customers. Others carried plates of cooked apples or well-done fowl and meat steaming on huge platters. The place smelled of the cooked food with a strong force comingled with body odors and stale beer.

As with the Turtledove Inn, tapestries of hunting scenes hung from the walls. Here, there was a fullface portrait of Queen Elizabeth, much younger than we had just seen her, hanging over the fireplace. As the three of us nudged and swerved through the crowd, I saw a man wearing a long apron making marks in chalk on a blackboard behind the bar. There was a name followed by so many 'groats' and 'shillings'. I assumed that was how they kept the running tabs.

There were no electronic diversions for the patrons, unlike O'Leary's Sports Bar, but the place did have live entertainment, consisting of three men and one woman standing on a low rectangular stage perpendicular to the fireplace. One man played the recorder, another a violin. The other musician played a small piano-like instrument. The woman was a small breasted redhead with long stringy hair. She was singing a song in a soft, reedy voice that only those close to the stage could fully hear above the general din.

Because of me getting directions from one of the servers, we discovered that the Lord's Room was located upstairs. We were escorted to the room after Shakespeare told the young man his name. There were three people waiting for us there, all of them Strunks. Sherwood Strunk III, his blonde bombshell wife and a rough potato-faced replica of the father.

The room was spacious and the decor featured square recessed panels on all three of the walls. The fourth side of the room was a balcony that looked out over the downstairs. There was an overhead candle-powered chandelier that dropped little spots of wax on the dark oak table in the middle of the room. The table was set with pewter glasses, plates, flagons, and baskets filled with fruits and shelled nuts.

I got my first up-close look at the politician/ billionaire, and the deep, pale-white scars that ran about his puffy face. Sherwood Strunk wasn't wearing his glasses and squinted at us as we entered the room. Strunk stayed seated, a glare on his face, his mouth pulled back to reveal the upper bridge of his perfectly straight front teeth and, below that, the front of his tongue hanging slightly over his lower lip.

"I said for you to come alone, Shakespeare," Strunk said in a tinny, barely masculine tone. His voice was testy. This was not the public, smiling, would-be Governor of California, and standard-bearer of his Truth Party. This was Strunk the hard-core businessman. He had his arms folded over his shiny baby-blue silk doublet and I would've bet that, somewhere on his person, below the ruff and the fancy jacket, he was armed with something more advanced than some one-shot wheel lock pistol.

"You are not alone, I see," Shakespeare said. "Wherefore should I be?"

"Sherwood, shut the door," the patriarch said. Sherwood the Fourth complied. I kept my eye on the kid as he stood and pulled the cord that closed us off inside the dining area. The kid was packing a gun, for sure: I could see the bulge on his hip. I kept my eye on him until he sat down again.

"I told the management I didn't want to be disturbed once Mr. Shakespeare arrived," Sherwood III said. He looked at me. "My son is armed. I want you three to know that."

"I'm armed, too," I said. "It's the American way. Do you let your kid have bullets or does he just like to play cowboy?"

The younger man gave me a sneer but didn't go beyond it. The three of us took seats on the bench opposite our hosts. I sat on the outside of the bench, closest to the door, and Bonnie sat on the other side of Shakespeare.

After the six of us were all seated, Strunk reached into the silken cuff of his shirt and pulled out of piece of plain white paper. He unfolded the paper and spread it out on top of the table. It was a miniaturized version of the blueprints Major Trubshawe had confiscated off Southampton at the falls.

"I'm afraid it's just a rough sketch," he said, addressing himself to Shakespeare. "I'm no architect. We can do the theatre in the design of The Globe, only bring it up to modern specifications. It will be at the center of my complex."

Shakespeare barely gave the paper a glance. "What about Edmund? What about my brother?"

"He's fine," Strunk said curtly. "You don't have to worry about him. You'll get him back Friday night after you make your speech at Grantum Hall, just before the play starts."

"What speech?" Shakespeare asked.

"The one that acknowledges William Devant as the author of the plays attributed to you," Strunk said. "We need to get that taken care of. I promised my friend, Trevor, we'd get that done. After that, we can get to the benefits resulting from your sacrifice." Strunk took a quick gulp from the mug in front of him, then continued speaking.

"Here is the deal, Mr. Shakespeare. I'm a fan of yours and I'm rich. I have a private park in Northern California a few centuries ahead of here called The Forest of Arden. I want to set a similar park here. I picture it as a grand theme park, a literary Disneyland. I'm sorry, I forget you don't know about these references I'm using."

Shakespeare sat back, a look of grim determination in his face. "Nor do I want to know the references, Mister Strunk. You are a pirate. You steal my brother, and now you tell me you want to steal my plays and give credit to another man for my labors. I care not about your parks or what you—"

"Hear me out," Strunk said patiently, lifting his hands, palms down, over the table. "Just hear me out. I am from the future. I have designs for a park here where I want to bring certain friends. I want you to be a part of my organization. I want you to provide me with your works, which I will pay you handsomely for. Add to that some personal appearances I'd want you to make and it will be a nice package for all concerned. Who's your agent?"

Shakespeare crossed his arms. "I have no agent. My brother Gilbert represents my business interests in Stratford. I have the advice of Francis Bacon on legal matters. There is a small project I might do for my own friend from your time."

"That would be Jack Benchley?" Strunk said.

"Aye," Shakespeare replied.

"Forget him," Strunk said. "He's minor league. I'm going to be the one doing things here. I'm the guy to be affiliated with. You will be the greatest attraction in show business history. Thousands of your future admirers will shuttle back here to see your plays and to see the Lord Chamberlain's Men and to see you. I'm going to build a township which will be a perfect replica of Elizabethan Civilization. When this super-retro thing goes public back in modern time, it'll be big. Really big. Now, Shakespeare, you can get in on it now or, frankly, we can do it all without you. But I feel like I should give you a shot at the big time because you're the guy who first got me thinking about making money out of big-time drama."

"A theme park," Bonnie said disgustedly. "You jerks are

going to build a stupid, sanitized themepark and bring people here to spoil everything these people have. Why?"

"Why not?" Ms. Strunk said in a squeaky voice. She waved her fingers idly on either side of her square chin, wiggling her digits as if to show off their length and thinness. "We have the technology. Jack Benchley has kept the invention to himself long enough. We have two of the STUMP machines. In time, Sherwood will bring in scientists to duplicate the schematics of the device, make sure it's safe and all for our friends. We might even let common people know about it and use it—eventually." She stopped the finger exercises, and stuck her small square chin and pug nose up in the air, as if daring Bonnie or one of us to take a swing at her.

"I hate tourists," the younger Strunk said blandly.

"There will be *select* tourists, Sherwood," the father said. "The long term plan is to bring in scholars and builders and engineers from various corporate power centers. No damn bureaucrats of course, or anyone else who's ever had a paycheck cut from the United States Treasury. The scholars will mingle with the major writers and thinkers of this period, and study them firsthand instead of relying on the random anecdotes of diarists and the odd scrap of a letter or a business record. We're going to really get to know you, Mr. Shakespeare, and all your important contemporaries. The playwrights and poets: Ben Jonson, Thomas Dekker, Thomas Kyd, Philip Sidney, Edmund Spenser, Christopher Marlowe, all the big name actors like Burbage and Kempe and—"

Shakespeare shook his head. "Thomas Kyd is dead, sir. Spenser, I am sad to report, has just died. Sidney breathed his last on a battlefield in the Lowlands, long before I even came to London. Marlowe is dead these six years: he took a knife through the skull in a tavern brawl. If you wish to meet any of these gentlemen, Master Strunk, it would be best to bring a shovel and a strong back."

"Let me work on that one," the Senior Strunk said. "Once we get the schematics this egghead Ryskind character set up, we can break this time-space thing wide open. I might just save Kit Marlowe from that tavern brawl in Deptford. I'll bet there's a lot of good poetry left in him."

Shakespeare shook his head. "You are trifling with things that no mortal man has business dealing in. This is not in the obedience of God or nature to pull the dead from their graves and change the course of people and nations to suit your fancies. We writers of this age have enriched your world with thought and beauty. Let that be enough! You are mortal beings. Do not pursue us like the Furies for secrets of our lives we may not have ever intended you to know! Take your infernal machines and your impious desires and leave us to the prideful posturers of our own time. Why not be satisfied with your own world and its wonders and diversions and challenges? One world was enough for Alexander and Ceasar: surely you cannot be more ambitious than these Worthies? Suffice to make the most of that gift given each of you by your Creator: the gift of time, prealloted and precious, not fungible and manipulated by mortal whim."

There was a long pause, then Strunk the Third spoke: "Okay, those are noble sentiments. I'd expect that from you, Shakespeare. But here's the deal, see. I'm building a new Forest of Arden Theme Park, bigger than the one I have back in California. I already have a site picked out in Middlesex Forest. Once I can get three of the STUMP machines together, then we move the heavy equipment in. By then, our friends will be in control around here and I won't be offering you another deal after tonight. Frankly, we have all your plays already: all the ones you've written and the works that you still have to compose." He swept an open hand over the blueprint on the table. "We can do all this without you. I produce television shows and movies for my cable stations so I can bring in my own actors and directors. I can freeze you out. There are no copyright laws to worry about, not for another 300 years. Your company will be the featured performers. All you have to do is acknowledge that the Earl of Grantum wrote the main part of your stuff and good things start to happen. I'm going to take it all anyway, whether you join up or not. What's it going to be?"

Shakespeare said nothing. Nobody said anything. I looked at Strunk's son, watching his folded arms stay folded. Then I glanced at Bonnie. She was looking at Shakespeare stare down at the table.

"What it be, Shakespeare?" Strunk said. "In or not?"

Shakespeare slowly looked up at his questioner. He leaned back, scratched his pencil-thin mustache, then told

Strunk, softly and firmly, to go fuck himself.

"What?" Strunk said as if he had been addressed in Icelandic. "What did you say?"

Shakespeare lifted the blueprint off the table. He tore the paper neatly in half, then in quarters, then in eights, then in sixteenths. Then he casually tossed the pieces into the air. They fluttered back down on the table, one bit landing on the top of Ms. Strunk's hat.

"Let me put it more direct," Shakespeare said. "I am saying, *ex necessitate rei*, go fuck thyself!" The last part was intoned loud enough to cause the Strunks to wince. The playwright continued: "I trust that four-letter word is still in use in your time. You, my dear Strunk, are a Machievel. You kidnap my brother to extort my false confession and give away my life work to some cheap masquerader, and then you call this a bargain? You tear my heart and brain out and offer in its place the chance to be studied by your courtiers. By my troth, I will slay myself first."

"It's part of the deal," Strunk said defensively. "When Trevor Warbeck came to me with the time travel opportunities—look, I made a deal already. You need to write a statement he can take back to his own time that supports the premise of this book he's written. I went along with it and now, if you want to see your brother in a reasonably short length of time, you go along too. Christ, you can go to the future if you want. You get to live in a house with electric light and flush toilets and video recorders and computers. You can write a whole new set of plays on an IBM laptop if you want. Hell, you have almost twenty years of life left, more years even if you start working out like I do and lay off the red meat and swallow a few aspririn now and then. So what's the problem here? I don't understand all the negative feedback I'm getting here."

Shakespeare made what almost sounded like a growling noise, put his elbows on the table, and joined his hands by intertwining his fingers. He rubbed his two thumbs together as he spoke, giving me the impression he was trying to maintain control of himself.

"The Proverbs say that the recompense of a man's hands will be rendered unto him. The Earl of Grantum, the real Earl of Grantum, was a man I long considered a friend. William Devant and the Devant family are the rightful heirs to

Grantum Hall by sanction of Good King Harry and his royal heirs. I do not know what you have done to the real Devant, or with Edmund, but I know this. I have written comedies in the style of Platus and Terence; I have written tragedies in the style of Seneca; I have taken the work of other men and added, if I may be bold, marked improvements on their ill-fated lovers or differing sets of identical twins or scheming villans or reckless heroes. I brought back to life the heinous, crookbacked Richard of Gloucester, the brave and hearty Talbot, the meek and pious Henry the Sixth, and his scheming virago Queen, Margaret of York. The shrill Kate of Padua was given words befitting her choler; the vengeful Shylock was given his just reward; the fair Juliet given a heart-rending demise that filled the galleries with tears. I have given the rougish Falstaff and his saucy minions to the hearty men and women who come and pay their coins and suffer the smells and ruffians of the grounds that abutt the stage. They and their betters expect a pleasant or moving two hour diversion for their time and travel. I have almost always rewarded them. That, and my pastoral poems and sonnets, are my legacy to this world. They are from my hands, my mind, my sweat, my worry, my passions, my agonies, my folly, and the grand stage of life that enthralls me and gives me substance to create characters that hold the mirror up to man and nature. They are mine. You ask me to give up my life—my very life!" He pounded the table so hard the plates rocked.

"We have your brother," Sherwood Strunk III said softly.

"Indeed you do," Shakespeare said in a tone of anger. His eyes closed tightly, his right hand went to his florid face and swept across the brow.

"Indeed you do," he repeated, now in resignation.

The elder Strunk ran an index finger across his bushy eyebrows. "It's damn hot in this place," he said. "That damn fire down there—heat always rises I guess." He took a long drink out of the cup in front of him, then set it back down. He drummed his stubby fingers across the tabletop. Then he lifted up his cuff to reveal a gold Rolex watch. He glanced at the face. The bushy brows tilted upwards. Now he appeared anxious.

"I want to get out of here pretty soon," Strunk said to Shakespeare. "So what is your answer. Spare me any more dramatic recitations. You know the situation. I know you want your brother back. Talk to me here."

Shakespeare spoke meekly. "What would you have me do?"

"O.K, here's the deal," the patriarch said quickly. "Renounce all the plays you have written up to this time. Do it before the performance of *Merry Wives of Windsor* at the wedding, in front of the Queen and everybody at Grantum Hall Friday night. Then give Warbeck a paper, in your own handwriting, to that same effect. After he's got that, your brother is returned unharmed."

The doorway that separated the private room from the rest of the mezzanine opened. Jack Benchley was in the house. He looked pale, but at least he was standing on his own feet.

"Hello, Strunk," Benchley said in jocular fashion to his adversary. "Hello Madame Strunk and hello to you, too, Junior." He nodded to Shakespeare. "William, I can't say I approve of some of the company you're keeping these days. Nor you, Bonnie. And Wells, I must admit I thought better of you as well."

"We were just leaving, Jack," Shakespeare said, standing up. "Your terms for the latter portion of the bargain are acceptable, Master Strunk. I will not welch on my end of it, pray you are honorable enough to hold up your end."

Strunk Senior rose from the table, a jaundiced expression forming on his face as he eyed Benchley. Benchley returned the hostile look with a cheerful gaze.

"Oh, didn't Warbeck tell you, Strunk?" Benchley said. "I busted out of that nasty little cell you and your co-horts threw me in. You are a most ungenial host, sir, both in this century and in your own. I thought I was to be treated as a guest at your Forest of Arden. Instead, I'm kidnaped as I try and take my leave, drugged, shanghaied on a private plane across the Atlantic, sent back in time without my consent, then tortured." Benchley turned to Sherwood the Third. "You, sir, are a dirty, inbred sadist with the ethics of a pimp."

The junior Strunk stood up. He took a step toward the old man, but his father grabbed the son's slender wrist and retarded his progress.

"We're leaving, Sherwood," the father said in his high-pitched voice. He turned to his wife. "Get yourself together, Sugar," he said. The lady rose regally and moved out from the table with a rustle of her taffeta farthingale brushing against the woodwork. She followed the two men out of the room. After Benchley watched them (to make sure they were headed down the staircase, I suppose) he then leaned over the table and gave the now-standing Shakespeare a brief, but firm, hug, which was reciprocated. Benchley took a seat across from us. I took a glance over the railing at the tavern below. The Strunk party was going out single-file through the throng of patrons.

"You lost your eye," was Shakespeare's first remark to his friend. "Is there no act of depravity beyond these people?"

"I'm just lucky to be alive," Benchley said. He grabbed a dark red apple out of the bowl on the table and took a healthy bite. His breathing looked regular again.

"How did you get here?" Bonnie asked. "I hope you didn't tax yourself on a horse."

"I hired a coach," Benchley said after swallowing enough of the apple to allow speech. "It's an ample vehicle, with two stout English hackneys to pull her with. Bacon's man, Geoffrey, is my coachman. He went to the dock just below the bridge to await his master. I hope you three haven't eaten dinner yet. How did the play come off?"

"My brother has been seized by the same faction who held you prisoner," Shakespeare said bitterly. "I was dealing with them, Jack, when you arrived."

"The bastards have Edmund?" Benchley said hotly. "Damn! What do they want?"

"They fancy themselves a brace of Norman dukes and wish to make a conquest of this realm. From me, all they desire is the forfeiture of my work, in writing and in voice, two days from now. Otherwise, I suspect I will never see my brother again."

"We have to think on this," Benchley said. "Let's order something to eat, shall we?"

We had dinner in the Lord's Room. I had some kind of roast beef I made sure from the waiter was going to be throughly cooked, and some small-beer. Our conversation centered on Warbeck, Essex and the Strunks. None of us had a way to stop them. The only way to checkmate their schemes was to somehow steal back the time machines they possessed from deep inside Grantum Hall and leave the lot of them stranded. Benchley wasn't sure how many AK-47s and grenade launchers they had, but at least without the second STUMP the Essex's would-be rebels could not be reinforced and Strunk couldn't build his new, sanitized, electrified and computerized Elizabethan town.

"What are we going to do now?" Bonnie asked Benchley, after we had exhausted all plausible schemes for keeping the status quo in place in this age we were 'visiting.'

"Go home," Benchley said. "We will find out what Bacon has managed to do at Greenwich Palace as to forwarning the Queen, then we will leave the morning after tomorrow. Trubshawe will be out of the hospital. He and I will return to this time frame in the remaining STUMP with as many weapons as we can bring through time. Then we will volunteer ourselves directly to the Queen and her Privy Council to train her soldiers in how to combat Warbeck and his group. That's all we can do. Bonnie, you and Wells are going back to the States. You've gone above and beyond for me, but this mess is not of your making. I'll finish it or it will finish me."

Both Bonnie and I gave silent acquiecense to Benchley's plans.

We left the tavern shortly afterward. It was dusk now and, except for candles in the windows of homes and shops, the street was rapidly falling under a deep-blue gloom. A ground fog had settled in around the area, so thick that the gateway to the bridge (and the severed heads of the two-time felons) could no longer be seen. The air was moist and cold.

"Oh," Shakespeare said to Benchley as we came out onto the street, "I nearly forgot a request you made of me the last time you came to visit."

"Considering the travails you've been through, I'm not surprised," Benchley said as he retied the strings of his cape over his ruff. "But, whatever it was, it is no matter now."

"It is the translation of Ovid's *Metamorphoses* by Arthur Golding. You said there were no extant copies of the original printing available on the market in your time. I managed to secure one a few months ago at the Green Dragon Book Stall at St. Paul's. It is rare even in this time. I trust you could auction a few more quartos as well and secure funds for your festival?"

"I could probably use it, yes," Benchley said enthusiastically. "The Festival, your festival really, needs a new maintenance building. We're bursting at the seams at the storage facility we have behind the Lizzie. The Lizzie is our name for the Elizabethan Theatre."

"Indeed," Shakespeare said. "Perchance, if you ever meet the Queen, do not inform her of that particular moniker."

Benchley gave a thin-lipped smile. "You know me, Will. I have the manners of a courtier."

"A courtier who frequents the taverns," Shakespeare said in on easy manner that told me the two men were well acquainted. "You have never seemed out of place here as long as I've known you, but the Court is a bit more formal than, say, celebrations of Middlemass at Grey's Inn. I need to make my way to the Mermaid over in Cheapside this evening. I understand you will be meeting Bacon there this evening after he returns from Greenwich. Why not accompany me to my apartments? I can change my doublet and shirt, get you the copy of Ovid, and we can take a wheeryman's craft across the Thames."

"That way I can get my horse and Harvey can get his mule," Bonnie said cheerfully. (I had almost forgotten about the damn mule.) "I'd love to hear you do your poem and Mr. Jonson's poem, as well, if there is room for us at your party."

"Of course, milady," Shakespeare said. Then he sighed deeply. "I hope Edmund will come safely out of this."

We waited for a coach to pass along the street, then headed back toward the cluster of townhouses around the theatre area.

"I wonder if The Mermaid has nice rooms?" Bonnie whispered to me.

"What kind of rooms," I whispered back, intrigued.

"Ones with nice big beds, with client sheets, and big four-poster frames. Maybe a maid to heat some water so we could get a bath before we retire for the evening."

"Yeah, I wonder," I said.

"The word retire is a euphemism, by the way." she added.

We were halfway across the wide street, with Benchley and Shakespeare walking ahead of us toward a narrow alley maybe big enough to drive a Volkswagon Beetle through. I was contemplating the possible pleasures of the later evening when I heard the clatter of hoofbeats coming our way.

They came down the street, all six mounted men coming to a stop in front of 'The Anchor.' Four of the men were soldiers, and they charged into the bar like I used to do with my comrades in Sutter City whenever we had a judge's signature on a warrant and a nice drug lab we needed to secure before the evidence could be broken up or flushed down a toilet. I said there were four soldiers. The two men on horseback who stayed behind were familiar. One was the dwarf, Geoffrey, the guy who was supposed to be down at the dock in the coach waiting to pick up his boss. The other man was his boss, Frank Bacon himself. It was hard to recognize them at first from the heavy mist that blanketed the street.

Certainly, Bacon had no trouble recognizing us.

"Yonder!" he cried out, pointing to us with one hand and shouting back at the open door of the tavern. "Yonder lies the spies. Do your duty, subjects. Hue and cry! Hue and cry!"

This was not the same Francis Bacon I had come to know and generally dislike. He had transcended arrogance. He was now flat-out inhospitable.

I turned toward Benchley and Shakespeare. Shakespeare was no longer there. "Run, Goddamn it, run," Benchley said. "Split up and run." He took off down the narrow alley, moving as fast as his weary, unstable legs could go. Bonnie looked to me. I grabbed her hand.

"This way," I said. We took off in another direction, down the main street. I didn't look back, but I could hear manly shouts of voices and hard-soled steps on the paving stones, coming on toward us.

I glanced at Bonnie. She was looking back, and from her expression I could tell we needed to be moving a lot faster.

"Horses. We need horses," she said anxiously. Bonnie tripped on a stone, falling against me and nearly tripping me up. I helped her back to her feet. The shouting and footsteps behind us were now accentuated by hoofbeats. I spotted another public gathering place, probably a tavern of some kind with a good number of horses tied up to a hitching post in front of the place. At Bonnie's urging, we became horse thieves. She jumped on one, and I was trying to mount the horse tied at the railing next to hers.

"Forget that," Bonnie said, holding out her right hand.

"Get on mine. Hurry up."

She was right. I could barely ride a half-dead mule and I didn't want to be left behind. I swung up behind Bonnie and then we took off down the road. A man emerged from the tavern where we had purloined the beast and yelled for us to stop.

I looked back from my spot on the back of the saddle. From what I could tell in the dimming light, we had several horses behind us. Men were running alongside the horse-backed soldiers. They were ordinary men in plain clothes. It was a good turnout.

Bonnie turned down a narrow alley between two houses. The only light in the thoroughfare was a lantern hanging outside a sign in a doorway. A woman was in the doorway. I had a hasty look at her, and she was no Sunday school teacher.

The woman in the doorway yelled out something incomprehensible just as Bonnie said something to me. In retrospect, what Bonnie must have said was along the lines of, 'duck!' I didn't duck. The next thing I felt was open space under me, followed by my body making contact with the stones that lined the street.

I had hit my head against something, probably an unlit business sign hanging opposite from the establishment we had just passed.

As for me, the jig was up.

Bonnie stopped the horse from galloping and whirled the animal around to see what had happened.

"Hue and Cry! Hue and Cry!" the woman in the doorway was shouting. Out of the fog I heard hoofbeats getting closer. I was still on the ground. I had landed on my side and the pain was bad.

"Go!" I shouted out to Bonnie. "Go!" I repeated. Bonnie had an expression of fear on her face. Then she whirled the horse about with a sharp tug to the reins and vanished into the fog.

I had no Bonnie. I had no horse. I did have my Baretta. I undid the safety and, barely taking aim, fired at the oncoming mob. I succeeded in hitting the neck of an advancing horse. The shot sent the mounted rider sprawling off the rapidly-collapsing animal. I tried to fire again but the weapon was knocked from my hand by a long lance from another rider. The gun was now somewhere on the ground and I had no time to look. I drew my sword, but I was well outnumbered. I soon had another horseman plunging toward me, a long sharp lance pointing right at me. I dove downward. The lance hit the stones just in front of me. The tip caught in a small break in the stonework. The next time I saw the soldier he was flying over the top of me like a pole vaulter on his way down from the bar.

I scrambled to my feet, intending to run. Horses were now circling around me. I ran backward, through a gap between two men trying to dismount. One of them was carrying a harquebusier. That was the last image I saw, that soldier coming off his horse with that musket.

Something must have hit me in the back of the head. It must have been from something hard and blunt. Any running I was going to do from then on out would be in my dreams.

Chapter Fifty

My first conscious sensation was of water. It was all around me, lapping up against me in the darkness. But I wasn't wet. I heard the rhythm of waves coming close to me. For a moment I felt I was on a beach somewhere. Maybe the whole time travel biz was just a dream. Perhaps all this jockeying about was just a dream.

Perchance to dream.

No such luck. I thought my eyes were opened but all was darkness. Slowly a few more things entered my realm of senses: the murmur of men's voices, the squacking of birds, the flickering cast of a torch bobbing up above me like a giant firefly. Then came the headache. My first words were the familiar four-letter variety.

"He wakes," a hard, gruff voice said.

I heard the sound of wood knocking against wood. I saw part of a rounded-off wooden pole before my eyes, held diagonally by a hairy hand. An oar, perhaps?

"He needs a psychic," another voice, also gruff and hard, replied to the first man. "We are at the gate, and I'll not be burdened with carrying him to the wharf."

"Furnish the papist dog your psychic, if ye have any to spare, sergeant," the first man said.

It began to rain. Or, rather, to spray. It was warm, much warmer than the cold air, and the scent was pungent. I was being peed on from a short distance above my head. The stream was aimed directly at my face. Laughter accompanied the shower. I scrambled upright, trying to ward off the vile spray with my hands. (A funny thing about my hands and arms: they were joined closely together by something heavy.) The hoarse laughter from the two raspy male throats joined now with the sound of the birds—it was a cawing sound, the kind that crows make. The piss kept coming so I kept my joined hands above my face, enduring the foul liquid to flow down on my shirt and inside my cuffs.

The stream finally stopped.

"You are now baptized, Jesuit," one of the voices above me said.

My fuzzy vision now turned to triple fuzzy vision, or so I thought. That one big firefly of fire was now joined by two other fireballs looming up toward me. I heard a horse whinny. I was sitting up, holding still, yet whatever I was in was still rocking. I had to be in a boat, a small boat similar to the one I had been in earlier when I crossed the Thames with Bonnie.

"Bonnie," I said, hoping for a moment to get a reply, then a moment later I fully realized how bad a situation this had to be. Someone did reply to me.

"Oh, you'll have a bonny time here, good sir," a gruff voice said. "It will not be as cozy as your old cell at that English College for Jesuit Spies in Rome, but we promise you'll be snug as a babe in a cradle. On your feet now, seminarian."

I was in no hurry to get up. My head hurt, and I figured my next stop was not a clean, comfortable room with a hard mattress for my aching back nor any clean sheets, or cable television or a complimentary supply of Tylenol. Suddenly we abruptly stopped. "Land ho!" one of the wags shouted. I could now make out two ugly, bearded faces with the helmets and raiments of soldiers. The two men grabbed me, one taking an arm and jerking me upward and forward.

I saw a low archway done in heavy brick and mortar. I smelled the smells of stagnant water and the body odor of men who rarely bathed. Some of the smell might have been mine at this point.

"Bring the prisoner up the steps!" It was another voice, further away than the two men who escorted me. I saw the body that the voice belonged to. He was a short, barrel-chested man in a red uniform that looked like a robe cut at the knee, with a red and gold belt about his ample midsection. He was holding his gaze on me as I was led up the twenty or so stone steps to his level. I saw more torches, and more soldiers, standing around him. From his central position, and from the piping and elaborate patches on his duds, I got the impression he was in charge of the welcoming committee. I was stopped a couple steps below him, and allowed a good look at his face. The face matched his body. He looked like Charles Laughton from his *Mutiny on the Bounty* period: a pumpkin-headed man with wide nostrils, thick lips, and a heavy, bushy browline that hung like a crag over deep-set and unforgiving dark eyes.

"How now, sirrah?" the short stocky man said to me.

My head was splitting in pain. I looked down for a moment, taking in the reason my arms felt so heavy. I had heavy iron handcuffs on my wrists, separated by a few thick links. I was grabbed by an ear and my head yanked back up by one of my escorts.

"Look at the Chief Warder, papist!" one of the soldiers growled.

The Chief Warder repeated the question.

"Where am I?" I asked. I could barely recognize my own voice it was so weak. I tried to clear my throat and didn't get very far.

"You are at Traitor's Gate," the officer said. "I am your innkeeper, Chief Warder, Robert Harkins. Welcome to Her Majesty's Tower. You are a prisoner of state, and as so you may look forward to the barest mercies."

I heard birds cawing again, then, from the light of one of the torches, I saw a moving shadow passing across the high stone wall in front of me.

"Can we take the Jesuit pig on a tour, sir?" one of my escorts asked. "Can we show him the managerie?"

Some of the other soldiers laughed. A couple offered to help the two men take me to this 'managerie,' which, judging by all the enthusiasm, must have been a real gas.

The Warder shook his head. "No antics, corporal. Take the prisoner to his cell. Be quick about it." He turned about to the assembled men and cried out, "Return to your posts!" Accompanied by two soldiers who followed him a few steps behind, the Chief Warder walked away toward an archway. I was propelled in the opposite direction.

There followed the journey to my new abode. I heard gears creaking as I was marshalled along up a stairway. There was enough light for me to see that the walls around me were high enough to discourage either gate-crashers or guests leaving early. Castle-like merlons stood in long rows on the battlements at the top of each wall.

The next stop was a massive archway blocked by a porticullis, a massive grate of iron bars with spike-shaped points at the ground level.

"Prisoner for the Bell Tower!" one of the escorts shouted out. I took a look at his profile. He, like Benchley, was short an eye. Instead of a patch, this fellow went with a cloudly bluish marble-like substitute for the empty socket. He had more beard than face, the black tuffs of hair sprouted over whatever it was that he wanted covered from his jawline practically up to his temples. The phony eye clashed a bit with the red splotches on his nose, but I didn't offer any cosmetic tips. His voice told me this was the lout who pissed on me. The other guy was a hatchet-faced younger man with a long and bushy mustache. This guy shaved now and then. His weak chin, coloring and profile reminded me of Russ White.

I heard gears creaking again: the massive porticullis slowly raised up. I saw another uniformed man pushing on a crank that turned the metal cylinder that took up the rope. I turned and saw another man doing the same thing opposite him. From there I was led up a narrow vaulted stairway. And then another stairway winding in an opposite direction, and then another the same direction and angle as the first. I caught a bit of starry sky as the stairs ended and I was led from a portal to another walkway. We were on a parapet. I knew we were high off the ground, but with the high battlements, there was no telling how high up. At the other end of the parapet was a soldier. Next to him, leaning against the wall, was a battleax. The soldier stood next to a lit brazier mounted on a tripod. Dark smoke emanated from the fire. The air was heavy with the scent of coal. As we got closer, I saw that the soldier was young, maybe seventeen or so, with friendly brown eyes, and a pointy chin with a bit of beard under the lip. The eyes were warm but the face betrayed no expression. The red doublet seemed to hang on him rather than fit and his helmet was a couple sizes too big for him, held above his eyes only through the intervention of his ears. His buff-colored gloves were laying on a crenel and he was warming his hands against the fire.

"This is a fellow called Wells, a traitor," the hairiest of my escorts announced to the man on guard. "He's to join his friend in the Bell Tower this evening."

My friend? That was probably Jack Benchley. I was glad he didn't say friends. Maybe Bonnie had gotten away. Maybe.

The other guard nodded, quickly put his gloves back on, took up the battleax, and motioned me to go forward. I could see the blade on the weapon was big enough to decapitate a horse, so I fell in behind him.

We were only a few steps away from another archway leading into another tower. I waited for yet another porticullis to creak and grind upward. The redhaired escort helped the guard pull the chain up that raised the barrier, then lowered it back down after the guard and I got under the arch. Then it was up another winding, vaulted stairway which was low enough for me to conk my head on, then I was in a corridor wide enough for the aisle on the tourist section of an airplane. The smell of that corridor was like an untended barn. The only light was on a table at the end of the corridor, where a dark curly-headed man sat reading a book. His light source was a lantern that was hanging on an iron hook in a niche just behind his head.

"Cell number five," my newest escort said.

The other man put down his thick book and stood up. I saw the hilt of a long knife in a leather scabbard on one hip and, hooked on his belt next to the knife, a round metal loop with several ridiculously large keys attached to it by ridiculously big eyelets. The turnkey took the lantern off the hook and I was (not roughly, surprisingly) turned about by the guard and led back down to the middle of the corridor.

"Here you are," the jailer said as the three of us got to the front of a a narrow metal door. There were two slits in the door, one at eye level and one about the same height as my kneecaps. A key was produced by the jailer that undid the shackles about my wrists. The door opened outwards and I went in. The door closed behind me, the iron hinges crying out for lubricant. I heard the swift grinding of metal that told me I was locked in the dark room. At first I couldn't even see two feet in front of my face but I knew I wasn't alone.

Jack Benchley was with me.

I had seen him from the lantern light just as the door closed. He was lying on his back on a twin-sized cot that took up about a quarter of the available space in the cell. His one pale blue eye took me in but he didn't try and get up.

I felt my way against the wall opposite the wall, then bumped into what I hoped was a stool. I felt with my hand to distinguish it. It had a flat surface, so I sat down on it. I noticed there was a hole in the middle of the stool. That, and a pungent smell, told me I had no need to ask Benchley where the bathroom was.

I was incarcerated in the Tower of London. In 1599, no less. My back hurt, my head throbbed, everybody around thought I was some kind of spy, and now I felt a shiver of cold wind coming from somewhere on the wall opposite the door. It was an unsettling cold wind coming from right off the river.

"This is bad," I said to Benchley.

"I've been on a couple hunting trips that were pretty bad," Benchley replied evenly. "But I have to admit this is looking real bad." There was a pause. "I'm sorry, Wells," he said finally. "What the hell else can I say?"

"It's not your fault," I said. "I got myself into this."

"I should have known better than to trust Bacon," Benchley said ruefully. "He craves power and high office. I should've known he wouldn't want to wait for that. Warbeck must have wooed him over to his side, probably promised him the Lord Chancellorship when Essex becomes the local tyrant. Bacon would have had to wait years to get King James to grant him that office. Bacon played us for suckers. I'll wager he never went to the Queen at all."

"What about Bonnie?" I asked. "Did she get away?"

"I haven't seen Bonnie," Benchley said. "Wasn't she with you when you were arrested?"

"Last time I saw her she was riding off. I fell off the horse we were on. Then I got my head busted." I felt the sore spot a couple inches above my left ear. It gave me a jarring pain just to touch it.

"I hope she got away," Benchley said. "Bacon has had us labeled as Jesuit spies, part of some fifth column group working within the kingdom to bring down the Queen."

"I'm not even a Catholic," I said. "How did they get that crazy idea?"

"Planted evidence," Benchley said before breaking into a coughing fit. After the hacking subsided, he spoke again.

"Bacon, or that dwarf in his employ, planted a bunch of anti-Anglican pamplets in our saddlebags. They were signed by Robert Campion. Campion is a Jesuit *provocateur*, the most wanted man on this island. He wants to tie England up in a pretty package and deliver it to Rome and the King of Spain. I know about the pamplets from the Chief Warder. I got to chat with him before they dragged me up here."

"How did Bacon get ahold of these pamplets in the first place?" I asked.

"Warbeck probably furnished it to him. They probably had a couple of the surviving pamplets stolen out of a museum in modern times, then copied them onto fresh parchment to make them appear new. I'm sure a computer and a printer could create a resonable facsimile." Benchley coughed up a storm again.

"Do you know any good lawyers? Besides Francis Bacon, that is?"

My eyes were better adjusted to what little light we were getting from under a small crack in the door. It was enough light to see Benchley shake his head.

"It's no good, Harvey. I won't lie to you. I don't know if you're a praying man, but I've said my prayers several times tonight since I got here. Warbeck has us bagged. And if his plans with Essex succeeds, his crowd will be in control of this fortress in less than a week. Even if Elizabeth can hold out for a time, she'll be quick to put her enemies—any enemies—to death. That'll include us. I told you what happened to my friend Morton Ryskind. We'll get the same treatment he would have had if disease didn't get him first—hanging, disembowlment, the whole nine yards."

I racked my brain for an idea, a shread of hope, a trick, anything to get us out of here. I thought about my automatic pistol, and, stupidly, checked to see if I still had it. I had forgotten it had been taken from me. The soldiers now had the gun and Benchley's too, no doubt. I wondered what the local natives would make of a double action semi-automatic.

"There's a bucket over there, under the window," Benchley said feebly. "You're sitting on the toilet. There's another bucket under the stool. I'd give you a portion of this cot but it's rather narrow."

"Forget it," I said. "You were here first." I crawled over to the bucket, took the water out with a laddle, then drank it as best I could. It tasted horrible, and I was probably going to come down with dysentery, but at least my thirst was slacked. I crawled back over to the stool, moved it and the bucket out of the way, and stretched out onto the stone floor. There was a small amount of straw along the edge of the wall and I used my arms to create a pile of bedding. Then I folded my arms to create a makeshift pillow.

Suddenly, a thought crossed my mind. I articulated it a split second after it flashed into my brain.

"The Trubshawes," I said. "The Major's bringing the STUMP back to that grove in Hampstead in about a day, right? He's an army officer, right? One of his sons is a Royal Marine. They gotta have connections. If he knows you're locked up in here, maybe he'll let the modern military back in London know about this time travel business—"

"I doubt it, Harvey," Benchley said. "Truffie might go to Whitehall and tell the government, but would they believe him?"

"What if he demonstrated—"

"You forget we've only got one of the STUMPs. So, even if he wasn't locked up in a rubber room, even if he did demonstrate the thing, then what? One STUMP has too small an energy field to send heavy equipment back through time. The only way to take the Tower of London would be from the air—a paratrooper assault. That takes planes, helicopters. Same for Grantum Hall. But Warbeck has the other two STUMPs. It might take years to get another STUMP out of a laboratory. We probably have days before we'll be put to death."

We didn't talk very much after that. I turned over on my back, concentrating the straw right under my aching spine. I stared upward into the darkness, eventually falling off to sleep. I kept waking up and falling back to sleep, each time still hoping this mess was a dream. I did have a dream—it involved hooded figures staring down at me. My limbs were tied, I was facing up at them from a horizontal, prone position. Torches and red-hot irons were in the grasp of their bony extra-long fingers. I couldn't see their faces, just empty darkness under their hoods. Fire and branding equipment passed over my face, closer and closer.

I woke up yelling. It was still dark. Benchley said we were alone and told me to go back to sleep. I turned myself to the wall, balled myself up in a fetal position to sustain what warmth I could and tried to sleep.

I didn't sleep much. I didn't need any more nightmares. Instead, I laid down in the straw until daylight thinking about everything that had happened back to the night that my best friend Dave McCreedy filled me in on the Benchley case. It took me a couple hours, and took my mind off dreadful thoughts of the future.

Chapter Fifty-One

Nothing happened to us the next morning. We stayed in the cell and talked and worried about what would happen. For what it was worth, there was a nice view of the river from our window and the boats and barges plying up and down the Thames. We looked to be about four stories up. I could take a quick view of the place, before my acrophobia kicked in. There were six vertical irons bars across the window and it would have taken a high-intensity arc welder to cut through them. Getting past the bars would leave us with a forty or fifty foot drop to the ground below. And then we would find ourselves in a small enclosure surrounded by high walls. A couple soldiers trooped back and forth on the ramparts just below our cell. I imagined the Powers That Were had a 24-hour guard all over the place.

Occasionally I would hear a series of deep growling noises, sometimes several in unison. Benchley told me the beastly sounds were full-grown lions who were kept in a keep we could not see but, according to Benchley, we were just across a stone viaduct from them. The place had a pit where the animals roamed and a jetty above the pit where paying visitors could see the lions. It was called the Royal Menagerie, which had to be where the two soldiers wanted to take me the preceding night before their commander vetoed it. The growls of the lions and the foul scent from the brackish water in the nearby moat did nothing to help my disposition.

"They even have part of the Tower open for tourists at this time," Benchley added. "The last time I was in London I took in the Tower Armouries and saw the lions. The place is very similar to the way it's going to look 400 years from now. I wish they would have drained that damn sewer of a moat long before this."

Benchley knew a lot about The Tower of London: what fortifications were around us, when they were built, and what would be added later on. He told me Sir Thomas More and a few others, including Queen Elizabeth, had been housed in the same tower we were held in. (She had gone in as a princess, when her half-sister Mary was on the throne.) He knew the Tower of London was in reality a series of towers and the oldest one was a castle-like structure smack in the middle of the fortress called the White Tower. That tower had gone up after William the Conqueror and the Normans had invaded and subjugated the Saxons. That was around 1066, of course. A millenium before, the Romans had some type of fortress here, built by the Emperor Claudius when he did his own invasion. But all of that was buried now, waiting to be dug up when serious archeological explorations were undertaken. For now, all the buildings and walls and towers within sight were all put up by the crowd of inbred regal types who followed old William the First.

"There's probably nothing like it for security and design in Northern Europe," Benchley said as if he were a modern Beefeater giving me a tour. Yes, Jack Benchley knew a lot about the Tower of London, except the one thing I wanted to know: how to get the hell out of it alive.

Breakfast was brought to us by the jailer, who handed it to us through the lower slit on the cold iron door. Our meal was cold porridge and unbuttered bread, with a small cup of what Benchley called small beer. I drank it, having little worry about falling off the wagon since my days might be numbered anyway. The beer, if that's what it was, was served lukewarm and was weak. The porridge was cold and lumpy and might have been cooked from the water in the moat from the smell, and taste, of it. The bread was chalky. The whole repast only made me hungrier than before. "What's going to happen to us—specifically?" I asked Benchley. "You can leave out the very last part. I don't want to hear that again."

Benchley paused from his efforts to scrape the porridge out of the wooden bowl with the thick wooden spoon, set it aside, then stared up at the barred window for a few moments. Finally he spoke, his deep voice just above a whisper.

"We will be interrogated. I will probably be the first to undergo it since the Lord Lieutenant will see me as the ring-leader. The Lord Lieutenant is a fellow named Waad, William Waad. If I tell him the truth, about the time traveling and all, he won't buy it. If I was in his shoes, I wouldn't either. He'll think his pal Bacon has uncovered a secret nest of Jesuit spies. I'm just glad Shakespeare got away before he was seen with us—that would have put him in the same spot we're in now."

"So that meeting Shakespeare had with the Strunks—that was just a trap set up by Warbeck and Bacon. Once the Strunks were clear of the tavern, Bacon and whatever soldiers he had at his disposal went in to nail us."

"Strunk knew what time to leave 'The Anchor,'" Benchley said. "That's why he checked the watch under his sleeve. Bacon must have gone to Greenwich Palace, but not to urge the Queen to stay away from Grantum Hall. He went to Robert Cecil, the Lord Secretary, and asked him to issue warrants against us. Bacon no doubt offered to track us down, if Cecil dispatched some soldiers along to back him up."

"Shakespeare was with you the last time I saw him."

Benchley nodded. "He saw the trouble coming before I did, and warned me. We took cover under a wagon parked on the road. Bacon must have seen you and Bonnie. That's when he raised the hue-and-cry and all the male civilians joined the troopers in tracking you down. That gave the two of us some time. I persuaded Shakespeare to flee down the backstreets to his lodgings. He urged me to go with him, but I knew I was too feeble and I'd only hold him back. I was caught a few minutes after he'd snuck away."

"What's the deal with this 'hue-and-cry' stuff? On top of the soldiers, we had this mob of citizens chasing us down? What the hell is all that about?"

"The 'hue-and-cry' is what passes for back-up law enforcement these days. A sheriff or a member of the Queen's guard will shout and point out a suspected criminal and all able-bodied men in the area—apprentices, shopkeepers, every man below the local gentry—are immediately deputized to run him or her down. It makes up for not having a formal police force. But, back to what is ahead for us. Waad will want names. We don't have any to give him. I'm going to try to get by with some Ultra-Catholic conspiracy angle: that Essex and Warbeck have imprisoned the rightful Earl of Grantum in his own estate, which is true enough. I'll also casually mention a few dozen times that Essex means to take the Queen captive Friday night and either rule the kingdom himself or invite Phillip of Spain to put his daughter on the throne. That should worry the Lord Lieutenant. Maybe it'll buy us some time."

"So, we won't pass for innocent tourists from 400 years in the future," I said. "So suppose you leave out the Strunk angle. Suppose this guy Waad won't buy that. Then what?"

"Then the Lord Lieutenant will send some officer to court to ask the Privy Council to ask the Queen for permission to torture us. Since we are Jesuits, permission will be forthcoming." The old man, who had lost his cape somewhere, picked up his blanket and wrapped it about his shoulders like a shawl. "Then we will face a variety of excruciating physical torments to get the supposed truth out of us."

"Such as?" I asked, feeling my stomach churning up burning acid.

He talked about them: a small room called 'Little Ease' which they put people in so they couldn't lie or sit down for long periods of time; we could be stretched on some contraption called a *strappado*, which, from Benchley's description was the rack they used to stretch people until their limbs left their sockets (the same device, I suspected, that Warbeck showed Bonnie and I at the Tower of London exhibit back in San Francisco.) There was the thumbscrew, which got your attention through the fingers, or we could just be chained to the wall and have hot irons applied to various parts of our bodies. All these torture devices were over in the dungeon below the White Tower, waiting for use.

I stopped wanting to hear about what was in store for us.

After some prodding, Benchley told me a few anecdotes about his life as a filmmaker. (The subject was not pressing on my mind, but I thought, since other subjects like escape seemed academic...)

I asked questions about his career for hours. It was not like we had anywhere to go.

"What about *The Long Twilight*?" I said, referring to the

first American film to make a statement against the Vietnam War.

"That was supposed to sell the Vietnam War," Benchley said. "I did that for President Kennedy. By the time I actually started it he was dead. I was in a hotel in Saigon when I heard about the shooting in Dallas. I made it, but I put in my personal reservations in the narrative. The United States Information Agency didn't want my reservations. So the film got canned. It was Bobby Kennedy who got it away from the bureaucrats. That was in 1967, when he was beginning to change his mind on the war. *Long Twilight* actually was a modest success. The longer that war went on, the more people lined up to see it. It made the most money in 1972, even though I stopped shooting it in '65. You probably know I took a lot of flack for it. The American Legion put up a boycott of my films. I was kicked out of the VFW down in California. Even some of the guys in my old bomber group, guys who knew me and who had been through hell with me, called me Un-American for the benefit of the media. That hurt. I wasn't against the men who went over there to fight; I was trying to get them home alive. The reaction I got from my old air corps buddies hurt me deeply. It hurt almost as much as my dad being blacklisted. It hurt as much as my having to name Silvio Malatesta as a Communist to keep myself from being blacklisted."

That last part took me by surprise. I leaned away from the cold stone wall and looked at Benchley to see if he'd suddenly laugh and say that his last remark was a jest.

It was no jest.

"Warbeck is right," Benchley said, his blanketed shoulders drooping. "What he said back at the tavern, what he told Jack Picasso about my little visit to the Senate Internal Security Committee—that was true. I sold out a good friend: a friend of my father's and a friend of mine. It was name a name or be denied work in Hollywood. No equivocations allowed. I had a nice house, lots of alimony to pay, and I had bills galore because I had expensive tastes back then. So, I sold out my friend. It was him or me, and I picked him. I saw what being blacklisted had done to my father. He was doing dinner theater engagements and getting damn little of that. He lost his house. He damn near had his Cadillac taken back by the bank. I couldn't get on the blacklist and go live in some cold-water flat in New York while I tried to write plays or novels. I needed to work in the film business. I couldn't fight the whole United States Government. Shit, we were up to our eyeballs in a war with the Chinese in Korea. Who knew when this internecine hysteria would lift? Warbeck was right: Jack Kennedy got me a secret session with Joe McCarthy. I gave him Malatesta's name. It was Silvio who had to lose it all and go to Europe and seek out a living. That same year I gave holy hell to the House Un-American Activities Committee. My friends and my daughter know about that Jack Benchley. But the only reason I could oppose HUAC was because I had already carried wood and water for that rat Joe McCarthy." He paused, looking up at the ceiling, then continued.

"When Silvio came back to the States in the Sixties, I tried to make it up to him. I made him my screenwriter and a co-producer on a few films. I made him Artist-In-Residence at the Shakespeare Festival later on. I helped him make his anti-fascist picture to get back at Mussolini."

"Did Silvio Malatesta ever know you sold him out?"

Benchley shook his head. "No. I was there in his bedroom when he died, and I never had the courage to tell him. I wrote myself up as a stalwart defender of Freedom of Speech, as some big Crusader against Nixon and McCarthy and Roy Cohn and that crowd. Those guys only let me alone, let me catawaul against the establishment, because I had put out for them. I was just another sell-out."

I noticed his right hand was shaking. He put his left hand to his right wrist, closed his eyes and visably shuddered.

"Your daughter told me the FBI bugged your phone when she was growing up. Is any of that true?"

"No," Benchley said. "Part of the deal was that I could keep working, stay off the *Red Channels* blacklist, if I reported in to an FBI Special Agent. The fellow was named Farnum, one of J. Edgar's men in Hollywood. He reported right to Hoover. I did that a couple times every year, from '53 to '61. I never named anybody else, but I went along with the program. I even made little speeches at the Directors Guild Meetings against the blacklist. I signed petitions. I gave money to help men and women who couldn't get work because they had been fingered by their fellow artists. The FBI didn't care because they already had their pound of flesh from me. I was just a trusty in the great big prison of the National Security State."

"Why are you telling me all this?"

Benchley's response was immediate. "Because I think I'm about to die, Harvey. If not today, then very soon. I want to get this off my chest to somebody. Now that Jack Picasso knows what I did to his father, all the demons are dredged up again inside me."

Someone close to the Tower we were in barked out the command, "Fire!" The sound of a cannon boomed out, the echo everberating about the high walls and towers. Then another command and another blast. And then another series. Each explosion was followed by an echo, the last shot followed by the sound of something heavy landing in the river.

"Target practice," Benchley said calmly. "The troops are firing a fusillade, probably to sink some decrepit barge. Remember that videocassette, the one Warbeck gave me, the one that is supposed to concern Ann?"

"Yes."

"I managed to hang onto it. It's in this boot." He reached into the one of his leather ankle-length boots and pulled out the microcassette.

"Be interesting to know what's on it," the old man mused, "and if it could have been used in a court of law to incriminate Warbeck. But I suppose it hardly matters now."

I agreed, but didn't say anything because I was too depressed. Neither of us spoke for a time. Not being a priest, I tried to segue any further conversation away from another confession on Benchley's part. I decided to focus on his artistic projects.

"Mr. Trubshawe told Bonnie and me you were working on a documentary about this age we're stuck in."

"That was going to be my next project. I brought in some lightweight videocameras to clandestinely shoot various sites. You may have seen the footage we took on our last trip: various shots in the rural stretches of Middlesex, the bustle of London, the lost landmarks like the original Globe Theater, St. Eleanor's Cross, and the Royal Exchange, people scurrying about up and down Cheapside and the Strand. I wanted to document what Truffie and I had seen. We bought a large wagon, covered it with hay, and drove it around while Truffie took the video from a small coffin-sized box concealed under the hay. He stretched out and filmed from a knothole on one side of the wagon. Eventually, I was going to edit all the raw footage—possibly have it tranferred to film stock if I could get the equipment and do it myself. I also wanted to get Will Shakespeare to talk about his life—on video. We would have to shoot that secretly, too. The problem is that Shakespeare doesn't like talking about himself. He soaks in what I tell him of the future avidly, although he's not into collecting books from the future the way Bacon is. But his private life—except for the basic details of his life as an assistant schoolmaster and a player—is a closed subject with him. He just won't talk. He won't recount the episode of his giving away his son to me when he had no other recourse. I've tried to get him to come to the future and see his son but fears the experience would be too painful. He lost his legitimate son, Hamnet, a few years ago and I suppose he believes Tyler will remind him too much of the other offspring. No, as far as Shakespeare's contribution to the project, I've about given up."

I thought about Bonnie. It had not taken her long to get Shakespeare to open up on his life in our journey across the Thames. It was too bad he hadn't let her in on the time travelling. I'll bet Shakespeare would have opened up to Bonnie.

Bonnie. Was she somewhere safe?

Benchley continued: "I was thinking about putting the footage into some form and just putting it out for release—anonymously. Maybe just send it to the American Film Institute and see what kind of shitstorm starts up from it. Just sit back and watch all my younger peers and the snotty critics wonder how in the hell this stuff was taken, where it was taken, how somebody did it. I think that would have been a kick." He managed a short snort of a laugh.

I was going to ask him more questions about his work, but there was the sharp noise of metal on metal from the cell door. I held my breath, wondering what was next.

What was next was Jack Picasso and Trevor Warbeck stopping by for a visit.

Chapter Fifty-Two

"Stand," a red-coated guard with an emotionless, Buster Keaton-like Stone Face said. He was holding a staff with a very sharp-looking spear head on the top and a metal ball on the bottom. He struck the ball on the floor three times. We stood up. The jailer who had dealt with me the previous night entered the room, edged his way around Picasso and Warbeck, and put thick manacles on my legs, which were tight enough to cut off my cirulation. Any thoughts I had of dashing for the door, punching and kicking my way past the guards, grabbing a brace of pistols and shooting my way out of the Bell Tower, then jumping over two high walls, crashing Traitor's Gate and swimming to freedom across the Thames, flew right out of my mind.

Benchley was about to get the same treatment but Warbeck intervened.

"No, no," Warbeck said in a casual voice. "Do not shackle the elderly one. He had a rather trying evening last night. And please have these miserable men take their ease. I am willing to forego the usual courtesies accorded my rank." The jailer shrugged and wedged his way back out of the cell. The guard stepped gingerly around the two visitors as well, but stayed in the cell, his back against the door, which had been left open a couple inches.

Warbeck's girth took almost all the space between Benchley and myself. The pale-faced Jack Picasso, dressed in an outfit similar to Warbeck's garb was taking in the narrow cell and then taking in me. I noticed he had a bulky black leather satchel under his arm. The satchel was supported by a leather strap slung over his right shoulder.

"A cozy nook, eh, Benchley?" Warbeck said. The fat man walked to the far wall and craned his flabby neck toward the barred window. "Your view of the river is somewhat obstructed. Pity. If you prefer I could see the Chief Warder and have you moved. A pleasant vista can be such a good tonic in trying circumstances."

"It's suitable to our needs," Benchley said dryly. He carefully sat back down on the cot, using his shaky arms to help absorb his collapse at the end of the effort.

"Come to gloat, Warbeck?" Benchley asked.

"Actually, I came on official business. I brought the Lord Lieutenant of the Tower the Official indictments against the two Jesuit spies that Mr. Bacon apprehended last night. Mr. Bacon and I had a nice, if all too brief, breakfast with Her Majesty. There we presented the evidence of Popish treasons found on your horses at the stable of the Three Cranes Dock and in the coach old Benchley hired."

Warbeck spoke of only two captured spies. Perhaps Bonnie had gotten away.

"You mean planted evidence," Benchley growled. "Planted by the treacherous Mr. Francis Bacon of Grey's Inn. I took the little ferret for a scholar and a philosopher. Instead, I find he's just another grasping, back-stabbing politician. The next time you see Bacon, tell him for me that everything he ever wrote about honesty in his essays was hypocrisy, and not worth a bucket of warm piss."

"Leave us," Warbeck said to the guard. The guard complied.

"I'm sure he would acknowledge the deception," Warbeck said. "But I would suspect he would remind you of a certain phrase attributed to King Solomon: *'Prudens adverti ad grossus suos, stultus divertit ad dolos'*."

Benchley sighed. "'The wise man looks where he is going; the fool strays into the snare'." His light blue eyes cast a steely look at Warbeck. "I hope you used your rank Latin pronunciation in your audience with the Queen. It's *'gressus'*, man, not *'grossus'*. The real Earl of Grantum was educated at Jesus College in Oxford under the finest Dons in the Kingdom. He didn't speak Latin like a state school dropout."

Warbeck chuckled. "My cousin the Queen and I conversed entirely in English. And take me for her good and loyal cousin she did. I may be rusty in Latin, Benchley, but I know enough to get through the wedding ceremony I'm undertaking in two days' time. I told the Queen you were an elderly man and she asked that I would see you on her behalf. She wants me to personally implore you to confess your treasons and name all other Jesuit spies and lay traitors in your network. If I were you, Benchley, I'd start dreaming up some whoppers. A quick death will be your reward, as opposed to the gamut of slow tortures the Tower is justly famous for."

"Either way the outcome is the same," Benchley said stoically. "I'd just as soon tell the Lord Lieutenant the truth and see if he'll check out thoroughly to make sure you are the real Earl of Grantum."

"Oh, but he wouldn't dare!" Warbeck intoned in his deep, resonant voice. "I am a cuz of Her Majesty herself. I need not fear scrutiny. Who in this kingdom will believe the word of a desperate Jesuit spy, posing as a tradesman, over that of an earl and Knight of the Garter?"

Picasso sneezed, then blew his nose into a handkerchief he pulled out from inside one of his lace-trimmed cuffs.

"Hello, Jack," Benchley said. "Feeling good about yourself today?"

Picasso spit at Benchley's feet.

"The Lord Lieutenant will have free rein to deal with you two as he wishes," Warbeck said. "A student of history like yourself, Benchley, will know what that means." He turned to me, focusing those dead black eyes on mine. "As for you, Wells, prepare yourself for a few rather trying moments of physical mayhem in your near future."

"Better prepare yourself, Warbeck. We still might get out of here."

Warbeck laughed at that remark, a laugh that seemed to start at his guy and roll up to his plump face.

"And I have a good idea Jack Picasso here had more than something to do with Ray Harrison's murder."

That got Picasso's attention. He leaned back against the wall opposite me, patting his satchel like something important was inside. "How do you figure that?" he asked me.

"You got a minute, guys?"

"Depends on how interesting your theory is," Picasso said. "You said at that crummy inn you were going to nail me for killing your pal McCreedy. I said I *knew* who killed Dave McCreedy, that's all. You got nothing on me except some imaginary notions you can't prove. But, since you aren't going to live much longer anyway, why don't you run your little scenario by me."

"You sure your horse isn't double-parked down at the drawbridge?"

"Tell me," Picasso said smugly. "I could use a couple laughs."

"Okay," I said, stretching my legs out and rubbing between the slight gap between the shackles and my ankles. "Here goes. Bonnie told me this business about the Belle Killroy movie you were planning to make with Ann Benchley," I said. "You needed Ann Benchley because she starred in the first film and has the audience identification with the part. Plus, she owns the rights to the Belle Killroy books. Your last three pictures didn't make money, right?"

"So this deal is the best thing you have going. You need a hit film bad. You know Ann Benchley is only going to let a hack director like you do a sequel to her biggest hit if you can charm her into it. She agreed to do the *Forget Me Not* movie with you, but you really need her to green light you for the *She Came to Europa* sequel and you weren't sure if she was going to let you direct that one because the script you and your pals came up with on *Forget Me Not* is weak. So one weekend Mr. Benchley here invites you up to his ranch. Is that right, Mr. Benchley?"

"It must have been the weekend before Thanksgiving," Benchley said. "That was the last time you were at the ranch." He looked up at Picasso. "You seemed rather upset, Jack, that Ann wasn't staying around for you. I told you about her and Dave. You were not too partial to their relationship."

I took up from there. "You come up and you find Ann Benchley hanging out with this Dave McCreedy guy. This is not good for your career path. You need time with your ex-girlfriend and she's slumming with some local shamus. That's disappointing to you."

"O, my! Look at that." It was Warbeck commenting on some carving on the wall next to the cell window. I had not inspected it owing to the dire situation pressing on my mind.

"This looks like a fresh inscription," Warbeck said. "Probably the last wretch in this cell made it before he was hanged and quartered at Tyburn Hill." The fat man turned and looked askance at me. "Oh, but I'm interrupting this fascinating theory, aren't I? Go on with your theory, old boy. I promise to be quiet."

I continued, keeping my gaze on a spot right between Picasso's dark brown eyes.

"You go to your old film-making buddy from the 1980's, Ray Harrison. He has the solution to your problems: he knows about the time machines. He went back in time with his then-wife, Susanna when her father was a prisoner awaiting execution in this little Renaissance Resort here. You think he's nuts, babbling about time machines and such, but still you're a desperate guy. And you know Morton Ryskind was a physicist, so maybe..."

I let my voice trail off.

"Go on," Picasso said, motioning his gloved right hand at me to keep talking.

"So you and Harrison get Ralph Bates, the security manager and Ray's barfly friend, in on the deal. He goes snooping around Mr. Benchley's private offices, either at the festival or in the basement of his ranch. That's when he finds evidence like a journal or photographs that Mr Benchley here is keeping of his trips to the past. So you no longer think Ray Harrison is totally nuts, he really is onto something big."

"Maybe I do," Jack Picasso said with a thin-lipped smile.

"So now here's where I think your fat friend fits in," I said, not sure I was right but willing to take the theory all the way out. "You were invited to attend one of the Forest of Arden Festivals, the one held the year before last. Warbeck was there, too. My guess is that Warbeck showed you the papers he had from Roy Cohn's private files, the files left from Joe McCarthy's Senate Internal Security Committee back in the fifties, the files documenting how Mr. Benchley here sold your father and his friend out so he could keep directing movies. That upset you more than a bit."

"Damn right," Picasso said.

"But you pretend to stay loyal to the Benchleys. At least you don't tell Mr. Benchley here that you know about his little confessional back in 1953. Maybe it's because of Ann Benchley. You and her go back a long time. Maybe she was your first girl or something. Maybe you wanted her back in the sack with you. But my bet is you're just a cold-blooded shit and all you want her for is to make that *Belle Killroy* picture. But when you find that Ann is preoccupied with Dave McCreedy, then you decide to get a little drastic. You go back to Warbeck, who's been wanting to do something drastic to Mr. Benchley for a long time."

His nose only a few inches from the wall where the barred window was, Warbeck read aloud from the inscription carved into the stone work. "'He that endureth death to the end shall be saved. This from the faithful hand and heart of Thomas Haverstock. Anno, 1586'. Hum, quaint sentiment. I'm sorry, Wells. Don't mind me."

I continued: "So, you go back to San Francisco and meet Warbeck, and show him the evidence Bates acquired on the time machines—my guess is either film or photographs. Warbeck is up enough on his history to know that a lot of the buildings and landmarks in the photographs no longer exist in England. He also knows Benchley's best friend was a physicist, and scientists have funny ideas about fooling around with time and space. Warbeck here knows something else. He knows his pal Sherwood Strunk owns Sobel House, which is on top of the ruins of Grantum Hall and where he found the forged journal William Devant's grandson tried to pass off as grandpa's. The false journal was nearly published, but the printing shop that was going to do the work was burned down in the Great Fire in London of 1668 or whatever."

"1666," Warbeck said, not taking his eyes off the inscription. "The Great Fire swept through most of London in September of that year. It started in a bakery."

"Whatever," I repeated. "Anyway, Warbeck here uses the forgery as the basis for his *Shadow On the Crow* book. Then right away Mr. Benchley comes up with a portion of William Devant's real journal. He and Mr. Trubshawe stole it from Grantum Hall a few months ago, the last time he and Trubshawe went back into time. So, Warbeck suddenly sees that Mr. Benchley here can refute the basis for the anti-Shakespeare book. A newspaper article comes out and shows that the handwriting on the journal and the paper used comes from a later time—that comes from document experts and graphologists. But no writings of William Devant survive, you think, so how did Mr. Benchley come up with this stuff? You've scoured the foundations of the old castle and you didn't find it? And then along comes Picasso here with strange evidence: pictures of buildings and monuments that haven't existed for 300 some years, and Ray Harrison's story about a trip 400 years back in time."

Picasso put a thumb and two fingers to his face, and gave the wispy proto-beard along his jawline a good scratch. I could tell he was very interested in what I had to say.

"Meanwhile, back at the ranch, Ann Benchley breaks it off with Dave around the first of this year. So you go up there and rekindle the relationship. But by now you probably got the idea you don't need Ann Benchley to make a hit movie, All you need is the rights to the *Belle Killroy* books and you can get another actress, one who will work cheaper maybe. Probably the movie was going to be produced by Sherwood Strunk's company. Tell me where I'm wrong here, Jack."

Picasso said nothing. I looked over at Trevor Warbeck. His head was cocked to one side, mouth slightly open like a black slit. He looked interested.

"So Warbeck here gets Sherwood the Strunk to invite Mr. Benchley to the Forest of Arden for a supposed debate on who wrote Shakespeare's plays," I said. "Then you guys have Dromio and Charles Lindsay Aarons I'd guess kidnap him and Carolyn Mason. They kill Mason and bring Mr. Benchley to London, all drugged up, in a Strunk private jet. Somehow you get the old guy through customs. Maybe you put him in a trunk or something. Sherwood Strunk's a multimillionaire so British Customs isn't going to open every bag the guy takes off his own plane."

"It was a trunk," Warbeck said offhandedly. "A large one, with airholes of course."

"Then, Mr. Picasso," I said, "just when you think Dave McCreedy is out of Ann's life, she pulls him back in to look into her father's disappearance. You find out he's getting close to the Institute for Factual History, and you're afraid he's going to steal your girl from you. That upsets you, right?"

"You're kind of close," Picasso said dismissively.

"So," I said to Picasso, "you or your old pal Harrison rig

up a phony message cut from snatches of dialogue from some of Ann Benchley's movies. That lures Dave to his fishing spot on Cramner Creek on his way back to Rogue Falls from San Francisco. He goes there, thinking he's going to meet Ann, thinking maybe she's going to dump you and go back to him for a romp in the hay. You get somebody, maybe Bates or Dromio or Ray Harrison, to kill him. Tell me if I'm going too fast for you here, Jack."

"Wrong on the last part, pal," Picasso said, smiling broadly. He omitted any judgement on the other details of my theory. Maybe he spoke the truth or maybe it was another lie.

"Okay, but somebody else kills Dave McCreedy, and he or she is somebody who has your interests in mind. With Dave no longer in the picture, and Ms. Benchley's dad kidnapped or dead, she's going to need a shoulder to lean on. Enter you, Jack Malatesta Picasso. You were supposed to be up in Washington State scouting locations for that prison movie you and Ann Benchley had in pre-production. But you had someone down in Bowman setting up my friend."

Picasso just looked at me for a few seconds. I stared back, then resumed.

"A couple weeks later you show up to see Ann Benchley at the Shakespeare Festival. Later that same night you have an argument with Ray Harrison in the corridor of the Ryskind Theater during the play. He's got you pushed against the wall when I come looking for you. Would you mind telling me what that little argument was about, Picasso?"

Picasso seemed to contemplate a bit, then shook his head.

"Okay," I said, remembering what Richard Allen, the editor of the Rogue Falls paper, said to me over the phone back in modern London. "Try this, Jack: you had somebody slip into Ray's house after the two of them got back from the play—somebody like Ralph Bates maybe? He pulls open a window in Ray's house, knocks Kathy Quisted unconscious somehow, then sets her up to look like she was Ray's murderer. You also have Ralph Bates put some methamphetamine in the bathroom to make it look like maybe the killing was over drugs. I don't know if Kathy Quisted was clean or not but Bates could have put some meth in her system—by injection probably—so she'd be sure to test positive for junk in her blood when the state police nailed her. Must have been easy for a rich drug addict like yourself to get hold of any kind of dope you might have a use for."

Picasso sniffed again. It struck me he didn't have a cold. More likely he had recently taken a hit of cocaine. I continued.

"Once Kathy Quisted is quietly out of the way, Bates goes into the back bedroom and surprises Ray. He drills him from close range then carries or drags the lady in the bedroom and puts the gun in her hand. Bates shoots Ray like a professional would, a nice ugly job that a supposed junkie couldn't pull off, but that's Bates' mistake, not yours. Kathy Quisted is alive to take the rap after she comes around and who's going to believe she was framed if there's so much direct evidence piled up on her? That was why her fingerprints were on the blood smear and the doorknob. You figured she'd panic and run out of that place and then hit the road. What else could she do? She had no alibi, she's probably still strung out on drugs, and her prints were all over the gun. A good plan, Jack. I don't know why you had Ray killed, but I do know he had you pushed up against the wall inside the Ryskind Theater. You guys had a little falling out that night, I guess."

Picasso smirked. He looked up at the narrow, flat stone ceiling, and then back at me.

"Yeah, I put Bates on that job. He already helped that other redneck mercenary Charlie Aarons kill that Mason bitch down in Frisco. Ray and I had a deal and Ray reneged." Picasso puffed out his cheeks then exhaled. "Stupid bastard."

"You guys were together at the play that night. You two looked none too happy together. Why was that, Jack? Ray told me it was because you called him a loser, so he put you up on the wall. But I think that's just a story. Was Ray not living up to his part of the bargain on something?"

"The bastard set me up," Picasso said matter-of-factly. "He had something on me and something on a friend of his who helped us out. That jerk didn't know when he had it made. He wanted me to send a videotape to Ann Benchley that very night, a certain tape that I wanted to send later on. He wanted to cut Mr. Warbeck and Mr. Strunk out of the deal and do our own blackmail job on Ann. He was way out of his league. I got plenty of friends in L.A. who would have wasted him for a lot less than he was hitting me up for."

"Warbeck snorted out a laugh. His paunchy stomach vibrated a bit and, without his dark eyes, his face almost looked jolly.

I remembered now. Ray had wanted me to pick up a videotape from him and get it to Ann Benchley. It was supposed to be an audition video for Kathy Quisted for the movie star's next film. Jack Picasso would not help Ray get it to her. I was supposed to pick it up at Ray's house the morning I had found him murdered. Ray had said Ann Benchley would be "very interested in it."

"What was on that tape, Jacko?" I said.

Picasso took a look at the cell door, then undid the leather strings that held shut the flap of the satchel. He pulled out a video camera, one that looked specially designed. The camera featured a 5 inch video monitor built in to the back of the unit.

"Stand over there Wells, you too, old man," Picasso said to Benchley. "I got something to show both of you. You want to see the tape, you'll get your last wish." The younger man motioned him up but offered no assistance. Benchley got up slowly and came over toward the other side of the cell. I got myself to my feet, wobbling a bit from the added weight about my ankles. Warbeck squeezed by Picasso and blocked the narrow entrance with his considerable bulk. He also pulled his trusty rapier out of his scabbard.

"Since you'll never get another chance, I think you should see what really happened to Dave McCreedy up in Bowman," Jack said. "Ray shot this bit. Mr. Warbeck gave Benchley the edited version of what went down with Dave McCreedy back in Bowman. What you are about to see is the unedited version. Don't make any sudden motions at the equipment, Wells, or I think Warbeck here will impale you."

"Indeed," Warbeck said to me, turning hilt and blade up and down with a few sharp flicks of his wrist. "My story to the jailer will be that you would have tried to rush me, and I had to defend myself. Bear it in mind."

Picasso held the small screen on the camera up to us. He pressed a button on the console on top of the camera and the screen went from bright grey to an image. It was a moving image: a tall dark red-haired woman standing on the bank of a creek. The woman looked like Ann Benchley. She was standing right at the edge of what looked like a river or a creek, her feet on a couple large rocks at the water's edge. I recognized the place: Cramner Creek, just outside of Bowman. It was a wide shot, probably taken on the other side of Cramner Creek, which I remembered from my perusal of the crime scene as having a thick stand of young fir trees. Thick enough to hide a video cameraman and his equipment. The lighting was natural and of a high resolution, a combination produced by good video stock and the camera being pointed the same way as the setting sun. It was a soft, romantic light—the light called "the golden hour" by the filmmakers of D. W. Griffith's era—and the woman standing there looked lovely bathed in it.

The woman who looked like Ann Benchley was smoking a cigarette. She dropped the smoke on a rock and squashed it with her sneaker-clad foot. Next she reached into her purse, with her left hand, and pulled out a small object that looked like a handgun.

"That's not my daughter," Benchley said. "Ann doesn't smoke cigarettes."

"Come on, old man," Picasso said. "Don't make me give the twist to the movie away."

Picasso pressed a button and the picture sped up fast. He tilted the camera up so he could see where he wanted to stop. He stopped at a point where the camera was no longer on "Ann Benchley." It was now fixed on the steep foothills above the creek: a shot of the tree line and the outcropping of boulders. A large bird flew across the screen. It looked like a nature shot. And suddenly the camera panned down in a wobbly, jerking fashion back to the woman at the creek side.

Another figure entered the frame from the top of the steep bank. It was a man riding a motorcycle—a Harley V-Twin. The man took his helmet off. I could see and identify my friend Dave McCreedy as the other figure.

"Enter Dave McCreedy," Picasso said, as if either Benchley or I needed to know.

The action happened very fast. The woman turned around and walked the few feet toward him. There was an embrace. Then Dave seemed to pull back. The camera zoomed in. I could see Dave's face better. He had an expression of puzzlement on his face, his eyes wide. He knew something was wrong. I tried to will him to turn around and run. But he stood still.

From behind Dave and the woman, all of a sudden, came a familiar red glow. One of the STUMPs was materializing into view a few feet behind the pair. Suddenly I could see winds whipping up the sand and rocks on the ground. Dave turned around, but before he could run away, the force of the energy coming from the STUMP knocked him backwards, his body twisting like he was caught in a mini-tornado until he fell face-first to the ground. He fell down just as I did back in the alley in San Francisco, when Ralph Bates surprised me after I handcuffed Charlie Aarons. The woman in the picture fell down violently from the force of the STUMP's breaking through time. She landed on her back, apparently stunned.

And here, standing inside on the platform of the cube-shaped STUMP was both Ralph Bates and Jack Picasso. They were both dressed like cowboys, with wide-brimmed hats and bandannas about their necks. Picasso stepped off the platform when it stopped glowing. He moved quickly to Dave and pulled out a small gun, a Golan automatic no doubt, out of his coat. With a suddenness devoid of mercy, he stood over my best friend's prostrate body, the gun to Dave's right temple, and pulled the trigger. Blood and matter squirted out of the side of Dave's head. It wasn't as gory as watching John Kennedy take his head shot on the Abraham Zapruder film, but it had quadruple the impact on me. My friend's head, shot back-wards like a doll's head. From the helpless position he was in, I saw Dave's arms and legs twitch spasmodically for a few sec-onds as his limbs got the signal from his damaged cerebellum that this was the last reflex activity they need ever perform. Now he was still, on his back in a heap, with Picasso and Bates standing over him.

Picasso looked down at the body and then directly at the camera, mouthing something right at the point of view. There was no sound on the tape but I'd swear Picasso was saying the word 'cut' as he waved his arms across his body. The camera continued to run, however.

Picasso bent down next to Dave and rolled up one of the victim's pant legs. I knew what he was going to do even before he did it. Picasso took the nine millimeter Golan automatic that Dave kept in an ankle holster, his back-up gun, and pulled it out of the holster. He aimed the gun and fired one shot to the right of the camera. The bullet fired had to be the one which wound up embedded in the trunk of a ponderosa pine on the opposite side of the creek, the one the deputy sheriffs found. That was the slug the ballistics team determined was fired from Dave's gun and had different grooves and lands from the bullet that blasted into his brain.

Bates lifted up the woman who looked like Ann Benchley, then shook her awake and sat her down on a rock. She shook herself a bit to come to completely, then, seeing Dave's body, covered her face with her hands. I guessed from her reaction that the woman had no idea beforehand that Dave was going to be killed.

Picasso situated the gun he had fired into Dave's limp right hand. The director was wearing black gloves that matched his jacket. I could see him press the digits of Dave's right hand onto the butt of the gun. Then Picasso checked over the area.

The woman got up and looked over her shoulder to the camera. She looked very upset. She seemed to say something to the camera or toward someone near it. Then she tugged at the crown of her head. In a few seconds the auburn hair was peeled off. What was revealed underneath was a mop of brunette hair, held down by the thin web of a hair net. The hair net came off, and the woman pivoted her neck back and forth until her real hair—a long mane of chestnut brown tresses—came loose. Then she pulled with both hands at her face. Off came some sort of skin-like latex around her cheeks and nose.

The skin revealed from the peeling was slightly darker than the skin, or make-up foundation, that still clung around the edges of her face. With the front of her face exposed, I could tell the woman who had done the shooting was Ray's girlfriend, Kathy Quisted, not Ann Benchley.

An explosion of anger went off inside me. I looked away from the camera to Trevor Warbeck. His sword was a few inches from my stomach. All I could do was ask Picasso "What the hell did you do it for?"

"Dave McCreedy was too nosy," was Picasso's cold reply. "Just keep watching."

Most of what I saw next I knew was coming. Bates and Picasso picked up the limp body of my friend. They tossed him over the ledge. Then they waited about half -a-minute, then the two "cowboys" went back to the time machine. Picasso punched some buttons on a small console. Suddenly the bright glow of pure reddish light came into the picture from the background, putting a ghostly cloud just behind the trio. Bates and Picasso climbed up on the STUMP platform. They shortly vanished. A charred patch of earth was all that was left. Then the video display went dark.

Benchley had apparently been watching the video as closely as I had. He asked Picasso, "What time period did you travel to when you left Bowman?"

"We landed in the exact same spot, roughly 150 years into the past. Early September of 1851 to be more precise. That put the three of us near the earliest settlement at Bowman, when it was still called Kentville. There was nothing there but a small frontier settlement and we were a couple miles away from that. Gold wasn't discovered there until 1853. The guy who discovered gold at the creek there, Ernest Bowman himself, wasn't even there yet."

"What about when you left San Francisco, after you jumped out of the apartment window?"

"The alley on Church Street was an empty horse stable back in 1851. The proprietor of the place had closed up his business to head out for the gold fields. It was deserted so we just took it over. Before that, we had been in San Francisco, taking in the historic sites and people of the Barbary Coast. Amazing how cosmopolitan San Francisco had become just three years after the big gold rush started. The town could have used more women, I'm afraid. Anyway, Ralph Bates and myself posed as newly-arrived Easterners looking to set up a dry goods store to fleece the miners. I put together some frontier costumes out of old material I had from the festival. We passed for eastern dudes quite easily. Once I found out where you were, Wells, it was just a matter of going back in time and using an old map to determine the best place to get at where you were staying."

"When did Ray Harrison tell you about his blackmail plan, the one that didn't include Warbeck here?" I asked.

"When I got back from that prison up in Washington," Picasso said. "He called me on my cellular phone, said we needed to meet. He said to be on the landing in the second tier of the stairway at the Ryskind Theater, between the first and second acts of Ann's play. That's when he told me he didn't shut off the camera, that he had me on videotape fooling with McCreedy's body and he had that Millman chick pulling off her disguise. It was Ray who put that face and hair on her, and padded her boobs and hips up a bit to make her look better, good enough to fool that dumbass McCreedy so she could get a shot at him."

"Are we talking about Ray Harrison?" Benchley asked weakly. "That's the porno film guy I had to fire from the Costume Department a year or so back."

"You're sharp, old man," Picasso said. "You were sharp enough to sandbag my father back in '53, too."

Another volley of cannon shots pierced the air, echoing on top of each other. It gave me time to think. I thought about Wendy McCreedy sitting in jail for Dave's murder, a murder Jack Picasso committed.

Picasso spoke after the rumble of artillery died away. "Ray said he'd take the tape to the cops if I didn't cough up serious money for him in 48 hours. That's when you showed up on the landing, playing the errand boy for Ann. I had offered him a job as Art Director on my next two projects. That was a ticket back into the business for him. I thought we had a deal. But the bastard wanted to hold me up instead. He wanted to skim my bank account and do a fast fade with his girl back to England."

"So where's your friend, Ralph Bates?" I asked.

"Poor guy fell out of the top of the castle keep at Grantum Hall," Picasso said casually. "Dromio was the only person who saw him fall. Guess all the time travel didn't agree with him."

"Time travel is not for everyone," Warbeck said in a bored tone. "I rather liked Mr Bates in some ways."

"You liked him so much you let Dromio kill him," I said.

"Why not?" Picasso said. "Mr Warbeck here couldn't afford any loose ends, anybody tracing him back from Charlie Aarons to Bates to him—and then maybe me. Hell, Ralph played the game and he lost. Too bad but so what?"

"Why did that woman do herself up like my daughter?" Benchley asked with trepidation in his voice.

"I needed some leverage," Picasso said. "I needed to get my hands on the rights to the *Belle Killroy* books. Ann would never have let that go unless she came in with the package. 1 needed the rights but I could do without Ann. There are three Belle Killroy novels about her when the character is in her twenties. I have a hot actress in mind, Cindy Greco, who's just the right age. Ann's too old."

"So you were going to blackmail Ann," Benchley said. "You made up this second-rate prima-donna to look like my girl and cut her out of her investment. You were no better than a mafia hood."

"We have to get going," Warbeck said.

"You needed Ray for the make-up job," Benchley said. "He had done the life mask for her when she was Queen Hermione in *The Winter's Tale*. That bastard must have stolen the spare mold from the museum when I fired him."

"Boy, are you two boys swift," Picasso said mockingly.

"And where was Ann when all this happened?" Benchley asked.

"Ann always went off for a ride on her Harley after a matinee, and she always tried to go way up on the roads up in the mountains. She had given Bates half the day off like she usually did and he joined me in the Bowman of 1851 via the STUMP. Ann probably didn't care for Ralph. He could be a trifle vulgar around good-looking women. But I figured she wouldn't fire him because Ralph's dad was your friend back in your studio days. What you didn't know was that Ralph had become my friend, too, until that unfortunate accident he had."

I wished I could have killed Picasso then and there.

"Anyway, I got the edited videotape and Ray's dead," Picasso said. He turned to Benchley. "Guess what, old man? I'm going back to modem times after the Grantum Wedding and pay a little call on your daughter. She'll get to see the tape. She'll cough up the rights I want or I'll do her dirty just like you did my dad. I'll see her cute little butt go down for first-degree murder."

Benchley reached out to get Picasso by his doublet. The younger man pushed him back against the wall. What was left of my reserve gave way. I got Picasso by the neck, hoping I could break it for him before Warbeck could get to us.

I got a good grip on my target, who was slightly off-balance from pushing Benchley down. I held him by the skin around his throat with one hand—my thumb pressing as hard as I could into flesh and arteries—and tried to thrust the lower palm of my other hand against his jaw hoping to hear a sharp snapping sound. My blow was too high and caught him by the cheek. Picasso spun away from me. In the next second I saw Warbeck lunging at me, leading with the tip of his rapier. I fell backward against the wall.

The tip of Warbeck's rapier was a couple inches from my own throat. From the deadpan look he gave in his lifeless eyes I couldn't tell if he was going to skewer me or not. The guard came into the room. I thought his appearance and the shocked expression on his face would be the last thing I'd see.

Seeing that the guard was a witness, Warbeck was satisfied with cutting me just under the chin with his rapier. It was a superficial wound but it still stung. He turned away from me, allowing me to crouch down and try to stop the bleeding with both my hands.

"Let him die slow," I heard Picasso say between ragged coughing jags. "I want them to die slow, especially that one." I guess he meant me, but I didn't bother to look up as the three of them were leaving. As I didn't kill him, I didn't want to look at him.

The last words in the encounter belonged to Trevor Warbeck. I glanced up at him as he squeezed his way out the door, then stuck his head back in. I saw some of my blood glistening on the tip of the rapier he held downward. He said what he wanted to say casually, but it hurt worse than the slash he had just made under my chin.

"The gentlewoman, Bonnie Noel is at Grantum Hall, by the way, old boy," he said. "She was found by chance along the road in Hampstead by some of Essex's men. The Earl himself was along and recognized her. She is currently accommodated in the keep. She will stay at Grantum Hall until her health is restored. I fear without the right physic she may not stay well. The angels above may call for her in a few days, such is the brief voyage of this life. All flesh is grass. Life is but a walking shadow and all that. Fare thee well, heretics." He nodded, then the top half of his fat penguin body bobbed back out of sight behind the cell door.

That was it. Without Bonnie to lead Trubshawe and whomever he would bring to rescue us, we were lost.

The guard with the stone face came back into the cell. He gave a fairly clean rag to try and stop up the blood coursing out of my wound. I thanked him for it. I helped Benchley back up to his cot. He said nothing. I said nothing. I sat back down on the straw bundle and held the cloth to my chin.

About an hour later, three soldiers came for me.

Chapter Fifty-Three

The next twenty-four hours are hard to recall.

After being relieved of my first set of chains, another set of leg irons, shorter in chain size and equally constrictive, was attached to me. I was escorted by the Chief Warder—the one who wore the fancy derby and looked like Charles Laughton—and the guard who had given me a rag to stop the blood from my chin. I followed the warder, with the ax-wielding guard bringing up the rear, out of the Bell Tower via a couple flights of winding stone steps. Again, I had to duck to keep from braining myself on the low ceiling of the archways. Then it was out into the battlements and down an exterior stairway to a small plaza of brickwork. I saw a group of soldiers standing in formation on a greensward. They were armed with matchlock rifles and were engaged in loading their muskets (with barrels as long as the height of the soldiers) under the watchful eye of a burly-looking fellow with a couple strips on his sleeve. I recognized him as the man who had urinated on me.

The powder they put into the barrels of the muskets came from horn-shaped containers that looked like they were made from bone. "Powder in," the sergeant barked, "now your shot and be in haste you devils."

Our procession stopped. I watched as the men rammed the little circular ball each had in one hand down into the barrel with a long metal rod, just as I had seen Jack Benchley do a few days earlier on the road to Grey's Inn. The men then mounted the long barrels of their muskets up on stakes with fork-shaped tops.

"Now, pull back the serpentine and load your priming pan," the sergeant said. "Come now, be quick lest you want a pikeman's lance in your gizzard.

The soldiers brought the weapons to a horizontal position, the ends of the barrels resting on the stakes. They pulled back on the long curved hammers, the serpentines, of their weapons then poured shot into the small holes in the stock of the weapon, I thought it was the firing squad for me for a few seconds, then I looked up and saw that the target was a scarecrow against the stone wall about fifty yards across the yard.

The soldiers all had rope-like wicks, lit and smoking, hooked to their belts by a metal bracket. They now took the wicks from their belts and lit the tips of their serpentines, then steadied themselves with legs apart and the butt of the muskets resting against just underneath their right shoulders.

"Aim...Fire!" said the sergeant. The muskets erupted in flame, first at the top of the rifle, where the hammers sprang forward and hit the powder holes, and then came a sharp report of noise as the shot blasted out. The scarecrow took some hits—straw flew about, I could see the cloth about the dummy ripped apart—and some just hit the already pocked stone wall. The sergeant turned about and gave me a nasty look.

I knew now why we had stopped. It was practice for the soldiers and a lesson in intimidation for the prisoner being led away. One of the guards prodded me in the back and we continued on.

"Tell them the truth, Harvey!" shouted Benchley from the tower above me. I looked back over my head and saw his haggard face between the bars of our cell.

Tell them the truth, Harvey. Great advice, old man. The truth would not be believed and, even if it was, it would not set me free.

My throat ached. I wanted a glass of orange juice and maybe a couple strawberry breakfast bars (the low-fat kind) and maybe some hash browns because I had been such a good boy. I wanted to be back in the tower of London in the year 2001, with those retired military lifers who posed for pictures with the tourists and told them where Anne Boleyn or my buddy the Earl of Essex got beheaded. I wanted those nice, affable old soldiers who turned history into a cozy recitation of other people's misfortunes. Instead, I was stuck with the real deal bad-smelling younger guys in Conquistador helmets who wore the funny red uniforms and carried the funny hats and poleaxes and thick pistols for real and not for show.

We walked diagonally across the brickwork and onto a dirt trail that led up a moderate-sloping knoll. We were in front of the White Tower, the largest building in the complex. I knew it was the White Tower because Benchley had already pointed it out and told me that morning. The fact that the trim around the windows and keeps were whitewashed made that easy to remember. (If I cared, which I didn't.)

We went up an outer stairway and entered the fortress. From somewhere up above me I heard a beautiful sound. It was a chorus of high-pitched male voices singing something that sounded like a hymnal. The echo of the voices gave me a brief sense of calm. For a brief moment I might just be forced to hear a sermon and then be let off with a warning. We climbed up a narrow stairway and the voices got louder. As we passed down a hallway, I looked through an open set of double doors and looked into a small barrel-vaulted chapel supported on three sides by thick pillars. I briefly glimpsed the source of *a capella* tones: a group of about a dozen boys in ankle-length black robes were singing in front of the small altar at the opposite end of the chapel. In front of the choir was a minister in a grey cassock, his head bowed in what I took to be reverence, and in the foreground of the chapel were a group of caped men and long-skirted women. They were all kneeling, on pillows I imagined. The rattle of my legirons across the stone floor caused a couple bowing heads to look up and out the doors. I was by them before I could even see their faces.

"The Lord Lieutenant putting on a display of piety for the visitors from Hanover," said the Charles Laughton's look-alike to his subordinate.

"There's no end to this train of German nobles," grumbled the guard. "London is swelled enough without more foreigners. A plague on the Lutheran dogs."

Now we descended down another stairway, this one even more narrow than the ones in the Bell Tower. At the bottom of the passage was a landing and then we came face to face with a small door, made from wood planks, probably oak, and reinforced by iron hinges and an iron frame. The bottom of the door was two feet above the landing, and was the size of an old-fashioned ironing board cabinet. The Chief Warder stepped in front of the guard and opened the lock. He swung the door out. I did not like what I saw.

I was expecting one of those Gothic torture chambers, the kind set up like a recreation room for sadists, the hospitality staff inside consisting of a pack of slack-jawed, clubfooted jokers who came off like lab assistants in a Vincent Price movie. But there was no room for any local color at all. It was a warped-looking little room, maybe big enough for a crooked ironing board. My irons were not removed.

"Up with you, Jesuit," the guard said, poking me in the ribs with the sharp end of his pole.

I stepped up into the little space. At first I thought I wouldn't fit, then I was being pushed so I would fit. I found out from the design of the place that it was impossible to stand up or sit down.

"You weasels will be hearing from Amnesty International," I said as the guard slammed the door shut on me. Instantly I was in pitch darkness. The mechanics of the lock clanked back into place. The door was so thick I could barely hear the footsteps of my escorts as they went back up the stairway. I heard the muffled sound of another door closing from somewere.

It was sensory deprivation, Elizabethan-style. This was bad. The only thing that could be worse, with my acrophobia, would have been suspension from a cage over some great height. It was the 'Little Ease' room Benchley had spoken about, designed to bring out the claustrophobic in any mortal. I thought of Bonnie, who had told me of her claustrophbia the first time we met. Or was it the second time? Bonnie with her beautiful smile and sharp wit and that infectious laugh that was so familiar a short time ago but now was hard to simulate in my memory. Bonnie, her turqoise eyes and smooth mouth and maybe smoother body that I got to experience only—at best —twice. Bonnie, whom I almost certainly would never see again.

There was no room to do much other than wiggle my fingers and toes and pivot my neck. I could already feel my legs getting heavy, with no way to take a load off those feet. I could not sit down or even crouch down. I could only stay just as I was.

Time dragged by. I thought a lot at first, random notions rolling around inside my skull like marbles on an upturned garbage can. I talked to myself, coherant at first. Then I started on just talking to try and stop thinking. I did the Preamble to the Constitution and most of what I could remember from the Gettysburg Address. I thought about Civil War battles I had read about, wondered what would have happened to the Republic if General George McClellan had had guts or better intelligence from Alfred Pinkerton on the Peninsula Campaign. I wondered what would have happened at the First Day of Gettysburg if Stonewall Jackson hadn't been killed two months earlier at Chancellorsville, or if young Jeb Stuart would have had his cavalry for Lee's disposal instead of joyriding his men around Pennsylvania trying to steal some beer or whatever it was Stuart was doing. I decided it was very good the Civil War turned out the way it did, an opinion I knew would not sit well with Sherwood Strunk and his Truth Party, but so be it.

I talked some more to myself. I whistled. I sang old Sam Cooke songs. The song *Chain Gang* got an encore because I remembered all the words. I sang Sinatra songs. I did Elvis Presley's *Blue Christmas*, even though it was out-of-season. I sang Electric Light Orchestra songs I remembered from the jukebox in the cafeteria at Prospect High School. I next did a stirring, full throated, off-key rendition of 'America the Beautiful.' I did snatches of songs I didn't even know who originally performed. I thought about movies I'd seen. I wondered why so many people like Frank Capra's, *It's A Wonderful Life*. My parents liked it. I tried not to think about my parents, that didn't help. I needed to stick to trivia. My body ached. My head was swimming in pain.

I thought about music. Disco music had pervaded the popular culture of my youth. I could actually remember liking the late Van McCoy's, *The Hustle* but, after that, the deluge. I thought Streisand had the best vocal range for a white chick, but I had put off renting the *Live In Concert* video that was released a few years back. Probably too late now. I thought about Bonnie, who was just under all my thoughts. What were

Warbeck's bastards doing to her? It sounded like she was going to be bargained for; Bonnie goes free in exchange for the third STUMP. Trubshawe would have to deal with that one. I thought about all the reports I had done as a cop, all the court appearances, all the sweating I did the night before I qualified on the firing range at the Sutter County Police Academy, how proud my retired cop of a dad was when I followed right along in his path. I remembered some of the busts I had made, some on people who were scared and crying, some who practically spread eagled for me before I walked up to them. I remembered the busts I had made on drugpushers, bathtub methamphetamine chemists, crackheads, and the general breed of punk I knew I would bust again and again until they ran out of money for sharp lawyers or some new prison opened and the judges stopped letting punks out because there wasn't enough prison space. Some of their fellow punks did the taxpayers a favor and shot their own dead. I remember the boredom of those 12 hour shifts in a patrolcar, or on a Kawasaki Police 1000. I remembered all the whiny drivers I gave speeding tickets to. I remembered trying to give cardiopulmonary resuscitation to a cat after an old lady called 911. The cat didn't make it.

I remembered my partners. I had liked most of them but only one of them stayed in touch with me after I lost my job. That was my first and best partner, Barry Haskins. Haskins smoked like an early industrial age smokestack. I couldn't picture the fat bastard without a cigarette. It was Haskins who taught me all the practical stuff the academy had not prepared me for when it came to surviving on the street. Haskins was an Oakland Raider fan, and fifty pounds overweight, but somehow stayed on the force. He ate everything organic that was put in front of him, constantly talked about those damn Raiders unless we were responding to an incident, farted proudly whenever he felt the need (even when testifying in court) and he was a good cop. After he got me street-wise, they moved him over to another partner. I had heard last year he had died of a heart attack at all of 48, two years from retirement. How thoughtful of old Barry. Once again, the overburdened taxpayer was spared the problem of renumerating a man who kept the peace for twenty years. Exercise, I told Barry, exercise. But I didn't exercise enough, either. Would I have made twenty years, or would I have busted my heart or blasted myself in the head one night? A moot point.

I thought about the little girl I ran over in the squad car. That had broken the camel's back. I had no business being a cop. I should have gone into computers, become a lawyer, a butcher, baker, candlestick maker, golf pro, anything, not a cop.

I tried to decide if the Designated Hitter Rule in Major League Baseball was a good thing or a bad thing. Ditto inter-league play. Trouble was, there was nobody to argue with. I tried to piece together the line-up the San Francisco Giants were using the last time they were in the World Series. I went on to the line-up of the 1976 Cincinnati Reds, the 1961 New York Yankees, the 1953 Dodgers, and some other teams I had never seen but had read about. My spine was aching to the point that thinking wasn't much good anyway. My legs had started to go numb. I couldn't feel anything below my knees and so I stopped trying to wigggle my toes. I thought about how good it would be to get out of here. My mouth was dry, my stomach was rumbling. It got cold. Very cold.

How many hours had gone by? I just knew I couldn't sleep for any amount of time. I knew people in POW camps and such had survived in these situations. Just don't think negative thoughts. Put aside those negative thoughts. Just because I was 400 years back in time and not exactly playing on my home court was no reason not to think positive. They'll take me out of here. They have to. They'll want answers. They'll want to question me, soon.

But they didn't take me out. Not after all my limbs seemed to go numb and could barely move my neck. I must have been in that place two, three days. I was aware only of how bad I smelled and how bad the air was. There must have been a point where I did sleep because I had nightmares. They were all nasty, as nightmares are, and yet I still regretted it when I came around again. The last dream had me on rollerblades. I was flying around the curves of a winding two-lane mountain road. It was like I was skiing. I was holding on to a rope. At the other end of the rope was a man on a motor-cycle. The helmeted driver looked around. Dave McCreedy was on his Harley/Davidson. He drove faster, veering me into the other lane. I narrowly missed a honking car coming from the opposite direction. The driver swerved out of the way. Then another car came and another swerve and another miss. Then came a truck. I yelled or thought I yelled. The rope that held me to Dave's bike suddenly broke. A horn blew. I headed right for the front grill of the truck. I saw my arms go out, and then my momentum carried me around the truck. There followed a steep embankment. I hit the guardrail and fell end-over-end, gaining glimpses of the enormous open space before me. Blue skies rotated with jagged rocks, getting closer and closer as I dropped. Then everything faded away. I wasn't going to hit the rocks. I felt water coming down on my face. Where did the water come from?

And then I woke up. At first I thought it was another dream. The room, wherever it was, was dark, dank and musty. My eyes could not focus on anything. I was lying down. Thank God, I was lying down. But my body was not touching anything. My ankles and wrists were aching. But I could at least feel my limbs.

I felt the water. It came from a thick, soggy sponge. A hand wiggled the sponge close to my face, causing a few drops to drip down. The sponge was real, and I greedily stuck my dry tongue out to trap what moisture I could from the shower. It was just a few drops to wet my tongue and give me some idea how much dry film had built up inside my throat. I heard voices. I saw forms in the darkness. The pain to my limbs was getting worse and worse.

A face leaned over me. It was an ugly face with one continuous eyebrow over heavy lids, protruding Bugs Bunny front teeth, and a flat nose that looked like it belonged to an old fighter. There came another fellow in my face. This was the fat, thick-lipped Charles Laughton clone. He stared at me like I was a specimen.

There must have been other people in the room because I could hear footsteps, the echo of which told me the room was large, and more mumbling voices. I figured out that I was hanging horizontally from my wrists and ankles. I looked back by craning my neck back as far as it could go. There was a thick rope around my left wrist. My hand was white. I couldn't feel my fingers. I was on the rack, a contraption like the one Warbeck had shown Bonnie and me at the Tower of London exhibit back in San Francisco.

"Confess your deeds; confess your designs," the Chief Warder said. "Give forth the names of your confederates."

I told them the truth. I told them about getting through time and trying to get Jack Benchley out of Grantum Hall. I knew they wouldn't give a damn about that, so I threw in the part about how Essex was planning to crash the upcoming wedding at Grantum Hall, snatch the Queen, then use weapons from the future to mow down all the Queen's men.

"Believe this," I said. "Believe me. You know my accent is strange, but I speak English, or something like English. I'm from another time, a time with weapons worse than you can even dream about. I'm no Jesuit, not that being a... oh forget it. Look, I'm a patsy. Francis Bacon is the guy you need to question. Or that Essex guy. Did you run him down yet?"

The questions were only repeated. I repeated my story. I heard the sound of gears grinding. The ropes that held my arms and legs were tightening. The pain shot through my body from all the sinews I had—everything was stretched to the maximum. The gears turned more. I heard a scream. My mind thought it was somebody else but, looking back, I was the screamer. The Chief Warder carried on.

"Confess your deeds; confess your designs; name your confederates. We don't wish to stretch you to further, eqivocating papist, but we'll do so. Fantastic stories will not grant you mercy. Your soul is already damned; look to your body, Jesuit. We will cripple you. You'll go to the hangman in a tip-cart lest you heed my counsel."

My tormentor looked up and nodded his head at someone. The gears turned and the rope tightened. Then something burned into the side of my left hand. It was unbearable. The pain was beyond any agony for what seemed a long time. I screamed and howled. Everything after that was in a fog of pain and pleading.

I signed my confession with my right hand, which was the wrong hand for me. I guessed they assumed I was right handed, and set the left arm up to take the worst first. My left hand had been branded by a hot iron right on the fleshy side of my left hand opposite the thumb. What was left of my little finger was a charred limp mass. I didn't feel as much pain as the look of my hand would indicate so I knew that under that blackened flesh my nerves were gone. I can't tell what I signed.

The desk I was seated at had only a candle to illuminate the scroll, and the calligraphy was so strange it could have been in Arabic lettering for all I knew. The now thoughtful attendants dipped the quill in the inkwell for me when it came to the signing. Then I was allowed to stand up, then allowed to fall down. I was taken up by the arms and brought back to my feet. I could actually feel the ground under my feet after several hesitant steps. There followed the climbing and descending of stairways, two guards behind me and one in front, until they marched, and I staggered, out into the harsh daylight in front of the White Tower. I figured the time, judging by the shadows cast on the cobblestones by the trees and buildings around us, to be late afternoon.

Just before I was led onto a greenspace, the guards took me past a wooden scaffold supported by four thick timbers. It was situated in the middle of a square. The top of the scaffold was flat as a tabletop and covered with straw. Above the straw matting was also a wooden block, concaved in on the side facing the greenspace. The block was big enough for a human to lean down next to it. If I had any doubts about what it was for, the long ax leaning up against the block removed all doubt.

"Don't fear that ax, papist," one of the guards said. "That is reserved for men of nobility who have fallen from grace. You'll be hung and disembowled on Tyburn Hill. Your entrails will be plucked from your guts before your very—"

"Still thy tongue," one of the other guards said. "The man has confessed. He knows the gravity of what he faces."

That I did.

I was taken inside a two-story brick house, into what looked like a meeting room, and put in a chair at one end of a long, heavy-looking, polished wooden table. The curtains over the windows were drawn shut, the only light—so far—from a chandelier above the table. There were paintings on the wall, faces in some frames, and frames with lots of fancy wording etched into copper. I never bothered to look very long at any of it, and then I couldn't if I had tried. A lantern was placed on the table right in front of me. The glass door was opened and the wick inside was lit. The lantern operated in a way similar to a film projector, casting an intense light out from the glass with the aid of a mirror behind the wick. The focus of the harsh light was on my face. I would have looked away but two of my escorts had put a thick, restrictive collar on my neck. The collar must have been attached to the back of the chair because I could hardly move my head.

I brought my left hand up to try and loosen the collar. A stinging pain came to my hand. I had forgotten, momentarily, that I had what was probably a severe third-degree burn and not all my nerve endings were gone. I dropped my favored arm to the armrest and positioned it so the burnt flesh would not touch anything.

I could look up for what that was worth and glanced at the thick beams protruding out of the A-frame ceiling. Then my head was thrust into place by a hand so I could take in more of the lantern light.

A door behind me opened. At least one other person besides myself and the two remaining guards was now in the room. There was the sound of a heavy footstep, followed by a sharp knocking sound, wood upon wood. There fell a step, then a knock, a step, then a knock.

A face leaned over me, deflecting the lantern light. He was wearing that wide-crowned derby like the Chief Warder had, but there was also a thick-linked chain about his high red collar and just under his wide, multi-layered ruff. He wore a short, trim goatee, long mustache, dark hairs flecked with grey, and just enough beard to cover his chin. He was almost popeyed, the color around his pupils a rich brown, the eyebrows high like they had been plucked. He was no sunworshipper: the cheeks, creased with age, were pale. Only the tip of his nose showed some ruddiness. Surprisingly, his expression was benign, certainly not unfriendly. This fellow had a kind face. He looked me over like a doctor performing an examination: an intelligent, weary old doctor who had seen too many patients this month and looked forward to a two-week vacation in the Bahamas.

"I am William Waad, Lord Lieutenant of the Tower," the man said.

"I am...Dog House Riley," I said, remembering a line from an old movie and not caring what I said.

The man smirked, one corner of his thin lip turning up slightly. "We have your confession, Wells," the kind-looking, brown-eyed man said. "I do not wish to do anymore to you than our devices have already done." He got up and I got the light in my eyes again.

"Sounds good to me," I said, blinking my eyes rapidly and expecting a 'but' or 'however' to come out of his mouth.

"However," Lieutenant Waad continued, now somewhere beyond the harsh light, "I feel you know many more details you are not furnishing us. Now is the time to unburden yourself and reveal all you know. It will go well at your trial if you do so. It may even spare you a protracted process of dying."

"Whatever I signed, I signed," I said. "You're going to kill me, anyway, after some kangeroo trial. Why should I talk anymore. You won't believe me."

"Unburden yourself," Waad said mildly. "Give me the truth or I will ask the Queen's permission to send the older man you bound yourself with to the rack. It is your choice." Footstep, then a knock, footstep, then a knock.

I gave him the truth. The whole truth and the only truth. Lying would be too taxing and I was feeling almost resigned to getting this all over with. I told the one-legged fellow behind the nova of light exactly where I was from, what I did for a living, how I got back in time, who was behind the kidnapping of Jack Benchley, and how this same guy was helping the Earl of Essex to overthrow the Queen and the whole ball of wax that went with her.

Again, I was surprised. The guy seemed to be listening to me. Above the light, I could see him puckering his dry, thin lips. I felt, for a moment, like he might even believe at least some of what I said. This impression was helped when he told one of the guards to blow out the lantern. The drapes on one side of the room were flung open by another guard, revealing a large rectangular window and a stream of light coming through the window panes.

With the light off, the room seemed cool. After the red flashes of light disappeared from my sight, I looked up at my interrogator. He was holding one of the nine millimeter Baretta pistol taken either from Benchley or myself. The weapon made a strange juxtaposition when matched with Waad's uniform. His other hand was holding onto the back of a chair.

He ejected the ammo clip with a dexterity that told me he had examined the weapon well. "Where did you get this?" he asked.

"Where I came from," I said. "That gun is a double action

Baretta M92. It's an automatic. That means it fires every time you squeeze the trigger. It's the official sidearm of the United States' military and a few other official military outfits, too. It replaced the Colt M1911. There's a few million more guns very similar to that one where I come from. Warbeck, the guy who's pretending to be Grantum, has some of those multi-shot pistols. He also has rapid-fire muskets that leave your black-powder guns in the dust."

"Fantastic fables," I heard a voice behind me say. I recognized the voice. It belonged to Francis Bacon.

"His tongue speaks false," Bacon said in an oratorical manner. "They are the ravings of a man who means to disqualify himself from revealing the fount of treachery within the kingdom." I heard footsteps moving behind me and soon I could smell Bacon's heavy cologne behind me. Suddenly, I had Bacon in my face.

"I say put him to the rack again," Bacon said, looking at me, but addressing the Lord Lieutenant. "He is a link to a network of Jesuit spies. I know the man Benchley knows even more of what their masters in Rome have in store for us. I observed Benchley closely on his visits, at some risk to my personal safety, to be sure. They were part of a cypto-Catholic plot to harm the Queen. I say rack him again and rack Benchley as well."

"The Queen has forbidden the torture of the older man," Waad said.

"Look," I said, addressing Waad, "this guy is in league with the Earl of Essex, and with this actor, Warbeck. He was the one who planted the documents in our saddles. The guy set us up."

Bacon laughed, then straightened up and walked toward the window. "A farcical accusation," he said, gazing out on the greenspace. "All London knows that I was attacked by the Lord Deputy before hundreds of witnesses in front of St. Paul's three days past. Come, Waad, seal his mouth lest he wither our patience with more falsehoods."

"That is the truth," I said, trying not to sound too desperate. "The attack was a put-up job so Bacon here could be Essex's inside man. He's been getting favors from Essex for years, am I right? Essex has been giving him and his brother houses and trying to promote him with the Queen. Am I right?

And now, lo and behold, Essex attacks him in a place where he can get a ton of witnesses to make it look like the two of them are on the outs. I saw the wounds Essex gave this guy. He was barely scratched. You think this little..." I gulped for air. "This little weasel here would have had a chance against Essex if His Earldom had wanted to take him down?"

Waad looked over at Bacon. I could not read what was on his mind, but the fact that he looked at Bacon—and Bacon turned about from the window to gauge his reaction—told me there was at least one guy in the room worried besides me.

"Have you ever seen firearms like those that were taken off Jack Benchley and myself?" I asked Waad. "You've never seen anything like them, have you? Nobody has. That's because I'm telling you the truth. I know it may sound fantastic, but it's the truth. You listen to my accent? Who do you know talks like this? And it's English I'm talking here. Ever hear some Englishman or Welshman talk like I do? Do I sound like some guy who's been hanging around the Pope's Super Catholic Spy School or whatever it is? You need to get over to Grantum Hall with some soldiers and—" I then realized I had lost track of time.

"What day is this?" I asked.

"'Tis Friday," Waad said.

"The wedding of Grantum and the Queen's Lady-In-Waiting is this very evening," Bacon hissed to me.

"Did the play—?"

"A play is being presented at the Globe this afternoon," Bacon said. He glanced up at a large wall clock with roman numerals. The hands indicated it was a few minutes past four o'clock.

"The play should be concluding," Bacon said. "Several of the notables at the Lord Chamberlain's presentation will go on to Hampstead and attend the festivities at Grantum Hall. The Queen is on progress with her hundred Gentlemen Pensioners and the rest of the court to attend the betrothal."

"You need to get what troops you got in this place and get up to Hampstead," I said to Waad. "Essex is going to come out of hiding and seize the Queen. I'm not lying. There's a woman there named Bonnie Noel. She's being held by Warbeck and this other guy Strunk who's in on it. Get her out of there and she'll tell you just what I told you, word for word."

"You say you are something called a detective," Waad said. "And you were paid by this family from a future time to find this man Benchley?" Waad shook his head, but I could tell he was wavering a bit from his original estimation. He looked at the gun in his hand. "I have fired this weapon. The mechanics are most strange, most strange." He looked up at me, folded his arms and gave me that searching look similar to when I had first laid eyes on him.

"Most strange," Waad said almost under his breath. He stroked his beard with his free hand, looking contemplative.

"Just rescue the woman," I said. "Just do that. You can always kill me later. I can tell you all you need to know about guns and how to make the damn things so you can shoot all the Irish guys and Spanish guys you want. Just go to Grantum Hall and get Bonnie Noel out of there. And bring lots of cannons. You'll need to be loaded for bear to get your Queen out of there when all this goes down."

"Tell us the truth!" Bacon said, stepping forward and slamming his fist onto the table. His face was beet red. "Waad, stop giving attendance to this muck. Rack the heretic! Rack him! As Council Extraordinaire to Her Majesty, I demand that you—"

"Still your tongue, templar!" Waad shot back. "I am in charge of this investigation. This man speaks strangely. I know not what we have in our midst but I will not be hasty here. I brought the old man Benchley to this chamber yesterday before you arrived. His speech is unique as well. I will not be hasty in exploring these matters. And I remind you, Bacon, you are at my pleasure. Do not offer me further advice on my duties unless I solicit it."

I gulped and took a deep breath. There was a pinprick of light at the end of the tunnel. If it would be enough to rescue Bonnie...

"I'm notifying the Lord Secretary," Waad said. "These prisoners speak strangely, carry strange implements. They do not speak in the cant of Jesuits. This is not something—"

A knock came at the door. I twisted my neck about as best I could and saw a skinny guard enter and salute the Lord Lieutenant. He handed him a large brown envelope with a large wax seal holding the flap closed. The guard saluted again and walked out.

Waad opened the envelope with a long slender knife he picked up from a desk that was against the wall. His lips moved ever so slightly as he read the once-folded letter inside. He kept his head down as he carefully placed the letter on the table. He looked at me, his countenance more somber than before. The look made me feel uneasy.

"Your fate is sealed, Wells," Waad said in a stiff, formal tone. "You are to be taken forthwith to the block across the greensward outside. You and your compatriot, Benchley, are to be beheaded. There will be no further interrogation and certainly no trial. The Queen commands it. God have mercy on your soul."

I heard Bacon, from behind me, sigh deeply. Then a buzzing noise started in my head. A minute later, hardly able to think or react, I was picked up under my armpits by two guards. The pair had a good grip on me as we went out of the meeting room. Their support was almost the only thing holding me up.

Chapter Fifty-Four

It was near dusk outside, a golden light irradiating any part of the courtyard that shadows had not already consumed. I stood in a cobblestoned walkway, chained hand and foot now, watching several ravens hopping about the gold-tinted green space in front of me. They were poking their beaks between tuffs of grass in a search for food. One wing on each bird dangled a bit below their bodies, indicating the wings had been clipped. One of those fat birds looked at me for a moment, cocked its head, then went back to foraging. At that time, I would have traded places with that peanut-brained creature in a New York minute for all the gold that ever was.

I was waiting for my last request: a cup of water. They had sent a soldier back to get it, along with a bandage for my burned left hand (as if I really needed it). I did not look upward, I did not look past the ravens on the green. I knew to lift my head meant looking at the wooden scaffold and to see that would have meant another look at the wooden block and the ax set up on a bed of straw on the platform. I had plenty of time to look at that later. My stomach was twisting up, my lungs burned as if they were catching fire, and my heart pumped so hard I thought I might die standing right there.

Standing a few yards away from me were the two men I assumed were the messengers. One man, a skinny fellow with long shoulders, wore a uniform similar to what the guards wore only with fancier epaulettes and a large letter 'E' and 'R' running from right to left on the front of the uniform. The man had dark facial hair so thick it almost covered his face. The man next to him was dressed in a black tunic and black hose. The full morbid effect was completed by a black hood over his head. I didn't need to guess what his job was going to be.

There were also two men near me. One was a guard who was making sure I didn't fly away. The other was Francis Bacon. The latter man was closer than the redcoat. He wasn't close enough for me to lunge at him—he was too smart for that, good old Frank—but he was close enough for me to get a good whiff of that irritating musk he poured on himself, and for him to talk quietly to my shock-deaf ears.

"We have apprehendeth the woman, Bonnie Noel," Bacon said. "She was captured in Middlesex Forest yesterday. The only reason we caught her was that I remembered Benchley telling me the appproximate location that he and Trubshawe used to enter this time. Essex himself and a small party captured her. I suppose she was waiting to join up with that odius man, Trubshawe."

I said nothing. Nothing I could think of was worth saying.

"We have her now," Bacon continued. "I know this Major Trubshawe will be back and when he does we will trade the woman for the third STUMP. That will make operations here much easier."

"Has she been hurt?" I asked. My whole body was shaking.

"No," Bacon said. "If Trubshawe does not deal for her, however, she will be turned over to the High Sheriff of Middlesex. Sufficient evidence will be supplied to him through testimony that she was caught practicing witchcraft. Do you know what is done to a woman convicted of witchery in these times? She will be hanged."

"Inhuman bastards," I muttered.

"She is being held with Master Shakespeare's younger brother," Bacon said. "He will be released pending Shakespeare's acknowledgment that Grantum is the author of his works. Otherwise, he will also be dealt to the High Sheriff and tried as a co-hort in her sorcery. I will prosecute the cases myself, on behalf of the new government."

Bacon then babbled on about what the last words of some ancient Roman hot-shots were, but I paid no attention to him. The shackles on my arms were getting heavier. I didn't think I could muster enough strength now to wrap a few links around Bacon's neck. The guard would get me off him before I could do much anyway. I looked back over at the hairy-faced man in the crisp, colorful uniform. I decided that it wasn't his shoulders that were wide, it was the cut of his doublet above the armholes and the flared look of the rope-trimmed epaulettes that made them look wide. His sleeves were puffed out wide so you could see no definition to his arms. I might not have been looking at this fellow so closely but he kept looking at me—looking at me with an intent expression.

Then he winked at me.

And smiled.

It was a fast smile, but for a second I caught a familiar look to 'him'. The way 'his' eyebrows arched.

The jig might not be up after all, I thought.

"Where is the old man?" the black-hooded man next to the disguised Ann Benchley asked.

"The Lord Lieutenant has gone to fetch him from his cell," the guard next to me said. "It is customary when a death warrant has been delivered for the condemmed man to be escorted by one of the superior officers."

Just then I saw Benchley being escorted down from a rampart. He was walking in a slow, schuffling fashion down the stone stairway. I could see he was in bad shape. Waad, whose peg-leg made his negotiating the stairs no easy matter personally, had ahold of Benchley's right arm as they carefully descended together. Two guards marched slowly just ahead of them and, bringing up the rear, was the fat Chief Warder.

"What kind of prison is this if a condemmed man can't get a cup of coffee?" Benchley said as he came across the green. He was putting up a brave front.

"Coffee is a rare thing," the Lord Lieutenant calmly explained, as if he were a Front Desk Manager dealing with a miffed guest. "We simply have no supply on hand."

"Jesus, if you can't even get a cup of coffee around—" He stopped talking when he saw the young bearded man with the elongated shoulders.

"It's no matter," Benchley said. "I'm sure there's coffee in heaven. Even espresso, perhaps even latte."

Ann Benchley spoke up. Her voice was on a high level, but it still sounded male. Too male, really: like a coal miner who smoked non-filtered cigarettes. I was afraid the game might be up before whatever the plan was could be implemented.

"If I were you, Jesuit," Ann Benchley said, "I would request to repair to the chapel and pray for your misquided soul. Your reckoning hour is at hand."

If there was to be a break-out for us, the chapel had something to do with it.

Now the headsman, whoever he was, spoke: "Both these wretches need to square themselves before God."

"To the nearest chapel then," Ann Benchley said, turning to Waad. "That would be the Chapel of St. John in the White Tower, would it not?"

Waad nodded. "The warrant says to swiftly dispatch the prisoners, Sir Thomas. It says nothing about recantation before a holy altar. The Queen herself—"

"I know the Queen herself very well," 'Sir Thomas' said. "She is my godmother. A minute of prayerful repose for these men in the chapel will not be an affront to Her Majesty's judgement. Even a heretic should be allowed to make his peace before a righteous altar of God."

"This is most irregular," Waad said. "These are treacherous men, indeed, but not the normal run of spies that skulk about our kingdom. There is something strange here and only further interrogation will bring it out. I'm surprised Her Majesty would execute a death warrant in so sudden a manner. We have only one prisoner's confession. Besides, a formal Star Chamber proceding should take—"

Ms. Benchley interrupted him: "Would you wish to personally explain to Her Majesty why you failed to carry out a state document bearing her signature and seal?" Her voice broke on the last word. She coughed several times to cover herself, then continued.

"After Her Majesty returns from the wedding at Grantum Hall tomorrow, she plans to go to Whitehall Palace. You can gain audience to her Presence Chamber and explain your actions. I hope you'll find the Queen in a sanguine humor, for your own sake."

Waad literally threw up his hands. "Take the condemmed to St. John's then to the block. I wash my hands of it."

The guard next to me delivered a shove and I walked forward to the green, taking a place next to Jack Benchley. Ann Benchley walked just ahead. She turned around and gave her father a quick glance, but no more. Even close up, the facial disguise—the cheeks and face covered with must have been a wide flesh-colored latex also had a surface area of artificial beard stubble to heighten the facade of masculinity—looked convincing. The high ruff she wore covered for her lack of an Adam's apple.

What with Bacon near, I was now very glad Jack Benchley had never taken his daughter on one of these trips to the past.

Jack Benchley's last request was that my chains be undone. That was granted by Waad. With two guards on either side, and myself helping the older man saunter along, we walked behind the headsman and 'Sir Thomas' toward the White Tower.

"Is the headsman to pray as well?" one of the guards asked as we approached the wooden stairway to the White Tower.

The headsman, whose voice I couldn't recognize, spoke: "A man about to draw blood, even from the neck of a traitor, needs to ask absolution for his deeds."

"Wait a moment," Bacon cried out from behind us. "I wish to see that headsman with his hood off." We stopped. The little philosopher ambled forward.

"So it shall be," the headsman said when Bacon came face to face with him. The man revealed himself with a quick jerking off of the hood. He looked a bit like Stephen Trubshawe, but younger and more intense about the eyes. Bacon studied his face, then turned about to face Waad. The latter man was still standing on the green where I had last seen him.

"Who is this man?" Bacon asked excitedly. "I have seen the Queen's headsman before. He is a French Hugenout named Dumont. This is not the man."

"I am Richard Vernon, lance-knight and late of the Royal Fusillers at Dover Castle. I was assigned to the duty this day. Sergeant Dumont has the sweating sickness. I will carry out his duties until he recovers, if he recovers."

Bacon practically screeched. "I have never seen this man in the Queen's service!" He looked over at 'Sir Thomas', giving the lady a scrutiny that concerned the hell out of me. He turned back to Waad to say something but Waad beat him to the punch.

"I care not if the Lord Secretary himself performs the deeds at hand. Bother me no more, Bacon. The two men must die. The quicker this bloody business is over, the quicker I am to supper."

Benchley noticed the large bandage over my left hand.

"Torture?" he said to me.

I nodded. Then we were turned around by the guards and marched again toward the main tower.

Out of the corner of one eye, I noticed Bacon was coming along a few paces behind our group.

The narrow high-vaulted ceiling was dimly lit by long-necked candelabras that were placed under the heavy Romanesque columns and archways that surrounded three-quarters of the room. The altar was covered in the same red cloth that had been there when I passed by three days ago. There were a few small gold-tassled pillows in front of the wooden base the altar was situated on. I helped Benchley down to his knees. As I did this, the fellow playing the headsman (his hood off) assisted me. He took the opportunity to whisper something in my ear.

"Keep Mr. Benchley down. Whatever happens, don't move until I want you to." He then knelt down on a pillow close to the one I was using.

'Sir Thomas' stood behind us. Next to her was Bacon. I looked back at them both as they knelt behind us to pray. The senior Benchley began to pray out loud. He spoke in something akin to the deep, resonant voice I had first heard him speak in the day I got the autograph from him at the book-signing in Rogue Falls. The timbre of his voice was helped by the acoustics of the chapel.

"'The Lord is my light and salvation. Whom shall I fear…? And now shall mine head be lifted up above mine enemies: therefore will I offer in his Tabernacle sacrifices of joy…. Deliver me not over unto the will of mine enemies, for false witnesses are risen up against me, and such as breathe out cruelty.'"

Benchley paused. Whatever was supposed to happen next wasn't happening.

"'How long will thou forget me, O Lord?'" Benchley said

after the pause. "'Forever?'" he added, now sounding less reverential than anxious. I saw Benchley glance over his shoulder at his daughter. I could not see her reaction.

"This is reverence enough," I heard Bacon say. "Let us get to—"

The blinding light came, right in front of us, just a few feet in front of the altar. It was, if anything more intense than when I first saw it in the alley back in San Francisco. The light faded and there stood two men, Major Trubshawe and son, Stephen. They were dressed in green and black battle fatigues and were both sporting automatic rifles.

"Jesu! Jesu!" I heard one of the guards behind us shout out, just before the chapel was raked with ear-splitting multiple fire. They were firing over our heads, and over the heads of the escapees. I turned around and saw the guards running, bent over like twin Groucho Marxes, leaving their spears and helmets behind them. They were out the wide chapel door, unharmed, in a flash.

Closer to me, Ann Benchley had Francis Bacon in a headlock but she was having problems. He landed an elbow to her head, sending her falling backwards, then, after slipping from my grasp, hightailed it out the door. I had reached out for him with my badly-burnt left hand in a reflex move, but I couldn't hold unto his cape. The 'headsman,' whom I later found out was Trubshawe's youngest son, Malcom Trubshawe, tried to stop Bacon but the small man wheeled around on him and fired a fat antique pistol he had concealed under his cape. The shot whistled past the intended target. A burst of automatic fire narrowly missed Bacon as he scurried behind the big oak doors and out into the passageway. Malcom looked keen to follow him, but his father told him to "secure the bloody doors!" instead. I helped the dazed Ms. Benchley to her feet.

Malcom Trubshawe, a Lieutenant in the Royal Marines and the one who had been on some operation in Labrador, slammed the doors. "I need help," he shouted out. His hands were pressed, one on each door. "Some bugger fetch me those lances."

I was the bugger. I picked up the two disgarded lances and gave them to Malcom, who put them in the U-shaped iron handgrips that substituted for knobs. At his behest, I also went and shoved a heavy chair up against the door to provide some extra weight to the impromptu barrier. After I did this I turned around and saw Ann and Jack Benchley inside the shell of the time machine, being positioned by Major Trubshawe. I then put my attention to holding the doors. A few seconds later I looked again and I saw both Benchleys vanish through the cloud of brillant red light generated by the STUMP.

As I slid one of the pews across the floor (to further secure the door) I could hear all hell breaking loose in the hallway outside. Shouts could be heard, along with the clatter of heavy footsteps coming nearer to us. A few moments later, the doors that Malcom and I were holding were being pushed harder from the opposite side.

“Open in the name of the Queen!” I heard a fierce voice shout out. With every push I could tell there were more guards joining in the effort.

I looked back at the altar. Major Trubshawe was now making his getaway. “Hurry up, you stupid buggers,” he said just before he vanished, absorbed in the red light. I hoped very much that the STUMP would be back soon.

A real surge of power smashed against the door, causing our make-shift defenses to slide and opening the doors enough so a few inches now separated the frames of the doors. Malcom was muscular, but he was not much bigger than me, and we needed to fall back.

“Open in the name of the Queen,” the same voice shouted. A bullet zinged past our heads through the crack, followed by the thick smell of black powder. Stephen Trubshawe, standing behind one of the columns, fired back at a rapid clip. Bullets tore into the oak walls a few feet above our heads. This, more than the barriers, seemed to keep the guards at bay.

“We’re going,” Malcom Trubshawe said in a shout I could barely hear above the din of fire and the confusion of voices on the other side of the doors. His eyes had that wild intensity I had only seen before on men and woman who actually drew and fired weapons on a place other than the practice range. I supposed I looked the same. He took a semi-automatic pistol out of a belt holster and handed it to me, then brought what looked like some type of AR-15 rifle about (tugging at the shoulder strap that held it to his back) to his front and jammed a new magazine in place of the one he discarded in a flash. I undid the safety on my gun, wishing I had what he was packing.

We waited until the red glow returned. When it faded, along came the STUMP. I could see the control panel on the inside of the thing with a bright red row of numbers flashing away.

The remaining Trubshawe barked out orders, "Move your arse when I hit three," he said. "On three now. One—two—three!"

I covered the ground from the door to the altar running backwards and letting off a round every couple seconds. Malcom made up for my single shots with a heavy rate of fire. Both brothers were still firing when I squeezed into the left side of the STUMP. I wondered if three people had ever made it through a journey in this contraption. Two or three more bursts of fire were all the brothers had out of their rifles. I was out of ammunition as well. No soldier had come over the threshold of the chapel but now I could see the doors splintering apart from the work of heavy axes. Another long musket came through the widening gap between the doors. The musketman took aim at me. He had a dead bead. I ducked down as best I could. There came a spark from the top of the weapon, obscuring the musketman's face, then everything went suddenly red.

The red light engulfed us. I quickly developed the dizzying sensation in my head and the nausea in my stomach from my first time trip. I felt ready to vomit. But I hadn't been shot—nor had my two companions.

A few seconds later we were in the same place: St. John the Evangelist's Chapel in the White Tower. But we were not facing adversaries. There were the Benchleys, Truffie Trubshawe, and a group of redcoated Beefeaters much older-looking than the rowdy pack we had just left. One of the beefeaters had his mouth open like he was trying to imitate a pelican. There were also five middle-aged men in thick green sweaters with insignias on their shoulders. All five of them were staring at us; one of them was shaking his head.

I vomited again. The three of us untangled ourselves from one another and got off the platform. I saw a collapsible metal hospital gurney off to one side. I wanted to jump on it and stay on it until I could get on a plane to Heathrow Airport. But Bonnie still had to be rescued.

I found out we were back in modern London, four days after we had first left. I found out that the five men in green sweaters around us were officers from a Royal Marine Commando Unit.

“The cat had to come out of the bag,” I heard Truffie Trubshawe say to Jack Benchley as he helped the older man to sit down on a folding chair.

“I hope Mortie Ryskind will forgive us,” Jack Benchley answered.

Chapter Fifty-Five

I sat in the backseat of Truffie Trubshawe's Range Rover, with a new bandage on my left hand. I had received a shot of pain-killer as well. Ann Benchley was sitting next to me in the backseats. In the time it took her father and me to tell her that Jack Picasso had a videotape that, if editted properly, would send her to prison for life, the Rover left the Tower via a non-public underground tunnel. The actress at first expressed incredulity at this news about her Jack, but our adamant conviction of what we saw won her over. Her father was up front in the passenger seat of the vehicle and Major Trubshawe was driving. The burnt portion of my hand had been treated with ointment, gauze and the bandage courtesy of a Royal Marine dressing kit. I no longer wore my ragged Renaissance wear. I was now back in the clothes I had left behind at 'Trubshawe's Curiosities,' including my green felt bush hat. I was also eating—slowly—a chicken sandwich and a liter of water from a plastic thermos. I felt a great deal better than before, but my good fortune was tempered a bit by the thought that Bonnie was still a prisoner and we had a limited time to get her out.

We were headed north, up a congested four-lane street, not counting the turn lanes called Commercial Road. The time on the dashboard clock read 4:44 and the lanes were filled with Londoners trying to beat it out of the city in cars and minivans. Behind us was another Range Rover carrying the Trubshawe brothers and some of the Royal Marine Commando Officers. Behind that was a red and white ambulance carrying some medical team that was going to patch us up when —and if—we got back from the next excursion to the past. The plan as I had grasped it from Truffie on the way out of the Tower of London was to make it to Sobel House, the modern site of Grantum Hall, near Hampstead Heath. The modern estate, until recently the property of the Strunk family, had been donated to a private preservation group called the National Trust. I learned the estate and the public golf course nearby had been closed—obtensibly because of a gas leak —and we were going to meet up with two helicopter crews, each flying an attack chopper called a Sea Lynx. The course had been chosen, so Major Trubshawe said, because it was quite close to the site of Grantum Hall.

"The government is giving us complete cooperation," Trubshawe said as he weaved in and out of the traffic. "The sad part is that, if any of this comes out, the damnable Admiralty is going to get most of the credit. I wanted it to be a job for one of the army paratroop units, but the old deskjockeys at Joint Intelligence Command display a rather disgusting preference for the Senior Service. They thought I was a complete nutter at first, of course, until I managed to get my brother officers to come out to Hampstead and see how the thing works. After I gave them each a trip to Merrie Old England, and they got over the initial shock, I started getting cooperation very quickly."

Jack Benchley used his pinkie finger to rub under the new, sanitary eyepatch he was now sporting. "How many people know about the STUMPs?" he asked.

"You might as well say anyone in Whitehall that needs to know, Jack," Trubshawe said. "The Prime Minister, the Minister of Defense, all the high mucky-mucks in the Joint Intelligence Committee, some brasshats I had to cross swords with to even get into the JIC.... If we want to stop Warbeck, this is the only way to get the job done—"

"They have Bonnie," I said.

"She must have been waiting at the original place we dropped the three of you off. I brought the STUMP back to a spot a couple kilometers away. I figured using the back-up site would be safest. I found one of Bonnie's cigarette lighters on the ground when Ann and I reconnoitred over to the primary site. We might have just missed Bonnie. I'm sorry, Annie."

"We're getting her back," Ann Benchley said adamantly. "If we go back, we get Bonnie out of Grantum Hall—alive. That has to be top priority."

"That's phase one," Trubshawe said. "Once we get Bonnie secured, then we have to get the two STUMPs that Warbeck has out of the keep. That's phase two. Once we have that, we'll have all three time machines and the capability to set the Sea Lynxes back into time. Strike Command has authorized an air attack. The ground crews will have them loaded for bear. If we can get back before Essex and Southampton come out of the woods and attack the Queen's forces, we can blast into the rebels, land a commando unit or two on 'em when they get softened up and relieve them of their weapons. That's phase three. Then we're to back on out and leave our remote ancestors in the legitimate government to mop up. But before any of that, we have to get some people into Grantum Hall."

"I'm going to be one of those people," I said.

"This is going to be an Official Royal Marine operation, Wells," Trubshawe said. "Malcom is going in with some handpicked—"

"I'm going in," I said firmly. "Your son and his handpicked commandos can get the STUMPs. I'm getting Bonnie out, hell or high water. If I screw up, then it's my funeral."

Trubshawe turned back to look at me, giving me a hostile glare. "Understand this, Wells, this has to be—"

"Understand this, Major," I shot back, trying not to raise my voice above a shout. "I was good enough to risk my neck when we took the STUMP back to get Mr. Benchley out. I killed some poor kid and damned near bought it myself. Bonnie put her life on the line, too. She saved both of us when we were jumped by those two robbers. You owe it to her to have somebody going in specifically to get her out. Don't bullshit me about this operation, Major Trubshawe. Those guys in the Admiralty or whatever want to get their mitts on the time machines so they can find out what military value they might have. Getting Bonnie out is a secondary goal. Let me go in with the first group or I'll spill the whole fucking story to every newspaper from here back to the States."

"Wells is right," Ann Benchley added. "The marines can do what the brass hats want done. He can concentrate on Bonnie. I want her out alive, too. I don't want her lost in the shuffle. Let the man try."

Ann Benchley won that battle for me.

"Very well," Trubshawe said with a sigh. "Wells goes in with me. Understand, Yank, if you get left behind when the time comes, then that's the fortunes of war. Period."

"I understand," I said, getting the first pang of fear in my gut since I had narrowly missed losing my head.

"Francis Bacon betrayed us," Jack Benchley said. "He went over to Warbeck's side."

"I know," Trubshawe said. "Shakespeare told us when we made it back into time. I wished we'd captured him back at the chapel. Then we could have traded him for Bonnie. I went to Southwark looking for you gents. I found out from Shakespeare that his younger brother is a prisoner in Grantum Hall as well. Bill Shakespeare's a wreck. I saw him the day before the play Essex paid his company to perform for his followers. Apparently he was ordered by the Queen to substitute *The Merry Wives of Windsor* for the Richard the Second play that Essex wanted. He knows Essex and his mob will be madder than hornets. It's a horrible dilemma: risk your imprisoned brother or get your absolute monarch mad enough to send you to the block."

"Would Essex try and get Shakespeare's Company cancelled out for the wedding play then?" Ann asked.

"Not while the Queen wants the Lord Chamberlain's Men to perform after the wedding," Major Trubshawe replied. But now, tonight—that is 398 years' worth of tonights ago—he has to go to Grantum Hall and annouce to the Queen and her Court that the Earl of Grantum is the author of practically everything he's written professionally. He's got to put it in writing."

"And, after that," Jack Benchley said. "Trevor Warbeck can use the forced confession in Shakespeare's own hand to prove to the world that the 15th Earl of Grantum wrote the plays. Then he gets to go back to the early 1600's and play the Earl while the real man languishes in a cell. It's damn abominable."

Benchley turned around and looked at his daughter, who was sitting diagonally from him in the back seat. He put a shaky hand back toward her and she clasped it in her two hands.

"I'm sorry I lost my temper with you, Annie," Jack Benchley said. "Please forgive me. I had just been through too much. I said things that were—"

"Don't worry about it, Daddy," she said. "I love you. I'm just glad you're safe. Don't worry about Avalon, either. The doctors say she's going to fully recover. She lost some muscle in her arm, but she'll be able to move it—hell, she'll do anything she wants."

"Just like you," Jack Benchley said.

"Damn," Trubshawe said, trying to pass a small car that suddenly swerved in front of him. He turned to Jack Benchley and spoke: "We have to get back into time before that weasel Bacon can ride from the Tower up to Hampstead and warn Warbeck. I know he's headed up there right now. Where's our STUMP, by the way?"

"Waiting for us near the present estate," Trubshawe said.

"How'd you and Stephen get into the old Tower of London?" I asked Ann Benchley as Trubshawe gunned his vehicle and us past a red double-decker bus that had a beer advertisment between the first and second deck.

"It wasn't easy," Ms. Benchley said, turning about to face me as best her shoulder belt would allow her. "I fell apart for awhile there after Avalon got shot, but I got my shit together well enough for Truffie to take me back with him."

Ann Benchley went on to explain that Shakespeare himself had come up with the plan to spring Benchley and me out of the Tower. It revolved around a young man named Sir Thomas Marbury, who was a godson of the first Queen Elizabeth. Marbury is, or was, a detizen of the Mermaid Tavern and Shakespeare had a miniature portrait of the young man. His official duties at court included delivering messages and warrants from the Queen to military posts like the Tower. He had, as Ann Benchley put it, "an androgynous appearance," a look he tried to compensate for with a good deal of facial hair. She went on.

"Truffie and I went back to this time now and got Dylan, that's the lady who picked us up at Heathrow, to put together a make-up job to make me look like Marbury. About that time Malcom got back from Operation Northern Lights in Labrador. We got a death warrant and put your names on it, went back into time, then Malcom and I went to the Tower of 1599. We put a black suit and hood on Malcom so he'd look like an executioner. I was scared when Bacon told him to take his hood off, but he thought fast with that bit about the officer executioner being sick and saved us. The only thing that was worse was actually riding up to the Lion's Gate at the Tower and presenting the warrant to the guards. That had me scared shitless."

"How did you get death warrants signed by Queen Elizabeth?" I asked.

"We didn't, Wells," Trubshawe said. "Once I proved the STUMP worked, we had access to everything in the Prints and Drawings Department at the British Museum. They had a copy of the death warrant Elizabeth signed off to Essex in 1601. We just had a facsimile drawn up, a nice forgery job courtesy of a nice scholarly lady the museum has on hand to check for fraudulent documents. Apparently, she could have had a second career making fakes because the warrant passed muster going in. Stephen and I had synchronized the STUMP to appear at the Chapel of St. John right about the time we figured Annie and Malcom would get the two of you up there for your last rites."

"You could have been a couple minutes earlier and it wouldn't have hurt," Jack Benchley said.

Truffie chuckled. "Sorry, mate. We synchronized as best we could. Your little girl back there was slightly ahead of schedule. The Beefeaters you saw gawking at you back in the chapel helped us carry the STUMP up into the White Tower. We had to close the Tower up for a couple hours—offically the tourists were told there was a gas leak at Waterloo Barracks—until we got everything done and got out of there. All in all, we muddled through fairly well."

"You'll get no complaints from me," I said.

After a few miles along a two-lane road, scooting around boxy compact cars and the occasional storty roadster, Truffie turned down a one-lane paved road that led to a graveled stretch of narrow road flanked by tall, gnarled oaks with leafy green leaves that took us up over a rather steep hillside. At the apex, he turned the utility vehicle down a trail. Just around the corner from the roadside, I saw two soldiers in fatigues and black berets guarding the trail. They were carrying assault rifles. Both men offered Trubshawe a salute as he slowed down and rolled down the window.

"Another Rover like this, then an ambulance," Major Trubshawe said after returning the salute with a whip-like motion of his open right hand to his browline. "After that, sergeant, put up the barricades going out. I trust the hillside has been sealed."

"Yes, major," the young soldier Trubshawe addressed replied. Another saluting session and we travelled on down the trail.

The trail ended in a small dirt turnabout. After the other officers got out of the second Range Rover our entire party proceeded single-file down a switchback trail wide enough for a nimble hiker or a dog. We came up on a large clearing, maybe fifty feet across, that must have been the top of a bluff. Beyond the bluff was a view of Sobel House.

This was not the Grantum Hall of the late 16th Century that Trubshawe, Bonnie and I had crept up upon a few days earlier. Instead of a medieval keep surrounded by four towers that were inter-connected by a Tudor-style manorhouse, this estate had a smaller, symmetrical Neo-classical main building with a flat roof fringed by a jutting cornice with an extended terrace above that. Behind the terrace were two small circular-domed Grecian temples about twenty or thirty feet apart from each other. There were two smaller buildings of the same variety on each side of the main house, connected to the larger structure by a covered walkway supported by slender white pillars that matched the color scheme for the whole complex. Nothing moved down below. I assumed that, like the Tower of London, the government had asked The National Trust to shut the place down. We faced west and watched the rays of the setting sun behind us ebb into a batch of darkening clouds that blanketed the eastern horizon.

I stood between Jack Benchley and his daughter. Malcom Trubshawe, dressed in his Royal Marine commando uniform, and his older brother, still in the fatigues he was in when he surprised Bacon and company back at the Tower, came up to us. I now had time to examine Stephen's countenance. He looked very different from his sober, almost drab and business-like appearance back at the family shop.

"Hello again, Harvey," Stephen said, his large eyes radiating life and energy like he was up for whatever was ahead.

"Things a bit less hectic now, eh?"

"Good to see you," I said. I had already thanked both men for rescuing us from the tower. As I talked with Stephen, telling him I was coming along on the mission, I took note of the STUMP situated behind us in the clearing. Major Trubshawe was working on the panelbox, punching buttons that put numbers up on display. The officers stood around him, taking it in with undivided attention. There was a helicopter already on site. It was a small open cockpit thing that could only carry one adult. The small chopper was in two pieces: the fuselage and main rotar blades of the machine and, resting on two sawhorses, the metal gridwork that supported the tail and rear rotars.

Benchley explained to his daughter how he had Major Trubshawe swipe part of William Devant's journal during one of their time-trips to help prove the Charles Devant forgery.

"We needed specimens of William DeVant's handwriting," he said, finishing up, "to prove his grandson was behind a hoax. I'm going to give Devant back his letters—if he's still alive after all this. It was wrong for Truffie to steal into the man's library and make off with part of DeVant's journal and his letters, but it was for a good cause."

I nodded.

"It might have been unethical, but it was for a good cause, Daddy," Ms. Benchley said. "Besides, you haven't done very many unethical things in your life."

"Don't bet on it," Benchley said. "There's one or two things even you don't know about me, Annie. I'll have to tell you about them after this is over with."

About the time Jack Benchley, with a glum look on his face, wondered aloud where the helicopters were, I heard the mechanical whirl of rotating blades chopping through the air above us, drawing nearer and nearer. It was a loud, heavy sound, the type of turbulance in the air that military rotarcraft make when they land. And land they did, after swooping in from behind us. The action of the rotars caused the bystanders to hold on to their berets.

The Sea Lynxes, large green Huey-sized choppers with big cargo sections and an extended fusleage that bore the lettering 'ROYAL NAVY' on the sides, both landed on the edge of the bluff right in front of our group. Through the windscreens above the nose of each chopper, I could see they were each manned by a helmeted pilot and co-pilot. On either side of the attack helicopters, just under the cargo hold, were torpedo-like missile batteries attached to the small wing-like projections. The side doors rolled open and a team of about a dozen commandos, each dressed in green camouflage jumpsuits and sporting green and black facepaint, dislodged around us. On the sides of the helicopters, just behind the nose, were the business ends of the machine guns. The barrels on the guns were quite wide. They were quite impressive but, as Benchley told me once the rotars stopped, without all three STUMPs operating and synchronized with the one we already had they would be unable to get back to the point in time where they were needed.

After the soldiers deployed around the area, I noticed a few other crewmen inside the choppers. They simply stayed in their jumpseats inside the cargo area, as did the pilots up front. Malcom and Stephen went off to join the other soldiers.

The military officers gathered in a circle. I noticed that two of them were females. The only one not in uniform was Truffie Trubshawe. Even though he was inactive, Major Trubshawe (Retired) seemed to be in charge of the operation. On the table in front of us was a copy of the book that I had seen back at the Northwest Shakespeare Festival, the one which had a sketch of the old Grantum Hall and the landscape around it. Trubshawe was relying on the artist who made the sketch that the hill we were on was little changed from our time to theirs so it would be safe to transport ourselves via the STUMP without hitting anything solid. I thought the plan Trubshawe laid out (and was endorsed by the other officers) had merit. I was surprised at the part William Shakespeare was going to play in the scheme. He and the Major must have conferred on what was going to go down. The first 'group' going in would only be Major Trubshawe, former Lieutenant Stephen Trubshawe, and myself. My job was to stay close to them and shoot anybody with my pistol if things went wrong. There were two more Sea Lynxes standing by at a nearby aerodrome to support the two that had already landed.

The major suddenly looked over to me, then spoke sharply: "Being a civilian, Wells, I'm giving you a chance to back out of this now. If you slip up at your end of the operation, you get left behind. That's the way it's going to be. Even if we try another operation later, chances are that Warbeck or Essex will have you or any other prisoner killed on the spot. You remember old Jack here talking about all the dead shot up and buried back at old Grantum Hall, right? So this is your last chance to—"

"Save it," I said. "I'm in it, major. You just tell these other men what they need to know."

Trubshawe gave me a brisk nod of the head then, in the dimming light, he verbally laid out the rest of the plan to those assembled.

Chapter Fifty-Six

It was an outdoor wedding being performed against the rays of the setting sun. Major Trubshawe watched it through binoculars while Stephen and I tied up the soldier we had surprised when we transported back into time. We had sent the STUMP through once as a drone, to make double sure we would not transport into a tree or a large boulder. When it came back unscaved, Stephen and his father went ahead. I followed, showing up right after the soldier had been snuck up upon and knocked senseless.

"Mom gave into Dad for the sake of getting Jack Benchley back," Stephen said to me as he tied the feet of the guard. "She didn't like it but Dad talked her into it. Of course, Mom had no idea we'd have to go in with guns blazing like that. You didn't acquit yourself too badly, Wells."

"Thanks," I said. "But next time bring me an AR-15, too. Are those made by Colt or Olympic?"

"Actually, what Malcom and I used back at the Tower were PM lightweight assault rifles. Accuracy International puts them out for our boys in the field. Damn good British-made design," Stephen said off-handedly.

Our new prisoner had been armed with a matchlock rifle which made him one of the Queen's soldiers and, technically, on our side. But the operation had to be kept quiet so a blow to the back of the head by Stephen from the butt of a rifle rendered him a non-combatant for the duration. There were no signs of soldiers with AK-47's and grenade launchers but, according to the major, only men with matchlocks and swords were in sight down at the wedding party in front of Grantum Hall. Trubshawe said that the Queen usually travelled with a hundred or so personal bodyguards—the Gentlemen Pensioners. The presence of a soldier on the bluff made it clear she had brought along some regular or conscripted soldiers to add to her security, he added. Essex had not made his move—yet.

We were back in the early evening of September 26, 1599, A.D. After the groggy guard's hands and feet were bound, and his mouth sealed with ducktape, Stephen and I crawled over to where Major Trubshawe was laying prostrate scanning the wedding scene.

"I see the Queen," he said without emotion. He handed the binoculars to his son, and then Stephen pased them to me.

The wedding party was divided into two rows, with a wide red carpet making an aisle down the middle of the lawn at the front of the estate. There were several score of well-dressed ladies and gentlemen on both sides. I could see the bulky form of Trevor Warbeck waiting at the end of the carpeted aisle, standing in front of a man in a black robe. Just behind them, seated in a throne-like chair in the first row and surrounded by an array of men dressed in shiny blue doublets, was a woman with a stark white face, her hair a big red bird's nest. She was wearing some type of transluscent collar that shimmered in the retreating amber light coming from the western sky. It was an enormous ruff with long points of what had to be very starchy fabric jutting up like a lion's mane around that clown-white face.

"The men around her are the Gentlemen Pensioners," Major Trubshawe said. "They have swords and matchlocks and those damn single-shot petronels. They won't know what hit 'em if our boys can't neutralize things. I know that bastard Essex is out in the woods somewhere around here. He's going to make his move when it gets dark, when the whole wedding party can be trapped inside the manor. We have to be squared away and moving as soon as this light goes down."

Twigs snapped behind us. All three of us whipped about to the sounds. I dropped into a barricade stance behind a tree trunk, my Baretta pistol set to shoot.

A horseman came through the brush behind us. I recognized the man and relaxed. The major signaled William Shakespeare over to us. Seeing we were all crouched down and could possibly be seen if he rose to full height, Shakespeare tied the reins of his horse to a tree and duck-walked over to us. He was dressed in a long-flowing black robe like a judge. His head was covered with a large black skullcap with flaps down over the ears. His feet were covered with red shoes that curved back at the points. He was wearing red stripe 'venetians' with moss green piping. The whole of his attire combined to convey a comic look.

Our contact, after being introduced to Stephen, got right to business. "A messenger has just arrived," Shakespeare said, addressing the Major. "He went right to the queen just before the ceremony. I crept as close as I dared to the Royal Presence without arousing suspicion. I overheard that a band of armed men, perhaps two or three score, have been spotted by scouts not three miles from the hall."

"Where?" Major Trubshawe asked.

"Three miles to the east I heard say," Shakespeare said. "I heard Essex's name mentioned. I also heard the messenger say the band his platoon scouted possessed strange firearms the likes of which he had never seen."

"So the Queen has been informed," Stephen said. "Do you know what she is planning to do?"

Shakespeare shook his head. "She probably thinks the extra company of soldiers she has brought up from London will be sufficient to ward off Essex if an attack is made. She does have a great numerical advantage...." Shakespeare's voice trailed off as he saw the uniformed man lying tied up on the ground. He was conscious now, and staring back at us.

"One of that numerical advantage," I said.

"Is there no way to warn Her Majesty what she is really up against?" Stephen asked.

"I know the full measure of the forces against her, as does Kempe," Shakespeare said. "But you have to understand, I am just a player at court. None of the players are allowed to even speak to Her Majesty or disturb her in any fashion. I may get a chance when she enters the Great Hall and we stand in line to pay homage. But even then, Warbeck may be near. If I try to warn her in public, what will happen to my brother?"

"What about the play after the wedding ceremony?" the

major asked.

Shakespeare glanced down at his outfit. "*The Merry Wives of Windsor* will commence after the dancing that's coming up. The Queen no longer dances, so that will not be long as she detests watching the galliards without being able to take part. There is only one way to get Mister Wells and your Stephen into the manor. They must be disguised as late-arriving players for the performance. We can do that. The problem will be the bringing in of weapons. All of the company was searched for armaments before we were let near the courtiers. Secretary Cecil apparently takes the threat from Essex more seriously than does Her Majesty."

"That's not good," Stephen said. "We need our pistols, otherwise how the hell do we get into the keep and get the time machines? We have to have both STUMPs out of wherever they are now and up on those battlements for the mini-copter to airlift out. We need those guns."

"You'll have pistols," the major said. He pointed to a green satchel lying on the ground next to him. You won't be able to ramble into that place with rifles or even regular sized semi-autos. But Mr. Shakespeare has some costumes for you, and the costumes have a place to accommodate a short-barreled Beretta 21." He opened the satchel and removed the blue matted guns from the bag, handing them to us along with one seven-shot clip.

"The Model 21 is small enough so you can stash the guns where the Queen's bodyguards won't think of looking," the major said. "While you're infiltrating the castle, and getting ahold of Warbeck by hook or crook, Malcom and Captain Thompson will be back here assembling the two pieces of the mini-copter." He glanced at his watch. "I have to go back and get Malcom in five minutes, along with the first piece of the mini-copter. You have to be on the battlements exactly one hour from now. Mr. Shakespeare, I trust you've brought the men the costumes they'll be needing."

Shakespeare nodded then duckwalked back to his horse. He returned with a large carpetbag containing what we were to where to the infiltration. He told us they were costumes ordinarily worn by fools, which seemed appropriate.

There was a faint round of cheers and clapping from the people at the wedding. Music was struck up. Through the binoculars, I saw Warbeck kissing his new young bride. I handed the binoculars over to Stephen to let him survey the scene.

"The fat bugger!" the son exclaimed. "That girl Warbeck's hugging is barely past childhood. That's not a marriage; that's statutory rape."

It was about ten minutes later that Stephen and I emerged from the bushy hillside. We were both wearing pointy white hats with thick red stripes, large eyeglasses with Coke bottle lenses, and a pinocchio-sized wooden nose glued at the edges to the glasses. A bristly false mustache which smelled like horsehair completed our facial camouflage. The main article of clothing was a 'motley' coat, which consisted of a multitude of loosely sewn patches of cloth, each a different color. A rope sufficed for our belts. We had on loose-fitting breeches and tights with codpieces situated over our privates. Stowed away under the codpieces (so far out of fashion in this time that only fools would wear one) were our Barettas.

Shakespeare had left to rejoin the crowd at the manor a few minutes ahead of us. Before he left, he gave us some tips in trying to pass ourselves off as zanies, jockeying about during the merriment that led up to the play.

It was dark now and, since we carried no light, we managed to get within fifty yards of the manor. I could see into the rows of large multi-paned windows that had been cut out of the smooth grey stonework. The ground floor was lit up by what must have been an enormous supply of candlepower. Inside we could see the backs of people pressed against the windows while couples danced round and about each other. I looked away from the front entrance—a double doorway with a sculpted lion in sphinx-like repose guarding each side of the broad stone staircase—to the small lake across the green. There was so much light coming inside the manor that I could easily see the bridge where I had exchanged Jack Benchley for the Earl of Southampton a few days earlier. I was actually less scared now than that in past experience. Maybe I really was a fool, I thought.

A few more paces and we were challenged by a single soldier, brandishing a musket. I could see the piece of thick rope he carried coiled about his forearm, the end lit and smoldering in readiness to set off the long barreled matchlock.

"Stand!" barked the soldier who, like many of his ilk was quite thin and young. He was wearing a morion helmet and had a sword to go with the musket, the latter of which wavered back and forth at each of us.

We stood.

Another soldier came up to support him. He was carrying a lantern in one hand and was being pulled by a large, aggressive, and thick-furred dog that could have passed for the Hound of the Baskervilles. He was probably some kind of Great Dane/ Irish Wolfhound mix. The dog tugged at the leash the other soldier held onto and barked like we were mailmen.

"What brings you here?" the second soldier asked in an unfriendly tone.

"Fear not, good gentlemen," I said in a voice that I hoped sounded local and perhaps the worse for the effects of drink. "We are men of the Lord Chamberlain's Company. This is where they are to entertain, is it not?" I bowed deeply to the men, almost losing my nose and glasses in the process.

"There you rascals are," came a loud voice from behind the soldiers. It was William Shakespeare, advancing toward us on the lawn. He had to have come from the main doorway and down the dozen or so steps and then advanced quickly across the lawn. The playwright came right up to me and boxed me upside the head. It was a light box, glancing off an ear, but the quick motion of his open hand probably made it look like a severe blow to the soldiers. "'Ods Wounds," I shouted after the blow struck. I threw my hat down in mock disgust and then made an extended backward motion with my left arm to avenge the strike. (My hand was so badly burned that, even with the bandages under my glove, that very motion seemed to reignite the burning. The painkillers were wearing off.) Shakespeare, having time to see the haybailer coming, ducked. He caught me under my arms as I spun about, my exaggerated swing carrying me off balance. I was tossed back on my feet. Stephen was now involved, attempting to kick Shakespeare. The kick from his long pointy shoe missed and he fell on the lawn, toppling me over as he went. We had only walked through this mock horseplay once, but the execution was enough to get the guards laughing.

"These are company men," Shakespeare explained to the soldiers. "Humphrey Staggers and Erra Pitt, our fools. I have been waiting for these dawcocks for over an hour." He next helped Stephen up, boxing one of his ears for effect. "Dogs, what has detained you? Where are your horses?"

Stephen, employing an accent coached to him by his father, told of an unpaid bill we had run up at an inn somewhere between London and Hampstead and the necessity of leaving our horses at the inn for security. This was our excuse for lateness.

"A pox on you cranks," Shakespeare said indignantly. "More's likely you were cozened out of the nags by a couple cony-catchers. Come, get thee toward our tent by the buttery. Follow me."

The guards insisted on frisking us first, but did not handle our codpieces. We had passed the first phase. Now the three of us headed across a gravel path that adjoined the side of the manor.

"The play commences in a quarter hour," our inside man said as we rounded the pinnacle-topped rook. Young men passed back and forth of us, each boy either carrying a wooden chair from off the lawn or two boys assisting one another in bringing a bench in from the outdoor wedding. It was a warm, cloudless night. The main windows on the side of the manor were open. Various scents wafted into my nostrils as we passed: burning candlewax, some type of potpurri, cooked meat with an aroma of lamb predominating and, further down our path, the strong stench of human excrement and body odor. The source of this smell was apparent when we saw a woman in a plain smock and skirt balancing two buckets on each end of a pole across her shoulders. She was transporting the noble excrement from the blessed event.

There was a large tent erected next to a wagon, illuminated by candleight from the inside. We stepped inside the half-open flap of the tent. There were men preparing their faces with chalky make-up, and putting on costumes. The shadows from the artificial light cast earie figures along the canvas sides of the tent.

William Kempe was there, along with several other men I recognized from the tiring house at The Globe. Ben Jonson was seated in a small chair, wearing a gown similar to Shakespeare's and scribbling something on a long sheet of paper. Two slender young boys were dressed as ladies, and were applying the thick rouge to their cheeks and lips. One lad was adjusting his wig. On the small table in front of him was a thin-crowned lady's hat, a purple scarf, and one of those purses women wore that dangled from their waists. Kempe was patting his stomach and adjusting his belly in an unnatural show of intestinal flexibility. I realized his stomach was padded. He took a brief glance at the other William and ourselves, then lifted himself up from his seat and came over.

"Am I fat enough?" he asked Shakespeare. "Is this your wastrel knight?"

Shakespeare pushed down the front hem of his doublet. "Your peascod jacket is almost too tight for the stuffing. We will lose the deception if your straw pillow protrudes. Have you tried on the stag horns for the final scenes?"

"Aye," Kempe said, "Alas, Sir John Falstaff will be made the total fool. I liked his sharper wits when he bandied with Prince Hal in the Henry of Bolingbroke plays."

Shakespeare acknowledged the criticism from his colleague with a glum expression, then acknowledged us to the players. "These men are strangers to you," he said, "But I assure you they are trustworthy. I have told you of the deceptions of the man who calls himself the Earl of Grantum. And I have told you of the plans of the Earl of Essex. Many of you believe my mind is disordered, that my wits have flown. By my troth, I speak the truth. You have all heard the rumors of Essex hiding in Middlesex Forest. You can believe them. He is headed here, and his aim is treason."

Shakespeare looked about at the dozen or so men assembled around him.

"God's Wounds, what a tale," a man said. It was Richard Burbage, his hair again perfectly combed, every bit of beard in perfect trim, the scowl on his handsome face indicative of skepticism as was the tone of his voice.

"This is my company, William," Burbage said. "Mine and my brother Cutbert's that is. My father, God rest him, built the first permanent theater London ever had. I will not have my family's work destroyed by rash actions against our betters. It was bad enough we angered Essex's friends by substituting the *Richard* play for this Falstaff bauble."

"That was at the behest of the Queen," Kempe said. "Queens trump barons and earls, Richard."

Burbage said, "Would it that the Queen's Master of the Revels had issued a writ banning the play and I might not have been so hotly berated by Sir Gelly Meyrick and Sir Christopher Blount, nor forced to part with the advance money Essex's men gave us." Burbage then turned and scowled at Stephen and myself.

"I do not want these men mixed up with our business. We are actors, Shakespeare. We are not rogues, spies, nor dabblers in statecraft. Away with these men."

Shakespeare raised his right hand, palm open, at Burbage. "There are greater matters at stake here than our little company: Lord Essex means to tear the lions out of England's Coat, and rive all good men into the trenches to do battle with an unholy usurper. Are we to stand by and wait until our homes are ablaze and our wives and children placed by the whim of a foreign-armed militia, led by men with weaponery we cannot hope to overcome? That man in the grand hall is not my old friend Grantum. He is nothing but a player himself, a strutting demagogue from a future age, an age as flawed as our own, with machines of shell and fire that your worst nightmares cannot imagine."

Burbage shook his head. "I spoke some of those last lines myself, as Gloucester in one of your *Henry the Sixth* plays."

"And I know you must believe them," Shakespeare said. "If I am a liar, then I forfeit my share in this company, to be divided among the other sharers. There is no more surety I can give. My brother is a prisoner within the keep of this very estate. Richard, I will fight these diabolical men with or without you, but the better with you and our fellows."

"Are you certain your brother is somewhere within these walls?" Burbage asked.

"I am certain," Shakespeare said. "As I am equally certain that the real Grantum lies a prisoner within the stone walls of the keep as well. But I see I must further assay my cause 'gainst your doubting minds. Therefore, take the measure of this."

He reached under his robes and revealed a small flip-top cellular phone Major Trubshawe had given him earlier for a communicator. He opened the cover, pulled up the antennae, punched the 'power' button which activated the now-glowing number pads, and punched in a few random numbers which set off the electronic beeps he knew would be strange to the ears of his friends. "'Tis witchcraft," Burbage said, a startled look in his eyes.

"'Tis a fantastic device," Shakespeare interjected, "but 'tis not the product of witchcraft. This device is from a future where men can contact one another with unseen currents in the air. The man who gave this to me is an ally of the two men I have brought before you. They are allies who can stop Essex from usurping the Queen's throne. The man who calls himself Grantum lays a false claim to the plays our company owns. He means to steal our rights as free Englishmen."

Burbage shook his head.

Kempe interjected, spreading out his arms as he spoke: "You are warned by the most articulate among us, yet you do not hear."

"*One* of the most articulate," Ben Jonson chimed in. The burly man stood up. "This business is strange and I know not the origin of Will's strange device. But I do know something is amiss at Grantum Hall. I spoke to the man who claims to be Grantum just before the wedding. His son, young Devant, and I attended university together. I visited this very edifice a few years past. The elder Devant was a great connoisseur of Horace's Odes and Epodes. He particularly enjoyed the Roman poet's, *In Praise of Wine*. That Grantum of several years ago gave me a copy of Horace's Odes he had personally translated and had printed up for friends. When I met him briefly before the ceremony, I spoke a few lines of the wine poem to him. This Grantum thought I was quoting Seneca! I further questioned him in the universal language and found myself barely understood. His Latin syntax betrays a poverty of knowledge. My talk flustered him. He moved away from me as if I suffered from plague. The more I think on it, the less convinced I am that the man I met as a student is the same man who is the host of this event."

"You believe the two Williams then?" Burbage asked Jonson.

"I believe them with the buttress of my recent experience," Jonson replied.

"Listen to our young friend, Richard," Will Kempe said. "Listen to Master Shakespeare. Have any of us been the less for his efforts or his judgement?"

One of the actors, standing near the tent flap, called out, "The Lord Grantum is coming."

Warbeck was coming and, with that, came phase two. I moved around the ample Kempe, putting myself out of direct sight. Stephen went behind Shakespeare.

Trevor Warbeck swaggered his fat carcass into the tent, with an assist from the obliging Dromio. The thick hand of the giant appeared at the edge of the flap, then lifted the cloth up high and wide for his boss to make an entrance. Then Dromio came in with his customary pigeon-toed walk, half wobble and half stride. He was dressed in livery, with an insignia on his blue vest. Warbeck was dressed in a vertical-stripped black and white doublet, pleated breeches of a similar color and a broad white cape. A white hat with a black band completed his look. The fat man wobbled a bit himself, I suspected from the effects of the liquid wedding refreshments. He walked right up to Shakespeare, paying no attention to anyone else in the tent. Shakespeare stood his ground in the center, surrounded by his fellow actors.

"Do you have the paper prepared?" the imposter asked the playwright.

Shakespeare handed him a folded paper from a pocket under his judicial robes. Warbeck unfolded it and held it up close to his face. I watched his dead slate-grey eyes look the document over, his thin lips slowly vibrating as he read. He let out a deep bass chuckle. The paper was refolded and handed back to Shakespeare.

"It will serve as an adequate concession," Warbeck said. "I expect you will announce to the Queen and the other guests the true authorship of these works your company has performed these many years. May the tone of the speech match the humility set forth in your letter."

"When will I see my brother?" Shakespeare asked.

Warbeck arched an eyebrow. "When I will it. Perhaps tonight, perhaps tomorrow, perhaps the next day."

"I want Edmund released tonight," Edmund's brother said emphatically. "This was the compact. You will not renege on—"

"Still your tongue, player," Warbeck spat back. "You have a speech to make, Shakespeare, then my comedy to perform. I am wasting time away from my bride by even talking to you.

Bother me not with these trifles. Set your mind instead to presenting a performance. Make it worthy of my munificence and your brother will come to you in time."

At this point on African lady dressed as a scullary woman entered the tent. She was Anita Shumpsky, Warbeck's ladyfriend from San Francisco, and the lady who Bonnie and I saw at the museum in San Francisco. The Assistant Editor for the Institute for Factual History was slumming it (to put it mildly) at the wedding of her boyfriend. Warbeck heard the tent flap open again and turned to the intrusion. Ms. Shumpsky spoke in a halting, frightened tone of voice, a far cry from the confident woman who had carried herself confidently in modern times.

"My Lord, I—I—" Ms. Shumpsky said in a halting tone of voice. She curtsied in her ragged dress that had the look of burlap. Her torso was covered by a short white smock, a length of rope about her waist. She had a haggard look on her erstwhile calm, beautiful face. Large beads of sweat ran down her forehead. Streaks of flour were smeared across her forehead. "My lord, I beeseech you to intervene on my behalf. There are common women in the kitchens who called me the vilest of names. Surely you could—"

"This is not your place, slave" Warbeck shouted to her. "What care I what name you are called by. You do my bidding and I bid you to the kitchens. Dromio, get this Ethiope back to her work. Have her see to her cooking."

Anita Shumpsky was the wrong woman in the wrong place at the wrong time. Warbeck had reduced her to the status of a slave by bringing her back to the England of this time, no doubt to show her who was boss in the relationship. She gulped hard at the nastiness delivered upon her. Dromio grabbed her roughly by the arm and led her out of the tent.

As Warbeck turned about he caught a glimpse of me. Even in my Groucho Marx-like disguise, something about me triggered an alarm in his head. I could tell it from his eyes. His face registered surprise. That made sense since I was supposed to be reposing uncomfortably in the Tower of London. Something else registered with Warbeck: the barrel of Stephen's Beretta being put to his temple and a forearm locking around the fat man's bulging neck.

"Not a bleeding word," Stephen said. "Not a bleeding

sound, Mr. Warbeck. There are seven little bullets in this gun and all I need is one of them to send you off."

Warbeck said nothing.

I threw off my facial disguise, made my way around Kempe, and used the opportunity to pat down the bridegroom for weapons. Under his doublet, I came across a bulge that felt like a pistol with a holster. I tore the doublet open with my right hand and found a Walther PPK .22. I yanked the gun out and showed it to the assembled.

"Ever see anything like this?" I said, holding up the firearm before I handed it to Shakespeare.

"Or this?" Stephen said. He pulled out a small flashlight from some pocket on Warbeck's person. He pressed a switch on the battery powdered penlight. I moved the light about, holding it in the three still-functional fingers of my left hand, to allow the beam to shine in the faces of the actors. Then I got a good close-up look at Warbeck's stern face. I reached up and, after a strong tug, ripped Warbeck's false goatee off his chin, and then tore into the bridge of his nose, pulling away a sponge- like piece of flesh-colored coating that was designed to make him look more like the man he was impersonating.

"This big lunchgut is no more the Earl of Grantum than I'm the King of France," I said. "He's an actor, just like you guys are, only from another time. He's in with Essex, like Mr. Shakespeare says. He's a front for a whole pack of bastards that are going to move in on you and rip this country up one end and down the other. These guys make those Jesuits you're so scared of look like..um..." (I was going to say boyscouts, but I changed it to "choirboys.")

"Help us," Shakespeare implored. "Help us. I have a guarantee from a Major Trubshawe that the time machines will be destroyed and there will be no more invasions from the future."

Trubshawe had lied to Shakespeare. Ends justifying means.

I heard the heavy tramp of feet coming back toward the tent. It had to be Dromio. Stephen pulled Warbeck toward a corner of the tent. I then looked to Burbage. He was the leader of the outfit. The others, except for Shakespeare and Kempe, would wait for him to make a call on our case.

"The giant returns," was all Burbage said.

Dromio came through the tent a moment later. He looked around for Warbeck. What he got was the butt of my gun slammed upside his head, courtesy of me. I had hit him as hard as my right arm could, half-expecting that the sapping would kill him, but I was being optimistic. The blow only staggered the giant. He moved slowly about, one hand cupped to the point on his skull above the left ear where I had struck, the right hand swinging about trying to ward off any further attacks. I didn't wait for him to reach for his sword or gun. I jumped on his back. Another actor, whose name I never knew, grabbed him by the feet. Burbage, Kempe, Shakespeare and Jonson waded in after that. We needed all the help we could get. I gripped his mouth, and took a nasty bite for my trouble, but after a few seconds the gang tackling paid off and Dromio was flat on the ground.

Rope from the company propwagon was fetched to tie Dromio up. He struggled like a pig with a knife to his throat. We finally quieted his muffled groans and breathless huffs by jamming a scarf from one of the boy actors into his mouth and securing it with a thick leather strap tied behind his head. We stripped him of his livery. Stephen put the larger man's uniform on quickly, stuffing the extra large doublet and shirt into his breeches. Dromio struggled until he finally was stripped. More leather was used to secure his hands and feet.

Another man came around to the tent. I never saw him because I was crouched down behind a trunk with a gun to Dromio's head to keep him from making any noises. Stephen had Warbeck in a similar position, although both men were vertical and standing above me. The man was looking for the bridegroom at the request of the bride. He never got beyond the entrance to the tent. A quick-thinking Ben Jonson said that the earl and his bodyguard were in the main keep, seeing about "procuring a special vintage of wine for the Queen's enjoyment." According to Jonson, Grantum/Warbeck would be returning to the Great Hall shortly.

"Have your men ready to stand for the Queen's procession to the Viewing Throne," I heard the man say. "The play must commence sooner than expected. The Queen wishes to see more dancing when the play finishes."

"The Queen must be in a gay mood then," Jonson said.

"And I'm to make sure Her Majesty remains so," the man

said, then apparently walked away.

"Leave matters to myself and these gentlemen from here," Shakespeare said to the troupe.

Burbage looked over at Warbeck. Warbeck's expression back was burning hatred.

"God help us if we are mistaken in this," Burbage said to Shakespeare.

"You are not," Shakespeare said. "You will be affirmed as patriotic men when all this resolves itself. Leave the summing up of this to myself, these gentlemen and their friends."

"The history of this kingdom is filled with men who thought themselves in a patriotic cause and then wound up hanged and gutted at Tyburn," Burbage said. He exited the tent followed by the rest of the other actors. Shakespeare snuffed out all the candles left burning. He saved the last lit candle to destroy the letter he had written for Warbeck's benefit. By then I had double-checked Dromio's bindings and gotten off his back. I stood up next and got right in Warbeck's face. The only light we had was from the small penlight Shakespeare was holding. My one good hand held onto the Baretta.

"Essex and Southampton are headed this way with their forces," Warbeck said with an assurance I thought too casual for a man with a gun to his head. "They are poised to strike. I have to ride out and communicate with Essex at a set location. If I am not there, he is to assume that the plot has been compromised. Then he will attack in full force. He will have shoulder-carried anti-tank weapons at his disposal. The first target will be those in the keep: your brother, Shakespeare, and the charming Miss Noel. The battlements on the keep will cave in and all in the cells will be killed. Then the weaponry will be turned on the manor house around it. Then there will be a charge. One way or another, Essex and Mr. Strunk—"

I jammed my gun into the folds of Warbeck's chins. "Listen to me, Warbeck," I said. "You're going to tell me where Bonnie Noel and Edmund Shakespeare are right now. Do it or you're dead." I tore off my left glove and showed him the brand on the palm of my hand. "See this?" I said. "I got this in the Tower. This hurts. I don't like pain. It puts me in a very bad mood. Now I want to kill you as bad as you've wanted to kill me."

Warbeck cleared his throat slightly. "Essex has a—"

"*Fuck* Essex," I said. "I'm going to give you five seconds to tell me where Bonnie is. Five seconds." I pressed the barrel harder, ramming it into his jaw bone.

"The—the keep," Warbeck stuttered out. "In one of the cells just below the top battlement. Jack Picasso is with her, conducting an interrogation."

Jack Picasso. I had almost forgotten that bastard.

"Oh, I hope you're right," I said. "You're taking me there now."

We went with Shakespeare's plan after all.

I heard Dromio struggling with the knots that were binding his wrists together and the muffled noises of frustration emitting from his clogged mouth. My frustration was not emitted. I was worried about Bonnie and getting out alive, in about the same priority.

The four of us left the tent and walked across a cobblestone walkway, then through a modest doorway into a large pantry area I took for the 'buttery.' There were four rows of shelves with a variety of jars and corked bottles being stored. The air was filled with the scent of cooked meat and spices. We reached the kitchen. Piles of plucked bird feathers littered the floor. Wooden barrels of flour and salt were left half opened next to the preparation tables. A line of skinned rabbits lay on each of the tables, as did a pile of plucked and headless chickens. A brick oven was going full blast and men and women were scurrying about, some bringing in empty trays of food, others going out with steaming plates of meat or bowls of vegetables. Shakespeare walked in front of our group, followed by Stephen, then Warbeck and then me. The servants nodded at Warbeck as he passed.

When we were out of the kitchen, there were two corridors that bisected one another. The four of us were alone in the hallway. Stephen asked Warbeck which way to the courtyard. Warbeck was slow to reply. Stephen was not slow to twist his right arm.

"To the right, through the door at the end of the other hall," Warbeck said through clenched teeth.

"Save my Edmund," Shakespeare said imploringly to me before we turned right and he headed down the other dimly-lit corridor.

Chapter Fifty-Seven

The fife and drum group were playing music on the stage. The grim-visaged ancestors of the rightful Earl of Grantum adorned the walls in gilt-edged paintings, the biggest one hanging over a huge unlit fireplace with a Grecian-style portal adorned with gigantic stone roses on intertwining stems. There were two rows of subjects lined up for the Queen's entrance. One row was for the well-dressed ladies and gentlemen of the nobility and the gentry. The ladies wore hoopskirted farthingales with stomachers across their fronts from their half-exposed breasts to their shoes, the latter barely seen under the lengthy skirts. Mixed in the row were the gentlemen, dressed in a gaudy fashion that rivaled the women. Stephen and I could see that line through our hiding place next to a stone buttress near one of the windows. Warbeck was with us, sitting cross-legged like Buddha, head to the wall and hands behind his back. He was told not to make a sound—yet.

The windows were open and the smells of bodies, sweaty from dancing, were intermingled with the aromas from food the servants were bringing in from sidedoors and setting on the tables. Everyone was standing, including Shakespeare and the players who were in a straight line at a right angle to the row of the invited swells. Shakespeare looked nervous. All the players looked nervous.

There were children playing about in a few places. Even a few dogs were present, romping with the children. Younger women, plainly dressed as you would expect nannies to be, chased them about apparently trying to get the kids into line.

I got to take all this local color in because, although we had made it into the courtyard, the trio of us were being held up by four soldiers who were standing at a doorway just a few paces ahead of us. They were facing inside the door that opened onto the courtyard waiting, I hoped, to go inside when the Queen entered.

On the side of the room opposite the stage were two immense double doors. The doors seemed to glow from some type of heavy varnish. They were side-by-side, at least thirty feet high and half that wide. Standing right next to the doors were footmen in red and gold doublets and long venetian-style knickers. Next to them were the trumpeteers, two to each side. The trumpets were long and thin. Suddenly a man entered the double doors. He was dressed in a red uniform that reminded me of the gang at the Tower. He was carrying a staff and he banged it three times on the floor.

There came a fanfare from the trumpets. The doors were swung open fully. Everyone bowed. The Queen entered the room, her Gentlemen Pensioners lined up a few paces behind her. She was now wearing a bright red head of hair, much fuller and darker then the wig she had worn at St. Paul's. The powder that had been on her face was gone. (Maybe the powder was some primitive form of sunscreen.) Queen Elizabeth's eyes looked directly forward, her lips wearing a coloring that matched her hair. She was walking slowly into the room, a small brown dog held in her wrinkled and withered hands, clutched to her jewel-brocaded bosom. The dog kicked and squirmed in her arms. She bent down, a widow's hump visible on her back, and let the dog down on the carpet. Other dogs joined in greeting the new arrival. The Queen smiled. Those black teeth were something else.

There was a man directly behind her. He was a long-faced, beak-nosed man in his thirties, decked out in a flowing black robe with a thick-linked gold chain about his neck. He had a little goatee that was no more than a little tuft of chestnut-brown hair from the middle of his lower lip to just below his chin. He was closest to the Queen, just a few paces behind her. He was also hunched-over like some underqualified chiropractor had practiced on him one or two sessions too many. I guessed this poor guy was the Principal Secretary, the 'pygmy' Robert Cecil that Bacon had made derisive mention of.

Something happened that I didn't think was on the program. A soldier ran into the room. He ran up to one of the Gentlemen Pensioners and whispered in his ear. The other man looked astonished.

The other man went to whisper to the Queen. The small, hunchbacked man came forward to catch the conversation. Suddenly, the Queen swatted Cecil with an open hand across his face. Her voice, husky and reedy, followed up the assault.

"I am informed by the Earl of Essex's messenger that I am to surrender my guard and soldiers and put myself into his protection. I am to be taken to the Tower. To the Tower!" (Another swat. The Secretary ducked this one.) "Cecil, I was told Essex was not even in Middlesex. Yet, here is his writing and here is a man from his outlawed band. That man Bacon assured me he had crossed the Thames yesterday and was hiding deep in Surrey. Am I right in thinking you have failed to grasp the madman's wherabouts? Am I right in thinking I am under siege?"

The assembly let out a collective gasp. Murmurings of alarm followed.

The Queen clenched her gnarled hands up to her face, then barked an order: "Assemble a force, Cecil. Gather arms and men. Let no man go without musket or sword. Find Grantum and bring him to me. I will have him in my grasp this very minute."

"I told you,Wells," Warbeck whispered, his face still to the wall. "Essex is near the manor. He's sent a messenger in telling the Queen she has to surrender. Bacon has fooled the Queen and Cecil. They're organizing a defense. It will be hopeless, of course."

"Shut up, you bastard," I said. I looked to the soldiers that had blocked our way; they were no longer in front of us or even in sight. It was time to make our move for the keep.

There was no way that a hundred sword-carrying Gentlemen Pensioners and a company of troops armed with single-shot muskets, pikes and black-powder pistols were going to stop Essex, Southampton and probably fifty to seventy-five men armed with grenade launchers, machine guns, automatic rifles and, if Warbeck wasn't lying, hand-held anti-tank weapons capable of firing missles. Stephen and I had to get the STUMPs out to the battlements and airlifted away in Trubshawe's copter. If we didn't, our own chances, including Bonnie's, were nil.

Warbeck walked up the stairway to the keep. Stephen, with his appropriated uniform, came right behind him with his pistol only a few inches from our captive's back. In my fool's 'motley' I brought up the rear. I had my arms behind my back as if I were shackled. There was one guard stationed at the front entrance to the keep, a horseshoe-shaped doorway framed by thick stonework. He had been gnawing on some type of meat when we came around the corner, but snapped to attention and grasped for his matchlock when he saw the 'Earl' coming up the stairs. A lit torch was hanging from a curved metal flange attached to the stonework. He wore a uniform similar to the one Stephen had on. It was time for Warbeck to put on his act.

"We have a prisoner for the cells above," Warbeck said convincingly. "This fool here was caught stealing. Open the door, sirrah, and be quick."

The guard nodded and, after cradling his musket against his body with a forearm, put one of the keys he had hanging from his belt into the door lock. As he did so, Stephen reached over with his free hand and grabbed hold of the torch, keeping Warbeck where he was by putting the gun right against his back. As soon as the door was open, and I could see from the firelight there were no other guards inside the foyer, I stepped around Warbeck and Stephen and delivered a kick to the guard's left leg, right behind his kneecap. His body buckled, giving me the chance to throw my left forearm around his neck and choke off any loud noise. I knocked the musket to the ground with an elbow smash then jammed the butt of my pistol against his temple.

"This is a gun," I said. "Make a sound and I'll kill you."

He seemed to understand.

Stephen and Warbeck came in next, the first man hustling the other across the threshold. Stephen left the door partway open.

I tied the guard up while Warbeck, at Stephen's orders, settled himself Buddha-like on the stone floor. Stephen used a walkie-talkie to check with his father. Their conversation was brief. My partner said, "Hold on, Dad. We've got someone coming." I had barely finished hog-tying the guard when I had to leave him and take charge of Warbeck. Stephen grabbed the musket and went back outside. With Warbeck on the ground, I held the torch with three fingers of my wounded hand and kept the gun pointed on him. We were less than a yard apart. The fat man faced me, the fire from the torch casting a long shadow across the floor behind him. From the firelight I could see a narrow stairway under a peaked arch, leading upwards. It was so narrow I wondered how Warbeck ever got up it. Outside, I heard Stephen talking to another man, but I could not make out the words.

"Where is Bonnie and Shakespeare's brother?" I asked him. "Don't raise your voice when you speak." My Baretta was right at his head.

"Top level of the keep," he said softly and calmly. "That's where the cells are. Picasso is with them, trying to get information from the young lady."

"Where is the room where you keep all the video equipment and the tapes?" I asked. I figured that was where the tape showing Ann Benchley shooting Dave would be. Warbeck did not give an answer. I lost it, stepped forward, and pistol-whipped him across the face.

"No more games," I said just above my breath. "Answer my questions."

Warbeck told me. The chamber with the electronic equipment was next to the cells. I asked him where the STUMPs were, and made a motion like I was going to jam the barrel of the gun down his mouth. Turned out the STUMPs were in the same chamber. The trace of fear in his voice made me believe him. I watched a trickle of blood ooze down his bruised cheek at the point where I had struck him.

The door opened behind me. I stepped back from our prisoner. Stephen came through the door, alone. There was good news: he had told a lance-knight he was assigned to watch the keep while the first guard went to reinforce the troops defending the eminent attack from Essex. The story had been bought. He reconnected with his father over the phone.

"Dad's crew has the chopper air-worthy," Stephen said as he pocketed the phone. "He'll be over the battlements in five minutes." He took over the torch from me. "Get him up," he said, pointing to Warbeck.

I next heard what sounded like a rumble of rolling thunder outside. Then a high-pitched, inhuman whistling sound. The next minute there was a blinding light and the world went upside down. An explosion was ringing in my ears as I picked myself up off the floor. I was no longer holding the gun I had in my hand, and I was at least ten feet away from where I had been. Smoke filled the room. Jagged splinters of heavy crossbeams dangled from the roof. There was a beam that completely dislodged from the ceiling. It was lying across the doorway. The torch that Stephen had been carrying was lying on the ground, still lit, a few feet away from the beam. Under the beam had to be what was left of Stephen's head. His skull had been crushed, his arms splayed out in front of him. I could see his blood seeping across the floor toward the torch.

And where was Warbeck?

He was still alive. Through the smoke I could make out him making a dash for the stairway. I had no gun. Then I found it. I took aim at the fat man going up the stairs. My shot took out a chip of the archway instead.

I dug into my pocket and pulled out the flashlight. I went over to Stephen to see if my first impression was wrong. It wasn't. His torso and his feet looked untouched. He had never felt anything. I went on up the stairway, after Warbeck.

The further I climbed, the smokier the stairway became. I pawed upward, bounding three steps at a time, my eyes trying to detect any movement in front of me. Sounds of whistling and then explosions reverberated about the castle. One blast knocked me against a wall and small chips of stonework rained down on my head. I covered my head and prayed. Nothing big came down on me so I kept going.

It also got hotter as I climbed. Something was on fire above me. Then I came up to an entry point for a large barrel-vaulted room. I stopped at the threshold, trying to see as much as I could through the concentrated smoke before I stepped quickly backwards into the room. Seeing no one, I turned to face forward again. There were tapestries on the inner wall. They were being consumed by fire. There were several slits, shaped like crosses, along the outer wall. One part of that wall had a large hole that something stronger than a cannonball had to have made. Next to the tapestry furthest from the entrance was another archway. I took off at a run and fell down on my side at the base of the entryway, ready for anybody waiting for me to come up.

But there was nobody. Only more stairs to climb.

There were the shouts of men drifting up from the courtyard below me. They sounded like the local crowd. I needed a compliment of modern Royal Marines, not the natives with their popguns and oversized cocktail forks. Anyway, the shouts below conveyed a sense of panic. I doubted any soldiers would try to go up into the keep since it was geting the full brunt of the bombing. I got to my feet, coughing hard enough to make me clutch my ribcage. There followed another rumble, another whistle, and then the floor rocked underneath me. A bomb had landed somewhere above. More chips of stonework fell on me, more smoke and dust took up the atmosphere I needed for air. Something large hit me on of my head. It hurt like hell.

I went up the stairs, putting myself against the wall—gun drawn—as I turned the bend in the passageway. For the first time I heard voices above me. Male voices, shouting for help in unison. Then another voice, feminine and familiar:

"Let me out! Somebody let me out!"

Bonnie was alive.

I held upward, steadying myself against the wall with my left hand. The brand on my palm burned as I slapped my hand against the stones, but my system blocked a lot of pain out with adrenaline. I tripped once or twice due to the smoke and smacked my head against the low passageway. I climbed quicker now, wondering when I would run out of steps.

I ran out of steps. Then I tripped over something. It turned out to be somebody: the body of a guard, his head and torso smashed by two large chucks of stone that had caved in on him from the ceiling. The wide-eyed, bloody corpse was still holding a long matchlock rifle in one hand and a small ammunition pouch around his neck. I scrambled over the body then called out Bonnie's name. Bonnie answered, calling for help. Her voice was coming from behind an iron-framed door. I kicked at the door once or twice. Whatever was holding it in place gave a bit. I backed up and gave it everything I had with my left shoulder leading the way. It was almost enough, but something hard was still holding me from getting in. I took the gun and fired into the keyhole. Another bodyslam. Nothing came of it. Then I fired again. At last I swung the door open.

I got down on one knee, in a barricade stance, at the doorway. No smoke was coming from inside. It was dark, except for what looked like a large television screen at the end of the room. A soft blue light emitted from it. That wasn't enough light to see anyone. My right hand gripped the gun. My left held the flashlight just above the barrel. The first thing I could make out was one of the STUMPs. It was to the right of the television. The male voices that were crying out were clearer now. There were doors with bars on small windows on each side of the room. Edmund Shakespeare's face was looking out of one.

I called out Bonnie's name. I heard a muffled cry coming down from somewhere above the television. I focused my beam upwards. I discovered a flight of steps. Warbeck was dragging Bonnie up the stairway, using her for a shield so I couldn't shoot him. She was terrified—I could see it in her face—and I didn't have a shot at Warbeck. Then the two of them disappeared through a doorway at the top of the staircase.

Someone jumped out from behind the television screen. It was Picasso. I saw him and the AK-47 he was cradling and ditched my flashlight as I hit the floor. Then I rolled against the wall with the pop-pop-popping sound of automatic fire in my ears. I scuttled on all fours into an open cell door. More gunfire. I fired back from the corner of the cell. I shot three times. That gave me two bullets left against probably a few dozen slugs for Picasso.

I was in a dark cell, cornered like a rat. Any thoughts I had that I might have hit Picasso was wiped away when he spoke: "Throw out your gun, Wells," he said. He sounded healthy. I had two bullets from a little Baretta against a military assault rifle.

"Let me out," I heard some older-sounding man say.

Picasso must have pressed the trigger because a few more rounds went off. I could see the flash from the barrel. A torrent of bullets were fired. He had aimed his shots at one of his cells. Nobody asked to be let out after that.

I used my last two bullets to take a quick aim at Picasso. I took out the damn television screen then, with things nice and dark, I crawled to get something near the door. By the time I was headed back, electric lights from somewhere had illuminated the room. Then more popping noises and a nasty whizzing sound going off next to my ear. A near miss.

I had gone back for the long, fat matchlock musket the dead guard had on him. I examined the long barreled weapon. I pulled back and cocked the serpentine and, with the flashlight, checked the hole that led to the priming pan.

There was powder in it.

The cell I was in had to have been Bonnie's cell. I could tell that because my flashlight fell on a package of her cigarettes on a stool next to where I was situated. Inside the cellophane wrapper was a butane lighter. There was a pouch attached to the musket. I tried hard to remember how Benchley had loaded this musket back at that hill when we were headed toward Camden Town.

"Throw out your gun and come out, Wells," Picasso said. He wasn't coming in after me; he was afraid I still had bullets in my weapon.

I looked down the barrel of the musket. My guess was it wasn't loaded. I opened the pouch that I had also taken off the guard. I used my right hand to pour powder down the barrel. There was also a round metal ball in the pouch. I dropped that down the barrel. I had nothing to jam the shot down into the barrel so I shook the musket up and down with my 'good' arm, my thumb jammed down the barrel, hoping to get the ball lodged as close to the powder as possible.

"Throw out your gun and come out, Wells," Picasso said. He was beginning to sound like an English-Made-Easy tape.

"I can't," I said weakly. "I'm hit."

"Throw it out, fucker." Picasso was sounding closer.

I threw the Baretta out of the cell. I already had Bonnie's lighter in my other hand when I did that. Covering the little bud of fire from her lighter with my hand, I lit the wick that was fixed on the end of the serpentine. I then stood up, raised the musket, got right up to the corner of the door, and gauged where Picasso was by the sound of his voice, once more asking me to give it up. I then hoisted the weapon up horizontally, planting the butt of the rifle against my left shoulder, balancing the barrel upright as best I could, which would only be for a few seconds. I made sure the wick was well-lit. Then I pulled up on the trigger and charged out.

Picasso had not expected this. His weapon was at his side, not ready to fire. He brought his weapon up to fire, but by then the serpentine had hit the priming pan, the charge had ignited, and a blast of light and smoke came out of the musket barrel. When it cleared I still had Jack Picasso in front of me. His doublet was covered in black powder and he was shaking like he was hooked up to some old-fashioned vibrating machine. The ball of lead I had shot him with had hit him in the chest. He was staggering backwards, trying to get his bloody, broken body to work enough to bring the barrel of the assault rifle up to shoot me.

I turned my matchlock into a club, hitting him across the face with the butt of the musket. He took two blows from the butt of the antique gun before he went down on his back. He dropped the AK-47, then fell backwards. I bent over him, planting my knee on his chest.

"I wasn't going to kill you," were the last words that came out of his mouth. Then he coughed up a good amount of blood. His eyes rolled back, and he died.

I helped myself to the AK-47, fought my pain to get it in firing position, and headed up the stairway. I still had three fingers of my left hand. I could still operate the rifle. At least that was what I hoped.

I pushed the hatch at the top of the staircase open. I heard the sound of a helicopter somewhere overhead and saw the open sky and a field of stars through a thin layer of smoke that was coming up from the direct hits of missles that the keep had taken. I was at the battlements at the top of the keep. It was a faint sound from a helicopter without much power. All around I could hear the sound of ordnance going off around the estate. Also small arms fire. Major Trubshawe's little egg-beater of a flying machine was getting nearer, but I could not see it.

"Picasso, is that you?"

It was Warbeck's voice. I knew Bonnie was up there with him. There was no time for diversions or plans. This was the endgame. I took a breath and came up as fast as I could out of the hatch. Warbeck had Bonnie pressed against him, the barrel of a pistol to her head. They were maybe twenty feet away from me, backed up against the parapets.

"Throw down the weapon, Wells," Warbeck said defiantly.

"Throw it down or she dies."

"Five seconds, Warbeck," I said. "Five seconds to let her go, or you die."

"You have no choice," Warbeck said. "I'll kill her before you can do anything to me."

I could feel my whole body shaking, my heart going like a jackhammer against my chest. The top of my head burned with pain. Warbeck held her so her feet were a foot off the ground. I was afraid she would be strangled, but I couldn't risk the shot. Bonnie had saved my life twice and I couldn't save her. I couldn't risk the shot. Warbeck knew it. From the light of fires dancing around us I could see the confidence in his face.

I noticed something else: helicopter noise from right above me. Just then a bright white light lit up Bonnie and Warbeck. It was a hard, concentrated daylight-bright ray and it caused Warbeck's eyes to squint. Bonnie took her chance. Somehow, she got one of her pinioned arms loose and rammed her fist up and into Warbeck's gunhand. The gun went off, but in an upward direction. She wiggled loose and ran forward, towards me. I yelled out: "Duck!"

Warbeck tried to recover and fire again, but his eyes weren't adjusted to the light. Bonnie had ducked and there was Warbeck lit up like he was the star at some World Premiere. I squeezed off the trigger, drilling him with several slugs across the chest. He fell down against one of the stone blocks that rose above the parapets. Bonnie was down too, but she was getting up.

I got to her and wrapped my arms around her, then had to let go because of the pain.

"Thank you for not being Jack Picasso," Bonnie said as she worked on me. "Your head is bleeding. We have to get you to a hospital."

"Not without you," I said.

"Is Picasso?"

"He's dead," I said. "So is Stephen Trubshawe."

Major Trubshawe and his helicopter landed. He told me he had seen Bonnie and Warbeck through his infa-red glasses as he approached the keep with the helicopter.

"I decided to go in without lights at first," he said. "I knew it was a risk but I had to take the chance to see if I could draw

Warbeck's attention. Good to see you were in position, Wells." He examined the wound to my head from the piece of stonework. "You'll live," he said off-handedly. I told him Picasso was dead. He looked over at Warbeck's riddled body, then asked me what I didn't want to answer.

"Where's my boy?" he asked.

"Stephen was hit by a beam," I said. "It had to be a missile that hit the floor above us. He was dead before he knew it happened. I'm sorry. I'm so sorry."

"I knew it when he wasn't on the battlements," Trubshawe said. His body trembled. His fist slammed into the side of the helicopter. Then he reached inside the cockpit of the copter. Out came a Thompson machine gun. Warbeck's body was peppered with some extra rounds.

The major gulped, dropped the gun to his side, then spoke: "Where are the STUMPs, then?"

I told him.

"Help me get them out of here," he said to Bonnie and me.

While she was down in the room below, Bonnie found a leather pouch near to where Picasso had first fired at me. One of the things in it was an eight millimeter videotape cassette. I hoped it was the tape of Dave being killed by Kathy Quisted in her Ann Benchley get up. And I hoped it showed her taking the disguise off.

No soldiers came up to the level we were on, so we assumed that Elizabeth's forces were—for now—holding their own.

We let Edmund Shakespeare out, and a man who looked like Trevor Warbeck, but wasn't. He was the Right Honorable Earl of Grantum.

"What manner of men are you?" the earl asked as he walked out of the cell dressed in a dirty nightshirt.

"I don't have any time for explanations," the major said. "You," he said to Edmund, "help Wells and I get the STUMPs up to the roof."

"Am I right in thinking I am a free man?" the earl asked.

"As free as a bloody toff with his own castle, mate," Trubshawe said. "Go down and help your Queen. Essex is loose and he's gone nuts."

"Essex," the earl said as if he suddenly remembered a trauma. "He's the one who locked me away and slaughtered my servants. What of the old man who was imprisoned with me?"

"He's fine, your Lordship," Trubshawe said brusquely. "Now, if you'll excuse us..."

"Essex and the whole lot of 'em will pay," the major said grimly as Bonnie, Edmund and I, using my left hand for what it was worth, helped Trubshawe to carry the time machines back up the stairs.

The major hooked the time machines up to a pair of thick towlines, tying it around the imitation knotholes that Morton Ryskind had put on the devices so it could pass as a dead tree.

Trubshawe got back into the cockpit. "Sorry we can't take you out," Trubshawe said, his voice numb, his mind on other things. "We have nearly too much load as it is with the STUMPs and myself in the cockpit.

Trubshawe took off. I was left with Edmund Shakespeare, Bonnie, and a fully-loaded Thompson machine gun, courtesy of the Royal Marines. Bonnie took over the AK-47.

She also gave me a kiss to keep me warm.

In the next few minutes, a pair of SeaLynxes made their appearance over the dark eastern sky. They launched missiles into the woods around Grantum Hall. The helicopters made a second run and now lines of tracer fire from the front machine guns pierced the darkness. I guessed they had night vision equipment because they were only bombing and strafing certain areas. Fires broke out, spreading all over the forest. After that initial attack another two attack helicopters came from the same place as the first two. More missiles and tracer bullets flew from the sky. The fire that had been directed at the manor had stoppped completely. There was more battle. Several more helicopters came in. These were larger, big as a Sikorsky Blackhawk. Edmund and I could see groups of Royal Marines jumping to the lawn as the big choppers hovered a few feet off the grounds. Some of the marines fanned out around the perimeter of the forest. A bullhorn coming from one of the choppers told the inhabitants inside the Grantum Hall that, "you are now under the protection of the forces of Her Majesty Queen Elizabeth the Second. There is nothing to fear."

"Providence has saved us," Edmund said to me.

"No likeness of man could hope to conceive of such a

sight," a voice behind me said. I turned and saw William Shakespeare and some of the other of the Lord Chamberlain's Men. He embraced his brother.

One of the transport helicopters came and hovered over our space a few minutes later. Bonnie and I said our good-byes and thanks to the men who had aided us and then I was pulled inside the fuselage by a young man wearing a flight helmet and a blue jumpsuit. We took a seat amongst a group of marines, their faces painted with camouflage.

"It's like something in a bloody comic book," a white marine with his full moon face in heavy camouflage said to his black compatriot. "A bloody comic book."

I asked the black marine how the battle had gone.

"It was a walkover," he replied with a relaxed smile. "Most of them must have thrown down their weapons and ran for it before we even got on the ground. The rest are charred."

"Do you know where the hell this is?" the other fighter asked me. "They got us in the copter and blasted us with some red ray and the next thing you know we're here. Where the hell is here?"

"You're in England," Bonnie said. "We can't tell you anything else. I don't know how much you guys are supposed to know. What we know ourselves might put us in the Tower of London when we get back."

I hoped she was kidding.

I had just killed two men but I didn't feel bad about that. They had killed, and would have been responsible for killing many more, if they hadn't been stopped.

Epilogue

The London hospital I went into was a private medical facility the Royal Family used to have their heirs slide down the birth canal into the cold, real world. I got the niceties of relative privacy not accorded to the average National Health in-patient at a government-sponsored hospital.

The doctors had a look at my burned hand and said I'd need skin grafts. I also had a concussion. Bonnie visited me several times, leaving me books (one a new biography on Audrey Hepburn) and even some flowers, before she and Ann Benchley went back to America.

Meanwhile, an 'anonymous' caller told the local constabulary that they had seen a man wandering about Hampstead Heath, a man who bore a distinct likeness to an American film director whose picture had been in the London papers in connection with a murder case. That was how Scotland Yard got hold of Jack Benchley. The director claimed he had escaped his captivity in Warbeck's house after his captors had fled. The police found a broken window leading to the basement—courtesy of Major Trubshawe—that led credence to Benchley's story.

Jack Benchley had to spend some time in a British courtroom, going through an uncontested extradition process because he was still a suspect in Carolyn Mason's murder. A couple weeks later, when the old man was in custody in California, the DNA tests on the traces of blood found in research came back. Benchley was cleared of the crime;

Charles Lindsey Aarons wasn't.

Major Trubshawe made sure the incriminating videotape Ray Harrison had taken of my friend's murder got into the hands of Scotland Yard. The tape was not Jack Picasso's 'cut'. This was an honest version, one that incriminated Kathy Quisted. The major had planted the tape in Jack Picasso's car, which was parked in the driveway of Trevor Warbeck's rented mansion in Hampstead. It was easily done since all the former occupants of the house were either dead or unavoidably detained in the late 16th Century. After planting the evidence, the British military authorities took care of the case, tipping off Scotland Yard to secure a warrant to search Warbeck's residence on the possibility of a kidnapping. They didn't find Warbeck or his associates, but the police did find the video tape that showed how Dave really was killed. That tape freed Wendy from jail.

Wendy McCreedy told me she had indeed been in front of the convenience store in Bowman shortly before Dave was shot. Wendy had heard the doctored phone message with Ann Benchley's voice on it the night after her mother came out of the hospital in Klamath City. She knew Dave spent a lot of time fishing up near Bowman and had a hunch that was where he would meet someone clandestinely. Dave had stopped at The Bowman Store, apparently to get some cigarettes. Wendy confronted him in the parking lot and she was pushed to the ground. That was what the Sheepman had witnessed. Sheepman also watched Wendy drive down Cramner Creek Road, in the direction Dave had rode off in.

"I got a mile or so down the road," Wendy said to me. "I was going to confront both of them. But I stopped. I decided to just let it go. I drove back to Klamath City. I wasn't planning ever to go back to Dave. Never. I was so shaky driving out of there it was a wonder I didn't drive off the road."

Wendy was a free woman, reunited with her daughter Jill. I suspected that either the late Jack Picasso or, most likely, the deceased Ralph Bates, had planted the gun in Wendy's Honda Civic late one night. If Ann Benchley had agreed to Picasso's blackmail demands to sign over the movie rights to the Belle Killroy books, then I suspected the police would have been told where to find the murder weapon, sealing Wendy's fate.

Rochelle Millman and LeRoy Millman, my old nemesis, patched up whatever was going wrong in their marriage. LeRoy was now his political party's official candidate for the Congressional District that included Middleburg and Rogue Falls.

Sherwood Strunk and his party had managed to make it back to the present day—sometime while I was stuck getting the work-over in the Tower of London I suppose—and, with Jack Benchley unwilling to reveal the real story of his ordeal to any more authorities than possible, they were still in the good graces of the law. The blame for the kidnapping, therefore, stopped at Trevor Warbeck. There had been a manhunt for Trevor Warbeck in the United Kingdom for a few weeks. His body, needless to say, had not been found. The Strunk News Network was rather scant in their coverage of the story I noticed. The coverage of the story was ebbing away from a lack of new information.

The case of Ray Harrison's murder had taken a good turn for Kathy Quisted. District Attorney Peter Masterson decided not to charge her with her boyfriend's killing, owing to the blow to her head that collaborated her story of being knocked out by an intruder at Ray Harrison's house. Not that she was free at all. When Scotland Yard had discovered the videotape—carefully edited by Jack Benchley and Major Trubshawe to eliminate showing the STUMP in operation—Masterson had the evidence to have her booked as an accessory to murder in the death of Dave McCreedy. Police in all of the United States and several countries were on the lookout for Bates and Picasso. I could have saved them the trouble.

Jack Benchley did pay well for what I'd done for him. I got a final check in the mail for my services around the middle of May. There was a long interval where I rather expected an invite to the Benchley Ranch. But I heard nothing personal from the director until the First of July, two days before his wedding.

It was a sultry Thursday afternoon and I was in the office of McCreedy Investigations (I had kept the name). There was a thunderstorm in progress outside the McLoughlin Building, a humid sort of activity unusual in this part of the West. I had no air-conditioning and, despite the precipitation, I was wiping sweat off my forehead with a cloth drink coaster as I typed away. I was pecking away on Dave's Dell Computer. After getting some initial treatment at a private hospital in London (courtesy of Jack Benchley) I had taken my left hand to a burn specialist in Middleburg the preceding month. He had taken some skin from my leg and grafted it to my hand. It would be scarred but I'd be able to use my index finger when the bandages came off.

I had recently been out of town for a couple days, staying overnight 175 miles up the road in Eugene, working on a private case. A woman had hired me to watch her husband, a high school principal, while he was out of town up there. It was a case of presumed marital infidelity. His wife was afraid he was going to use an Oregon Educators Association Convention up in Eugene to shack up with his female office manager. That's what his wife thought and the wife, my client, turned out to be only half-right. He was shacked up, but with a young lady who bore no resemblance to the picture I had of Mrs. Elaine Speckles, the school office manager. This lady was more like a young lady. Seventeen years to be exact. I had photos of this man going into his motel room near the conference meeting place with this girl. She was posing to the motel staff as the principal's daughter. Mr. Andrews had three offspring, all boys.

I happened to take a break to stretch my legs. I stood next to the halfway-open window, watching the rain fall and looking to see if I could see lightning. A couple cars went by on the street below; sets of tires hissed along the wet asphalt. Those sounds and the sounds of water pelting the top pane of the window gave way to the sharp beeping tone of a car alarm being set. I saw Benchley walking away from a dark blue Ford Mustang. He was wearing a knee-length grey raincoat and a tweed Irish rainhat. He looked up at the building, then down at a slip of paper in his hand. Bonnie must have written down the address for him.

He looked younger than the first time I saw him. His face had a ruddy tint about the cheekbones that had looked almost paper-white that last time I'd seen him last month when Bonnie and I had gone to pick him up at the Middleburg-Rogue County Airport. He had been surrounded by a pack of local television crews and, after he made a brief statement thanking the San Francisco police for catching the real murderer of Carolyn Mason, the two of us—along with the groundskeeper, Mr. Kincaid— ran enough interference to get the old man out of the terminal and to his vehicle.

We shook hands. I helped get his coat off. He wore a golf sweater underneath the coat. A small roll of fat now hung over his baggy pleated slacks. He announced that he had shot a 46 that morning playing in a foursome at the Oak Lane Country Club.

"We only played nine holes," Benchley told me. "Too damn hot for the back nine. Do you play golf, Harvey?"

"Once in a while," I said. "My dad and I play when I go back to California."

"Terrible thing, golf," the old man said. "They talk about banning boxing. Hell, hundreds more men have dropped dead from the stress of trying to improve their golf game than ever died in a boxing ring. Ban golf I say; there's the real killer. Thank God for this little bit of rain." He looked about the office.

"Glad to see you cleaned it up a bit," he said. "Dave showed me this place once. He was a great fellow but he was sloppy. You got rid of all that sports junk on the walls. Good. Didn't this hole in the wall used to have air conditioning?"

"I'm getting a replacement AC as soon as some of my accounts receivable come in," I said, trying to exit my computer without losing the report I had been working on. "Dave's old window unit went down. I got a fan going but that doesn't seem to help."

Benchley slowly sat down, gripping the arms of the chair with the shaky hands and quivering arms of a man approaching his 76th year. He accomplished the sitting phase, then took out a neatly folded red handkerchief out of his breast pocket. He dabbed his brow, then patted his almost-bare crown of pinkish-white skin. He smoothed the wispy patches of white hair around his ears with a couple strokes of his right hand to each side. "God, I just got here," he said, "and I'm sweating like the horse that ran second in the Belmont Stakes."

"Sorry, Mr. Benchley," I said. "I've got some Dr. Pepper in the compact refer over there. I also have some cranberry juice left."

"Call me Jack, Harvey. And I will take some juice, please.

Went in for my check-up last week. Doctor Wilson says I've got a prostate gland the size of a baseball. It's cancer, but it's a slow cancer so it'll just be getting around to full-blown metastasis when something else kills me. Anyway, the doctor wants me to give up booze and cigars and become a health nut. Might as well put some juice in the old bladder for what it's worth."

I brought him back a glass of cranberry juice with ice, and myself a can of Diet Dr. Pepper. I then congratulated Benchley on his impending nuptials.

"The ceremony was Ann's idea," Benchley said, sounding perturbed. "Beatrice and I just wanted to fly to Vegas and elope but Ann wouldn't hear of it. She's planning a big gig at the Lizzie after the 8:30 show. Ann wants all the guests to light candles around the theater at the stroke of midnight and then Beatrice and I get hitched."

"I thought William Shakespeare would never come to the modern world. He told Bonnie he was staying in his own time. What brought the change?"

"He wants to see his son," Benchley said. "I guess that last picture Bonnie showed him made him want to see the boy. He lost his only legitimate son, Hamnet, in 1595. He won't announce his parentage to Tyler. He promised me that. But William is not the problem. Edmund is going to be the problem."

"What's happening with Edmund?"

Benchley took a sip of the cranberry juice, pursed his lips like he had swallowed cough syrup, then set the glass down on the front of my desk. He shook his head as he did so, then spoke.

"The little twerp wants to stay in what we call the present, which is the future to him. Apparently, he got hold of a biography of William I left with his brother a couple visits ago. The bio mentions Edmund Shakespeare dying of some malady in the winter of 1606. He'll be all of twenty-seven years old. Naturally, he's not pleased at the short spin he's getting on Fortune's Wheel. He wants to fake his death back in the London of 1600 and get in on the Third Milleneum."

"And do what?" I asked.

"Be an actor, of course," Benchley said sharply. "A man with a bizarre speech pattern and no real idea what post-industrial society can do to somebody wants to emigrate through time. His elder brother wants me to employ him at the theater and ease him into modern civilization. In exchange, he'll give me more nitty-gritty details about his life and let me stage any new plays he writes."

"So you agreed to this?"

Benchley nodded. "William is up at my ranch right now, examining all the twenty or so plays he still is supposed to write after *As You Like It*. He's going to take copies of the newer plays back and rewrite them in his own hand onto paper from that period. Once that's done, he'll release them to be performed by the Lord Chamberlain's Men and, later, the King's Men at the court of James I. Since that's the plan, he now doesn't have to write *King Lear* or *The Tempest* or any of the later plays. So now he's got time on his hands. So now he wants to write a bunch of new plays from material in Plutarch and Boccaccio and Chaucer and the work of a smaller literary fry he's been reading back there in Old London. He told me all this last night after dinner."

"Is that such a bad thing?"

Benchley shook his head. "Artistically, it's a great thing. William could write a dozen, maybe two dozen more plays. The Western World, hell the whole world, would be enriched greatly with stories and themes he had wanted to develop, but didn't have time to create. Prospero gets a new chance to conjure up literary magic."

"Sounds good to me," I said.

Benchley rolled his eyes. "Stop and realize, Harvey: Shakespeare has a fixed canon of works that are attributed to him. If you don't count the longer poems and sonnets, he's got thirty-seven plays in that canon. That's all that is recognized by serious scholars and it's been that way since the publication of the Second Folio. Now, it's one thing for me to clear up this hoax Trevor Warbeck tried to buttress with the phony diary Charles Devant wrote and attributed to his grandfather. I got away with that. But what if I say to the world, 'Hey, gang, I've just found an old trunk full of Shakespeare plays everybody else has overlooked?' No matter how good the plays were, I'd be held up to public ridicule as perpetrating a fraud. The Festival would lose all credibility."

"You've got a problem there, Jack."

"I asked William to write the new plays and submit them to me in another name. I could say they were lost plays of some lesser playwright of his time—John Fletcher or John Webster or Ben Jonson. Ben Jonson wants to come to the present too, by the way. He wants to come soon."

"Oh, brother."

"Oh, brother is right. I haven't put on a Jonson play at the Festival in a dozen years. Wait until he finds that out. Wait until he finds out Shakespeare has eclipsed him in the modern stage. He'll be one pissed-off puppy, that's for sure. But to the matter at hand: William wants no one else, alive or long dead, taking credit for these new plays. I could turn his work down, of course. But I know it will be wonderful work: he's at the height of his powers. The thought of turning down a new Shakespeare play offends every fiber of my being."

"I wish I could help, but I don't see how."

"You've done more than your share already, Harvey. I'm grateful."

The rain was coming down harder, and now at an angle that was getting the sill of the open window wet. I got up and shut it to let in just a small amount of air. While I was up, Benchley asked me if I had kept quiet about the existence of the time machine.

"Yes," I said. "I just hope those Royal Marines that took out Essex and his pack can keep their mouths shut."

"Truffie thinks none of them will talk," Benchley said, "not while they are in the service at least. Those marines were part of an elite anti-terrorist outfit. I suppose some of what happened will wind up in the tabloids over there. Somebody will defy the Official Secrets Act for a fat paycheck and hope to get away with it. But since Truffie and I have the one and only remaining STUMP, only gullible people will buy it and there will be no proof. God, that was too bad about Stephen."

"Sure was," I said. "I heard you turned down Queen Elizabeth's several million pounds to turn the STUMP over to her government. Queen Elizabeth II, that is."

Benchley nodded. "I don't want any government spooks or military brass hats getting their mitts on the STUMP. That goes for the Brits or the Americans. It stays with Truffie and I, come hell or high water. When I go, Ann can decide what to do with it. The only reason to keep it working now is to let the

Shakespeares go back and forth to visit each other. Even that is risky. You know about the other STUMPs being destroyed, right?"

"Yes," I said, recalling Bonnie telling me that the British government did insist on two of the machines being destroyed to prevent another incident such as happened with Trevor Warbeck.

"Mankind can barely handle the proliferation of nuclear weapons. It's only been in the last few years that the Americans and the Russians stopped building up masses of nukes to blow Civilization into a heap of rubble and cock-roaches. Man is too predatory for a time machine. Our own country has fouled up even democratically-elected regimes in this hemisphere and everywhere else. And we're the best of a bad lot. The STUMP would become just another weapon. Imagine the mischief that presidents, prime ministers and their spooks could get up to running people back and forth in time, fouling up unfriendly governments and planting little traps on their political rivals."

"They might undo some of the mistakes we've made. Save lives."

"Or fuck things up worse," Benchley said somberly. "That's the more likely scenario. The Queen could have offered me twenty or thirty million pounds for it and I still would have said no. No, no, and no. Oh, hold on, there was something I wanted to show you."

Benchley reached into a pants pocket and pulled out a newspaper article he had, clipped out of a copy of *The London Record.* The headline for the story was as follows:

'MODERN' ASSAULT WEAPON MAY BE 400 YEARS OLD, EXPERTS SAY

The article began with details on how a telecommunications outfit in Britain was laying fiber-optic cables underground at a site near Hampstead Heath. They had come across the remains of a Russian-made AK-47.

> Scientific tests on the firearm indicate its approximate age at 375-400 years, according to Arthur W. Evans, head of the Archeaology Department at the

> University of Birmingham.... There have been a variety of other opinions
> expressed in the scientific community, from flawed testing procedures to allegations of a deliberate hoax along the lines of the 'Piltdown Man' hoax that occured just before the First World War. Professor Evans himself is at a loss to offer a personal explanation to the mystery.
>
> 'In an era that knew only matchlock muskets and wheel lock pistols, it seems impossible to do anything but dismiss my findings,' Evans says. 'I myself cannot see how a 20th Century weapon could be found to have the same age as the sword fragments, human bones and other objects in that layer of earth. But the decay of the metal on the muzzle and the trigger mechanism is consistent with the metal objects found around the automatic rifle....'

"Wow," I said after finishing the article.

"Wow, indeed," Benchley remarked.

"Did the Shakespeares bring any news about how Essex and the other survivors fared after the Royal Marines rolled them up?"

"Essex was beheaded last month inside the confines of the Tower. He had a brief trial before the Star Chamber. It was a closed court but the rumor was mad: kept talking about being visited by beings from the future. Lord Lieutenant Waad and his troopers must be sworn to secrecy because, according to William, all of London just assumes Essex is off his rocker. Southampton had apparently been spared, as he was originally. Lady Southampton, his mother, made a personal appeal to the Queen, and I guess it worked otherwise he would have gone the way of his older peer."

"Has Queen Elizabeth said anything to William Shakespeare? I mean, she must have seen her and those Gentlemen Pensioners were saved by the men in the helicopters."

"He tells me he met privately with the Queen in Whitehall a couple days after the event. Basically, the Official Tudor policy is that the Gentlemen Pensioners fought off Essex's forces with conventional weapons of the time. Anybody who suggests otherwise in some pamphlet will find their rump in a cozy little cell like we had. Shakespeare was told to inform the other members of his company to keep their mouths shut and their quills dry on the subject or face great peril. The Queen wanted to hear nothing of the future by the way. Now that her last love, Essex, has betrayed her I don't think she much cares about anything. Poor old girl."

"What about Francis Bacon?" I asked.

"He's locked up in the Tower as well," Benchley said. "He misled the Queen and that's not a good move when you're dealing with an absolute monarch. I'm sure James the First will let him out in three years when he gets to the throne. He'll probably make Lord Chancellor yet. Elizabeth will spare Bacon, if only for his mind."

"Bacon in the Tower, eh? Couldn't happen to a nicer guy." The noise from the pelting rain had stopped. The storm had passed over us. The rumbles of thunder seemed ever more distant than before. I got up and reopened the window to let cool air in. I asked Benchley if he wanted a refill of cranberry juice. He asked if I had any whiskey.

"Sorry," I said.

"Not good for me, anyway," Benchley remarked. He got up slowly and walked over to the open window. He asked me how my business was doing.

"I have a couple cases," I said. "I'm doing a sordid little domestic matter. I'm also working on some potential phony injury claims for an insurance company. Plus my part-time job at the County, that helps. I've got a pretty good lease agreement here. It'll be close for a few months but I'm going to make it."

"Good," Benchley said, leaning out the window. "I'll bet you'll miss Bonnie when she goes down to San Francisco in a few days."

"I miss her already and we see each other regularly now."

Bonnie was indeed leaving Rogue Falls. She had resigned as Ann Benchley's secretary and had accepted an offer by the American Conservatory Theater in San Francisco to play the part of a "ghost-wife" character named Elvira in *Blithe Spirit*, a comedy by Noel Coward. I was partly happy that Bonnie had gone back to acting, and partly worried on the effect it would have on our budding relationship.

Jack left shortly after that. He said he was afraid he was rambling and started to bore me. I denied it, but I knew I had an appointment coming up with a woman who was going to get to see a photograph of her husband going into a motel room with a kid who was probably her daughter's schoolmate. I helped him on with his coat and watched as he cocked his rain hat. From my window, I watched a stoop-shouldered old man carefully maneuver his old body down the sidewalk and, after deactivating his vehicle alarm, climb slowly back into his Mustang.

The wedding went off two nights later at the Elizabethan, right on center stage. I wore a dark business suit that satisfied Bonnie. The bride wore a long shimmery beaded beige dress that made her look like the last of the Romanovs, but for a lady pushing seventy she looked in good shape. Benchley had on a black tux and looked genuinely happy.

Peter O'Toole had flown in to be there from Europe, as had Jack Benchley's ex-wife (number four) Bebe DuPont, a glamourous fifty-something lady. She wore a low-cut lemon dress that Bonnie thought looked like some deranged fashion designer had cut the fabric off a slightly-used naugahide sofa to make. There were a few other older actors and fellow directors up from L.A. who had either worked with or been pals of Benchley.

Truffie Trubshawe was conspicuously absent. He was still too distraught over the loss of his eldest son, Stephen, to make the trip. Bonnie told me his wife Jo had walked out on him after she found out that Stephen had been sent back into time and would not be coming back alive. (The commandos had recovered his body before leaving 1599, A.D.)

Ann Benchley looked radiant in her outfit, all black taffeta and ruffles. I am probably biased, but I think Bonnie had her beat in a red Chanel suit, the hem coming up above her knee and showing off a very nice set of legs.

We all held up candles during the ceremony. Someone played a flute during the ceremony. It was a bucolic little ditty, no Wagner 'Wedding March' for the Temple of the Universal

Spirit. The priestess announced that the two seniors were "enjoined in the ideal of divine love" at the finish of her speel. The bride was kissed, and then everybody lined up to shake hands and/or peck the cheeks of the newlyweds.

Elizabeth Taylor, whom Benchley had directed in a forgettable domestic drama back in the early seventies, had come up from wherever to see her old friend married. While Bonnie and I stood in line, I noticed Ms. Taylor in line a couple dozen guests ahead of us. She had a small entourage of people around her, creating a second receiving line. And one fellow I did recognize, standing close to her. He wore a dark suit like mine, with his dark brown hair pulled back and tied with a ponytail at the nape of his neck. I was too far to hear what he was saying, but whatever it was Ms. Taylor let out a deep-throated laugh.

It was about midnight after the reception at the smaller Blackfriars theatre (a cozy theatre-in-the -round thing) was finally over that Bonnie, William Shakespeare and I went over to The White Cliffs English Pub on the plaza named after the latter. (I no longer went to O'Leary's Bar. There were too many bad memories there.)

Bonnie had a Zinfindel, I had a Seven-Up, and the Bard had a Red Rock Ale.

"What did you think of Elizabeth Taylor?" Bonnie asked her admirer.

"A woman glorious in all particulars," Shakespeare replied. He was speaking in a different accent, more modern-sounding, the result of some coaching from Jack Benchley, I expect. He talked about the sheer terror he felt flying and he vowed never to repeat the experience after that.

"How did the people at Grantum Hall react to the strange weapons going off and the helicopter appearing?" Bonnie asked.

"The Queen says it was divine intervention," Shakespeare said in a hushed tone. "An act of providence such as the storm that blew up the Channel in '88 and helped to scatter the Spanish Armada. She also forbade her subjects from discussing it, lest it be construed as the fantasy of an aged woman. She had lost her Essex, not that she ever really had him, and the pain of signing his death warrant has drawn the life from her. She may die earlier than expected now. I feel a heavy burden, too. Poor Mr. Trubshawe lost his good son in an effort to secure my Edmund's rescue. I am forever beholden to him."

I made no mention of the business of the new plays Shakespeare planned to write and wanted presented in modern times. Somehow, listening to the man's gentle voice and seeing his elegant demeanor, I knew he and Jack Benchley would come to some agreement that would satisfy both parties.

"I have given Jack a brief sketch of my younger days," Shakespeare said. "He wants me to read it, a chore from which I will receive no billing, as part of a narration in the documentary about myself. When that's done I am back to England for a bit of a sojourn to see what has become of Warwickshire and then back to my own time."

"What is your opinion of this world?" Bonnie asked. She was sitting next to Shakespeare, her whole body turned toward his, her hair glistening from the green-shaded neon light fixture hanging above us.

"Too much hurly-burly, my lady," Shakespeare said. "I've seen London. It is no longer a city as I knew it. It is a cosmos. Save for the Tower and the Abbey of Westminster, I hardly recognize a stone of the city I know. And such horseless machines as clog the streets and run underground? It is a wonder dead men and women do not litter the curbsides. I will try and take back some books, but I can only scratch at all that is new and stimulating here."

"Are you surprised so much of your work has endured?" she asked.

Shakespeare shook his head. "Modesty fails me here. I knew so long as men could breathe or eyes could see, my works would be recalled. I only wish more of the nimble minds of my age and place were equally blessed. In smaller, discerning circles of men and women perhaps they are." He paused to listen to the music that was coming out of the speakers around the pub. "Ah, that music has a sweet strain," he said, referring to a solo from Miles Davis' *Sketches From Spain*. Then he continued.

"I admit it is unnerving to come to a village and see my visage embossed somehow on shirts and drinking mugs and etched into little busts sold in the curiosity shops. I much prefer the station of a gentleman of flesh and blood rather than an icon."

"Is there anyone else in this time you want to meet?" I asked. "Besides Liz Taylor, I mean."

"Yes," the Bard said, after telling the passing waitress to please bring him another ale. "There is a certain Irish journalist and playwright I would have liked to cross paths with. Bernard Shaw is the fellow. The rogue claims in the preface to one of his plays that I never understood virtue or courage. He claims to despise my work more than any other writer possessed of the sort of keen intellect he claims to himself. I have read some of Mister Shaw's one-act plays and one of his longer pieces, including the essay where he puts hot coals to my memory. I saw his *Major Barbara* at the Ryskind Theater last night. The man is clever, God grant him that, but he is a disparager of humankind. I created such a man in Apemantus, my cynic in *Timon of Athens*. He is a a clever man who grasps ideas and knows how to make maxims. But he is so full of hubris that his characters are but trumpets to blast out his philosophy. They live only to please him and disparage ordinary mortals. I mean to read more of this Irishman, this iconoclast of every noble idea I ever put to pen, then I would like to pay a gentlemanly call on him. One scathing appraisal methinks deserves one in kind."

"Shaw died in 1950," Bonnie said. I noticed her speech was becoming slower and shorter in length; the effects of wine consumed here and at the reception.

"Yes, died a very old man so I'm told," I said.

"Perhaps Benchley's time machine can be enhanced to make a visit to an earlier year in this century." Shakespeare said. "I would like to meet this Shaw in a quiet place and discuss his views, perhaps offer a few views my own on the pompous stick-figures he calls the heroes of his own plays."

"Where is Edmund?" I asked.

"Working on his vocal training back at the ranch," Shakespeare said. "He is listening to the radio and the television receiver, trying to perfect his speech. He wants to pass as an American. He will stay with Jack in the coming months and get used to his new surroundings. It will be sad to leave him here and then to lie to my homefolk that he has passed on to heaven's gate, but then he faced an early death anyway. At least here he can eventually wive and have progeny of his own."

"Maybe he'll marry Ann Benchley," Bonnie said. The wine was definitely affecting her.

"Where do your friends and family think you are?" I asked.

"The North of England," he replied. "Edmund, Ben Jonson and I are supposedly on a walking tour about the Lake District and the suurounding peaks. Alas, Edmund will go off alone on a sojourn and accidentally fall from one of the peaks. That is the lie I am telling to his friends and our family. That is the ruse we came up with. Only Jonson is actually in the North. He's visiting a fellow scholar in York."

We drove our friend back to the Benchley Ranch. Jack Benchley's Mustang was in the circular driveway, festooned with a large 'Just Married' sign on the back bumper. There were also all colors of streamers attached to the hood, side windows and rear of the vehicle. The next day Benchley and his new bride would be flying off to honeymoon at an island resort up in Washington State.

Bonnie saw Shakespeare around the ranch for the next couple of days. He read and went for walks in the nearby woods while she got Ann Benchley ready to fly south and start shooting her movie. I saw Shakespeare myself only once more, and in a surprising situation.

Two days after the wedding came Rogue Falls' Annual Fourth of July Parade. Bonnie and I went early in the morning to secure curbside seats in the grassy triangular park that sat in the middle of Shakespeare Plaza. Several marching bands from all over the state and Northern California marched down Siskiyou Boulevard passed the Plaza, along with various colorful floats representing the Rotary Club, the Kiwanas, the Masons, the Rogue County 4-H Club, the Chamber of Commerce, etc. There were also flatbed trucks decorated in patriotic red, white and blue bunting.

Randy Noel, Bonnie's brother, was situated next to us, along with his wife, and their four kids. The family, visiting Bonnie from Austin, Texas, spent a great amount of the time putting sunblock creme on the faces, arms and lower legs of the two boys and two girls. Bonnie and I helped out in making sure the younger kids did not get run over by the floats or the trucks in their pursuit of wrapped candy being thrown at them by people dressed as standard frightwigged clowns, enormous playing cards, old time streetcar conductors, and by a group of hairy legged men dressed in pink ballet tutus.

The Governor of Oregon, riding in a purple 1930's era Oldsmobile convertible with a running board and a shiny grill above the front bumper, got a lackluster reception from our area (as did the other state and local politicos who waved and smiled from the backseats of antique cars. Old men in Shriners fezzes rode about in miniature cars, jugglers and acrobats were on the parade route as well.

A parade of former mayors went by, chauffered in open-top vehicles, as did the city's oldest resident (age 102). She was seated in the back of a Ford Model 'A' and from the look on her face she could have been back at the nursing home for all she knew.

Then came the Northwest Shakespeare Festival Float. It was a stucco and paper maché castle with the Three Witches from Macbeth. The actresses, garbed in grotesque facial make-up, were busy stirring a large black cauldron that occasionally shot up sparks and smoke. At the far end of the parade, two men dressed in chain mail and pointy helmets engaged in what looked like a pretty friendly fencing contest.

"Lay on, Macduff, and damned be the first that cries, 'Hold, enough!'" one of the fencers said. It was a hot day and I imagined the duelers were glad the parade was winding up.

There followed another float featuring the actor who always played William Shakespeare in public events and television advertisments for the festival. He sat on a wooden bench, quill in his hand, large book on his lap. Behind him, also dressed in Renaissance European garb, were the dancers and musicians from 'The Green Show' that opened each outdoor production. I had thought the real Shakespeare would have played himself in the festivities and I whispered as much to Bonnie.

"He's coming up next, with Ann," she said.

And indeed he was. The final group in the parade was the local chapter of the Harley/Davidson Club. He was on a motorcycle, riding it like he had been doing it all his life. Ann Benchley was on the 'Hog' in front of him, making her first appearance in the July Fourth Parade. She was wearing a white helmet with her name in multi-colored letters on each side. Ms. Benchley was riding point, along with Shakespeare, and about twenty other helmeted cyclists were riding in two phalanxes behind them. She got a good round of applause from the on-lookers, indicating that the frame-up had fooled neither the legal system nor the public. Shakespeare picked us out and waved to us. We waved back.

"Mr. Benchley wanted to do a Cleopatra float, but she turned that down." Bonnie explained to me after the loud roar of the exhaust pipes on the cycles died away. "She did like the idea of being the Honorary Leader of the Pack."

"She's been giving him riding lessons?" I asked.

"Took to it like a duck to water," Bonnie said.

"Who was that guy riding next to Ann Benchley?" Bonnie's brother queried.

"Her fitness trainer," Bonnie cheerfully replied. "She has to get in shape for the next Belle Killroy movie. He's been working on her abs and glutes."

❖ ❖ ❖ ❖ ❖

Bonnie and I skipped the booths and distractions offered in Pioneer Park after the parade. Instead we went to her apartment and stayed cool and spent quality time watching a video of Bette Davis and Paul Henreid in *Now Voyager*. It was one of Bonnie's favorite movies. We played Scrabble while watching the tape. It was only a few more days until Bonnie left for San Francisco and, with my schedule, it was the last full day we would spend together for a few weeks.

Later, after dinner, we watched the fireworks going off about a half-mile away at the Rogue High School football field. Her apartment balcony offered a great view of the pyrotechnics. We were dressed for bed, Bonnie in a sheer chiffon robe I had given her, and me in a pair of blue two-piece pajamas she had given me.

A cool breeze came off the mountains and we cuddled together against the railing and each other. I kissed her long and hard. Whatever would happen or not happen in the future between us, I was damn grateful for this moment in time.

THE END